BLACKTHORNE

ALSO BY STINA LEICHT

The Malorum Gates
Cold Iron

The Fey and the Fallen
Of Blood and Honey
And Blue Skies From Pain

THE MALORUM GATES
BOOK TWO

BLACK
THORNE

STINA LEICHT

SAGA PRESS

LONDON SYDNEY **NEW YORK** TORONTO NEW DELHI

SAGA PRESS
AN IMPRINT OF SIMON & SCHUSTER, INC.

1230 AVENUE OF THE AMERICAS, NEW YORK, NEW YORK 10020

SAGA PRESS and colophon are trademarks of Simon & Schuster, Inc.

For information about special discounts for bulk purchases, please contact Simon & Schuster Special Sales at 1-866-506-1949 or business@simonandschuster.com.

The Simon & Schuster Speakers Bureau can bring authors to your live event. For more information or to book an event, contact the Simon & Schuster Speakers Bureau at 1-866-248-3049 or visit our website at www.simonspeakers.com.

Also available in a Saga Press hardcover edition
The text for this book was set in Adobe Jenson Pro.
Manufactured in the United States of America
First Saga Press paperback edition August 2017
2 4 6 8 10 9 7 5 3 1
Library of Congress Cataloging-in-Publication Data
Names: Leicht, Stina, author.
Title: Blackthorne / Stina Leicht.
Description: First Saga Press hardcover edition. | New York : Saga, an imprint of Simon & Schuster, Inc., 2017. | Series: The Malorum gates ; book 2
Identifiers: LCCN 2016044036 (print) | LCCN 2016055186 (eBook) | ISBN 9781481442893 (hardcover : acid-free paper) | ISBN 9781481427807 (softcover : acid-free paper) | ISBN 9781481427821 (eBook)
Subjects: LCSH: Imaginary wars and battles—Fiction. | Good and evil—Fiction. | GSAFD: Fantasy fiction.
Classification: LCC PS3612.E35554 B57 2017 (print) | LCC PS3612.E35554 (ebook) | DDC 813/.6—dc23
LC record available at https://lccn.loc.gov/2016044036

For Ian MacDonald, Enid Crowe, Brian Magee, Joe Monti, Barry Goldblatt, William Shunn, Bo Bolander, Ellen Kushner, Deliah Sherman, and last but nowhere like the least, Kari Sperring. Thanks so, so much for NYC, Brooklyn, Cambridge, Oxford, and most of all, Northern Ireland. That adventure was the experience of a lifetime. I totally couldn't have done it without y'all.

As always, to Dane Caruthers . . .
as you wish.

THE CONTINENT
OF
VÄSTMARKE

KALE

MASSILIA

BLACKTHORNE

❧ C A I U S ☙

28 August

The Twenty-First Year in the Sacred Reign

of Emperor Herminius

"That is not good," Cadet Warden Fortis Caius muttered. The stench of death assaulted his nose. His heart chilled, and his stomach seized into a tight leaden knot.

The tan brick walls lining the narrow alley off Five Sisters Road were splashed with blood. The ground, comprised of dried piss, old shit, and assorted city grime pulverized by time into something resembling dirt, was black where the gore had pooled. Insects buzzed in the damp mud. His gaze kept skipping over the primly arranged body lying at the center of it all.

He didn't want to look too closely at her ruined, eyeless face.

How can one person have that much blood in them? he thought.

Warden school, as rigorous as it was, hadn't prepared him for anything like this. He listened to the thudding of his heart while a metallic taste slimed the back of his tongue. His partner, Tavian, choked and turned away.

Caius swallowed an urge to be sick too. He took a long shuddering breath. *Focus. Remember your training. Follow procedure, and you'll get through this. Show no weakness. Remember Tavian is watching.*

Glancing at the hunched and retching Tavian, Caius reconsidered that last thought. Still, this was their first corpse in the field, and Caius was determined not to give Tavian any opportunities for advancement at his expense. *Not like poor Severus.*

Steeling himself, Caius resumed an air of professionalism. "This can't have been a malorum attack. There's too much blood." He scanned the ground for an assassin's token that might explain the body, but didn't find one. His gaze drifted over her eyeless face once again. Her lips formed a serene smile.

This is the work of a rogue.

His gut muscles knotted yet again. To combat the nausea, he checked the roof line for trouble. Lamps bolted to the alley's walls cast long shadows thinned by a full moon.

He told himself he was calm, and with the exception of his stomach, he discovered with a shock that it was true. Having only recently graduated from the Academy, he wasn't certain if he had training to thank or the unreality of the situation. He forced himself through the next steps nonetheless. Making note of the time for the report, he checked his pocket watch.

The lid snapped shut with a precise click that seemed far too loud.

A quarter to eleven. Wiping palms slick with sweat on his uniform coat, he stepped closer to the corpse. He was sure it *was* a corpse. He wouldn't bother checking for her breath with a mirror.

No one can live through that much violence.

She seemed to have been laid out for her funeral. She lay on her back with her legs straight and together. Her stained and well-worn dress had been smoothed in a tidy arrangement around her. Her wounded left hand rested on her chest. Her right arm lay at her side, ending in a fresh stump at the wrist. Her severed right hand rested a foot or so away. The two shortest fingers ended in jagged wounds. A short distance from that, a tiny gold earring glittered in the lobe of an amputated ear. The ear was pointed.

It seemed odd to Caius that so much care would be taken in arranging the body but not those stray parts. It was as if they'd been discarded and forgotten once they were no longer attached to the whole. At last, he let his gaze travel up her bruised neck to her ravaged face. Not only were her eyes missing, but both ears had been removed as well.

He turned his attention back to the lone, severed ear. *Why take one and not the other?*

Malorum never take trophies. Neither do assassins.

At that moment, the race of the victim registered. *An Eledorean slave. What was she doing out alone at night?*

With a jolt he understood that he'd been so intent on what he was seeing that he'd forgotten where he was. *There may be malorum nearby. Check your partner. Your partner is all you have in the field.* Those words began to make sense in ways they hadn't before. "Tavian?"

"Just. Give me a moment. Please."

All right. What's next? Valarius, their supervisor, wouldn't be far. Caius set the hooded lantern he'd been carrying on the ground near the remains before wriggling out of his pack. "Tavian?"

Tavian spat and wiped his mouth on the sleeve of his coat. "What?"

Caius avoided gazing at Tavian's weakness. *That could've been me*, Caius thought. *But it wasn't.* "Do you have the spare lanterns?"

"Of course."

"Get them out." Caius waited for Tavian to protest. Tavian was of higher social rank, and it was his place to give orders, not Caius's.

To Caius's surprise, Tavian closed his eyes, swallowed, and nodded.

They worked together in silence as they unfolded, assembled, and arranged five camp lanterns in a half-circle near the body. The additional light would make the alley safer and would provide illumination for the investigation. With that done, Caius half-checked the small, barred windows above for witnesses. Anyone who hadn't lived in Novus Salernum for more than a week would wonder why the neighbors weren't awake. The Eledorian girl would most certainly have screamed for help, but Caius knew perfectly well why the windows had remained dark. No honest person would risk themselves and their family by indulging their curiosity. Anyone out after curfew was either a criminal or stupid, and therefore deserved what they got.

We must finish before daylight. It was clear the alley was going to require a great deal of cleaning. *We should start now.*

Or should we wait for Valarius? Undecided, he thought to consult Tavian but hesitated.

Tavian's marks were the highest in the cadet class. Caius himself hadn't placed nearly as high. *Maybe Tavian will get better with time?* But Caius knew there was little chance that Tavian would have the luxury of time. If Caius knew it, Tavian certainly did.

Be careful. He'll turn on you. But looking into Tavian's eyes now, Caius understood otherwise, and in that instant, he knew he would forgive him.

Tavian's face was pale, and his uniform collar was unbuttoned.

His expression bordered on panic. The unspoken question in his eyes was obvious. "Caius?"

Annoyed with himself, Caius already knew what he would do. *How often have I longed for an advantage over Tavian?* And now he had one, and he wasn't going to act on it. *I'm so sorry, Severus.*

Out loud, Caius said, "Don't worry about it."

"But I was the one who reported—I'm the reason they reassigned Severus."

Caius blinked. Severus was—*had been*—Caius's closest friend. The news that Tavian had been the one to speak to the Director wasn't shocking. Caius had known that for more than a month. What was surprising was that Tavian was admitting it. Honesty had been the last thing Caius had expected from Tavian. That, along with the past month's assignment, altered Caius's perception of Tavian. Caius didn't like it.

And that's why the lieutenant inspector assigned him as my training partner, Caius thought. *Mithras's blood.* He hated feeling manipulated. "I know."

Tavian said, "But now you can—"

"I said, don't worry." *Revenge won't bring Severus back. The* thought reminded Caius of his father's lectures on ethics. *Only Severus has that power now.* And knowing Severus, that wasn't going to happen anytime soon. Caius said, "Just . . . forget it."

"Thanks," Tavian said. "If I wash out, my father—he won't understand. Me being a Warden means everything to him. He—"

"Just pull yourself together before Valarius sees you." Suddenly, it occurred to Caius that he hadn't followed procedure as well as all that. "Shit."

"What's wrong?" Tavian asked.

Caius rushed to the street. Reaching for the brass whistle hanging from a chain at his neck, he blew into it with one short and two long bursts. He paused for a count of five and made the signal again. *A body has been found.* With that done, he returned to the alley.

A series of distant whistles echoed in answer. *Delayed, but on our way.*

Caius signaled acceptance and returned to the alley. Tavian was lurking a few feet off, keeping his back to the body. One look at Tavian, and Caius knew Valarius would guess Tavian's failure. Caius gave the situation some consideration. There were regulations for every scenario in the field, and it wasn't long before he had an idea. The only problem was that Tavian had to be seen as the one to act.

Caius said, "This is a special case."

Tavian blinked. "Are you sure?"

"Sure enough." Caius gestured at the remains. "No assassin would do that. Not to a slave. Not without a very large fee. Who would pay that much to dispose of a slave? Anyway, there's no token. And if an assassin did anything as showy as this, there would be a token."

"Oh."

Caius waited for Tavian to come to the appropriate conclusion. When it was clear he wouldn't, Caius continued. "Someone should fetch Captain Drake from the Watch House."

"We're cadets. You know the rules."

"We're Academy *graduates*—"

"Not yet."

"This is our second-to-last field exercise. We're supposed to act as full Wardens."

"You're my partner. I'll get into trouble for leaving you alone."

"Not if this is a special case. Anyway, the moon is full. The alley is well lit. I'll have my weapons at the ready." He drew his pistol and began loading it. "The Inspectors will be here soon." *And you don't want them to see you like this, Tavian.* "I'll be fine."

Tavian paused. He wiped his mouth with the back of a hand. The unbuttoned collar of his Academy coat gaped, and the hem was stained with his own vomit. It was clear he didn't want to be anywhere near the body.

Caius took the opportunity. "It'll get you away from here." Naturally, it would also mean that Tavian would be the one to pay Captain Drake, and Caius decided he was fine with that. Tavian could well afford it, and the Brotherhood would reimburse him anyway.

Eventually.

"All right." Tavian took a deep breath to steady himself. Then he fixed his collar and combed his fingers through his hair. "How do I look?"

"You'll pass. You know the Watch. It's not like they're all that observant."

"And you won't tell anyone I was sick?"

"Are you going to make me swear?"

"Thank you," Tavian said. "I'll remember this. And you must have something in exchange. Father says one should never leave a debt unpaid. Oh, I know. My new mare?"

"The blood bay?"

"End of the week, she is yours if you want her. I'll talk to Father. It's as good as done. I promise." He then sprinted to the street and was gone.

Maybe Tavian isn't so bad after all, Caius thought. Of course, his mother wouldn't approve. Horses were expensive to keep, but a horse would mean more frequent visits home. In the end, she'd be thrilled.

He walked back into the alley. Alone, he decided to gather as much information as he could while he had the chance. He got down on his knees next to the corpse's head. Next, he set his pistol on the ground nearby, careful not to dislodge the shot in the barrel. Then he patted the pockets of his greatcoat, locating his graphite holder and sketchbook, and prepared to take notes.

He started with the face. The wounds in and around the eye sockets were narrower than the ones in the torso, indicating they had been made with a second, smaller blade. Studying the bruises around the neck, he could make out handprints. He stuck the graphite holder behind one ear and measured them with a tailor's tape. He hoped it might indicate the size of her killer. When he was finished, he moved on to her torso. Based upon the diamond shape of the cuts on the chest and the abdomen, he deduced that the second blade used was double-edged.

"Cadet Caius, where is Cadet Tavian?"

Caius dropped what he was doing, grabbed his pistol, and hopped to his feet. He spied an older Warden with a solid build and thinning grey hair under his tricorne hat. He stood in the street with his arms folded across his chest. *Inspector Warden Lucrosa Valarius.* "I'm sorry, sir," Caius said. "I didn't hear you coming."

Valarius frowned.

Shit. Caius inwardly flinched. *That's going to mean a demerit.* "Tavian went to get Watch Captain Drake."

"And why would he do that?" Valarius asked, and waved his partner over.

"It's a special case, sir," Caius said. "Come. Look."

Valarius's expression remained flat. He gave a nod to his partner before joining Caius in the alley. The second Inspector Warden stationed himself at the corner of the building to the right.

"You two are not full Wardens, Cadet. You've broken regulations and endangered yourselves."

"I know, sir," Caius said. "But I—he felt it was necessary. I'm armed and—"

"Don't make excuses," Valarius said. "Do you understand how few cadets survive their first year in the field?"

"Yes, sir."

"A pistol is very little protection against a malorum." Valarius stooped over the body. "One bullet won't stop an adult. It takes silver shot to bring one down. You weren't paying attention to your surroundings. If I'd been a malorum, you'd be dead now."

"Malorum don't venture out during a full moon, sir."

"They've been known to risk the light when hungry enough." Valarius paused, leaning closer to the corpse. "Ah. Been at it again, has he?"

"He who?"

"We don't know yet," Valarius said. "He left the first kill two weeks ago. Near the Sector's northern wall."

"Is there a problem?" Valarius's partner asked in a loud whisper.

Valarius made a few hand signals in reply. Caius caught a piece of what was said before Valarius moved. *Watch is on the way.*

Caius asked, "Sir?"

"I told the Inspector Captain we had a rogue hunter on our hands," Valarius muttered. "It seems you did well to send for Drake after all."

"Is it really a rogue?" Caius asked.

Valarius's expression softened. "I wouldn't go repeating that, if you know what's good for you."

"Yes, sir," Caius said. "What did the Inspector Captain do when you told him?"

"My partner and I were assigned to cadet training. That's what happened." Valarius hunkered down next to the body. "Interesting. No rogue ever left anything like that before. What do you think it means?" He pointed to Caius's leather-bound sketchbook. It had landed on the girl's bloody chest.

"Sorry, sir." Caius retrieved his sketchbook and then searched for something with which to wipe off the cover.

Valarius asked, "More scribblings? Haven't you been cautioned for that?"

"I don't know what they're so afraid of," Caius said. "How is reading signs left on a kill any different from tracking targets in the field?"

"It is different," Valarius said. "Hunters are citizens. They pay a great deal for their privileges, and privacy is one of the things for which they pay. What they do is their business, not ours."

"But if there are signature differences between hunters, such information could help catch rogues," Caius said. "We should keep records of their methods."

"Which would only cause trouble for the Brotherhood in the long run." Valarius got to his feet and dusted off the knees of his breeches. "Besides, no rogue has escaped the Brotherhood of Wardens since it was founded. And neither will this one."

"But such information could be used to prevent repeat offenses."

"I don't think you understand the situation," Valarius said. "There are no repeat offenses. Ever."

"Officially."

"Officially."

"But you have to—" One look at Valarius's face told Caius he'd made a mistake. He lowered his gaze. "I'm sorry, sir."

Valarius sighed. "I can't fault you for enthusiasm." He lowered his voice. "But you're making people uncomfortable. Take care, or you'll never rise above Patrol Warden."

"Who said I wanted otherwise?"

"Trust me. Your purse will. And if you've any expectation of a long, happy life, you will too."

"You survive. And it seems to suit you well enough, sir."

Valarius's half-smile was a little sad. "Never love an ideal more than your career, boy. Principled men are rarely happy in this world." He took a deep breath. "Now, it seems we have a bit of a problem. A rabbit was reported less than a mile from here. We tracked him to Jackson's Mill Road, but Quintus and Noster are also on his trail. Bastards will collect the reward if we're not quick about it. And I have some hefty debts to pay." Valarius looked up at the night sky and then scanned the alley. "Can you take care of yourself until Drake arrives?"

"I think so." *Wouldn't leaving me here alone break regulation again?* Caius bit back the question lest he antagonize his superior once more.

Valarius nodded. "All right. Blow an alarm if anything seems out of place. You hear? I'd rather lose the reward than a cadet."

"Yes, sir."

"And Caius?"

"Yes, sir?"

"Inform Tavian he's been issued a verbal caution."

"What for?"

Valarius pointed to the puddle of vomit. "Loyalty to one's field partner is admirable, but do it again and you'll both go on report, understand?"

"Yes, sir," Caius said. "How did you know it wasn't me?"

Glancing over his shoulder, Valarius said, "Patrol Wardens survive on their ability to observe details. And I *have* been in the field for twenty years, Cadet."

⊰ BLACKTHORNE ⊱

Novus Salernum
The Regnum of Acrasia

—⊰◆⊱—

Midnight
28 August
The Twenty-First Year in the Sacred Reign
of Emperor Herminius

Stylish lamps corralled the Commons park in a ring of protective light. Blackthorne hazarded yet another glimpse at the time, cupping his pocket watch in both hands before releasing the catch. He tilted the black enamel face to better read its mother-of-pearl hash marks and then wiped fingerprints from the cover on a worn sleeve before returning the timepiece to his breeches pocket.

A quarter to eleven. The Lucrosa was late for her appointment. *Again.*

Watchmen will make their rounds soon, he thought.

A cool breeze tugged at his greatcoat, causing it to flap around his knees. He made no move to pull it closed. Instead, he shut his eyes and breathed in, savoring the dusty scent of dead leaves. Behind the pleasant odor he detected the gritty specter of coal smoke and river fog. Thunder rolled in the distance. The storm it announced might pass to the south or north. He hoped for the south. If it was headed northward, the bad weather would add complications.

He used a passage from the Retainer's Code to calm his nerves. *The ideal Retainer lives in the present. The present is where control lies. The past is of no consequence, and the future does not exist.*

When he was a Cadet Warden, he'd volunteered for evening patrols. His partner had thought him mad. Most preferred to make their rounds during the day, expending a great deal of money and influence to do so. It was but one of the many differences between him and the rest of the Brotherhood.

That life is finished. And you would not want to go back, even if you could. As was too often the case lately, he couldn't decide whether it was reassurance or justification. *The past is of no consequence. The future does not exist.* The greatcoat pulled tight across his shoulder blades. He stopped stretching to avoid ripping the back seam. It wouldn't withstand yet another round of his inexpert stitching, and it needed to last him through the winter.

The insects abruptly stopped their singing. The stench of grave dust deposited the taste of tin in the back of his throat. He knew the creature—*the malorum*—was there without hearing or seeing it. He always did. He tried hard not to consider why. It was a useful skill. One he told no one about, because doing so would endanger his life.

The monster risked a full moon? Is it because there's a storm coming? There was no knowing why, really. Malorum were unfathomable.

Holding his breath, Blackthorne concentrated on blending in

with his surroundings. His stomach tensed, and a tingling sensation crawled over his scalp. Discarded leaves strewn on the grass snapped into sharper focus. Behind and to the right, he sensed the malorum relax. Using gradual movements as he'd been trained to do at the Warden's Academy, Blackthorne settled a shoulder against the trunk of a large oak tree and laid a hand on the hilt of his knife. At the edge of his vision, a spindly form ventured from the shadows. Dressed in rags and a floppy hat, it toed moonlight like a reluctant swimmer testing the water. The outstretched foot was misshapen and coated in spiny fur. Lurching on two crooked legs, the creature limped closer. Then it passed behind a cluster of trees. The metallic taste flooded Blackthorne's mouth, and he fought an urge to spit. Inching his dagger free of its sheath, he listened to the stealthy crunch of its offbeat step until it reemerged a few paces away.

It drew in a sharp breath when it spied him.

He launched himself at it with his knife drawn, driving it to the ground. The thing's hat fell off, and a patch of moonlight hit the malorum full in the face. Its nose slits snapped shut, and the too-wide mouth tightened in pain. The creature's visage blurred, and an old Eledorean male with pale hair struggled beneath him in the grass. For a moment, Blackthorne couldn't breathe.

Oh, Mithras. It's Esa.

"Have mercy." The words rasped through too many teeth.

When Blackthorne didn't react, the creature let out a piercing discordant cry. Blackthorne trapped its howl with his forearm. The malorum bit down, and a bolt of pain shot up Blackthorne's left arm. The malorum struggled, and a muffled scream pressed against Blackthorne's skin. He rammed the silver-laced blade under the creature's chin. Its hide resisted the knife for an instant before the blade sank home. Elph-black eyes bulged. Blackthorne gagged on both the stench of the malorum and the horror of what he'd done. Cold blood spurted from the wound, soaking his clothes.

In Mithras's name, why did the thing have to choose Esa?

Drunken singing echoed off the ancient city wall and down the street—rich toughs staggering their way to a fashionably coarse alehouse or salon.

Swiving hells. That's all I need. Fighting revulsion, Blackthorne trapped the malorum with his body until the creature finally stopped twitching. Then he rolled off and crawled back to the oak tree. Resting his back against its trunk, he sat between the roots and attempted to get control of himself. His arm was agony. A deep voice called out.

"You there! You are in violation of Senatorial Safety Edict number three seven five. Please return to your homes at once or face arrest for curfew violation."

Curious, Blackthorne peered around the base of the oak for a view of the street. The drunken rowdies had halted, and a woman dressed in loose black clothing had positioned herself between her charges and the Watchmen. There was no need to look for the black fur trim on her coat. Her air of lethal expertise was enough. Someone within the group could afford to employ a titled Retainer.

The Watchman with the lamp gave her proffered identification a bored glance. The Retainer tilted her head down by way of a curt bow. Blackthorne knew she would've kept her eyes on the Watchman. No well-trained Retainer would do otherwise.

"My patron appreciates your concern for his safety and would like to express his gratitude with this donation." She tossed the Watchman a small cloth bag that clinked on the paving stones.

Silver. Not paper or pewter, I'll bet. Blackthorne's estimate of the group's worth increased.

The Watchman bent to retrieve the bag, and the exchange

reached its standard conclusion. The two Watchmen continued their rounds. With the exception of the Retainer, who scanned the Commons for potential trouble before proceeding. No one had so much as glanced in Blackthorne's direction during the entire transaction. He took a deep breath and slowly released it. When he returned his attention to the malorum, he saw it had resumed its original form.

Esa is dead, Blackthorne thought. *Malorum steal images from the minds of those nearest. Images with strong emotional resonance. You know this.*

He waited until his hands had stopped shaking before cleaning and sheathing his blade. Checking the wound, he saw the left arm of his greatcoat had been shredded, but not so badly that it couldn't be patched. The bite burned and throbbed up to the elbow. Blood oozed down his arm, tickling as it went. He felt above the wrist and found a broken tooth lodged in the bite. He shoved up the tattered sleeve and pinched the fang out of his own flesh with stiff fingers. Then he retrieved the Acrasian soldier's pack he'd left at the base of the oak and searched for the vial of antivenom he'd mixed himself. As he stooped to open the pack, he felt cold wind toy with the fresh rip in the back of his coat.

He sighed and in resigned frustration applied the medicine to the wound. He waited until he felt the concoction begin its icy work. Then he returned to his pack for a bandage. With his coat in rags and the Eledorean wastelands in his near future, there was nothing he could spare. So, he resorted to cutting his shirttail. Once the bandage was secure, he hid the dead malorum under a pile of damp leaves. He purposely avoided looking at its face during the process. Straightening, he wiped his hands on the grass and then checked the time. *A quarter past twelve.*

It was obvious the Lucrosa wouldn't keep her appointment.

He'd have to remain in Novus Salernum until another meeting could be arranged. It would be a great risk, but his orders were explicit. For reasons he wasn't significant enough to know, the Eledorean boy named Tobias Freeson was important. Unfortunately, the barkeep at the coaching inn had begun to ask uncomfortable questions. Blackthorne didn't have any coin to spare for a bribe. That meant that soon the landlord would report him, and Blackthorne's forged identification papers weren't going to hold up to an official inspection. The way the situation was going, Freeson would cost contacts it had taken him months to cultivate.

Blackthorne bit back his frustration and forced himself to settle once more in his chosen waiting place. *Calm yourself. You cannot afford mistakes.* He would remain for an hour and then return to the coaching inn.

It wasn't long before he heard two sets of footsteps echoing down the street. He paused, focusing on the sounds. With a sick twist in his gut came the knowledge that Lucrosa Aurelia was one of the two who approached. He shouldered his pack and skirted the edge of the clearing in the middle of the Commons park until he came to a more advantageous position.

"He's not here. I told you we shouldn't have waited to say goodbye to your sister." Lucrosa Aurelia's aristocratic voice came from the trees to Blackthorne's left.

"Shhh," Tobias said. "Get out of the light. If there's a Warden near, he'll see us."

Blackthorne waited a count of one hundred. When it was clear no one followed, he shifted to a place where he could observe the pair. Aurelia, he knew. This Tobias Freeson, however, was another matter. He'd never met the boy before.

Freeson removed his tricorne hat, dropped his heavy pack and then scanned the clearing with a worried look. The angular marks of elpharmaceutria ancestry were plain in his face. However, that was where the influence of his lineage ended. He was broad-shouldered and solidly muscled. Pure nonhumans were becoming a rarity in the city, but Blackthorne had been told to expect a full-blooded elph, not a quadrane or a semivir, and he'd made his plans accordingly.

Mentally, he cursed his superior, the Lucrosa, and every Eledorean god he could name—which, all told, wasn't that many, since Eledoreans kept such things secret.

"You're late," Blackthorne said in a quiet voice frosted with irritation. He reached into his greatcoat for the established token—a signed letter outlining their agreement. Most of it was a lie designed to deal with questions no one actually wanted answered.

The Lucrosa paused, staring at what was in his hands before she retrieved the document. Again Blackthorne waited while she examined the letter with some difficulty in the dim light. Then she returned it without touching him. If she could've managed it, he knew she'd have looked down her nose. He understood her attitude for what it was—a futile attempt to assume authority in an uncertain situation. He had done it himself often enough when younger. *As if that was all that long ago.*

A lot can change in a year, he thought. And it had.

"What assurance can you give that Tobias will be safe?" She exaggerated the tones of Regent Street in her voice.

Blackthorne remained unimpressed. "None. You'll have to trust me."

She sniffed as if she smelled something unpleasant. Given that his clothes were stained with malorum blood, he was relatively certain she did.

"I don't like you," she said. "How do I know you didn't steal that letter? Who's to say you won't hand him over to the Brotherhood?"

Tobias raised a hand. "Aurelia, don't." He measured Blackthorne with his elph-black eyes.

Blackthorne knew what Tobias would see—a human face with the coloring of Gens Aureus. Skin somewhat darker than that storied gens tended to favor, but passable nonetheless. Grey eyes, small scar in the right eyebrow, black hair tied back with a ribbon, angular features shielded by a mustache and goatee. He was only nineteen, but the beard did a good job of hiding Blackthorne's age. All in all, he would appear respectable, if a bit rough. Tobias would accept the exterior without question. *Everyone did.* And then Blackthorne's confidence in his disguise was abruptly shattered by a tingling sensation so powerful that not only did it make his skin crawl but his stomach tried to heave itself up his throat as well.

Magic. He fought panic. *This Tobias Freeson has magic.*

Tobias gasped. "You're not human."

Struggling to keep his face blank, Blackthorne swallowed. *Only noble elpharmaceutria wield domination magic. There's nothing to fear. This one is only a peasant.*

And what if he isn't? Are you willing to take the risk?

Is this why Slate wants Freeson?

"What *are* you?" Openly curious, Tobias took a step closer.

"Late." Blackthorne stood his ground, using impatience to bolster his courage and deflect the question. "Can we start? I would rather not miss breakfast in addition to supper."

Aurelia's brows pushed together. "Wait one—"

"It's all right," Tobias said. "I'll go with him. He can't possibly be a Warden. He's one of us."

Blackthorne bit down a denial.

"But how will I know you're all right?" she asked.

Tobias shrugged. "I'll send you a message as soon as I can. I promise." He paused and fidgeted with the hat in his hands. "I guess this is it."

Blackthorne watched the two stand in awkward silence before Aurelia disrupted it.

"I hate this. Who am I going to get into trouble with when you're gone? I wish you didn't have to go. I wish I could go with you."

Tobias nodded in misery and stared at the pewter buckles on his shoes.

"It's not fair." She started to weep.

Reaching into his waistcoat pocket, Tobias pulled out a handkerchief. "Shhh. It's okay. Once I get to Eledore, I'll send for you."

"The Haunted Lands." She sniffed and accepted the cotton square from Tobias. Wiping her eyes, she smiled through the tears. "What an adventure! Wouldn't *that* make Father furious?" She laughed and hugged Tobias. When she stepped back and blew her nose, a shadow from a tree branch made a blindfold over her light-colored eyes.

Blackthorne surveyed the woods while Aurelia and Tobias finished their parting words. When they were done, Aurelia handed a folio of sterling notes to Blackthorne with a forlorn hiccup.

Tobias stooped to grab his pack.

"Leave it," Blackthorne said.

Tobias gaped. "But . . . I can't."

"We had an agreement, and the agreement stated there was to be no baggage," Blackthorne said. In his anger, Regent's Street slipped into his voice.

Aurelia tilted her head as if noting it.

"You have a pack; why shouldn't I?" Tobias asked. "I won't leave without my books. I haven't finished researching—"

"I thought you were a journeyman blacksmith," Blackthorne said, not quite making it a question.

"I'm to be a gunsmith," Tobias said. "Well . . . I will be. Once I'm out of Acrasia."

An elph with such knowledge would be considered a great danger to the Regnum—one who wields magic even more so. Slate's orders and choice of courier suddenly made terrible sense. *Anyone found in possession of Tobias and those books would not merely be punished for attempting to smuggle a registered nonhuman outside of Acrasian borders—they'd die a traitor's death.* Blackthorne hid his shock at Slate's ruthlessness by turning his face away. He tucked the money folio inside his greatcoat and fought a sense of betrayal. *Who else can Slate afford to lose? Who else can he trust to withstand any amount of torture?*

The reply that Blackthorne forced up his throat was terse. "You carry them. I won't."

Tobias hesitated before giving Aurelia's cheek a bashful peck. She gasped and then impulsively returned the kiss full on the lips. Blackthorne walked away, trusting Tobias would follow.

A freezing wind poured down the street, carrying old paper in its wake. Blackthorne shivered. One corner of a seditious one-sheet pasted on a wall fluttered and flashed its bold and hopeless declarations at the empty street. It was the same call to action Blackthorne had spied in various places across the city. Its twin was hidden deep inside his pack, an added offering for his superior. He walked the cobblestone street with bold purpose. It was an old burglar's trick—a Warden wouldn't fall for the pretense, but a casual observer might. Tobias caught up with him. Unfortunately, it became apparent that he wasn't following Blackthorne's example. He skulked from shadow to shadow, exuding terror with every movement.

When Blackthorne reached the corner, he whirled, grabbing Tobias's arm and yanking him into the moonlight. "Walk as I do, or I'll put a collar on you."

"I'm a freeman. Who do you think you are?"

"The man who was paid to get you out of Acrasia. I have no preference as to how."

Tobias yanked his arm free. Resentment blazed across his face before he spoke. "Fine. You know your business."

Blackthorne turned his back to Tobias.

"Your coat is torn," Tobias said.

"I know." Blackthorne resumed walking, and attempted to ignore the cold wind pouring through the rent.

"For what you were paid, you'd think you could afford another," Tobias muttered.

You're assuming I'm the one for whom the fee is intended, Blackthorne thought.

After that, Tobias followed instructions without further protest. As they neared the border of Novus Salernum's North End, the brick houses with their modest white pillars gave way to closed and barred inns, coffeehouses, and merchant shops. Blackthorne led Tobias into a crooked alley and dropped his pack.

"When we're stopped at the gate, do not speak. No matter what happens," Blackthorne said. Once again, he searched through the contents of his soldier's pack. Finding what he needed, he tossed filthy rags at Tobias. "Bandage your face and hands."

"What is this?" Tobias asked, making a face. "It stinks."

So many questions. Blackthorne selected a filthy bandage and wound it around own his head. "Leper's bindings."

Tobias dropped the rags onto the cobblestones in disgust.

"Be certain your ears are covered," Blackthorne said. "And look no one in the eye."

"I'm not putting that on my face."

"Elpharmaceutria are immune to leprosy. I fail to understand your concern." Blackthorne knotted old cloth around his hands.

"One of my parents was *kainen*."

His disguise complete, Blackthorne retrieved the cloth Tobias had discarded. "I was informed I would be transporting an elph—" He cut the word short when he spotted Tobias's glare. "*Kainen.* If you have concerns, perhaps you should take them up with your friends, the Lucrosa." He shoved the bundle back into Tobias's hands. "Accept the danger or not. Make the choice now, and stop wasting my time."

It was a bluff. Blackthorne couldn't return to Slate without Tobias, but Tobias didn't know that. However, he'd run out of time. The guards at the gate were due to change in a quarter hour, and if he missed Sergeant Fisk, they'd have to wait another day. The way things were going, he didn't want to take the chance.

Tobias stalled, glancing around the alley. Finally, he sighed. Blackthorne waited until Tobias finished with the rags. Then Blackthorne limped into the street, putting a finger to his lips. Tobias's bandaged head bobbed a reluctant yes in return. A few hundred feet from the gate, Blackthorne paused to listen. He heard a sneeze and a sniff. Someone cleared their throat and spit. The sound echoed off the twenty-five-foot wall ahead.

Four guards. Two more on the wall. Again, the information came to him with an uncomfortable ease. He had sharp ears, always had. *It doesn't mean anything else.* He took a deep breath and staggered to the portcullis.

"Here, you! Gate's locked! It's dark. Ain't nobody getting out, see?"

Blackthorne changed direction at once, targeting the guard who'd spoken. He wheezed in a cracked voice, "We've no shelter. Please. Let us stay in your guardhouse."

"Lepers! Get them away from here!" The shout came from the right.

"Malorum took our friend. Please." Blackthorne reached out to the nearest soldier, who jerked away in disgust.

"Shoot him! Now!"

Muskets clicked as hammers locked into place.

Heart hammering in his ears, Blackthorne hoped Tobias had enough courage to stay silent. *Damn it, Fisk. Where are you?*

"Wait! Paulus, old friend? Is that you?"

Through the narrow opening afforded by his disguise, Blackthorne recognized the fat sergeant with thinning braids on either side of his face. The hairstyle was one adopted by the emperor's shock troops, and legally, only those who once served in their ranks could wear their hair that way.

Blackthorne bowed his head. "Yes, sir. Sergeant Fisk, sir."

"Lower your guns." Sergeant Fisk waved the guards down. "It's only Paulus. He means you no harm."

"You know him, Sarge?"

"Of course I do. He served with my poor brother Jori in the Eledorean campaign," Fisk said. "Never you mind what he is now. He was a Retainer with a Gens name once. Killed hisself a bear in the games, didn't you, Paulus?"

Blackthorne carefully straightened his shoulders in tattered pride. "That I did, sir."

"What happened to you?" one of the other guards asked. His face was set in disgust and disbelief.

"A swiving elph gave him the rot. That's what happened," Sergeant Fisk said.

At the edge of his vision, Blackthorne saw Tobias tense.

Fisk continued, not noticing. "—poor devil. Mark my words, same could happen to any one of us. The legion will cut you loose just as quick too. That's why we look out for our own. Got it?" Sergeant Fisk stopped at a safe distance. "Shouldn't you be in a bolt-hole, Paulus?"

"Full up when we got there, sir. Planned to start for Archiron in the morning." Blackthorne shrugged. There were moments when he felt guilty for taking advantage of Fisk's sympathies and moments when he didn't. "Plans changed."

"Who's that with you?" Sergeant Fisk asked.

"Don't know his name. Rot took his lips and tongue. You want to inspect him?"

"No need. No need. I can smell him from here," Sergeant Fisk said, "You got anything for me?"

Blackthorne reached into his greatcoat and brought out two pewter coins embossed with wheat stalks. "Today's takings. Only a couple of pennies, I'm afraid. Will it do?"

"Civilians don't give veterans proper respect. Not like they used to." Sergeant Fisk wiped the pewter wheat stalks on the front of his jacket. "Private Cullen, get the gates."

The portcullis creaked open just wide enough for Blackthorne and his charge to pass through. He made a point of limping along the road to Archiron until they were out of sight of the wall, and then ducked into the trees. Releasing the breath he was holding and stretching, he resumed his normal posture.

"Can I take these filthy things off now?" Tobias asked.

"Give them to me," Blackthorne said, stuffing Paulus's bandages into the military pack. He stood straight and filled his lungs with clean air. He didn't enjoy playing Paulus, but terror of disease meant lepers weren't searched nor were they asked for identification.

Tobias ripped the cloth from his face and tossed it onto the ground with a shudder. "Where are we going now?"

"We must avoid populated areas until we reach Aurivallis," Blackthorne said, gathering the discarded rags. "We'll cut through the woods over to the road. Hard ground will make tracking more difficult." He looped his pack on his shoulder. "Keep quiet while I listen for patrols. We can't chance resting until we're at least five miles outside of the city walls."

The patches of sky revealed between the tree branches were black velvet jeweled with pinprick stars. It seemed the weather might hold. That was good luck. Blackthorne arranged the wide lapel of his greatcoat in front of his nose to prevent breath-clouds and fell into the rhythm of a long hike, letting its cadence soothe the tension in his stomach. He remembered his early training and focused on keeping his shoulders loose and his weight centered in the pit of his stomach.

"You walked in the middle of the street, bold as anything, before. Why hide now?" Tobias asked.

"Because there is now cover worth hiding in."

When they reached the main crossroads, Blackthorne headed north. A nagging feeling something was wrong gnawed at him.

"I've never been as far as Aurivallis before," said Tobias in a cheerful tone. "Well . . . I've never been out of Novus Salernum, actually."

Blackthorne stopped and gave Tobias a sharp glance.

"What is it?"

Tilting his head, Blackthorne strained to hear. *The woods to the right. One man. Medium build by the sound. Horse not far. Too careless for a Warden.* He drew his pistols.

"Blackthorne?"

"Hide over there," Blackthorne whispered. "Now."

The voice that drifted from under the trees was crude. Its friendly East Side tone stretched over menace like an ill-fitting waistcoat. "Here, now, why would you want to go and draw weapons for? All I wants is a friendly chat."

⊰ ✠ D R A K E ✠ ⊱

ONE

Novus Salernum
The Regnum of Acrasia

———⊷•⊷———

Quarter past Midnight
28 August
The Twenty-First Year in the Sacred Reign
of Emperor Herminius

"Captain? You awake? Captain?"

Captain Drake mumbled a drowsy curse. *That would be Gilmartyn, the new recruit, damn him.* One of the others must have put him up to it, knowing her disposition when her sleep was interrupted. Based on the tremor in his reedy voice, she surmised Sergeant Benbow must have related an account of her predecessor's fate. There were at least three different versions circulating the Watch House. Which rumor was to blame for Gilmartyn's newfound timidity was of little consequence. She let Benbow have his fun with the recruits. Occasionally, his embellishments were useful.

"There's a Warden here to see you," Gilmartyn said. "Says it's urgent. Captain?"

"Stop that incessant banging." She sat up, hunching to avoid slamming her head into the empty bunk above. A dreadful ache settled into her head the instant she was upright, and she squeezed her eyes shut against agony.

Mithras, I hate this job. The original attraction had been the money and respect the uniform brought. For the daughter of a common street harvester, she'd achieved a great deal. However, at the moment, she would've traded it all for a decent night's sleep. She swung her feet out of bed. The clock on the mantel read twelve-thirty. The fire was out in the hearth, and the kettle hung cold on its swivel hook.

"Gilmartyn? Blast you, are you still there?" The effort of shouting plunged a fresh bolt of pain through her temples.

To Gilmartyn's credit, there was only a slight pause. "Yes, Captain. What do I tell him?"

Pushing both hands through her hair, she made an unsuccessful attempt at smoothing the fingers of agony clawing at the inside of her skull. "Tell him I'll meet him in my office. And Gilmartyn, there'd *better* be a cup of hot tea on my desk when I get there."

"Yes, ma'am!"

She flinched as Gilmartyn thundered down the stairs. Taking her time getting presentable, she gingerly scraped a comb over her tender scalp and then made a face in the mirror. When a quarter hour had passed, she threw on her captain's jacket, not bothering with the buttons, and made her way downstairs. A cadet Warden stood at attention in the middle of the room, secreting urgency like stale pipe smoke. After only two hours of uninterrupted sleep, she didn't give a toss if he was in a hurry or not. *It isn't even daylight.* She shoved past and caught the faint stench of vomit and rotting corpse. Fighting down a reflexive stomach clench did nothing for her mood.

She spied the mug of steaming tea in the center of her desk.

Gilmartyn just might see corporal one day.

The door slammed. Sergeant Benbow assumed a position next to the shut door as if on guard. His pox-scarred face was set in a disgruntled glare, and the left leg of his breeches gaped free of his boot.

Where's Jaspar? Drake thought. *Benbow should be in the bunkhouse snoring loud enough to rattle the floorboards.*

"Am I addressing Captain Drake?" the cadet Warden asked.

She detected a sneer as he pronounced her last name. *It's an Ytlainen name, not an Eledorean one, damn you.* Her father hadn't paid to change it to something more suitable, because it hadn't been necessary, not in his line of work. However, she couldn't afford to do the same. It was high on the long list of items she needed to tend to soon.

She dropped into her chair with more enthusiasm than was wise, given the state of her head and stomach. Half-awake, she had enough self-discipline to keep her retort to herself—just barely. *And you can see the stripes on my sleeve. If you're too stupid to figure out who I am from that, then you don't belong at the Academy.* Instead, she grunted an acknowledgement.

"I'm Cadet Warden Lucrosa Tavian. You're needed. I'm to take you to an alley off of Five Sisters Road. This is a special case."

"Benbow, check the door," she said.

Benbow obliged. The captain's office wasn't secure—nowhere in the Watch House was, but it was wise to check that Gilmartyn wasn't listening in. Not that she expected him to understand what he was hearing if he did. Opening the bottom right drawer of her desk, she fished out the bottle she kept there. After pouring a measure of cheap whiskey into her tea, she replaced the cork, deposited the bottle in the drawer, and gave it a hard kick. The bottle rolled and hit the inside of the drawer with a clank. *Gordan said the Brotherhood might come calling, and that it'd mean extra pay.*

A special case, though. At this hour, I knew it wouldn't be good news.

Unable to delay any longer, she looked up at Cadet Lucrosa. Insignia embroidered on the lapel of his black greatcoat indicated he had attended the Warden's Academy for four years. His brown hair was shaved off the back of the neck in the outdated Academy style—she understood the Academy barber used an inverted bowl to measure what would be cut. The fringe was normally groomed back from the face, but sweaty hair hung in the cadet's pale green eyes. There was also a stain on the hem of his coat. Everything else about him was clean-shaven and regulation.

She took a long swallow of spiked tea, waited for it to appease her hangover, and then sighed. "Messy one, is it?"

Cadet Lucrosa blushed faintly and frowned.

"Look, this sort of thing isn't within my jurisdiction. Need a review, Cadet? Fine. The Watch protects the citizenry. *Your* duty is to keep the nonhuman scum from overrunning the Regnum; therefore, hunters are the Brotherhood's concern. *Your* concern. Not mine." She leaned forward and whispered. "You lot are the ones issuing the damned hunting licenses." *What in the hells am I doing? This puppy has a gens. He can have me killed.*

Cadet Lucrosa dropped his formal posture and bunched a fist. His jaw visibly tightened. "I was informed that your predecessor maintained an equitable agreement with the Brotherhood."

She knew exactly what the cadet meant but kept to her pretext of innocence nonetheless. Looking to Benbow, she saw him nod.

Damn it, Gordan. Sometimes I wish I had killed you. She pinched the bridge of her nose and took a deep breath to get control of her emotions. "All right. What is it *exactly* that you want from me? Understand, this is going to cost you."

TWO

Drake surveyed the street while Benbow set the brake on the Watch's feed wagon. Tavian jumped down at once. The road was clear. It had rained the day before. Luckily, the alley was far enough from the cesspools at the corners that the smell wasn't overpowering. *At least this parish has sewers. Gibson Road is a perpetual offal-filled bog this time of year.*

Five Sisters was where the middling sort lived and worked. Respectable red and tan brick structures competed for space along the street. Their doorways were unadorned and narrow, their roofs sensibly angled to prevent snow from accumulating in the winter. The windows were shrouded with lace curtains, and the mullions supporting the glass panes were lead instead of silver. In the spring, regimented gardens of vegetables and flowers appeared in the fenced plots behind the buildings. No nonhuman sullied the neighborhood unless they possessed citizenship, an appropriate amount of sterling, and the demeanor to match. It was the kind of area that set Drake's teeth on edge. Everything and everyone in its proper place and arranged in a façade that said nothing bad happened there. Yet, if one looked closely, one would notice the streetlamps left to burn, the sensible sterling pieces hung in windows for protection, iron bars. Malorum were as feared there as they were in other parts of the city.

The alley Tavian had indicated ran between two businesses, a potter and a tailor. Their owners slept peacefully ignorant in the uppermost floors. She glanced at Benbow's ugly face and caught his determined frown. He didn't relish this kind of work any more than she did, but he'd been included in Gordan's bargain. Given that the agreement stipulated that the Brotherhood paid in silver coin, only a fool would turn it down. It usually involved mopping up a bit of blood before the public noticed. She'd done a great deal worse before buying her stripes.

Cadet Lucrosa waited near the wagon, obviously unwilling to chance another eyeful of the body.

A Warden with a weak stomach, she thought. *His parents must have a great deal of money and very little sense.*

She wasn't surprised when a second cadet Warden with longer black hair knotted into a non-academy-regulation queue met them at the corner. Wardens traveled in pairs, particularly the cadets. There was something attractive about the second cadet in spite of the scowl. *His eyes? Or perhaps it was his jaw?* She couldn't make up her mind in the dim light. He had a nice build. Like the Lucrosa, his collar indicated he'd been at the Academy four years, which meant he was seventeen or eighteen. She took in the whole of his demeanor and decided he was at least eighteen.

Older than Cadet Lucrosa, anyway, she thought. *Four years younger than myself. Interesting. I wonder how much he knows of the world? Might be fun to teach him a few things. He'd certainly have the stamina for it.*

He turned, and she glimpsed the gens name Fortis embroidered on the right breast of his greatcoat. At that moment, she decided she didn't like the line of his jaw after all.

It has been too long. Her boyfriend, Gerald, had abandoned her after she'd confessed her plans for buying a captaincy in the Watch. A street harvester moving up to burglar was one thing, but the Watch? She might as well have declared herself to be malorum. Unfortunately, the business of dishonest trade was strictly regulated by the Syndicate, and the Syndicate was as fussy as the wife of a silversmith when it came to bloodlines. Drake didn't look it, but her mother's mother had been a navigator on a Waterborne ship. She could change her name, but she could never change her ancestry. The Syndicate would never grant anyone with tainted ancestry membership. While she hadn't told Gerald about her grandmother, it'd been easy enough to put together once she'd explained why she was hiding sterling from her father. There were few employment options left to persons of mixed blood. The prisons employed anyone willing to take on the job of guard. The Watch was the second more pleasant, more respected option. Therefore, she'd put in her application at the nearest Watch House.

Naturally, Gerald had vanished the next morning. The fact that he'd done so without taking the hidden sterling with him had proved just how much he'd cared. That had been over a year before, and her nights were getting longer by the week. *Must do something about that itch before it gets me into trouble.* She thought of her friend, Mallory, and considered a visit after she'd been paid. Of course, her father would've insisted she marry, but she'd seen what that'd done to her mother, and she wasn't about to follow her dull but brutal fate. So, Drake swallowed the expensive tea she secretly bought from the Eledorean apothecary, did what she could for herself, and kept her feelings and memories of Gerald buried deep.

Love is a pretty ribbon used to tie a knot on a terrible box of goods.

Anger flashed across the Fortis's haughty face. "This is an important matter of the Regnum." Blocking the mouth of the alley, he folded his arms across his chest and planted his feet shoulder-width apart. "Cadet Lucrosa should have explained you were the only one permitted. Your sergeant must leave."

An older pair of Wardens waited across the street.

Oh, hell. He's strutting for his superiors, Drake thought. "Benbow's been in on this deal longer than I have," she said. "He knows what to do. He works fast. And he's capable of keeping his mouth shut. He's here to do the real work. I didn't become Captain of the Watch to clean up *your* messes." She waited while the Fortis considered his options. "Is it a human?"

His voice was flat and businesslike. "Elpharmaceutria."

A human would've meant more money, and she would have to split with Benbow. *Still, hard cold silver is hard cold silver.*

The first cadet produced a book with a leather cover, wrote in it, and tore out a page. "Sign this."

When the receipt was verified and witnessed, he gave her a handful of sterling coins.

"Don't worry," Drake said. "The cobblestones will be soaped off before anyone sees."

In the distance, thunder rolled. She hoped they'd finish before the storm hit.

⊱ BLACKTHORNE ⊰

ONE

Novus Salernum
The Regnum of Acrasia

———⊱◆⊰———

28 August
The Twenty-First Year in the Sacred Reign
of Emperor Herminius

A short man armed with mismatched pistols and dressed in a grubby coat stepped onto Old Aurivallis Road. His gap-toothed smile looked like a gash in his pox-scarred, unshaven face. He was hatless, and his silk waistcoat had clearly been tailored for someone with a much smaller circumference. The white cuffs of his clean linen shirt were much too long. It didn't help matters that he smelled like the exterior of an alehouse at dawn. Cloud-shadowed moonlight drenched him in blacks and greys.

"What I'd like to know is how you cogged I was there. Me, being quiet as a church mouse and all." The highwayman nodded at Blackthorne's pistols.

The knot between Blackthorne's shoulder blades tightened. "What is it you want?"

The muzzles of the highwayman's pistols were steady. "Dismissing with the pleasantries, are we? Fair enough. If you're legit, show me your papers. Otherwise, there's a toll for illegally leaving the city. And I'm here to collect it."

Tobias moved from the safety of the tree and stood at Blackthorne's side. "If we're illegal, you are too."

Blackthorne spoke to Tobias over his shoulder, keeping his eyes on the highwayman. "I told you to stay where you were."

"Awww, what's this?" the highwayman asked. His predatory smile now expanded into something positively cheerful. "A halfbreed? What you doing outside the Sector this time of night, boys? There's a reward for the likes of him. Trade in escaped slaves, do you? Gots me a Syndicate permit for this road, I do." The smile became a leer. "Show me yours, and I'll show you mine."

Blackthorne said, "Name your price. And we will be on our way."

"You've no pretty little pass to flash me?" the highwayman asked. "You're not Syndicate, boy. That's clear. You going to work this route? Fine. You pays for it. I wants my cut."

Taking up a defensive position in front of Tobias, Blackthorne purposely stepped on Tobias's foot. Tobias stumbled backward with a loud protest.

"Now, now, don't be making a row," the highwayman said. "Will draw the wrong sort of attention, that will."

Blackthorne blinked once before he pulled the trigger. The blast sounded like a cannon after so much quiet. Smoke billowed out of the barrel. The recoil jerked his left hand up and back, numbing his arm to the shoulder. A lightning-flash of fire illuminated the cloud like a small storm. Hot gunpowder particles hit him in the face. He tasted salt, sulfur, and grit as the highwayman collapsed. With a vengeful kick, Blackthorne rolled the gasping thief onto his back. Blood darkened the dirt road in a large, spreading patch while Blackthorne searched the highwayman's pockets. He grabbed a folio of paper notes, the pistol, and a silver snuffbox.

"What are you doing?" Tobias asked.

"If he'd possessed a permit, he wouldn't have cared about the noise," Blackthorne said. "It's unfortunate he didn't. I could have used it." He pointed his second pistol at the dying highwayman's head, but a final shuddering breath spared Blackthorne the shot. "We'll have company soon. Get going. I'll be along in a moment. Follow the road north, and stay to the ruts where the dirt is hardest."

Tobias gazed down at the body and swallowed. "You killed that man."

"Yes," Blackthorne said.

"He's . . . really dead."

"Didn't you hear me? A Warden Unit is sure to have heard that shot. Get out of here."

Clearly shaken, Tobias turned and headed north. The moment he was out of sight, Blackthorne cut the dead man's throat and tossed an assassin's token next to the body. He considered stealing the robber's coat but knew at a glance it'd be too small across the shoulders. He could take it anyway and sell it, but the cloth was as worn as his own. In any case, he'd already wasted too much time. He left the highwayman where he was and caught up to Tobias after a short run. The young smith's face was pale, and his unease was palpable in the silence. Blackthorne knew of nothing useful to say. He'd only done what was necessary. He was certain of it.

He spent the rest of the evening watchful for signs that the Warden Unit hadn't been satisfied with the explanation provided. When dawn revealed a newly mowed field to the right of the road, he headed for an isolated group of haystacks. Selecting the tall-est, they spent the daylight hours sleeping concealed under the hay while the mail coaches roared past. Blackthorne slept to the sound of pounding hooves and blaring horns, dreaming of battlefields and blood.

TWO

Time passed as they travelled north. Nights blended, one into another, in a footsore haze of cold food, hard ground, and white-knuckled vigilance. Freeson's chatty enthusiasm had faded into an anxious quiet after witnessing the highwayman's death. More recently, that reserve was interrupted only by a worrying cough. Thus, Blackthorne was relieved when at last they arrived at the first planned stop.

He tensed against the near-freezing rainwater trickling down his back in the dark and studied the farm house. Lamplight poured through the open front door and cast a welcoming glow on the solitary white pillowcase hanging from a laundry line in the dooryard. An old woman in a rocking chair teetered in and out of the shadows thrown onto the front porch. Dark-streaked white curls escaped her mob cap, framing her pale face. A musket leaned against the wall within easy reach.

He closed his eyes and listened past the hiss of rain slapping mud. A few feet away, Freeson's teeth chattered. A bird high up in the branches shook water off its feathers. A porch plank rhythmically creaked with the weight of the rocking chair. When the unsettling twitch in Blackthorne's stomach had passed he was certain all was as it seemed.

"Come on," he whispered, stepping from the brush just as Tobias let out yet another booming cough.

Mrs. Mandilynn Holton ceased her rocking at once, snatched up the gun, and peered into the darkness.

"It's only me, Mrs. H," Blackthorne said.

"Oh." She lowered the musket and beckoned with one hand.

Elbowing Freeson, Blackthorne gave a sideways nod toward the house. He watched the smith's listless progress across the dooryard and frowned. Obtaining the services of a physician had been out of the question. So, Blackthorne had done what he could during the twenty-day journey to Aurivallis. Unfortunately, his education didn't cover medicines. He hoped a few nights out of the elements would be enough. He didn't want to think about what would happen if Freeson died while in his charge.

Mrs. Holton tugged a wool shawl tighter over her thin shoulders. Then she handed Tobias a blanket from the mending basket at her feet. "Get in front of the fire, you two, before you catch your death." Her kind, strong voice carried no hint of age.

Shivering, Freeson stumbled into the house with a nod of thanks. Blackthorne used a branch to obliterate their tracks in the dooryard, tossing the tree limb aside when he reached the steps. Then he perched on the stoop and removed his muddy boots. The smith's prints on the porch planks might pass for Mrs. Holton's, but his certainly wouldn't.

"Home Guard is in Aurivallis this week. Arrived day before yesterday," she said. "Your timing isn't the best."

Blackthorne froze. "Have they searched your farm yet?"

"Of course they have. Wouldn't have put out the laundry in

this if they hadn't," she said, waving him inside. "You think I'm a fool?"

The scent of grilled onions and rosemary filled the cabin, making Blackthorne's mouth water. Tobias had collapsed into one of the chairs in front of the fire. He sneezed and wiped his nose on a damp sleeve. Blackthorne closed the door and then pulled off his soggy stockings on the rug so as not to track water on the clean floor. Already at the hearth, Mrs. Holton was spooning food into a bowl. She handed it off to Tobias.

"Sergeant Brown is rather fond of my apple tansey." Mrs. Holton turned her attention to a loaf of fresh bread, cutting thick slices. "No leavings this time, I'm sorry to say. But the better fed he is, the less likely he'll give the place a thorough look. So, I don't complain." She balanced a bread slice on the edge of Freeson's bowl. "Says no one with my hand at cooking could possibly harbor runners. They'd never leave."

Freeson shoved the food into his mouth with a contented moan.

"Do come to the fire, Joshua. You've come a long way in the muck, and I'm not expecting any other visitors."

Blackthorne carried his muddy boots and stockings to the blue-tiled hearth and settled onto a stool half-facing the door. She gave him a bowl the moment his hands were free and set a mug of hot tea on the floor next to his bare foot. He breathed in the rising steam from the bowl, savoring the warmth.

In the firelight, Freeson's face appeared flushed. His voice had a nasal quality as he whispered, "Joshua?"

When Blackthorne had first met Mrs. Holton, she'd insisted on giving him a name if he wasn't going to offer one. *Joshua Archer* was as good as any other. She had introduced him to the townsfolk as her nephew. His skin was light enough that it hardly mattered. He assumed the real Joshua Archer was dead—if such a person had ever existed in the first place—and was unable to object. Ignoring Freeson's raised eyebrow, Blackthorne took a bite of savory potato tureen. He couldn't argue against Mrs. Holton's culinary reputation. It was one of the reasons he relished this leg of the journey. After cold travel rations, anything hot would've been marvelous. As matters stood, it required strict control not to bolt his food. He reached for the warm mug.

Mrs. Holton said, "That coat of yours looks like it's ready for the rag men."

"It only needs repair and a wash," Blackthorne said. He burned his mouth on hot tea and winced. "I'd be grateful for the loan of a needle and thread."

"They're yours, as much good as it will do," she said.

"Thank you," Blackthorne said.

Freeson had another of his long coughing fits.

"And I'll brew some coltsfoot tea," Mrs. Holton said. "I'm no healer, but it should soothe that cough." She went to the door and pulled her shawl over her head. "But I'd best bring the laundry in first."

THREE

The hidden room behind the fireplace was all of six feet by ten and windowless. It also smelled faintly of soured barley. The only furniture was a cornhusk-stuffed bed tossed onto the dirt floor. Regardless, the space was dry and, above all, safe. Blackthorne stationed himself next to the narrow door and then began to repair the rent in his filthy greatcoat by the light of a candle. He found sewing frustrating. The mechanics of it seemed simple enough, but it eluded him. He considered it but one of the many necessary skills in which he hadn't been trained. However, the future for which he'd been prepared was different from the one in which he found himself. He was free. He told himself that this was the most important thing to remember. The more he tried to focus on the immediate as his training dictated, the more difficult it became to remain calm.

The fireplace bricks were warm and scratchy against his back while he struggled with his frustration. Still, tension knots in his muscles brought on by weeks of extended vigilance began to loosen. With the immediate danger gone, he found it hard to keep his eyes open. He let them slide closed. *Just for a moment. Do I have to fix the coat now?* But he knew the answer to that question. Although he'd travelled with Freeson for weeks, he didn't trust him. In truth, there were few people that Blackthorne trusted, including himself.

"How long will we stay here?" Freeson asked.

Blackthorne started awake, blinking.

Freeson stood wrapped in three blankets and was holding a clay mug with both hands. His nose was red, and his eyes had narrowed to exhausted slits.

"Two days," Blackthorne said. "Perhaps three. It depends upon how long the Home Guard will remain in the area." He continued sewing until he finished the last stitch, knotted the seam, and bit off the thread. Spitting, he tried to get rid of the taste of filthy wool. "They should move on to the next town soon enough."

Freeson looked relieved. "Oh. Good."

Blackthorne paused to examine his handiwork. The thread was brown, not black, and the stitches sketched an uneven, drunken line, but given the coat's overall state, he didn't think anyone would notice. Joshua wasn't supposed to be prosperous. Therefore, all Blackthorne cared about was that the coat covered his back.

Freeson let out a series of deep, chest-rattling coughs.

"Take the bed," Blackthorne said without looking up. "And try to keep quiet. I don't know how much sound carries outside these walls. It will be good practice. There's no guarantee the guard won't return for an extra inspection. It's happened before."

Downing the last of the coltsfoot, Tobias made a face. Then he stretched in pained movements. This brought on yet another coughing fit, which he covered with a hand. Blackthorne hoped Freeson's illness wouldn't become debilitating. The journey up the slopes of Grandmother Mountain was going to be difficult enough without carrying a delirious sixteen-year-old smith on his back the entire way.

"Blackthorne? What's it like in the Haunted Lands?"

Blackthorne considered his answer. The truth of the matter was that he'd not seen much of Eledore—not since the war. The colony established in Jalokivi had been abandoned by the Regnum—or had vanished, depending upon which story one believed—not long after it'd been conquered. More than likely, like himself, Tobias would never venture much beyond what was considered the borderlands. "It's cold."

"All the time?"

Dredging up memories of the war, Blackthorne just as quickly tamped them down. "In spring and summer, it's warm enough. The winters are hard." The Regnum's retreat had left a trail of broken-down equipment and frozen dead. That much of Eledore's vengeance, he'd witnessed himself.

Tobias shifted, and the cornhusks crackled. "Aurelia said the Acrasian colonies disappeared overnight. No one knows what happened. Is Eledore really haunted?"

"Quite a few el—Eledoreans live rough in the north. The plague didn't kill them all." Although it'd come damned close, from what Blackthorne had seen. In his opinion, Acrasia had disease to thank more than destiny for winning her war with Eledore. Of course, that hadn't stopped the emperor from declaring otherwise. "Spirits weren't to blame. Nor was it a curse. It was probably an attack. The rest is exaggeration."

"How do you know?"

"I've seen what was left behind."

"Oh," Freeson said. "But the priests say the settlement was found abandoned, not burned. And there was no sign of battle."

"There could be any number of reasons for that. Eledorean

domination magic, for one. Why fight when you can simply order your enemy out into a blizzard?"

Freeson looked uneasy. "I thought that was just stories."

He knows he has magic. He's hiding it. But what sort of power does he have? "Domination magic isn't as commonplace among Eledoreans as the Regnum claims. It's rare." At least, that had been Blackthorne's experience. *So far.*

He'd never understood the priests' conflicting logic. Either the Eledoreans were as powerful and evil as they claimed—the defence that the Regnum had used to justify genocide—or the elphs were the weak, less intelligent race deserving of slavery. He didn't believe elphs could be both. Such reasoning stank of self-serving, slippery lies, and Blackthorne had no patience for lies.

Even though you live them?

"Are there malorum in Eledore?" Tobias asked.

"Malorum seem to prefer Acrasian cities."

"That doesn't answer my question."

"It is the answer I have to give. I've not seen malorum in Eledore. But that doesn't mean they aren't there."

"How many people live there?"

"Approximately two hundred or so live in the settlement where I'm taking you," Blackthorne said. *Not including the Ghost and his men.*

"Isn't that enough to attract malorum?"

Blackthorne gathered the last blanket and positioned his pack so he could use it as a pillow. The floor was cold, so he opted to use his greatcoat as a barrier against the chill. "I've never seen malorum north of Kylmapuro River. I don't know why. No one does. Perhaps they don't like the mountains."

"Do you think I'll be able to send for Aurelia?"

Blackthorne paused. He didn't want to lie to Freeson any more than he had to. "Do you want the truth?"

"The truth."

"You can never contact her. And if all goes well, you'll never see Aurelia again."

Freeson sat up, frowning. "Why?"

"She's the daughter of a noble. Think about what that means. Her father wouldn't give up the search until he'd found her. And as a member of House Lucrosa, he has enough money for a thorough search. Lives depend upon our not being found." *A little over two hundred of them, to be exact,* Blackthorne thought.

"I hadn't considered that."

Blackthorne blew out the candle and settled into his makeshift bedding. "Go to sleep."

Listening to the sound of Tobias's phlegm-clogged breathing, Blackthorne stared into the darkness. He was beyond exhausted now, but without the distraction of constant vigilance, he found he didn't want to face the insides of his eyelids. He wiped a hand against the wool blanket with a shudder. If he let himself, he could still feel the release of pressure as the point of his knife had penetrated reluctant skin. Novus Salernum was weeks away, but the words of the malorum who'd worn Esa's face echoed in his head just the same.

Have mercy.

He wasn't sure he knew what that was anymore.

FOUR

Blackthorne spent the next day helping Mrs. Holton with heavy chores. She couldn't afford to hire a regular farmhand. Thus, her neighbors had been made to understand that this was the reason for Joshua's irregular appearances. It worked well enough for them both. It was a hardship on her—his drain upon her resources. So, he did as much of the farm work as he could manage during his stay. He made a point of offering to pay her for the extra blankets and fresh provisions, but she refused as she always did. Ever careful of his increasingly scant resources, he couldn't argue.

The morning sun hadn't cleared the horizon when he started on the list of things she needed done before he left. He didn't mind. It passed the time and kept his thoughts in the present. He was an hour into his chores when she approached with a basket of eggs.

"I need to go to town tomorrow," Mrs. Holton said. "I'm short on a few things. And I want to visit with Ruth—that is, Mrs. Brown. She's been ill. Any chance I could persuade you to go with me?"

Blackthorne jammed the dung fork into the manure pile and tugged down the handkerchief tied over his face and nose. The stench was particularly bad because of the rain. Fertilizing the fields was hard work, made worse by all the water. Chances were, dirt and manure would stick to the plow rather than mix into the soil.

"I'd like the company," she said. "But I know you've more important things to do than chat with an old woman."

He gave the sky a quick glance. There wasn't a single cloud. "I'll go." A break might give the fields time to dry. "I should look into the price of a horse."

She paused. "You've need of one?"

Blackthorne looked to the house where Tobias was convalescing. Although they were alone, he made a point of not directly speaking of his charges outside the cabin. It was safer. "A horse would make the remainder of my journey easier."

"It would at that."

"I must . . . make sure of a few things first." He wanted to check on Tobias. If it looked like his health was taking a turn for the worse, Blackthorne couldn't risk leaving him.

"There's no rush. We can go in the morning."

The fields had their coat of fertilizer by the end of the day. He decided to delay the plowing. He supposed there wasn't any harm in doing so, but then, he wasn't much of a farmer. Tobias, for his part, had spent the day next to the fire, studying and making notes in a stained journal with a borrowed quill. He seemed stronger. Warm food, substantial shelter, sleep, and periodic doses of coltsfoot all seemed to be doing their work. Unfortunately, the cough didn't seem to be dissipating.

Mrs. Holton woke Blackthorne for breakfast after the sun had crested the horizon. Leaving strict instructions for Tobias to remain hidden while they were away, Blackthorne grabbed his things and headed to the barn. Then he drove Mrs. Holton's wagon into the dooryard where she waited. He helped her up onto the wagon's bench. Settling next to her, he took up the reins, and they started on their way. Per usual, she made no attempts at conversation. He appreciated the fact that she didn't pry. It meant he didn't have to lie. Over time, the day grew warm as the sun rose higher in the sky. He shed his greatcoat and rolled up his sleeves. He didn't worry about Mrs. Holton seeing the scars around his wrists. He knew she wouldn't bother with questions he wouldn't answer. He could keep his mind blank.

A balmy wind gusted through the forest with the roar of an ocean. A herd of reindeer bounded across the road. Their dolphin leaps manifested in an unearthly grace. It was simple to focus on breathing, to imagine he was in a place where who he was supposed to be no longer mattered. It was the closest thing to privacy and meditation he'd had since leaving Novus Salernum.

He waited until they were within sight of Aurivallis before shoving down his sleeves and shrugging on his coat. They reached the gates at a quarter past noon and were allowed entrance without the requisite identity paper check. Everyone knew Mrs. Holton. More importantly, everyone knew the deceased Mr. Holton's reputation as a staunch loyalist.

"If it's all right, drop me off at Mrs. Brown's first. Come fetch me once you've seen to your business, and then we'll pick up the supplies together," Mrs. Holton said. "Turn here."

Blackthorne left Mrs. Holton at a prim, whitewashed house with green trim and a bright red door. Returning her wave goodbye, he headed for Aurivallis's only coaching inn, where he paid the stable hand to look after the horse and wagon. He passed under the painted sign depicting a sandaled foot stamping upon a snake and through the door of the Crushed Serpent. He was welcomed by a fog of stale pipe smoke and deafening cacophony of local gossip and laughter. Braving the din, he tensed until his sensitive ears adjusted. With that, he located an unoccupied table. A large serving maid arrived for his order. She left, revealing the two men who'd been waiting behind her.

"Why, hullo, Joshua. How's the auntie?"

"Payton. Austen." Blackthorne nodded in a cautious greeting and kept a frown from forming on his face.

The pair seated themselves opposite without being invited to do so. The smaller of the two, Payton, was blond, balding, and unshaved. His eyes squeezed into triangles of mirthless glee. The bigger man, Austen, was darker and dwarfed the first. A crooked scar traced a crooked line across his crooked nose. His sullen, rough face was so standard to his profession that Blackthorne found himself wondering whether the scar was the result of his vocation or the vocation had been the result of the scar. Of course, since Blackthorne didn't think he'd ever heard Austen speak, he wasn't sure Austen had the capacity to provide an answer even if he did ask.

"Don't suppose you got the money you owe?" Payton asked, scratching his cheek. "Austen here has been concerned ever since you up and vanished like you did. I reassured him. Him being prone to worry and all. I told him you're a family man, you are. Wouldn't want nothing happening to your auntie. Her being all alone."

"You overcharged me," Blackthorne said.

"Then do your buying from someone else," Payton said, and then leaned forward. "Only, someone else is likely to ask why a carter from Greenleaf is in need of that much barley on the sly, now, won't they?"

One day soon, Payton, I'm going to have to silence you, Blackthorne thought. *At this point, I may even enjoy it.* He paused for an instant before reaching into the pocket of his greatcoat. Producing the silver snuffbox he'd taken from the highwayman, he set the little box on the table's surface with a resigned thump. He had hoped to trade it when he got home—perhaps even acquire a new greatcoat in the bargain.

The snuffbox had rested on the table's scarred surface only an instant before Payton snatched it up and examined it. There was a greasy gleam in his eye. "Fine work, that. Won't ask where you acquired such a thing. That would be impolite." By his expression and tone, it was clear Payton was asking nonetheless.

"I won it in a card game," Blackthorne said.

"That's real silver by the mark, or I'm a duchess." Payton made a *harrumph* sound. "I'm supposed to believe the likes of you plays at cards with swells?"

"Your beliefs aren't any of my concern," Blackthorne said. "Is the debt settled?"

"Sure." Pocketing the treasure, Payton then shrugged. "For now."

The serving maid set a full mug and a plate of sausage and onions on the table. She took Blackthorne's offered paper note and vanished into the crowd again.

"Do you require something else?" Blackthorne loaded his fork and bit into a sausage. The gaminess of the meat wasn't even thinly disguised by the over-salted gravy.

"Home Guard is real keen on finding a rabbit for the Brotherhood," Payton said, snatching the bread from the edge of Blackthorne's plate.

"Viviforam or elpharmaceutria?" Blackthorne asked between mouthfuls.

Ever concerned with bloodlines, ancestry, and racial purity, Acrasians had a myriad of terms for nonhumans, slang that classified them by place of origin, purity, skin color, profession, and religion. "Viviforam" had its roots in the old tongue and meant "hole-dweller." He understood it was due to the mistaken impression that kainen with darker skin lived in caves. "Elpharmaceutria" implied "sorcerer." None of the expressions were complimentary.

"Do you think they'd be turning up the countryside looking for a brownie?" Payton snorted breadcrumbs. "Like a brownie can hide the color of its skin. No, this one's elph."

Blackthorne suppressed a twitch. "And what makes you think I'd know anything?"

"You're a carter. You travel." Payton sat back and shrugged. "Was wondering if you'd heard or seen anything odd. You know, on the road, like."

Blackthorne didn't answer. He didn't like the direction the conversation was headed.

"This elph is carrying a load of books."

Blackthorne swallowed the mouthful of onions before he choked on them.

Payton didn't seem to notice. "Stole them right out of his owner's library. The reward is big enough for a gens membership," Payton said. "Reward is for the books, mind you. Lucrosa don't much care about the runner, long as he gets dead. But Austen here figures on having some fun. So, a live rabbit is best for us, if you get my meaning."

"What kind of books?"

"I don't know. Austen says it's not listed in the notice," Payton said.

Blackthorne often found it perplexing that the uncommunicative Austen was the more literate of the pair.

"Just says 'books.' Must be important. They're old, I'm thinking. The sort with pictures."

"Then, I'm certain you won't need my help in locating them," Blackthorne said.

Payton placed a hand on Blackthorne's right arm. "You owes us. You find that elph, we get half."

Blackthorne stared at Payton's filthy hand until it was removed. "Am I incorrect in assuming you were just paid?"

"Awww." Payton gave him a nasty smile. "Gone all fancy in your talk." He turned to Austen. "Always does when he's put off. Don't he? Has ambitions of his own, I'm thinking."

Austen nodded in silent agreement.

Payton lowered his voice until it could just be heard above the crowd. However, the menace in his words came through with no trouble at all. "You don't look fine enough to be brewing beer legal, my friend. Hells, you don't look fine enough to be brewing it illegal. No matter. You know the rules. You scratch my back, and Austen don't knife yours." He got up from the table. Austen followed.

Too bad I can't take the time to deal with you now, Blackthorne thought as he watched them leave. Waiting until he was certain they were gone, he finished eating and gave his resources some consideration. If the stableman was in a generous mood, he might stretch his dwindling funds to cover two horses instead of one. He didn't think one horse would bear the weight of two. *Not up a mountain. Not quickly.*

FIVE

"You stole books from a Lucrosa's library?" Blackthorne asked. He kept his voice quiet. *Controlled.* But the chill of rage crept in nonetheless. "What was I thinking? Of course you did."

With no more space in which to retreat in the tiny hidden room, Tobias bumped into the fireplace bricks. "I didn't think—"

"Your Lucrosa told me you were a freeman. *You* told me you were a freeman."

The red in Tobias's cheeks went darker yet. "I'm a bonded apprentice. I was—I was to be free in a week!"

"You couldn't have waited the week?"

"He was going to burn them!"

"Who?"

"Watson and Simons!" Tobias seized one of the books scattered on the pallet bed. "Don't you understand? This is David Watson's notes on metallurgic tolerances, trajectory, and the effects of barrel length. There are only ten copies in existence! And this! This is Walton Simons's theories on corning gunpowder and moisture-proofing!"

Blackthorne shoved hair out of his eyes one-handed. He needed time to think. Time to plan. But the weather was turning, the Home Guard were on alert, and Tobias was still ill. Blackthorne had to act before the situation got any worse. "We're leaving here as soon as it's dark."

Tobias nodded. He dove for his pack and placed the tomes with care on the bottom, cramming spare clothing on top. Blackthorne stooped to get through the short sliding panel and rammed the top of his head into the doorsill. The explosion of pain made it very difficult not to put a fist through a wall.

Mrs. Holton paused in front of the fireplace, an iron pot lid in her hand. Whatever it was she was cooking smelled fantastic. "Is something wrong?"

Get control of yourself, Blackthorne thought. "We must leave tonight."

Mrs. Holton resumed stirring. "All right. Then you'll take my wagon."

"I can't—"

"The pair of you aren't going to get far on that nag you bought. Mrs. Brown said the Home Guard is camping along Jackson's Creek. It's the only area with good cover between here and Greenleaf." She replaced the lid.

He fought to keep surprise from his face. It was doing enough to his stomach.

"Don't fret yourself. You didn't let it slip. Still, it isn't difficult to puzzle out where you're headed. Wyeth isn't an option. The Eastern Sea is too rough this time of year. We both know there'll be no Waterborne ships until spring. No, if it was sea passage you were looking for, Archiron would've been your best bet. But you've gone two weeks out of your way. The mountains are the only option, and the closest bridge over the Kylmapuro is at Greenleaf. Of course, you could be up for a swim, but that boy isn't." She settled into a chair, resuming her knitting. The bone needles in her hands clicked. "Trouble is, if I can suss things out, Sergeant Brown can too—that is, if he's been told the boy will pass through here. And I have to assume he has, since he's focused on Jackson's Creek."

"We can't stay," Blackthorne said. "The weather—"

"It's going to turn. I know. The pain in my hip is telling me, right enough. But Toby won't make it—not on his feet, he won't. And you know it. That cold of his will run to lung fever before long. You don't have to be a healer to see that. It's a miracle you made it this far without that."

Blackthorne stared at the now-open hidden door. His shoulders dropped with the weight of the problems he faced.

"How do you think I came by that little room?" she asked, not looking up from her knitting.

The abrupt subject change threw him. "I—I'm sure I don't know." His stomach executed another flip. *What am I going to do now? If they find us here, I won't be the only one they'll hang, draw, and quarter. She'll be right next to me.* Suddenly, he wished he'd decided to risk the journey north rather than stay at the farm.

"My husband, Lee, was a loyalist through and through—except when it came to his drink," Mrs. Holton said. "He smuggled Eledorean whiskey. There's a secret compartment in that wagon big enough for three hogsheads. It'll be a squeeze for the boy, but you can hide Toby inside. Take the road. It'll be faster. Safer. But not without that wagon. We both know it."

"It isn't likely I'll be back until spring. Maybe later."

"That's fine by me. I won't have need of a wagon until then, and if I do, I can always ask one of the others for help. It's what neighbors are for. Anyway, why do you think I laid in so many supplies?

That nag of yours will suit me fine. And don't you worry about Payton, neither. My Lee did business with him during the war. Thick as thieves, they were. And I've known Payton since he was in clouts. I can handle him. I've no qualms against using a dung fork on him until he gets some sense. Worse comes to worst, I'm a damned fine shot."

Someone pounded on the front door. Blackthorne pressed the second blue tile on the hearth, shutting off the hidden room and Tobias's frightened face. The knock sounded again. He picked up Mrs. Holton's knitting and pushed it into her hands, waited for her to resume her knitting, and then answered the door. A paunchy man with two days' beard growth and a grey-dyed handkerchief tied around his right arm stood on the porch. Three others, each sporting a grey handkerchief, waited in the dooryard, holding their horses by the reins.

Home Guard. Four of them, Blackthorne thought. *Why didn't I hear them approach?*

"Who the hell are you?" the first Home Guardsman asked.

"Joshua Archer. Who the hell are you?"

The Home Guardsman squinted at Blackthorne for a moment before he stepped up with his chest out. He had terrible breath. Blackthorne judged the man had at least ten years on him and possibly another seventy-five pounds. "And what are you doing in Mrs. Holton's house, Joshua Archer?"

Blackthorne stood his ground. "Visiting my aunt."

"Don't recall Mrs. Holton's got a nephew."

"Quinton Halsey, is that you?" Mrs. Holton called from the hearth. "Joshua, quit bowing up like a young rooster in front of the henhouse. I got no time for that foolishness."

Stepping back, Blackthorne allowed Mr. Halsey through the door. The older man snatched off his tricorne and gave Mrs.

Holton the sheepish expression of a schoolboy. Fuzzy brown hair retained the shape of the hat's interior.

"Sorry, Mrs. H., but Sergeant Brown says we're to search your barn."

"Didn't you just do that four days ago?" she asked.

"We're to look for an elph," Quinton said. "Might be dangerous."

"Nonsense. Even if such a creature would be stupid enough to set foot on my property, I'm a dead shot and you know it," Mrs. Holton said.

"What if he uses magic on you?" Quinton asked. "What would my mum say, I go and let that happen?"

Mrs. Holton sighed. "Make yourself happy, then. You will anyway. Don't you disturb Bess, though. You know how upset she gets. There'll be no milking her until tomorrow afternoon if you're not careful."

"Yes, missus," Quinton said and tugged a lock of greasy hair on his forehead before fleeing.

While Quinton and the Home Guard descended upon the barn like bloodhounds after a fox, Blackthorne watched through the window. The muscles in his back tightened. *Damn, damn, damn. Why did Slate give me this assignment? Why didn't he simply put a musket ball in my skull? It would've been less dangerous for everyone else.* He took a deep breath, held it, and then released it. *This isn't about you.*

Mrs. Holton whispered, "Damn it."

"It isn't dark yet," Blackthorne said. His voice held a disinterested quality he didn't feel, but there was no point in worrying about things over which he had no control.

Mrs. Holton moved to the windows and pulled the curtains. He returned to the fireplace and stared into the flames, willing himself calm with a rigid jaw. Mrs. Holton slipped a bowl of stew through the darkness of the hidden door before settling onto one of the chairs at the hearth. When supper was done, she gathered the dishes. Blackthorne went out to the well in the dooryard for a bucket of water. The noises from the barn indicated that the Home Guard was being thorough—far more thorough than he liked. He wondered how long it would take before they decided to take the same care with the house. When he returned with the water, Mrs. Holton was in her bedroom, rummaging for something, by the sound. He set the bucket by the fire and started on the dishes. It gave him something constructive to do.

"You didn't have to wash up," Mrs. Holton said.

Toweling the last plate dry, he set the clean dish on the sideboard and shrugged.

"I'm—I'm going to give you something, and I want you to take it," she said.

Turning, he saw she held up a black greatcoat. The wool was thick and new, but the cut was familiar. Blackthorne swallowed shock.

She whispered, "I cut the gold braid off and dyed it. Emery never lived to wear it. No one will know it used to be blue. Eledorean blue."

An Eledorean officer's long coat, Blackthorne thought.

"He was promoted just before—before . . . He was . . . Emery was at Virens," she said. Her sharp eyes were shiny.

Virens. The image of a muddy battlefield filled Blackthorne's mind. Thousands of crows. Their calls mixed with the agonized cries of the wounded. The stench of death. Sulfur from powder smoke. Prisoners shot with musket balls they'd bought themselves with coins or trinkets that would only have been stolen later. Of the group whose executions he first witnessed, only one prisoner had braved the bayonet. It had been enough to convince the others that a bullet was the better choice. The duke had pulled him from his studies at the Academy in order to serve on the front lines. The duke had insisted he—

"Is something the matter?" she asked. "You look like you've seen a ghost."

Blackthorne blinked and swallowed again. *Perhaps most in Aurivallis wouldn't know that coat. But others would, regardless of the dye.* "It is a gracious offer and deeply appreciated, but I cannot accept it."

"I know you're proud. I got my own pride. But this isn't meant as charity. Consider it payment."

"I'm deeply honored you think me worthy of such a gift."

She frowned. "You know as well as I do this wouldn't be the first time one of these has seen use after a bit of dye." She gave him closer scrutiny, then tears welled up in her eyes.

He didn't speak. He didn't trust himself. She sighed and then turned on her heel. The quiet sniff before she shut her bedroom door was like a dagger in his chest. He almost reconsidered but knew he'd be killed if the coat was found in his possession.

And if I weren't a coward, that wouldn't matter. Blackthorne stared at the shelf on the sideboard. A tiny masculine face in a scorched miniature stared back. The serious expression was topped with a shock of black hair. Before thinking, he snatched it up and flipped it to see what was on the back. The lettering was singed but legible.

Dearest Mother,

Father won't allow my likeness in the house, I know. But I thought you could keep this in the garden to frighten badgers. Ginger always did say I had a face that could stop a clock.

Your loving son,

Joshua Emery Holton

Blackthorne read the name with a start, then returned the

picture to the shelf before Mrs. Holton could discover his intrusion. *Joshua*, he thought. *You stupid bastard.* He didn't know who he meant it for—the young man in the picture, or himself.

The last of the daylight gave out. The Home Guard finished with the barn but seemed to have decided to camp in the dooryard. Quinton Halsey hadn't swayed in his determination to inspect every inch of Mrs. Holton's farm. Blackthorne didn't dare look out the curtain, but he passed in front of the windows anyway in the hopes of hearing signs of their leaving.

"Hard to be too angry," Mrs. Holton said from her spot in front of the fire. "The damned fool thinks he's protecting me."

"We can always depart tomorrow."

"Then perhaps you should stop pacing like a caged wolf and get some rest," she said. "I'll wake you once they've gone."

⚔ DYLAN ⚔

ONE

20 AUGUST, 1783

Thunder punched the air. Flashes of lightning stitched crooked seams into billowing black clouds. Dylan Kask staggered out onto the quarterdeck just as an eighteen-foot wall of water crashed into the side of *Coral Star*, scouring her boards. Unsecured fishing traps washed over the side, and the deck violently tilted forty-five degrees. Unfortunately, he hadn't yet fixed himself to the lifeline. So, he scrabbled for a handhold before he went the way of the vanished traps. Cold seawater finished the drenching the rain had begun. Lost in the chaos of water and wind, his grip slipped. He slammed into the platform ladder. Pain exploded in his shoulder, arm, and back. He opened his mouth to scream and swallowed seawater. The ocean pulled at his body as if hungry to devour him. He fought for purchase on the ladder rail, finally anchoring himself with both hands. He hugged it with all his might. At last, the wave moved on. The ship righted herself, and he was dropped onto the boards with stinging eyes and nasal passages. Coughing and spitting, he fought to acquire his balance on chilled bare feet. Shoulder-length spirit knots hung in clumps in his face. The clatter of the prayer tokens sewed into his braids was lost in the screaming wind. With his free hand, he searched his belt for the heavy metal clasp used to hook onto the lifeline.

It wasn't this bad when I went to my hammock, Dylan thought. *What happened?*

The weather had been unseasonably calm over the summer months. That had meant a prosperous fishing and trade season for Clan Kask. However, August marked the start of storm season. Now was the time when Aegrir, for whom that eastern ocean was named, demanded her due.

We wouldn't be here, but for the Acrasians, drown them. He felt a little guilty for that sentiment, given the news.

The Waterborne Nations avoided open hostility as a matter of policy. For Clan Kask, that friendly facade had lasted until the Emperor of Acrasia had discovered Clan Kask's support of the deposed Eledorean queen. Thus, *Coral Star* had found herself the target of a vengeful Acrasian fleet. Captain Brian Magaodh had gambled on turning into a squall to lose their tail, and Dylan Kask, serving as weathermaster for this venture, had exhausted himself getting them safely away.

But this was no squall. *It's a typhoon.*

I won't let us sink, Dylan thought. *Not as long as I have any power left. Coral Star* was Kask, and Clan Kask was his family. *I can't let Dar die. I won't.*

A loud, splintering crack ripped the air. Broken oak pounded the deck beneath his feet with a force he could feel in his teeth. Someone screamed. Another wave pounded the boards—this time from a less dangerous angle. The crew waded in water up to the knee until it passed.

Captain Magaodh shouted, "Drop the lightning rod chains! And reef the mainsail! Clear that deck! And get that broken hatch secure! Now! Drown you! Now!"

First, the message, Dylan thought. *Nothing I do will make a difference, if I don't get the message to Dar or Captain Magaodh.*

Sailors rushed to comply with Captain Magaodh's orders. Dylan squinted against wind and rain, searching among them for the one face he'd risked the storm and his weakened state to find. One of Dar's message birds had announced its arrival with a crash against the cabin's window glass. Dar, whose main responsibility was ship's messenger, hadn't been present to receive the bird, since there were no idlers during bad weather with the exception of the weathermaster. Dylan had saved the poor creature before the storm had claimed it. However, the bird had returned the favor by depositing a great deal of water into the cabin in the process.

Rain lashed Dylan's face, blinding him yet again. He felt someone grab his arm and then a tug at his waist as a tether was anchored to his belt. Dylan flipped long wet braids out of his eyes. That was when he spied Dar's lighter brown face. His hair, with its short tufts, made him easy to recognize even under these conditions. Dar was the only practicing Leaudancer onboard above the age of twelve with such short spirit knots.

He'll never grow them past his ears, will he? Dylan thought with a warm inward smile. *My Dar will be forever doing penance.*

Dar glared, his spiked hair emphasizing his displeasure. "What in all the gods' names are you doing up here?! And without a life-line?! You know better than to—"

Dylan shouted against the wind. "You have a visitor!"

Dar paused. "In this?"

"Whitewing. She's half drowned, but she made it, all right."

"Must reward her," Dar said. "Did the message scroll make it?"

"It did."

"I assume it's urgent."

"Captain Argall says *Emperor's Crown* foundered. We can finally get out of this swiving storm!"

"Thank the gods and goddesses and all the seas! Get any rest?"

"Some."

"Enough?"

Dylan knew what Dar was asking. This was no time for the truth. "Enough."

"I know you. That means no. Get yourself safe below," Dar said, resolve lending a hardness to his expression. "*Coral Star* can weather this. It isn't as bad as it seems."

In truth, they had weathered worse, but only because Magaodh had been lucky. Dylan didn't think Aegrir was with them this day. He swallowed Dar's lie and then gave him a kiss. They both knew the odds. Dylan could feel it in the intensity of his lover's lips. He tried not to make it too obvious a goodbye. "Be careful!"

"You too," Dar said.

"I love you."

"And I love you. Now go!"

Once Dar had gone, Dylan prepared himself to begin his ritual. His feet were already bare, and he was tethered. He found an out-of-the-way place next to the ladder and put his back against a wall. He didn't want to interfere with the work of the crew. With that done, he stretched his arms wide, took in a deep breath, and began.

The first law of magic is thus: energy does not vanish. It transforms.
All are born of water. All shall return to water.

Using the sea washing across the ship's boards, he extended his consciousness across *Coral Star*'s wooden surface and around her spotless hull. This close, he could sense the woodmaster at her work as she battled the sea to keep the ship sound. Her workings involved both hardness and flexibility. Beneath her hands, *Coral Star* was a living entity bound and knit together without nails. They exchanged a quick, wordless blessing, and then he left her to her duty. Feeling his way, he invoked the tension between seawater and hull to anchor his body to the deck through his feet and back. With that done, he let his awareness rise above the ship. He passed through dense clouds as he floated and sensed various air densities. It got colder the higher he got—not that he could've said why or how he felt this. His body remained on the ship. He shouldn't have felt anything at all, yet he did. It wasn't consistent, these senses. For example, wind had no effect on him, which was a good thing, considering.

He moved upward through banks of swiftly moving fog until he reached a place where the storm was divided into two parts— the broadest part, stretching out for miles above him in a dense spiral. He felt his heart drop into his stomach. From his new perspective, he understood the typhoon was too big for him to control. The best he could do was to shift the worst of the storm's force away from *Coral Star*. Those energies would transfer to another part of the typhoon, forming larger, more dangerous waves and winds.

Using a distant part of himself, he lowered his arms, widened his stance and pushed his palms out in front of himself with focused grace. Then he tucked in his elbows, bumping them against the ship. He barely registered the pain.

The second law of magic is thus: the tide which goes out shall return, bringing with it all energy collected in its wake. That was why it was important to keep one's intent pure. One could choose to ignore the second law, but too much carelessness exacted a high price—one that could be unpredictable. Ultimately, he hoped any nearby ships would have the wherewithal to save themselves. Such phrasing didn't guarantee to eliminate negative effects. He was only a mortal being, after all, and some forces were far more powerful than the will of one Waterborne weathermaster, but it was best to make allowances in one's working nonetheless.

May the Mother of All Waters bless the souls circled in her holy embrace this night. For all are worthy. I, Dylan Kask, beseech the Great Lady Aegrir for her favor. I make this request for Coral Star *and her crew. I weave the winds and dance the seas with the intent of the best outcome for those touched by my will.*

With that, he shoved his arms forward and used all the magical energy he had to wedge the heaviest winds away from the ship.

He'd once tried to explain what it was like to weatherwork to his friend, Suvi. He'd told her it was like walking the main royal yard without a tether while carving. During a storm, it was even more intense. His consciousness drifted up and up until the ship seemed like a lost toy. Clouds gathered around him. The wind swirled west-southwest. He'd created a hole in its current like dropping a stone in a fast-running stream. He formed the space around the ship and then extended it into the surrounding water. He flattened the area across the ocean and stretched it bigger and bigger until the violent waves near *Coral Star* began to dissipate. He steered a helpful wind into the reefed sails to pilot the ship from danger. *Coral Star* seemed to jump at the chance. She moved with nimble grace northward and away from the worst of the storm. To Dylan, it took no time at all, and he was ready to return to his body when an unexpected shape caught his attention. A kainen shape.

Aegrir.

The goddess threw her head back, laughing as she danced among the winds—whirling counterclockwise. Her black hair was cast all around her dark head. Her bare brown arms were likewise flung wide to the storm. She was one with the clouds and yet not. Her gown matched the color of her surroundings and faded from dark to light and back again in patterns Dylan recognized from his mother's paintings. Flashes of lightning glittered all around her like white-hot silver. Majestic, Aegrir was all at once young and old. She portrayed a sensual beauty and power in her joyfulness that no mortal could've matched.

Not even my Dar can dance like that.

Dylan had sensed her presence before. As a Waterborne and a practicing Leaudancer, it couldn't be avoided. He lived on Aegrir's waters, after all. She embodied crest and trough, expanding and contracting tides. She was both the world's blood and the world's heartbeat. However, he'd always visualized her as an abstract concept—the spirit of the ocean, not an actual entity. To see her was a shock. Transfixed, he couldn't bring himself to turn away. He drifted closer. Mid-whirl, she paused, and turned her attention to him. All at once, he felt caught like an insect on a pin. Her black gaze was brimmed with a presence so vast that he fought an urge to flinch. Terror spurred his faraway heart to beat faster.

What do you want, little one?

Her voice was huge in his mind. Stunned, it took him a moment to form a response. He knew he couldn't show her his terror. She would dismiss him, and he had need of her good will, more so now than ever before. *Great Lady, I am here to protect my family and my home.*

Aegrir cast her gaze down at the ocean surface. *Why would you venture into my storm? Surely, my children would know better.*

He didn't want to argue. He had a feeling it wouldn't go well. *We did so to avoid an enemy who wished to drown us. We had no desire to do the same to them.*

Ah. The landwalkers. I sensed their deaths. They should've had more care.

Dylan didn't move. To agree would give the impression that he wished the Acrasians ill. To disagree might mean that he disapproved. He could afford neither.

She floated closer, and as she did, he became acutely aware of his insignificance. Again, he controlled his fear. He didn't wish to risk Dar's safety. *I can't. I won't*, he thought.

You are brave.

He stayed silent.

Your spirit-name, it is Lord of the Sea.

It is.

She smiled. *That is brash.*

He swallowed and held her gaze.

I like you, little lordling. Perhaps you will stay with me for a time.

Shock sent yet another chill through him. He executed a respectful bow. *Great Lady, I regret that I am not free to do so.*

You are bound to another?

I am, and I wish to return to him.

I see. She smiled again. *I forgot your kind are concerned with appearances. If this were my form, would this still be your answer?* She transformed into a handsome Waterborne male with hip-length spirit-knotted hair, dark eyes, and a sexy grin. His smooth bare skin was a healthy dark brown. His muscles were firm and strong, and in an instant, Dylan knew what it would be like to slide his hand down that perfect thigh—to feel those teeth sink into his shoulder.

Dar. Remember Dar.

This man was bigger, more perfect, even more attractive than Dar. Dylan found himself staring. The urge to touch the stranger sent a shiver through his entire being. *Stop it. Think of Dar.* In truth, it was the first time in all the years he'd been with Dar that he'd been tempted to this extreme—even when he'd lived as an exile. *I made a vow.*

It wasn't until he began to sense an intense cold that he understood his danger. He was losing contact with his body. *It's late. Please forgive me, but I must return now.*

The stranger pouted, and Dylan found it very difficult to turn away.

You are very loyal.

Dylan said, *I'm in love, Great One.*

Loyalty and love, these are worthy things. She transformed into her previous shape and returned her gaze to the lower half of the storm. *This working you have wrought. It is . . . weighty. It will be expensive.*

I am aware. I will make a suitable offering, Great Lady. I will not forget.

She smiled again. *I know you will, little lord. You are and always have been a wise and respectful child. This, too, pleases me. Return to your family.* She made to go back to her dance, but before entirely withdrawing, she spoke over her shoulder. *One last thing, Little Lord of the Sea.*

Yes?

I claim you, Dylan Ardan Kask son of Judoc Kask, Sealord of Clan Kask. You are mine. And with that, she reached toward him and placed a finger in the middle of his forehead. *Bear my mark as well as my blessing.*

An astounding shock ran through him and then the sensation of a sickening fall from a great height into unconsciousness. He awoke with Dar stooping over him. The deck was hard and dry under Dylan's back. Steam rose from the boards, and rain poured into his face.

"Don't you leave me, drown you! You can't do this!" Dar's handsome face was marred with panic. "Don't you dare! You promised!"

Too stupefied to do much of anything, Dylan forced two words past his lips. They came out in a jagged whisper. "Not gone." He was smothered in a hug at once.

"What did you think you were doing?" Dar asked.

"My duty?"

"You scared me!"

Dylan carefully glanced around him. A headache the size of an Acrasian dreadnought was building up behind his eyes. Movement made it worse. "Is the word given?"

Once more, Dar hugged him tight. "It's given, drown you. It's given."

"Good," Dylan said. "I think I'd like to sleep now." His teeth began to clatter together. It didn't do his headache any favors.

"Let's get you below, then," Dar said. Turning, he shouted over his shoulder, "Get Jade! Tell her to meet us in our cabin!"

Dylan breathed in the scent of Dar and smiled. *I'm home.* The thought was accompanied by a sense of guilt. *I refused the offer. I came back. I kept my word.* Still, he'd been more sorely tempted than he'd been in his life. The idea shook him. He'd never even thought such a thing was possible. *I can never tell Dar, can I? It would hurt him.*

Dylan felt himself lifted from the deck and set on his feet. Dar positioned himself under his shoulder to provide support. Together, they staggered belowdecks and through the common area until they reached their cabin. Dylan could feel bruises swelling on his shoulder, legs, and back. Pain shot up his left leg and ran the length of his spine. He winced and shifted his weight.

"There's not much farther to go," Dar said. "Can you make it? Or do we need to stop?"

"Let's get this over with," Dylan said, gritting his teeth.

Dar slid open the pocket door to their narrow cabin with one hand—larger accommodations were reserved for crewmembers with children. The door trundled into the wall with a loud thud. Dylan lurched inside with Dar's help. The door slid shut. Dylan took small pride in noting that the ship's movements were less drunken than before. His bare feet crossed the rug with a squish, and damp wool prickled under the sole of his right foot. He'd forgotten to clean up the water puddle. Dar wasn't going to be happy about what that'd done to his mother's rug, but Dylan supposed they had more important things to worry about. Closing his eyes, Dylan let Dar help him undress and change into a dry nightshirt.

All the cabins on this level were temporary shelters, but some were more temporary than others, particularly during a battle. Since theirs was one of the cabins positioned at the end of the row, it had a door and one solid cabin wall—not counting the side of the ship. The wall shared with the next cabin was a divider made of heavy canvas. It flapped and swayed with *Coral Star's* movement. The action seemed to fan the sharp ammonia stench of bird.

Wooden cages, six of them occupied, were stacked and secured against the ship's side under the window. The occupants protested the unsteadiness of their surroundings. It didn't matter how much Dar cleaned, Dylan could smell bird shit. It was the one downside to bunking with Dar.

It could be worse, Dylan thought. *We could be bunking with the guns. We have our privacy at least.*

There came a knock on their cabin door.

Dar asked, "Who is it?"

"It's Jade. May I come in?" The ship surgeon's graceful Tahmerian accent held an edge of tension.

"Yes," Dar said. He then grabbed a blanket, folded it on top of a trunk, and then returned his attention to Dylan. "Sit."

Dylan sat. "Dar, give me your knife."

"Later," Dar said.

"I need it. Now," Dylan said.

"Why?" Dar asked.

Rain pelted window glass. Lightning brightened the cabin's interior. Thunder, less immediate, rattled the window.

Jade Kalyani entered, balancing a cup in one hand and carrying a leather bag in the other. She was a compact and middle-aged woman with tan skin. Her face was tattooed with small, precise circles—two above her eyebrows, one close to each ear. The backs of her hands were also marked. Each circle contained a tiny dot-pattern inked in reds, blues, and greens. Dylan understood that the marks were related to her medical practice. The top of her head barely reached Dar's shoulder. Not a Leaudancer, her grey-streaked hair was bound into one thick braid that fell down the length of her back. She was dressed in baggy brown breeches, a white linen shirt, and a painted silk waistcoat of purple, red, and blue. Her hair was wet. She smelled of medicine and the ocean.

"Please, Dar," Dylan said. "The knife."

"You can't even stand," Dar said. "What makes you think handling a knife is going to be a good idea?"

"I need to take care of something. It's important," Dylan said.

Dar sighed. "Fine." He handed over his knife.

With weak and trembling hands, Dylan reached under his hair and cut two of the braids there. Each represented a connection with an ancestor forged over more than a decade. It would cost him an equal number of years' meditation and sacrifice to regrow, but the price was well worth the survival of *Coral Star* and all aboard her.

"Oh," Dar said as understanding dawned on his face.

Laying the shorn braids on top of the trunk next to him, Dylan planned to dispose of them properly after Jade left.

"How are you feeling?" Jade asked.

"Like I was hit with a wine barrel," Dylan said. "A full one. Lashed to two other wine barrels packed with lead. What time is it?"

She placed the cup and saucer on Dar's trunk. "Three bells. Middle watch."

No wonder it was so dark. He blinked. It had been morning when he'd gone to bed. "You let me sleep that long?"

Dar answered with a frown on his full lips. "If I hadn't, you'd be dead right now. As it is, you very nearly killed yourself. Again."

"You're not going to persist in arguing about this, are you?" Dylan asked.

"All right," Dar said. "All right."

Jade reached into her bag and began mixing ingredients, which she poured into the dish with expert motions. "Drink," she said, handing him the weighted stoneware cup.

"What is it?" Dylan asked.

"You've weakened yourself. We can't have you getting sick, can we?" she asked.

Dylan drank, winced, and almost spit it back into the cup. "That tastes terrible."

She took the dish from him. "Don't be a baby. Darius says you took a fall. You're in pain?"

He nodded.

"Let me see."

Pulling up his nightshirt, he turned his back and displayed his injuries.

She whistled. "It's a good thing you didn't land on your head." She poked and prodded his back. "Your leg hurts?"

"Yes. Left one. I didn't break it. At least, I don't think I did."

Placing a warm hand on his bare back, she said, "Breathe deep for me. Slowly."

He followed her instructions as best he could in spite of the hurt. She said nothing for a few moments. He felt a gradual, tingling warmth radiate from her palm. Knotted muscles, tense with pain, began to relax under her touch. Eventually, it spread down his spine and through his whole body. He breathed out in relief.

Finally, she replied, "You wrenched muscles in your back. Maybe something is pinched. It's difficult to be precise in this weather. Nothing is broken." She sat, returning her attention to her bag. She lined up a row of bottles and jars and mixed a new concoction. Once the necessary ingredients were inside the cup, she paused, placed her right hand over the brim, concentrated, and then whispered a blessing in Tahmerian. Tracing a holy symbol in the air above the mixture with a finger, she then poured hot water into the cup. She stirred its contents and then handed the finished product to him. "Drink this, too. For the pain. I didn't remove the hurt. I can't right now, but I blunted it. Unfortunately, that won't last long."

This time, he downed the medicine all at once. Its bitterness gave him a shudder, which sent a flash of agony through his spine. He blinked back tears. After three breaths, the ache faded until it became more tolerable.

Packing her things, she said, "I'm afraid that's the best I can do for now. How do you feel?"

"Better," Dylan said.

"Think you can sleep?" she asked.

"Yes. Thank you very much." He got to his feet.

Dar waved him toward the hammock they shared. "I'll pay. Sleep. Now."

"All right." Dylan carefully did as he was told. His aches and pains seemed to drift away. The need to sleep grew even more powerful.

Retrieving a smooth black stone from inside his own trunk, Dar then closed the lid. Jade, like any other member of the crew, was paid a wage for her services. However, Leaudancers were required to give of a gift in exchange for magic done on their behalf. It didn't have to be valuable, only meaningful. "Please accept this small stone. It's jet. It came from a beach in Eledore." In fact, Dylan had given it to Dar as a love token. "Keep it with you for protection."

Jade accepted the stone and then placed it in her waistcoat pocket. "Thank you." She turned and left.

Dylan prepared himself to be jostled as Dar joined him. He closed his eyes.

"I'm going topside," Dar said. "I'll check on you later."

Dylan felt Dar plant a kiss on his cheek and tuck the blankets in tight. "Sleep well, my love."

And with that, Dylan was lost to his dreams.

TWO

"You don't want that tile," Dar said, frowning down at the game board.

"Why not?" Dylan asked.

"You already flipped it. Remember?"

"Oh."

The third bell on the dogwatch had sounded, and they were playing a game of vuelta before going to bed. It was a child's game, but Dar enjoyed it, and Dylan was in the mood to indulge Dar.

A whale oil lamp gave off a not-unpleasant warm, fishy odor. Its light filled their cabin with a yellowish glow. Supper had consisted of spicy seafood and rice stew, fresh bread, garlic, and butter. Dylan's belly was pleasantly full, and he was comfortable, his injuries having already healed, thanks to Jade. That is, all but one. Idly, he brushed a finger across the healing bruise in the middle of his forehead. It itched. Jade said it was going to scar. All in all, he didn't mind. *It could've been worse.* His thoughts drifted to those final moments like a pin to a lodestone. Over and over, the image of Aegrir as that muscular, attractive—*naked, so very naked*—young man sprang to mind. Over and over, he felt guilty and willed it away. Worse, he'd dreamed all night of what might have happened if he'd accepted that invitation and had woken with a fierce cock-stand. He'd whispered things into Dar's ear until a sleepy smile had crept across his face. Then he'd made love to him. That'd been good, but it felt strange somehow—as if there were a third person in their hammock.

"Don't pick at it," Dar said, not looking up from the game board filled with colorful thin metal tiles. Each was magnetized to stay in place.

"What?"

"Your forehead," Dar said. "So . . . are you going to tell me about what's wrong, yet?"

Dylan kept his gaze on the game. *I can't tell him. His feelings will be hurt. Mine would. I can't do that to him.* "There isn't anything to tell."

"There's something, all right," Dar said. "You could start with that mark. You didn't get that when you fell. I would've noticed."

Turning over a tile, Dylan slumped when he spied the yellow star set in a blue box. It didn't match the green-and-black anchor with the purple flower wreath. It was the third time in a row he'd picked the star. "It's nothing. My mind isn't in the game, that's all."

"No wonder you lost so much at five-card bluff when you served in the Eledorean navy," Dar said. "You're a terrible liar." He turned over two tiles and matched them. They were red roses. He flipped another piece that revealed a crescent moon. The next one was a clock.

Why not trust in him? If you don't, he will only guess. Dylan didn't know which was worse. *I don't want to lose him.* After years apart, he was only getting comfortable with Dar again. In so many ways, it had felt like starting over from the beginning.

"All right." He looked away. "The mark came from Aegrir."

Dar blinked. "The real and actual Aegrir." It was one part disbelieving statement and one part question.

"Yes." And with that, Dylan explained everything, including the proposition. "I—I refused her . . . I mean him. You don't have to worry. I kept my oath. I know it doesn't mean anything. It doesn't. But . . . I felt I should tell you I was—I am attracted."

"Long hair? Big with dark eyes?" Dar snorted and shrugged. "No shit. She knew your type. It's not that difficult to figure out."

Dylan reached toward Dar and brushed his cheek with his fingers. "*You're* my type."

"Of course I am," Dar said with no sign of insecurity. "You have more than one. There's nothing wrong with that."

"You're not upset?"

"Why would I be?" Dar said, moving closer. "You refused a goddess to keep your oath to me. I'd say that was drowned romantic."

And just like that, the overwhelming power of attraction as well as the guilt and fear were gone. Relieved, Dylan kissed Dar. "You're wonderful."

"So are you," Dar said, kissing back.

Dylan's hand drifted to Dar's lap.

Dar's voice acquired a low note that could almost be a purr. "Don't start something you don't intend to finish."

"What? The game?"

THREE

The setting sun cast glowing embers across the gently rolling ocean. Gazing out at the expanse of water from the gunnel, Dylan heard yet another series of clanks and thumps indicating opened and closed message boxes. He waited while Dar refilled the reward containers and indicated it was time to move on. Then Dylan lifted the sacks of crumbs, fish scraps, and other treats intended for Dar's partners in the messenger business and followed Dar to the next station. It was tedious work, but Dar enjoyed it. Anxious, Dylan had joined Dar in his twice-daily check for messages as a distraction, but it seemed the perches and cages would all be empty, and Dylan had started to wish he'd chosen to go aloft and read a novel instead. His duties as weathermaster often came in short bursts of fierce, exhausting work spaced with longer periods of inactivity. Rest being a requirement for recovery, it was necessary. Unfortunately, Dylan tended toward fits of unease during long calms. He knew this about himself. His senses would grow sharper with each passing day, making him twitch with vigilance at any hint or sign in sky or water. And that was why he hadn't said anything when he'd felt that odd empty flattening sound and raising the hairs on the back of his neck.

Am I making trouble where there is none?

Dar stopped at yet another empty cage and began the process of scrubbing it out with seawater. Dylan set down his burdens so that Dar could access them when he was ready. Studying the clouds and finding nothing of interest, he placed one hand over first one ear and then another, testing his hearing. It made no difference. The dull heaviness remained.

It's as if I've cotton wool in my ears. That was when he realized that filling his lungs was becoming more difficult. It was as if the air were somehow too thick to breathe. At the same time, it smelled as it always did—of salt and sun and good ocean water.

Turning his attention to *Coral Star's* deck, he saw that all was normal. Children played and laughed and sprinted across the boards. His ship-brothers and -sisters and elders sang Clan Kask's histories as they worked, naming the captains all the way back to the first Sea Mother in time with the rhythm of ropes and block and tackle.

He told himself that he wasn't the only one—or at least he hadn't been last night. The night before, Angelique, the highest ranking Leaudancer priestess onboard, had read *Coral Star's* fortunes for the week. The first card drawn had been *The Storm.* Alone, Dylan knew it wasn't necessarily a danger. Technically, it indicated disruption and violent change, but that could mean anything from a minor family quarrel to a clan-wide disaster, depending upon the surrounding cards. It was best to take such signs as temperate warnings, not dire emergencies. However, *The Ten Iron Nails* had appeared next. The final card had been *The Cuttlefish.* Angelique had left the galley to inform the captain of the result with a frown, and Dylan had gone to his bed worried. They were headed deeper into Acrasian waters, after all, and they'd already been attacked once.

Captain Magaodh had taken the warning seriously. In the morning, more extensive safeguards were put into place. Clan Flounder's insignia replaced the Clan Kask flag and half of *Coral Star's* name was painted over. As an extra precaution, her sail plan was in the process of being altered. Soon, Clan Kask's frigate, *Coral Star*, would vanish, and Clan Flounder's barque, *Star*, would take her place. Such changes wouldn't fool Waterborne—all the clans knew what the sign of the Flounder meant. However, the Acrasians didn't. They weren't exactly observant when it came to non-Acrasians.

Unless they were at war, Dylan thought. *Their generals can be frighteningly observant.* Technically, they weren't at war with Clan Kask and never would be. Acrasia couldn't afford to anger the Waterborne Nations. They relied on Waterborne whale oil too much for such a thing.

The morning's fishing nets had returned empty and no porpoises leapt in the ship's wake. Even the gulls, a constant nuisance this close to the Acrasian coast, were absent. Jet, one of two of the ship's dogs, trotted across the deck and leaned into Dylan's leg.

Jet was a black Sakurajiman water dog that he'd raised from a puppy—that is, until he'd been exiled. When he'd returned, she'd re-bonded with him as if he'd never left. Therefore, Jet had shipped off with him and Dar. Dylan was even happier to have her with him now. Her shoulder thumped against the outside of his thigh. He wasn't sure if she was reassuring him or herself with the gesture. He reached down to pet her.

The muffled feeling in his ears was suddenly joined by a strong taste of metal in the back of his mouth. He spat over the rail and frowned. Jet let out a worried whine and pointed her nose starboard. The feeling of dread twisted a knot in his stomach. He had noticed such a thing only once before. It'd been during the duel with Isak Whitewater. It meant only one thing.

A soulbane is near. But where? Dylan hadn't noticed any other signs. *Not onboard. Could a soulbane get onboard and no one notice?* He glanced down at Jet and knew the answer to that question was a resounding no. Sensing magic was what Sakurajiman water dogs did—not that they were the only breed with that ability. This was why Waterborne ships kept dogs in addition to cats.

Dar spat and made a disgusted face. "My stomach feels as if I've swallowed lead." Dar tilted his head and paused. When he broke the silence, his voice was distant. "Nothing swims within a two-mile radius of our ship. Maybe more. The water has never felt so . . . desolate." He shuddered.

"How can you be sure if you don't touch the water?"

"I am as sure as I want to be for now." Dar blinked as he came back to himself and pointed at the sea. "I'm not sticking my hand in that. Not now. I wouldn't recommend you do it, either."

Again, Dylan searched for some solid sign of danger in the sky. "Do you know what's wrong?"

The boatswain's pipe whistled an alert, announcing a ship sighting to the east. Dylan got out his glass and scanned the horizon. It didn't take long to spot her. Her size and sail configuration indicated she was a brigantine. The blue, white, and purple striped flag indicated it was one of Clan Kask's.

Dylan scowled as he watched the sister ship's progress. *Why is she sailing this close to the coast without precautions?* "Is *Sunset* still our only brigantine?" *Sunset* was one of only three whalers operated by Clan Kask. A wise clan diversified, and Kask concentrated on four key items—fishing and Eledorean imports, primarily whiskey, whale oil, and spices from Tynnyri Island, Clan Kask's home.

For years, whale oil had been the most profitable. The clan traded heavily with the Acrasian Regnum, after all, and whale oil fetched a good price on the Acrasian market. Acrasians consumed a great deal of oil, keeping their lights burning at night. The wealthy were known to do so even when the moon was full. However, since Kask's relations with the Acrasians had soured, it had placed certain restrictions on Kask's whaling interests. Priorities changed. A new focus was found. However, the whale oil market hadn't been abandoned entirely. Nothing prevented Kask from selling to another clan and then, in turn, that clan selling to the Regnum. Doing so did, however, cut into one's profits due to broker's fees.

"As of the last convocation? Yes," Dar said, motioning for the glass. "May I? My cousin Ada should be onboard."

Pausing before handing over the spyglass, Dylan said, "Don't drop it in the water."

"I won't."

"It's expensive. A gift. And I can't get another one like it, as the manufacturer is probably dead. So, be careful unless you plan on replacing it."

"When did you become so distrusting?" Dar stopped his teasing and raised the glass to his eye. A concerned line appeared between his brows. "It's *Sunset*, all right." He paused. "That's odd."

"What is?"

"I don't see her whaleboats. There should be at least four."

"Let me look."

Dar returned the glass.

It was Dylan's turn to frown. *Is this the soulbane I've been sensing?* "Her rigging is fouled."

Dar reported this information to Captain Magaodh. Given Star's incomplete sail plan change, Magaodh decided to send a boat over to check on *Sunset*'s crew. While the boat crew assembled, Magaodh repeatedly used the horn to hail her, but there was no reply.

"That's it," Dar said. "I have to find Ada."

Dylan said, "And I'm going with you."

Sunset's sails were torn and hung slack in the fading light. She bobbed and rolled from side to side like a drunk—listing more to port than starboard, exposing her hull below the waterline. Barnacles and weeds clung to her bottom—something no Waterborne crew would have allowed. Such growths slowed a ship down, and Waterborne ships depended upon speed.

A skiff was lowered with a great splash, and those so assigned climbed down the pilot ladder with their weapons and a number of lanterns. Jade had been added to the crew of seven, in case a sickness was to blame. It would be up to her to make the final determination as to whether it was safe to board. If the problem was disease, they didn't want to risk exposure.

Dylan took a place at the oars next to Angelique and began rowing. They worked against the current, lengthening the journey. A horrible stench blew toward them from the ship. The closer they got, the worse the smell of death and decay became. Dylan tugged his scarf up over his nose and mouth. His ship-brothers and -sisters did the same. It helped some but it was hard not to gag. Finally, the skiff thumped against *Sunset*'s starboard side. Jade called out while Dar attached a grappling hook to *Sunset*'s gunnel. No answer came.

Jade laid a hand on *Sunset*'s side and closed her eyes. "I don't think it's sickness."

"Then we board her," Dylan said. *If it is a soulbane, let it be only one. One, we can handle.*

Dar was the first, and Dylan followed him up the knotted rope onto the ship's deck. As he did so, he had to make his way past the tangle of chains, pulleys, and rope. Standing on the slippery hull, he edged onto the slanted gangplank and held onto the gunnel while lanterns were passed up. There were signs that the crew had been missing or dead for some time. The boards were filthy. The rigging hung in knotted clumps. The wind beat chains, ropes, and tattered sails together as the water lapped at *Sunset's* hull. The port gunnel was only a few feet from the water's surface, and the higher waves washed up to the mainmast.

He scanned the deck for any sign of life. *Dar is right. The whaleboats are missing.* Dylan supposed that must have been where the crew had gone. *Still, why would they have abandoned the ship?* There was no evidence of a fight—no blood, no holes left by cannon shots. There was only that putrefying stench. That was when he spied the masses of taut rope leading into the water. *Sunset* appeared to be tied to something huge and heavy.

"What is she anchored to?" Dylan asked.

"I don't know," Dar said, and crawled down to the main deck. He inched to the mainmast and then half-slid to the opposite gangplank.

Dylan followed Dar's lead as did the others. Only Jade kept her distance.

"Hello? Captain Leticia? Hello?" she asked again.

Staring down into the water from the port side, Dylan spied the body of a sperm whale. It lolled as it floated, secured lengthwise along *Sunset's* side with loops of ropes and chains. One stumped, ragged fin seemed to point at the clouds in accusation. Its deathly pale flesh had been torn by scavengers.

Dylan searched the darkening sky. *Where are all the gulls?* Looking into the water, he didn't see any sharks, either.

"I don't like this," Dar said.

"I don't either," Angelique said.

"What do you think happened?" Nathan asked.

As if in answer, a loud, shuddering moan filled the air. Its resonance seemed to contain all the sorrow and agony of the world. The backs of Dylan's eyes stung, and he swallowed a lump of emotion. *Where did that come from?*

The whale corpse's stunted fin twitched once and then the great bulk of its body moved. Angelique let out a surprised yelp. *Sunset* shuddered in kind, and Dylan began to understand her previous drunken sway. He staggered backward to keep his balance. The great whale rolled toward the ship, its white belly revealed as it loosened its shroud of ropes and chains. It revolved a handful of times until it stopped and lay panting on its side. Again, the gnawed, stumped fin flapped ineffectually in the air. Dylan listened to the creature's labored breathing and wondered how the thing could possibly still be alive. Its eye opened, and what gazed back at him sent a bolt of ice through his heart.

It's dead. It has to be dead.

The outer edge of the whale's eye was bloodshot and yellow, and the flat pupil took up the entire iris. Arching its back, the whale opened its enormous mouth—a mouth big enough to swallow their skiff whole—and bared jagged rows of huge teeth. It had no tongue. Instead, long, sickly-hued, suckered tentacles shot out and swept the gangplank. One of them clamped onto Angelique's leg. She screamed in pain and horror as she was yanked onto her back. A spray of something wet plopped against the boards, and Dylan felt something slap him in the chest. He staggered backward in shock, glanced down, and saw the sticky white substance covering the front of his shirt and waistcoat. It stank of rot like the whale, and his skin stung where he'd made direct contact with the substance. While he wanted to be sick, he wasn't hurt. Therefore, he put that information aside and then searched the deck for anything useful. Meanwhile, Angelique was being slowly dragged toward the dead whale's jaws. Dar, Nathan, and Wester drew their cutlasses and began chopping at the tentacles in an attempt to free her. Dylan hopped down to the main deck. It didn't take long to find what he was looking for.

"Malik, Lesia, Diego! Here! I've got the harpoons!"

Dylan distributed the weapons among the others, selected the last for himself, and then climbed back onto the gangplank. He stabbed at the thing repeatedly. However, it didn't take long for him to discover that the harpoons weren't going to do much good. The more he cut at the thing, the more it slammed itself against the disabled ship. He heard movement behind him. Turning, he saw that they weren't alone. For a moment, he beheld the image of an uneven creature coated in spiny fur, hobbling on two crooked legs. Its arms were too long and thin to be human. Its face was flat, and its mouth was wide. Then his vision blurred. When it cleared, Dylan saw the impossible—a young kainen woman with light brown hair and pale skin dressed in her older brother's cast-off clothes. Of course, she didn't dress like that now. She was much too dignified for that. *Queen Suvi?*

Wester asked, "Captain Leticia?"

A second creature emerged from belowdecks through the captain's skylight. Its movements carried the eerie grace of a large insect. Within the blackness of the open hatch, Dylan thought he could see more of the things making their way to the main deck.

They're soulbanes! All of them! "The ship is infested! We have to go!" Dylan brought his harpoon down in a great arc, finally slicing through a cluster of tentacles. The whale-creature roared, and the deck shifted beneath his feet. "Run! Now!" He helped Dar get Angelique up off the deck just as the last of the sun's light faded. They rushed to the opposite side of the ship and made it to the grappling hook before the soulbanes could get between them and the skiff. Nathan and Diego went over the side first in order to help Angelique. Wester kicked at the closest soulbane, hitting it in the chest and knocking it into the others behind it. Dar dropped his harpoon and grabbed tar-coated ropes, lumping them into a pile. He added shreds of sail and bits of broken wood—whatever he might find.

"Come on, Dylan!" Dar shouted.

"Almost ready!" Dylan snatched the first lantern that had been left on the starboard gangplank and hurled it at the pile Dar had created. The sound of breaking glass joined Dar's cries.

"Dylan, it's time to go!"

Looping his fingers around the handle of the second lantern, Dylan tossed it neatly down the main hatch. The things in the hold below howled in unison as the flames caught.

"Drown you, Dylan! I'm not leaving without you!"

Dylan whirled and ran to Dar. "Ready. You first."

Dar scrambled down the rope. *Sunset* shuddered beneath Dylan's feet as he looked back one last time. Black smoke filled the air and the scent of burning tar joined the stench of decay. Through the haze, he thought he glimpsed *Sunset*'s crew, members of his clan, his *family*, writhing in the flames.

"I'm so sorry," Dylan said. And, whispering a prayer for the dead as he went, he scrambled over the side before the powder stores caught.

⊰ SUVI ⊱

Twenty-Third of Korjuukuu, 1783

Assuming a chair opposite that of Councilor James Slate's, Suvi silently agreed to Ilta Korpela's offer of a cup of tea. Nervous, Suvi kept her face otherwise impassive. The expression was wearing thin after traveling the whole of Västmark in order to conduct nine months of fruitless negotiation. She was finished with begging for her people. *For now.* That said, she wasn't entirely sure how she should interact with this former Acrasian. On one hand, she had every right to hate Acrasians. Their war had destroyed Eledore and her people. Worse, she understood that Acrasians had begun hunting kainen for sport. Still, this particular Acrasian had joined forces with her Silmaillia, Ilta Korpela, and saved hundreds of kainen refugees.

I've found it in my heart to forgive Ilta for grave mistakes she made—mistakes that killed Mother; why not extend the same to this Acrasian? Suvi thought.

Ilta is kainen. He is not. She returned the Acrasian's stare, listening to the clink of silver against porcelain. His eyes were shielded with polished dark-lens spectacles that made him seem all the more aloof. His weathered, clean-shaven face was drawn in pale, broad Acrasian lines, and his expression revealed nothing. The challenge was implied, but it was there nonetheless.

What if he wants to retain rulership? she thought. She glanced to her korva, Jami Rautio, standing next to the door with her back to the wall. She seemed unconcerned, at ease, but Suvi knew Jami— had seen her in action. She knew all it would take is a nod. *Am I prepared to assassinate this man?* She kept back a sigh. She had other alternatives for handling the situation, and they were ways that wouldn't require the use of Jami's blades. *Hasn't there been enough death and struggle for power in Eledore?*

I will do what I have to do. Is Eledore not my home? The questions were weighted with months of exhaustion. She had been far too long living in uncertainties. It was time for that to end. *One way or another.*

James Slate turned to Ilta when she placed a hand on his arm. For a moment, the lenses of his dark spectacles reflected the light shining in from the high windows overhead like a mirror.

"The tea is ready," Ilta said. Her voice was informal, almost a whisper. "It's directly in front of your right hand. Be careful. It's hot."

Suvi looked to Ilta. *Is he blind?* Ilta hadn't mentioned it in her letters.

After a short pause, Ilta seemed to catch her unspoken question and nodded.

Why hasn't she cured him of it? Suvi thought. *Is it possible she can't? Or is it that she's too afraid to try?* Before the war, Ilta had been the former Silmaillia's impulsive apprentice and had been rumored to be the most powerful healer in the country. She had been passionate and unafraid of her power, but a great deal had happened since then, and one of the consequences was that the queen had died of variola. *Has Ilta grown more cautious? Surely, that is a good thing, isn't it?*

Suvi watched Ilta prepare the tea as if her motions might reveal some secret. Ilta looked up from her task, and Suvi lifted her gaze to the windows. She thought she recognized their shape, but she couldn't place where she'd seen them before. *Probably scavenged from one of Father's buildings he was so obsessed with.* Of course, those buildings were now rubble for the most part—thanks to Acrasian artillery.

And now here I am. Examining the room, she had to admit that James Slate had done a wonderful job of disguising the stronghold's original purpose. The forced neutral expression began to hurt as she willed away the beginnings of a bitter smile. The idea that she was now inside what had once been a grave mound held a certain symbolic correctness.

"Please permit me to formally welcome you to the Hold, Your Grace. Are your accommodations to your liking?" Councilor Slate asked, picking up his cup with expert care. His grey-peppered brown hair was neatly gathered with a black ribbon at the nape of his neck. He dressed like an Acrasian professor of philosophy—in austere blacks and browns—which was, she told herself, as it should be, since that was exactly what he'd been until a little over two years earlier.

"I'm quite comfortable for the moment, thank you," Suvi said, relaxing her face. If the man was blind, there was no point in maintaining her control.

She wondered if he knew about the former Eledorean taboos surrounding death and anything and everyone associated with it. If so, her father would've been offended to the point of making the Councilor throw himself on his own sword. Staring at those dark lenses, she found it was difficult to read the man's intent. *Perhaps that's the point?*

Is he as blind as he pretends? Surely, there is an advantage in being thought more blind than one is?

If so, I must be careful. She caught herself almost smiling at the thought of the challenge of getting to know his unspoken cues. It'd been one of the things she'd enjoyed about court—the little intrigues, at least the harmless ones. She'd been very good at reading people, and on some level she already liked this James Slate.

As for the choice of lodging . . . does it matter? Times change, she thought. *And those who beg do not have the option of choosing. Of course, this isn't the first time the people have had to hide in barrows underground.*

She had grown tired of living like an unwanted guest—an unwanted *outlaw* guest, to be more precise. *How does Nels do it?* As much as she loved *Otter,* she craved a space of her own with a real bed. *Oh, goddess, you've become a landlubber. Four years before the mast, and this is what has become of you?* "My trunks are being transferred from my ship as we speak."

"Good," Slate said. "The Hold is yours, Your Grace. Please feel free to make yourself at home."

I shouldn't delay, Suvi thought. *I should seize control and leave no question as to who is in charge.* Yet all the time spent negotiating with no actual power made her reluctant to adopt a direct approach. "Forgive my rudeness," she said. "I find myself overly tired."

"Would you rather postpone this meeting?" James Slate asked.

"No. Thank you." The longer she waited to assume her place,

the harder it would be to battle the Acrasian for political power. *He hasn't given a sign of resistance yet.*

A worried look passed over Ilta's fine features, marred by a single variola scar high on her forehead. It was clear she was as concerned about the outcome of this meeting as Suvi was. Ilta moved close and whispered, "I promise. Everything is as I wrote to you."

Suvi nodded and granted her a small smile. She regretted hesitating. It displayed distrust in her Silmaillia, and she didn't wish to make the situation with Ilta any more uncomfortable than it was. In any case, Suvi knew the Waterborne were highly skilled at hiding their vessels when forced to conduct their business on land. Dylan had been the one to first repurpose the Hold as a Waterborne warehouse and business office, and in truth, it'd been Nels's idea to house the refugees in this place, not James Slate's.

Stop being a coward, Suvi thought, and took the plunge. *I hate treating anyone like this, but it's necessary.* "I find myself in the need to be frank, Mr. Slate. I hope you won't be insulted. It is not my intent. You have done my people a great service."

James Slate's serene expression didn't change. Suvi found it unsettling.

"I highly value honesty, Your Grace," James Slate said, seeming to address the whole of the room and not merely one individual within it. "I'm flattered by your candor."

"My Silmaillia has informed me that you're a man I can trust," Suvi said. "Are you?"

"I believe I am," James Slate said.

"Do you know what a Silmaillia is, Mr. Slate?" Suvi asked. "Did Ilta tell you?"

"She's your chief counselor," Slate said. "My Eledorean is not terribly good, but I believe it means 'Eye of the People.'"

"That's close enough." Suvi nodded. "However, there are some details about the Silmaillia of which you may not be aware. For example, Ilta can hear the thoughts of those near to her." She watched James Slate's expression for any sign of surprise or dismay and saw none. *Unless you count that twitch of an eyebrow? He's very good.* "She also has visions about the future. These abilities have been most useful to the Eledorean crown in regards to palace intrigue. Do we have an understanding?"

"We do, Your Grace," James Slate said.

"One last thing," Suvi said. "I assume you've heard of command magic?"

It was at this point that she noticed him grow pale. "I have."

"All the stories are true," Suvi said. "Would you care for a demonstration?"

He cleared his throat. "There is no need, Your Grace."

"I'm glad to hear it," Suvi said. "Because I am not my father. I don't believe in abusing those who work for me. However, I wouldn't recommend taking that as a sign of weakness." *Are you going to fight me for control? Even a Silmaillia can be wrong.* Of course, he didn't need to know that.

"I give you my word as a gentleman, Your Grace." James Slate folded his hands in his lap. "I have no lofty aspirations. My interest in governance is strictly an academic one, I assure you. We had need to organize while you were away. I thought a democracy based on the philosophy of the humanist Charles Davidson would serve—"

"I'm familiar with Davidson's works," Suvi said. "They bear a striking resemblance to certain Waterborne texts."

"Miss Korpela indicated that Your Grace is well educated in a broad range of political and philosophical subjects," James Slate said.

"My mother believed study of political theory to be of great benefit for a queen. In truth, she hoped I would institute radical changes in the Kingdom of Eledore. Improvements for the sake of all the people, not merely the nobility. She was Ytlainen, after all, and her politics were those of an Ytlainen. Mine, to be frank, aren't much different from hers." Suvi didn't use the words "constitutional monarchy". She assumed James Slate knew enough of Ytlain to be understood. "Unfortunately, due to certain circumstances, that didn't happen."

Ilta looked away.

I meant due to my uncle, not you. Suvi said, "Traditionally, a queen's position of power in this country isn't exactly stable. Therefore . . . I hope you'll forgive my being blunt."

"It's quite all right," James Slate said. "In truth, I would've been disappointed if you hadn't."

Suvi let go of the tension in her shoulders. "I'm finally home."

Ilta smiled. "You are." Having finished serving the tea, she took a seat in the green chair to Suvi's right.

"Mr. Slate," Suvi said. "May I call you James?"

"You may," James said.

"All right, James," Suvi said. "Tell me about this council of yours."

He nodded. The round lenses of his spectacles once again reflected the light from the high windows. "The council currently consists of myself, Ilta, Jyri Ingersson, Maarit Vinter, and . . . one other."

"Who? What other?" Suvi asked.

"Nels," Ilta said. "However, we haven't convinced him to take the seat."

"I see," Suvi said.

"He claimed that he didn't want to assume your place. He's not interested in ruling," Ilta said. "We kept telling him that this wasn't the intent of—"

"I'm quite familiar with my brother's recent attitude toward responsibility."

Ilta said, "It isn't that."

"Isn't it?" Suvi asked. She took a sip of tea. It was exactly how she liked it—with milk and a small amount of sugar. Ilta had done so without asking. *She reads minds, and I've no protection, no souja, thoughtshield.* Where once that would've frightened, even angered her, now Suvi decided to take the comfort offered instead. "Speaking of Nels, where is he?"

Suddenly uneasy, Ilta turned her attention to the tea things. "He's on a ship bound for Ytlain by now, I think," James said.

"Ytlain?" Suvi asked, getting to her feet. She felt her brows draw together and her mouth tighten. *He did not do that. He wouldn't.* "Why?"

"He's meeting with King Edvard to—"

Suvi addressed Ilta. "I expressly told him not to!"

Ilta said, "You know how he is. He wanted—"

"I don't care what *he* wants!" Suvi's shout bounced off the glass above. "I'll not allow him to waste his life on such a stupid, obvious—"

"He saw it differently," Ilta said.

"Well, he's wrong!" Suvi began to pace.

"I'm sure he'll be perfectly safe," James said.

"He's not safe! If the Acrasians don't kill him, Cousin Edvard will!" Suvi turned, the force of her anger sending her skirts in an arc all around her legs. "And if Cousin Edvard doesn't, I will! I swear! That stubborn mule of a—a—"

"Brother?" Ilta asked.

Suvi resorted to a Waterborne curse. "Drown it all!"

❧ N E L S ❧

ONE

TWENTY-THIRD OF KORJUUKUU, 1783

Prince Nels Hännenen collapsed on the *Lorelei*'s railing and longed for death. Pitching overboard seemed the best solution. It would end his misery as well as save his sister the trouble of beheading him for a traitor.

And leave Suvi alone among foreigners? Leave Eledore a smoking ruin?

Hero. Military genius, he thought, mocking himself. *Good thing what's left of the court is on Treaty Island and can't see me now, or they'd be lining up for lessons in Acrasian grammar.*

A low female voice spoke his next thought for him. "Are you often this pathetic?"

Shite. "I hate boats," he said, too weak to move.

A slender arm, bared to the elbow, appeared on the rail. Its smooth skin was darker than his own. The hand dangling over the side was callused, and the fingernails had been bitten to the quick. He let his gaze travel upward and discovered a feminine form dressed in a homespun shirt, a waistcoat of somber missionary grey and a pair of breeches. He got the impression of shapely calves bare of stockings. In spite of that powerful motivation, he didn't have the energy to lift his head for a look at the rest. His stomach stopped him dead with another knife-edged cramp.

"*Lorelei* isn't a boat. She's a frigate. A ship carrying thirty-two eighteen-pound guns and six six-pounders," she said, clearly offended. "*My* ship."

She's right. He had no excuse for making such an error. He damned well knew the distinction. His twin sister, Suvi, had been obsessed with sailing from the time she could crawl, and as a result, he knew more about ships than he'd any right to.

Well, haven't you made a fine start as an ambassador? he thought. *Damn you, Edvard. I'm no swiving diplomat. Surely, another would have made a more suitable courier?*

Why did Cousin Edvard insist upon me?

Don't be stupid. It's a trap.

However, King Edvard of Ytlain had been a trustworthy ally. *For the most part.* What remained of the Eledorean army couldn't have survived the previous winter without his support. Edvard had made another offer. As the leader of that army, Nels needed the monies promised. With funding, he had a chance of restoring Suvi as Queen. Without it—

Something is wrong, and you know it. In previous dealings with Edvard, the money had arrived via courier at a predetermined location. This time, Edvard had requested that Nels meet him on a small outpost named Norman Island off the southern shore of Ytlain. Suvi couldn't come up with a solid reason outside of paranoia to refuse, and neither could Nels, but that didn't mean he was comfortable with the situation. Still, it wasn't as if they had a choice.

Nels swallowed nausea and frustration. *Lorelei* was a Waterborne ship. In that sense it was safe enough, possibly safer than anywhere else he could be, including the Hold. The Waterborne Sea Mother, in spite of Clan Kask, was known to have taken a neutral position in what had come to be known as the Eledorean War—although in Nels's experience, it hadn't been started by the Kingdom of Eledore. That didn't mean history would agree with him because the historians in question would be Acrasian. To his knowledge, no Eledorean historians had survived. Of course, the Waterborne Sea Mother took a neutral position in all wars. As an ocean nation with no land, the Waterborne survived through equitable trade. Since no other country had control of the oceans, everyone treated with the Waterborne or conducted their trade within the continent of Västmark via the Chain Lakes and the connecting rivers. For Eledore and Ytlain, this was only possible in the warm months. Ultimately, if one wanted to do business, one did it through contracting with the Waterborne Nations.

The Waterborne, themselves, were divided into clans. To Nels's knowledge, the clans did not war upon one another without permission from the Sea Mother, and such permission was rarely granted. Each clan had their specialties, loyal customers, and individual contracts. Suvi had close ties with Clan Kask through her friend Dylan Kask. Nels's passage to the meeting place had been arranged through Dylan. However, *Lorelei* wasn't a Clan Kask ship, and these weren't Clan Kask waters. *Lorelei* was a Clan Gannet ship, and Clan Gannet maintained a close relationship with the Acrasian Regnum.

For that reason, Nels had never intended to speak to anyone

related to *Lorelei*. Given the situation, it was best that he remain belowdecks and out of sight, but his tiny cabin reeked, and he'd been desperate for fresh air.

"*Lorelei* doesn't take kindly to insults." The woman with the husky voice gave the ship a pat and, speaking to it, said, "You'll forgive the elph for mucking up your sides, won't you, my love?"

As if in answer, the deck lurched and then dropped two feet. Nels fought for balance and failed. The woman clamped onto his arms. He staggered, and his face met the front of her shirt. The steadying force of her grip vanished, and for a moment, he pillowed his head in the scent of rosewater. Firm, breasts pressed against his cheek.

She's not wearing stays.

She coughed. He snapped upright, and fierce human eyes the green of spring leaves took his measure. Dark hair parted into a hundred tiny braids curtained a crooked smile, and a scar traced a pale, narrow line up one cheek.

"You're a fine specimen. Big, too. I understand elphs have a certain reputation. Might be fun to see if your equipment measured to standard." She lowered her voice even further. "However, my crew is watching, and I value my post more than a good swiving—no matter how good." Her face went hard, her pistol bored into his tortured stomach, and the hammer on the flintlock clicked into place.

He raised both hands in the air.

"Time for introductions," she said loud enough for the others to hear. "I'm Captain Gaia Julia. I don't give a shit how much your man is paying. Touch me again, I'll kick you overboard and settle for the half he's paid. Understand? Or do I need to translate it into Eledorean for you?" Her finger didn't move off the trigger.

"I apologize," Nels replied in Acrasian. "I hadn't intended—"

"Good." She uncocked the pistol and secured the scrap of oiled leather protecting the pan from the damp before returning the weapon to her belt.

It's a long way to Norman Island, Nels thought. *Too bad I can't swim.* After a lengthy uncomfortable pause, he bit back his resentment and gave her his most charming smile. "Call me Gunnar."

She stared at his open palm as if he'd offered her a rotten fish and stalked off. "Get the hells below before this slop turns into a full-fledged squall."

TWO

Nels dreamed of home. Laughter and music from one of his father's many parties drifted through the glass-paned doors to his right. He was outside on a palace balcony, leaning against the cold marble wall in an effort to lose himself in the shadows. His only company was a stolen bottle of his father's best whiskey. A waltz—presumably from Kaledan, based upon the preponderance of bass string instruments—drifted from the ballroom and into the garden. Staring at the hedge maze, he considered fleeing to his barracks house. But before he could make good his retreat, Suvi swept through the doorway. A purple mourning ribbon was knotted around the right arm of her pale yellow ball gown. Her hair swung around her shoulders and waist in thick curls one or two shades lighter than the night sky—the same shade as their father's. Once again, Nels thought she looked more his mirror opposite than his twin. Unlike Suvi, he'd been marked with their mother's moon-pale coloring.

A strawberry bounced off the front of his uniform coat.

"That's going to stain," Nels said without much concern. He uncorked the bottle and took a swig of whiskey.

"I'm angry with you," Suvi said in Acrasian. No one at court bothered with anything as vulgar as Acrasian. Therefore, he and Suvi employed it for conversations they didn't want overheard. Even so, her Acrasian was often barely adequate to the task. However, that wasn't the case this evening. He decided she must've practiced while he was away. That struck him as odd.

"Why are you out here?" she asked. "You're the guest of honor."

"Father is capable of making a show of mourning me without setting the family disgrace out on display," he said.

"You're no changeling. You're a late bloomer, that's all."

He blinked. It was just like her to use an expression normally employed to reference young girls. It shamed him for reasons he didn't want to explain, because it would only anger her, and he wasn't up for a fight. "I'm twenty-one, for the goddess's sake. If my magic were going to manifest, it would have when I was fifteen. Like you." That was another thing wrong, of course. He was twenty-one *now*. The night of that particular ball, he would've been sixteen, but dream-logic slipped past that detail with little resistance.

He took another long swallow.

She frowned. "It upsets Mother when you drink."

"Soldier's prerogative. And anyway, last I checked, she wasn't here. Unless you're taking on her role for the evening?"

"Oh, stop it." Her scowl transformed into a slow conspiratorial smile. "May I try some?"

He handed off the bottle.

She grimaced. "That's awful! Why drink it?"

"Wait a few moments and ask again."

"Wine works just as well." She gave it back. "And tastes less like tar solvent."

"How would you know? Have you acquired yet another filthy

habit from your sailor friends? Father didn't react well to the pipe, I recall."

"To hell with Father."

"Oh, my. Acrasian curses too? *Tsk, tsk,* Little Sparrow." He used their father's pet name for her out of spite.

"I do as I please. Just like you." She gave him a gentle shove, making room for herself in his shadow-refuge. Half her buttercream-colored skirts pressed against his legs, making it impossible for him to move. The other half protruded into the doorway, and the exposed fabric shone like a beacon. He didn't have the heart to tell her that ball gowns weren't designed for stealth. She grabbed the whiskey from him and drank again.

"I thought you didn't like it."

"Changed my mind. It stops the pain."

"My thought exactly." His skin tingled.

Stop. Please, Nels. Make it stop.

The scene blurred. The darkness reflected a more sinister hue. Suvi and the balcony were gone. He staggered down a familiar passageway. He knew this dream. He'd had it before, and he didn't want to have it again. He didn't want to hear her crying. He definitely didn't want to see the blood.

Inching forward down the hall against his will, he reached a place he knew from childhood. A nook outside the nursery. He stooped. His hands shook as he tugged a small section of the baseboard free and reached inside. His fingers found the cherrywood box his sister had tucked inside as she always did when they exchanged hidden messages, but the lid felt different. Sticky. The sparrow carved into its surface was changed. Darker. Hollow sobs echoed in his head. A bolt of dread shot him through. He didn't want to look but found himself lifting the lid anyway. The stench of death and stagnant saltwater filled his nose. He looked upon the contents and choked.

A severed sparrow's head lay inside. Its delicate beak gaped. He could see the tongue had been torn out. His skin prickled with energy again.

"Please make it stop. Nels, please." Suvi's voice. Suvi's tears.

He snatched his hands from the box as if it'd burned him. His mouth mimicked the bird's. Like the bird, no sound came from his throat—only forced air. He tried to feel his teeth with his tongue and couldn't. His mouth flooded with pain and the salty taste of blood. He gagged.

The falling box sank from sight, drowning in the darkness. He woke with his heart crashing against his chest. The hiss of rushing water reminded him of the smothering weight pressing the timbers at his back. The cabin was as lightless as a cave. Its dead lantern squeaked on its hinge on the ceiling. With a deep breath, he blinked the nightmare into oblivion and waited for his stomach to quiet. Aboard ship, rest didn't come easily. He wasn't certain how long he'd slept, but judging by the headache, it wasn't nearly long enough.

He focused on the sound of Sebastian and Viktor's breathing and had almost drifted off to sleep again when a potent blast of magic flooded the stale cabin. Nels sighed in exasperation. *Gods damn it, Viktor.*

Viktor's voice pierced the blackness. "Sorry. I was listening for—"

A distant, deep thump brought Nels up into a sitting position. It was followed by a loud splash.

"That would be cannon. Knew I heard another ship." Viktor's even tone was contradicted by the nervous pop of cracking knuckles. "Thirty-two-pounder is my guess. Acrasian naval issue."

"Warning shot," Sebastian muttered from his blankets on the floor.

"I thought Eledorean magic didn't work on the ocean," Nels said. *Have we been betrayed?*

He started as the alarm rang out. Hundreds of feet thundered across the decks. There came a second cannon blast. Closer. Grabbing the edge of the bunk, he shivered with a need to fight, to do something, anything but sit and wait for the inevitable. Another cannonball smashed into the water somewhere off starboard.

"My mother's father was Waterborne," Viktor said. "Sometimes my magic works. Sometimes it doesn't. It costs nothing to test. Why wait until it's needed? Anyway, I've found the calmer the water, the better it works."

"Thirty-two-pounders," Nels said. "Those are . . . big. You're sure?"

"I am," Viktor said.

"Why waste thirty-two-pounders on warning shots?" Nels asked. "Doesn't that bitch carry anything smaller?" *Calm yourself. You're the damned colonel.* He considered what should be done, but there was nothing. He wasn't in charge and this wasn't his ship. In truth, he'd accepted Edvard's offer against Suvi's specific orders. Nels hadn't wanted her to take out her anger on anyone else. Thus, when he'd left, he'd told no one where he was headed, only that he'd be gone for a few weeks. *On second thought, there were certain aspects of this plan that could've used rethinking. Ilta probably knows where I am, anyway.* As she was a powerful Silmaillia, it was impossible to keep the truth from Ilta, and he'd given her a kiss goodbye.

"We're slowing," Viktor said.

The ship let out fresh protests. The water's hiss against the hull changed pitch. Someone grunted.

"Watch your step, Lieutenant," Sebastian growled.

"Sorry, sir," Viktor said.

The rasp of a sulfur match tore at the darkness. Blinking, Nels shielded his eyes from the light. A knock sounded. Sebastian abandoned his blankets and hopped up from the cabin floor. The door slid open, and a fresh aroma-cloud of sheep shit wafted in. Based upon the smell, the sheep didn't enjoy sailing any more than Nels did. The sailor standing in the doorway hefted a lantern, peering inside. His dark brown face was a tattooed mask of indigo swirls and shadows. Thick hair hung to his waist in small ropes—the badge of a Waterborne spiritual sect, Nels had recently learned. Scars ringed the sailor's neck and wrists.

"I'm to warn you. We've visitors. An Acrasian ship of the line, she is. Navy regulation down to her pins. They're boarding us. Lights out, and keep quiet." The sailor whirled, sinking into the darkness and taking his lantern with him.

The panel snapped closed on its own.

"Your orders?" Sebastian asked, grabbing his breeches from the floor.

"Are you up for plan B, Viktor?" Nels asked. "Do you think the magic will hold long enough?"

"I think so." Viktor's face brightened. "Oh, how I enjoy playing royalty. In spite of the little inconveniences, you're afforded the best accommodations. Is that bunk as comfortable as it looks?"

"A coffin would be more spacious." Nels regretted his words at once, but he pressed on, hoping to cover. "Damned box is too short. My legs cramp, and the bedding is crawling."

Sebastian pulled a sailor's cap over his greying head. It would do nothing to disguise the black of his eyes, Nels knew, but Acrasians demanded meekness from inferiors, and a downcast gaze would not arouse suspicion.

"We'll only go with this plan if there's absolutely no other option, hear me, Sebastian? It's too risky. And I don't want to spend the next year searching Acrasian prisons for Viktor's sorry carcass," Nels said. That was the more pleasant of the possible options if they were caught, they all knew, but now wasn't the time to focus on the worst. "Here's hoping this visit is up to chance and that Dylan was wrong about our informer."

"Yes, sir." Sebastian opened the door panel and shut it after passing through.

Viktor said, "Now, your clothes. The good ones. Not those rags you normally wear."

Nels handed off his kit and then frowned as Viktor pulled his last silk shirt from the bag and sniffed it.

"I hope you're not for the executioner," Viktor said. "Your sense of timing isn't always the best, you know."

"Are you implying I'm unreliable?" Nels asked.

"When was the last time you wound your own damned watch?" Viktor asked. Her eturned the closed lamp to its hook when he'd finished dressing.

Blind, Nels lay still on the floor and listened to water lapping the hull, the creaking of the ship, the rapid thump of his own heart, Viktor's breathing—anything that might prove a sign of what was ahead. A door slammed the deck. Nels felt the vibration through the boards beneath him.

"—reward." The word may have been Acrasian, but there was no mistaking Sebastian's voice.

Plan B it is, Nels thought. *Damn it.*

"I assure you, you'll be granted your request should your information prove correct. Now, where is he?" The speaker's officious Acrasian could have rivaled Eledorean court speech, and although it lacked the power of domination magic, the voice sounded no less menacing.

"There," Sebastian said. His Acrasian was limited, but he was learning. "Behind the crates."

Heavy boots shuffled closer to the door panel. The muffled clatter and bang of guns being made ready filled Nels's ears.

"We know you're there. Discard your weapons and come out."

Nels took a deep breath.

"They're only Acrasians. Marines, by the smell," Viktor whispered in Eledorean.

Nels didn't ask how Acrasian Marines smelled any different from any other Acrasian—nor how Viktor was able to smell anything beyond the sheep shit.

"I can take the twelve in the back if you'll dispatch the first eight."

"They sent twenty marines after little old me?"

"If my ear is any judge," Viktor said. "And we both know it is. Well? Shall we go out fighting?"

"You'll get bloodstains on my good clothes."

"Hrmph. These? You really should find a new tailor."

"On what remains of my allowance? That isn't likely." Nels kissed the Ytlainen medal hanging around his neck from a silver chain. Its raised surface bore the image of a running horse, Hasta, patron Goddess of cavalry soldiers. He couldn't suppress the thought that Hasta was out of place on the open sea, but then, so was he.

The voice on the other side of the wall lost patience. "You have until a count of three until we force our way in. One—"

Nels shoved open the door and was met with a row of musket barrels and men in dark grey uniforms. *Acrasian Marines. Eighteen of them.*

Viktor was off by two. He's never wrong. Bad sign, that. Again, he thought, *Will the magic hold?*

"Nels Hännenen, you are hereby under arrest for inciting rebellion among the people of Eledore, a protectorate of the Acrasian Regnum."

Are there enough Eledoreans alive to call the kingdom a protectorate? Nels thought.

Viktor reached for the cabin's ceiling, and Nels did the same. It was a short stretch, given that neither of them could stand without smacking his head into a ship's beam. As planned, Viktor passed in front. Nels placed a hand on Viktor's shoulder and focused on giving him a boost. Based upon how such things were judged in Eledorean circles, it was nothing, this magic of his, but Nels had begun to understand that it came in useful from time to time. The release of magical power prickled against the skin of his palm, and he felt tired at once. With that, he assumed it'd worked. Still, something didn't feel right. Too late, it occurred to him that it would've been better to have direct skin-to-skin contact for the transfer of energy.

No one seemed to know why the magic of land-dwelling kainen was so very unstable on ocean waters. Waterborne certainly didn't have any problems, and this was the source of their dominance on the world's seas. Since land-bound kainen had fewer problems on fresh water, some thought it had to do with the amount of naturally occurring salt. Salt did have a grounding quality when it came to magical power. This was why it was so often mixed with water for blessings in rituals. The current Ytlainen theory was that it had to do with the mutability of the sea. Nels didn't have an opinion either way. All he knew was that he hated water.

From behind their canvas wall across the hold, the sheep bleated nervousness into the stench-crowded air. From past experience, Nels knew he'd be the only one to discern the charge of magic thrumming in the mix. He just hoped it was enough to help Viktor.

The marines paused, confused.

Viktor had two magical talents: exceptional senses—mainly hearing and sight—and personal glamour. Even in the dark, it was apparent what had happened. Viktor had made himself conspicuous, more *there*.

"Slippery bastard, got you at last," an Acrasian marine said, grabbing Viktor's arm and yanking.

The action broke Nels's contact with Viktor, but it was apparent that the marines had taken the bait. Nels's relief was cut short when he was shoved face first against a wooden box, and his hands were bound behind his back.

"Make certain he's the one. I want no mistakes."

An overstuffed Acrasian marine lieutenant with porcine eyes grabbed Nels's jaw and wrenched his head into an awkward angle toward the light. The Acrasian stank of stale rum and pipe smoke. Nels's foot slid, and the edge of the rough wooden crate bit into his stomach and chest.

The lieutenant squinted. With a growl, he turned to the marine restraining Viktor. "Sergeant Marius, get the creatures out of here. Can't see a Goddamned thing, and this place reeks of sheep."

"Yes, sir," Sergeant Marius said.

Herded up the stairs, Nels stumbled from the hold into the moon-shadow of an Acrasian dreadnought half again the length of *Lorelei*. Three rows of gun ports pierced her side. Members of Julia's crew were being escorted across the boarding planks. Someone shouted a warning, and a heap of knotted line slammed the deck. Acrasian sailors swarmed *Lorelei*'s yards like flocks of battle crows, picking apart the rigging. Sails lay in tangled heaps on the deck. Severed ropes whipped the air as they were cut and the tension holding the ship's vital parts in place was released. One brave soul attempted to snatch a holed lump of wood the size of a person's head from a surly Acrasian marine sergeant. She was rewarded with a punch in the face for her trouble. The sergeant tossed his prize to another sailor and joined the others restraining Nels.

Dragged to the stern where a marine commander waited, Nels read the name MUNITORIS stitched in black thread on the commander's coat. The kerchief was yanked from Nels's head, releasing a cloud of ash. His scalp felt gritty, and the sea air was cold against his ears.

Commander Munitoris scowled at Nels's ash-coated hair and then Viktor's brown curls. Nels stumbled into Viktor, once again lending as much power as he dared to Viktor during the impact. Another charge of energy weighed in the air. Commander Munitoris shook his head, and the filthy kerchief slipped from his hand. Nels hunched. Viktor stood straighter; he was still a good four inches shorter than Nels in spite of both of their efforts, but then Viktor tilted his chin upward in exaggerated royal defiance.

Commander Munitoris blinked and appeared to awaken. "Well, well. I believe we've resolved our elph problem."

"May I be granted my request now, honored sir?" Sebastian asked.

Right on cue, Nels launched himself at Sebastian. "Traitor!"

He was yanked back. A marine punched Nels in the stomach. Bent over, he gasped for breath as his eyes watered with the pain.

"Take both of them, sir?" Sergeant Marius asked.

The lieutenant glanced to his commander.

"The stench of one elph on board will be quite enough, Sergeant. Leave the other as agreed."

The lieutenant tossed a small leather folio to Sebastian. Then he made a sideways nod at Nels. "A quick sale at a slave market will make up the difference."

Commander Munitoris addressed Captain Julia. "It's apparent you didn't know what you were hauling, or you'd have cashed in on the bounty yourself." He gave Julia a self-important bow with a sweep of his hat. "The Acrasian Navy appreciates your cooperation as well as your donations, dear lady."

"I didn't donate a rutting thing," Julia said.

"Keep silent, Captain, or I may decide to dismantle more than your ship's precious rigging."

"Your emperor may have something to say about that when the Regnum's contracts with Clan Gannet aren't renewed," Julia said. "Be a shame you couldn't take that ship of yours out of the harbor without her sinking, her being new and all."

"Is that a threat?" Commander Munitoris asked. "Because if it is intended as such, I will report your behavior to your superior. I understand Sea Lord Gannet isn't much for half-breeds from Archiron, no matter how much money they have."

Julia changed the target of her scowl to the deck. Nels saw the muscles in her jaw tighten.

"Are you going to apologize?" Commander Munitoris asked. "Or do I invite you aboard as well and have the apology beaten out of you?"

"I regret my words," Julia said through her teeth.

"Very well," Commander Munitoris said, signaling to his lieutenant. "I accept."

A bosun's whistle announced the imminent departure of the Regnum's finest. The flurry of objects hammering the deck as they rained from the rigging intensified like a sudden deadly storm, then the Acrasian sailors abandoned their lofty sabotage.

When it was obvious the danger was past, the Commander said, "And now I leave you to your ship, such as it is." He fished a snuffbox from the interior of a jacket pocket and partook of a pinch. "Good day."

Viktor whispered in Eledorean, "Don't be late."

"I won't," Nels whispered back.

"Gag those creatures now," the Commander said. "I don't want them using any of their tricks."

Nels thought, *If any of us had domination magic, you'd be*

nibbling the end of your pistol right about— He choked as Sebastian crammed the kerchief into his mouth. The ash-laden cloth tasted foul. Nels looked on with stinging eyes as the marines dragged Viktor away. He wished there had been any other alternative.

Changeling. The word probed old wounds, and the barb in its syllables hadn't dulled with time. *I did what I had to do. I did what I could. We'll find Viktor before anything bad happens.*

Somehow.

The dreadnought yanked up her boarding planks, and Viktor vanished in a crush of disgruntled marines.

Please, Hasta. Let me find him before anything bad happens, Nels thought.

"Swiving officious pricks. May the sea rise against them. May the abyss take them, and the sharks chew them to bits before they drown," Captain Julia muttered and spat. She waited in barely restrained fury until the dreadnought had distanced herself enough that her crew were no longer visible in the dark. "Bastard pressed half my crew and tore out the rigging."

Sebastian pulled the cloth from Nels's mouth. "Apologies, Your Grace."

"Just get my hands free," Nels said, and spat to clear his mouth of ash. "How much did they give us?"

Captain Julia's eyes narrowed and a frown tugged at her full lips.

Sebastian said, "I told him you were worth six hundred sterling."

Nels whistled. "The reward is up that high?"

"I may have exaggerated." Sebastian shrugged. "Thought if we were only getting half...."

"You're getting as bad as Viktor." Nels stretched and then rubbed his bruised wrists. Sebastian handed over a folio of Acrasian paper notes.

"You sold your friend for the reward?" Captain Julia asked.

"Correction: I sold *myself*," Nels said. "It isn't my fault if the leadbellies can't tell the difference between an Eledorean infantry scout and a prince." He counted. "Hrmph. Shorted us by a hundred. Typical. Still, if we're careful, two hundred Acrasian sterling will get us enough flour for a month or two. If we're very careful— should we ever get back." He scanned the decks. "Too bad it doesn't look like that will be anytime soon."

"You think I'd let the Acrasian navy get the best of me? It's not like they're terribly creative in their sabotage. This?" Captain Julia motioned toward the unstrung rigging. "It's an old Waterborne trick." Captain Julia put her fingers to her lips, letting out a shrill whistle. "You can stop your cowering! The leadbellies are gone! Time to get to work!" Her crew began sorting through the tangled lines. "Marley!"

"Yes, sir." The scarred woman with grey hair who'd fought with the marine stepped forward. Her nose had been badly bloodied. She sniffed and wiped at her face with a stained sleeve.

"Did they take the fetch with them?" Julia asked.

Marley winked. "Stole it right out of the rigging. Activated it per your order."

"Excellent," Julia said with a vindictive grin. "That'll slow them down for a while. If we're lucky, they'll not figure out what's wrong until they've sunk in a storm. Clan Gannet won't be held accountable. Was the Commander's choice to take the thing onboard, after all. Hells, you even tried to stop him." She turned her attention to Nels. "Don't look so glum. We should have the rigging sound in a few hours."

"In that case, are you still willing to continue on to Norman Island?" Nels asked.

"You're not swimming right now. That alone should demonstrate where my sympathies lie." She folded her arms across her chest. "So. *You're* the Ghost?"

Nels nodded. *Dylan did say Julia could be trusted even if she was half Acrasian.* And he trusted Dylan. So did Suvi.

Captain Julia looked away and lowered her voice. "Sorry about the elph crack yesterday."

"It's all right." Nels shrugged. "I've heard worse."

She paused. "I suppose you have."

"Mind you, not much worse," Nels said. "And usually not while I was being so charming."

She grunted. "What of your friend?"

Nels turned to the horizon and watched the dreadnought slip away into the darkness. "We must meet Cousin Edvard first. Even if *Lorelei* could take on an Acrasian dreadnought—"

He saw Julia's eyebrow twitch in surprise.

"—we couldn't take the time to run her down. We wouldn't arrive at Norman Island in time." He turned his gaze to the Acrasian ship and tried not to imagine what might be happening to Viktor at that moment. "Chances are he'll be fine until they get to Rosavallis. They'll want him alive. And that's the closest Acrasian port. If we're at the docks to meet them, I might be able to arrange an escape." *Please let them be headed for Rosavallis.* "Sebastian tells me we're a day's sail from Norman Island. That's two days early. Am I correct?"

"And three days from Harper's Mill, where we're unloading the sheep," Captain Julia said.

"Your ship is fast?"

"The fastest you can afford," she said with a smile. "We could make both ports, unload our cargo, *and* beat that overweighed, leaky scow to Rosavallis by a whole week even if they didn't have to contend with that fetch. Provided we don't dally. Of course, that assumes that I'd be interested in going to Rosavallis."

Nels asked, "What is a fetch?"

Julia smiled again, and this time, her eyes wrinkled at the corners with vicious mirth. He was beginning to like that smile. "It's a type of curse used to sabotage a ship whose captain is stupid enough to bring one aboard. The effects vary with the creator and grow more powerful over time. It feeds on negative energy. Anyway, I began taking the precaution of keeping one woven into the rigging after the first time they pulled that gull-shit stunt on me."

"And what does that particular fetch do?" Nels asked, gazing once again at the dreadnaught's retreating shadow and worrying again for Viktor.

"For now?" Julia asked. "It only prevents their sails from catching the best wind. But it'll get stronger. More so as it becomes clear that something is wrong. You see, the more tension builds up on ship between crew members . . ." She shrugged. "In my experience, the Acrasian Navy is comprised of the most superstitious excuses for crew on the Aegrerian Ocean or any other. Of course, they have had a small amount of encouragement in that capacity from . . . well . . . the Waterborne."

"Really?" Nels asked.

Julia said, "Just because Clan Gannet trade with Acrasians doesn't mean they actually *like* them."

"Oh," Nels said. "Would you be willing to sail to Rosavallis after Harper's Mill?"

Again, Julia hesitated. "I've commitments to keep. Sea Lord Gannet doesn't trust me yet. As long as I'm on probation, *Lorelei* doesn't have the full benefits of Clan membership. That said, I don't truck with the Acrasian Syndicate, either. Which means I'm an independent, Mr. Ghost. I'm not sure you understand what that means, so I'll spell it out for you. Me and mine live on the edge of a strap razor. Me keeping my word is largely what keeps us alive."

"I know we only booked passage for Norman Island and then Merta," Nels said. "But I'll pay whatever—"

"Don't play me the fool by floating me a lie. I know you don't have any money except for what you've collected by selling your friend," she said. "It would be pointless to give up what little you've gained by hiring me to get him back."

"I won't leave Viktor to them," Nels said. "I can't. I'll pay whatever it takes."

"Then, I think I've learned something about you," she said, tilting her head. "Something that our mutual friend Dylan didn't mention."

"You have?"

"You're quite a bit more loyal to underlings than most Eledorean nobles are reputed to be."

Nels frowned. "Viktor is no underling. He's my friend."

"You're still an Eledorean noble."

"Royal, if you want to get specific."

"Ah, I see," Julia said. "Eledorean *royals*, on the other hand, are infamous for being stupidly rash."

"Nice that I live up to some aspect of the reputation."

"That said, by the time we're finished at Norman Island, they'll be dead in the water," she said. "I think we can easily enough make a case for breaking the curse in exchange for one extra prisoner in addition to my crew."

"You'll be able to find them?"

"Absolutely. That fetch has a number of purposes," Julia said. "Location is one of them. It costs a great deal in the way of headaches and the occasional nosebleed to create, but it's worth it when done well. How do you think I was able to afford this fine ship without the help of the Syndicate?"

"You made the fetch?"

"I did," she said, and then appeared to notice the look on his face. "Do you have something to say?"

"I suspect that I didn't thank you enough for the reprieve regarding my, ah ... earlier misstep," Nels whispered.

"Are you referring to the moment when you landed face first in the front of my blouse?"

He did his very best not to let his gaze stray from hers.

"You know, I do believe I'm starting to like you, Mr. Ghost."

"Call me Nels."

"Wasn't your name Gunnar yesterday?"

"Gunnar is one of my names." Nels shrugged. "But my friends call me Nels."

"Are we friends now, *Nels*?"

"I hope so. Otherwise, I'm going to owe you one very large sum of money before the end of this journey."

She raised an eyebrow at him again. "Maybe I'll give you a chance to work it off. How are you at tying knots?"

"In case you haven't noticed, I'm a terrible sailor."

"Who said it'd be in the form of working the ship?" With that, she turned her back on him and walked away.

"Oh," Nels said.

"You know," Sebastian said. "If I didn't know any better, I'd say that woman has designs on your virtue."

"Shut up, Sebastian."

"Yes, sir."

THREE

The setting sun cast orange and red across the ocean's surface. *Lorelei* dropped anchor in an inlet surrounded by white cliffs. True to her word, Captain Julia had pushed both ship and crew and had managed to make Norman Island long before dawn. Both the ship's dinghies were lowered into the sea for the visit landward— the second crew was intended to refresh the ship's water supply. Nels clambered into the first boat and settled in the prow, shaking. He took a deep breath to steady himself. The near-constant nausea that plagued him whenever he set foot aboard a ship had been tolerable until then. Sitting nearby, Sebastian gave Nels's white knuckles a pointed look, and Nels forced himself to release the boat's side. Unfortunately, the dinghy violently rocked at that moment as the last crew member hopped from the main shroud into the boat. Nels's blood chilled, and his gut clenched. Putting down his stomach's latest revolt cost him a whispered curse. He squeezed his eyes shut.

"I thought you were remaining on board, Captain?" he heard Sebastian ask.

Nels once again let go of the boat's side. Captain Julia thumped down on the bench, squeezing between himself and Sebastian. Sebastian moved over to make more room.

"Only making sure of my bargain," she said. "You still owe me for the last half of your passage."

The crew set the oars and began their rowing. After the initial jostling, the dinghy glided to shore in confident, predictable surges. Nels let himself breathe and searched for something, anything steady to concentrate upon for his stomach's sake. He scanned the horizon and decided Norman Island would be a good idea—that is, until he noticed the beach. Surf roared and clawed at the shore. With that, he clutched at the boat's side once more.

Swive it. It's only water. You'll not drown. Not this close to land. If the others don't see a danger, you shouldn't. Aware he was being watched, Nels decided to focus on the activity inside the boat. "We don't need you."

"Is that so?" She arched her eyebrow. "Do you have other specialties besides bouts of nausea?"

"You're human—"

"My mother may have been human, but my father was kainen."

"—and those present will be kainen. Kainen *royalty*—"

"—from Ytlain," she said.

"It's still too dangerous for you," Nels said. True, Ytlain didn't have the same abusive history with humans that Eledore did. The Ytlainen simply didn't go in for crude displays of power. In his experience, they were more subtle and thus more capable of living among others. *But equally as dangerous—possibly more so for all that.*

"You're concerned for *my* safety?" she asked. "I'm not the one knowingly walking into a trap."

"Who told you about that?" Nels asked.

"Dylan," she said. "And then your friend Viktor. And sometime during the last dogwatch, your man Sebastian."

Nels leaned forward to speak to Sebastian. "You told her?"

Sebastian shrugged and turned away.

"He thought you might be in need of help. I can't imagine why," Julia said. She made no effort to hide her sarcasm. "For the record, I don't believe in the absolute power of command magic."

"You don't?" Nels blinked, confused.

"Would I endanger my ship by allowing you on board, if I felt you represented a threat? Most of my crew—even before the Acrasian Navy made off with half of it—are human. Although not if you go by the Regnum's racial purity standards. Like I said, Acrasians are a superstitious lot. They also tend to exaggerate, particularly when it comes to their fear of magic."

"I can't believe what I'm hearing," Nels said.

"You're a royal," Captain Julia said. "And yet we've been safe. Absolutely no evidence of this terrible domination power everyone's so damned frightened of."

"Tell me something," Nels said. "You've met my man, Viktor Reini, before they took him away?"

"Of course."

Nels gestured at himself. "Did he look blond and six foot tall to you?"

"Acrasian marines aren't selected for their brains. They made a mistake."

"That was one big mistake," Nels said.

"I don't disavow the existence of magic. Only command magic," she said. "You've yet to pay me in dead leaves or force me to do anything against my will." She paused. "On second thought, you *have* nearly made me sick against my will."

"I'm different."

"How?"

Sighing, he debated what to tell her and came up with nothing. If he admitted his defect to her—if he told her he had no real power of his own, she'd know him for a weakling, and for reasons he wasn't willing to acknowledge even to himself, her opinion mattered.

The dinghy lurched as the bottom scraped sand. Nels could say this much for her: she had made him forget he'd been sitting on a narrow plank in the middle of a fickle ocean. He staggered out of the boat, splashed to shore, and resisted an urge to kiss one of the trees. *Land, sweet land.* Then the world tilted a bit to the left, and he caught himself before falling. *Swiving hells! Hasta, why must there be oceans?*

Captain Julia ran to catch up with him. "Don't play games with me."

"You know what you're doing on the sea. I respect that. I trust you to know your business," he said, taking another stabilizing breath. "But I know mine. Edvard is a kainen royal with royal powers. Do the smart thing. Stay with your crew. Fill your water casks. The stream should be far enough away from the meeting site that you can get what you need and back to the ship without being noticed." He continued to the tree line.

"Hells, no. This island belongs to the Kingdom of Ytlain. You can't order me off of it." She marched up the beach, hands on her hips. "And like it or not, I've an investment in you. I'm going."

"Suit yourself," Nels said. "But I reserve the right to say 'I told you so.' Provided you're alive to hear it."

"I can take care of myself. Can you say the same?"

She might *think you a weakling?* he thought.

Embarrassed, Nels motioned for Sebastian to follow him and plunged into the trees without turning back. He heard Captain

Julia issue orders to her crew before leaving them to their tasks. It wasn't long before she was tagging behind. He ignored her labored breathing as she fought the underbrush he let slap backward every few steps along the path, and spoke only to Sebastian, who cut their way through the thicket with a hatchet.

Norman was a small island with several coves and played host to only one tiny Ytlainen fishing village of the same name located near the northernmost bay. Nels didn't know how it'd come to be known as Norman Island. Unlike his sister, Suvi, he hadn't spent much time studying the history of their mother's home country. He'd focused on their enemy, the Regnum of Acrasia. The map he'd acquired from Dylan had all the information Nels needed as far as his plans were concerned. According to the map, Norman Island was a scant hundred miles across at its widest and twenty-five at its narrowest. There was one hill, a former volcano, where one could easily spy the ocean surrounding the whole landmass. Of course, this wasn't Nels's goal. The meeting with his cousin would take place near the easternmost cove, named Coral Bay. *Lorelei* would anchor on the opposite side of the island because as much as he wanted to like and trust Cousin Edvard, Nels simply didn't. He didn't have a reason other than the standard distrust the powerful have for one another. Suvi liked to refer to their extended family as a nest of bad-tempered spiders. Nels disagreed. In his experience, spiders didn't actively seek out their own to destroy. Although they were known to eat their young.

He supposed the differences were slight after all.

Once they'd located the most advantageous spot from which to spy on Edvard's camp, they'd bivouac nearby. When the meeting was done, they'd hike back across the island with their silver and take a dinghy to *Lorelei*. It meant more of a risk to himself and Sebastian, but Julia and her crew would go free if they ran into trouble.

Nels glanced over his shoulder. At least, that had been the original plan.

It took several hours to locate a well-concealed place with the desired view. It wasn't long before he regretted his gratitude for reaching solid land. The predawn light was clogged with mosquitoes. None, it seemed, had eaten in days. Their buzzing and biting were enough to make Nels want to scream. He had finally resigned himself to their feasting when he spied Julia's teasing lopsided smile. Lying in the undergrowth, he borrowed her spyglass.

Four tents flanked a pavilion furnished with a table, chairs and three large chests. A cookfire burned in front of the main pavilion with an attendant cook. Royal guardsmen and servants patrolled the campsite—two of which remained near the chests at all times.

"It would seem we're not the only ones who have arrived early," Nels whispered.

Sebastian crawled up, slapped at his arm, and then wiped sweat from his brow. "I counted fifteen guards."

"Only fifteen? Good old trusting Edvard," Nels said. "Always did like him in spite of the miasma of garlic."

"It looks like the entire palace guard is encamped on the beach north of here," Sebastian said. "Far more troops than I'd deem necessary for a quiet chat with a cousin."

"Terrific," Nels said.

"And no fewer than four ships in the harbor. All are flying the Ytlainen cross and crown."

"Four? Are they ships of the line?" Julia asked, clearly worried.

"I'm artillery . . . er . . . was," Sebastian said. "I wouldn't know a frigate from a rowboat."

"How many troops?" Nels asked.

"About two hundred," Sebastian said. "Give or take a few. I don't have Viktor's eyes. But . . ." He let the last sentence trail off.

"All right. What is it?" Nels asked.

"I don't think they're all Ytlainen," Sebastian said.

"Are they Acrasian?" Nels asked.

Sebastian shrugged. "Perhaps. Perhaps not. Is it possible there are a large number of humans in the Ytlainen Royal Guard? And would they be carrying Acrasian muskets?"

"Anything is possible," Nels said. "It's Cousin Edvard."

Sebastian said, "Well, sir?"

"Shit." Nels shoved stray hair from his eyes. "I don't like this."

"I never have," Sebastian said. "Dylan was right."

"We don't know for certain that Cousin Edvard sold me out," Nels said, and then sighed. *And here I've angered Suvi by going against her orders.* "All of you were right. This was stupid."

"I could've told you that. So, why, in the name of Mithras, did you decide to come here anyway?" Julia asked.

"If I hadn't shown up, Cousin Edvard may have guessed that we knew this was a trap and that we knew about his dealings with Acrasia," Nels said.

"And what difference does that make?" Julia asked.

"He would've searched for the spy before Clan Kask could get their contacts safe. I bought them time to cover their tracks by coming here. It's the least I could do in exchange for everything they've done for us. Still, I wanted to believe that Edvard hadn't abandoned us," Nels said. "Anyway, you never know. It's possible Sebastian and I might get away with the silver."

Julia glanced down at the valley and the beach below. "You two must be a great deal faster, smarter, and stronger than you look."

Nels scratched at another insect bite. "If Viktor were here—"

Sebastian said, "He'd tell you the same. Don't do this."

"Another winter is on its way, and the troops aren't going to weather it eating raw roots and sleeping in the snow," Nels said.

"Then send them to Treaty Island with Suvi and the rest," Sebastian said.

Nels asked, "And leave the refugees? What of the Hold?"

"We aren't there a majority of the time, anyway," Sebastian said.

"How much energy and expense do the Acrasians waste chasing us through the mountains?" Nels asked. "Time they could be spending hunting refugees? It's better this way. Small raiding parties are harder to track. We know Eledore better than they do. We take them unaware, and we fade away into the forest. Leave them no solid targets."

"We're only three hundred now," Sebastian said.

"Three hundred and twenty-three," Nels said. "And how many have we killed in the past year alone? Don't we have the leadbellies jumping at their own shadows?"

Sebastian shrugged. "Your tactics are sound, sir. But we can't hold out forever. The Acrasians have hundreds of thousands of troops."

"We only have to hold out until they start another war. And they will. You know they will," Nels said. "I won't abandon Eledore. Not if there's a single chance. Suvi can stay where she is with what remains of the court. Safe. She has to. If she dies, the kingdom dies with her. My duty is to keep the weeds from taking root while she gathers her strength."

Sebastian opened his mouth.

"I don't want to discuss this anymore," Nels said, holding up a hand. "Not now. We've other problems." He gazed down at Edvard's camp. He wished for anything substantial to work with. Anything at all. *How are we going to get down there and back with the silver without getting caught? If only I had troops in reserve, they could cover us while I negotiated.* Nels lowered the glass and rolled onto his back. *Damn. Damn. Damn.* Once again, he was forced into doing everything with nothing. It was getting to be a bad habit. Gazing up at the pine trees, their trunks seemed as broad as cannon as they stretched to the stars.

Damn it all. If only I had something, anything to—

Suddenly, he was reminded of something Julia had said earlier. *You've never paid me in dead leaves.*

Dead leaves. Ah, now that is something. Nels spoke to her now. His voice was calm, quiet. "How much gunpowder do you have onboard?"

"Quite a bit. Enough for thirty-two eighteen-pound guns and six six-pounders," she said. "Are you planning on buying it from me?"

"Maybe," Nels said.

"With what money?" she asked.

"Never mind that. Do you have black paint? Brown will do, if it's dark enough."

"Have you lost your mind?" she asked. "What do you need paint for?"

"Do you have it?" Nels asked.

"We do." She shrugged.

"Good." He waved away a mosquito. "How about saws?"

She said, "No ship sails without carpentry equipment. At least not one planning on staying afloat for long."

"May I borrow a few members of your crew?" he asked.

"That depends," she said. "Will they be in danger?"

"I don't think so," he said.

"You'd best be certain. Because after the Acrasian Navy's last visit, I can't afford to lose a single crew member," she said. "That is, unless you plan on taking their place. Although it might be fun watching you vomit from *Lorelei's* topgallant during a storm."

"Point taken," Nels said. "All right." Rolling onto his stomach, he searched for a stick and gave it to Sebastian. "Draw the troop positions."

FOUR

Nels pinched the bridge of his nose. His eyes burned, and he ached from a long day and night of hard labor. He'd been able to catch a few hours' rest, thanks to Julia and her crew. Otherwise, he didn't think they'd have finished in time. He resisted an urge to check his pocket watch. He'd been at sea too long for it to be anything approaching correct—Eledorean magic wasn't the only thing on which the movement of the sea wreaked havoc. Instead, he looked to the sky. The blinding sun was positioned directly overhead. Of course, Cousin Edvard hadn't established a time for the meeting, only the date.

A trickle of sweat itched as it oozed its way down Nels's back. In honor of the occasion, he was wearing his best uniform. That is, the parts of it that Viktor hadn't scavenged for his disguise.

Worries for his friend again surfaced. Would the Acrasians treat Viktor well? It wasn't likely. They wouldn't kill him. The price on Nels's head was too high for that, and the Acrasian Emperor would want him alive to make an example of him. They wouldn't know Viktor wasn't who he claimed to be until they reached port.

Unless Viktor's powers wane on the water or they sail into a storm. Then they'll kill him. After they torture him, of course.

Damn, damn, damn, Nels thought. *Why didn't I just let them take me?*

"Shit," Julia said, rubbing her temples with her eyes closed.

"What is it?" Sebastian asked.

"You'll never guess where that dreadnought—the one with your friend on it—dropped anchor," Julia said.

"Where?" Nels asked.

Julia indicated the other side of the island with an annoyed nod.

Nels said, "I suppose I should thank them for not making us sail all seven Waterborne oceans in the search for Viktor." *Is he still alive?*

Sebastian borrowed Julia's glass and vanished into the underbrush. After a moment's thought, Julia followed after him. They returned not long afterward, scratched and sweaty.

"Five more ships in the harbor," Sebastian said.

"All Acrasian dreadnoughts, no less," Julia said, and then responded to Sebastian's unspoken question. "Ships with guns that will tear apart my *Lorelei* should they corner her. She's rated a ship of the line, but she can't stand against that kind of opposition. We're dead the instant they know we're here, if they don't already."

"And they've more Acrasian marines," Sebastian said. "This just gets better and better."

"I guess that definitely answers the question about Cousin Edvard," Nels said. He looked up at the ridge and hoped Captain Julia's people were in position. "All right. Let's go."

"You're still going in?" Julia asked. "We should run. Now. While we have the chance."

"I'm not leaving Viktor to them," Nels said. "If they're here, they

know he's not me. How long do you think he has to live after that?"
Whispering yet another prayer to Hasta for luck, he buttoned the
collar on his wool jacket and then strode toward the path that led to
the clearing. Sebastian trailed two steps behind, carrying a pack containing a bottle of wine, some bread, and hard cheese. Captain Julia
reluctantly followed. She might not believe in domination magic, but
Nels had spotted her furtively plugging her ears with cotton wool.

Smart, he thought.

It wasn't long before he saw green-dyed tent canvas billowing
in the sea breeze. One of the guards spied them and scurried off,
vanishing inside the main pavilion. Within moments, the tent flap
flew open, and King Edvard of Ytlain stepped out. His hair was wet
and freshly combed. He finished fastening the buckle on his belt.

"You gave no warning of your arrival, cousin," Edvard said in
Ytlainen. Although there were more wrinkles around his eyes and a
few grey hairs among the black, he hadn't changed that much since
Nels had seen him five years before.

"I've been away from court," Nels said, also in Ytlainen. "I suppose I've fallen out of the habit. In any case, I seem to have left my
page in Jalokivi. About four years ago. The army tends to frown on
such things. Some silly rule about baggage limits."

Edvard gave the purple ribbon bound around the left sleeve
of Nels's uniform a raised eyebrow. "Still in mourning for your
parents, I see."

Nels kept silent, but the knot in his stomach grew cold.

"Terrible thing, what happened," Edvard said. "But you didn't
come all this way to discuss the past. At least, not that aspect of it."
He motioned toward the pavilion.

"You're right," Nels said. "I've come to discuss the future."

Settling into the chair offered by Edvard's servant, Nels
glanced at the chests sitting next to the table. They looked heavy.

"Will you have some wine first?" Edvard asked. One of the servants opened a bottle and poured the contents into two glasses.

Nels had expected this test and had come prepared. Bringing the crystal goblet to his nose, he breathed in the bouquet. *Cherries. Raspberries. A hint of apricot. Port. A fine vintage.* The best vintage he'd seen in years. It smelled wonderful. *More than wonderful. Exquisite.*

Edvard leaned forward. His lips moved, and his piercing black eyes grew ever more intense. Nels registered a tingling sensation in his fingertips.

The wine was more than mere wine. It was an open symbol for an unspoken offer—one Nels intended to reject, but the blatant force of its temptation surprised him. Drink, and the pressures of the past year would fall from his shoulders. *Eledore's survival. The responsibility. The deaths. The guilt.* The lives of three hundred twenty-three soldiers now weighed directly on him. Would he gamble their fates well? Or would he fail them as he'd failed his father?

Changeling.

Drink. Drink from the glass, and his sister's problems were no longer his own.

Their father had cut Nels off when he'd fallen from grace and became a soldier. Still, Suvi had given her twin her support. She had been the only member of the family to openly do so in spite of their father. Their mother had also helped in every way possible, but her position was more tenuous than Suvi's. A foreigner and a queen, their mother couldn't take the same chances. Therefore, her assistance had come through Suvi. *Always Suvi.* Sometimes, Nels wondered if his mother would've defied their father at all if he hadn't had a twin sister. He wanted to believe that his mother would've. Still, it'd been Suvi who had seen to it that he hadn't starved or been murdered in his sleep. And when he'd been intent on self-destruction, Suvi had sent her personal bodyguard to drag him out of the gambling houses when he'd passed out. It'd been Suvi who had hired the fencing instructor, who'd paid for the lessons that had saved his life in duel after duel during that first year of service. It'd been Suvi who'd paid for Loimuta's stabling when he couldn't afford the price of a bucket of oats. *Suvi. Always Suvi.*

Had she done it out of a sister's love, or was it because she'd sensed all along that he'd prove useful?

Forget. Drink. Rest. Let someone else deal with the responsibilities. Someone will. And they'll do a better job of it, too. You aren't that important.

Nels teetered on the edge of that terrible decision.

Magic-laced sea air crackled all around him. It dulled his senses as his cousin's intent bore down on him. Nels's sight narrowed into a tunnel. His brain ached. He was dizzy with the weight of the magical power, even if it didn't affect him in the way it was intended. He didn't want to imagine what it'd be like to endure the pressure otherwise. *Domination magic and a great deal of it,* Nels thought. *Edvard treats me as if I were an animal to be directed as he chooses.* Those who knew of Nels's weakness often made that mistake.

You are a defective. You should not have been permitted to live. You should've lived out your days in the dungeon beneath the royal palace. You should've been used for sport. Discarded.

Changeling.

You will drink, and declare loyalty to Ytlain.

With his vision blunted by crushing magical force, Nels felt more than saw Sebastian take up a protective position behind him. Nels heard weapons clatter, and Captain Julia let out a surprised grunt. Nels didn't need to look. It was Edvard's next trap snapping closed.

"Take Ytlain's offer. It is the only way you'll leave this place without leg irons, Ghost." The words were in Acrasian.

Nels recognized the voice. It was the overstuffed Acrasian marine lieutenant who had arrested Viktor.

"You came here? For me?" Nels asked switching to Acrasian without effort, not turning around. "I'm flattered. But are you certain it's me this time? I can wait until you fetch your spectacles."

"Make your jokes, if you will. I won't fall for your games again," the Acrasian marine said, and snapped his fingers.

Nels heard something thump onto the ground. Someone grunted, and Sebastian made a small angry noise. Nels finally turned. The dizzy feeling vanished.

Viktor lay in the dirt face down, his back a bloody mess. Nels kept his face blank against the shock. Viktor shifted—agony evident in the hiss of his breath.

He's alive, at least, Nels thought.

Smug triumph curled the corners of the Acrasian's lips. Nels struggled with an overwhelming urge to punch it off his mouth.

"You're making deals with the Regnum now, cousin?" Nels asked Edvard without turning from Viktor. He stuck with Acrasian, knowing that Edvard would have no trouble understanding. "That doesn't usually go well for anyone but the Acrasians. You'd be wise to learn from my uncle."

"I've done everything I can for you," Edvard said. "The Emperor knows you can't inherit the throne of Eledore. You'll be safe in Ytlain, you and your troops. I can offer you refuge. Your sister, I'm afraid, is another matter."

"Is that so?" Nels asked, switching to Ytlainen.

"What did he say?" the Acrasian commander asked.

Edvard ignored him and continued the conversation in Ytlainen. "There's nothing to be gained with further bloodshed, Nels."

"But there's certainly something to be gained in selling me to

Acrasia, isn't there?" Nels asked. "I hear the price on my head has gone up recently."

"Do you think the Acrasians can offer me enough?" Edvard asked. "If I sell you, I betray your mother's memory. You must know I won't do that. She was like a sister to me. We were close until the day she died. She looked after you. She asked me to do the same if I could. She was a good person. She wouldn't want—"

"She found that being good has very little to do with survival, I'm afraid," Nels said.

"Nels, please," Edvard said in Ytlanen-accented Eledorean. "Let me do this for you. Let me save you. Give up this nonsense."

"It isn't nonsense," Nels said, answering in the same language. "It's my home. Suvi is my *sister* and my queen."

"Hopeless idealism," Edvard said. He kept his voice low. "Be realistic. Save what you can."

"And accept my place like one of father's automatons?" Nels asked in an angry whisper.

"I didn't intend to insult—" Edvard cut himself off. "Your mother said you were proud, self-destructive, and willful. I was merely attempting to do what was best for you."

"I'm not a child," Nels said. "I'm twenty-one."

"I apologize. I didn't mean to treat you as such."

"No. You treated me as if I were less. You tried to control me like an animal. Well, Mother didn't tell you everything about me, did she?" Abandoning the chair, he poured the wine onto the ground.

Edvard blinked.

Nels's left hand twitched into a fist. He switched to Acrasian. "Thank you for your most generous offer, cousin. But I find I must decline."

"Then you are under arrest," the Acrasian commander said. "Bring the irons."

"Not . . . so fast," Nels said. "Perhaps you should have a look at what I have positioned on that hill first?" He pointed.

Growing up without discernible magical power in an environment that was deadly to those without had forced Nels to compensate for his lack in other ways. It had forced him to lie. It had forced him to cheat. In short, he'd learned to fake it.

He'd only recently come to understand that such a thing could be used as an advantage. Of course, tricks learned from Acrasian street harvesters and mountebanks didn't suffice in all instances, but he found people tended to see what they expected to see. Especially if they were told to see it. And if the commander's expression was any indication, he saw exactly what Nels hoped: eight cannon bearing down on the clearing. In truth, they weren't much more than Captain Julia's dead leaves. *One swivel cannon, a number of hidden powder barrels primed to explode, and seven carved and painted tree trunks, to be exact.*

The marine's face turned bright red, and he pointed to Edvard. "You said he would be defenceless! Where did he get those guns?"

Edvard shrugged. "It seems my cousin's spies are better than yours. Does it matter? You have made the gamble and lost. We both did."

The commander drew a pistol and pointed it at Edvard.

Nels said, "Oops."

Changing targets, the commander aimed at Nels.

Nels's heart dropped into his stomach, and his blood froze in his veins. *This is it. I'm going to die.*

"Commander . . . pardon me, but I seem to have forgotten your name," Edvard said.

The commander frowned. "Munitoris, Commander Munitoris Ulpius." He emphasized his gens name in a way that indicated Edvard should be impressed.

Edvard clearly wasn't. "Commander Munitoris." His tone was measured and calm, almost bored. "Are you personally negating the treaty between the Regnum of Acrasia and the Kingdom of Ytlain? Because it would appear to be the case at this moment."

Commander Munitoris hesitated. "You are hardly neutral. You're helping him."

"I arranged this meeting, did I not? I told your general that the rest was up to him. You have lost the encounter," Edvard said. "So. Again, let me ask, are you personally negating the treaty between the Acrasian Regnum and the Kingdom of Eledore?"

Commander Munitoris shook his head.

Edvard said, "In that case, would you kindly put away your weapons?"

Signaling to the others first, Commander Munitoris lowered his pistol.

"Now I think you should leave," Edvard said. "You have nothing left to achieve by staying. You have six hours in which to vacate Ytlainen waters. Linger an instant longer and the relationship between your country and mine will be damaged."

Nels waited until the Acrasians were gone. "Thank you."

"Don't thank me. I'm not doing you or the rest of the world a service by furthering your cause," Edvard said in Eledorean, his voice weary. "The more you antagonize the Regnum, the more diffi-cult you make it for the rest of us to live peaceably with them. Don't ask anything more from me. Please take your money and go."

Biting back an angry retort, Nels bowed and then went to Viktor. He knelt and laid a gentle hand on Viktor's bloody shoulder.

Viktor whispered, "Next time, you visit with the nice Acrasians."

"Done." Nels shut burning eyes and for the first time admitted something to himself. It destroyed the last vestige of a hope that had haunted the back of his mind for three lonely years.

I'd have made a terrible king.

"Sir?" Sebastian asked.

"Julia, if you will help Viktor? Sebastian and I will see to the chests. We've got what we came for."

⤙ I L T A ⤚

"Good afternoon," Ilta said, pausing in the doorway. Although she'd been sent for, she wasn't sure if she was interrupting.

"For a philosophy professor from the University of Novus Salernum, James Slate seems to have a talent for spying," Suvi said. Thumbing through the thick stacks of papers neatly piled on a dining table serving as a second writing desk, she didn't look up from what she'd been focused on as she spoke. "I've the names of the Acrasian military leadership and their relations. This is a list of the five gens and their spheres of business influence. Here's a log of active navy ships as well as a list of new vessels being built and advancements made in their construction. I've read several papers on Acrasian weapons technology. And this is a report on the Brotherhood of Wardens. That one is proving to be a frightening read, I must say."

Suvi then pointed to another sheaf of papers. "I've also lists of artistic salons and political discussions patronized by the nobility. I've counted four different reports on the malorum. Just how many spies does that man employ? And what can you tell me about him that you haven't already?"

Ilta nodded a greeting to Jami, Suvi's korva, and then shut the door. "You're not even going to say good afternoon?" Her voice echoed off the walls of the nearly empty trunk-littered room.

"Sorry," Suvi said. She finally pulled her attention away from her work. Her thick mouse-brown curls had been gathered in a disordered knot on top of her head, her feet were bare, and she was wearing a white silk nightdress with a yellow robe thrown over it. She held a half-eaten apple in her ink-stained fingers.

Getting to her feet, Suvi abandoned the apple to a small plate and gave her a hug. "I've been up all night, trying to get caught up with what's been going on around here."

"I think this is the part where I'm supposed to remind you that you need to take care of yourself," Ilta said, returning the hug one-handed because of the basket in her other hand. "Why so much reading? Hasn't Jami been any help?" She settled into a padded chair near the fire and set the empty basket on the chilly stone floor.

The interior of the Hold tended to stay cold even in the summer months. Now that it was autumn, Ilta's feet already felt like ice. She toed off her slippers and shifted closer to the hearth. The room smelled of blessing candles and burning oak. She eased into the disordered coziness. *Thank the gods for thick rugs.*

"Jami is a more-than-adequate sneak," Suvi said. "However, people don't tend to enjoy being spied upon. Particularly if the someone in question is someone with whom one is attempting to form a trust bond. Not that she isn't good enough to escape notice."

Jami, the sneak in question, shrugged.

"So, gossip is better?" Ilta asked.

"Does it count as gossip, if it's a queen asking?" Suvi winked. She retrieved her apple.

"Only if she says it does," Jami said in a bored voice.

Suvi pointed at Jami. "See?" She joined Ilta at the hearth, collapsing into the second wingback chair with a less-than-ladylike thump. Suvi bit into the remains of her apple.

The rooms that had been reserved for Suvi were spacious, far more spacious than the limited furnishings—a writing desk, a large Waterborne rug, and two wingback chairs—transferred from the ship required. However, Suvi had indicated that she was planning on taking up permanent residence. Therefore, Ilta had done her part to make the place welcoming—even providing wall hangings, blankets, and rugs from her own collection. She'd created a number of them herself. Birch had installed the stained glass in the top half of the rows of north-facing window sashes. Each had been scavenged from Ilta's grandmother's house now abandoned on the other side of the mountain. The bedstead and wardrobe, which had been moved to the apartment, had been salvaged from Gardemeister. Trunks of books that Nels had smuggled from the now-abandoned summer palace in Järvi Satama months ago had been shoved against the far wall near the bookcases. Other tomes, Ilta knew, had been rescued from other cities, now ruins, as was Nels's habit. Some of the trunks had been unloaded onto the shelves, but not all.

Will everything ever be easy between us? "I don't know the exact number," Ilta said, continuing the conversation.

"What?" Suvi asked. There were dark circles under her eyes.

"Of spies. I don't know the exact number of spies James Slate employs," Ilta said. "I've never asked. Perhaps you should, since they are now yours by extension. As far as I know, James has been working on his contacts for a year and a half. Possibly longer. He did live in Novus Salernum for most of his life.

"You should talk to him about the communication systems he's invented," Ilta continued. "They're brilliant. There's a woman in Novus Salernum who sends him messages through swatches of lace."

Suvi leaned closer. "How?"

"The patterns are a code that only he and the spy in question can decode," Ilta said. "The Acrasians merely see an old woman and a basket of lace. They never give it thought. Nickols buys the lace from her once a month and doesn't even know its importance."

"That is incredibly smart," Suvi said. "I wish I'd thought of it. How did he?"

"It was on a day when he wanted to read and couldn't. He found that if the typesetter used a particularly heavy press, he could make out some of the text by feel. That's when he had the idea of a code meant to be felt, not read," Ilta said. "The Acrasians can't see a message that's intended to be read with one's fingers. All of his spies report to him in a similar manner—not with lace, mind you. But with items related to their daily lives. There's a carver who works messages into wooden toys."

"That is amazing," Suvi said.

"He's very intelligent."

"Philosophy seems an odd background for a spymaster," Suvi said.

"I suppose," Ilta said. "But then again, maybe it isn't. I thought you liked him."

"I do," Suvi said. "I just don't know if I trust him yet."

"That's understandable," Ilta said without stating what she

knew bothered Suvi the most. *He's Acrasian.* "These things take time."

Jami grunted.

"What do *you* think of James, Jami?" Ilta asked.

As the Queen's korva, Jami had a mind that was refreshingly unreadable.

Jami said, "He seems quite a competent korva for an Acrasian."

"That's high praise," Suvi said, the sarcasm evident in her tone.

"She asked," Jami said, and shrugged.

Suvi leaned back in her chair, stretched, and closed her eyes. "Ilta, I'm sorry we haven't talked alone until now. And I'm sorry I haven't thanked you for everything you've done to make me comfortable here."

With Jami in the room, Ilta knew they weren't exactly alone. However, they were as alone as they were going to be.

"It's all right," Ilta said, and smoothed her skirts. She couldn't help feeling nervous. There had been a time when Suvi had hated her and with good reason, Ilta had felt, but they had sorted out their differences, or at least found peace with one another. *No one lives a perfect life, free from error. Especially those who wield power.* However, sometimes the old unease crept in, and she found her insecurity formed obstacles. She was aware that Suvi had her own self-doubts—largely because of her inability to shield her own thoughts. Nonetheless, they were slowly becoming friends, and Ilta was pleased by that knowledge. She told herself that the fact that it was taking so long was for the best.

"We've both been busy," Ilta said. "So, how *did* the negotiations go?"

"As you predicted. Terrible," Suvi said, and sighed. "They're afraid of the Acrasian Regnum. Everyone. And yes, that includes Cousin Edvard—although he'd never admit it. Not that I saw him. His prime minister made excuses to cover Edvard's having left before I'd arrived. The Zhelezokholm visit was much more profitable. The Queen of Kaledan donated a thousand gold pescas, which amounts to five hundred or so Acrasian sterling. So, the trip wasn't entirely pointless."

Ilta got the sense that Suvi was far more frustrated and frightened than she let on. *She's worried about Nels. Well, she's not alone in that.* Rather than drawing attention to the source of her anxiety, Ilta kept the conversation directed elsewhere. She knew Suvi would find it more reassuring. "And were you able to locate Trygve Blomgrin? Or at least some indication as to where he might be?"

Trygve Blomgrin had been the Royal Swordmaster during the Acrasian war. Rumor had it that he knew the secret of Eledorean water steel. Suvi didn't believe that this was the case. However, she did know that he understood the blades better than anyone alive. Unfortunately, he'd disappeared during the evacuation of Jalokivi.

"I'm afraid not. But I did find fourteen blades in Kaledan and three more in Ytlain," Suvi said. "They aren't currently useable, but the Waterborne have swordsmiths. They should be able to repair them."

"That isn't nearly enough to pay what we owe," Ilta said. "Sea Lord Kask won't be satisfied."

"I know," Suvi said, an unhappy expression on her face.

"Dylan will be here soon," Ilta said.

"I know," Suvi said. "Jami told me."

"What are you going to do?" Ilta asked.

"You're my Silmaillia," Suvi said. "I was hoping you'd have some ideas."

Ilta shook her head. "Sorry. I'm all out of aphorisms today."

A weak smile appeared on Suvi's lips. "I wish I knew what the Acrasians did with the swords they took when they invaded."

Ilta tried not to take that as an accusation. *You're the Silmaillia.*

You should know these things. But visions weren't something one could control, and Suvi knew that. "Me too."

"I've one bit of good news," Suvi said. "I was able to locate a swordsmith in Kaledan. One with a great deal of experience."

"That's something, anyway."

"Her name is Pasha Kuznetsov," Suvi said. "And she's a metal-speaker, I understand. I don't know how powerful. But if she can learn how to replicate water steel, our problems are solved."

"If only it were that easy," Ilta said.

"She's motivated to experiment, at least. And in the meantime, she'll keep the troops in serviceable blades by repairing what we have," Suvi said.

"You mean what Nickols is able to steal."

Suvi shrugged. "That should reduce our dependence upon our allies. The only problem is, Kuznetsov speaks Ledanese. She doesn't know Eledorean or Acrasian, and her Ytlainen is limited."

"She'll learn fast enough, I assume," Ilta said. "I can help." Not that she spoke Ledanese, but at least she could better guess Kuznetsov's meaning through her feelings and thoughts—provided Kuznetsov was a person who associated ideas with images. Of course, it was likely that Nels did speak Ledanese. However, bringing him up wasn't the best idea at the moment.

"And when will you have time for that?" Suvi asked.

Ilta returned her smile. "I can find someone else to help too, but as far as I know, no one here speaks Ledanese, much less the southern dialect."

Suvi winced. "I didn't mention which dialect."

"Oh, goddess, I'm sorry," Ilta said.

"It's all right," Suvi said. "At least you're the only one I have to worry about anymore. The Hold isn't exactly populated with thought-readers."

"I do try to not act like I can hear," Ilta said.

"I was able to adjust to Piritta. I'll get used to you," Suvi said, remembering her former souja. "At least you don't interrupt my thoughts with a constant commentary on courtiers' mode of dress." *Oh, Piritta. I do miss you, my friend.* Suvi changed the subject. "What about our new gunsmith?"

"I don't know yet," Ilta said. "He should be here soon. The good news is we've three volunteers interested in apprenticing. None are metal-speakers, but they can help with the labor."

"Excellent," Suvi said. "Dylan and Dar should have the last of the equipment we traded for. Do you think one forge will be big enough?"

"It'll have to be," Ilta said. "What do you think about Kuznetsov?"

"She seems excited about the prospect of experimentation," Suvi said. "I don't think she got much leeway for creativity in Zhelezokholm. I suspect one enthusiastic boy won't hinder her much. She's old enough to know how to manage herself and him if necessary. Nonetheless, Acrasians aren't terribly open when it comes to foreigners. If problems evolve, I'll leave it to James to sort out. Freeson was his idea."

"I'll talk to James. I'm sure it'll be fine."

"And the surgery?" Suvi asked. "How are you doing?"

"We're busy. I delivered another baby yesterday. My eighth. A girl," Ilta said. "Everything is working out well enough. I've one assistant. Kaija Westola and Sergeant Wiberg have been helpful when they're not traveling with Nels. But we need an assistant for Kaija. Unfortunately, she keeps driving them off."

"Really?" Suvi asked.

"Have you ever met Kaija Westola?"

"I can't say that I have," Suvi said.

"She's one of the best surgeons I've ever worked with," Ilta said.

"Unfortunately, she's a grumbletonian with the personality of a wet bear in Nälkäkuu. She doesn't bother me because I understand her. But Kaarina refuses to be in the same room with Kaija, and well . . . she punched Cassian in the face. Not that he didn't ask for it. But still."

Suvi paused. "Don't bears usually sleep in the winter?"

"Not wet ones. Not unless it wants to freeze to death."

"Oh."

There came a knock on the door. Jami answered it, and Valerri, Suvi's servant, entered with a tray of food and wine.

"Would you like to join me for lunch?" Suvi asked.

Ilta stood up. "I can't. I told James I'd treat his eyes this afternoon."

"How is that going?" Suvi asked.

"As well as can be expected," Ilta said. "If he were kainen, he'd have been treated sooner. He wouldn't have to worry about becoming blind. I could've stopped the progression, but now? All I can do is slow it."

"I'm sorry to hear that," Suvi said.

"Me too," Ilta said. "At least I can give him another year or so of sight, a few days at a time."

"All right," Suvi said. "I'll see you later." She got to her feet and gave her a hug. "Are you free for dinner? I'd like some company."

"I am," Ilta said, and hugged her back. Then she gathered her basket and left.

❧ S U V I ❧

The Hold
Grandmother Mountain
New Eledore

Third of Verikuu, 1783
Midnight

Clár Oibre Rúnda, with her charcoal-black hull and matching sails, was difficult to spot in the dark. Watching the two-masted sloop of war glide to her berth next to *Otter,* Suvi briefly wondered how many ships the Waterborne had that were similarly designed. *Probably quite a few,* she thought. Although honorable, not every movement the Waterborne made was above the waterline—as Dylan would phrase it. *Useful. Maybe we could have a few of the same sorts of ships one day? If New Eledore survives.*

That's a big 'if.'

The Eledorean corvette and the Waterborne ship were of

similar size. Side by side, they looked like two beautiful sisters—one light, one dark.

Her relief at seeing her friends safe was mixed with anxiety. She had missed Dylan, of course. He had been one of her closest confidants since her first posting in her father's navy—years before she'd become queen, but the news she had for him wasn't positive. She hoped this wouldn't spell the end of the only positive political alliance New Eledore possessed. Her chest ached with that thought, and she told herself for the hundredth time that a queen could ill-afford self-pity.

When Dylan spotted her waiting, he secured the sloop to the dock with one last rushed knot and scrambled down the short rope ladder. Smiling, he held his arms out wide. "Suvi! You met us at the dock in person?"

"Of course, I did!" She grabbed him in a tight hug, her face hitting him in the chest. He smelled of fresh air, ship tar, salt, and spices. "You certainly took your time getting up the river."

He lifted her into the air like an indulgent big brother, and she couldn't help letting out a girlish squeal. That was when she noticed the white mark on Dylan's forehead. She held her questions for later.

He set her back on her feet. "Sailing only at night has its disadvantages."

"Why bother? Didn't you travel the whole way from the coast by the Kristallilasi River? The Acrasians don't have any fortifications west of Trecoli, not on the river. They haven't resumed moving westward, have they?" Suvi asked.

"They haven't," Dylan said. "But there were complications."

"Complications? Are you hurt?" She pointed to the white mark. It was the size of a thumbprint. She'd never seen anything like it before. "Should I get a healer?"

An embarrassed expression passed over Dylan's features. "Not now," he muttered.

"My turn." Dar dropped two seabags onto the dock with a thump that echoed off the cave walls, and held out his arms for a hug. "River navigation isn't any fun. The wind is always in the wrong direction this time of year. Do you know how often we had to resort to towing *Clár* like a barge?"

"Why didn't Dylan make some wind?" Suvi asked, and released Dylan.

Dylan said, "Even I don't have power enough to pilot a boat the length of the Kristallilasi."

In the midst of changing targets, Suvi spotted a shaggy brown Eledorean pony eating oats from a bucket on *Clár's* deck. She wrapped her arms around Dar. "Good thing you remembered to bring a horse."

"Who says we did?" Dar said.

"Then where did that come from?" Suvi asked, stepping back from Dar and pointing to the pony.

"Oh. That's Anu," Dar said with a grin.

"Did you steal Anu?" Suvi asked.

"Why, dear lady," Dar said. "What are you implying? Water-borne are merchants—"

Suvi said, "I know. I know."

"—we'd never ever do—"

"—any such thing," Suvi said. "I know."

Dar leaned closer. "Poor Anu was living in an Acrasian work camp north of Wyeth. She was pining for Grandmother Mountain. How could we refuse?"

"I see," Suvi said. "And that didn't have anything to do with your need to travel only at night?"

Dylan said, "Not as much as the noise Dar made when he stole her."

Suvi said, "I thought you didn't—"

"I was quiet!" Dar made his defence to Dylan. "The dogs were the noisy ones. Can I help it I don't speak Acrasian guard dog?"

"Information that would've been good to know before you wandered into an Acrasian work camp," Dylan said. "Filled with armed Acrasians, I might add."

"Admit it," Dar said, giving Dylan's cheek a kiss. "It was fun."

"It may have been fun," Dylan said.

"Come on, you two," Suvi said. "It's cold out here."

"What about poor Anu?" Dar asked.

Suvi motioned to one of the troops guarding the river gate. "She'll be fine. Private Olhouser will see her to the stable," Suvi said, linking her arms through both Dylan and Dar's elbows. "Now, let's get your things to your rooms. I've a bottle of Kaledan port that needs drinking."

"Oh?" Dar asked.

"We should take care of this rather unfortunate circumstance, Dar," Dylan said. "For the sake of friendship."

"I admire your noble selflessness," Dar said. "A trait I find I share."

A little over half of an hour later, she was once again sitting in front of the fire in her rooms, this time with a glass of port. Anu was happily munching oats in a clean stall with the few horses kept in the Hold, and Dylan and Dar's baggage had been taken to the apartments next to hers.

She kicked off her slippers and dug her bare toes into the thick rug. "How was your journey?"

"The river portion of the trip was dull, for the most part," Dylan said. "The Acrasians haven't made much progress colonizing Eledore."

"My brother's efforts do seem to have lessened their enthusiasm." Suvi detected guilt in Dylan's face at the mention of Nels, and frowned.

Dylan looked away. "What's wrong?"

"You convinced him it would be safe to meet with Cousin Edvard, didn't you?" Suvi asked.

Dylan held up his hands. "As I recall, *I* tried to talk him out of it. I merely supplied passage to Norman Island."

"You did what?!" She jumped to her feet. "Dylan Ardan Kask! I don't know that I'll ever forgive you!"

"It was safer than letting him do it himself," Dylan said. "Do you know how much the Acrasians are willing to pay for his head right now?"

She began to pace. She reached the end of the rug and whirled. "That doesn't give you an excuse to—"

"Look," Dylan said. "He's only doing everything he can to keep you alive."

"He's reckless and—"

"I know what you're doing. Don't think I don't," Dylan said. "You're angry with him, not me. And in all honesty, you're probably not even angry with him. The person you're actually angry with is King Edvard. But you can't scream at him. So, you're taking it out on me. I wish you wouldn't."

Suvi sighed. "Shit." The mantel clock ticked nine times before she fell back into her chair. "I'm sorry."

"Apology accepted. Please don't do it again," Dylan said. "Now, what's really bothering you? You can tell me."

"And me," Dar said. "I promise not to tell a soul. Unless it's something really juicy."

"Dar, you're not helping," Dylan said.

Dar held his hands in the air. "It was a joke!"

Dylan said, "Some things aren't funny. Particularly when it involves leaders of foreign countries."

"Right," Dar said. "Shutting up now."

"I *am* sorry," she said. *This is Dylan and Dar. You can say what you feel.* "I'm—I'm terrified."

Nodding, Dylan said, "Any sensible person would be."

"Every door has closed against us," she said. "And I'm running out of options. Let alone ideas." Tears blurred her vision and a painful lump formed in her throat. She struggled to voice things she didn't dare say even to her brother, Nels. *Especially Nels.* "I—I'm failing my people—have failed. Oh, goddess, I don't know what to do." She began to sob. "I'm so tired of everything going wrong!" She took out her frustration on the padded arm of the chair.

Dylan stood up. "Come here."

She held him tight and cried in a way she hadn't dared to do in front of anyone in more than a year. It felt wonderful to not have to worry about what anyone thought.

When she'd finished, she fished a handkerchief from her sleeve, stepped back, and blew her nose. "I'm sorry."

"Don't be," Dar said. "I honestly don't know how you keep from constantly weeping."

"Suvi is a strong one," Dylan said.

"No, I'm not." She moved back to the chair, her face heating.

Dylan let her compose herself before continuing. "I take it your search didn't go as well as planned?"

She waited, attempting to find the right words, and gave up. "The swordsmith, Trygve Blomgrin, is still missing. I was able to trace him as far as Ytlain, but he took a ship for Zhelezokholm a month later. The vessel never reached the city. Pirates are being blamed."

Dylan frowned. "My father isn't going to be happy to hear that."

"I found seventeen water steel blades," Suvi said.

"That isn't what you promised," Dylan said.

"I know. I—" She sighed. "I didn't lie to your father. I'd do anything to get them to him. I know you need them. I know why."

"The soulbane problem is getting worse. We've lost six ships in the past eight months," Dylan said.

Suvi said, "If I had them to give, I'd—"

"I've two options," Dar said. "But you're not going to like either of them."

Suvi said, "As long as they don't involve letting down the only ally that Eledore has left, I'm open to hearing them."

"The first," Dylan said, "is a proposal my father pulled together in the eventuality that you wouldn't be able to meet your agreement."

"Now I really feel terrible," Suvi said.

"It's all right. Listen," Dylan said. "He's willing to sponsor your application for clan membership as an independent clan. He is willing to take your request directly to the Sea Mother. In exchange, he would like to form a close partnership."

Suvi blinked. "Why would he do that? What could he gain? We have nothing."

"Not nothing," Dar said.

Dylan said, "You have several thousand acres of virgin ironwood forests north of Mehrinna which, should Clan Kask partner with your clan, could make us both a great deal of money."

Eledore was the only source for ironwood in the whole of Västmark. That had been one of the reasons Eledore had enjoyed favored status with the Waterborne in the past. *Before Uncle Sakari destroyed that relationship.* It was also one of the reasons Eledore had once been known for her navy. "I see," Suvi said. "And what prevents him from simply taking whatever he wants?"

"The Acrasians, for a start," Dylan said. "If a member clan had a legitimate claim to those lands, there is very little the Regnum could do. All the Waterborne would stand united with you. And the Regnum of Acrasia cannot afford to anger the whole of the Waterborne Nations."

"They need our whale oil," Dar said.

"I thought the Waterborne as a whole didn't take sides in wars," Suvi asked.

"It's rare, but there are exceptions," Dylan said. "In this case, the ironwood alone would be reason enough."

"The Waterborne don't openly hold land," Suvi said, already knowing this wasn't the case.

"Not within the continent of Västmark," Dylan said.

Dar said, "Dylan—"

"Suvi isn't stupid, Dar," Dylan said. "She's been to Treaty Island. She's lived there for a few months. She already guesses the homelands exist."

Suvi noted that Dylan didn't give the name or hint at the location. "And that information is safe with me," she said, and paused. "That's the other reason for the offer, isn't it?"

"It would keep that knowledge where it belongs," Dylan said. "Within the Waterborne Nations." He paused. "This isn't the first time such an offer has been made, you know."

"I see." Suvi nodded. "That's why you're the Waterborne Nations."

Dylan shrugged. "Well?"

"And if I refuse?" Suvi asked. "You've shown me the carrot. Where's the stick?"

Dylan looked away. "Something will have to be arranged, one way or the other. Obviously, my preferences don't feature in the matter."

I thought as much. The pressure of ever-narrowing options intensified. Suvi swallowed her panic and asked, "And your second proposal? I'd like to know all my options before I give you an answer."

"What if I told you that there's a large cache of water steel swords that the Acrasians took out of the vault in Jalokivi? And what if I said I knew where they are located?" Dar asked.

Suvi sat up. "You do? How?"

"'How' isn't the right question, is it?" Dylan said with a smile.

"All right," Suvi said. "*Where* are they?"

"You're not going to like it," Dar said.

"I don't give a shit," Suvi said. "I'm desperate."

"Novus Salernum," Dar said. "In a closely guarded military depot owned by Consul Numerius of Acrasia."

Suvi slumped. "Shit."

"I told you you wouldn't like it," Dar said.

She bit her lip and stared into the flames. "Do you know exactly where this warehouse is?"

"We do," Dar said. "Thanks to a very curious, and as luck would have it, chatty quartermaster. I bet you never thought you'd be glad of the Acrasian's unreasonable fear of Eledorean magic."

"What?" Suvi asked.

Dylan said, "The swords were recently collected and moved to a single location. Some were even removed from warehouses under the Brotherhood's control. Strangely, the Brotherhood attempted to refuse the order."

Suvi said, "So, the tension between Emperor Herminius and the Brotherhood has been worsening."

Dar said, "Apparently, enough that a number of Wardens were executed."

"Consul Numerius has the Emperor's sympathy as well as his ear," Suvi said. "What happened to the blades?"

"They were packed into crates marked FOODSTUFFS and stored in a restricted room. No one is allowed in or out. Our man decided to have a look, since the depot in question is his responsibility. He was rather disconcerted by what he found."

"Oh."

"Well?" Dar asked.

Suvi gave the situation some thought. "Those aren't great choices."

"I know," Dylan said. "What do you think?"

"I think I need to have an Acrasian military depot burgled," Suvi said.

"And the other option?" Dylan asked.

"Tell your father that—that I'm giving his kind offer serious consideration," Suvi said.

"You're not going to accept," Dylan said.

"Probably not—not now," Suvi said. "But I can't reject it outright. If our situation gets any worse, I may not have any other choice. I am a realist, you know."

Dylan nodded.

"Why did the consul take custody of the swords? For that matter, why would the Brotherhood refuse to hand them over?" Suvi asked. "Aren't Acrasians afraid of Eledorean magic? Aren't the Brotherhood charged with protecting Acrasia from kainen?"

"It makes no sense to me, either," Dar said. "Unless they plan on using them. But they wouldn't possibly do that. Would they?"

"Who knows?" Suvi asked. "They're Acrasians."

"Then you'd be willing to steal them back?" Dar asked.

"What other choice do I have?" Suvi asked. "But there's one problem."

"And that is?" Dar asked.

"I don't know any thieves," Suvi said. "And neither do the Waterborne."

"And who says the Waterborne will have anything to do with breaking into an Imperial military depot?" Dylan asked.

"I thought you—"

"Clan Kask can't be anywhere near this," Dylan said.

"Right," Suvi said.

"However, Dylan, best friend of Suvi Hännenen, wouldn't miss it for the world."

Dar said, "Me neither."

⊰ BLACKTHORNE ⊱

ONE

FOURTH OF VERIKUU, 1783

The campfire popped. Blackthorne placed fresh wood in the flames to reheat the tea water. A cold wind gust blasted through the camp, and he waved smoke from his face and coughed. He'd spent a good part of the morning replacing the fuel he had used from the hidden cache the night before, and his muscles twitched. He'd needed the physical exertion after the long, dull ride. The journey was nearing its end at last. Mrs. Holton's wagon had seen them to safety. He stood and turned. The view of the valley below was breathtaking, and had he been in the right mind, he'd have meditated in preparation for the day ahead. He had need of his usual routine, but he told himself there wasn't time, and in any case, he wasn't alone.

Another hour or two up Grandmother Mountain, and he would be home.

"I'm not crawling back into that coffin. It stinks." Tobias sat on a log next to the fire with a handkerchief tied over his eyes. "Haven't heard anyone pass us in ages. We can't be near a town. I counted six days since we crossed the river."

It'd been nine, but Blackthorne wasn't about to correct him. Disorientation was normal under the circumstances. He knew from experience, but he'd also deliberately changed the meal routine and driven the wagon through the night—only stopping when necessary to save the horse, or when his or Tobias's bladder required it.

"I can't know where we're going. I understand that," Tobias said. "But isn't the blindfold enough? Can't I ride next to you in the wagon? You'll have to trust me at some point. Right?"

Pouring the last of the tea into a tin cup, Blackthorne made a decision and dug for another of the vials in his pack. Then he poured half the bottle's contents into the tea. With that done, he placed the cup in Tobias's blind hands. "Drink while it's hot."

"I heard wolves howling last night," Tobias said with an edge of unease in his voice. "They sounded close."

Blackthorne raised an eyebrow. "Wild animals are to be expected. This isn't the city." However, he was certain the wolves that had prowled outside the camp walked on two legs, not four, and wore the remnants of Eledorean uniforms, not fur. "There was nothing for you to fear." In truth, there wasn't—not for Tobias, anyway.

Tobias sipped. "This is good. When did you get honey for the tea?"

"I could drug you." Blackthorne returned to his breakfast. "It would make the remainder of your journey more comfortable." He didn't know why he said it. The smith's answer wouldn't change anything. *Not now.* Blackthorne's words were a cheat and wouldn't soften the repercussions. The friendly portion of their association was now ended, and he damned well knew it, even if Tobias didn't.

Emptying his cup in one gulp, Tobias shook his head. "I want to be awake when we get there."

Unfortunately, that isn't an option, Blackthorne thought. *Not if you wish to be outside the hidden compartment.* Using a stick, he broke up the still-burning coals and moved the largest piece of wood out of the fire now that the tea was gone.

"What's the town called again?" Tobias asked. "Can you tell me that much?"

Blackthorne rinsed the kettle with water from his canteen. Tobias had been uncharacteristically quiet since he'd become ill. Blackthorne took the fresh show of curiosity as a good sign. "It doesn't have a name. It isn't a town. It's a honeycomb of warehouses once owned by the Waterborne. They call it the Hold. Are you finished?"

"Yes, sure." Tobias held out the tin cup. "What does the Hold look like?"

"You'll find out soon enough. We arrive tonight."

Kicking dirt into the fire first, Blackthorne emptied the water bucket on hissing ashes and stomped. He hadn't slept well in more than a month, and he was dead on his feet. The nightmares had been getting worse, more vivid. They were strongest when he spent any time in Novus Salernum. It wasn't until he'd come to live on Grandmother Mountain that he'd known any relief from them.

He pushed aside trivial worries and focused on clearing the campsite. By the time the packing was finished, Tobias was unconscious in the back of the wagon. Blackthorne took the steep trail as slowly as he could, for the sake of the horse. The last four hours of the journey were accomplished in fits and starts. He had to stop, move a deadfall or some brush from the path, pull the wagon forward, stop again, and then replace the path-obscuring brush. Once, he reached a stream and had to place wooden planks across it to form a temporary bridge. There were checkpoints as well. Sentries who didn't offer to help him with his charge or the wagon. Done alone, it was hard work, but necessary. He wouldn't and couldn't be the one to bring the Wardens or the Home Guard to the Hold. It was almost dark when he spied the Hold's carved mountain face.

Before the site had been leased to the Waterborne, it had been constructed by ancient Eledoreans as a burial site. A fifty-foot edifice complete with columns had been sculpted into the canyon wall. Centuries ago, a branch of the ever-shifting Kurainen River had washed away the lower half of the carvings. During certain times of the day, the remains of the pillars appeared to float above a natural cave entrance. At some point, a door had been installed at the back of the cave. It was the only indication that the place hadn't been long abandoned.

Blackthorne applied the brake, hopped down, and went to the back of the wagon.

"Who goes there?" The question was accompanied by a loud click.

"Blackthorne." He held his hands high in the air and waited. This was the third sentry he'd met in two hours. Since news of his impending arrival had most certainly been communicated to the Hold by now, he knew the repeated identity check was unnecessary. However, he complied anyway.

The scent of pipe smoke filled a long silence. Exhausted and hungry as he was, Blackthorne didn't move. Depending upon who was on watch, the guard might choose to mistake him for an

Acrasian soldier. It'd happened before, and he was in no shape for dodging musket balls.

A tall figure slid down from a hidden niche, and Blackthorne recognized one of the Ghost's soldiers by the blue greatcoat.

Swive me, Blackthorne thought.

The Eledorean officer with long blond hair and a pox-scarred face let out a loud whistle using his fingers and then moved closer until his musket muzzle touched Blackthorne's chest. Then the gun suddenly swept the air, knocking Blackthorne's tricorne off his head and into the dirt. "Assume the position, crow."

Gritting his teeth, Blackthorne got down on his knees and moved his hands to the back of his head.

"That's right," the pox-scarred Eledorean said. "Flap those wings. Now give me the pass phrase."

Blackthorne focused on the ground. The cold gun barrel tapped his cheek. He lifted his elbows higher and turned his head away from the muzzle. *He'll grow bored. Can't do much more than this.* Blackthorne's heart raced, and his jaw clenched. He closed his eyes and attempted to still his rage. *You'd better pray our places are never reversed.*

But the truth was, they had been.

Swallow it. It's only pride. And the true Retainer cannot afford pride.

"The pass phrase. Quit stalling."

Blackthorne forced out the question. "May I polish your boots?"

"Brotherhood of Wardens. Pride of the Regnum. *Pure.*"

Warm spittle hit Blackthorne in the face.

"Not so haughty now, are you?" the pox-scarred Eledorean soldier asked. A quiet sound signaled the musket was no longer cocked. "On your feet, crow."

Wiping his cheek, Blackthorne picked up his hat. His legs

were unsteady as he dusted it off and returned to the wagon for his pack. He also shouldered one of the sacks of corn that had been used to cover Tobias's hiding place. The others would take care of the new arrival. They would see to it Tobias found a comfortable place in the community. It was how things were done.

As Blackthorne moved past, the guard hissed a guttural phrase. Blackthorne didn't speak Eledorean, but the emotion fueling the words was enough to understand the meaning. As usual, he let it pass without comment. The muscles between his shoulder blades tightened another notch.

He was home.

TWO

He decided to leave the corn in the kitchen larder rather than walk all the way to the granary. Then he'd go straight to his pallet bed and sleep for a few days. No one would miss him. He knew he should report to Slate first, but Blackthorne didn't trust himself to maintain self-control, let alone speak coherently. Slate's betrayal cut too deep. Still, Blackthorne was unsure if "betrayal" was the correct word. He was an underling—*a Retainer*. He was expendable. Therefore, it was important to be careful. Still, the rage lodged itself in his gut.

He took a deep breath and used that emotion to fuel the remaining steps to the kitchen.

Upon entering, he found that the scent of baking bread, coffee, and warm food hit him like a mule kick. He remembered that he'd not eaten since breakfast. His stomach let out a loud growl that sounded huge in the empty room. Heat from mounds of hot coals in the twin cooking hearths gave the kitchen a welcoming air.

Coffee, then, he thought. *A slice or two of bread.* He owned a toasting fork, a frivolous item he'd purchased on a whim in Novus

Salernum. He would warm the bread at the hearth in the privacy of his room. As a meal, it wouldn't compare to Moss's cooking, but it'd suffice. Blackthorne would rather not risk another encounter with the Ghost's men. He didn't trust himself. *Not now.* There were always a number of soldiers around. They protected the Hold, after all. He understood that when they weren't doing so, they travelled throughout the north, collecting what they could from the ruins of Eledore and her dwindling supporters, or harassing Acrasian troops.

They'll take a break from the raids soon. There will be more and more of them sheltering here. With winter coming, it makes sense.

He wasn't looking forward to his first winter in the north. It would present certain dangers that he didn't think Slate had considered when he'd ordered him to stay. Blackthorne didn't want to let more than one of the Ghost's men corner him. It'd happened before. *Once.* And if it hadn't been for the Reclamation Hospital, he would've ranked the beating he'd received with the worst of his life. It was a circumstance he sincerely wished to avoid repeating. As a Retainer, his life wasn't his own to squander.

He set the heavy grain sack next to a wooden crate and dropped his pack with a grunt. A dizzy spell almost knocked him off his feet. Placing a hand against the chilly stone wall, he breathed deep. Alone, he didn't bother pretending the vibration in his limbs was due to the weight he'd carried. It was against everything he'd been trained to be, but he'd long understood that knowing a thing and doing a thing were two different matters. He had been afraid—more than that. *Terrified.* He was weak—always had been. The duke would've said that it was his tainted blood that made him so. The best Blackthorne could hope for was to put off the emotional reaction until he was alone. It was but one of the many reasons he'd been a failure.

He slapped dirt from the knees of his breeches and allowed the release of delayed terror quake through him. *One of these days, the Ghost's men will kill you.* He didn't understand why he cared. He never had before.

Breathing deep, he mentally recited a line from the Retainer's Litany he'd memorized as a child. *Acceptance of the inevitable grants clear thinking in crisis. A true Retainer does not cling to life. Such thinking makes one vulnerable. It opens the mind to cowardice. A Retainer exists only to kill and die at the Master's whim, and the true Retainer dies only at the most advantageous moment. A Retainer is not bound by family, friends, or lovers. There is only duty—*

Footsteps drummed on the steps behind the larder door. He tensed, waiting to see who would emerge.

Moss, one of the Hold's few volunteer cooks with any talent for it, exited the larder carrying a tiny kitchen tin. Naturally, anything appeared small in Moss's massive hands. Clad in flour-dusted breeches and a cook's apron, he had the intimidating form of a massive foot soldier—provided foot soldiers were six and a half feet tall and weighed three hundred pounds. If such an infantry existed, Blackthorne never wanted to meet it. Moss's skin was pale and mottled with shades of grey. His hair was white and thick and knotted into a gentleman's pigtail. His eyes were an unsettling, colorless grey. It was said that when he'd first arrived, he'd given his name as Aleksander Jedediah Moss. No one used his full name. Slate said Moss came from the far north—farther north than even Eledoreans dared venture.

The Eledoreans had a name for Moss's kind. Slate had said it meant "people of iron and stone." Blackthorne didn't have a name for what Moss was. Moss's people weren't listed in the Brotherhood's registry of nonhuman races. As far as anyone in the Hold knew, they were unintelligent, cannibalistic, and mute.

Why are you here, Moss? Where did Slate find you? Are there others like you? As many times as Blackthorne had asked himself those questions, he hadn't dared to speak a single one aloud. If he didn't want others prying into his own past, then he couldn't justify prying into theirs.

"Welcome back, young Master Blackthorne. I understand your journey was a success?" Moss asked. His deep, rumbling voice matched his stone-like frame. However, the friendly yet formal tone didn't.

Blackthorne gave a polite nod in answer. He assumed the Ghost's men had informed everyone of his imminent return. News traveled fast in the little community, and a new resident was definitely news. Unable to move without staggering, Blackthorne stayed as he was with one hand against the cold wall.

Moss set down the tin container with care. It released a puff of flour nonetheless. Then he went to the big sideboard where most of the communal dishes were stored. Retrieving a bowl and wooden spoon, he placed them on the table as in invitation. His movements were graceful and quick in spite of his massive frame. "You must be hungry. Dinner was served an hour ago. However, there's stew left in the pot. When I heard you would be returning, I thought you might have need of it." The warmth of his expression became lost in incisors filed to sharp points.

Hesitating, Blackthorne asked, "Stew?" The word "cannibal" leapt to mind again before he could stop it. His stomach gave out a noisy protest, and he swallowed.

"The meat for the evening's repast was lamb," Moss said as if in answer to the thought. However, his demeanor didn't indicate that he'd understood Blackthorne's misgivings.

Blackthorne looked away before Moss could spy shame in his cheeks.

"I prefer not to handle meat. However, I've been instructing Slate's ward, Kat, in the culinary arts. It was one of her lessons. She won't mind if you consume the remainder. I imagine that if the stew isn't gone by the time she returns, she may be insulted." With that, Moss returned to his baking.

Armed with bowl and spoon, Blackthorne went to the iron pot heating over the grate in the first hearth. Glowing coals warmed his hands and legs. He bunched up the tail of his ragged greatcoat in one hand and used it to lift the iron lid. After filling his bowl with brown gravy and large chunks of mutton, he settled on the bench facing the door. The trembling in his knees slowly diminished. After a few bites, he forgot about insults and relaxed—as much as he could with a stranger in the room. Soon, his eyelids grew heavy, and he fought an urge to rest his head on the table. The gentle thumping rhythm of Moss's bread kneading drifted over Blackthorne, and his thoughts dissolved into a comfortable haze. His eyes fell closed. His room seemed an eternity away.

I'll rest here. Only for a moment, he thought. He'd begun to dream when a loud bang jerked him awake. His right hand flew to his pistol.

Moss pushed an old game board across the table toward him. "You were once an Acrasian patrician, were you not?"

Blackthorne's sluggish mind struggled for a response. It was the first time that anyone other than Slate had asked him a personal question. Shocked, Blackthorne glanced around the kitchen.

Noble. No one uses the word "patrician" anymore. And once more, Blackthorne wondered where Moss had learned to speak Acrasian. "And if I was?" The question came out in a hoarse whisper.

"Then you might be familiar with vendetta. I understand it's an Acrasian patrician's game."

Blackthorne swallowed a dull ache. He hadn't seen a vendetta board in well over a year. It brought up memories of the few pleasant aspects of his former life. He stared at the board. It'd once been expensive and would've been highly prized. Carved from cherrywood and oak with gold and silver inlay, its abused surface was now coated with dirt.

"Where did you get it?" Blackthorne asked.

"Slate gifted it to me some months ago. But I have been unable to find anyone who knows how the game is played. Do you?" Moss reached into his pockets and produced marble game pieces that didn't match the board.

Blackthorne paused. In a community of refugees, castoffs, undesirables, exiles, and escaped slaves, Moss was only slightly less feared than himself. This, regardless of the fact that Slate had declared Moss to be worthy of trust. It was the same reason Blackthorne was tolerated—Slate's word. That tolerance stretched a bit from time to time, Blackthorne knew more than anyone. Moss, like Blackthorne, kept himself apart. Although Blackthorne couldn't imagine that Moss felt threatened.

He must be lonely.

I shouldn't become involved, Blackthorne thought. His palm itched, and he rubbed it against his thigh. *Keep your distance. It would be safer for Moss.*

A Retainer is not bound by family, friends, or lovers. There is only duty to one's Master. Blackthorne gazed at Moss's expectant expression—at least, that's what Blackthorne hoped it was. Sometimes it was difficult to tell with Moss.

I've exchanged one cell for another, Blackthorne thought. *Is that what I want?*

"I apologize. I shouldn't have disturbed you," Moss said. Disappointment crested the wave of hope. "You are quite tired, I see. Please forgive me. I am still learning the social graces."

Blackthorne found himself reaching out to the chipped pieces, hesitantly at first. Then he righted the board, setting each figure in its proper place. "Why should you wish to learn?"

A shy smile tugged the corners of Moss's mouth. "Slate felt vendetta would be mentally engaging."

"I see." Blackthorne swallowed. He didn't understand why he was doing this when there were so many reasons why he shouldn't. "Black or white? The player who selects white moves first. It is also the aggressor—"

The kitchen door flew open, and a short, heavy man barged in. He stank of sweat, and his clothes were dirty. Stomping to the fireplace, he left a careless trail of mud and dead leaves on the clean kitchen floor. Blackthorne went rigid and dropped a hand to his pistol under the table. Technically, Jacob Nickols was human by Brotherhood standards. Blackthorne wouldn't have stretched the definition that far.

Damn my luck.

"There better be more than a few scraps left around here. There ain't, I'll— What in the hells is going on?" The Gibson Road in Jacob Nickols's voice often made it difficult for the others to understand him. Blackthorne understood Nickols perfectly well and so was certain it wasn't worth anyone's effort.

Nickols stepped toward the table, glaring.

"Mr. Blackthorne has generously offered to teach me to play vendetta," Moss said.

"He's teaching you what?" Nickols's mouth hung open.

Blackthorne prepared for a fight.

Moss said, "If you're hungry, there's stew available within—"

"Making friends with the Warden, are you?" Nickols asked with a laugh. "Right. The Warden hunts the extra nonhumans. And you pop them into the cooking pot? Is that it?" He put a dirty hand on Moss's arm. The area under the nails was black with grime.

Grabbing Nickols by the wrist, Blackthorne kept his voice low. "Leave him alone."

Nickols yanked free in disgust. "So, the Warden's gonna defend the monster? That's rich." He swept the game board off the table with one hand. Glass and marble pieces skittered across the floor.

Blackthorne hopped to his feet. Glass shards crunched under his boot as he stepped around the edge of the table and snatched up a handful of Nickols's filthy collar. Ramming his pistol under the man's chin, Blackthorne locked the hammer with a loud click.

Nickols choked and sputtered. "Was only funning."

"I don't appreciate your sense of humor," Blackthorne said. His whole body shook as he fought an urge to pull the trigger. *He isn't worth it.* Then he mentally counted to ten and released Nickols with a shove. "Get what you need and leave before I feed you your own gizzard."

Scrambling backward, Nickols put a hand to his throat as if the barrel had drawn blood. "I'm reporting this. Slate'll have you thrown you out. See if he doesn't." He edged to the door and scrambled through.

Blackthorne didn't breathe until Nickols's footsteps had faded. Putting away the gun, Blackthorne looked down at the remains of the game. *Why did I do that? What is wrong with me?* He blinked. *Is it because he attacked someone else?* "I shouldn't have interfered. I should've let him hit me and have done with it. That was stupid—"

"And unnecessary," Moss said. "But I thank you. No one has defended my honor before." He grabbed a broom that'd been leaning against the wall and began to sweep. "I had understood human males usually reserve such actions for potential mates." There was an undercurrent of mirth in his words. "In which case,

I feel I should inform you that my sexual preferences do not include humans. I hope my refusal does not damage our potential friendship."

A smile tugged at Blackthorne's mouth. It felt strange and nice all at once—this mutual exchange of humor. He couldn't remember the last time he'd done such a thing. "I should go." His head ached, and his eyes burned. Still, he knew it didn't matter how tired he was; he wasn't going to sleep, not now. "May I borrow a candle?"

"Of course, you may. And please return. Tomorrow. I would enjoy continuing the lesson, if you feel you can spare the time."

"I look forward to it," Blackthorne said, cursing himself for a fool.

THREE

He set the oak plank he used as a bolt against the door to his room. There was no other lock on the door. The Hold prided itself on having no need of them; therefore, he hadn't the heart to install one. Still, he found he couldn't rest without the bolt set. Having been away for months, he next took the time to see that everything was exactly as he'd left it. He didn't know why he bothered. He didn't keep anything in his apartments worth stealing—the stand for his pocket watch on the mantle, a three-legged stool, a pallet bed, and a homespun shirt hanging from a hook. What little else he owned traveled with him. The burgeoning community founded itself on the principle that what was needed was freely given. Thus, the Hold's citizens looked out for one another regardless of class, creed, or race.

Provided the person of that class, creed, or race isn't a former Warden. He bit down on resentment he didn't normally feel. *What is wrong with you? All is as it should be.*

A Retainer is not bound by family, friends, or lovers. There is only duty to one's Master.

Located on one of the lowermost levels, far from the others, his apartment was a former storage room and still smelled of scorched oak and fermented barley. With no windows, the room had no outside source of warmth or light. It became dank and cold when he was away. Dropping his pack for the last time, he went to the hearth. He couldn't rest until the fire was lit. His hands trembled as he stacked the wood and then used flint on the dried pine needles he stored for tinder. It didn't take long. He could do so without thought. The estate's hearth fire had been his first responsibility as a child.

Next, he removed his boots, knelt, and then rested his buttocks on his ankles in the Retainer-student position. Taking a deep breath, he smelled the warm scent of burning oak and pine. He focused on distributing his weight evenly on his hips and ankles. When he was sure of his balance, he closed his eyes. Breathing slow and deep, he attempted to release the tension in his shoulders and back with each exhale while keeping his head up. He visualized each intake of breath moving slowly up into the sky and then down his spine and into the earth with the outgo as if it were an ocean's tide. *Breathe in. Breathe out.* These were the first steps in centeredness. Each breath was to empty the mind, leaving only calm and clarity.

What have I gained by attacking Nickols? Nothing. I've left myself open for trouble.

I wouldn't have made that mistake before. I'm losing myself. Piece by piece. Who am I now? Is anything left of me? Stubborn tension anchored itself in his shoulders and stomach.

Why does this matter?

There is only duty to one's Master.

A silent vibration from his pocket watch marked the half hour. *Half past five.* There was no need to look. He gave up on meditation.

Carefully retrieving his watch via the leather thong he used in lieu of a watch chain, he got to his feet and placed the timepiece upon its wooden stand on the mantle. He was exhausted. Still, he couldn't bring himself to lie down.

He removed his ragged coat and carefully hung it on one of the hooks set into the wall. He stared into the fire and gave reading some consideration. Rejecting the idea, he resumed the student pose. This time, he did so closer to the hearth. His muscles at last began to unknot themselves. Unfortunately, it wasn't long before footsteps echoed in the passage outside the door. At once, Blackthorne shifted from the seated position to kneeling on one knee. He turned to face the door with a hand resting on the butt of his pistol. It was done with fluid grace and practiced skill, and his teacher would have been satisfied but for one vital mistake. His gun wasn't loaded.

Rather than focus on self-disgust, he tilted his head to listen. *One heartbeat. Two.* The footfalls echoing in the hallway were accompanied by the tapping of a cane. *Three heartbeats. Four.* His guts twisted, and knowledge came to him with a prickling sensation under his skin.

It is Slate, and he is alone. Blackthorne let his hand fall away from the useless gun. He went to remove the bolt before the anticipated knock landed on the door.

His ability to know a person by the sound of their steps had been something for which the director of the Warden Academy had praised him. Although it was one of the characteristics Wardens were reputed to have, the reality was that Wardens weren't superhuman. The myth was one of many designed to make citizens feel more secure. He had long thought it ironic. The Regnum cited the threat of magic as justification for its treatment of nonhumans and yet at the same time used myths verging on the magical to bolster its sense of righteousness.

"Blackthorne? May I come in?"

Blackthorne said, "Yes, sir." He stepped aside, allowing his superior admittance.

"Still bolting the door, I see." Slate was dressed as he usually was, in the prim but shabby tailoring of a professor. He was also one of the few residents, other than Blackthorne, who openly wore black, because Eledorean custom dictated that only soldiers wore that color. He held a wooden cane with a round silver knob on the end in his left hand. Although he was a robust fifty years old, the grey in his brown hair had grown more noticeable over the past year.

Blackthorne detected a frown on the man's face in the dim light. *Nickols has registered his complaint.* "Yes, sir."

Slate entered and almost immediately tripped over the abandoned pack. Without thinking, Blackthorne reached out and caught Slate by the elbow. Slate turned to him and squinted displeasure.

Blackthorne released his arm at once. "I—I'm sorry, sir."

"It's quite all right."

"Permit me to light some candles." Blackthorne preferred to navigate by the light of the fire when he was home. However, he understood that Slate's blindness wasn't complete, and the man seemed to see better in brighter light. At the same time, the glare seemed to pain his eyes.

Going to the trunk, he fished out the three beeswax candles that a grateful Holder had given him. That had been before Nickols had told everyone that he'd once been a Warden.

"You haven't had time to unpack," Slate said. "It is I who should be sorry. I can return tomorrow."

Blackthorne set the first candle in a small pewter holder and lit it with a twig from the fire. "I should have given you my report before retiring, sir."

"It can wait."

"Please stay, sir. There are things I must say," Blackthorne said. He finished with the last candle and motioned to the three-legged stool by the fire. "It is important for me to do so now rather than later."

Slate's frown returned, but he moved to the stool, leaned his cane against the fireplace, and sat. "Were you discovered?"

Resuming the student posture on the floor, Blackthorne said, "No, sir. I would have come to you at once if that were the case."

"That's a relief." Slate reached inside his coat and produced a silver flask. "Care for a little something to warm up?" The fire's glare caught his steel-rimmed lenses. Circles of yellow hid clouded eyes.

Accepting the flask, the sweet aroma of fine whiskey drifted up Blackthorne's nose. *Is this one of his tests?* He paused before taking a sip. "I understood you don't approve of alcohol, sir."

"There are exceptions to every rule," Slate said. "In any case, I thought you could use a drink after chatting with Nickols. I know I often do."

Blackthorne drank. He'd thought Slate to be a practicing member of an Acrasian religious sect that was strongly against any sort of vice, including drink. They called themselves Moralists.

"I apologize for my behavior, sir." Blackthorne kept his gaze lowered. His throat pleasantly burned as he returned Slate's flask.

"This isn't a reprimand," Slate said. "Let's hear what happened. I want your side of it."

"I drew a pistol on Jacob Nickols in the kitchen."

"You did what?"

"He insulted Moss. I shouldn't have, sir. I understand the rules about weapons within the confines of the Hold. I—"

A short laugh burst from Slate's throat. It was joined by several guffaws. It took a while for him to stop. "Oh, God. No wonder he was so damned angry and yet was unwilling to state the cause. You got the jump on him. I wish I'd seen it." Slate shook his head and sighed. "There have been times I wish I could've done so myself. Still, that was probably not the best idea in the long run."

"It won't happen again, sir." Blackthorne felt his face heat.

"How did he get under your skin? That isn't like you."

Blackthorne tried to think of an answer and couldn't—at least none that didn't sound as stupid as he felt. His hand tightened into a fist, and the knot between his shoulder blades sent a bolt of pain from his spine to the back of his head. *So tired.* He stared at the offered flask in Slate's hand but made no motion to accept it.

"Look. This isn't as bad as it seems. You need allies. Friends. More than myself. You aren't going to survive here alone. You need the others. And they need you. We all must work together." Slate sipped from the flask and swallowed. "Besides, I can't always be there to protect you."

Protect? Blackthorne bit down hard on a flash of anger. "Then don't."

"Severus—"

"If I'm fit to live, I will."

"Don't spew Brotherhood dogma at me. I know you don't believe that horse shit, or you wouldn't be here."

Blackthorne blinked. The words hit him like a slap.

Slate said, "I believe in justice—"

"Then you should've left me to die."

"You've had plenty of opportunities to kill yourself. If that is what you wanted, why didn't you? You're a free man. You can leave whenever you like. Why come back?"

Because you aren't the only one who believes in justice, and death would be too easy, Blackthorne thought. *Perhaps I should've done the honorable thing.*

A Retainer's life is not his own to spend. "Why did you bring me here?"

"Because you needed sanctuary."

"That isn't the whole of the reason. I'm not stupid."

"Do you want me to tell you that you have skills and knowledge we need? That I need you to keep this community hidden from—"

"Colonel Hännenen needs no assistance from me."

"And what happens when he's killed or captured?" Slate sighed. "Do you know how many people live here? We were only a little over a hundred last spring. More than forty of them have you to thank for getting here in one piece. You've managed this in the six months you've been here. Not only that, you've made the journey less dangerous for those you don't escort. Nickols couldn't have brought in that many in a year. Not without tipping off the Wardens. Neither could Nels, much as he would've wanted to. Do you understand what I'm saying?"

I'm useful to you, Blackthorne thought, and nodded. *And I am safe as long as that is the case.* The knowledge was reassuring in its familiar brutality. He didn't know why he felt the sharp pain in his chest. Slate's ruthless estimate of his purpose was no different than anyone else's had been. *"To fulfill one's purpose is to be content." A worthy Retainer is absolutely loyal to his Master.* He took a deep breath in an effort to release the rage he felt. *All is as it should be.*

"Content? Bullshit. You aren't content. What do you want? Tell me. I'll arrange it, if I can. We don't have much here, but you should get something in exchange besides a few meals, a rickety pallet bed"—he cast his gaze around the room and motioned toward the rest of it—"and an—an empty storage room."

Blackthorne's throat closed, and for a moment, he felt trapped. It wasn't that he didn't know the answer—he'd dreamed of it as often as he'd dreamed of freedom. He wanted to live as the others lived. He wanted to live without hiding, without fear. He wanted to be himself—whatever that was. He even briefly considered what it might be like to not be alone. It'd been a very long time since he'd spoken with a woman with the intent of getting to know her, let alone bed her. *Two years?*

You want to know what will make me happy? The resentment he'd kept in check since discovering Tobias's little library overflowed its bounds. *Horse shit. Is that why you sent me to collect Tobias and his books without warning me first? Because you want me to be happy? I am a tool to be used and cast off. No more. No less.*

"Talk to me," Slate said.

Unsettled by thoughts he knew he shouldn't have, Blackthorne once again directed his gaze to the floor, cleared his throat, and muttered, "I don't know."

"You don't know?"

He clipped his reply. "No." It was hard to breathe beneath the weight of his anger and confusion.

"All right. I knew I shouldn't have asked such a personal question." Slate shook his head and sighed. They sat in silence for a few moments before he spoke again. "For the record, I sent Jacob Nickols away to Greenleaf. It was the plan before your little altercation. Doing so a week or two early isn't going to make a difference around here. If the weather goes bad, we'll not see him again until spring. No one will be the worse for it. Forget about it."

"Jacob Nickols won't."

"Then I'll deal with Jacob Nickols when he returns. He knows the rules."

"And his brother?"

"Jack knows the rules too."

Blackthorne swallowed and nodded.

"You have something else to say. Out with it."

"House Lucrosa is offering a substantial reward for Tobias Freeson."

"I suspected they might be more motivated to look for him than usual. He was a trained apprentice. I took the gamble anyway because of his relationship with the Lucrosa's daughter. He would've been removed eventually anyway. It is how the Lucrosa will see it." Slate shrugged and took another sip from the flask.

"He's a weaponsmith, sir. Not a blacksmith."

"I'm aware."

"Sir, he also has *magic*."

It was Slate's turn to register surprise. "He's from peasant stock. I checked. You're sure?"

"I'm sure," Blackthorne said, hoping that Slate wouldn't ask him how he knew. If Blackthorne were honest, he couldn't have said. It was one of the things he purposely didn't dwell upon.

"Interesting. What sort? Do you know?"

Blackthorne stared at the floor and shook his head. *Please don't ask me for more.*

"I'll set Ilta to finding out, then."

"The Lucrosa will not stop. Not this time, sir. Freeson stole rare books from his weapons library. Books containing the latest research on gun manufacture—"

"Where are they now?" Slate sat up straighter. "Are they *here*?"

"Yes, sir."

"Son of a bitch." Slate stood up and began to pace. "I had no idea that he would do something so stupid." He walked to the pallet bed and turned. "How did he manage it?"

The open shock on Slate's face loosened the tension in Blackthorne's jaw. "He didn't. Not on his own. The Lucrosa's daughter, Aurelia, took them from the library herself. Freeson insisted they were a gift."

"Then she's the one who committed the crime, isn't she?"

"We both know that isn't what Gens Lucrosa will have reported."

He watched Slate continue to pace the width of the small room with increasing unease.

"Tobias claims the Lucrosa had intended to destroy the books," Blackthorne said. "I'm fairly certain this makes the situation worse rather than better."

"I agree," Slate said. "It means they contain information the Lucrosa didn't want any other gens to have."

"Alone, each of these factors isn't of much importance. Together, they make Freeson dangerous. Gens Lucrosa is already looking to the north. Word had reached as far as Greenleaf by the time we got there. They don't know anything for certain. I'm willing to bet that they're casting their net wide out of desperation. I've been as careful as I can, but it won't take long for them to find a trail that will lead them here."

"I'll look into it."

"There isn't much time. If they aren't satisfied soon, they'll hire a Brotherhood Unit, sir," Blackthorne said. "If they haven't already. If that happens, they *will* find the Hold. And they will uncover everyone who supports this place and helps get refugees here."

"No one smuggles kainen out of Acrasia without knowing the risks."

Blackthorne thought of Mrs. H and decided it might be best to never see her again. The idea weighed on him. *She should be warned at least.* "I—I've done my best, sir."

"Your best is enough."

"No, it isn't," Blackthorne said. "I've seen Warden Units in action. I've trained with them. And that isn't the worst of what might happen. If they send Missionaries up the mountain—"

"The situation requires consideration." Slate stared into the hearth. A long silence stretched out. "We must know how much Gens Lucrosa knows in order to convincingly misdirect them." He seemed to be thinking aloud. "You've already risked much in getting Freeson and those books here. We should take advantage of that as soon as possible." He didn't shift his gaze from the flames. "We'll strip the covers. Create decoys. Burn them in such a way as to leave no doubt what they are. Dump the remains in the south. Plant enough evidence to make it look like the boy was killed and robbed. It's what they'll expect. Even better, if we can pin the blame on another gens . . ." He took a deep breath. "The books are what they want, even if they only retrieve proof of their destruction. This is Gens Lucrosa. Gens Fortis is their most active enemy in the senate. We'll focus on that."

"Yes, sir."

"Maybe we'll need only to sacrifice a few pages to make the decoys," Slate said. He paused and his frown deepened. "We have another problem. Aurelia Lucrosa knows what you look like. We'll have to assume she's told them everything she knew."

"That isn't much. She can lead them to the coaching inn where I stayed. They won't find anything there," Blackthorne said.

"Good."

"I am more concerned about the initial contact," Blackthorne said. *The one you support, sir.* He didn't know the details of how Aurelia knew to reach him. It was best for him not to know, should he be captured. "It is a weakness."

"Point taken." Slate didn't continue right away. "I suppose we needn't worry about your cover until next spring. Nonetheless, to be safe, no more journeys outside the compound vicinity until further notice. You hear?"

Blackthorne shrugged. "Blackthorne is a persona. I can switch to another. Shave. Cut my hair. Alter my voice." He'd done so often enough over the course of the past year. "In any case, I suspect they'll be looking for a kainen passing for human."

Slate raised an eyebrow in question.

"The Brotherhood have certain . . . ideas as to what that means, sir," Blackthorne said.

"I see," Slate said. "I'll arrange an interview with Tobias the moment he wakes. We need to know what Aurelia will tell them. I'll send for you. It should make him feel more relaxed. He doesn't know me."

Did Slate forget I drugged Freeson against his will? Blackthorne thought.

Slate said, "As for the rest, I'll send out a few birds to warn our contacts." He went to the door. "In the meantime, get some rest."

⊰ ILTA ⊱

ONE

Ilta exited the Hold via the riverside gate. A large cave enclosed the main dock, and Suvi's *Sea Otter* was moored to the pier next to the Waterborne sloop of war, *Clár Oibre Rúnda*. They were of a similar size. To Ilta's right, sunlight poured in and a brisk fall wind blew dead leaves into the water. She waved to the crew working on *Otter* and made her way out into the woods. Almost at once, the weight bearing down on her began to lift. The air was crisp and fresh, and she took a deep breath in relief.

"Afternoon, Miss Korpela!" a voice called from above. The greeting echoed off water and solid rock.

Ilta whirled. Gazing up at the spy perch set into the canyon wall near the cave opening, she waved at the older man dressed in soft brown deerskin. His dark brown hair was grey at the temples, and he wore a patch over the left eye that gave him a rascally demeanor.

"Jeremiah Birch?" she asked. "Aren't you supposed to be bruising tree trunks with wooden swords?"

In case of an Acrasian attack, Nels had recommended that every resident of the Hold learn something of weapons, and James Slate had taken that suggestion to heart. It was a dramatic break from Eledorean blood custom, and for that reason, most Holders were reluctant to comply. With the exception of Nels's troops, native Eledoreans saw the order as an affront to their culture. They weren't the only ones. Some of the individuals most vocal about Eledorean traditions were the ones newest to them.

"Training was canceled today. The Ghost is away, and Erkki went to Gardemeister with a squad of soldiers last night. He should be back soon, though," Jeremiah said, talking around the stem of a pipe. One hand rested on his rifle.

"You know Nels doesn't like being called 'The Ghost.'"

Jeremiah said, "And that would be why we only do it behind his back."

She let sarcasm seep into her reply. "*That* makes it better."

"Nobody means any harm by it, miss," Jeremiah said. "It's a compliment."

I'm fairly certain it isn't, Ilta thought. *But then, ghosts have different associations in Eledore than they do in Acrasia, don't they?* And Jeremiah had been Acrasian. "I'm sure Nels will keep that in mind when he finds out."

"You planning on telling him?"

"He won't hear it from me. But I'd watch yourself around Viktor. He'd jump at any chance to mock Nels."

"Actually, *I* heard it from Major Reini."

"And why am I not surprised?" she muttered.

"Don't suppose I could convince you to bring back some sassa-fras root while you're out?"

"Are you feeling ill?"

Jeremiah shook his head. "My grandmother used to make sas-safras tea, and I got a taste for it. Anyway, I've run out. Since I'm doing two turns at guard today, I can't harvest more, not today."

She put a hand against her forehead to shade her eyes. "You're taking an extra turn at watch? How very community-spirited of you."

Jeremiah snorted. "Kat has been teaching Erkki to play tetra, blast them both. Was either this or lose my last bottle of rum. If I didn't know any better, I'd swear the cards were marked."

"Rum? You've been smuggling rum into the Hold?"

"We're forbidden the whiskey. So, Nichols brings in a drop of rum here and there," Jeremiah said. "Would take it kindly if you didn't let on to Mr. Slate, miss."

"That's two secrets you've asked me to keep. You're not very good at duplicity, are you?"

"Not unless it involves cards."

"I see," Ilta said. "I'll look for the sassafras. If not, I'm sure I have some in the herb stores."

"Thank you, miss." He balanced his fowling piece on his knees and reached into a pocket. "So, where you headed?"

"I need some fresh air. And I thought I might as well gather a few herbs while I'm walking," she said. "We're running low on willow."

"All right. You be careful, now," Jeremiah said. His tone switched to quiet amusement. "Keep your eyes open. I may have seen some-thing down the river path."

"Something dangerous?"

"May be it's a nice sort of danger," Jeremiah said. "You're young."

Ilta frowned. *Now, what does he mean by that?*

"You call out if you need anything. You hear?" He blew out a mouthful of smoke with what Ilta was sure was a wink. When he didn't offer further explanation, she decided it wasn't important and continued on her way.

The forest crowded both sides of the river. It'd rained earlier in the day—a light mist that still managed to soak the ground. The path was sticky with mud, not enough to make it too messy but enough to make it slippery. Listening to the quiet crunch of damp grit under the thick soles of her boots, she felt the persistent tension between her temples gradually fading away.

As much as she loved her community, for her, the Hold represented a constant, overwhelming morass of dissonant thoughts and images. Sometimes she found it difficult to protect herself. Stone walls provided insulation when she was alone, but they also intensified a crowded room—like echoes off a cliff face. The winter months were particularly trying. Still, she couldn't help thinking her Gran would've been proud. This would be Ilta's second winter spent in close quarters with a large group of people. Not long before, that would've have been impossible, not without going mad.

And now Suvi is living here. Ilta looked forward to spending time with Nels's sister, not merely in her capacity as advisor. It would be good to have an actual friend.

A breeze ruffled Ilta's hair. Tree limbs clattered against one another. She paused, smiled, and turned her face up to the sun before returning her gaze to the path. It was then that she spied the boot tracks on the muddy ground. It seemed she wasn't the only one with a need to escape. *Or maybe that's from earlier?* In all honesty, she wouldn't have known. She wasn't a tracker.

The path took a sharp, rocky incline. She hooked her basket

handle in the crook of one arm and lifted her skirts one-handed to pick her way to the bottom. It wasn't long before she arrived at her destination: the willow grove. It wasn't the best time of year for harvesting willow bark. That would be the spring. However, she could make do with newer branches. Setting her basket on the ground next to a candidate willow, she whispered a prayer of gratitude before beginning her work. Content and focused, she hummed an old tune her Gran used to sing and then began paring bark from a small branch. She didn't sense she wasn't alone until it was too late. She turned, leaned to see better through the willow vines, and her heart stumbled.

Blackthorne sat with his eyes closed on a flat rock several paces from the shore.

Think I saw something dangerous down that way. The nice kind. You're young.

Very funny, Birch.

Blackthorne didn't stir or indicate that he'd been disturbed by her presence. She began to suspect he might be asleep. She didn't know how that was possible—he was sitting on cold rock. Then she spied the folded horse blanket beneath him. From what little she could catch, his thoughts were still and empty—which explained why she hadn't noticed him before. She folded white cloth over her cuttings. Knowing he couldn't possibly be unaware of her with all the noise she had made, she pushed through the curtaining willow. When he still didn't move, she debated whether or not she should say something or simply leave him to his privacy.

Largely, she stayed away from him for the same reasons the others did. *For the most part.* There were those who didn't shun him, like Birch for example, but even Birch didn't seek out the ex-Warden's company. There was a lot that Holders could forgive—everyone had dark pasts or shameful secrets of one kind or another. It was understood that war tended to force one into hard choices, but the line was drawn when it came to the former Warden. The rumors about why James Slate had taken in Blackthorne were as inventive as they were broad. Some bordered on the ridiculous. Having been consulted at the time of James's decision, Ilta damned well knew why, and yet she still wasn't comfortable.

It occurred to her that James had wanted her to interview Blackthorne when he first arrived a few months earlier. For one reason or another, he'd been scarce, and she'd been too busy. *What would be the point now?* She assumed there wasn't anything Blackthorne hadn't already revealed in his written report. Unless James had wanted her to look into Blackthorne's mind.

Surely James knows I can't do that, not on purpose. It would be unethical.

The trouble was, most people didn't shield their minds. Sometimes, she had difficulty remembering what she had been told versus what she had seen or heard in a vision. Over time, she'd learned it was best not to know things that people weren't ready to reveal, or at very least not to let on you knew.

Looking at Blackthorne now, she noticed sunlight brought out blue highlights in the black waves of his hair. His skin was a light tan. His lips were plump beneath the beard, and his eyebrows traced graceful arches above his closed lids. His right eyebrow was intersected by a L-shaped scar.

You're attracted to him.

I can't be. I'm with Nels. And anyway, Blackthorne is Acrasian. Before she could turn away, he opened his eyes. They were the pale blue-grey of a storming sea.

Have some dignity. Quit mooning at him like a girl in pigtails. Not that she'd ever been prone to mooning at men when she'd been a girl in pigtails. She spoke as calmly as she could with ears deafened by her heart's drumming. "I—I'm sorry to have disturbed you."

He said nothing in return, and his expression was impassive.

She stumbled on. "This is a lovely place. I can see why you would choose to pray here."

She'd heard it said that Wardens were part shadow, but in her experience, that wasn't the case—except perhaps in their nature. Blackthorne was different. *Or maybe I merely want him to be.*

"I wasn't praying." He shifted his gaze to the river.

Without warning, the ravine blurred. Her vision was consumed with an image of masks within masks, and a bone-deep yearning for the freedom of water. *Not water. More. Bigger . . .*

Oh. The ocean. Her shoulders were heavy with a great weariness. Confinement. Hopelessness. *Loneliness.* She shook off the vision and with a deep breath focused on the solid feel of the ground under her feet. *Stay present. Don't get lost.*

She knew what it was to be alone. Her Gran had kept her from others when she was little for the sake of her sanity. It was one thing to be apart when no one was near. It was quite another to be separate from those who connected and entwined with each other around you. His loneliness ran so deep, it'd become physical pain.

Where did he come from? Did he leave a family behind? What drove him here? Why does he stay when it's clear he isn't welcome? She was certain a forbidden love tryst with a kainen was to blame. It was a romantic notion, admittedly, but the only one that came to mind. He was handsome for an Acrasian. Studying him now, she noticed something out of place. It was subtle, and if she hadn't been so close, she'd have missed it.

He gave her a sideways glance.

Suddenly, she remembered Grandmother Sophia's white-

ILTA

handled knife and slipped it into the leather sheath she kept at her waist. "This is a good place to think, then." She inwardly cursed the tremor in her voice. Her nerves weren't helping her conversation skills.

He nodded, again intent on the river.

She struggled to find words that would provide a legitimate path behind his barriers. At the same time, she felt guilty for wanting it so much. *I love Nels.* That was true, but there was something about Blackthorne. Temptation nearly overcame her propriety. One touch, and the privacy of his skull wouldn't be so private. She had that power. However, she'd made that mistake before, and it'd ruined everything. She wasn't about to do it again.

For a long time, there was only the gentle rush of the wind through dying leaves. Then Blackthorne ventured nine more syllables.

"You are the healer, Miss Korpela." Anxiety flashed across his face.

"I'm so sorry. I didn't introduce myself, did I?" The thrill of his recognition gave her heart another flutter. "Yes, I'm Ilta Korpela. You can call me Ilta."

Didn't you discuss the idea of seeing other people with Nels? I didn't really mean it, did I? She bit her lip.

He stretched. His body was long and slender. And for an instant, her hands twitched to touch him. *Ilta Korpela, what is the matter with you?*

"May I inquire how long you have known Mr. Slate?" he asked.

She blinked. "About two years." She requested to sit beside him with a motion.

He got up, unfolded the blanket, and made room for her.

"I found him during a winter storm. He'd been tracking a reindeer and had gotten caught out. He was lost and couldn't find his way back to camp. Did you know he used to hunt?"

Blackthorne shook his head.

"This was before he started having problems with his eyesight, you see," she said.

He nodded.

Ilta smiled, pleased at how well things were going. "He visited once or twice afterward. Then one day, he brought Katrin to me. To keep her safe."

"Is Katrin his daughter?"

Nodding, Ilta said, "Adopted. She was an orphan living on the street in Novus Salernum. He caught her stealing a man's handkerchief."

"She was a street harvester?"

""Is that what they call it?" Ilta asked. "After that, James approached me with the idea of bringing others. That's when I spoke to Suvi and Nels. James has this dream of building a new republic from Eledore's ashes." She shrugged. "It wasn't too far off from Suvi's plans. So, the Hold was born. I'm beginning to think James intends to transport refugees here one at a time, until no one's left in Acrasia except the Emperor and his cronies."

She allowed herself another smile, feeling more confident. Her palms had quit sweating, and her stomach had stopped its fluttering. "How did *you* meet James?"

"Three freebooters seeking membership in the Syndicate attempted to rob him outside an alehouse. The Green Dragon, I believe it was," Blackthorne said. "I convinced them to find an easier target."

"Lost in a winter storm and then attacked outside an alehouse? Who'd have thought James so feckless?" When Blackthorne didn't laugh, she felt her cheeks grow warm. She fought to find a worthy change of subject and failed. *Goddess, I'm terrible at this.*

Once again, the sound of the trees swaying in the breeze and the flow of river water were the only things to pierce the silence. It became increasingly clear that if she didn't say anything, he wasn't. She had so many questions but didn't know how to phrase them in a way that wouldn't cause offense.

She took a chance. "Why did you retire from the Brotherhood?"

Her heart stopped when she felt him blink up internal barriers and then turn away. "No one retires," he said. His tone held an edge of bitterness. "I was decommissioned."

"Decommissioned?"

"Dishonorably discharged."

The emotions behind his answer made Ilta uneasy. She had assumed he hadn't enjoyed being a Warden—that he'd left of his own volition. His hand strayed to his hair, and suddenly she knew his formal demeanor for what it was. Her eyesight blurred again and a mix of feelings invaded her thoughts. *Shame? Despair? Anger?* A secret lurked close to the surface. *So close.* She didn't want to press. She couldn't, but it was so difficult to resist the urge. "You went to an alehouse after being decommissioned? To drink away your grief?"

"No. The Green Dragon was later. Before being decommissioned I was arrested, and sent for treatment at the Reclamation Hospital."

"Wait. Were you injured or ill?"

He frowned. "The Reclamation Hospital is where they send you to be retrained, if you can be. If you can't, you are killed."

Again, she blinked. "I don't understand. You were retrained? But . . . how did you get to the alehouse?"

He reached for a stone and threw it violently at the river with an intent she knew wasn't meant for the water. The accompanying thought pierced her head with red-hot hate, and she winced. *Coward!* "I escaped before I could be executed."

"Oh." Shaken, she focused on breathing until his emotions dissipated. She said, "I'm sorry. It was wrong of me to have pried."

He took a slow, measured breath. Words muffled by strong emotions drifted to the surface of his mind with the feel of a long-practiced ritual. Again, it reminded her of a prayer. With that, his demeanor resumed its former placidity.

"I should go." She slid off the rock and retrieved her willow cuttings. "I must collect what I can before it gets dark."

"You would go alone? Aren't you afraid?"

"It's daylight."

"What of wild animals?"

Her eyes narrowed. "I lived alone on this mountain long before the rest of you came here." She didn't tell him that it was only for a few months and that she'd been terrified the entire time. "I can protect myself."

"I apologize. I didn't mean to imply you were defenseless."

Ilta felt her mouth relax from its tight frown. "I'm sorry. It's a sore subject. All beings harbor the capacity for good and evil. Some people seem to believe that healers are the exception. As if healing powers couldn't have a negative application. No one is pure—"

She saw the word trigger another negative reaction behind his eyes and regretted her word choice at once. "—not even pure evil." It was a gift to him, her guilt. She wanted to show him that he wasn't the only one to have done wrong, but then she spied the horror as it flashed across his face. It struck her as odd until she remembered Acrasian superstitions regarding magic. *How can he have lived this long among us and not understand?*

She caught another glimpse of his despair and loneliness. Her heart went out to him. "I should get back to what I was doing." She still didn't move. "My work would go much quicker if I had help. Would you like to come along?"

A hint of mild surprise touched his brows. "If you wish."

She made her way back to the shore with him tagging her. Using stones in the rushing water to cross, she glanced back and found herself drinking in the way he moved—graceful, powerful—the set of his shoulders revealed by the ridiculously tight rag of a coat.

Why am I so attracted to him? She still loved Nels with all her heart. She was as sure of that as she was of the ground beneath her, but she'd been feeling anxious of late. They had reached a point in their relationship where she needed to make an important choice— whether or not to bed him, and she didn't know what to do. She was terrified of losing herself in Nels. It'd happened before. Ever since that day, Nels had been so patient and kind and careful, but the truth was, she didn't know if she could ever bed him, no matter how much she wanted it. *What if I go mad? Is the problem Nels? Did that happen because we're so close? What if I can't have sex with anyone?*

She forced herself back to the present.

Blackthorne is alone and hurting; that's all this is. I'm a healer. Helping those in pain is what I do. For the most part, he gave off a quiet calm. *Steadiness.* She had to concentrate to pick up much else. It was part of why his emotions hit her so hard when they did surface.

Pointing at a tree with rough bark, she said, "Wild cherry."

His eyes never left her face. "Black choke."

Surprised, she smiled again. "That's one of its names. When soaked in alcohol and combined with honey, young thin bark makes a syrup that is used to suppress coughs. It has other uses as well. But you must be careful when harvesting wild cherry bark. The sap is poisonous."

Blackthorne recited, "One of the main ingredients of The Hagg's Kiss. Causes drowsiness, difficulty breathing, staggering, convulsions, and death. Results can be rapid but dependent upon dosage. Preferred method of administration: ingestion. However, it may be applied to blades and used—"

She gasped. *Warden. Murderer.*

Do I honestly have any room to judge him? How many died because of my actions?

But does he regret what he did?

Standing close, she caught the pleasant scent of him—leather, wool, and a hint of what she could've sworn was Eledorean funerary incense. *That's not possible*, she thought. Its main components were frankincense, amber, and myrrh. All hailed from distant Tahmer. None of which were easily acquired, not any longer. She brushed aside her thoughts and focused on locating a suitable tree. Like willow, wild cherry was more potent in the spring. However, willow and cherry could be harvested anytime, which was good, given their usefulness. They also didn't store well for long periods of time.

She selected a branch, whispered her gratitude to it in Eledorean, and began paring.

"What did you say?" he asked.

"I thanked the plant for its gift."

"Why?" He seemed genuinely curious.

"Grandmother Saara taught me that it takes away negativity from the process," Ilta said. "If you're going to create a potion to heal, the ingredients should be as free of harmful intent as they can. Anyway, it's the least one can do before hacking away at another life."

He frowned. "But it didn't give anything. You *took* it."

Ilta smiled at his literal-mindedness. "I prefer to think of it as a gift out of respect for the plant."

"Is it respectful to take from that which can't speak for itself?"

She blinked. It was obvious he felt strongly, but it made no sense. They were talking about plant life, not people. "Do you eat food? Drink water?"

"Of course."

"Do you have these same objections when you do? I'm curious."

"Of course not," he said. "But I am not the one claiming to be respectful to them."

"I see," she said. Her lips clamped down on a hurtful retort, and she took a slow, deep breath to get control of roiling emotions. When she was calm again, it was easy to see that Blackthorne wanted to ask a question but was now hesitant. "Yes?"

"Is this an elph—a *kainen* practice?"

"Really?"

"I'm sorry." His face darkened with embarrassment.

"Nels would be more than happy to beat you for a slip like that." She took a long breath to calm herself again. He was Acrasian, after all, and it was clear he was trying to overcome his prejudices. James himself fell prey to the stray ill-considered Acrasian word. Thinking back on her initial discomfort about being attracted to Blackthorne, she had to admit she had her own prejudices. *All are one.* It was difficult to root out negative ideas when they were so ingrained in language and custom. "Never mind. What did you want to ask?"

"Forget it."

She tried one more time. *Be patient. Healing happens through knowledge.* "I won't let this go until you answer me. I'm very stubborn that way. Just ask—" She'd started to say *Just ask Nels* but reconsidered. "Ask anyone. What was it you wanted to know?"

He hesitated. "This talking to plants before harvesting them? This is a kainen practice?"

"It was an old *Eledorean* custom among healers." She attempted to make a distinction between kainen as a race and Eledorean as a culture. *Surely, he knows the difference.* "But almost no one remembers it. Especially not now." Feeling awkward, she plunged onward. "Ytlain, Kaledan, Marren—all have their own beliefs and practices regarding the healing arts. But I'm not familiar with them. Gran was my teacher, and she was an Eledorean Traditionalist."

"Can you tell me more about kainen? Do you know anything of—of the people of Marren?"

She lost control of herself. "Didn't you make enough of a study as a Warden?"

A frustrated line reappeared between his brows, and he turned away. "That was different. They taught us . . . We never learned. . . ." He frowned again in consternation, but almost as soon as the emotion registered on his face, it vanished. "It was unthinkably offensive of me to ask such things. I beg your pardon."

For an instant, the barriers he so carefully maintained slipped. She glimpsed him as he saw himself—shaded with swirling black and red—barely contained self-loathing, rage, and despair. The image vanished right after it was revealed. *Not steadiness. Not quiet,* she thought. *Blank. He keeps himself blank to hide what he is.*

Sudden knowledge loosened her grip on Gran's knife. She caught it with her other hand before it hit the ground. "You're kainen."

His face went grey, and panicked, he scanned the riverbank for witnesses. "You're mistaken."

"How can it be?" She bit her lip again. "I've seen you a hundred times and would never have guessed." She put out a hand to touch him.

He stepped out of reach at once. "You are mistaken. Wardens are not in the habit of accepting elpharmaceutria within their ranks. Such an abomination would be killed the instant it was discovered."

It? Warden. Oh, goddess, he was a Warden. "How could you? How could you murder your own kind?"

His hand shook as he pushed hair from his eyes. Blushing even more fiercely, he stared at the ground. "I must insist—"

"You murdered them. And willingly. You actually miss it!" *I must tell Suvi or James. Someone must know.*

"I don't! I—"

Her foot slipped. He caught her by the elbow before she could fall.

"Don't touch me!" She jerked from his grip and backed away, pointing Gran's knife at him. It wasn't intended for fighting. The blade had been consecrated. She could use magic but didn't have a soldier's training, and using magic offensively meant dropping one's emotional defences. She couldn't count on having the discipline to avoid incapacitating herself with whatever pain she inflicted. *I'm a fool.*

Blackthorne leaped toward her. "Wait," he said. "Please."

That's why he keeps himself apart. He didn't want me to know. He doesn't want any of us to know. "You should never have been allowed to stay here. Get away from me!" Again, she brandished Gran's knife at him. When he didn't heed the warning, she brought it down in an angry arc that slashed his coat and pared away one of the buttons. He moved back, then he lost his purchase on slick stone and stumbled into the near-freezing water with a loud splash. She didn't wait but took the opportunity to run. Before she'd gotten three steps, he had captured her elbow again.

He's too strong—too fast. If I don't do something, he's going to kill me. Even if she screamed, Birch would be too late. With no other option, she slapped a hand on Blackthorne's face. Her palm became engulfed in a warm tingle before his essence flowed through her in an overwhelming surge of raw intimacy.

He wrenched away as if burned. His expression filled with sickened horror before he dropped to his knees, choking.

Oh, Goddess, I didn't think I hit him that hard. I didn't want to kill him. She moved to return the energy she had siphoned.

He gagged once more and shook his head. "Wait. No more. Please. I won't hurt you. I—I merely wanted to . . . Slate knows."

"What?" She gaped as his words registered.

With obvious effort, he straightened and put both hands up in surrender. When she made no move to run or attack, he slumped and let his hands fall. Then he sat on the riverbank with his back against the wild cherry tree. Wet hair fell into his face, hiding his eyes. He shivered. "I told him before he brought me here."

"How? How did you do it? Why?"

He took a shaky breath and then wiped his mouth with a soggy sleeve. Again, she sensed ritualized verses in his mind. He seemed to gain control over his stomach, and she saw him glance at the top of the ridge. "I'll tell you, but you must promise not to say anything to the others."

"I won't promise any such thing." She wanted to run but knew she couldn't bring herself to use magic against him again. She might kill him, and she couldn't break her Healer's vow. On the other hand, if she didn't, she'd never reach the top of the ravine alive. It was then that it came to her that after all her bravado about being able to take care of herself, she simply didn't have the courage to kill him. *Is "courage" the right word?*

"Slate—they'll never trust him again."

"Perhaps that's for the best." She didn't mean it. She knew they needed James Slate, but she was angry.

Blackthorne's clothes were soaked, and he was shivering. She decided not to care.

"And after? Will the others live as they do now? Or will they regard each other with suspicion?" He sighed. There was bitterness in his words. "What happened to accepting any who come here, regardless of their past?"

"We don't have to accept spies and traitors."

"I am no spy, not for the Regnum. Nor am I a traitor to your cause."

"Only your own people," she said. She let her anger slip into her voice.

"Give your word. Then I'll explain."

Ilta glared down at him. This was it. This was his secret he'd been hiding. She felt foolish for having liked him—more than anything else for not knowing, for thinking about him all those long nights and wondering. She should hate him, spit in his face and leave, but she couldn't, and she hated herself for it. "If Slate knows, then there can be no harm if I speak to him about this."

Blackthorne shrugged with one shoulder. "If you wish."

Why didn't I know?

Blackthorne was right. She couldn't tell anyone. Still, she wanted to understand why James had risked so much.

"All right," she said. "I won't tell the others." She kept Gran's blade drawn just in case.

"Thank you."

"Don't even try to lie to me. I'll know."

Blackthorne nodded and then began unbuttoning his coat.

"What are you doing?" She backed up and prepared to run. *I'll never win out, but at least I can make him wish he'd never touched me.*

He gestured, pleading for her to stop, "No. It's . . ." He sighed. "I suppose proof should wait." He dropped the hand from his collar.

"You better tell me what's going on before I run back to the Hold, screaming my head off." Her intuition conflicted with her emotions. *If he meant to harm you, you'd be dead or worse already.*

"I am not what I seem."

"I think we've established that." Ilta crossed her arms, hugging herself and glared.

"My father was a duke."

"I know. Everyone does."

"He was also a semivir."

It took her a moment to understand what he meant. She'd heard that Acrasians used "semivir" to mean half-kainen. Nels had told her that it literally meant "half-animal". She found it disturbing that Blackthorne would use such a word in reference to his own father.

"I'm one-quarter human. My mother was a kainen slave. I understand her people were from Marren. I lived with her until I was taken away when I was small. I assumed I was to be groomed for the games, but I was sent to a sorcerer. You would call him a healer—"

"A powerful Eledorean *healer* lives in Novus Salernum?" she asked.

"Lived. He died of river fever ten years ago."

"Oh," she said. "Go on."

"I was given a potion, and I slept. When I woke hours later, I was different."

"How?" Ilta asked. She watched his hand stray to the rounded top of one ear. There was no scar to indicate it had ever been pointed. His eyes, although not black, were tilted like her own and his skin had a dusky undertone. *Like many natives of Marren did.* She wanted to be sick. "Why would anyone mutilate their own son?"

"To give the duke the heir he wanted. To make me human."

"And that can be done so easily?"

"You have *magic*." He filled the word with disgust and hate. "You tell me."

"I've never heard of anyone doing anything like this. Even if a healer could bring themselves to do it, why would your father go to so much trouble? Couldn't he simply marry an Acrasian?"

"He was still a . . . kainen, even if he had the good fortune to be born passably free of the characteristics. He had noble status and the wherewithal to obliterate public record of his ancestry. But any family worth the match would investigate further. A blank record is telling. And the Brotherhood won't sell false lineages, no matter how large the bribe. An heir would still carry the taint. He needed proof of his purity. So, he had me fashioned into what he wanted."

"Where are your grandparents? You said one of your father's parents was kainen."

"I never met them, and the duke didn't speak of them. Especially not to me."

"Then how do you know about them?"

"The sorcerer told me."

Healer. She almost corrected him, but it occurred to her that what the Acrasian healer had done was against every ethic her art held dear. "Then how did your father become a duke?"

"Titles are bought and sold in Acrasia like gens memberships," Blackthorne said. "The cost is sufficiently high that most nonhumans cannot take advantage of it. Sometimes, they're inherited. But there's a price for that, too. Naturally, it is less, but . . ." He shrugged.

She shut her eyes and focused on breathing in the scent of damp forest. Her feet were freezing, and her skirts clung to her legs in wet clumps. Like him, she was shivering with the cold. She wanted to get inside where it was warm. "All right. What is it you were going to show me?"

"A slave mark." He tugged at his clothes until he bared his left shoulder, revealing a rough circular burn scar.

She had heard they removed slave tattoos with branding once freedom was granted. Raised red scars laced his shoulder and wrapped over his collarbone. She automatically reached out, but he shrugged the shirt back into place and moved away.

Why take so much care with his ears and then leave that burn?

Perhaps it wasn't considered important. Debt slaves were common in the Regnum, from what she'd heard. A mark like that could hold many meanings. She shivered again. "That could be faked."

"Yes. But it is the proof I have."

She knew he was telling the truth, as much as she didn't want to believe it. "Why become a Warden?"

"Nothing garners acceptance like a son trained at the Academy."

"You went willingly?"

"I wasn't consulted," Blackthorne said. "Not that it would've mattered. The duke granted me his name but could discard me on a whim." He paused. "I passed for human. A high-ranking noble. Do you know what a powerful thing that is? Once you've lived as a slave, you'll do anything to keep from wearing a collar again. Anything."

She sat in silence for a moment before he quietly added, "I did what I did. It doesn't matter how much I wish otherwise."

"And the Academy found out."

He shook his head. "I graduated with honors. When Gens Aureus granted the duke membership, he declared me his heir. All was well until I was given my first field assignment. I argued with the Huntmaster about a—a case. I was put on report for insubordination. They sent me to the Reclamation Hospital. Twice. I—I escaped after the second time. I met Slate two nights later."

"Wouldn't your father have intervened?"

"Upon the first reprimand, the duke emphasized the extent of his investment. Then he stated I couldn't expect his assistance if I failed to cooperate." Blackthorne looked away. "It was easy to see he was afraid. I half-believe the reason I rebelled in the first place was to torment him. Not merely because I believe that what the Brotherhood does is wrong."

"Still, you rejected everything. At great cost."

"I agreed to murder nonhumans to maintain the Censor's quotas. I supported a system that issues licenses for murder to the rich."

"What made you stop?"

She watched him run his fingers through his hair. "I . . ." He closed his eyes and sighed. She thought he might lie but sensed one of his internal walls fall away. "He was only nine or ten. An escaped slave. He was kainen. He'd run after being sold to the Church as a sacrifice. I tracked him into an alley, but I couldn't . . . I handed over my knife, some food, and told him to flee the city."

"That was brave."

"It was foolish." His eyes opened. They smoldered with anger and self-loathing. "A Warden Unit caught him an hour later. Fed him to the Huntmaster's dogs. I had to watch while they ripped him apart. He would have been better off had I cut his throat. At least it would have been quick." *Coward!* This time, the thought held an edge coated with poison.

"Please don't do that," she said with a wince.

He took a breath and the mask shifted back into place. His lips were beginning to look a bit bluish-green, and his shivering was becoming ever more violent. "I do not wish to discuss this any further."

"I've heard enough." *We need to get inside before we both freeze to death*, she thought.

Blackthorne got to his feet with no small amount of effort. He clasped his arms around himself. "I am Slate's Retainer. I will venture into Acrasia as many times as he wishes. And I will do everything in my power to see that every person I'm assigned to retrieve arrives in Eledore safely. But ultimately, I don't expect to survive."

"Is it because you'll be recognized?"

"I'm confident I can disguise myself. I have done so often enough. People see what they prefer to see," Blackthorne said. "What is more likely is that your prince will cut my throat when he returns. I only ask that he wait until I've served my purpose. If it comes to that, can you convince him to wait?"

She didn't know what to say. So, she said nothing. She watched Blackthorne stare out into the forest while the sounds of snarling dogs echoed in her mind.

TWO

Running up five flights of stairs, Ilta paused long enough to catch her breath at the top. She set her surgeon's bag down for a moment, grabbed her knees, and took in great gulps of air. The muscles in her legs twitched. She was an hour late because of having to set Frikk's broken arm—an accident in the stable. She supposed it was pointless to rush now. However, two days had passed since her encounter with Blackthorne, and the conversation had been preying on her mind. She needed to vent her frustration and confusion. She still didn't know what to think, but it was time to talk.

She retrieved her bag. Rushing through the ironbound door leading to the first of the tiered gardens, she scanned the rows of plants for James Slate.

With so many mouths to feed, there were several gardens tucked around the Hold. However, the topmost garden was James's favorite. Ilta assumed this was because it was the least frequented by the others. Five flights of stairs tended to deter casual visitors.

The garden was quiet. It smelled of damp black earth. Most of the fall vegetables had been harvested. Still, some plants remained among the rows of small dirt mounds. James tended to find his way there at first light, and it was now nearing dark. She had a hunch that he would've waited, given recent tensions. There'd been a fight between Jack Nickols and Eli Karstensen, not that that was anything new. There was always some fight going on between one of the Nickols brothers and Eli Karstensen. Sometimes she wondered why James let the Nickolses stay. They were often more trouble than they were worth.

Don't judge. Everyone deals with loss their own way, she thought.

When she rounded the first wall, she spied James sitting in the dirt between two rows of winter roses, sketching. His serene expression was marred by a squinting frown as he concentrated on his drawing. He shifted nearer to the rose plant. Removing his spectacles, he leaned in close enough to touch his nose to the leaf. After a moment or two, he returned to the image on which he was working. He moved the paper as closees he had the leaf and rubbed at it with a blackened finger.

As she watched, she noticed a charcoal smudge on his nose near the bridge of his spectacles. He wore an inexpertly knitted blue scarf looped around his neck, and his coat hung open. That was when she understood he was wearing the same rumpled clothes from the day before. Briefly, she wondered if he'd remembered to eat. His duties often distracted him from self-care. Still, Ilta often envied his skills with people. *And he does so without magic.*

Before approaching him, she closed her eyes and focused in an effort to make sure they were alone. James preferred to keep his treatments private, and she respected his wishes. All at once, she knew he was upset and worried. The depth of his feelings hit her like a slap. She shoved them back before she could understand details. When she didn't sense anyone else nearby, she gathered her skirts and squatted in the dirt next to him.

James started. "You're late. Is something wrong?" He closed the large portfolio, but not before she caught a glimpse of what he was working on—a striking black-and-white sketch detailing the rose plant's parts in formal Acrasian.

"Not really. Not anything urgent, anyway," Ilta said. "Frikk broke his arm helping shoe the grey stallion. Something is going to have to be done about that beast. He'll have to be gelded or sold."

"Jack Nickols doesn't want to geld him."

"Well then, perhaps Jack Nickols should take care of that creature himself and risk having *his* head kicked in," Ilta said.

"I know you don't like either of the Nickols brothers, but they are part of the community."

"You're right. I know. I'm sorry. I only wish either of them would think of others first once in a while." She sighed. "Speaking of . . . are you ready?"

He nodded and winced.

"Headache?" she asked.

"A bit."

"Well, let's see what I can do about that." She opened her surgeon's bag and fished out the half-full bottle of medicine she'd prepared. "Drink this."

He accepted it from her. "All of it?"

"All of it."

Sipping, he grimaced but didn't comment on the taste. Next, she produced a different concoction, soaked a cloth with the liquid, and instructed him to place the cloth over his eyes while they were open. Ilta had been trained as an Eledorean Traditionalist by her grandmother, and it was important for James to take part in his treatment—just as it was vital that she incorporated all her healing magic in the preparations and the cloth. Pouring one's magic directly into a patient was reserved for emergencies. To do so took dangerous risks.

When the treatment was finished, she checked his eyes. The cloudiness in their centers had vanished. He blinked in the sunlight.

"You can put your spectacles back on now," she said. It was important to protect his eyes from the light lest he suffer worse pain. If that happened, she wouldn't be able to do much about it.

"Thank you," he said with a smile. "I'm feeling much better already."

"Good."

"Now you can tell me what's wrong."

"I told you—"

"Not with the others," he said. "You."

She focused on securing the contents of her surgeon's bag so that the assorted bottles wouldn't break. When he didn't interrupt the silence, she decided to finally say something. "Blackthorne," she said. "He's kainen."

James's expression was impossible to read, but the spark of panic was easy to detect. "And?"

"There is no 'and,'" she said. "He was a Warden, and he hunted his own people."

"He did."

"You aren't outraged?"

"The past is the past. That *is* what we agreed, isn't it?"

"We didn't agree to harbor murderers!"

"Interesting. I wonder if Jacob Nickols, Franklin, and Carter are aware of that. And I believe Birch is wanted for—"

"Don't you change the subject!"

"We need Blackthorne," James said. "He smuggles refugees out of Acrasia. And he's more successful at it than anyone else who's ever tried."

"I know, but—"

"But what?" James set the portfolio on the ground and wiped his charcoal-stained hands on his trousers.

She drew up her knees, wrapping her arms around them. It was difficult to find words for what she was feeling. James's copper-colored eyes bored into her through his lenses. She released the breath she was holding. Sorting through her emotions, she focused on the clearest. "I feel so . . . foolish for not having known. I just . . . I can't believe it."

"Who would? It's unthinkable," James said.

There was a long pause. She waited, confused and unable to contribute anything useful.

He continued. "The only explanation of which I can conceive is that certain persons are predisposed to follow authority. Most people do tend to look up to and even identify with societal power bases, particularly when it's dangerous not to do so. Of course, this is an extreme case—"

"He told me he didn't choose to attend the Academy. He said he'd been a slave. That he didn't have a choice in the matter."

"I was thinking more of his father, the duke."

"Oh."

"It's difficult to even imagine the twisted logic involved," James said, and then paused. "Did you know there's a naturalist term for when one species disguises itself as another for survival? They call it mimicry."

"Mimicry?" she asked.

James gazed off at the horizon. "Maybe it's a form of mental mimicry?"

"Would you listen to yourself?" Ilta asked. "You're referring to people, not animals. It makes you sound cold and calculating, and I know that isn't you."

Blushing, he looked uncomfortable. "I was merely examining the situation in a scientific sense. I want to understand why."

"You believe understanding would make it less . . . frightening."

He nodded. "Evil is . . . perplexing. Small evils are one thing. Everyone gets angry. Everyone is selfish from time to time. But something on this scale? Requiring so much commitment, energy, and time? How did it not occur to him to question? Even once?"

"I know," Ilta said. The subject troubled James to the core of his being. She suspected it could mean only one thing. *What terrible choices did he make before leaving Acrasia?* "But I wish you would be more careful. I can sense your emotions and intent behind your words. The others can't."

"And that is why I only say such things in front of you."

"Oh." She hesitated. She didn't want to upset him further, but she had to know. "May I ask you a question?"

"Certainly."

"Why did you bring Blackthorne here?"

"Where else can he go? He would've been dead within a week. Possibly less."

"Nels would say he'd be better off dead. I'm not sure Blackthorne would disagree."

James pushed his spectacles up his nose. "What happened?"

She stopped hesitating and took the plunge. "We chatted for a while by the willow grove."

"He went with you to the willow grove?" Slate's face suddenly reminded her of the depths of a murky pond. The only thing to surface was the tiniest hint of a smile.

Willing away the sudden warmth in her face, she tightened her jaw. "He was already there. Praying, I think."

"Blackthorne isn't religious," James said. "After what he's been through, I can certainly understand why." He paused. "Wait. You went into the woods alone?"

"It was daylight, and you know I need solitude to clear my head."

"Did you take a gun with you?"

"I can't shoot. Why waste the ammunition?" Ilta asked. "Anyway, I have other means of protecting myself." The unwelcome image of Blackthorne grabbing her cropped up, contradicting her words. She looked away. "And I can sense the presence of bears, snakes, and lions far faster than anyone else can."

"You're not telling me something."

She paused. "Why didn't I see it before? You know—Blackthorne."

"Perhaps you've been trying too hard not to?"

"I have not."

James gave her an incredulous look punctuated with a raised eyebrow. It stopped her before she could deny it further, and she slumped.

"I've been avoiding him," she said.

"Why?"

She picked up a twig and drew circles in the dirt with it. "The same reasons everyone does."

"That's not true," James said. "You like him."

Ilta's stomach clenched, and she felt as if she'd just been caught without her shift.

"One doesn't have to have visions in order to read people, you know," James said.

So this is how it feels to have others know your thoughts before you do. Ilta studied the ground in an attempt to conceal her chagrin. "Is it that obvious?"

"I don't think anyone else has noticed."

"Birch did." *And if Birch knows, how long will it be until Nels notices?* Her face heated again. She didn't fight it this time. "Someone has been gossiping behind my back."

Slate snorted. "Gossip is currently the Eledorean national pastime."

"What's left of Eledore."

"What else do they have to keep themselves entertained? If you know a way to stop it, tell me. I'd love to know," he said, and then shrugged. "You like him. What's wrong with that?"

"Everything is wrong with it. How can you even ask? I love Nels, and I want to be with him."

"I would say that one does not preclude the other," James said. "In any case, it is possible to have a lasting relationship with more than one person. There are at least three different groups in our community that manage it just fine. Minor complications aside."

"Yes, but—"

"In this case, I'd agree with you. That isn't an option," James said. "Therefore, I have to ask, do you really want to be with Nels?"

"I do!"

"And Nels's opinion in the matter?"

"Nels loves me back. He's asked if I'd bind with him. It was a while ago, but he hasn't changed his mind." Beginning to feel the cold through her skirts, she got up and brushed off the damp earth.

"Then why aren't you together?"

"We're together."

"You know what I mean."

"Bound?"

"Did you refuse?"

"No. It's—it's complicated."

"Sure it is," James said.

"It *is*." She thought about all the bad decisions she'd made—all the harm she'd done. "I—I don't want to make any more mistakes. I don't want to hurt Nels any more than I have already."

"Well, I'm afraid that isn't an option. Mistakes and pain are part of life. They are a part of relationships, too."

"You sound like Gran."

"I'll take that as a compliment," James said. "So . . . what about Blackthorne?"

"What about him? He's a Warden."

"Was."

"Is there a difference?"

"I was a major in the Acrasian Army," James said. "I killed Eledoreans in the name of the Emperor during the war."

"That isn't the same."

"It isn't?"

"You never tortured anyone."

"Neither has he."

I watched while they ripped him apart. She shuddered. "How can you be sure?"

"He wouldn't be here if he had. I'd see to that."

"How well do you know him?"

"Apparently better than you, O Great Silmaillia, Blind Eye of the People. You didn't even know he was kainen." Slate stood and then retrieved his portfolio from the ground.

"You think you're funny?"

"A sense of humor is handy in my line of work." Then he gave her that patient, fatherly look he used from time to time. A touch of worry deepened the wrinkles at the corners of his eyes. "Well?"

Not for the first time, Ilta felt a twinge of excitement and fear. She had come close to taking the risk of bedding Nels once. The result had been horrible. Curious, she'd entered his mind and lost herself there. Nels hadn't known she was in a trance. *Not exactly.*

It would've been so easy for him to take advantage of her. *But he didn't.* After that, she'd chosen to remain celibate in a sense, and despite strong temptation and his frustration. *Poor Nels. Why is he so patient with me?*

Would it be less dangerous if I slept with someone I didn't love, first?

She had been content to wait, for the most part. That is, until the day she had seen Blackthorne hand Berlewen Bonner her five-year-old grandchild safe and sound from Archiron. *And how long ago was that? One hundred and eighty-seven very long nights, to be exact.*

After a couple of days' thought, she'd decided Blackthorne was like her. They'd both made terrible mistakes that had harmed other people. He would understand what that meant. He knew the day-to-day burden of guilt. He understood how it felt to remember the faces of those for whom one was responsible. She wasn't entirely certain that Nels could. She had tremendous magical power and then had misused it. Living with the knowledge that she was responsible for an untold number of deaths—

Well. Nels might understand that part. He's a soldier, after all. But it wasn't the same. It just wasn't. Blackthorne thought of himself as something monstrous. She could relate to that. *I'm a monster too.*

I miss Gran. More than anything, she wanted to talk to her about Blackthorne and Nels. Gran had understood the risks. Gran could've taught her how to shield herself if she decided to get closer, but Gran was gone. There was no one else.

How am I even considering bedding Blackthorne? He's a murderer. So are you.

I did what I did out of love, not hate.

James was giving her that patient look again. "Sounds like you have a choice to make."

Ilta sighed. "I don't know what to do." She shot him a hopeful glance.

"I can't tell you that. Ultimately, it's your heart. I understand that the fact that the matter affects others makes it more difficult to sort out, but sort it out you must. And soon."

"Why soon?"

James paused. "You've been putting this off since before I've known you."

Looking away, Ilta gave out a sad, short laugh. "We haven't known one another all that long."

"Two years," James said. "That's a very long, painful time to live with uncertainty."

"I've been confused this long, I think I can handle it for a while longer."

"Sure," James said. "But can Nels?"

Ilta blinked.

"He's suffering. He does his best not to show it, but if this continues with no resolution, it's going to cause trouble. And that's where I enter into things. Because this would be the sort of trouble that will get someone killed."

"Don't be ridiculous," Ilta said. "Nels wouldn't—"

"Blackthorne doesn't know that."

"So?"

"Let's suppose for the moment that Nels has enough self-control in an emotional confrontation to avoid killing Blackthorne," James said. "You're forgetting that Blackthorne isn't just anyone. He's a former Warden. A Retainer. You don't understand what that means, but I do. That makes him a professional killer."

"Well, sure, but—"

"And now you're making erroneous assumptions. Blackthorne won't hesitate to do whatever he has to in order to defend himself in a life-threatening situation," James said. "Think about everything he's already done to survive. Every. Brutal. Decision."

Ilta felt her blood go cold. "Oh."

"You're your own person. You owe it to yourself to do what will make you happy. Nels doesn't own you. No one does. And whatever those two do as a result of your decision, it won't be your fault," James said. "They're grown men. You don't control either of them. But I'm asking you to make up your mind as soon as possible. I want you to tell Nels what that is, even if it means you decide to be with neither of them."

Ilta lowered her head. "All right. I will."

"Look at me," James said.

She did as he asked.

He had a sad, wise smile on his face that reminded her even more of Gran. "Being young and in love can be a wonderful thing, if you let it."

"Oh, really?" she asked. "And how would you know?"

The images of two kainen rapidly blurred her vision, one after the other. The first was male. His long hair was brown and his pale features were narrow. The second image was female, with auburn hair and light tan skin. *Liisa.* Ilta reached inside her apron pocket and touched the watch she kept there. *It wasn't a long vision. He probably didn't even notice.*

"What did you see?" James asked.

It suddenly occurred to Ilta that Katrin bore a striking resemblance to Liisa. *He'll tell Katrin when he's ready. It's none of my business.* "Nothing important," Ilta said. She bit her lip. "You know that when Nels finds out that Blackthorne is kainen, he'll kill him, don't you? And afterward, he'll probably kill you, too." To cut the tension, she gave him a small wink. "I'm not sure I'd mind at the moment."

"Worrying about the lot of you killing one another is just one of my many duties." He yawned.

"Not sleeping again?"

"Of course not," James said.

She opened her bag. "Would you like some valerian or chamomile?"

He nodded. "But not too strong. I can't afford to feel sluggish. I need to be alert."

"No magic. Just herbal tea. I promise." She handed him a small tin of chamomile that she carried with her.

Hurried footsteps echoed up the stairwell. She turned in time to see the iron-reinforced door slam against the rock wall. A tall, blond kainen dressed in a threadbare Eledorean lieutenant's uniform loped into the garden. "There's been an accident at the forge. The new blacksmith—"

"Erkki? What's happened?" Ilta asked.

Erkki bent over. Between gasps, he sputtered, "It's Katrin. Something happened with the new blacksmith. Please come. Westola doesn't know what to do."

James bolted for the exit.

Ilta asked, "What exactly?"

Erkki shook his head. "Westola says Katrin has fainted and she can't wake her."

"Let's go, then," Ilta said, gathering her bag. "We have to get there before James does something he'll regret."

THREE

By the time she and Erkki had arrived, a crowd of curious bystanders had gathered at the forge. Taller than most, Private Wells did a fine job of blocking the doorway with foreboding presence. Her face was set in a mask of command, and her voice was calm but firm.

"There's nothing to see," Private Wells said. "Why don't you all go about your business?"

She stepped aside, allowing Ilta to pass. The acrid stench of terror and anger in the forge made her nose itch and her eyes water. Discharged magic crackled in the air. Ilta threw up a hand in defense and began shielding herself, but it was too late. Before she could finish, the room vanished behind an image of an elderly Acrasian. His face was twisted with hate. Panicked thoughts echoed off the stone walls like screams. *I'm cursed! Grandfather was right! Cursed! I've hurt her! What am I going to do? I've—*

Ilta staggered. When she felt the cold stone against her back, she drew energy from its strength and steadiness. She visualized a thick wall around herself and fortified it with rock energy. Her senses faded, even her hearing. She felt as if she'd been swathed in cotton. She hated feeling like that. It was why she didn't use such defenses all that much, but the shield did its job, and the assault on her mind ended. When she could breathe again, she blinked back the fogginess, released a majority of the energy back into the earth, and took stock of the room.

Katrin lay sprawled on the floor, unconscious. James pillowed her head and shoulders in his lap. Kaija Westola was packing her healer's bag. In a far corner, Corporal Horn spoke in soothing tones to the new weaponsmith, Tobias Freeson. The smith's eyes were wide with terror, and he paced like a cornered horse searching for an escape.

Kaija approached. "I did what I could." Her graying, fuzzy hair was twisted into its usual knot at the back of her head. She was short. Her face was set in surly lines, and her manner was brusque. "There isn't a swiving thing wrong with her physically."

"What is it, then?" Ilta whispered.

Kaija said, "I don't know. I can't wake her. Couldn't get anything useful out of the boy. He'd have run for it if it hadn't been for Wells. If I didn't know any better, I'd say . . ."

"What?" Ilta asked.

"I'd say it was the onset of magic," Kaija said. "But they're both too old for that."

"I think you're right about the smith," Ilta said. "Katrin, on the other hand . . ."

"I'll leave this to you, then," Kaija said. "I was distilling some herbs when I heard. Process is a bit finicky. Whole thing is likely to blow if I don't watch over it."

"All right." Ilta knelt next to Katrin and James.

"Can you do something?" James asked.

"Would you mind leaving her with me for a moment?" Ilta asked.

"Anything. Whatever it takes."

"Give us some room, then." Settling into place with Katrin's head in the crook of her elbow, Ilta said, "Stay back until I say otherwise. I'll need to focus."

As soon as James and his fear were at a safe distance, Ilta took a steadying breath and closed her eyes. She couldn't do anything without walling away the emotions filling the room. She first asked Terveh, the goddess of healing, for a blessing. Then she visualized a searing line of blue flames and, with that, mentally traced a circle around herself and Katrin. The fire grew hotter, higher in her mind until it arched and formed a bubble half-sunk into the floor. She paused long enough to check the boundaries one more time before opening her mind to Katrin's.

Katrin, are you there?

The blackness feels warm, like floating in the lake in summer. It folds her in the intense comfort of peace after pain.

Katrin.

The name is familiar. Yes. That is her name. And then the present sinks her. She chokes. It threatens to drown her. She thrashes against the memories.

He was kissing Deirdre! That horrible—

Katrin, calm down.

She pauses. She isn't alone. Afraid, she thinks of swimming away.

It's me, Ilta. You're safe. I won't let anything or anyone hurt you. Just tell me what happened.

She has come to the forge because Tobias asked her. He said he liked her. He said he was designing a special new musket just for her. She came to see the drawings. But he was with Deirdre. He was kissing her! Kissing that—

I understand. What happened next?

She doesn't want to listen to Tobias's lies. He's angry. He shouts. She tries to leave, but he grabs her arm. There is a flash of light and pain, and that is when the world goes away.

I see. No harm done. You were only frightened, then. Good.

She is confused.

Are you ready to come back? You've given your father quite a scare.

"Is she all right?" James's voice pierced the darkness.

For a moment, the raw smell of his worry leaves the sharp taste of uncooked onions in the back of her throat. She wants to gag. She doesn't like onions.

Ilta blinked. *That last thought wasn't mine.* She pressed her palm against the floor and began to focus on the chilly stone beneath her. The scent of burning coals lingered in her nose. Her eyesight slowly returned until fuzzy shadows formed faces. She let the invisible circle of protection sink into the floor along with a quick blessing. She would need to make an offering later.

Katrin sat up with a gasp. "Papa? Is someone cooking onion soup?"

James wordlessly asked permission to approach. Ilta nodded. James knelt, grabbing Katrin in a fierce hug. Ilta continued to focus on breathing and the feel of stone. The room darkened, and for a moment, she wondered if the floor would be enough to anchor her in the present. That was when she understood it was only Erkki standing over her. His body was positioned between her and the forge fire. His features were craggy, making him seem stern. She didn't know him all that well. Still, she sensed he was a caring person under the hard exterior.

He handed her a tin cup.

She swallowed half its contents in one gulp, focusing on the taste of tin and cold water, then glanced up. "Thank you."

Erkki nodded, but he hesitated.

"Don't just stand there gawking," Ilta said, reaching out to him. "Help me up." On her feet, she turned to Tobias, sitting in a defeated hunch at his workbench. His thoughts were quiet but throbbed like a deep bruise.

"Will the girl be all right?" Erkki asked.

"She'll be fine. It was an accident. The smith?"

"I'm not certain," Erkki said. "When I broached the subject of magic, he panicked. Given the circumstances, I thought it best to keep him calm and away from the girl."

"He's from Novus Salernum," she said.

"I'm afraid so," Erkki said. "Who knows how long he's been fighting it. Someone should teach him what to do with the energy before his skull explodes like a bad melon."

"Don't exaggerate. He isn't that powerful."

"He's strong enough to be a problem."

Goddess save us from Acrasian ignorance, Ilta thought. "Can you teach him? It should be a male who talks to him."

Erkki frowned. "Soldiers' rituals are all I know. And that would hardly suffice. He's a smith." And with that, he turned and left with Wells in tow. Seeing that nothing more interesting was going to happen, the crowd in the passage began to dissipate. The door was still open. Cool air drifted into the hot room. James whispered something in Katrin's ear and then tenderly brushed damp hair from her eyes. She nodded and pulled the coat that he'd wrapped around her closer.

Leaving her alone on the floor, James went to Ilta. "Is she going to be all right?"

"Yes," Ilta said. "Given the situation, Kat did the best thing possible. She hid herself away in her own mind. She was frightened, fainted, and couldn't find her way back. That's all."

"What do you mean, that's all?" James asked. "Tell me the truth."

Ilta paused. She really didn't want to add to James's worries. "It was uncontrolled magic."

"What?" James shot a worried glance at Kat.

"Not Kat. It wasn't her, not yet, and maybe not ever," Ilta said. "It was the smith."

"You're sure?"

"Absolutely."

"Is this . . . normal?" James asked, now giving the smith an uneasy look.

Feeling uncomfortable, Ilta paused. She hadn't discussed the facts of burgeoning magical power with James before and was reluctant to do so. Since he'd adopted Kat, Ilta had assumed he knew what he was in for, but now it was apparent that he didn't. Acrasians were terrified of magical power, and thanks to their history with Eledore, there were good reasons for that fear. At the same time, Acrasians frequently magnified the danger. "It's normal. But only for someone who is uneducated and unprepared." Of course, she didn't tell him that accidents occurred even when people were made ready. Magic was power, and power was dangerous when mishandled.

"What do you mean?" James asked.

"When kainen reach a certain age, their magical powers begin to manifest," Ilta said. "If your powers are very strong, if you aren't aware of what's happening, and if you attempt to repress them . . . it can be traumatic."

"Even dangerous?"

"For those without an equivalent amount of power and knowledge of shielding?" Ilta nodded.

James frowned.

"But understand, the power we're talking about isn't that common," Ilta said. "In your average kainen, it might manifest and no one but the individual might notice. Headaches are usual to varying degrees. Sometimes a small amount of bleeding—"

"Bleeding!"

"Nothing worse than a nosebleed," Ilta said. "Harming others has been known to happen, but not frequently. Not if all are aware. Anyway, you don't have to worry about the smith. I'll teach him how to keep it under control, but it might be best to isolate him until we know the extent of—"

"This is going to happen every time one of you acquires your powers?"

She paused. "Not really. But I'm afraid there's always a chance."

"Sounds dangerous."

"We have traditions in place to handle this. His father should've taught him the basics of how to ground himself when he was small. It's something every kainen child is taught, like learning to walk," Ilta said. "Usually, something like this only occurs among the powerful families. Nobles in particular. When children are old enough, they are assigned apprenticeships according to what powers are most likely to develop—"

"But we don't have traditions. I've never heard of this. Nor have most of the others. At least, no one who grew up in Acrasia," James said. "Everyone here is a refugee. Justiina, Henna, Miikka, and Sevri. They're all children. *Orphan* children. We have no idea where they came from because they were in shock when they were found. They could barely speak. You remember what that was like. We don't know who their parents were."

"I know."

"And they aren't the only ones, nor will they be. There will be more," James said, and took a deep breath. "We must come up with some sort of system to cope with this. And we have to do it now. I won't risk—"

"Calm down. We can start classes," Ilta said. "I'm sure others will be willing to volunteer. Westola and I can monitor their progress. Everything will be all right. The Ytlainen manage a mixed population without much difficulty. It can be done. Stop acting like—"

"I apologize. I didn't mean to . . .," James said. "I—I simply didn't expect . . . this."

"It isn't a problem if we're ready for it. And we can be ready," Ilta said. "Every kainen holds some kind of power. You know this."

"Not every."

"Nels does too."

"He claims otherwise."

"It didn't take the form he was raised to expect." She shook her head and whispered, "And I think he's committed to being defective because it makes being a failure easier for him to accept."

James glanced around the room. The weaponsmith picked up a sword from the workbench and began to run its edge along a sharpening stone. He seemed determined not to look at Katrin, who sat on the cold floor hugging herself inside her father's oversized coat.

The worry lines at the corners of James's eyes deepened. "How long will it take to stabilize Tobias? Will he be able to get back to work soon?"

"It depends upon how much of his upbringing I'll have to deal with," Ilta said. "Right now? I'd say it'll be a few days at least. He's been filled with a great deal of fear and shame."

"What if it's too much . . . power?"

"It isn't command magic," she blurted.

"How do you know?"

She sighed. *Because we're not scraping two sets of brains off the forge walls.* There was no point in saying anything. It would only serve to strengthen his prejudice, and there was nothing to worry about. *This time.* "I would know."

The lines in James's brow deepened.

"Why don't you take Katrin home? Tuck her under a blanket with a bowl of warm soup. After a few hours' rest, she'll be back to normal and getting into the usual trouble."

"That's what I'm afraid of."

Ilta felt a smile creep onto her face. Taking the opportunity to distract him, she whispered, "She's growing up on you, and you don't like it."

He glanced again at his daughter and then said, "Guilty as charged." Shaking his head with a wry smile, he said, "Will you let me know how Tobias is? Later, of course. Then we'll talk about what should be done. I need to get some sort of a plan in place as soon as possible."

"I'll come by," Ilta said. "Get Katrin home. And I'll bring two doses of valerian."

"Thank you."

"You're welcome."

James retrieved Katrin and they both left, a little worse for wear but safe and in one piece. The forge was quiet but for the crackling fire. Ilta went to the smith. Worry clouded his expression, and a spike of peppery anxiety pierced the air when she approached. He stopped fidgeting with the sword.

"Is Katrin all right?" he asked.

"She'll be fine," Ilta said. "Don't you worry. Your name is Tobias Freeson, am I right?"

He nodded.

"I'm Ilta Korpela," she said.

"Am I going to be punished? I didn't mean to hurt her. Will

Mr. Slate turn me out? I—I hope not. I don't have anywhere else to go."

"It was just an accident. Everyone understands that," Ilta said, settling onto the bench next to him. This close to the forge fire, she felt too warm. She unbuttoned her coat.

Tobias's face turned a deeper shade of red. "Deirdre said I'd killed Kat, but I only touched her arm."

"What happened when you touched Katrin?"

"I don't know. Something. . . . It . . . tingled." Tobias stared at the blade again. "Then she fell down."

"Has anything like this ever occurred before?"

"No. Never!"

"Did your parents have magic?"

Tobias's face went from red to white. "My parents weren't sorcerers. They couldn't make people see or do things. They never hurt anyone."

Goddess, please grant me patience, Ilta thought. "I mean, did either of your parents exhibit intuition or have portentous dreams? Did they have special skills? Was either of them particularly good with animals?"

His expression grew more alarmed. "Sometimes Mother got feelings about people. Father said I was like her. But he never said . . ." His voice dropped to a whisper. "Magic is evil. I'm damned, aren't I?"

"Don't be ridiculous. I use magic to heal people. Am I evil?"

"I didn't mean—"

"Give me your hand."

Exposing herself to yet another person's thoughts so soon was risky, but there was no one else to handle the matter. He flinched as she cradled his hand in both of hers. The familiar tingling began in her palms and raced up both arms to her elbows. A series of images blocked out the forge. Unfamiliar faces. Novus Salernum. Katrin.

The visions were spiced with the scent of terror, humiliation, and deep sorrow. His mind was in such chaos that it took Ilta a while to find what she was looking for.

An affinity for metal. Handy for a smith. Very strong, but not enough to be too dangerous. Dangerous enough, though. Releasing his hand, she blinked until the glowing embers of the forge fire were clear. She expanded her awareness to the smell of burning coal and lamp oil and finally the firelight dancing on the walls, the bellows.

"Tell Mr. Slate that I won't do whatever it was I did again," Tobias said. "Not ever." The last words came out in a rush.

Don't make promises you can't keep, she thought. "Like any talent, you have to learn how to use *and* control it. Everyone makes mistakes—even me, and I've been training my whole life."

Tobias sat with his head down and his shoulders hunched. "But . . . it's wrong."

"It's perfectly normal for you. You're kainen."

His horrified expression made her want to slap whoever had made him fear himself.

She decided to try a different approach. "You were born with the ability to hear. Is that wrong?" she asked.

Hesitating, he finally shook his head in answer.

"All right," she said. "How about being able to sing or paint? These things aren't any different. Magic is the force that flows through every living thing and every element in the world. Earth. Air. Fire. Water." She pointed to each. Then she laid a hand over her own heart. "Spirit."

He blinked but didn't protest.

She continued. "Magic connects us with the universe. And it most certainly exists whether or not one can sense it. Magic is part of what I am. It's also part of what you are."

Tobias's voice came out in a shamed whisper. "But everyone

knows what happened to Acrasians who came to Eledore before the war. The things that were done to them. You can't say that wasn't evil."

"The Acrasians invaded Eledore first," Ilta said, frowning. That much was true. Of course, it wasn't the whole of the truth. That was complicated. The border between Acrasia and Eledore had been disputed since long before she'd been born. Altercations had flared up on and off for a century. "People have a right to protect themselves."

Doubt hovered on the edges of Tobias's face, but he still didn't look up. "Yes, but—"

"Magic is a tool, like any other. It can be turned to multiple purposes like any tool can, including words." She stopped herself. He needed to trust her, and yelling at him wouldn't help. He'd been through enough for one day. "Magic is a powerful tool, and as such, it must be used responsibly. It's an important part of wielding power of any kind, knowing when to use it and how. Not everyone who is born with power uses it wisely."

"But—"

"Kainen are no more evil than anyone else. Every being is flawed," she said. "Therefore, I won't defend what was done to those who came to Eledore with peaceful intent. I won't deny it. I can't. Abuses occurred, and in truth, Acrasians weren't the only ones harmed."

"But . . . don't you do . . . spells?" Tobias asked the question as if it were going to bite him before it left his mouth.

"Do you know how spells work?"

Tobias blushed.

Ilta sighed. "Well?"

"Grandfather said . . . I mean . . . I hear you dance naked until a demon appears and then you ask it for help."

Ilta burst out laughing.

Tobias frowned. "What's so funny?"

"Who concocts these stories?" She laughed for quite a while, until she spied his face. Wiping away a tear, she took another deep breath. "It's simple. You've probably done it yourself and never given it a thought." She cast about for a suitable analogy that wouldn't upset him. "I can assume your father took you to an Acrasian church?"

He looked worried but nodded.

"What kind?" Ilta asked.

"Moralist."

I should've known, Ilta thought. "Tell me, when a blessing is given, what happens?"

Tobias cleared his throat. "The priest asks Mithras to watch and protect the person and makes a holy sign in the air or waves incense over them or anoints them with oil."

Ilta said, "There. That's a spell."

"No, it isn't!"

"The only distinction you can make between the two is terminology. Acrasians call it prayer, and Eledorean Traditionalists, like me, call it a spell," she said.

"Acrasians don't have magic."

"Well, not like kainen do. No."

"And kainen worship false gods."

"Tell me something," Ilta said. "Why are kainen gods considered false, more false than any others?"

Tobias blinked. "Well . . ."

"Acrasians only believe in one deity. I understand that. However, the rest of the world believes that there are many deities. There are even some people who don't believe in any deity at all."

"Humanists." His expression was filled with disgust.

"Eledoreans believe that you can choose not to ask any deity for help," Ilta said. "Or you can seek out one in particular who best embodies the type of assistance needed. It's even possible to ask for help from all of them at once. It's entirely up to you."

"But there aren't any other gods."

Ilta gave him a tolerant smile. "I'm certain there are, if there are any at all, but if you choose for there not to be others, there won't be for you."

"That doesn't make any sense."

"We'll talk about it some more later. Right now ... well ... you don't have to believe in anything for magic to work. You only have to connect to the source," Ilta said, touching his forehead, then his chest, and lastly pointing to the stone floor. "Every kainen has their own relationship with magic. Their own method of accessing and controlling it. You'll have to figure out what works best for you."

Obviously uncomfortable, Tobias turned to the saber lying on the table. It was then that she recognized the swirling pattern of water steel emerging from the black substance encrusted on the blade.

"Look what I found," Tobias said, snatching up the weapon and unscrewing the pommel. He pulled it apart and pointed to the Eledorean runes VT etched into the tang.

Ilta's jaw dropped. "Where did you get that?"

"Mr. Nickols brought it along with some others awhile ago. They're for the swordsmith, Pasha. She'll be here later. Most of them weren't much more than scrap metal. But this one is special. It's still sharp. Even after the blade was mistreated. See this?" Tobias pointed at a blackened section of blade. "Whoever owned it kept it coated in oily soot." He ran a finger along the dull top of the blade in awe.

"Why would anyone do that?"

"To keep others from seeing it for what it is. I think."

"Oh."

"Mother told me that long ago, Consul Sertorius sent spies deep into Eledore to find the great forge," Tobias said. "When Vihtori Tuomari wouldn't reveal the secret of Eledorean water steel, the Consul's men killed him and every apprentice and master smith who trained with him. Then they burned it all to the ground. The secret was lost. The Ytlainen smiths are good, but they'll never compare to Vihtori Tuomari."

At least he has some of his history correct, Ilta thought.

"Did Tuomari use magic?" Tobias asked, uneasy.

She nodded. "Just as I put magic into remedies I create, or the cloth I weave."

"What about guns?" Tobais asked, shy. "If Vihtori Tuomari placed magic in the metal of a sword . . . can I do so with a gun?"

"I suppose anything is possible," she said. "Unfortunately, I know nothing of weapons. I can only teach you what I know. Basic things that would be useful for a smith. Would you like that?"

"I don't know."

"Think about it." She got up from the floor. "In the meantime, please try to avoid strong emotions until you've learned some manner of control."

"You're telling me to stay away from Katrin."

"For the moment, sure. Overall? No," she said. "But I'm fairly certain her father will."

Tobias sighed.

Ilta paused, smiled, and then whispered, "However, if you really care about her, I wouldn't let that stop you."

❧ NELS ❧

ONE

MERTA
NEW ELEDORE

NINTH OF VERIKUU, 1783

Dizzy and queasy, Nels stumbled a few feet before he collapsed, landing hard on his backside with a wince. Merta's newly reconstructed dock planks let out a protesting creak. "No more ships. No more ocean travel. Never again."

He swallowed what he hoped was the last of his stomach's protests and tensed against yet another cold blast of wind racing up the river from the sea. It attempted to steal his tricorne, and he snatched it back before it could be lifted out of reach.

The air was bracing on Merta's sea-facing river docks. Freezing gusts plunged their way up the river, their force concentrated by the narrow canyon. The valley didn't widen until it reached Merta, where it slammed into several hundred feet of granite. He'd forgotten the wind. He glanced up at the city nestled against the mountains and spied a lone Eledorean flag slapping the grey sky. A weak smile tugged at the corners of his mouth. He couldn't fault his troops for their patriotism, but advertising their presence probably wasn't the best idea, strategically speaking.

Here's hoping they've made more progress since the last message bird. Before he'd left the Hold, he'd ordered Overlieutenant Larsson to gather most of the troops and meet him at Merta. There were shorter routes to Grandmother Mountain from Norman Island, but a visit to the mines had been the second reason he'd risked his sister's wrath.

Always prepare multiple plans. Life is a thimblerig. Never let anyone know which cup holds the pea. He'd not considered before whether or not this policy should include his twin sister. *Does she inform me of all of her plots?* He already had the answer to that question. *Suvi will forgive me.* But he knew that would only be the case if the gamble paid off.

On the other hand, the extra time spent in Captain Julia's cabin had been an unforeseen bonus.

Captain Gaia Julia bent next to him and whispered, "I hope I was able to make your journey more comfortable."

"Your surgeon's assistance was much appreciated," Nels said. As a result, his stomach had been fine until the journey ashore.

"I wasn't talking about that aspect of the voyage," Captain Julia said.

Nels heard Viktor's amused snort as he passed. Sebastian Moller was directly behind, carrying the first trunk. His face was set in an expression of determined ignorance. After a sideways glance, he focused once more upon organizing Julia's crew and unloading the supplies—food and clothing for the troops. Luckily, the Waterborne were still willing to grant Nels a more-than-fair discount.

Keeping his tone low, Nels said, "It was extremely pleasant and . . . educational."

"Educational?" she asked. "Somehow I expected quite a bit more from that tongue of yours."

"I deeply regret that I am operating under a significant disadvantage at the moment."

"There is that," she said.

His troops were otherwise occupied. So he motioned her closer. "I almost forgot I was on a boat."

"And . . . you ruined it," she said with a smile. "Good thing for you, *Lorelei* can't hear you."

"Can't we meet somewhere on land sometime?"

"The ports I frequent aren't ones you'll want to visit," she said. Then she got a thoughtful look. "Unless . . . How often can you sell your friend?"

"I don't think Viktor is up for another visit with the Acrasians," Nels said. "For that matter, neither am I."

"Then this is goodbye." Captain Julia put out a hand to help him up. "You're the only kainen I've ever met to react to water that way."

"Aren't I the lucky one?" Nels asked, took her hand, and got to his feet. Her grip was firm.

"Everyone adjusts eventually," Captain Julia said.

"And I did," he said. "Eventually. Thanks for being patient with me."

Captain Julia gazed off into the distance, and he caught a flash of something in her eyes that he would never have expected to see. *Vulnerability.* He found it as attractive as he had her tough exterior.

She asked, "You'll be careful?"

He moved closer. The top of her head reached his chest. With a smile, he whispered, "Permission to board?"

She tilted her chin up, raised an eyebrow, and just like that, her defenses shifted back into place. "Permission granted."

Stooping, he gave her the best kiss he could manage in spite of his twitchy stomach. Wrapping her gently in his arms, he pulled her close. Her full lips were moist and yielding, and her tongue brushed against his. She tasted of the apples and cinnamon they'd had for breakfast. It wasn't unpleasant.

Julia's crew is watching and so are Viktor and Sebastian. Nels prepared to let her go.

At that moment, she grabbed his buttocks and pressed herself against his burgeoning cockstand, and all at once, he forgot about possible witnesses.

Oh, gods.

After what seemed like an instant but was probably far longer, she broke the kiss and left him gasping. Her voice was so low it was almost a purr. "Too bad there's no time for another good, long docking." She winked. "Call me Gaia."

His heart thundered in his ears, as loud as a herd of runaway horses. Images from the past week seared his veins. For a moment, he couldn't speak. He cleared his throat. "Not if you want payment before the tide turns, Gaia."

She paused, confused. "Didn't you already spend all you had on those supplies?"

Half-turning from her, he motioned to the remains of the city behind him. "Before the war, this land was to be mine. And in the time of my father, Merta was famous for one thing."

"And what was that?"

"Silver mines," Nels said.

"Ah." One side of her mouth curled up in a wicked smile. "In that case, I would give the matter longer consideration," she said. "But in all fairness, I must choose your money. There isn't enough time for you to service my whole crew, even if you were so inclined."

"You do have a point."

She laid a hand on the front of his shirt, gathering the fabric in her fist. "May I have another kiss on account?"

"I suppose that—"

She yanked him tight against her by his shirt, the second embrace even more energetic than the first. He'd lost track of time when a polite cough brought him up for air.

"Sir?" Viktor asked.

"Yes?" Nels answered, not moving from Gaia lest Viktor see how much she'd affected him.

"Overlieutenant Larsson would like to make a report," Viktor said. "She's waiting at the gate."

"Were they successful?" Nels asked.

"Based upon her grin, I believe the answer to that question is yes," Viktor said.

Nels tried not to show his relief. "All right, tell her I'm on my way."

"Yes, sir," Viktor said.

Nels tugged his greatcoat closed and gave Gaia the crook of his elbow. "Shall we go see what Merta has on offer?"

She slipped her arm through his. "I believe we shall."

Making his way up the mountain slope, Nels noticed that the roadway leading to the city bore evidence of the Acrasian Army's futile attempts to open Merta's gates before those inside had sabotaged the mines. It'd rained before the battle. Heavy artillery wheels had plowed ruts into the hard-packed earth. Large sections of the city's outer and inner curtain walls had been pounded into rubble by the Acrasians' new, more mobile cannon. More than two years had passed since he'd last set foot anywhere near Merta. He hadn't been looking forward to it. Memories of death, destruction, and betrayal weighted the air, as thick as cannon smoke. He could almost hear the screams of the dying as he mounted the last few steps to the outer gatehouse. He kept his back to the former battle-field. Yet his nose captured the faint scent of burnt gunpowder long past. He wasn't entirely sure it wasn't his imagination. The city was empty and had been for some time. Merta, once the Kingdom of Eledore's second most prosperous city, was a ruin like the rest, but there were signs of new life. The smell of fresh-cut ironwood over-whelmed his memories when he reached the castle's newly replaced wooden doors.

Overlieutenant Larsson waited for him in the shadows cast by the portcullis. She stepped forward and snapped to attention, her dark young face set in a professional soldier's mask.

I don't think anyone who knew her before would recognize her now. She's changed a great deal, he thought. *But then, haven't we all?*

Larsson said, "Merta is ready for inspection, sir. The barracks repairs are complete, and we've started work on the outer walls."

Nels returned her salute. "At ease." He readied himself for her answer. "And Jarvi? How far was he able to get?"

Relaxing, she grinned. "The tunnel leading to the first mine shaft is cleared. In truth, the Acrasians did half the work for us. Sergeant Wiberg has a surprise for you."

"Is that so?"

"We stored it in the inner gatehouse great hall." She indi-cated where with an over-the-shoulder nod. Then her expression grew more serious. "That's the good news. Now for the bad. If the records are accurate—and none of us would know for sure, since we're not miners—the first tunnel is at the end of its usefulness. It's the second shaft that's the active one. It's also the problem."

"What is wrong with the second shaft?"

"It's set to blow, should it be tampered with. We expected that. But somebody got clever," she said. "Jarvi says the trap contains a long series of complicated triggers. Amazingly, the Acrasians were smart enough to leave it alone."

Gaia cleared her throat.

Larsson continued as if she hadn't heard. "Jarvi says if he knew who sabotaged it or even if we had anyone who understood mining, it'd make removing or working around the thing easier. However, we don't. So the dismantling process is going to take some time."

Shit. Shit. Shit. "How much time?"

"A few months. Maybe more. Certainly not before winter. He says we may have to abandon the tunnel and dig a new shaft."

Nels frowned. He muttered more to himself than to Larsson: "We're not wintering here."

"Well . . . that's one of the things Jarvi wants to talk to you about, sir."

"Fair enough. Where is he?"

"In shaft two, working. He's been at it day and night since we arrived," she said. "That is why I'm giving the report and not him."

"Without rest?" Nels asked. "Isn't that a little dangerous?"

She shrugged. "Master Sergeant Tane Jarvi isn't someone I argue with. I know better."

"And Wiberg?" Nels asked.

"He's upstairs," Larsson said. "I recommend talking to him as soon as possible."

"All right," Nels said. "Have Jarvi meet me in the gatehouse great hall. Immediately. I'll be there shortly."

"Yes, sir," Larsson said. She saluted, turned, and left.

"Gaia," Nels said. "Follow me. I suspect there may be something in the inner gatehouse relevant to your interests."

"If you say so," Gaia said.

He led her through the huge double oak doors, under both portcullises, and inside the outer curtain. There they entered the outer ward and then the second gatehouse, with its set of new doors and portcullises. Once they were inside the inner ward, he turned to the left and took the stone steps up to the inner gatehouse's great hall. Along the way, the rasp, clatter, and thump of construction echoed inside Merta's walls. Troops repaired the barracks, groomed and exercised the horses, and otherwise prepared for the journey to the Hold. Upon reaching the gatehouse great hall, Nels laid a hand on the ornate iron door handle and gave it a twist.

Wiberg, seated behind a writing table laden with treasure, dropped the quill in his hand, jumped to his feet, and saluted. The corps healer was shorter than Nels but taller than Gaia and Larsson. His hair was light brown, and his brown eyes sparkled with happiness. "Good afternoon, sir."

Gaia took in the contents of the big room and choked.

Nels felt his jaw drop open. "Oh."

"I suspect all this is going to come in handy," Wiberg said.

Nels said, "Where did you find—"

"The citizens hid everything they couldn't carry and wanted to save from the Acrasians in the first tunnel, bless them," Wiberg said. "I had all the most valuable items stored up here. Lieutenant Larsson thought it best, considering."

Stepping to the writing desk, Nels stuck his hand inside a small chest filled with gems and jewelry. Sacks of silver coins lined the walls, along with various items made of gold. He didn't remember seeing anything like it outside his father's treasury since long before the war. He finally remembered to return the salute. "Good work."

"Thank you, sir," Wiberg said.

"Captain Julia, I believe we can now discuss the second half of your payment," Nels said.

Gaia gave out a low whistle. "Don't take this personally, but I made the right choice."

"I thought as much," Nels said.

Someone knocking drew his attention away from the treasure. A dirt-smudged and weary-looking Master Sergeant Tane Jarvi entered the room.

"Welcome back, sir," Jarvi said.

"Thank you," Nels said, and then motioned to the contents of the room. "You all have been busy, I see."

"Yes, sir," Jarvi said. "Unfortunately, the other mine shafts have been less profitable."

Nels said, "As it is, this is more than what I'd hoped for."

Jarvi nodded. "About that—"

"You want to stay. I can't let you," Nels said. "I need you with me."

"You can't leave Merta unattended. There is no knowing if or when the Acrasians will return. That's a gamble we can't afford to take," Jarvi said. "Also, there is no way we can transport all this back to the Hold. Not without risking unwanted attention."

"You've a point," Nels said, and paused. "And once the walls are repaired, how many troops do you think we'll need to leave behind to effectively guard Merta?"

"In order to continue the work in the tunnels—"

"We don't have anyone qualified to work the mines," Nels said. "Not yet. I'll talk to Slate about . . . acquiring someone with the necessary experience."

"Good," Jarvi said.

"I intend to leave only enough troops behind to hold Merta," Nels said. "How many?"

"Once the walls are finished?" Jarvi asked.

Nels said, "You were artillery. You'd know."

"Half a company," Jarvi said.

"Leaving me with the other half to protect what we take with us." Nels gave the situation some thought. "Should work. Send for Larsson. It's time to pack."

TWO

Nels woke to a gentle kick in the side.

"Get up, sir," Viktor said. "We're about to have company."

Nels sat up and took in his surroundings. The ground beneath his folding camp cot was damp, and outside his dog tent, it was dark and raining. During the time he'd been asleep, the temperature had plummeted. It was cold, bordering upon freezing. *At least there isn't much wind,* he thought. Reaching for his trousers, he already had a bad feeling regarding his day. "It isn't morning, and I haven't had my coffee yet. Tell me, who has come to visit?"

"Remember that Acrasian outpost we passed yesterday?" Viktor asked. "They're sending troops our way."

"They didn't know we were here. We made very certain of this before we camped, did we not? So, why are the nice Acrasians not sleeping?"

A guilty look passed over Viktor's face. "It may have to do with the matter of a few missing cattle."

"Damn it," Nels said, moving faster than before. *Who needs coffee when you've news like this to wake to?* "We have with us enough money to *buy* our supplies from the Waterborne for the next three years. We don't have to steal." *Maybe not ever, if we get that mine working.*

"Where's the fun in that?" Viktor asked.

"Getting home in one piece *with* our money?"

"Honestly, the longer you remain in charge, the more dreary you become."

"Being responsible for a few hundred lives will do that to you." Nels rushed to finish dressing while Corporal Mustonen began packing.

"Don't you have fun anymore?" Viktor asked.

"Being chased through half the countryside in the rain isn't my idea of fun," Nels said. "It never was."

Viktor said, "Well, you can't blame me for this one."

"It wasn't you?" Nels asked.

"If it had been, I'd have been a swiving lot quieter about it. Also, I'd have passed it by you first," Viktor said. "You know this, right?"

"Maybe," Nels said.

Viktor gave him a hurt look filled with imaginary indignation.

"All right, all right. Whose brilliant idea was it, then?" Nels asked. His fingers were stiff with cold, making the buttons on his jacket a bit of a challenge.

"I can't say, *exactly*," Viktor said, helping with his overcoat. "But Groop, Kurri, and Lassila went for a late-night stroll about two hours ago and came back with ten new friends."

Outside his tent, Nels could hear the hushed sounds of the camp being rousted out on the quiet. He also thought he heard the calls of anxious cattle.

"That's just swiving fantastic," Nels said. "Remind me to have a chat with Groop, Kurri, and Lassila later."

"Yes, sir," Viktor said, stepping outside and holding open the tent flap for him.

Nels crammed his tricorne onto his head. The camp was a soggy sketch in organized chaos. Private Nyberg ducked into the tent behind him—Nels assumed, to help Mustonen.

Nels asked, "Where's Moller?"

"With the cattle," Viktor said. "I thought it'd be best, since he can control them."

"Good," Nels said. Gazing at the night sky through the trees, he noted that the moon had already set. *That's good.* "Viktor, you, Jarvi, myself, and Corporal Mustonen's squad are with the treasury. Moller stays with the livestock. They'll be on their own. I'm not risking what we got out of Merta for a few head of cattle. Understand?"

"Yes, sir," Viktor said.

"We'll go with the usual. Give the order," Nels said. "We'll meet at Painted Rock tomorrow. Everyone knows what to do."

"Time to vanish without a trace," Viktor said. "Got it."

After more than a year's practice, Nels trusted his troops to handle the situation with efficient and, above all, *silent* grace. The camp was broken down, and the half-company that he'd taken with him from Merta divided into squads which, in turn, left the instant they were ready. All were on their way in less than a half-hour. In addition, he knew Master Sergeant Jarvi would see to it that there wouldn't be so much as a smoking fire pit remaining by the time the Acrasians arrived. It was all standard procedure, also one of the reasons why the Acrasians called him the Ghost.

In Eledore, ghosts were without power—ineffective, hopeless, and lost. In Acrasia, the word held more sinister meaning. Ghosts were ineffable creatures of unknown, uncontrollable power that came and went without a trace beyond that of the damage they left behind. In Acrasia, ghosts were the things that haunted the dark and fed on the living. Acrasians were superstitious, and Nels was more than willing to use that to his advantage.

Leading Loimuta by the headstall, Nels made his way as quietly and quickly as he could through the surrounding forest. Rainwater dripped from a corner of his hat. He'd checked twice but couldn't shake the feeling he'd left something behind. Shrugging it off, he continued. The sweat in his palms made the leather slick in his grip. *It's only the usual fear. No more. All is well.* It didn't matter how many times he encountered Acrasians; the terror of failure slammed him. He'd thought that the intensity of this feeling would fade eventually. However, he only got more practiced at pretending he wasn't afraid.

A line of thirteen men and women followed him, each holding the reins of a horse laden with valuables. Viktor stayed at the rear and used his powers to assure that they left no trace in the soft earth. A little more than three quarters of an hour had passed when an explosion brought Nels up short. Turning back, he caught a flash of Viktor's pale smile in the predawn murk.

"The Acrasians should learn to step more carefully when entering our camps," Viktor said.

Jarvi grunted. "As long as they don't, I am happy to provide the lesson."

Nels looked to the things tied to Loimuta's saddle and suddenly realized what was missing. "That was my dog tent, wasn't it?"

"What are you worried about?" Viktor asked. "You can buy another."

"And what am I to do for shelter until then?" Nels asked.

"Don't look at me. I'm not sharing mine," Viktor said. "You talk in your sleep."

"Do I?" Nels asked.

"And kick," Viktor said.

"And whose idea was it to use my dog tent for the trap?" Nels asked.

Jarvi, Mustonen, and several of the others all pointed at Viktor.

"Traitors," Viktor said.

"I believe the word you are looking for is 'intelligent,'" Mustonen said.

Private Horn said, "I prefer 'honest,' sir."

Viktor cut the next comment short with a signal for silence. Nels listened and thought he might have heard something to his right. He called a stop, holding up a hand then signaled to Viktor to investigate in that direction. In response, Viktor paused and tilted his head. He then vanished into the underbrush to the left. They all waited. Nels held his breath. A few moments passed before he heard a muffled noise. He drew his pistol and made it ready.

"Viktor?" Nels whispered.

No answer came from the woods.

Nels tried again. "Viktor?"

Two figures crashed through the foliage. Viktor parried two rapid blows from a smallsword and backed away from his shorter, more nimble opponent. In response, they leapt forward and executed a lunge. Viktor let out a yelp as the blade sliced through the fabric of his coat sleeve. His attacker didn't pause. They lashed out with a kick, knocking Viktor down. Viktor grabbed his opponent's boot, and they both tumbled across Nels's path. The other troops approached, gathering in a circle around the pair with drawn pistols and muskets. Loimuta tugged at his reins. Nels calmed the horse and then returned his attention to the fight. He didn't recognize the attacker, but whoever they were, they weren't wearing an Acrasian or Eledorean uniform.

Civilian. Kainen too. "Viktor?" Nels asked.

"Busy now. Can't talk," Viktor muttered, rolling away from another blow that just missed his midsection. "Why not do something useful?"

The fighters were moving too fast for guns. Nels was afraid of shooting Viktor. *Never mind the noise.* The pair rolled in the dirt again. Viktor ended up on the bottom. The stranger attempted another strike, two-handed. Nels took a chance. He kicked Viktor's attacker in the side.

"Ooof!" The stranger fell toward the blow rather than away.

Jumping backward, Nels only just avoided a slash to his shin. Loimuta let out a squealing protest and stamped the earth near the attacker's head. Momentarily distracted, they paused. Nels stepped on the stranger's torso and used only enough pressure to hold them in place. He tensed up, anticipating a cut to his leg.

Nels aimed his pistol. The others did the same.

"Stop! Stop!" Viktor scrambled to his feet. "She's a korva. Don't shoot!"

A korva? "Yield. Now." Nels kept his finger on the trigger.

Lying in the dirt on her back, the stranger dropped her blade. Now that she wasn't fighting, Nels thought she was underfed, by the look of her. Her long black hair with its thick streak of white was bound in a disheveled braid. He guessed she was in her forties. Even covered in mud, he could see she'd been beautiful once and still would've been described as handsome. Something about her reminded him of Jami, his sister, Suvi's korva. *What is her family name?* He couldn't remember. In fact, he wasn't sure that he'd ever known.

"Your name?" Nels asked.

"Natalia Annikki," she said.

"Your choice," Nels said. "Come with us or die."

She glanced at Viktor and glowered. "You brought the Acrasians down on my campsite."

"For that, I apologize. In any case, there isn't time to argue," Nels said. "Your answer?"

"I'll go with you," she said.

"We'll have to take your weapons. No insult intended," Nels said. "It's merely a precaution. Viktor?"

Viktor took care of securing Annikki's weapons. The process took some time, given that she'd secreted a large number of blades on her person.

"I'd have had you, you know," Annikki said to Viktor.

"Does it actually matter at this point?" Viktor asked.

"It does to me," Annikki said. "And that's all that counts."

Viktor pocketed the last of her knives. "Are you sure? Wrists, please."

She thrust her hands out, palms facing one another, and glowered.

❧ C A I U S ❧

ONE

Two second-year cadets shivered against a backdrop of waterlogged night on Caius's stoop. Cold air drifted across the threshold, and Caius could already smell the sewer—one of the disadvantages of living where he did.

The shorter cadet glanced at Caius's unbuttoned shirt and bare feet before fixing his gaze to the ceiling. "Senior Warden Valarius Tolerans urgently requests that you meet him on Ironmonger Lane," the cadet said. He lowered his voice. "It's a dumped kill, sir." In perfect Academy form, he then clicked his heels and tipped his tricorne. Rainwater poured from the front corner and splashed onto the dry floor just inside the doorframe of Caius's apartments.

The cadet's companion gasped.

Caius scanned the room for something with which to mop up the puddle and settled for the rag rug in front of the fireplace. "Very well. Give me a moment. Come in. And close the door behind you."

"Yes, sir." The first cadet's teeth audibly chattered as a fresh gust of wind blasted one and all.

It was strange, being the target of deference from a cadet. *Get used to it.* Still, Caius felt uncomfortable. "There's tea heating on the hearth. Help yourself." He finished mopping the floor and draped the now-damp rug over the hearth screen. Then he went to his bedchamber.

"Yes, sir. Thank you, sir," the second cadet said with relief.

Caius dodged the cramped furniture with practiced steps in the dimness, shedding his soiled shirt along the way. He'd completed his final pre-graduation cadet field tour a few hours before. His Letter of Assignment had been waiting for him. He was being transferred to Inspections. *Not field duty.* He assumed that was his mother's doing. *Again.* He'd been home for all of a half-hour. Officially, he wouldn't assume duties as an Inspector until next week, and if it had been anyone but Valarius, he would've told them he was off duty. He hadn't even had time to swap out his cadet collar tabs.

He changed into a dry uniform and then grabbed a last swallow of lukewarm tea before digging his discarded greatcoat from under a partially gutted pack. A shower of half-dried mud chunks clattered across the polished floor. He ignored an urge to stop and clean it. Carrying his boots to the drawing room, he saw the mantel clock read a quarter to two in the morning. Blinking, he pulled out his pocket watch. *Half past four. Housekeeper must have forgot to wind the clock while I was away. Wouldn't be the first time.*

"Please, sir, we must hurry," the second cadet said, leaving an empty cup on the hearth. "It'll be dawn soon."

Weary, Caius tugged his boots on and shrugged into his greatcoat. The instant he'd locked the door behind him, sleet slapped the top of his bare head. He considered going back for his tricorne but decided against it. If he didn't hurry, not only would it be too late for the cleanup to finish before dawn, the weather would probably destroy whatever it was Valarius wanted him to see. Tugging up the collar of his greatcoat, Caius rushed down the slick stairs.

The walk from his apartments to Ironmonger Lane normally took a little more than a quarter of an hour. He made it in half the time with the winded cadets in his wake. Valarius's partner, Lucian, signaled from his post at the corner. Two hooded lanterns rested at his feet. The Watch wagon was parked nearby, and Sergeant Benbow scowled from his perch on the wagon seat. Watch Captain Drake nodded as Caius passed. She was leaning against the side of the wagon, and her eyes and upturned nose were red above the dark wool scarf covering her full mouth. He thought she must have a cold until he caught her sour perfume.

Whiskey, he thought.

Rounding the corner of the brown brick building, he spied the victim. She lay on her back. Bloody handprints, large and small, painted the bricks in runny streaks. The scene was too much like the previous one. He tried not to imagine desperate pleas for help and pitiful attempts at bargaining echoing off the windowless, unsympathetic walls. He banished unwelcome memories with a shiver and let himself think what he hadn't upon reading his Letter of Assignment. *No more fieldwork. For once, I'm glad of Mother's meddling.*

Where's your sense of duty? Have you become soft?

"Thanks for coming." Valarius's breath fogged his words. He

stood next to the remains, his thinning hair dripping. Shoulders rounded inward against the cold, he appeared old, nervous, and tired. He stepped back, allowing access to the body. "It's against standard procedure, but . . . I thought I'd see if you'd returned from your tour." He gave Caius a furtive glance. The supervising Field Warden would want an explanation of the delay, Caius knew. Valarius was risking his career such as it was. "Is it our North End friend, you think?"

"Haven't they caught him yet?" Caius asked.

Valarius glanced to the end of the alley and shook his head.

"Why not send for the Inspector on duty?"

"You know what most Inspectors are like." Valarius looked away. The answer was written in the sneer on his face. *Corrupt.* "Perhaps I trust you to follow through."

"I thought you didn't believe in my methods."

"This is the *fifth*," Valarius whispered. "That's a huge revenue loss. And no one's doing a god damned thing about it."

"I'll compare the measurements to my previous notes." Caius reached into the pocket of his greatcoat for his sketchbook and then crouched next to the body. The eyeless face of a fifteen-year-old Eledorean stared back at him. Both forearms were slashed, and several of her fingers were missing.

Valarius coughed and covered his nose.

Eyeless face. "This hunter has similar habits, it seems," Caius said, purposely not using the word "rogue". "When did the rain start?"

"Approximately some time around four."

Nodding, Caius made a note in graphite and then leaned closer. By the condition of the girl's garments, he guessed she had been an orphan. As before, there was bruising around the neck and multiple stab wounds in the abdomen. He pushed away wet shoulder-length hair to check the rest of her face. Something was wrong with the shape of her mouth. He set down his notes, careless of the now-stained leather binding, and reached down to pry the jaw open.

Valarius stepped closer. "What is it?"

"I'm not sure." Caius forced her mouth wider and pulled out a square of yellowed paper embossed with bloody teeth marks. The paper was cheaply milled and torn along the top edge. Unfolding it, he discovered words scrawled in red ink. *Like the clock, keep a face clean and bright, with hands ever ready to do what is right.* Each letter *n* was reversed.

"Is it important?" Valarius asked.

"Has a . . . rogue left a note before?"

"You wouldn't believe some of the things rogue hunters do. A note would be the least of it."

"Interesting." Caius said, flipping the paper over to look at the stained back—he recognized it at once. A portion of the alphabet was printed in black with spaces in between each letter. The print had been embossed into the paper with movable type.

It was a page ripped from a child's hornbook.

TWO

Sleet melted in Caius's hair and oozed down the back of his neck. Hunching further into his greatcoat, he jogged across the Academy's grounds to a palatial four-story building with white columns—the Brotherhood of Wardens' Hall of Records. He took the marble steps two at a time, then tugged open the heavy door by its silver handle. His thoughts whirled in circles miles distant from his physical presence as he worked at the problem. *Why do some hunters become rogues while others don't? Why do rogues exist? Are they lunatics? Or is it an impulse related to cheating the Regnum of its due? Or is there another factor?*

What does that damned note mean?

Upon entering the building, the scent of aging paper revived memories of the receiving station late at night. Cadets were often recruited for unpleasant or tedious duties. It was considered a test of character. Receiving at the Hall of Records was one of the more pleasant of such tasks. Guarding the entry involved hours upon hours of staring at flower-printed wallpaper. The resulting boredom often led to infractions. Caius, himself, had used the time to study for toxin and antidote exams while no one was watching. Currently, a female cadet sat at the big writing table while her male counterpart stood guard at the door.

Women weren't often admitted into the Academy. As a result, they tended to be fanatics. Caius could sympathize to a degree. His own father hadn't wanted him to join the Brotherhood and had gone to much trouble to prevent it. This had resulted in a rift that had never healed. Caius's mother, on the other hand, couldn't have been more proud. She came from a long line of patriots, or so she claimed. Nonetheless, as he transitioned into active duty, Caius had begun to wonder if his father was right after all.

You swore to protect the Regnum. That is what you are doing. Keep up this line of thought and you'll end in the Reclamation Hospital next to Severus.

Stopping at the check-in station, Caius flashed his identification then signed and imprinted the record book with his thumb. Wiping ink off his thumb with the cloth provided, he waited until the young cadet released him with a bored salute. He stepped through the door before recognizing Tolerans Cornelius. Cornelius had the same thick curly hair, the same scar on the bridge of his nose from the day Caius broke it during fencing practice.

Cornelius gave him a nod and smiled.

"What are you doing here? Didn't you graduate last year?" Caius returned the smile. *I wonder if he still hums while under pressure,* he thought. It had been Cornelius's most annoying habit during exams.

"Ah, yes." Cornelius's tone was sheepish.

"I see," Caius said. "You're still holding favor with the director?" Cornelius had been notorious for taking unnecessary risks.

"I'm courting his niece."

"Ahhh," Caius said. "Some things don't change."

Cornelius shrugged.

"And is that why you've been assigned such a challenging post?" Caius asked.

"I—er—we haven't done anything to warrant it," Cornelius whispered. "On the other hand, we haven't exactly had the opportunity. You see, for some reason, I seem to have drawn the evening watch until further notice."

"Good luck. Sounds like you could use it."

"Thanks," Cornelius said. "Congratulations on the transfer, Inspector."

"You heard?"

Cornelius winked. "Of course."

Caius thanked Cornelius and continued on his way.

The ground floor of the Hall of Records was the only level accessible to the public. With the exception of the receiving area, it occupied the entire width and length of the building. Rows upon rows of shelves containing leather-bound ledgers formed a majority of the library. For the most part, the records stored on the ground floor were family genealogies—births, deaths, and marriages. Glass-enclosed lamps hung from iron chains above the central aisle. At night, they were the only light allowed other than the fireplaces. Buckets of sand were stationed near any fire source, and individual lanterns or candles were strictly forbidden lest they destroy the precious contents of the building. Of course, due to the curfew, no one but Wardens would have access at night.

He walked past the hulking wooden cabinets with their rows of drawers containing the Regnum's most recent, more mutable records. These were hand-printed on individual cards by members of the Brotherhood, arranged by date and filed. The records had been kept in this manner for centuries. Only the quality of the paper, ink, and cabinets had changed over time.

He reached the exit, exchanged salutes with the Warden guarding access to the upper levels. Again, he went through the ritual of signing in. His steps echoed up the stairwell. The smell of bound paper and leather was comforting.

It was said that the Hall of Records was a triumph of Gens Fortis design. It had stood for three hundred years and withstood two floods. Only one fire had ever violated the building, and that had been fifty years after the library had been built. The second floor had been created with vaulted ceilings and open aisles. The walls reverberated with each step and sliding page. Narrow windows at the tops of all four walls fed grey dawn light into the mirrors and glass lenses suspended from the ceiling. Each filigree-framed mirror redirected sunlight downward. Caius couldn't help a sense of awe every time he visited.

Every cadet was required to recite the rules for the Hall of Records from memory before they were permitted inside. Infractions were taken seriously. Nodding to a uniformed librarian wearing steel-framed spectacles at the checkout desk, Caius removed his soggy greatcoat. He sat on the bench beside the main fireplace and waited for the fire's warmth to penetrate his damp clothes. Loosening his hair from its queue, he took a drying cloth from the neatly stacked pile on the floor and used it. He left the used cloth on the bench to dry along with his greatcoat. After rebraiding his hair and assuring himself that his shirt was dry, he approached the pine cabinets containing the hunting records. He decided to begin with April of the current year and then work his way to the present. It was possible that the rogue hunter's license had expired—supposing the rogue had ever had one in the first place.

Caius pulled the first wooden card file and carried it to a nearby table. Then he retrieved his journal and graphite stick from his coat, drawing the attention of the spectacled librarian. Caius held up the graphite. The librarian nodded but continued his vigilance. Caius got as comfortable as the hard wooden chair would allow, pinched the bridge of his nose, and began flipping through records. When he proved himself worthy of at least limited trust, the librarian busied himself with putting out lanterns.

The morning sun cast bright patches on the table's surface. The light had crept halfway across the table's length before Caius discovered anything useful. The first possibility was a respected baron connected with Gens Lucrosa, the second a titled Retainer of lesser status who had recently acquired membership in Gens Tolerans. Both preferred young targets, and a search might determine whether either of them were cheating on their kill accounts. Caius jotted down names and addresses in his journal, and continued flipping through the records cards. When he glanced at the record card between his fingertips, he stopped automatically. Trained as a tracker, he sensed patterns without conscious thought. Therefore, at first he didn't understand why. Then he did, and he found he couldn't breathe.

The entry isn't consistent across the card. The ink doesn't match.

Public records such as those stored on the ground floor were easily altered, provided the client produced enough sterling. However, once a record was stored in the Brotherhood's main catalogs on the second floor, it was never altered. The information the Brotherhood maintained in the upper levels of the Hall of Records was inviolate. If a correction or change became necessary, procedure dictated that a second card be filed with the first. The policy represented stability in a tumultuous sea of bureaucracy.

He read the name: *Baron Munitoris Arion*. According to the card, Arion had renewed his license four months earlier. Exactly one month before the rogue hunter had begun illegally dumping his kills on the streets. The date was written in darker ink. Examining it more closely, he found abrasions on the paper and saw that the ink had bled. He could almost read what might have been written before. *July?* He set the card on the table and frowned. It was possible a lazy officer had forgone creating a new record for the catalog, but he didn't know anyone who would risk a court martial to avoid filling out two cards—one to be filed with the original and the other to be filed with the Record Adjuster. It was also possible that he wasn't correctly interpreting what he was seeing. He knew nothing of inks or documents.

Perhaps it is time I learned.

New to Inspections, he didn't know who he could trust, or even if the rumors of corruption were true. He wished he could consult with someone before going to his supervising officer. Once, he would've discussed the situation with his friend, Severus, and be confident that none of his suspicions would reach other ears. But Severus had been reassigned. Whatever Severus's duties were now, they were secret. Caius had received no word since the transfer and had been forbidden to attempt a search.

He made a carefully worded note and stretched. His belly reminded him it was past time for dinner. He was exhausted. His head ached from lack of sleep, and his eyes were dry. Finished with the August records, Caius returned the drawer to the catalog cabinet. To be certain, he made a cursory check for Baron Munitoris Arion in September and October.

Caius found nothing.

⊰ N E L S ⊱

ONE

THE HOLD
GRANDMOTHER MOUNTAIN
NEW ELEDORE

———◦◦◦———

TWENTY-EIGHTH OF VERIKUU, 1783

War and weather had taken their toll on roads that hadn't been all
that well maintained in Eledore's prime. The route up Grandmother
Mountain was dangerous enough in the warmer months. During
the winter, it was downright impassable. Of course, Nels believed
that these qualities were also what made the Hold an ideal hiding
place. Traveling the waterways was safer, easier, and, until the
King's locks had begun to fall apart due to neglect, faster. It was
why historically so much trade within Eledore had been conducted
via the rivers and lakes. However, now the rivers were more likely
to be patrolled by Acrasians for the same reason. Therefore, Nels
had chosen the overland route.

A light snow muffled the happy chatter of the troops. Everyone began unloading supplies, unpacking, and greeting loved ones and friends.

We made it. He began unloading his horse. Glancing back at his troops, he discovered a feeling of pride that warmed the numbing cold. They'd been pursued by the Acrasians as far as the northern banks of the Kristallilasi. After that, the weather had begun to turn against them. Still, they'd managed to complete the journey with six of the ten stolen cattle and the valuables from Merta that he'd dared take with them. Were it not for Master Sergeant Jarvi's pyrotechnics, Captain Sebastian Moller's affinity with livestock, Private Hanski's powerful sense of direction, and a bit of good luck regarding the weather, Nels knew they wouldn't have made it.

Once again, he'd gambled with all their lives and won. He'd have been happy but for one thing.

Where's Ilta? Why isn't she here? She usually met him at the last checkpoint and walked with him for a couple of miles.

"You seem less than enthusiastic about being home," Viktor said. "Would the reason why have to do with a certain blonde of our mutual acquaintance?"

Nels glanced over his shoulder to where the Holders were greeting their loved ones. His heart sank.

Viktor kept his voice low. "Maybe she had an emergency at the infirmary?"

"We both know why she isn't here," Nels whispered.

"No, we don't," Viktor said. "And if you're thinking about Captain Julia, you did the right thing."

"What do you mean by that?" Nels asked.

"Ilta told you that you should see someone else," Viktor said. "Correct?"

Nels shrugged. "What if she didn't mean it?"

"And if she changes her mind, you two can discuss the situation then," Viktor said. "You had to stop waiting for her. You were ready. She wasn't. You understand that. Right?"

"I could've—"

"No, you couldn't," Viktor said. "The simple act of your waiting has put pressure on her—"

"I never intended to—"

"—Pressure she didn't deserve. Your intent doesn't factor into it. The pressure was there. You did the right thing," Viktor said.

If that's the case, why do I feel so awful? Nels thought.

"Are you all right?" Viktor asked.

"I'm fine," Nels said. *You have far more important things to do.* His leg muscles throbbed with exertion, and his fingers and toes were numb. They'd walked the last stretch to save the horses, and his clothes were soaked through where his all-weather coat didn't reach. "Sebastian, get the recruits settled and the cattle to shelter."

"You heard the colonel," Sebastian said, projecting his deep growl over happy chatter. "Lieutenant Eld, you're in charge of the cattle. Lieutenant Wiberg, you've got the recruits. Get to it."

Lieutenant Eld groaned. Her red hair fell into her face. "Wouldn't Moller be a better choice?"

"Are you arguing with me about an order, Lieutenant?" Sebastian asked.

"Ah, no, Captain."

"Then get to it," Sebastian said.

Nels called out to his troops. "When you're done, grab some sleep. You'll need your strength for tomorrow."

"What's tomorrow, sir?" Private Hanski asked.

A smile stretched across Viktor's face. "The welcome-home party."

Laughter and whoops of joy renewed their flagging energy. Nels couldn't help thinking of those who weren't there. He missed

Major Lindström and Field Marshal Elzbet Kauranen the most. Both had been leaders Nels had admired. Although he wasn't sure their guidance would've proven helpful, given his defects. They'd each had the magic to back up their command, even if they hadn't used it. He did not, and while the troops had adjusted to his unorthodox methods, questions remained.

Unbuckling his pack, he dropped it to the snow-dusted ground. Then he handed Loimuta's reins to the private offering to take him. Loimuta would be stabled with the few horses the Hold maintained year-round. Extra mounts were sold off and replaced in the spring. Horses required upkeep and exercise, activities that left traces. Large numbers of horses were a giveaway that an army was near, and Warden Units patrolled the new border with alarming frequency, but Loimuta had been his companion since he was fourteen. Even if Nels could give him up, he had a feeling the gelding would only stubbornly make his way back to Grandmother Mountain.

Three blindfolded recruits stumbled to a halt at the entrance. The fourth turned to openly stare at him. Nels wondered how long each would survive under his leadership. Looking away, he set his jaw. *Stop feeling sorry for yourself. The troops are watching.*

Annikki in particular.

Natalia Annikki was the only recruit who hadn't been blindfolded. She was a veteran korva, and there wasn't much point. She was middle-aged, healthy, and strong, if a bit thin due to hiding alone in the Selkäranka Mountains for a year. She'd passed Viktor's tests, and Nels trusted her enough to bring her to the Hold. Still, there was something off about her. Most volunteers quickly relaxed into the familiar social order, letting the presence of others like them provide a sense of security and belonging. Such emotions were powerful. He understood why. It was intensely reassuring to see that everything wasn't lost. Recruits formed tight bonds fast. *But not Annikki.* She'd kept herself apart, with her eyes to the shadows. She gazed at him now as if he were the one under probation and not she. Feeling her hard gaze, Nels wished they'd opted to blindfold her anyway. She got on his nerves.

Does she know about my defect?

Imposter.

You've more important things to do than to worry about that same old horse shit. Swiving hells, stop it. "Viktor."

"Yes, sir?"

"The Merta chests are to be taken to my apartments," Nels said. "I'll secure them myself." His concerns regarding theft were minor. However, the haul was significant temptation, and their community was pushing the limits of one knowing every member on sight, if not by name. Trouble would come, one day. He hoped prudence might put off that eventuality.

Nodding, Viktor briefly left to take care of the matter.

Retrieving his pack, Nels had staggered a couple of steps toward the door when his twin sister appeared. He was brought up short. "Suvi? What are—"

"I see you've managed to avoid killing yourself *again*," Suvi said. Her voice was tight and flat. Her mouth was set in a firm line, and the irises of her eyes flickered from black to an angry red-tinged brown and back to black. She wore a plain light blue wool gown, and a heavy green cloak that protected most of her dress from the snow. Her hood had been pulled up over her mouse-brown curls.

He had known he'd have to face Suvi sooner or later, but he'd counted on it being later rather than sooner. She wasn't alone. First Ilta and then Dylan followed in short order. Ilta, clearly aware of Suvi's displeasure, held herself back. Dylan's face was haggard. Exhaustion traced circles under the Waterborne weathermaster's eyes, and his dark skin harbored a touch of grey. He and Ilta both smiled but glanced at Suvi with unease. The wordless message was easy to read: *I'm glad to see you. But take care what you say.*

"Hello, Suvi. It's nice that you're here," Nels said, mustering a light tone. "But you didn't have to travel so far to—"

"You're right," Suvi said. Her eyes narrowed. "I didn't have to. Or I wouldn't have had to, if you hadn't gone off on your own. *Against my wishes.*"

Nels stepped closer and lowered his voice. "Must we discuss this here? It's cold. My feet are numb, and I'm hungry."

Glaring, Suvi seemed to consider a more emphatic response. Instead, she nodded once and left. Ilta waited before enveloping him in a warm hug.

He held her close and breathed in the scent of her—all winter roses, mint, and whatever herb concoction she'd been brewing.

"I'm so glad you're back," she said, and then she surprised him with an open kiss.

And with that, he forgot all about his sister's rage for a while and lost himself in the one thing he'd been dreaming of. Her lips were warm and soft. Her tongue brushed his.

"Can't you two wait to do that in private?" Dylan asked.

With a laugh, Ilta broke the kiss and wrapped her arm around his waist.

Nels cleared his throat and tried very hard not to think of Captain Julia. "Why is Suvi here?" He kept his arms loosely wrapped around Ilta. "Isn't she supposed to be wintering on Treaty Island?"

Dylan kept his voice low and switched to Acrasian. "She came here right after Kaledan instead. Sent a message requesting that I meet her at the Hold to negotiate a new contract."

"She's the Queen. She can do what she wants," Nels said,

answering in the same language. Although the Hold was technically what remained of Eledore, Acrasian was swiftly becoming the default language. It was a hard-fought battle he'd so far lost to Slate, not that he'd entirely given up.

Dylan shrugged.

"She would say you can't afford recklessness, either," Ilta said. "And she'd have a point, you know."

Nels sighed. He released her and then hefted his pack.

Viktor came back. "What did I miss?"

"Want me to take that for you?" Dylan asked.

"Thanks, but no," Nels said. He stared up into the sky for a moment and then spoke to Viktor in Eledorean. "Nothing important. I'll see you tonight. We'll start the rituals at midnight. I should be done talking to Suvi by then."

"Yes, sir." Viktor saluted. "I'll bring the whiskey. I've a feeling you'll need something for the pain."

Nels returned the salute. "Grab some sleep in the meantime. Someone should."

"Taina might have other ideas," Viktor said. "At least, I hope she will."

"It's been three months," Nels said. "Who is to say she hasn't found someone else to warm her bed?"

"I don't mind," Viktor said. "As long as he isn't sharing it now."

Dylan said, "You're assuming it's a *he*."

"In that case," Viktor said, "I wouldn't mind the extra company."

"Oh, sure," Dylan said. "But will they?"

Nels turned to Ilta and whispered, "Are you free?"

She smiled. "Before or after your chat with Suvi?"

"After? I should have an hour or two." He considered adding that they needed to talk, but she was in good spirits, and he didn't want to destroy her mood.

"That depends."

"On what?"

"On whether or not there's enough left of you to be entertaining once she's done with you," Ilta said. "I believe the word 'keelhaul' featured strongly in her agenda."

"Ouch," Nels said.

"She invited me to watch. Don't worry. I turned her down."

"Whose side are you on?" Nels asked.

Ilta got up on her toes to give him another quick scorcher of a kiss. Then she slipped free of his arms and stepped back. "Gran taught me to stay far away from royal family arguments. They tend to be hazardous to one's health." She wiggled her fingers in a playful goodbye.

"You're not going to at least walk me to my execution?" Nels asked.

"I'll drop by later to tend to the wounded," Ilta said.

"That's just mean," Nels said to her retreating back.

Viktor asked, "You're surprised by this?"

Nels made his way to his apartments alone. Upon entering, he found that someone had lit a fire in the hearth and the room had been cleaned and aired.

Probably Ilta, bless her. It soothed the sting, even if it made him feel that much guiltier about his time with Gaia. The trunks from Merta had already been placed along the far wall. He dropped his pack by the door and then used the bootjack. His wet boots slapped the polished floor. The stone was so cold that it made his feet ache. Then he shed his all-weather coat and hung it on the hook where it could dry. Padding in his damp stockings to the hearthrug, he had time to discover that the kettle was full of fresh water and swing it over the fire before there came a knock.

"Who is it?"

"You damned well know who," Suvi said from the hallway. "Let me in."

Her Acrasian has improved. The thought didn't make him happy. Suvi had been content to limit her use of Acrasian to their private talks. Although, these days, they'd have achieved more privacy had they used Eledorean. In any case, her Acrasian had always been terrible. *I wonder what changed.*

He sighed. All he wanted was a bath, a shave, and to sit in front of the fire drinking and reading until Ilta dropped by—hopefully before the evening's scheduled rituals. He was tempted to tell Suvi to go away. Instead, he snatched a bottle of whiskey from his writing desk and took a drink.

What are you thinking? You're in enough trouble as it is. Still, he was furious, and he couldn't bring himself to go to the door. Therefore, he didn't—an insult for which his father would've had him imprisoned had he been alive. "It's unbarred."

Suvi barged in like a winter storm. Slamming the door, she whirled. Her skirts billowed. "I told you not to go! I *ordered* you! It was a trap!"

"Of course it was. What does that matter?" Nels asked, collapsing onto the cushioned green sofa next to the hearth—wet clothes, bottle, and all. He moved his feet and hands closer to the flames. The warmth didn't seem to make much immediate progress in penetrating his frozen digits. "I returned with funds enough to see us through another year or more, didn't I?" He jabbed a thumb toward the chests behind him. "Speaking of which, we need to talk about Merta." Rubbing his hands together, he blew on them.

"You can't openly disobey me like that! I'm your queen!"

He didn't face her anger. Instead, he took another drink and removed his damp stockings. "Which is it you want? One of

Father's automatons? Or someone you can rely upon? You can't have both."

"I didn't mean it that way, and you know it. You made me look ridiculous!"

"You should've trusted me." Of course, he should've trusted her, too. "The gamble paid off. I told you it would." He wiggled his toes and then stretched out across the sofa.

"You can't take chances like that with your life. We've lost so much. We've lost everything," Suvi said. "I—I can't lose you, too. I just can't."

All at once, he understood the strength behind her anger. "This isn't entirely about me, is it?"

"What do you mean?"

Family didn't mean the same thing for royals as it did for commoners, and he knew it. "Dylan mentioned a new contract. You were unsuccessful, weren't you?"

She sighed. "You always did understand me better than anyone."

"I'm your twin." He shrugged. "I'm sorry I caused you further embarrassment. But soldiers don't often make old bones. You know that. I am what I am. If I can face that, you can."

"Don't talk like that," she said. "I forbid it."

"Sentimentality isn't like you." He saw her wince, and frowned. "What are you really here for?"

"Stop trying to change the damned subject!"

He shrugged. "The truth is the truth."

"You want to talk about truth? Fine," she said. "The truth is, I'm worried you've reverted to your old ways."

"I haven't gambled since before Father died."

"That isn't entirely true. You're playing a different game, with higher stakes. You've been courting danger."

"What?"

"Don't deny it."

Nels bit down on things he knew he shouldn't say and looked away.

Suvi said, "You're too important to throw away your life."

"Horseshit."

"Has it not occurred to you that I can't perform my function as Guardian without you?"

He opened his mouth and then closed it. *Oh.*

"It hasn't? How is that possible? Do you remember when we went to Keeper Mountain together? Do you remember closing the gate against the Old Ones? Because I do. It takes all three of us—all of our powers—to protect the whole of Västmark, even the Waterborne. Me. Ilta. And *you.*"

He didn't say anything.

She continued. "I know you took the war with Acrasia personally—"

"I failed everyone."

"If you did, I did too." Suvi shrugged. "I still don't know why anyone would want me in charge, but here I am. And I'm going to do the absolute best I can with what little I have. And that isn't insignificant. Do you know who taught me that?"

"Who?"

"*You.*"

"Oh."

"Yes. 'Oh.'" Exasperated, she folded her arms across her chest. "Fine. What's done is done. Lucky for everyone you came back alive. This time."

"I'm . . . sorry."

"Apology accepted." She let her arms fall to her sides and then seemed to search for a place to sit. "On to the next order of business. What information were you able to get?"

He sat up, wordlessly giving her part of the sofa. "Edvard is determined to appear neutral. Or at least his idea of neutral. We can't expect any more obvious help. However, given the ease with which we got away with the silver, we know where his sympathies lie."

She rejected his silent offer and opted to drag a wingback chair across the room to a space in front of the fire at his left.

He'd gotten up to do it for her but had been too late.

"That's good, I suppose," she said.

Nels resumed lying on the sofa. "He seems to be gambling on the Acrasians being satisfied with conquering Eledore."

She tugged down the hood of her cloak and unhooked the decorative star-shaped clasp at the neck. Then she left the cloak draped over the back of the chair behind his writing desk and joined him by the fire. "For Ytlain's sake, I hope he's right."

"The Acrasians didn't stop with Marren, and they have yet to disband their army," Nels said. "You know, Edvard attempted to induce me to leave with him."

"His mistake."

"I considered his offer."

Suvi made a sound that was almost a snort from the comfort of the wingback chair. "You did not," she said. "He attempted to control you, and you told him to sod off."

Nels raised an eyebrow at her vulgar Acrasian. She held his gaze.

"You're right." He listened to the fire crackle for a while before continuing. "Why are you here? You know you shouldn't be anywhere near Eledore until spring."

"Maybe I wanted to spend the winter with my only living family member?"

"You can't be here. It's too dangerous."

"That hasn't stopped you. Why should it stop me?" she asked. "The Acrasians have quite the bounty on your head, you know."

"It hasn't helped them much in finding me so far."

"Dylan says this winter is going to be a bad one. By the way, you should thank him. Risking the trail this late in the season was a stupid stunt. He used a great deal of power to ensure that you weren't caught in that storm."

"Oh." *I should've known it wasn't luck.*

"What else did you learn?" She kicked off her slippers and propped her feet up on a pillow.

"Edvard gave me all the information he had on Acrasian troop locations and supply trains. After the Acrasians left, of course."

"That, along with the money," she said. "He *was* helpful."

"The silver was enough to make a payment on what we owe Clan Kask and buy some supplies from Captain Julia. Should help in your negotiations with Dylan."

"Where did that come from?" Suvi asked, motioning to the chests.

"Merta," Nels said. "The citizens buried their valuables in one of the mines. That is only a small part of what we found." Between the war and variola, no one was left to lay claim to it.

Suvi's face brightened for the first time. "Oh, my."

"Sebastian says two of the other mines are viable—at least, the records say they are," Nels said. "Unfortunately, all the tunnels are set to blow. Sebastian can handle the explosives, but we need someone with mining skills if we're to make use of what we've found. There's no one among the troops. I asked. Think Slate can find someone? Quietly?"

"It's possible. I'll ask."

"About the Acrasians." Nels paused before giving her the last of the news. "Something isn't right. They've abandoned the eastern coast, not merely Merta but Mehrinna, too."

Annikki had verified Edvard's report, at least the parts involving Mehrinna.

Nels said, "Edvard seems to think they've withdrawn from all our cities. And in a hurry, from what he understands. It makes sense of what I've been seeing. There's a great deal of activity along the Kristallilasi. Quite a few troops are holed up in Wyeth and Virens."

His sister's face grew suddenly pale. "Why? Did Edvard say?"

"I still think they're preparing to attack Ytlain. But Edvard insisted that the Acrasians are merely leaving Eledore. They blame demons and ghosts. Ill luck. They claim whole settlements have vanished. Crops have been ruined."

She smiled. "My, you've been busy."

"Not that busy, and you know it," he said. "I've not been as far north as Mehrinna, let alone Jalokivi, in months. I've focused my efforts along the new border." Memories of what lived beneath Keeper Mountain sprang to mind. He was reluctant to speak of his fears out loud, but he did it anyway. "Are you sure we closed the ga—"

"I'm sure."

"But not so sure as to stay away until spring?"

Apparently unable to hold his gaze, she turned aside and changed the subject. "I've been consulting with the Silmaillia."

At the mention of Ilta, he raised both eyebrows. "You're speaking to Ilta now?"

For Suvi to put aside her grudge meant she was seriously concerned about what lay ahead.

Or there's another reason, he thought. *Probably more than one, if I know my sister.*

"I've decided to forgive her," Suvi said. "What good comes from blame? It won't bring Mother back. It won't change anything. It won't make life any easier for anyone. It would only deprive me of my Silmaillia when I need her most."

"I'm relieved you changed your mind."

They sat in silence for a time. He'd thought she was finished speaking when she said, "You're right, you know. Something is wrong in the north. It's the same thing that is wrong in the south."

"The Acrasians?"

She shook her head and gave him a sad smile. "If only that were all." She bit her lip. "Ilta says it's the . . . Old Ones. They've broken through."

"You said—"

"Not in Jalokivi. Somewhere else."

Nels swallowed. "Do you know where?"

"May I have some tea? Is the water hot enough?" Suvi motioned toward the kettle hanging on the swivel-hook.

"It should be."

Proper black tea was one of the many items that would dwindle in supply as the winter wore on. Tea was imported by the Waterborne from the Republic of Massilia in the west. Ytlain imported Massilian tea as well through the Chain Lakes, while coffee and chocolate came from Acrasian plantations and colonies in the southern hemisphere. Acrasians loved their coffee and chocolate. Since a large number of the Hold's refugees originated from the Regnum, coffee was easiest to get.

Nels sat up. He then spotted the covered tray on the floor next to the hearth. Hungry as he was, he didn't know how he had missed it before. His stomach let out a loud rumble. "You had Ilta prepare all this before I arrived?"

"Ilta seemed to think you'd be more receptive with a full stomach. I'm surprised she isn't here."

"She wanted to permit you adequate space to verbally eviscerate me in private."

"How thoughtful." Suvi smoothed her skirts back, pulled up her sleeve before reaching for the kettle, and stepped to the hearth.

He jumped to his feet when he saw the hem of her voluminous dress brush the flames. Yanking her skirts from the fire before they could do more than scorch, he said, "You'd best let me do that."

"All right." She returned to her chair. Wrinkling her nose, she said, "You stink."

"Then maybe you should've waited until tomorrow to berate me."

"I—It couldn't wait."

"Why?" He went through the motions of preparing the tea in silence, allowing her time to get her thoughts organized. When he finally handed her a finished cup, he could see she was ready to talk again. His guts clenched. Whatever she was about to say wasn't going to be pleasant. He knew his twin. The line between her eyes was more prominent, and her jaw was tight. That expression never meant anything good.

Settling down once more, he reveled in the comfort of a fire and warm porcelain against his palms. His toes were no longer cold. He felt safe and somewhat relaxed for the first time in months. He relished it all the more, knowing it wouldn't last.

"I'm frightened," she said.

"More than usual? Why?"

"Ilta had a vision. The broken gate," she said. "It's in Acrasia."

"What?" He jumped to his feet again. "No!"

Suvi said, "We must seal it before they gather any more strength."

"No! Let the Acrasians rot! We owe them nothing!"

"We can't do that."

"We damned well can," he said.

"We *can't!*"

"And what about Keeper Mountain? Are you proposing we spend the rest of our days traipsing about the continent? Because I'm not saving the Regnum at the cost of what is left of Eledore!"

NELS

Suvi said, "We won't need to go to Keeper Mountain to perform the ritual, if we find the broken gate in the south."

"How does that—"

"First, you're assuming that the portal in the north is the important one. We did too, but we were wrong. It isn't. It never was. All the gates are linked, and because of this, when we close one portal against the Old Ones, we're closing them all. That's why it requires so much energy. That's why a Silmaillia is needed."

"How do you know?"

"I can have Ilta bring you the books we found in her grandmother's library," Suvi said. "You can read for yourself. They're quite old, however. You'll have to be careful."

"If Saara knew this, why didn't she tell Ilta?"

"We're not certain she did," Suvi said. "We're still looking into that. A great deal has been forgotten since the days of Kassarina Ilmari, the first Queen of Eledore."

"If it doesn't matter which portal we close, why can't we just close the one in Jalokivi? Why risk going south?"

"Because if that worked, the southern gate would be closed already," Suvi said. "It isn't. Ilta says she's seen it. Something is wrong in Acrasia, and the only way to fix it is to go there ourselves."

"All right. That's the first part. What's the second?"

"The Old Ones are already free in Acrasia. We don't know for how long. Nonetheless, if they're free, they'll want to open the way for others of their kind. The historical record states this. They'll travel north, if they haven't already. They'll attack the other gates. We must stop them before that happens. Because if it does, we will be traipsing all over the known world as Kassarina Ilmari did."

Nels swallowed. He thought of the troops he'd left secreted in the wilds, and shuddered. *Have I abandoned them to a worse enemy?*

"We have to do something." *We must get message birds out as soon as the storm clears.*

"I thought you'd agree," Suvi said. "I was hoping you would know what to do."

"Me? Why would I?"

"You're the one who is to save—"

His fist tightened. *Not you, too.* "That was a stupid rumor. If anyone should know that, it's you. I am not the savior of Eledore. That was a joke my first regiment used to mock a spoiled, impudent boy. Nothing more."

"The Silmaillia disagrees."

"We both know that Ilta is not infallible."

"That prediction wasn't hers. It was Saara's, her grandmother's."

He set his cup on the floor and stood up. "She was wrong, damn it! This is what we are now! A few ragged survivors hiding in our own burial mound! For the goddess's sake, don't put this off on me! I'll let you down! I let everyone down! That's it, isn't it? You don't want the responsibility. You're the one they crowned! This is your decision! Not mine!"

Wounded, Suvi looked away.

Shit, he thought. *Now I've done it.* "I'm sorry. I didn't mean—"

"Yes, you did." Her long brown curls hid her face. "You're right. I was never meant to be Queen. It was you who was supposed to rule. Not me. *You.*"

"Horseshit. You're a born diplomat and leader. You always were. I would've made a mess of everything. We both know that." He put out a hand to touch her arm, but she flinched away.

"I haven't given up. I can't," she said. "And I won't. This isn't over until the very last of us is gone. I refuse to see it any other way. And if you aren't with me, I need to know now. Because I can put someone else in charge of my army."

Army? We barely number enough to form a company. And who knows if that will be true after this winter? Nels thought. "I'm sorry."

"Don't apologize!" She turned to face him. Her eyes burned a fierce, hard bronze. "Either I have your support or I don't. And if I don't, you should've gone with Edvard. Because it's going to be a hard trek to Ytlain in the snow on your own tomorrow. I won't let Viktor go. I can't—"

"I'm with you," Nels said. "I'll—I'll do it."

Her eyes softened, and for a moment, she looked her age. It occurred to him that they'd had a great deal put on them when their parents died. Suvi had been pressured into leadership before she was ready every bit as much as he had.

She asked, "You really are with me?"

"I'm not just saying it." It was unsettling, seeing raw insecurity in her face. From the time they were both small, Suvi had been the one with the confidence and the power. He'd been the one who'd struggled. She was smart and politically adept. He wasn't and never had been, not like her. He didn't have the patience. As he looked at her now, it was the first time in his life that he understood she truly needed him, and not because he had command of the army. She needed him because he was her brother and she loved him. "I'll go to Acrasia if I have to, but I hope we can find another way. Any other way. If, as you say, it isn't the gate that is important . . . maybe we can go to a safer location?"

She folded her hands in her lap. "Your leaving made me realize something. You were right about Norman Island. I was being too cautious." She spoke to her hands. "Oh, goddess. What happens if I make another mistake?"

"Then we'll work with whatever is left. Better that than no decision at all."

Suvi nodded.

Nels said, "Being responsible for the lives of everyone around you . . . that's a terrifying thing."

"How do you do this? When they die? How do you go on?"

Her question, and the fact that it matched the one that had kept him awake too many nights, startled him. Oddly, it'd taken Suvi's asking for him to come up with the answer. "We do the best we can. No one can expect more than that—even you. Understand that those you're responsible for know this. In a way, they've given their lives that you might live. Don't waste that gift. Don't let the guilt consume you or stop you. To do so dishonors them and the price they paid. You have to go on. And you have to learn. You have to keep fighting and live as best you can. Be happy, too. They would want you to be happy. I would want that for you. If—if it were me." *Because one day it will be.*

And when that happens, how will Suvi and Ilta hold back the Old Ones?

Concentrate on the problem before you. The rest will work itself out. "I need you, too, you know."

She went to him and hugged him.

"I'll follow you to the end. No matter what," Nels said. "But that won't prevent me from telling you what I feel you need to hear—any more than it stops you from telling me what I need to hear." He felt her nod against his shoulder. "Nor will it stop me from doing what I feel have to do."

"We need the truth from one another—more so than from anyone else."

He gave her a gentle squeeze and released her. Turning away, he felt his thoughts going to the platoon wintering in the wilds. *At least a majority of them are in Merta, safe.* "We can't do anything about the breach until spring. By then it'll be too late to stop them from infesting Eledore. That's the truth, isn't it?"

"I—I'm afraid it's already too late."

"All the people left on their own . . . the ones living in the wild who haven't found their way to us . . . the troops I've hidden away in Holds elsewhere . . ." He let his words die. Natalia Annikki's guarded stare began to take on a new meaning. *I should ask her what she's seen. Maybe she'll know something that can help. She survived on her own for a year.* "That's why you're here. You're afraid we'll be overrun. And if that's the case, you've come to die with us."

Suvi didn't lift her head. Her hair hid her expression. "If you're not going to eat, at least have some spice cake. Ilta made it."

TWO

It was hours after the cleansing rituals when Ilta finally showed. He'd given up on her and gone to bed, but he hadn't been able to sleep. Her kisses burned too deep. Initially, he'd lit a candle and attempted to read. It did no good because he couldn't focus. So he'd lain on his back with his worries snarling into wince-inducing knots. He distracted himself by counting the blue and white star-patterned ceramic tiles on the ceiling. Then he mentally traced the constellation patterns. When the knock for which he'd been waiting came, he bolted through the velvet bed curtains and snatched his dressing jacket from the rug. He promptly stubbed his toe on a trunk.

"Shit! Shit! Shit!"

He went back for the candle. The stone floor was even colder than before—if that was possible. He got to the door and discovered Ilta waiting in the passage outside. One look at her, and he forgot all about his feet.

She was dressed but rumpled, as if she'd dozed off in her clothes. Her hair was unbrushed, her eyes were puffy and red, and her face was wet with tears. She huddled inside a soft blue knitted shawl. "I—I'm sorry. Were you asleep?"

Shit. She knows. She had the vision before I was able to talk to her about it. "Not really. What's wrong?" he asked. Unsure of what else he could do, he opted to step aside so that she might enter.

She came inside and waited long enough for him to shut the door. "I—I saw you," she said, and wiped her cheek dry with the back of a hand. The capital letter was implied. "I didn't mean to."

His heart caught somewhere in his throat and hammered against the roof of his mouth for freedom. *This is it.* "I wanted to talk to you as soon as possible. I waited for you to come by."

She shoved past and whirled. Her skirts whipped around her slim legs and then contracted in a graceful, angry movement. "I saw you with *her* on the dock!" Her fists were clenched at her sides. "And that—that ship's captain!"

"Wait just one—"

"Did you sleep with her? Oh, goddess. You did, didn't you?" She strode over to the fireplace. "I can't believe it. I just can't!"

He was glad she couldn't see his expression. With the exception of his candle, the room was dark, and the fire had been banked for the night. He had goose bumps along his legs and arms. He felt his lips press together in a tight line. With that, he bit down on his tongue and began the count to one hundred. Then he went to the basket where the spare peat was kept and placed a couple of blocks on the embers. He attempted to concentrate on building the fire and not on his feelings. He didn't want to say or do anything without thinking it through first. *I've learned that much, at least.*

"It's true, isn't it?" she asked again. "Don't lie! You can't hide it from me!" She paced the rug with heavy steps.

"Sit. Calm yourself," Nels said. He felt that if he could have a moment to think, if he could get her to—

She rushed at him in three swift strides, pointing an accusatory finger. "Don't you try to manage me! I know exactly what you're—"

"Thinking?" He spat the question out. "You promised me that you wouldn't do that to me ever again!"

"I can't help it if you're thinking too loud! You know that!"

"Am I?"

She put her hands on her hips, but she didn't look him in the eye. "You're . . . angry."

"Of course I am! We don't have a binding agreement, do we? And whose fault is that?"

His questions seemed to hit her like a slap.

"It's been a couple of months since I left," Nels said. "But I think your exact words were 'Nels, I don't know that I can ever have sex with you. Maybe you should find someone else to sleep with.' Or am I wrong?"

"You said you wouldn't—"

"I know what I said! But I changed my mind!"

She snapped her mouth shut and threw herself on the sofa. Then she folded her arms across her chest. He returned his attention to the fire. It took him longer than usual to get the flames going.

"Did you sleep with her?" Ilta asked in a quiet voice.

"I did. Not that it's any of your business."

"Oh." Ilta slumped and began to sob.

Nels sighed. He got up off his knees and jammed the iron poker onto its resting hook. It let out a sharp clang. As much as it tugged at his heart, he let her cry for a little while before he relented and sat next to her. Still sobbing, she grabbed him and pulled him tight. Her tears soaked the front of his dressing jacket.

"I'm sorry," she said. "I'm just—just so confused."

Again, he resisted the urge to soothe her, but not for long. "You aren't the only one." He sighed.

Ilta sniffed and sat up. "Now I know how Kat felt when she saw Toby with Deirdre."

Getting up, Nels went to his chest of drawers, retrieved a handkerchief, and handed it to her. "Here. Use this."

"Thanks." She blew her nose and then wiped the tears from her face. "Do you still love me?"

"I do. Very much."

"I don't know why. I'm broken and horrible."

"You're not broken and horrible," he said. "No more than I am, anyway." He paused. "Do you still love *me*?"

"Of course I do," she said. There came a long pause before she continued. "What is wrong with me? Why can't we just have sex?"

"You're scared."

"Why? You weren't."

He laughed.

Again, she sat up. Her expression was indignant. "What's so funny?"

"I was terrified," he said. "And I didn't have the prospect of losing my mind or my magic in the equation. Speaking as someone who lived with the idea of not having any power among people who murdered or used those without . . . Well, let's say I have some small understanding of how frightening that is."

She blushed. "What did you have to fear?"

He shrugged. He felt his ears grow warm. "Thinking on it now, it's stupid. But . . . I was afraid she'd laugh at me."

"Oh."

"Feel any better?"

"Maybe."

"Neither do I." He sighed and resumed his spot next to her.

"What are we going to do about it?" He readied himself to hear that she didn't want to see him anymore.

"I wish I knew." She relaxed into him again and wrapped her arms around him.

Something about her tone of voice told him that she wasn't exactly telling the truth. "What is it?"

She stopped breathing, and she didn't move. She spoke into his chest. "I—I have an idea."

"Go on."

"I want us to be together forever."

He paused. That wasn't what he'd expected to hear. "You do?"

She nodded.

"I fail to see an aspect of this proposal to which I might object," he said. "Wait. Are you saying what I think you're saying?"

Again she nodded. "But there's—there's something I want to do before we bind permanently." And with that she finally blurted out, "I want to—I want to have sex."

He raised an eyebrow and cleared his throat. "Technically, that's what we've been doing."

"You know what I mean." She let him go and stepped back. Her face was a brilliant red. "I want—I want you to . . . I want to . . . *swive* you."

He brushed a few stray hairs from her damp face and kissed her. There was something so endearing about hearing her attempt to be crude. "You're sure of this?"

"I am. I—It's . . . There's one problem," she said. "I'm not sure if I'm ready tonight."

"That's fine," he said, and for the first time he knew he truly meant it. "You can trust me. I'll do anything to make you feel safe."

"I love you."

"And I love you." Nels grinned. "That feels really nice to say."

"All right, then," she said, and took his hand. "Let's go to bed."

Again, he blinked. "To sleep?"

"What do you think?"

❧ BLACKTHORNE ❧

ONE

The Hold
Grandmother Mountain
New Eledore

———◆◆———

Thirty-First of Verikuu, 1783

Moss had spent some time the evening before explaining the First of Winter Festival in detail. As Blackthorne understood it, it was a last, joyful fling before the long fast of winter. It was also considered a holy offering. Eledoreans believed that joy multiplied in the sharing and that this joy would symbolically keep all in the community warm, fed, and safe until spring. Blackthorne told himself that attending the party was merely about following Slate's orders.

But it was a lie.

The meeting hall was decorated in bright red, orange, and yellow. The revelers crowding one another were dressed in the same colors. Enough were present that he could imagine what a

First of Winter had been like before the war. Movement and color combined as they danced, reminding him of flames. The scent of roasting meat, hearth fire, and lamp oil was thick in the air. Children snatched treats from tables loaded with food. Candles and festive lanterns carved from turnips and squash provided more light. The faces cut into the squash lanterns represented guardian spirits, ancestors, angels, and saints called upon for protection. A fire nestled in the stately fireplace at the opposite end of the room. Every so often, a lone seeker would move aside the fire screen in order to toss a folded note, a shred of cloth, or other prayer token into the flames. He'd heard that each represented a personal sacrifice offered to the gods.

Of course, the evening's revels weren't strictly Eledorean any more than the Hold's residents were. The music may have originated from Eledore or Ytlain, but most of the instruments on which it was being performed were Acrasian—violins, tin flutes, and drums. It was a homey setting, designed with comfort and celebration in mind. He drank in their warmth and laughter, understanding it was dangerous to do so.

The main problem was the alcohol. It relaxed boundaries and marred judgement. He observed Colonel Hännenen's soldiers with increasing anxiety. It was apparent that the troops had done the bulk of their drinking before the party. Many were openly drunk.

The knot in Blackthorne's gut tightened. *I shouldn't be here.*

His plan was to wait until Slate left and then withdraw. Slate tended to retire early. Blackthorne was tempted to stay longer, but he knew he had to leave the moment Slate did. Before trouble could start. Unfortunately, Slate didn't appear to be quitting the party anytime soon.

He was dancing with his daughter, Katrin. The tune the musicians played was one Blackthorne didn't know. Amusing verses accompanied brisk, jaunty music. People laughed and sang along. The dancers whirled. The mirth was loud enough to obfuscate most of the lyrics. Normally restrained, Slate freely cavorted. He was tender and open toward his daughter. It was a side of the man that Blackthorne wasn't used to seeing, and he wasn't sure he was entirely at ease with it. From time to time, Slate caught Blackthorne's eye and indicated in small ways—a sideways nod or an arched eyebrow—that he should join in the revelry. It was as if Slate were demonstrating an important lesson.

Blackthorne ignored the invitation and instead kept to the shadows like a wolf at the edges of a campfire. He began to feel the strain as multiple forces pulled him in opposing directions. He did what he habitually did in those situations. He laid a hand on the small leather-bound book secreted in the breast pocket of his waistcoat and mentally recited passages from it.

The worthiest Retainers have no need for love or friendship. Such mundane things distract one from one's true calling. A Retainer's life is not his or her own. One's life belongs only to one's Master.

—Duty. I've a duty to comply with Slate's wishes.

It isn't safe. I should leave now.

Safety for the self isn't a Retainer's concern—

This is the essence of the Retainer: neither fear nor love bar the path to death. Those sentiments are for others. This is the Retainer's sacrifice. Contemplate one's own death. Visualize it in every detail. Embrace it. Welcome it like a lover, for the lover does not bring terror. In this way, fear cannot splinter one's heart from duty. Grow numb. Feel nothing. Discard all that ties one to life. Thus, no cowardice can interfere in the crucial moment, and there will be no hesitation in the instant between life and death.

The ideal Retainer lives as if already dead. They are the master's sword and nothing more.

Blackthorne placed his back to the wall and kept the exit in sight. His pistols were in his room. Wearing them would've been an affront to Slate and to the community, but he felt exposed, defenseless. He'd taken the precaution of dining in his room before the party—an old habit from his years in the duke's court. Poisons were far too prevalent, and he'd been officially declared the duke's heir. There were—*had been*—ambitious plotters who had wanted him out of the way. He had known better than to hope that the duke would bestow his wealth upon the son of a slave, no matter how well groomed. He was—*impure*—not human, but they didn't know—*couldn't know*. Nonetheless, it hadn't stopped the plots.

He briefly wondered which of the duke's sycophants were most grateful for his disappearance and thus saved the cost of having him killed.

None of these things mattered. *Not now.* Still, he didn't take refreshments. If pressed, Blackthorne would've said that he needed to remain alert—someone had to, and it was a Retainer's duty—

A Retainer remains ever vigilant.

Slate would've admonished him for being paranoid. Still, Blackthorne leaned against cold stone, not drinking, eating, or in fact, reveling.

Without thought, his gaze drifted to Ilta Korpela. She approached the hearth fire with a token hidden in one fist. Her waist-length blond curls had been knotted into a thick silken braid and tied with a red ribbon. Her dress was made of a mix of fabrics, all of them muted red and gold. She turned, speaking to a young kainen woman beside her. He saw Ilta wore no shawl, and the neckline did a credible job of displaying the tops of her small breasts. Months ago, when he'd first noticed her, he'd decided that she wasn't a great beauty even for a kainen. Still, there was something attractive about her. Was it the graceful way she moved or her obvious intelligence? He sensed she was like him, separate from the others. *Different. Marked somehow.* He indulged in a fantasy that they were alike in that way.

She stooped and then tossed a small object into the flames. Firelight shone through and around her, limning her small form in gold. Her friend said something, and Ilta looked back over one shoulder. At that moment, she could have been an Acrasian saint from a painting. He longed to run his hands over her—

"Care for some punch?"

Blackthorne froze with his heart in his mouth until he recognized Slate. It didn't take terribly long, only an instant, but it was long enough to cause embarrassment. Blackthorne allowed himself to breathe and willed his heart to slow. *If you're so damned alert, how is it Slate surprised you?*

You're not worthy of life. Not—

"You're jumpy this evening," Slate said. He wasn't wearing his spectacles, and his eyes seemed to be clearer than they had the day before. "Afraid you might have a good time?"

Shrugging, Blackthorne didn't speak. *This must be one of his good days. I'm glad. It's a terrible thing to lose one's sight.*

In Acrasia, blindness without means led to begging in the street, not that the misery was long-lasting. Malorum feasted well upon the poor and infirm. There'd been a time when he hadn't questioned the rightness of it. Now he felt disgust for having believed such a horrible thing.

"Here. Drink this." Slate handed off an earthenware cup. "It will make the prospect of socializing less daunting."

A Retainer's honor is in following orders without hesitation. Accepting the drink, Blackthorne tasted apples, cloves, cinnamon, and honey. Then he raised an eyebrow. "The punch has a great deal of alcohol in it." It wasn't an admonishment, merely a statement of fact.

"Both cider and mead. I'm not supposed to know," Slate said, watching the dancers and tapping his foot to the music. "It's called apple snap. It's a First Winter tradition."

Blackthorne paused. "May I ask you a personal question?"

"Certainly," Slate said.

"Are you a Moralist?" The duke had been a Moralist, perversely enough, and Blackthorne had been registered as such, although he was no believer. He recognized the signs. Yet Slate danced and sang. He wasn't married, which would've been considered unseemly in a man his age.

Surprise lifted Slate's brows. "Intolerance isn't something I encourage in myself or others. Whatever gave you that idea?"

"Your public sentiments regarding alcohol." *For a start.*

Slate paused and then said, "As a naturalist, I'm more interested in science and philosophy than religion. I must say Humanism—"

Blackthorne controlled a wince.

"—is more to my taste even with its religious overtones," Slate said, looking out into the crowd. "Although I'm not much for the title. Humans aren't the only beings worthy of respect."

"Then why ban drinking and then actively ignore when it occurs?" *Or encourage it in me?* Blackthorne thought. "It's hypocritical." *Or depraved.* He noticed the judgemental tone and grimaced. "I intended no insult, sir."

Slate smiled a small knowing smile. "Sometimes, a little harmless hypocrisy is required to grease the day-to-day functions of a community. We are, all of us, complex creatures, after all. In any case, I never said I banned alcohol. I merely frown upon it. And as I am one of the leaders of this little band of refugees, frowning is all that is required. It's the most practical solution." He nodded at another resident as they walked past, heading for the refreshment tables.

"I don't understand."

"We distill a great deal of whiskey here. It would be best for everyone if we sold more of it than we consumed. Don't you agree?"

Blackthorne shrugged again.

"This way, the whiskey is used to support the Hold as intended, and consumption is kept to a moderate level, or at least a discreet one," Slate said. They both watched as one of Hännenen's troops stumbled and fell to peals of laughter. "Well . . . that's my theory, anyway."

To build one's actions upon lies is to build one's house upon wet sand and expect it to stand against the sea. Uneasy, Blackthorne frowned and then nodded.

"You should get out there, you know," Slate said with a motion to the dancers. "Show the others you're no different from they are."

"I don't dance."

"Are you going to lie to me and tell me that you don't know how?" Slate waved to a couple who shouted a greeting as they skipped past. "Oh." He paused. "Are you a Moralist?"

"Hardly, sir," Blackthorne said. His presence in church each Sunday had been mandatory. His whole life had been constructed of lies. Why should the afterlife be any different? He hadn't believed a single word. *Impure. Unworthy. Damned.*

"Well?"

Blackthorne was uncomfortable going against Slate's wishes, but he was also highly motivated to retain the ability to chew his own food. "I—I don't dance. Not anymore."

"I see."

Downing the contents of the punch cup, Blackthorne stared into the bottom. The paint used to color it seemed to pool there into a beautiful splash of bright blues, greens, and reds in the otherwise drab, handleless cup. For a fleeting moment, the sight dredged up a fuzzy memory of his mother, who had made such things.

"You've not wintered in the Hold before," Slate said. "We'll be trapped indoors for five months. That's a very long time to share a small space. They'll be afraid of you as long as you hold yourself apart. And that fear is not going to result in a comfortable winter for either of us."

Blackthorne nodded to indicate he'd heard.

"Right now you're an unknown quantity. If you don't give them something with which to fill in the blanks, they'll do so themselves. This isn't Novus Salernum, you know. We depend upon one another for survival. We have to. No one can do everything that is needed for themselves. There isn't time enough in the day. You won't be able to hide—"

Acting on an increasing need to flee the conversation, Blackthorne asked, "Do you want anything from the refreshment table, sir?" He turned before Slate could answer and walked directly into the one person he couldn't afford to be anywhere near.

"Oops," Ilta said.

"I'm sorry." Blackthorne struggled not to breathe in the scent of her hair and failed. *Winter roses, rosemary, and mint.* His heart hammered against his eardrums, and his skin tingled.

"My fault," Ilta said. "I should be more careful. Good thing my punch cup was empty, or I'd have spilled it all over my dress." She smiled up at him. Although she was nineteen—two years younger than he was—she seemed older. It was her demeanor, he supposed. Her features were angular, with high cheekbones and a stubborn set to her jaw. This close, he noted a small scar in the middle of her chin. Her nose was a touch too sharp and long, and there was a gap between her front teeth, but her eyes made up the difference. They were an intense black that practically sparkled when she smiled.

The fact that she was smiling at him made his skin feel tight.

"You're standing on my foot," she said.

He glanced down, registered the problem, and removed the offending appendage. The sole of his boot had scuffed the toe of her slipper. Lifting his gaze from her foot to her face, yet another apology lodged in his throat.

"No harm done," she said, as if reading his thoughts.

He nodded and then attempted a second retreat.

Blocking his escape in one graceful step, she asked, "Are you avoiding me?"

"A—avoiding?" His throat closed, and his cheeks heated. He was suddenly thankful he hadn't shaved the beard.

"Because, if that's the case, a girl could get the wrong idea, you know," Ilta said.

He blinked, unable to speak.

"Slate said you would like to dance but you're too afraid to ask," she said. "Is that true?"

Blackthorne felt his mouth drop open. He looked to Slate only to find that the man had vanished into the crowd.

"Well?" she asked.

"I . . . I don't dance."

"He said you'd say that." She now appeared to be mocking him. "However, he also said you wouldn't be familiar with Eledorean country dances. Don't worry. I'll teach you. It's easy."

She snatched the empty punch cup from his numb fingers and deposited it on a refreshment table in deft motions. She then captured his hand and dragged him into the dance pattern. Her grip was stronger than expected. For an instant, he tried hard not to think about where else that grip might be employed. She was close. *So close.* Her fingers were warm against his, and her perfume filled his nose. It threatened to make him dizzy. The spare grace with which she guided him stirred more thoughts he knew he couldn't afford. The other dancers whirled around them like a noisy stream, fluidly avoiding the obstacle they presented.

Blackthorne swallowed. *Congratulations. You're well on your way to getting yourself killed.* He could feel the others' stares as word began to spread.

Fear is the enemy. Fear hinders action in the final moment. Fear—

"You're shaking." Ilta positioned his hands so that one rested on top of her shoulder and the other was at her waist.

He could feel her warm, firm skin under the cloth. Another bout of heat spread throughout his body—this time nowhere near his cheeks.

"There's no need to be nervous. We'll take this slow. And don't worry about mistakes. Everyone is clumsy at first."

"I'm not nervous." *You might as well enjoy your last moments.*

"Sure you're not," she said. "Everyone trembles like a leaf when they're calm."

Deeply shamed, he cut off his feelings and scanned the room, alert for danger. "I can't do this," he said. The Ghost stood near the musicians, talking to a few of his men. He hadn't noticed yet, but it was only a matter of time.

"Sure you can. This is the easiest of the country dances. It's what we call a farmer's waltz," she said. "Skip three times in the same direction as the others and then turn together clockwise. One-two-three. Turn. One-two-three. Turn. That's the whole thing. Simple. Oh, and I'll let you in on a secret. Once you've got the steps memorized, Elen Stål would be thrilled if you asked her for a turn around the floor."

"You don't understand." Blackthorne glanced again at the Ghost.

Colonel Hännenen had abandoned his plate and returned Blackthorne's gaze with a hard glare.

Shit, Blackthorne thought. *I'm done for.*

"Pay attention," Ilta said, grabbing him by the jaw and turning his head so that he faced her.

Her fingers burned against his skin for an instant and then vanished.

"You're making this harder than it is," she said. "Here, watch my feet."

The noise level in the room noticeably diminished. A number of the dancers dropped out. The musicians played on as the atmosphere shifted from happy to tense.

"I thank you for the instruction," Blackthorne said as formally as he could. One of Hännenen's men was forcing his way through the crowd toward them. Blackthorne recognized him as the one he'd met at the entrance the day he'd returned. *On your knees, crow.* "But I shouldn't monopolize your time."

"Don't be silly," she said. "I'm having fun. Aren't you?"

Couples discreetly retired from the dance floor until only a handful remained. The crowd grew silent and watchful. When the song ended, it was met with abrupt silence. No one clapped or cheered as before. No one moved. A cough ricocheted off the high ceiling like a stray musket ball.

"Oh, well," Ilta said. "I guess we'll just have to wait for the next song."

The Eledorean officer with long blond hair and a pox-scarred face didn't halt until he stood uncomfortably close to Blackthorne's elbow. When he spoke, he did so in Blackthorne's ear. "I believe you're finished here." The underlying threat was obvious.

Blackthorne jerked his hands from Ilta and took a half-step back. His heart slammed against his chest six times while he withstood the officer's scrutiny. *Underlieutenant. He's an undernderlieutenant.* The underlieutenant leaned in. Blackthorne kept his back straight. He'd have to walk a thin line between subservience and defiance. It was a familiar line, one he'd long lived on. Stray too far on either side and he was dead. It didn't help that the death in question wouldn't be fast or painless. He yielded again, silently giving ground but holding the underlieutenant's glare with his own.

Slate said, "Perhaps we should—"

Blackthorne glanced to Slate, disrupting his concentration on the underlieutenant for an instant, but that was all it took. A blow slammed into Blackthorne's face. Someone screamed. Blackthorne hit the floor, blind. An explosion of pain flooded his senses. He registered something was out of place. *Wrong.* There'd been an odd sensation at the instant of contact. *Power. Magic. A great deal of it.* There wasn't time to ponder what that meant. Well used to violence, he rolled and then got on his feet. He forced his hands down to his sides. His left eye was already swelling. It was difficult to see. *Don't do anything that can be interpreted as a—*

Three more punches landed. One in the jaw and two rapid-fire hits in the gut. All the air went out of him. The pain was tremendous. He staggered. Bending over to empty his mouth of blood, he threw up. It took him a moment to find the strength to straighten. He tried not to flinch as the underlieutenant prepared for the next blow.

"Are you a coward?" the underlieutenant asked. "Fight me!"

Two more punches landed—one in the face and one in Blackthorne's bruised stomach. *A third. A fourth.* He lost count.

"Underlieutenant Nurmi, stop! That's an order!" It was Colonel Hännenen. The blows ended. Stooped over and wavering, Blackthorne paused and then straightened again. Wiping blood and vomit from his nose and mouth with the back of his hand, he spit out the vile-tasting mess coating his tongue. Then he gathered as much dignity as he could and, without a word, made to back away. Unfortunately, he was brought up short when Ilta grabbed his arm.

"Please don't go," Ilta said.

"What do you think you are you doing?" Colonel Hännenen turned on her.

"Only what Slate asked," she said.

"And what exactly did Slate ask you to do?"

"Blackthorne has proven himself a member of the community in good standing," Ilta said. "I suggest you learn to cope with his being here."

"Doesn't the queen get a say as to who stays and who doesn't? Did anyone consult her?" Hännenen gestured to a young woman in a bright red silk dress standing across the room. Her hair was light brown and swept up on her head in delicate curls with a matching red ribbon.

The queen is here? Why didn't Slate tell me? Blackthorne hadn't seen her before, and therefore he hadn't known what she looked like. She was much younger and prettier than he'd imagined. *I should've wintered with Mrs. Holton. I should've stayed in Novus Salernum—a cave—anywhere but here.* His already-bruised stomach did a slow roll. *This is bad. Very, very bad.*

"Is something wrong?" the queen asked, and stood next to Hännenen.

Blackthorne could see the pair had certain facial features in common, the nose, the chin—

Hännenen said, "This community harbors a—"

An alarm sounded. The crowd seemed to hold their breath in fearful anticipation as they listened to the pattern for meaning. *Two long, low bell tones followed by two short, higher ones.* The signal was repeated three times, then it was followed with three short low tones.

"Intruder. The river dock," Slate said. "Go! To your stations just as we practiced! Ilta, gather the children and take them to the larder. Your Highness, you should go with her. You'll be safer in the larder and there'll be food and water in case you must stay hidden for a longer period of time."

A flash of anger passed over the young queen's face. "You expect me to cower in a hole while the others fight for me? This isn't Eledore of old. Give me a damned pistol. I'm a passable shot. But I'm better with a cutlass."

"What?" Hännenen asked.

"You expected me to spend my time idling with my books and eating figs?" the queen asked. "I had Dylan teach me."

"There are weapons and powder stores in the larder, Your Grace," Slate said. "No cutlasses, I'm afraid. Ilta needs help protecting the children, if it comes to it. However, the choice is yours."

"I'll go to the larder," the queen said, glaring at Hännenen. "This time."

"We can discuss a better plan later," Slate said.

The queen nodded.

"Come on, everyone," Slate continued. "Stay calm. You know what to do. It's possible that this is only a drill. Do just as we practiced."

Blackthorne got up and dusted himself off. He was supposed to go with the troops, but he hesitated. He wasn't sure of the wisdom in doing so. *Now.* He felt Slate's hand on his shoulder.

"How bad is it?" Slate asked.

Blackthorne gingerly touched his jaw and winced. "Nothing broken," he said through swelling lips.

Slate said. "Change of plan. You're with me."

Relieved, Blackthorne nodded, and watched Hännenen's troops file out the doors. Hännenen lingered, apparently arguing with his sister, the queen.

"Colonel Hännenen," Slate said.

"Yes?"

"You and I will discuss this matter later," Slate said. "For now, I suggest you deal with the problem at hand."

Hännenen scowled. "You don't have to tell me—"

"Just . . . send someone back with a report about what's happening at the docks as soon as you can," Slate said.

Hännenen nodded at some signal from his sister and then said, "I will." The Ghost's mouth was set in a rigid line as he turned away.

With Hännenen gone and the hall emptied, Slate turned and sped through the passages. It didn't take long for Blackthorne to lose his bearings.

"Where are we going?" Blackthorne asked.

"Where we'll have the best view," Slate said. "The Lookout."

TWO

The Lookout was little more than a wide ledge positioned high above the ship access to the dock with an excellent view of the river and a large part of the surrounding ravine. There was space enough to shelter three or four guards and a grate for a small fire. The fire in question was out, presumably due to having been forgotten. Blackthorne shivered. His breath formed clouds. A guard was always posted at the Lookout, and the floor was kept clear of snow. At the moment, three of Hännenen's troops crowded the ledge, each armed with blunderbusses. Slate entered with no trouble. Blackthorne hung back. Should the guns need to be employed, things might prove a little too interesting for comfort.

All three soldiers scanned the area below. Shouts echoed off rock walls. Someone below was screaming.

"What's going on?" Slate asked.

"I don't know. I can't see," one of the men said. He was about fifty years old with greying hair, short and stocky for a kainen. It wasn't until he turned that Blackthorne recognized Captain Sebastian Moller by the deep scar on his left cheek partially covered by a beard.

"Who sounded the alarm?" Slate asked.

"I did, sir," one of the others said without turning away from the scene below. The voice indicated the bundled corporal was a woman. She sounded frightened. "Thought I saw movement. Heard a cry. Thought it might be someone who left the party for air and got lost. Sent the privates down to investigate. Lenkkeri was to stay at the door while Jauho was to check. I heard Jauho call the all clear. He said it was someone he knew from Rehn. The next thing I heard was the screaming. And that was when I rang the alarm."

"You didn't go down to help?" Slate asked.

"No, sir," the corporal said with a guilty look. "Lenkkeri went after him against orders. After that, I couldn't leave my post without endangering the Hold."

Blackthorne got the impression she yearned to be out there now, searching for the missing Lenkkeri and Jauho.

Slate nodded. "Can you see anything yet?"

A piercing animal cry sliced through the frozen air, and the skin along Blackthorne's arms bunched up in gooseflesh. The sound was at once high-pitched and low-pitched—hollow, shuddering, and altogether haunting. He recognized its otherworldly harmonics with a start.

"What in the abyss was that?" Moller asked.

Weaponless, Blackthorne bolted for his room. *The Eledoreans are facing a malorum unprepared.*

"Blackthorne? Where are you going?" Slate's question followed him down the passage. "Blackthorne?"

"I'll explain later, sir." Blackthorne shouted as he ran. *This is my purpose. This is why Slate saved me.* It was unfortunate that his vision was temporarily impaired. It would make fighting to the best of his abilities difficult. He cursed himself for allowing Underlieutenant Nurvi to injure him and thus limit his usefulness.

One's life belongs only to one's Master.

No one loitered in the passageways to slow him down. Throwing open the door, Blackthorne grabbed everything he'd need—musket, pistols, silver shot, and the ebony-handled Warden's knife. He checked his pockets for silver, grabbed the last of the coins he had stored in his footlocker, and then fled. When he reached the outermost exit, he paused. *No moon tonight. It will be very dark.* He spied the hooded lantern in a nearby wall niche and checked its oil reservoir before he stole it, closing the shutter out of concern for his night vision. He made for the river dock and hoped he wouldn't be too late. The lone malorum would lure the Eledoreans into the dark, split them up, and pick them off one by one. It's what malorum did.

Why didn't I warn them sooner? For that matter, why didn't Slate or one of the others? As much as Slate preferred to act as though the community was tight-knit, the reality was that there existed a dangerous rift between the Eledoreans and Acrasian refugees.

We depend upon one another for survival. We have to. No one can do everything. Suddenly, Slate's words took on another, more personal, meaning.

One's life belongs only to one's Master.

The first body Blackthorne came to had been drained and was little more than a shrunken husk. It wore an Eledorean private's insignia. *Lenkkeri or Jauho. Probably Jauho.* From there, the trail split off in several directions; one set of footprints led deeper into the woods while another went down the river path. He estimated there were eleven individuals patrolling the ravine. He glanced down at the corpse. The profane spice scent of the desiccated private made Blackthorne a little sick.

Turning away from the smell, he decided with some reluctance to take the time to concentrate on listening. He didn't like the way listening with intent made him feel, but tracks alone weren't going to be enough. He only had the use of one eye; the other was too swollen. It would be too easy to miss an important detail, and time was running out for the living. Gritting his teeth against the anticipated nausea, he closed his eyes and focused his will.

Knowledge came to him with an anxious, queasy twist in his gut. Three surviving Eledoreans were grouped together to the west. He opened his good eye and began following the tracks leading westward. It wasn't long before he discovered two more Eledorean dead—each had fallen about fifty feet from the other. Both had been caught fleeing. One of the victims hadn't been completely drained.

That's curious, Blackthorne thought. Malorum were crafty, careful, and exacting in their attacks. They were known to be vulnerable during feeding because they focused on their kill to the exclusion of all else. They never left a body undrained. This one appeared to have been in some sort of frenzy, as if it were brain-damaged or diseased. During his years at the Academy, no one had ever documented an instance of illness among the malorum. He wasn't sure what to make of what he saw. *Is it because it's feeding on kainen?*

No time. Think about it later.

He paused again to listen. The survivors' location was more difficult to discern now. *At least they're learning to stay quiet and in a group.* That was good. A malorum could only successfully glamour one victim at a time. However, without silver, the Eledoreans were still at a terrible disadvantage.

The trail led Blackthorne to a huge, jagged boulder in a clearing. Colonel Hännenen and two other Eledorean soldiers had taken up positions with their backs against the stone. Blackthorne recognized one of them, a lieutenant, as a close associate of Hännenen's but couldn't remember his name. Relieved to find survivors, Blackthorne took a moment to check the area again. The malorum wasn't in sight. That didn't mean it wasn't nearby. The Eledoreans had but one functioning lantern. Its light shone feebly against the darkness. The use of light and keeping the boulder at their backs was smart. The only problem was that it wouldn't take long before the malorum climbed up the dark side of the boulder. With that in mind, Blackthorne decided to circle the clearing.

"Who is there?" the lieutenant asked, and swung the end of his musket so that it pointed at him. "I hear you. Identify yourself."

That one has very sensitive ears, Blackthorne thought. He decided it would be best not to risk being shot. "It's Blackthorne." His jaw still ached, and his teeth felt a bit loose where Underlieutenant Nurvi's blows had landed. "Stay where you are. I must make sure of something." Not all malorum were capable of understanding speech. However, enough were that he decided to be cautious and not reveal details.

Moving silently, he left them to argue about the quality of their single reinforcement and made his way to the opposite side of the boulder. The rock appeared easily scalable. Unfortunately, climbing it while carrying a lantern wasn't possible. He didn't taste tin and grave dust in the back of his throat, not yet. *The malorum still isn't that close.* He tried not to think about what might be keeping it busy. With that, he placed two silver coins to make climbing the rock less attractive. Then he made note of their location for daylight retrieval and went to join the others.

He was halted by the lieutenant at the edge of the clearing.

Very good ears indeed, Blackthorne thought, and raised one hand to demonstrate he intended no harm.

"What are you doing here?" the lieutenant asked, not lowering his musket.

"Saving you," Blackthorne said. He slowly opened the shutters on the lantern. His night vision had been ruined, anyway. Not that he was that much use. The swollen eye was watering and painful. He resisted an urge to wipe it dry. With his good eye, he watched the others closely for signs of flinching from the light. *It never hurts to be doubly sure.* The lieutenant's eyes narrowed, and he looked away with a scowl. No one else reacted.

Frowning, Colonel Hännenen said, "We don't need your help."

"I believe the dead I passed on my way to you would testify otherwise," Blackthorne said. The words were slurred as he forced them past his swollen lips and aching jaw.

"The others are dead?" Hännenen asked.

"I'm afraid so."

"I'm to believe you got here by yourself?" Hännenen asked.

Blackthorne shrugged and answered before giving it much thought. "It is what Wardens are trained to do."

The third Eledorean muttered something in her own language with a sneer.

The lieutenant said, "Retired or not, he has more experience with these creatures. In this case, it's best to focus on the pragmatic."

"That swiving thing changes form at will. How do we know you are who you claim to be?" Hännenen asked.

You're learning. Blackthorne paused while he thought of a sign Hännenen might accept. "Underlieutenant Nurvi lowers his guard when he punches with his left."

Hännenen's frown deepened. "What?"

"He's right," the lieutenant said. "He does."

"Oh."

The lieutenant pointed the muzzle of his gun at the ground.

Setting down the lantern, Blackthorne laid out an arc of silver coins on the icy ground. He was careful to clear away the snow with his boot first for maximum exposure. He also made the circle as wide as possible for maneuverability. Without silver shot, the muskets wouldn't do much, but the noise might serve to startle it—particularly since he *did* have silver. The creature wouldn't know which gun would be harmful and which wouldn't. He straightened after placing the last coin and spied the others looking on, confused.

"What are you doing?" Hännenen asked.

"It takes silver to kill malorum," Blackthorne said.

Hännenen blinked.

"Well, there's a sound argument against debasing currency if I've ever heard one," Viktor said.

Blackthorne thought it best not to bring up that Acrasian sterling dollars weren't in public circulation and that most sterling coins hung in the windows of the poorer areas of Novus Salernum were largely comprised of nickel. It was a level of detail that the Eledoreans didn't need. *Not now,* he mentally added with no small amount of guilt. "In the future, it would be best to keep silver on your person. Even a small amount will give them pause, and that may provide time you need to escape."

"You're assuming there are more of those things," Hännenen said. "As far as we know, there is only the one."

"Where one is seen, others are most certainly in hiding," Blackthorne said.

Hännenen scanned the tree line.

"The naturalists say that malorum do not cooperate in groups," Blackthorne said. "They are competitive hunters with overlapping territories, much like felines. They also prefer darkness and are more active in the winter months." He didn't feel the need to add *And Eledorean winters are especially long and dark.*

"Those things never crossed the Kylmapuro before," Viktor said. "Why are they here now?"

"Is it because of the Acrasians? Did you bring them here?" the private asked.

Uncomfortable with the private's question, Blackthorne left them without answering. The truth was, he didn't know. He thought again about his nightmares and dismissed them. *Don't be ridiculous. If that were a connection, then I would've seen evidence of it when I was in Novus Salernum.* He started climbing.

Hännenen said, "Blackthorne, where did you go?"

Upon reaching the top of the boulder, Blackthorne searched the shadows. *Was that movement out there?* "Are we staying until light, or are you willing to risk the trip back?"

"We're killing that thing. And *then* we're returning," Hännenen said. "Not before."

"All right," Blackthorne said. "Hand up my lantern."

"Why?" Hännenen asked.

Attempting not to show his frustration, Blackthorne said, "To prevent the malorum from using higher ground for an attack. They are quite capable of climbing."

"Oh."

Once the lantern was in place, Blackthorne scrambled back down. The taste of old death and tin filled his mouth the moment he joined the Eledoreans. He glanced up in time to see the malorum rush the light.

That's not right, Blackthorne thought. He had time to draw his Warden's knife.

Viktor's gun fired. The creature didn't so much as pause. It bore down on them with a single-minded determination. One of the Eledoreans cursed, another screamed. Lantern light revealed the malorum's true form—or what Blackthorne had come to believe was such.

Its uneven arms and legs were bent at unnatural angles, and it moved with a rapid, otherworldly grace that reminded him of an insect. It had sharp, matted fur and spiny claws. These things he'd come to expect. The main difference between this malorum and the others he'd seen was that it was twice the size of a man. In addition, it hadn't attempted to clothe itself. Flat black multi-faceted eyes took up a large part of its face. They reflected no light. The thing had reindeer antlers weighing down its wolf-shaped skull. Its feet were bare of fur. That was when he saw they were fashioned like a human's. The creature reminded him of a newborn colt only now learning how to stand on its legs.

He registered all these differences in the instant before the creature's foot landed on top of one of the silver coins. The malorum leapt into the air backward, away from the silver, and crashed into a tree trunk. The monster thrashed and bellowed in agony as snow dropped from the shaken tree's limbs. Stench-filled smoke erupted at the point of contact.

Blackthorne put away his knife and loaded his musket with a silver ball. He took careful aim, using his good eye. At this angle, there was no way of hitting the thing in the skull. He pulled the trigger anyway. The butt of the musket slammed into his shoulder, and the explosion echoed through the forest. He tasted the grit of spent powder. Smoke filled the air. Temporarily deafened, he didn't wait to see if his shot hit. Instead, he went through the well-practiced motions of reloading. By the time he'd raised his weapon for a second shot, the smoke had dissipated.

The malorum had stopped moving.

"Stay here," Blackthorne said, handing his musket to Hännenen and then drawing his knife. "That's loaded with silver shot. Shoot the thing if it moves again." Blackthorne tried not to think about being shot in the back as he approached the twitching body. He inched closer. "I think it's dead." He stooped to cut its throat.

Something clamped down on his right leg. Turning to see, he spied the claw locked onto his thigh. The malorum's grip closed impossibly tight, and Blackthorne was yanked off his feet before he could shout a warning. The ground came up to meet him. He tasted snow in addition to the creature's taint. He spat.

The malorum righted itself. Its maw loomed huge above him. The interior of its mouth was fish-belly white. Poison oozed from its fangs. The smell was horrible. Gagging, he swiped at the malorum's neck with his knife, but its elongated jaw was in the way. The silver blade sliced across the malorum's chin and up to the snout. Cut by the silver-laced blade, it roared. A shot went off. The thing jerked and then slumped, landing on top of him. Suddenly overwhelmed with pain and the malorum's weight, Blackthorne's vision dimmed. The sound of his own heartbeat filled his ears. He couldn't move. He couldn't breathe. Soon, he was too tired to care.

"He's dead. Okay? We should get back now."

"Help me get it off him." It was Hännenen.

"But what if he's right and there are more of those things?"

"Don't argue, Private."

The weight was lifted. Blackthorne was able to gasp once for air before a wrenching pain exploded in his leg. He could feel blood and melting snow soaking into his clothes. His face was sticky with venom and grit. He made to wipe it away but couldn't move his hand. *Where's my knife?*

"He's alive. But I think he's been bitten."

"Get him out from under it, Viktor. I can't hold this thing forever. Filppula, bring that lantern over here."

Blackthorne felt himself dragged. White-hot agony blotted out the rest. When he came to, he was being carried with Hännenen's shoulder under him on one side and the private's on the other. A white linen tourniquet was tied tight around his thigh. His leg throbbed with the beat of his heart. The pain had been blunted by the venom but was no less awful.

"Can you walk?"

Unsure of his voice, Blackthorne nodded. *I'll damned well try.* He tilted his head to search with his good eye for his knife. A bout of dizzying nausea slammed him. He fought it, blinking back pain and tears. His vision cleared and he saw Viktor pull the blade from the malorum's throat.

Good.

His memory of the return journey was marred by patches of blackness. There was no second attack—at least, he didn't think so. His awareness centered on the snow-covered ground as he struggled to walk. The next thing he knew, they were met by Slate near the docks.

"Is that everyone?" Slate asked.

"All that are living, as far as we know," Hännenen said. "I won't risk anyone else to search, not now. It'll have to wait until the morning."

"What happened to him?" Slate asked.

Blackthorne felt Slate's hand on his shoulder.

"He killed that thing," Viktor said. "I think he was bitten."

"Get him to the infirmary," Slate said. "Someone wake Westola or Ilta. Tell them they've got a patient on the way! Now!"

⤝ CAIUS ⤞

ONE

"Close the door," Senior Warden Tolerans said.

Caius followed the order. The cavernous study became claustrophobic, and the pleasant scent of pipe smoke took on a sinister quality. *Valarius turned you in.* Caius's body completed the betrayal by revealing his terror. His hand shook as he reached for the door. His heart hammered a loud drumbeat in his chest, and his knees threatened to disobey him altogether. *Don't be ridiculous. It wasn't Valarius. They've been watching you since Severus was reconditioned. Standard procedure—to watch for a philosophical taint. Thoughts, if not regulated, can be like a disease. Severus was your closest friend, after all.*

You've been stupid.

Caius assumed his place on the large geometric-patterned rug before the Senior Warden's massive writing desk and resumed a rigid posture.

"At ease, Fortis," Senior Warden Tolerans said. His tone was flat, almost bored.

Caius dropped his shoulders and let his hands fall away from the small of his back. However, his heart continued its panicked gallop.

"We have a serious problem," Senior Warden Tolerans said. "One that cannot involve anyone else, including the Watch. Am I understood?"

Oh, Mithras, Caius thought, *will reconditioning be as terrible as they say? Will they tell my mother? What will Father say?* "Yes, sir." He was thankful that his voice didn't crack.

Senior Warden Tolerans said, "According to the census records, there is a discrepancy in the population numbers."

Caius blinked. That wasn't what he'd been expecting. It took him an instant to recover. "An error?"

"Not an error. A discrepancy," Senior Warden Tolerans said. "It would appear that someone is smuggling nonhumans out of the city."

"Sir? I thought—I thought *we* created that rumor." Such stories served two purposes—the first was to trap nonhumans who would attempt escape. The second was, to Caius's way of thinking, far more cruel. Naturalists and philosophers working within the Brotherhood claimed that nonhumans were more cooperative when they believed freedom a possibility. It was this meager hope that filled the arenas with fighters seeking a quick, inexpensive, and seemingly easy path to citizenship. For those without the strength, speed, and stamina for the games, there was always the possibility of running—of reserving a berth aboard a coffin-coach, so called because of the small spaces inside wagons used to secrete runaways. In either case, the official story was that a haven existed for those foolhardy or desperate enough. The logic seemed perverse to Caius. If no one returned to verify the haven in question, it only served to prove it existed.

Or had so far.

Senior Warden Tolerans said, "In this case, it seems someone co-opted our little lie." He went to a bookcase and retrieved a ledger from the rows of similarly black leather-bound volumes. Setting it on a table, he leafed through the pages.

"Begging your pardon, sir," Caius said, "but a percentage of inaccuracies shouldn't be unusual, surely. Statistically, we—"

"Are you suggesting that the census is inaccurate?"

"No, sir."

"Good." Senior Warden Tolerans returned his attention to the ledger beneath his fingertips. "Sixty-three nonhumans declared missing. This, from Novus Salernum alone. Other sectors have reported discrepancies, but the numbers are far less by comparison." He looked up from the tome. "There is a clever Rogue in our midst, Fortis. One who takes advantage of our little lie and is intelligent enough to hide the bodies. One who is familiar with our procedures. That makes him very dangerous indeed."

"Could it be one of our own?"

"That isn't possible. A relative, perhaps? That I might believe," Senior Warden Tolerans said. Using a quill, he made a note on a scrap of paper and blotted it with sand. "Nonetheless, there is one known witness. Interview her and report. Speak to no one else of your findings. You are to report directly to me and me alone." He offered the slip of paper.

Caius accepted it and read the name "Lucrosa Aurelia" and an address off of Regent Street in the Senior Warden's precise hand. "Yes, sir."

"And Fortis? Be polite. The witness is a high-ranking Lucrosa. The director will not want his alliances . . . damaged."

That meant that Caius couldn't use any of the standard methods for obtaining cooperation—no coercion, no threats. He had to manipulate her into volunteering the information he needed, which would be damned near impossible. *Why send me? Why not someone of more senior rank?* "I'll be careful, sir."

"See that you are."

TWO

The coach's iron step unhinged, announcing Caius's arrival with a heavy clang.

The Lucrosa's manse wasn't visible from the street. That wasn't unusual. Most of the residences in the area were situated on large plots in spite of being located within the city. Due to the malorum, it was considered safer. An ornate black iron gate twenty feet high and an equally imposing red brick wall shielded the property. He knew without looking that the tops of both were dotted with silver. On the other side of the bars, a private drive wound its way through a wooded lot.

One of the two guards stationed at the gate approached. Both were heavily armed and dressed in the loose black clothing of professional Retainers. Caius displayed his credentials and was granted access to the property. The rented coach drove off down the public street, rattling a goodbye on the cobblestones. The huge iron gate creaked before it slammed shut behind him. The crisp winter air filled his lungs as he gazed at the grey afternoon sky. A gusty wind rattled the naked tree branches, their dull clatter reminding him of bones. He tugged his scarf closer around his neck and pressed his tricorne tighter on his head lest it blow away. His boots crunched on an icy drive wide enough for three carriages and paved with thousands upon thousands of broken white shells imported from Archiron.

When he finally reached the building with its tall white columns and classical pediment, he noted that it was more palace than house. It projected a foreboding and impenetrable quality. Aristocratic rows of glass windows reflected the dull clouds, quartered by silver-plated mullions. It had been recently built, or had been remodeled, not that Caius was familiar with the minute distinctions between older buildings and newer ones. Unlike his mother, he didn't keep up with architectural fashion. Such esthetic endeavors were beyond his reach and therefore weren't worth the effort to study. For him, the telling details were in the brightness of the mortar and the fresh coat of paint.

The drive continued around the manse. He spied other buildings on the property, which he guessed were for servants. There were a stable and a large, white-fenced paddock. The carriage house was larger than his parents' home.

He approached the massive front door with a sense of helpless awe and resented it. There was no one on the grounds to greet him. So, he resorted to the brass knocker. The abrupt tap of metal against metal was invasive in the stately hush. After a long, oppressive silence, footsteps echoed on the other side of the white double doors, and a handsome elph with dark skin, wearing a powdered wig and a footman's uniform, appeared. He held out a silver salver. "The master is not receiving visitors today. Please leave your card on the tray."

"I am Inspector-Warden Fortis Modius Caius. I'm here to speak with his daughter, Lucrosa Aurelia, if I may?" It was best to make it sound as if there were a social call.

The footman bowed with a brief nod that only just satisfied modern standards of courtesy. "I will inform the mistress." He opened the door wider, permitting Caius access to an entry chamber. The floor seemed to have been fashioned from one huge piece of expensive white-veined black marble. "Remain here."

Removing his hat before entering, Caius felt insulted. No one spoke to Wardens as if they were barely worthy of the front door, particularly not nonhumans.

Careful, he thought. *Be polite.*

Recesses for the pocket shutters on the outward-facing windows were the only evidence of commonality between the classes—that is, the need for security from malorum.

When it became apparent the wait would be long, he entertained himself by examining the paintings on the walls. Several were hunting scenes. Others were portraits of aristocratic, alabaster faces with long noses and softened square jaws. All had varying shades of golden brown to blond hair. The women wore diadems, elaborate and fashionable wigs, and bright silk gowns. Quite a few of the men were dressed in military uniforms and equally intricate wigs. There were two Wardens in the mix. Both wore Director's insignia. Their pale grey eyes stared out of the paintings at him in faint disdain. Caius had edged closer to read the first name etched in the brass plate when he heard someone clear their throat.

Startled, he turned.

"My mistress will see you in the library," the footman said. "This way."

Following the elph footman, Caius was led beyond the vast upward curving staircase and down a wide hallway. They passed several dark oak doors with crystal and filigree silver doorknobs. Thick wool runners protected the polished wood floor, muffling the echoing rhythm of their steps. At last, the footman stopped at a set of open pocket doors, revealing a large room whose cathedral-height walls were lined with books. A blond girl sat reading in a large brown leather armchair with her silk slippered feet propped up on a matching footstool. Her soft buttercream yellow gown was the same shade as her slippers. She was about his age, beautiful and well groomed in a pampered way. He wasn't sure what it meant that he was more attracted to Drake, who was many years his senior and far less refined.

Aurelia didn't get up. She granted him a condescending smile and gestured for him to sit in a nearby armchair. "Father informed me that I wasn't to speak with you when you came calling." Her voice was cultured and prim like the rest of her, but an impish curl nested on the corner of her mouth.

"Is that so?" Caius asked, growing annoyed. "Then why did you have me shown in?"

"Because Father informed me that I wasn't to speak with you." Her pretty face pulled into a spoiled smirk. "Of course."

"Oh." *I see. So, these are the rules?* Caius thought. As he had spent a majority of his life among the children of the rich, it was a game with which he was far too familiar. *I'm not spoiled.*

Aren't you? Your family has money too. Remember that. They're just not as wealthy.

"Why do you wish to speak with me?" she asked.

"Your father owns an elph named Tobias Freeson." Caius retrieved his sketchbook and graphite holder in order to take notes, such as they would be. He suspected his time was being wasted, but an order from Senior Warden Tolerans was an order from Senior Warden Tolerans. One didn't argue with one's superiors. *Much.* He swallowed. *Perhaps Severus rubbed off on me after all.* "I've come to talk about Freeson."

"Toby wasn't a slave. He was an indentured servant. You would think you'd know that by his family name."

"Doesn't it amount to the same thing when they break contract?"

"Maybe for *your* purposes," she said.

That was risky, maybe even reckless, he thought. He reassessed the situation accordingly.

She continued. "But there is an important distinction."

"I stand corrected," he said. "What happened to this Tobias?"

"Don't you know?"

Caius held her gaze for what seemed an eternity. He knew he could out-stare her. She didn't have any discipline to speak of; that was obvious. He decided to let the tense silence stretch between them for as long as she wished. Right about the time he began to feel immature for having lowered himself to participating in one of her childish games, she broke the silence and glanced away.

"Toby quit working in my father's smithy. He . . . left without permission."

"How well did you know Mr. Freeson?"

"*Toby* is—was my *friend.*" It was easy to see she was daring him to say anything to her about her openly associating with a nonhuman.

Caius ignored the challenge. "Can you tell me if anything unusual happened before he left? Anything at all? Did he talk to anyone you'd never met before?"

She let out an impatient huff. "He took a few stupid old books from my father's library. So what? All that fuss over stupid books Father was going to destroy anyway. What is so important about that?" she asked, tilting her chin down so that the fringe of her curls hid her eyes. "They were recovered and destroyed, you know. Everyone knows." Again, she met his gaze. This time, a flash of worry creased her pout. Once more, she looked away.

"Is something wrong?" Caius asked.

"Do you think . . . Do you think Toby is safe?"

Her display of concern for someone other than herself caused Caius to revise his earlier estimate of her. Pausing, he decided to try a new tactic. "His chances aren't good."

"But they say . . . They say there are people who can help. People who can . . . you know, get people like him out of the country."

"Who says this?"

"You know . . . everyone."

"Did someone contact him claiming to be able to do such a thing?"

She stared down at her hands.

"What did this person look like?"

She bit her lip. "I don't want to say anything."

"Why not?"

Her expression transformed again into defiance. "You're a *Warden*. How stupid do you think I am?"

He shrugged. "You're assuming I hate nonhumans."

"Don't you? You hunt them when they escape the census."

"I don't hunt anyone. I'm an Inspector Warden." That declaration was, at best, a half-truth. He didn't hunt nonhumans. *Not anymore.* However, tracking down lawbreakers was a part of every Warden's training, and lucrative bounties saw to it that many continued the practice even when their positions dictated otherwise. "I became a Warden in order to protect Acrasians from magic. All Acrasians, including nonhumans." That was the truth; at least, that had been his original reason. Magic was said to harm the user as well as the target of the spell. If the nonhuman population, and thus their magical power, were controlled, then everyone would be safer. Unfortunately, after serving six months in the Brotherhood, he wasn't so sure of his vocation. *If*

*nonhumans are so powerful, then how is it they don't use magic to
save themselves?*

He returned his attention to the task at hand. "You care a great
deal for Tobias, don't you?"

She didn't say a word. Her expression answered the question
for her.

"He's in a great deal of danger," Caius said. "Runaways often fall
prey to the unscrupulous."

"He's *not* a runaway slave."

"Bounty hunters and Field Wardens don't care for distinctions
between indentured servants and slaves, not when a nonhuman
is involved. They'll profit off of him. Abuse him. Sell him, maybe
even kill him, if they haven't already."

"Why do *you* care?"

"Because nonhumans need our protection," he said. As puzzling as it all sounded coming from a Warden, it was how he felt.
It isn't the nonhuman that is the problem; it's the magic. It occurred
to him that he'd repeated that thought to himself a great deal over
the past year.

Caius argued with himself. *They don't sell hunting licenses for
nonhumans because of the threat of magic. You're the worst sort of
hypocrite. You're lying to yourself. And you're manipulating her.* For
an instant, he wondered what she would do if she knew what
he did—that her friend had probably been killed by an unlicensed hunter. And that the only reason the Brotherhood was
interested was because of the revenue loss. The fact that it was
a particularly fastidious hunter made it less of a priority, he suspected, in spite of the revenue loss. *No chance of the public finding
out about this one.*

"His name was Andrew Blackthorne. Worked out of the
Golden Swan on Headley Street," she said.

Caius blinked and then jotted down the name before he forgot it. "Description?"

"He was attractive, if somewhat rough. He was tall, kind of slender. Had straight black hair, a beard—just on his chin, a mustache, and light-colored eyes," she said. "He looked human."

"What do you mean, he *looked* human; wasn't he?"

"I thought Mr. Blackthorne was a Warden, but Toby said that he couldn't be, because he was nonhuman," she said. "Toby gets funny hunches about things like that. He's never wrong. So, I believed him. I let him go. Was I wrong?"

Pausing, Caius fought to hide his surprise. "Why would you think Mr. Blackthorne might be a Warden?"

She shrugged. "He was wearing boots like yours."

"Exactly like these?" Caius asked, stretching out a leg. While Wardens had been known to fall on hard times on occasion, no one would ever consider selling their boots. It was unthinkable. Anyone caught wearing them without the credentials to match would be killed on sight. It was one of the few instances when a duel didn't require a license or a fee. "Are you sure?"

"They were folded down at the top like yours," she said.

"You've just described hunting boots."

"Not black with tan tops. He'd covered the tan parts with boot black, but it's easy enough to spot. The blacks didn't match. And even if that weren't the case, I could see where he'd removed the emblems on the sides. It left holes that scarred the leather." She pointed to the outside and top of his right boot, where the two and a half inch–diameter silver Warden's roundel was set. "He was disreputable-looking for a Warden. Poor. Wardens aren't low-class, I know, but those boots were Warden boots."

The rogue is a nonhuman passing for a Warden? Caius swallowed. *Impossible. No nonhuman could penetrate the ranks of the*

Brotherhood. None of it made any sense. *Even if it were possible, why would a nonhuman do such a thing? How?*

Magic, that's how.

Nonsense. In six months of working around nonhumans, have you witnessed such powerful magic? The rogue had to be a human pretending to be an elph. There was a motive behind the action, a message. *But what?* The risks were too high. Rogues were clever. They rarely did anything without reason. Whoever it was had taken the boots from a dead Warden. *Oh, Mithras. What if it's a nonhuman rogue that hunts Wardens?* He felt suddenly cold at the thought.

"Is that all?" she asked, her bored, spoiled mask slipping back into place. "I've things I'd much rather do."

THREE

"Do you know a man by the name of Andrew Blackthorne?" Caius asked.

The alehouse floor was sticky beneath the soles of his boots. He hated to think of what he was standing in. It had been raining. He hoped it was only mud from the road outside.

Touching his bulbous nose, the landlord sniffed and blinked. His scarred face was spotted with boils, and his voice was hoarse. His breath stank of sour ale and garlic. "Why do you ask?"

"I wish to speak with him regarding an ongoing investigation," Caius said.

The air was thick with the merry roar of drunks, an out-of-tune fiddle, and the usual low-class alehouse stink. He'd ordered a drink, hoping this would help facilitate cooperation from the landlord, but now regretted the purchase. He set the mostly full glass down on the bar and swallowed the awful, watered beer, vowing to abandon it. The public room was cramped, made even more so by the rows of shabby, private snugs. The place overflowed with the pox-scarred, ragged, lame, and unwashed. Still, here and there, one could catch a flash of a bright silk waistcoat and white wig, or a cultured Regent Street accent. Headley Street was one of the areas frequented by rich young ruffians. Dueling was common and legal in Acrasia, provided one had a license. For those who didn't, or those who wished to gamble on them, the Golden Swan was rumored to host unlicensed duels.

"What kind of investigation is this?" the landlord asked, suspicious.

"One having nothing to do with you or your establishment, I'm sure, good sir," Caius said. He then paused, considering how much to reveal. "It is a matter related to the Brotherhood." He reached into his waistcoat pocket and showed the man his badge. "May I have your name?"

"I'm human. Got the papers to prove it," the landlord said. "And I support the Brotherhood and the Census. Everyone knows it."

"As I said, neither you nor your business are a part of my investigation," Caius said. "I only need your name to confirm who I'm speaking with."

"Name is Reggie Meade. I'm the landlord. You need to see my license?"

"There's no need for that."

"The Golden Swan is clean. I don't rent rooms to elphs," Meade said. "They can drink or fight, but only if they got the money, and they speak the Emperor's Acrasian. I'm no elph sympathizer."

"Noted," Caius said. "Now tell me what you know of Mr. Andrew Blackthorne."

"He's a duelist. One of my regulars. Fast," Reggie Meade said. "Not the best, mind you, but he's smart. He isn't in it for more than what he needs to get by, not like some of them others. Fools think fighting here will give them an advantage in the arena. Guess that's right enough, if you got training. Most don't, though. Most are the sort that can't afford dueling lessons, you know?"

Caius knew. Only the desperate resorted to the arena to gain citizenship.

"Is it my fault they die before they even get to the arena?" Meade asked. "I don't force them into it. They pay me for the privilege. Their choice to die. Not mine."

Caius felt uncomfortable about Meade's declarations but couldn't have said why. "So, Mr. Blackthorne is a citizen?"

"Don't know. Never asked," Meade said. "Easy to see by his fighting he comes from money, though. Must have fell on hard times. Happens often enough."

Getting out his graphite holder, Caius made notes. "What else do you know about him?"

"He's tricky and quick. Doesn't cheat, and he isn't a brute. Isn't in it for the kill. Doesn't prefer those sorts of fights. He doesn't do those unless he has to."

"Is he here?" Caius asked, scanning the room.

"I wish he was. Got a couple of matches I wouldn't mind having him in. Helps the odds."

"Any ideas of where I might find him?"

"Not really," Meade said. "He comes and goes. No timetable to it. Works as a Retainer, would be my guess."

"What makes you say that?"

"Wears a lot of black. Moves like one of them."

Good Retainers were highly valued by the wealthy. Caius didn't understand why someone with the skills wouldn't have a permanent patron. He wrote: *Has training. Lacks guild member-ship? Talk to Retainer's Guild.* on the blank page.

Meade continued. "Oh. And he keeps one of those little books with him. The one all the Retainers have. Thumbs through it a lot. I've seen him."

Caius felt the skin on his arms bunch up and his guts grow

cold. *It's a coincidence. Severus isn't the only person to own one of those.* He asked the question anyway. "Does he have a scar in his eyebrow? Shaped like this?" He drew an *L* on the page and showed it to Meade.

Meade's lumpy face bunched up in concentration. "Could be he did."

He'll say anything to make me happy at this point. "How long ago would you say that Mr. Blackthorne left?" Caius asked.

"I don't rightly know," Reggie Meade said. "I just know I haven't seen him in a while. A long while."

"A month? Two?" Caius asked.

"Two. Maybe three," Reggie Meade said in his gruff voice. "He'll be back, but not until spring."

"What makes you say that?" Caius asked.

"He always comes back. There's a grand lady left something for him," Reggie Meade said. "Paid me to look after it."

"A lady? Did she leave a name?"

"In this place? I think not."

"What did she look like?"

"Women like to watch the fights sometimes. Some of them like what they see and want to get an even closer look, if you know what I mean. Mr. Blackthorne impressed a few of them. He didn't go for that. She was different, though. He let her get a good look regular-like." He made a show of gazing upward at the ceiling. "Can't blame him. Pretty little thing. Good form. Dressed fancy but not too fancy. Don't know the color of her hair. She was wearing a real nice wig. Had dark eyes. Talked Regent's, like. Wore a mask. Most do around here."

"Anything else?"

"She had one of those little things on her face," Meade said. "A spot."

A patch, Caius thought.

"Was shaped like a heart," Meade said. "Had it high up on her left cheek, close to the corner of her eye."

Caius paused. He wasn't all that well versed in court styles. They changed with each season. However, his mother had taught him certain things to watch for in a woman's dress—things she felt would protect her son. Patches on the face were often used to hide blemishes—except when they weren't. The location and shape of the patch was often used to indicate a lady's politics or qualities she wished to display. He wasn't familiar with all the meanings. He didn't attend lofty social gatherings. Thus, he had no need to know. However, that particular combination was one that he *did* understand. He wrote out the word and underlined it before continuing with his questions: *whore*. And a high-priced one at that. *It might explain Mr. Blackthorne's employment habits.* Retainers did not regularly employ whores. They weren't known to form relationship bonds. *At least not the ones who held guild membership.*

"Interesting. And what did she leave for Mr. Blackthorne?" Caius asked.

"A chest." Meade finished pouring a pint of beer and passed it to one of the patrons in exchange for a few coins. Another patron requested and paid for a fresh pipe stem and tobacco.

When Meade was finished Caius asked, "And what's in the chest?"

"Don't know," Meade said. "Was told not to open it. Figured it was no business of mine. Since the lady paid me to make certain it stayed locked, figured it even more so. I'm an honest man."

Having tasted Meade's beer, Caius had his doubts regarding that statement but kept his opinions to himself. "May I see it?"

Meade's face acquired a thoughtful look. One of the

barmaids, a tall woman with short curly hair and dark skin, signaled a need to place an order. "A moment, sir." He went to the end of the bar.

Preparing himself to make another investment, Caius reached again into his pocket.

"You don't have to pay the man," a woman's voice said in a familiar, bitter tone. "He'll do it for nothing. Just to be helpful to the Brotherhood. Don't they teach you cadets anything?"

"I'm not a cadet." Turning, Caius saw it was Captain Drake. He moved his overcoat out of the way and tugged at his uniform collar. "I'm a full Inspector Warden now."

Drake raised an eyebrow. "Congratulations on the promotion."

"What are you doing here?" he asked

"What does it look like?" Drake asked. "I'm drinking."

"Why would you drink here?" Caius asked. "The beer is terrible."

"I know better than to order the beer." She swallowed the last of a short glass of what smelled like whiskey. "Don't let on you know it's bad. He'll only spit in whatever you order later. Pour it out on the floor or give it to someone else while he's not looking."

"Oh." *That explains the state of the floor,* Caius thought.

"If you're here for the fights, nothing starts until after dark," she said. "Makes it less likely the Watch will raid the place."

"Aren't you a Watch captain?" Caius asked.

"Not here, I'm not," Drake said, turning her back to the bar and propping her elbows on it. "Not for what I'm paid." She showed him her teeth.

Meade returned. "I see you finished your beer. Would you like another?"

"No, thank you," Caius said. "I'm on duty."

"Oh, I see," Meade said. "I suppose there's no harm in showing the chest to you. You being a Warden and all. It's me being a good citizen, like. I am one, you know." He signaled he was leaving to the dark bar maid. "Come with me."

Drake winked. She mouthed the words: *I told you so.*

In stark contrast to the public room, the alehouse office was tidy. It certainly smelled better.

"It's over here," Meade said and opened a large cupboard.

Inside, Caius saw a small, dark brown wardrobe trunk bound with sturdy black leather bands. Although not new, it didn't appear to be that old, either.

"She brought this in by herself?" Caius asked. "It looks heavy."

"She had a servant do it for her," Meade said. "I should return to my customers. If you wish, you may stay and . . . examine the chest. Just let me know when you leave so that I might secure the door." He placed a key on top of the trunk.

"Thank you," Caius said.

Meade left. As soon as the door closed, Caius knelt down on the floor and used the key. Inside, he discovered men's clothes of various styles, most were of the make those of the middling sort tended to wear. All in muted colors. Nothing too flashy. What was unusual was what he found in the bottom, buried beneath the clothes: jars and tins of different-colored pastes. He opened the first, dipped a finger into the greasy, black substance inside, and sniffed it. The scent brought up memories from childhood school holidays.

He'd hated doing so, but his mother had insisted he attend Church-sponsored theatrics. Caius muttered his surprise out loud. "Actor's pigments? Why would a duelist have need of actor's pigments?"

⊰ NELS ⊱

ONE

Thirty-First of Verikuu, 1783

With no free hand to open the door to the infirmary, Nels kicked it open. He was met with the scent of distilled herbs, soap, and medicines. Westola was right behind them, her surgeon's bag in hand. Nels staggered into the room and got the semiconscious Blackthorne onto the examination table with Private Filppula's help. It was then that Nels noticed that Ilta had anticipated their arrival. Everything had been readied. The kettle she used to boil water was hanging over the hearth flames. The unwelcome thought that Suvi had once been bitten by a malorum and had survived without the aid of the Silmaillia cropped up in Nels's mind.

Blackthorne saved us. I should be grateful. What in the abyss is wrong with me? Ashamed, Nels didn't like the person he was becoming, but he didn't know what to do with the unwanted emotions. They were too intense to ignore. That had been the reason he'd hesitated to stop Nurvi. War meant that no one came away clean. *Ever.* Atrocities had been committed on both sides of the fight. War changed people. It left scars. He knew this. He also knew that seeing past the damage done was the only way forward. Eledore could not continue to exist without the Acrasian refugees. *Nurvi will have to be reprimanded. Publicly. And soon.*

Ilta crossed the room with a bowl filled with steaming bandages. Her lips were tight, and she didn't meet his gaze.

Bemused, Nels watched her cut the leg of Blackthorne's bloodstained trousers up to the hip with a pair of scissors. Blackthorne was unable to protest, nor was he able to hear a word she said, for which Nels was profoundly grateful.

"Nurvi behaved like a bully," she whispered.

Her anger was so quiet that none of the others could hear.

He said, "I know. I'll handle it."

"Good."

Nels's thoughts raced back to those who'd died. *I'm in charge. The troops look to me for a standard of behavior. An undisciplined mob would be a disaster. Like it or not, Slate made the right choice to bring Blackthorne here. We need him. But can we trust him?*

Do we have a choice?

"Give me that cloth," she said. Her tone had softened. She'd switched her focus to her patient.

"This one?" Nels asked, lifting the bandage with the tongs resting on top.

"Yes. And then wash your hands and those tongs. Take off that filthy coat. I need an assistant," Ilta said.

"Isn't that what Westola is here for?" Nels asked.

That earned him another glare. "She's finishing the antidote.

Bring that basin on the table there. And that tray," Ilta said, pointing. "Hurry up."

He did as he was told. It wasn't the typical role of a soldier, but it wasn't the first time he'd assisted her, nor was it the first time he'd handled a bandage. Since he didn't have the standard powers of a leader, he collected every useful skill he could. However, that didn't mean he was comfortable. He hadn't had time to perform a cleansing ritual. The thought of tainting her work when Blackthorne's life depended upon it worried Nels.

After washing and shedding his coat, he returned. His left arm was now bare to the cool room. Feeling ridiculous in a one-armed shirt, he rolled up his right sleeve. Ilta used a damp cloth to clean Blackthorne's wounds in deft, expert motions. Unconscious, Blackthorne muttered something.

"What did he say?" Nels asked. He could've sworn it was something about eyes and blood.

"I didn't catch it," Ilta said. "He's delirious. It's not important." She seemed to finally notice Nels's missing sleeve. Her gaze traveled to the once-white linen scrap that had been knotted around Blackthorne's thigh. She blinked.

It wasn't until this moment that Nels understood he might've done otherwise.

Ilta laid her hands on Blackthorne's bare thigh and closed her eyes.

Immediately, Blackthorne sat up with a violent jerk. "No!" He would've fallen from the examination table if Nels hadn't caught him.

"Hold him!"

Blackthorne fought for freedom with all his strength. It was all Nels could do to keep him on the table. If Viktor hadn't grabbed the man's legs, they'd have landed on the floor in a heap. As it was, it took him, Viktor, and Westola to keep the ex-Warden stretched out on the table—and still he fought.

"Relax. You've been hurt. You're safe. I'm only checking your condition." Ilta spoke to Blackthorne in soothing tones. "You're going to be all right. But you must let me examine you."

"Get away from me! Don't touch me!" Blackthorne's unbruised eye was wide and unseeing. He didn't seem to understand. His face was at once gray and feverish. "Let me go!"

"It must be the poison," Westola said. "He's out of his head."

"Keep him still," Ilta said. "I can't do anything with him like this."

Westola grunted as she caught a knee to the face. "We're doing what we can."

Nels lay across Blackthorne's chest, anchoring him with his weight. Westola moved to Blackthorne's free arm and applied what force she could on the man's shoulders. Viktor had Blackthorne's legs. Still, he struggled to buck them off. Nels was stunned the man had that much strength left.

"You don't have to be afraid," Ilta said. "I won't amputate. There's no need. Can you hear me? Please don't worry. You won't lose your leg. Relax. Everything will be all right." She replaced her hands on his bare skin and made another attempt to read his condition.

Blackthorne's screams devolved into a coughing fit. Westola, well used to the signals, leaned back. Nels didn't. Blackthorne was violently ill before Nels had time to register what was wrong. He was only able to turn his head before warm vomit splashed his bare shoulder and soaked his clothing.

So much for this shirt, Nels thought.

Ilta stepped back, shock registering on her face. "Oh."

"What is it?" Westola asked over Blackthorne's fevered protests.

Recovering her professional demeanor, Ilta finally said,

"He—He's lost a lot of blood, but not too much. There's a great deal of venom in his veins, and his heart rate is high." She looked confused.

Nels asked, "What's wrong?"

Ilta said, "I don't know why he isn't dead."

Westola said, "Well, he'll resolve that himself if we don't get that gash closed. We can't leave that tourniquet on his leg forever."

Ilta nodded. "And I can't work on him like this."

"Should I try?" Westola asked.

"I don't know if the reaction is to my power or—or something else," Ilta said.

"All right. Do you want to knock him out, or should I?" Westola asked.

Ilta said, "You should do it. Use indirect magic, though. Just in case. Another strong response like that will kill him."

"What do you have prepared?" Westola asked.

Ilta bit her lip in thought. Then she indicated a set of shelves with a sideways nod. "On the shelf marked 'Desensitize.' The jar labeled 'Mixture Three: Strong.'"

"I'm letting go now." Westola released her hold on Blackthorne's arm.

Nels tried to capture it before getting hit and failed.

"I don't think the reaction is a physical one," Ilta said in a thoughtful tone.

"Feels physical to me," Viktor said with a grunt as Blackthorne's remaining boot twisted in his gut.

Closing her eyes, Ilta said, "I suspect it's emotional. But I'm not sure."

"You'd better be damned sure," Westola said, returning with the jar.

"He'll die anyway. We have to try."

Westola nodded. She spooned a portion of the mixture into a glass and then focused on the contents. Next, she laid a hand on Blackthorne's jaw. "Bite me, you brute, and you'll be sorry. You hear?" She pried his mouth open and poured the magicked mixture down his throat. Then she clamped his jaw shut with the same motions Nels had seen used on reluctant animals.

Blackthorne let out one last robust protest and slumped.

"Is he alive?" Ilta asked, and pushed stray hair from her eyes with the back of a hand.

"For the moment," Westola said. "Work fast. I don't know how long that will keep him down. I've never seen anyone fight a healing like this."

Ilta selected a surgeon's knife from the tray and began her work.

TWO

Blinking to clear his eyes of sleep, Nels slapped the seat of the chair next to his bed, where he'd tossed his clothes. The room was dark but for the light filtering in from the half-open door. His belt buckle clanged against the chair's wooden back, where he'd draped it the night before. His painful and blind attempts to locate his pocket watch knocked the belt onto the floor with a clank. At last, he found the watch and released the catch to open it. Tilting its face to the light, he read the time. He groaned and placed it on top of the rumpled clothes. "Is someone dying?" he asked in Eledorean.

"No," Viktor said.

"Then go away, you sodding bastard," Nels said, covering his ears with a pillow. "It's a quarter to seven! What in the swiving hells are you doing here?"

"I love you, too, my darling."

"Piss off before I gut you!"

Viktor worried at both pillow and blankets like a terrier. "Wakey, wakey, Colonel Sleepyhead."

"I didn't get to bed down until half past five. Why didn't Mustonen lock that damned door like I asked?"

"He's the one who let me in."

"Remind me to demote him." Nels rolled over.

Viktor prized the blankets out of his grip. "Mustonen made breakfast."

Chilled, Nels swatted at the missing blankets and got enough purchase to free them from Viktor. "It's only stale crispbread and cheese." Determined, he retreated once more to the warmth beneath layers of quilts and pillows.

"Blankets or coffee," Viktor said. "Which is it to be?"

Nels sniffed the air with his eyes half-closed. The nutty scent of hot coffee made his stomach grumble. He sat up and reached for the cup.

Viktor moved it out of reach. "Feet on the floor," he said. "I'm too familiar with your tricks."

"I'll have Suvi roast you on a spit!"

"You'll have to get out of bed to do it. Her Majesty will take my side, I'm thinking." Viktor moved the steaming cup under his own nose and breathed deep. "Mmmmm. Smells great. Maybe one little sip."

"That's mine! Don't you dare!" Nels leapt out of bed and snatched the cup with painful, stiff hands. Hot coffee scalded both his tongue and the roof of his mouth. Still, he cherished the bitter taste. "No honey?"

"First of Winter is over. We're back on rations."

Nels's knuckles issued painful protests in spite of the warmth. His head joined the chorus. *How much apple snap did I drink?* Suddenly, a bone-deep ache penetrated the soles of his bare feet. He leapt back onto the rug, spilling coffee in the process. "Oh, gods! Whose brilliant idea was it to live in a burial mound with stone floors?" A pair of stockings hit him in the stomach and landed in the cooling coffee puddle.

Viktor said, "Her Majesty has called a council this morning. We're to meet in Councilor Slate's apartments in a quarter of an hour."

Nels retrieved his stockings. Holding them by the tops, he checked how much liquid had soaked into the red wool. He decided to wear them anyway. "Why?"

"The queen wishes to discuss last night's attack."

Nels thought with a twinge of those they'd had to leave behind. "I won't have anything worth a full report until we can recover the bodies. And no one is going out there until the sun is up. She knows that won't happen until late afternoon, and only for a few hours."

"I don't think that's entirely what she has in mind to discuss." Viktor gave him a knowing expression.

Memories of the night before slid back into Nels's consciousness. "Oh. Shit," he said, flexing his angry and abused knuckles. "You had Nurvi confined to his apartments like I asked?"

"I had Sebastian take care of it."

"Good. Have him remain there until further notice." Nels threw on his cleanest clothes and stationed himself in front of the hearth to pull on his boots. The crispbread was laid out on a tray next to the coffee service. He forced down his breakfast between swallows of coffee.

"Now that you're awake, I've some good news," Viktor said. "Private Oramo stumbled in an hour ago."

"Thank the goddess. How did she manage to survive?"

"No one knows yet. She's reticent, but that's to be expected. I sent Sebastian to chat with her. If anyone can gently wedge details out of her, he can."

Nels nodded.

When he was ready, he walked with Viktor to Slate's apartments.

From the time James Slate had assumed the First of Council role, his drawing room had functioned as an audience chamber. Normally, it had a comfortable atmosphere. It was furnished with a writing desk and other mismatched furniture scavenged from the ruins of nearby Gardemeister. Rows of bookshelves crowded the walls, adding a studious aura. Some of the books Slate had brought with him from Acrasia. The others had been rescued by Nels himself from various ruins all over Eledore. A seascape of a Waterborne ship weathering a storm rested on the mantel. High above and on the wall to the right of the fireplace, many-paned windows traced a line under the vaulted ceiling. Their narrow black rectangles were half-covered with snow. A peat fire heated the room to a cozy temperature.

Two worn but serviceable sofas had been positioned near the fireplace. Blackthorne lay stretched out on one with Ilta at his side. *What is he doing here?* Nels caught Suvi's cool expression. As for Blackthorne, Nels thought a mountain lion dragged several miles behind a horse would've looked better. Wrapped in blankets and with the bandaged leg propped up on a stack of pillows, the ex-Warden seemed both weak and sick. The malorum venom was more to blame than the fight. *But it didn't help.* In truth, Nels hadn't expected Blackthorne to live to see the morning. Blackthorne's normally light tan face was grey, making the bruised eye stand out even more. Nels noted with a small amount of relief that while it'd been swollen shut the night before, now it was only slightly so.

Slate cleared his throat, and everyone turned to face him. He wasn't wearing his spectacles. "Welcome, everyone. Now that we're all here, we should get started. I understand we've a great deal to discuss."

Scanning the room for a place to sit, Nels chose a place next to Suvi and Dylan.

"Kat made some coffee, if you'd like it," Slate said. "I understand a number of you were up rather late last night."

"About that. We need to address last night's . . . altercation between Underlieutenant Nurvi and Mr. Blackthorne. We cannot tolerate such behavior in an officer of the Eledorean army. We cannot afford to let anyone believe that we condone ill-treatment of Acrasian refugees by our military," Suvi said.

Nels said, "I agree. Underlieutenant Nurvi is currently confined to his quarters until further notice."

"Is there a plan for further disciplinary action?" Suvi asked.

"He's being demoted to sergeant," Nels said. "A dishonorable discharge wouldn't resolve the problem. In fact, it might make the matter worse. And then there's the other reason."

"Yes?" Suvi asked.

"Our numbers are low enough as it is," Nels said. "And based upon last night, this winter we're going to need every soldier we have."

Suvi nodded. "Very well. I will consider the situation resolved." She turned to Slate. "Unless you have something to add, Councilor?"

"An apology would, I feel, be appropriate," Slate said.

"Very well." Nels attempted to think of Blackthorne as anything but a Warden as he turned to face the man. "My officer should not have acted as he did. I should have stepped in sooner. My deepest apologies."

"An apology is unnecessary." Blackthorne's voice was quiet and hoarse.

"I strongly disagree," Nels said, fighting another angry outburst. *Must everything the man does upset me?* "What happened was inexcusable."

Blackthorne swallowed. He was obviously uncomfortable. Nels watched him glance at Slate—subordinate to superior.

That's curious.

Slate nodded. And with that, Blackthorne ceased all resistance. "Your apology is accepted."

Nels nodded and hoped against hope that this would, in fact, be the end of it. He studied the former Warden for any sign of lingering antagonism.

Blackthorne lay with several blankets pulled tight over his torso. His legs were stretched out, feet propped up by the arm of the sofa. His lanky frame gave off a relaxed confidence, as if he were not overly concerned by any possible threat. He was tall for an Acrasian—only an inch or two shorter than Nels himself. His shoulders were broad, and the ridiculously too-tight rag of a coat he habitually wore made him appear even thinner. Shaggy black hair hung in his face, and his upper lip and chin were covered with a close-scissored beard. He hadn't shaved, and his cheeks were dappled with coarse stubble. Combined with the sober demeanor, it gave him a mature aspect. The color of his skin, the high cheekbones, the shape of his eyes, and his narrow face, all might have caused Nels to mistake him for a young kainen from Ytlain or Marren. With his hair hanging about his shoulders and hiding his ears, the never-changing pale grey eyes were the only giveaway that Blackthorne wasn't. The ridiculous coat excepted, his clothes were made of fine cloth that had been expertly tailored. All were shabby from too much wear. His feet were large and encased in finely made boots that had, like the rest of him, seen better days. Looking closer, Nels noticed that the decoration had been removed from the folded tops. A button, he supposed. That reminded him of something, but he couldn't remember what it was at the moment.

"Now that the matter is resolved," Suvi said, "we will move on to the next order of business."

Nels nodded, knowing perfectly well this wouldn't be the last he'd hear of it.

"Your Grace, not everyone has been formally introduced," Slate said. "Perhaps we should begin there?"

"Very well then," Suvi said.

"Your Royal Highness, Queen Suvi Ilmari of Eledore." Slate indicated each individual with a hand motion. "Colonel Nels Hännenen, Commander of the Royal Eledorean Army, and Dylan Kask, Ambassador from the Waterborne Nations. This is Mr. Andrew Blackthorne from Acrasia."

Nels asked, "And what is his real name?"

"Asylum seekers from Acrasia often take assumed names," Slate said. His face was expressionless, but his clenching jaw made it clear his patience was already wearing thin. "The Council thought it best to permit this under the circumstances. For everyone's protection. A fresh start is what we're all here for, after all."

Nels said, "Eledore is not ruled by a Council."

"You are correct. *I* rule Eledore," Suvi said. "However, the Council operates with my approval and oversight." Her words were cool and her eyes changed from a calm black to a hard copper. "And I have reviewed the Council's ruling in the matter, and it stands."

"But—"

Suvi asked, "Are you planning on fighting *me*, Nels?"

"Of course not."

"Eledore can't be what it was, and even if it could be, I wouldn't want it to. What it was is partly responsible for its collapse," Suvi said.

Opening his mouth to protest, he shut it again the instant his sister motioned for silence.

"Yes, the Acrasian Regnum invaded, but Old Eledore was crumbling to ruin long before that," Suvi said. "In the end, even

Father admitted his inattentiveness didn't help. He should've listened to you, for one thing."

Nels looked away and nodded.

Suvi continued. "That said, I've no intention of repeating Father's mistakes. We must adapt. We *will* adapt. New Eledore will be forged from what survives, and this Council is a part of that process."

"You're right," Nels said. He straightened and faced James Slate. "My mistake. I apologize."

"Apology accepted," Slate said. "You're only protecting Her Majesty's interests per your duty. I can see that."

"But not all the changes being implemented here are being openly discussed," Nels said, turning his attention to Suvi. "Some aspects of Eledorean culture are being discarded without thought. Shouldn't we give that more consideration?"

"Conservation of Eledorean culture is one of the reasons why we celebrated the First of Winter this year," Suvi said. "I've met with Councilor Slate, and we've begun a list of other projects. Do you have an item that needs to be added?"

Nels decided to bring up something that had been bothering him for some time. "Acrasian is becoming the de facto language spoken in New Eledore, and that can't happen."

Slate frowned. "I understood Acrasian was one of your interests before the war."

"It was," Nels said. "But that is very different from what is happening here now."

"I don't understand," Slate said.

"Language has a part in what makes a nation a nation," Nels said.

Suvi paused. "Nels is right. We should discuss the matter in detail. Of course, I'm not sure now is the time."

"Fine," Nels said. "When?"

Slate said, "It's a complicated subject."

"I disagree. The Acrasian Regnum destroyed Old Eledore. And the process of governing in New Eledore is being conducted in Acrasian. Do you not see the problem?"

"What language the people speak in the Hold isn't a conscious choice."

"Shouldn't it be?" Nels asked, interrupting.

"Acrasian is spoken because the Acrasian speakers outnumber Eledorean speakers when you and your troops aren't residing here. It's merely a natural result of a cultural difference in the population of refugees versus New Eledore's army—"

"I didn't say it was planned," Nels said. "What I am saying is that we must make active decisions about what aspects of Old Eledore will thrive in New Eledore. Before the decision is taken from us."

Slate said, "We're not taking—"

"You're not listening to me."

"You're making bad assumptions," Slate said.

"I disagree."

"If I hated Eledore and wanted to destroy it," Slate said, "I certainly wouldn't have left a comfortable life in Novus Salernum to do it. I'm attempting to help—"

"Why?" Nels asked.

"Nels, stop," Ilta said. Then she spoke to Slate. "James, I know you're a compassionate, thoughtful person. However, Nels is attempting to tell you something important. Do you remember our discussion about context?"

"This isn't the same thing," Slate said.

"I suspect otherwise," Ilta said.

"Then I'll illustrate. The Waterborne Nations have managed

to maintain their cultural identity in spite of an influx of a large number of asylum seekers throughout their history," James Slate said. "Would you agree?"

Nels shrugged.

Slate asked, "Ambassador Kask, how many languages do you speak?"

"Ten," Dylan said. "Not including three dialects of Ocealandic."

"Do you see?" James Slate folded his arms across his chest.

Nels didn't take his gaze from Slate. "Dylan, what was the first language you learned?"

Dylan said, "Ocealandic. North Aegrerian dialect."

"What is the language you speak on board your ship among your family?" Nels asked.

"Ocealandic," Dylan said. "North Aegrerian dialect."

"I'll go farther and ask one last question," Nels said. "Dylan, how often have the Waterborne Nations been conquered?"

"Never," Dylan said.

Nels turned to Slate. "Your example doesn't correlate."

"Ah." Slate sighed, and his face reddened. His shoulders dropped. "I ... begin to understand your perspective. The implication was unintentional. I needed to—to prioritize."

"And that was the right decision," Nels said. "The safety of those remaining had to come first. It's still the case. But if we lose our identity, ourselves, what is the point in surviving?" From the corner of his eye, he sensed a powerful emotional reaction from the ex-Warden, but before he could understand what it was, it was gone. *Interesting.*

Nels went back to his argument. "We cannot permit Acrasian to be established as the dominant language. If we do, New Eledore becomes a mere territory of Acrasia."

Suvi frowned. "I'm inclined to side with Nels in this," she said.

"We will meet again tomorrow and discuss what actions should be taken."

"Speaking of, I need to draw attention to a small matter," Ilta said.

Suvi motioned for her to continue.

"It's obvious that Nels has valuable contributions to make," Ilta said. "And our Council *could* use more members."

Oh, shit, Nels thought.

Raising an eyebrow, Suvi said, "Isn't he already on the Council?"

Ilta shook her head. "We asked him, but . . ."

"I see," Suvi said. "Nels, is there a reason you rejected the invitation?"

Of course there is. Nels shifted in his chair, uneasy about where the conversation was now going. "I wouldn't be of use."

"Really?" Suvi's eyes narrowed.

"I spend most of my time away from the Hold," Nels said.

Suvi said, "Absence didn't make Father any less responsible. Ruling was his duty."

"My duty is to lead your army, gather supplies, and harass the Regnum as long as they live on our land," Nels said. "Isn't that responsibility enough?"

Suvi said, "And what if I told you that I need you to serve on the Council, too?"

"I'd still say no," Nels said.

"Why?" Suvi asked.

"You know perfectly well why," Nels said. "I'm a soldier. Killers do not hold government power in Eledore."

"Are you going to pretend that Uncle Sakari was innocent of murder simply because he didn't shed blood?" Suvi said. Now *her* face was red. "There was more to blood custom than the literal meaning, and far too many nobles trod that crooked line in whatever way suited them. They abused the law, and that was a big part of what was wrong with Old Eledore."

Suvi spoke to Slate. "Did you know that there were very few criminals in Old Eledore?"

"I had heard that, Your Highness," Slate said.

"Eledore wasn't morally superior, I assure you," Suvi said. "It was due to the fact that the accused was given a choice between a dungeon or the military. And if Eledore's nobility hadn't spent a great deal of lives on frivolous infighting, we would've had a very large military."

"Interesting," Slate said.

Nels's face grew hot.

"It's also no coincidence that soldiers were ostracized," Suvi said. "That they lived in walled-off communities, not entirely different from prisons. And they did so without the full rights of other Eledorean citizens." She paused before continuing. "Blood Custom will not be practiced in New Eledore, Nels. I won't allow it."

By now, Nels was certain that even the tips of his ears were red. He glanced at Ilta and saw what he thought was the hint of a smile. *She's enjoying this.*

Ilta said, "You bet I am."

A bolt of frozen panic burst in his chest.

Ilta put a hand over her mouth. "Sorry."

"Perhaps the matter of Council membership should be tabled until tomorrow," Slate said.

"There will be no debate," Suvi said. "As its commander, Nels will represent the military on the Council."

With that, Nels resigned himself to doing what she wanted. *For now.*

An uncomfortable silence stretched out before Slate said, "Returning to the subject of assumed names . . . No one here is required to give information that might prove dangerous to their person. Blackthorne is no exception."

"So you're protecting him," Nels said.

"No more than I am anyone else in this room," Slate said.

"Yet he has our identities—mine and my sister's," Nels said. "I would hardly call the situation equitable. Both of us have a rather large price on our heads."

"As does Blackthorne," Slate said.

Nels said, "I hardly think his danger is the same as—"

Blackthorne's voice was quiet. "Aurelius Aureus Severus, recognized bastard of Duke Aurelius Aureus Corvinus."

Ilta started at the word "bastard."

"Do you need more?" Blackthorne asked. "I can name the estate where I was born." It was clear by his posture that he was holding strong emotions in check. Yet he kept the heat of his gaze directed at the floor in subservience.

It was at odds with everything Nels knew of Wardens. "I—I suppose that will do."

Placing a hand to his injured leg, Blackthorne winced.

"You're a duke?" Ilta asked. She went to him and began checking the bandage.

For reasons Nels didn't want to think about, the action sent a surge of rage through him.

"I didn't say that," Blackthorne said.

"This place is for Eledorean refugees, not the Acrasian nobility's castoffs." Nels saw Blackthorne's hand twitch into a fist and knew he'd hit a nerve.

Ilta's shocked expression made Nels feel like a bully.

Nels asked, "Why is he here?"

"In the Hold?" Slate asked. "The time for that debate is past."

"What is the purpose of this meeting?" Nels asked.

"I wished to begin plans for a certain venture," Suvi said. "This spring I will send a small group to Novus Salernum to retrieve a cache of weapons. A large number of highly valuable Eledorean water steel swords were stolen by the Acrasian Regnum during the war. And I want them back."

"I can inform Nickols," James Slate said. His quill scratched against the page in the ledger laid open on his writing desk. "When do you need him to leave?"

Suvi paused. "I would rather not give this to Nickols."

"Why not?" James Slate asked, looking up from his notes.

"Because Nickols, while useful, is a blunt instrument," Suvi said. "I need someone more . . . discreet."

"Do you have someone in mind?" James Slate asked.

Suvi said, "I do."

Nels prepared himself to hear that he was to be sent into the heart of the Regnum. *It's suicide,* he thought. *But she knows I'll go anyway.* He swallowed.

"Blackthorne?" Suvi asked. "Would you go—"

"Why him?" Nels asked.

"Because he knows Novus Salernum better than anyone," Suvi said. "Because he has proven that he can get in and out of the city safely and quietly."

"I will go," Blackthorne said. He looked like he was going to be sick. "Although I do not want to, but if it's what you require of me, I will."

Slate asked, "Where are the swords being kept? Do we know?"

"They're being stored in a secured military depot maintained by the Emperor," Dylan said.

Blackthorne choked.

"I made an agreement with Clan Kask, and I intend to honor it," Suvi said. "The Waterborne have need of them to combat malorum.

Therefore, one hundred of the blades will be given to Clan Kask to distribute as they will. The rest, we will keep."

Suddenly, Nels began to understand that this portion of the conversation had, in part, been staged for his benefit, and he wasn't the only one. He turned to Blackthorne. The Warden looked downright ashen.

Suvi didn't invite him here for an apology, Nels thought.

"Councilor Slate," Suvi said. "I would like a detailed report involving the layout of the depot and its security—anything Blackthorne will need to know in order to plan his assignment."

Slate nodded. "I will send messages to my contacts in Novus Salernum."

"Actually," Darius said, "I would like to volunteer my services, if Your Grace approves. I can ensure that Councilor Slate's messages get to their intended recipients safely, as well as their replies."

"Do it," Suvi said. "Mr. Blackthorne? I assume you won't be able to move several hundred swords alone. Once you have what you need from Councilor Slate, I want to see your proposal. I want your recommendations on who you'll need to go to Novus Salernum with you. My only requirement is that my brother be involved and consulted. Understood?"

"Yes, Your Highness," Blackthorne said.

"Good," Suvi said. "Now—"

Nels turned when a loud commotion erupted in the hallway outside. The door swung open, and Corporal Eriksson pushed past a still-protesting Lucy Mayfair, Ilta's apprentice.

"Mr. Slate?! Colonel Hännenen?!"

Nels jumped to his feet, and Viktor followed him across the room.

"What is it?" Slate asked.

Corporal Eriksson was hatless and there was snow in his hair.

"It's Private Oramo. She's dead, sir. Risku and that new korva are both missing."

"Annikki?" Buttoning his jacket, Nels asked, "Is it an . . . attack?" He was reluctant to name the creatures from the night before.

"I don't think so, sir. Looks like a fight. They found Oramo's body in the barn. Tracks lead into the woods." Out of breath, Eriksson added, "No one has gone out to look for Annikki. Your orders. But Lieutenant Sundstet sent me for you, sir."

"What happened?" Slate asked.

"Did Annikki kill Oramo?" Nels asked. He hoped not. Such a thing hadn't happened before under his command, but that didn't mean he didn't live in fear of recruiting the wrong person at the wrong time. He hadn't been too exacting in accepting volunteers. It wasn't as if the army had ever been comprised of Eledore's best.

"No one knows," Eriksson said. "That's why Lieutenant Sundstet sent me for you and Captain Reini, sir."

Nels moved to the exit. "Come on, Eriksson. We'll stop by my rooms. I'll need my all-weather."

Blackthorne struggled to get to his feet.

"Blackthorne, exactly where do you think you're going?" Slate asked.

"If it's a malorum, they'll need me, sir."

"Stay where you are," Slate said.

"Colonel Hännenen?" Blackthorne asked.

Nels turned. "What is it?"

"Malorum move fast. You won't know what you're dealing with until it's too close. Arm with blunderbusses," Blackthorne said. "And load them with the silver shot from my pack. Wherever that ended up."

"The infirmary," Ilta said.

"The infirmary," Blackthorne said.

"All right," Nels said. "Viktor, stop by the infirmary and get the silver shot. Eriksson, grab a couple of blunderbusses from the armory and then meet me in the barn."

"Yes, sir," Eriksson said.

The scent of animal dung and hay reached Nels's nose long before he arrived at his destination. The barn wasn't a separate building, not technically. It was, like most of the Hold, hidden inside the mountain and connected with winding tunnels. Also, like the rest of the Hold, it'd been built by Eledoreans centuries before Suvi had leased it to Clan Kask for a warehouse. There were quite a few such sites long abandoned in the mountain ranges of Eledore, and not all of them had remained burial mounds—evidence that the people had survived contact with the Old Ones in the past.

An outward-facing chamber on the ground floor, the barn was what Nels considered one of the Hold's few defensive weak spots. Horses, cows, goats, sheep, and reindeer needed access to grazing areas. They were an important part of the Hold's food supply. Unfortunately, large groups of domestic animals in one place were also a problem. *Wardens are trackers, after all*. Farm animals were also attractive targets for wolves and mountain lions. For that reason, he kept guards stationed in the barn. His troops viewed the task as the most boring and pointless of all possible assignments.

He rounded the corner and was brought up short by what he saw.

A harsh wind lashed the dim interior of the barn, and half the lanterns were out. The barn doors swung half off their hinges, creaking and banging against stone. Snow poured in. A wagon and several storage crates had been damaged. Three of the wooden stalls closest to the exit had been ripped apart. The sheep huddled inside their pen, but the goats roamed free. A dead mare and quite a few cattle lay in the debris. The living animals were terrified, and their panicked attempts at freedom echoed inside the room. The noise was deafening.

"Get some light in here!" *Loimuta? Is he safe?* Nels searched for a sign in the semidarkness but returned his attention to more important things.

He approached the first dead animal and knelt. The wound at the mare's throat looked far too familiar. They now had even bigger problems to hand. *Winter, even in southern Eledore, is going to be very dark indeed.* "Where's Oramo?"

Corporal Eriksson said, "Here, sir." He crouched in the snow near the door.

Kneeling next to Oramo's body, Nels spotted the knife wound in her throat with some relief. He checked for a pulse out of habit and then gazed into the blustery night. Pelted with snow and ice, he stood. Then he yanked the lapel of his all-weather coat up and buttoned it so that it covered both nose and mouth. "Viktor?" Nels asked. "What's the news?"

"Hard to say in all this," Viktor said. "There are three sets of tracks. Oramo, Annikki, and Risku. Risku is the only one who wears hobnails no matter the occasion. Like you do."

"But that was done by a malorum," Nels said, motioning to the mare. "Surely it left some sign?"

"The one we saw?" Viktor's question was more like a statement. "It had feet. If there was a malorum in this barn, it had hooves."

Nels nodded. Viktor gave him a look that was easy to read. He wanted permission to go out into the storm.

Risku and Annikki are out there. Viktor can handle himself, Nels thought. That only brought up images from the night before. He'd lost eight before he'd known it. *It'll be daylight soon.*

And exactly how bright is it going to get in this storm?

"I must go now while there's a chance of finding them," Viktor whispered. "I won't go far. Neither will they, I'm thinking. Not in this."

"How will you even know where to look?" Nels asked.

Viktor winked. "You're cute when you worry."

"Sod off," Nels said, and then whispered. "There's a malorum out there. It won't be friendly."

"And I have silver shot and a very nasty disposition," Viktor said, and then grew serious. "You have to let me go. This is what I do. I'll bring back Annikki and Risku. Alive. I'm the only one who can, and you know it."

At that moment, Nels knew that Viktor was terrified. Nels said, "I'll go with you."

Viktor gazed through the gaping barn doors. "If this situation required a sharpshooter, I'd be glad of the company. But out there? In that? You'll only slow me down."

"All right," Nels said. He paused. Reaching inside his coat and jacket, he found the silver medallion he wore under his shirt. It'd been a gift from his real father. "Put this on."

Viktor's eyes widened as he watched the medal swing on its chain. "I can't. That's *yours*. You know I—"

"It's silver," Nels said. "Do not argue with me. Put it on."

Nodding, Viktor accepted it and then looped it around his neck.

"When you return, give it back," Nels said. "Now go." He stood up and dusted the snow and dirt off his already-soggy trousers. He tried not to watch Viktor vanish into the swirling dark.

Hasta's blessing go with you, my friend, Nels thought. "Let's clean this mess and get that door barred."

Viktor returned an hour later with Annikki. Risku was lost in the storm.

⫷ DRAKE ⫸

2 DECEMBER
THE TWENTY-FIRST YEAR IN THE SACRED REIGN
OF EMPEROR HERMINIUS

For the third time that day, Captain Drake stared at a license card and compared it to the man sitting opposite her, with suppressed revulsion. Happily, this was the final interview and marked the last of the trophy checks. She'd had her fill after the first foul-smelling storeroom and wished she could send Benbow alone for the next inspection but knew that wasn't an option. It was simply too dangerous. She remembered well the Warden's warnings. After what she'd seen, they'd be impossible to forget.

Remember what you are. Remember who you are. And never be alone with a hunter if you can help it—not if you expect to live through this.

The current hunter perched on the hard chair opposite her appeared to be an ordinary citizen—perhaps too ordinary. His scant black hair had been worked into a tiny queue-braid at the nape of his neck. He had heavy eyelids, thin lips, and no visible scars. Oddly, his clothes were unremarkable for someone of his social stature, and his posture was submissive to the point of cowering. Nothing about him drew attention or revealed his status. More importantly, nothing outward indicated the monstrous thoughts that lurked inside his head.

She let the prepared speech roll off her tongue. "My Lord Baron, you've been summoned to my office for proof of hunting regulation compliance. This is a random check, and I am to inform you that your residence will be searched after this interview. As you know, you are required to retain a tag for all trophies per regulations. And you are to provide proper documentation of said trophies upon inspection."

Arion gave her a frightened nod from the chair. "I will gladly give whatever assistance is requested." His voice was nasal and breathy. He smelled of tobacco and something else she couldn't quite make out. Something unpleasant.

Drake said, "Thank you. Your cooperation is appreciated, sir."

As Arion stole glances around the room, his head bobbed like a wary bird. Drake was instantly reminded of one of her father's favorite tricks. Arion was memorizing important details of his surroundings and was doing an excellent job of covering for it. If she didn't know him for what he was, she wouldn't have been the wiser.

"You hold no lands, only a house on Oakwood Avenue," she said, reading the information off the license. She didn't have authority for much else. *Why would the Brotherhood require my help with the inspections?*

Perhaps they intend to dump the North End problem on me. The thought gave her a dull, throbbing pain behind her right eye before she dropped the card on the table.

No lands, she thought. At least I don't have to call him "my lord".

"I've no lands, Captain. It is true," Arion said.

She silently reread the last line on his record. "You work at the church school on Granger Road?" Disbelief slipped into her voice.

At that moment, his fearful demeanor slipped, and his words suddenly acquired a lofty, earnest tone she found deeply disturbing. "Charity work is the highest honor, Captain. Nonhuman children must be given the opportunity to learn to read, or they'll never grow to become proper contributing citizens of the Regnum. Without literacy, they will become a burden upon the state and the good citizens who pay taxes."

Drake set the record page down and again picked up the license Arion had handed to her upon entering her office. The word "orphans" filled the blank next to TARGET TYPE. Since hunters only legally preyed upon nonhumans, that meant Arion killed nonhuman children. *He studies his favorite targets without their knowledge and is given a modest stipend to offset the cost of his habit to boot.* The malicious efficiency of it all gave Drake a shudder.

"Your bag limit indicates ten kills per year," she said. The largest tally on a license she had yet seen was three. In spite of Arion's commonplace exterior, he was connected and extremely wealthy. But he held no lands with which to support himself. She wondered how he managed it. *Syndicate connections? Influential friends?* It was early in the winter season, and the record indicated his current total was nine, a majority of them female.

She glanced to Sergeant Benbow, who stood at the right of the closed door. The tension loosened slightly in her lower back. *We're nearly done.* To Benbow's left stood Arion's Retainer, a tall young man with brown curly hair. Retainers were always young.

Only the very best and, therefore, most expensive Retainers lived to an old age. This Retainer looked newer than usual. His traditional black clothing was pinned with quite a few silver baubles. *Is he showing off his wealth?* It was then that she noticed he seemed more focused upon Arion rather than potential threats within the room. It struck her as odd.

"Your license appears to be in order," she said, stalling.

"May I ask why an Inspector Warden isn't present?" Arion asked.

Drake frowned. She hoped Arion wouldn't be difficult. Using a polite but firm tone, she said, "You may ask, but I couldn't tell you for certain even if I knew." She'd been instructed not to mention the series of kill dumps in the North End. "However, I believe there is a backlog of some kind. I hope you understand that you aren't being singled out. This is a citywide investigation."

"Yes." Arion cringed in his chair and stared at the floor.

Something about the action made her stomach churn in disgust. Every aspect of Arion's manner said he was a victim of the most pathetic variety, and yet she knew from the records he was not. He disgusted and terrified her in ways that were difficult to comprehend. *He won't look me in the eye. It's more than a role he's playing. He's hiding something.* Holding the license by the corner, she handed Arion the card. "Thank you, sir. Please wait outside. We will accompany you shortly."

Benbow respectfully escorted Arion and the Retainer from the office. Drake waited until they were gone to reach into her desk drawer and pour a drink. She closed her eyes briefly and took comfort in the sound of the amber liquid filling the glass.

I hate this job. It's nothing like I hoped, but what else can I do? She gulped down the contents of the glass and gathered what she needed. Collecting a loaded flintlock pistol, she tucked it in her belt, then grabbed a second one just in case. Whiskey-laced courage burned in her belly as she opened the door. Arion hunched on a bench outside, flanked by the Retainer and a dour-faced Benbow. *How can Benbow sit next to him?* Across the room, Drake spotted Jaspar and Gilmartyn playing cards. Gilmartyn clutched his hand to his thin chest, not that it would do him any good. The deck was worn and dirty. The top left corners of two cards were torn and a third was bent. *Gilmartyn must not have noticed the pattern.*

His loss.

The Watch House walls were a dingy grey from years of coal smoke. A smoky fire heated the room. In spite of having had the damper fixed twice last week, it was apparently broken yet again. She glanced into the hearth and frowned. Someone had put too much coal on the fire this morning. Jaspar looked up from her cards and nodded, her dark eyes feigning innocence.

"Jaspar, you're in charge until Benbow and I get back." Drake turned to Arion, who instantly shifted his gaze back to the floor. "Come, sir. The sooner we get this done, the better. No doubt you have more important things to do," Drake said, and walked through the Watch House door. She paused to hold it open, waiting for Arion and Benbow to follow. As Arion's Retainer opened the coach for Arion, Drake asked Arion's carriage driver to take them to Arion's address. That's when she saw that not only was there a second token-decorated Retainer waiting inside but the driver was dressed similarly.

What's going on here? She blinked.

Benbow paused.

The young Retainer who had escorted Arion inside the Watch House motioned for her to enter the coach.

"No, thank you," Drake said, being very careful not to show her discomfort. "It's a nice day. I think Benbow and I will ride with the driver."

The Retainer didn't seem to register any surprise. He merely nodded and climbed inside. The coach step clattered back into place and the door thumped closed. Benbow raised an eyebrow in question.

Drake shook her head once. *Not now. Will discuss it later.*

Benbow shrugged and assumed a seat on the driver's bench. She scrambled up last. During the journey, Drake suppressed an urge to question the Retainer who was driving. She knew it would do no good. Retainers were notoriously reticent in general. When it came to the clients they served, they were even more so.

Arion's home was larger and more lavish than Drake had expected of a lesser noble. Fashionable marble columns supported a dentiled pediment reminiscent of the old country, and the windows were mullioned in what appeared to be silver plate. A filigree doorknob was set in the door. The topmost windowpane was arch-shaped, the white curtain inside reminding Drake of a lady's fan.

Perhaps Arion is a noble's second or third son.

The Retainer tapped a distinctive pattern on the door, and a servant with military bearing let them in.

Was that a warning? What are they hiding? She decided to make a mental note of everything she thought unusual so that she might bring it to the Brotherhood's attention. *They may even pay me for it.*

The spacious main passage revealed a curved stairway and a polished wooden banister. Two sets of sliding pocket doors, one on her left and the other on her right, led to separate rooms. Gazing to the right, she knew it for a formal receiving parlor. A stuffed couch and two wingback chairs upholstered in thick brocade squatted near a large fireplace. Another fierce-looking servant lurked in the archway between the drawing room and the room beyond it.

Sunlight from the window glinted off the pommel of his knife. There were fresh cuts healing across his right cheek.

An Assassin attack? She wasn't sure. Arion didn't seem important enough to warrant such an expense. He didn't seem the type to habitually insult or otherwise risk undue attention. She thought again of how she'd fought to keep her attention focused on him— how she'd wanted to dismiss him as unimportant. *Why would anyone want him dead?* On the other hand, she'd seen any number of people targeted by an Assassin for simply being at the wrong place at the wrong time.

"If you would wait here one moment, Captain," Arion said. "My private trophy rooms are in the cellar. It will be dark." He kept his head tilted down so that he seemed to speak to the floor.

Unease settled deep into her gut. *I do not like this man.*

The manservant with the military bearing made no move to fetch a candle for his master. Arion did so himself. The manservant remained where he was, facing the passage with his back to the open front door as if barring an exit.

Who's in charge here?

The original Retainer finally entered and swung the door closed behind them, shutting out the cold. Drake loosened her scarf. The house was warm, and once again she caught the scent of something unpleasant. *Sour.* She took a step backward, turned and was relieved when she felt the wall's comforting presence against her shoulder blades. She suspected her precautions regarding someone like Arion must seem absurd to Benbow. However, Benbow followed her example without question.

He knows more of what to expect than you do. Still, remember he doesn't know everything. She'd asked Benbow if her predecessor had been required to conduct inspections. He'd told her no.

We're both on unfamiliar ground. All the more reason to be careful.

Several minutes passed before the thump of a shutting door signaled Arion's return. He entered the hall passage from the receiving parlor. "No need to worry, Captain. The cellar is secure. The tunnels are kept in good repair," Arion said. He breathed out half-hidden amusement before leading the way.

They passed a wooden bench with a mirror set in the back and hooks along the top. A green greatcoat hung off the first hook. Beyond the second door on the left, Arion stopped and pressed a panel behind an oil painting. A hidden door slid open to the right of the landscape. The stench of dank earth wafted from the doorway, and the unpleasant odor she'd noticed before grew worse.

Something is rotting down there. Something dead.

Of course there is. Drake's stomach fluttered. She didn't care for cellars. They reminded her too much of childhood. *This is the last time, I swear. I don't care how much the Brotherhood pays. No more hunters.*

Arion took the narrow stairway first, the Retainer went next and then Drake, followed by Benbow. Once all had crowded into the narrow passage, the Retainer paused on the third stair. He reached back to press another panel. Drake did her best to avoid his touch as he did it, keeping her weapon side well out of reach. With the click of the shutting door, Drake felt the walls close in. She hated small enclosed spaces. She bit the inside of her cheek to give herself something else to think about. The back of Arion's head and his candle continued downward.

Benbow whispered, "I didn't sign up for this."

"Neither did I. But our orders are to check his tags. Jaspar knows where we are. The interview is on record," she whispered back with a confidence she didn't feel. *Of course, no one but the Brotherhood would know where to look for us, if something does go wrong.* She took a deep breath and forced her feet to carry her downward.

At the bottom of the stairwell, the passage took a sharp turn to the right. For a brief moment, she lost sight of Arion's candle. She put her hands to her flintlocks. Her heart pounded, and she scanned the blackness for any sound as she took a cautious sliding step forward. When Arion and the Retainer again came into view, the relief made her knees feel loose, but she didn't remove her hands from her pistols' grips.

Arion turned back and motioned for them to follow. "This way. It isn't far." He meekly bobbed his head, and it made her think of a child eager to show off his playthings.

At that moment, she couldn't help thinking they were far enough underground that no one could hear if she screamed.

Arion made a quick turn to the right through a roughly carved doorway. A makeshift curtain fashioned from an old tapestry hung over the open door. She pushed at the cloth and moved through. The acrid scent of lime and rot was thick in the air. She covered her nose and breathed through her mouth until she grew accustomed to the smell. Arion lit two iron candelabras, and slowly it grew bright enough to see. The room was approximately thirty feet long by twenty-five feet wide. Between the candelabras stood a roll-top desk. A folding pallet bed sat against the far wall, and three curio cases stood in a row to her left. Each case contained five shelves of trophies. The light was dim enough that it was easy not to focus on what was inside. Opposite the cases were several stained buckets, a rag mop, a narrow bedstead, and an ornate quilt. Chains were anchored into the wall, their ends resting on the featherbed.

"The tag information is in the desk," Arion said.

Reluctantly, she followed Arion. He opened a drawer, pulled out a sheaf of papers, and placed them in the middle of the desk. A small surgeon's satchel rested next to where he had deposited the papers. From the corner of her eye, Drake saw Benbow walk to the curio cabinets and gaze through the glass. Drake didn't feel comfortable with Benbow being that far away.

Don't be a coward. Just look at the damn papers and get the hells out of here. She moved around the desk and shifted through the documents. That was when something caught her eye. It was an expensive blown-glass paperweight containing the golden sunburst of Gens Aureus. It was tucked inside one of the little nooks in the top of the desk.

Arion is a member of Gens Munitoris, not Aureus. What is that doing here?

"I can read the tag numbers below the display, Captain," Benbow said.

I'm here to inspect hunting tags, not paperweights. "Read 'em out, Sergeant," she said.

With Benbow's help, the process went quickly. When she was done, Arion slipped the papers back into the drawer and locked it. She crossed the room and braved a look inside the cabinets, focusing on the first.

Mounted with care on a board covered in black velvet were nine small pairs of ears, each of them with pointed tips. Feeling a presence behind her, she whirled and bumped into Arion. He started. In that instant, she caught a good look at his eyes. The pupils were diamond-slitted like a snake's. A cloudy membrane nictated once, and Arion gave her a brief smile full of menace before he resumed his passive demeanor.

Oh, God. He's one of them. He's part malorum, she thought before the whiskey in her stomach turned to ice. *How is that even possible?*

⇥ CAIUS ⇤

Caius pushed his way through yet another alehouse crowd. A bois-terous fiddle, penny whistle, and drum combatted the low rumble of laughter and drunken conversation. Regardless of the press, his path to the snugs wasn't much impeded. The establishment's patrons were nonhuman and, upon spotting his uniform coat, fled to other parts of the alehouse. A pall of controlled menace blos-somed in the air. It occurred to him that he was without a partner and that any whistle-call for assistance would be answered too late. With that thought, a lightning flash of cold fear quickened his pulse.

They wouldn't dare attack a Warden. Would they?

The alehouse itself was every bit as disreputable as its clients.

The half-timber walls were a dingy tobacco-stained off-white. The dirt-encrusted floor was sticky beneath his boots, and the furniture had witnessed more than a few bar fights. It was the sort of place his cousins would've ventured into on a dare. Pipe smoke and the close stench of the unwashed formed a heavy miasma. Of course, the air outside on the street wasn't much better. Old Mercatur Road, located near the wharfs, was one of the city's poorest areas. It was also where a majority of the city's sewers terminated. The area was infamous. Old Mercatur was known for drunken brawling—the only entertainment for poor rabble outside of sex. There had been no less than three riots there over the past week. He didn't understand why Drake, a Watch captain, would select such a meeting place. Yet when he'd expressed unease, she'd given him his choice of alehouses—provided the establishment was located on Old Mercatur Road. He'd picked the Green Dragon because he'd liked the name. Now that he was there, he wondered if he should've asked for a recommendation instead.

I've given her another reason for which she can sneer at me. He couldn't help sensing her air of mild disdain whenever they spoke, and it struck him as odd. Most people, especially those associated with any type of authority, respected the Brotherhood. *Not her.* He wondered if she were nonhuman. The odds were good, given her job. *Why do I care what she thinks of me?* And yet, the truth was, he did.

She was nothing like any woman he'd ever met. She wore breeches, for one thing. Of course, he didn't know many women in positions of power. *If a Watch captain can be considered powerful.* It wasn't unheard of. Anyone with the means to buy a position was free to do so. It was one of the freedoms upon which the Regnum prided itself. *Everyone is free of restrictions to success.* While noble titles existed, they weren't limited to hereditary lines. It never occurred to him to think about why women and nonhumans didn't often invest their wealth in positions of leadership.

Why Old Mercatur Road? Captain Drake didn't seem the type to do much of anything without thoughtful motivation.

Her intent must be to keep me uncomfortable. He stood a little straighter and took a deep breath. *It won't damned well work. Not this time.* He gazed at the rough-looking patrons. At least, he wouldn't let her know it had. He held that thought close as he searched the snugs located at the back of the alehouse.

Each was partitioned off by high carved oak walls and frosted glass doors—a sign that the alehouse, and possibly Old Mercatur itself, hadn't always been as ill favored as it was now. However, the glass was the only aspect of the place that was well maintained. That detail stood out in his mind, and he pushed it aside for later consideration when he found Drake nursing a final inch of whiskey alone in the very last enclosure. Before entering, he paused to unbutton his greatcoat. As he did, the nearest snug emptied of its occupants. A number of the fleeing risked nervous looks in his direction on the way out. Ancient floorboards vibrated with the thud of heavy boots he could feel in the soles of his feet. A scruffy-looking youth in a dirty coat went so far as to tip his hat with a mocking smile before an elder tablemate shoved a hand in the boy's back, and they vanished into the crowd.

Caius let the snug's doors close behind him with some relief.

Captain Drake glanced up. She appeared annoyed, but then, Caius suspected she didn't tend to employ many other facial expressions.

"My message said to meet at one, Fortis," she said. "It's a quarter past three. Curfew is at four. I've other things to do than wait on you, you know."

"I regret having put you to the trouble of waiting," Caius said.

Resorting to formality when flustered was a habit he'd picked up from Severus. Severus had often said it gave a better impression than gawping. "Unfortunately, it was unavoidable."

Unimpressed, she said, "You should've changed out of your uniform. Green Dragon is Syndicate, you know. News of a Warden drinking with a Watch captain will spread like a company fire. And, I'll note, before we finish our first drink."

Oh. I should've thought of that. Caius sat down and rubbed his hands on his legs to warm them. The bench lacked padding. It was unforgiving against his back, and the smoky fire in the tiny, tin-framed fireplace across the room couldn't penetrate the snug's glass doors. He left his grey knitted scarf around his neck.

"What did you want to see me about that is so secret?" she asked.

He whispered, "I wished to discuss several persons you may have recently interviewed at the request of the Brotherhood."

"And I understood you people don't give a damn about the North End," Captain Drake said, matching his low tone. "How many bodies they have found so far? I've counted nine."

Nine? I thought it was only six. How is it that she knows more about my own case than I do? Caius tightened both fists to contain frustration. *Don't be so quick to take her word.*

The North End assignment was an independent investigation. His supervisor had stated it was to be a test. However, the same supervisor had apparently also ordered Drake to inspect hunting licenses without Caius's knowledge. The only reason Caius had found out was because his former partner, Tavian, had been assigned an administrative post, and Caius had asked Tavian to tell him about anything unusual. Tavian still owed him, after all.

Progress on the North End case had reached a dead end, and Caius didn't believe it was due to cleverness on the part of the rogue in question. *Someone higher up in the chain of command is tampering with the investigation.* Recently, he'd been informed that the director himself had taken a personal interest in the North End problem. The fact that Caius had been given the case without a partner was, in and of itself, a powerful statement, but until this moment, he'd naively let himself accept the reasons his supervisor had provided.

I'm expected to fail, Caius thought with an increasing sense of doom. "I'm not authorized to disclose such information to you." *This is a public place. A Syndicate place. Assume others are listening.* At least the two of them were well out of sight of the Brotherhood—his original reason for agreeing to meet her outside his usual haunts.

He repositioned the candle on the table so that he could talk to her without staring into the flame.

"Hmph. And maybe I'm not authorized to discuss the interviews with you either." She folded her arms across her chest and slumped against the bench with a thump.

Caius sighed. "I didn't intend for this to be an antagonistic conversation."

"Then perhaps you shouldn't have been two hours late. It'll be dark soon."

"Why are you concerned?" Caius asked. "The curfew doesn't pertain to you."

"That's true," she said. "But it does affect the market. And unlike you, I have to do my own damned shopping."

He frowned. *Damn it. I need allies, not more enemies. But I can't apologize. She's a Watch captain.*

"Don't look so damned helpless," she said. "Just . . . buy me a swiving drink."

"Very well," Caius said, standing and motioning for the landlady above the snug's swinging doors. "What would you like?"

The landlady nodded from across the room.

"Whiskey," Captain Drake said. "Not the cheap stuff."

"The best they have."

She blinked. "Do you mean it?"

"Will you tell me what you know?" Caius asked.

"Don't you damned Wardens talk to one another?" she asked. She paused for a calming breath and then returned to a whisper. "I thought you said you'd been assigned to the North End."

Someone knocked on the snug's frosted glass door. A young female voice asked, "Did you want something, my lord?"

Caius could see her blurred form through the glass, and if he'd been watching, he'd have seen her approach. The function of the glass occurred to him at the same instant as her honorific. *"My lord"?* "Ah, I own no lands. My father is—"

"I'll have a glass of the Eledorean, Fran," Drake said.

A blonde barmaid with elph features pushed the doors open wide enough for her to stick her head in. "Captain Drake? How are you this evening? Do you want something to eat?"

"I know what you put in that stew of yours," Drake said. "Just the *Eledorean* whiskey."

The barmaid gave Caius a sideways glance and then said, "We don't stock such a thing. That would be illegal. All our whiskey is of Acrasian make. Official tax stamp and everything."

Drake moved closer to the barmaid, Fran. "Have you seen his uniform?" Drake gave a sideways nod in Caius's direction. "Now, I have it on good authority that you do have Eledorean whiskey." She lowered her voice. "And you keep it in the storeroom under the crate labeled 'bar towels.'"

Fran went pale.

He shrugged and then reached inside a pocket to produce a ten-sterling piece. "Bring the bottle."

Fran's jaw dropped. "W—will you be needing anything else, my—sir?"

"A dish of chocolate," Caius said.

"We don't have chocolate . . . sir," Fran said.

"Then a pint of ale and a half-hour's privacy," Caius said. "Understood?"

She nodded, snatched up the coin, and left.

Captain Drake waited for the doors to stop swinging to lean forward. Caius caught a whiff of alcohol on her breath. She said, "You've just guaranteed the Syndicate's attention."

He tried to look unconcerned. "How long do we have?"

"I give it an hour or two," she said. "It'll take that long before George finds out Fran sold the Eledorean behind his back. Add a few minutes for him to beat that coin out of her."

"Then we'd best get started," Caius said in an attempt to hide his horror.

Drake got out her own notes while he retrieved his notebook and graphite stick from his waistcoat. She passed him a list of names—those she'd been told to interview.

"The last name on your list is Baron Munitoris Arion," Caius said. "What do you know of him?"

When she heard the name, Drake paused. "Arion is rich. Well connected. No visible means of support, but we both know that doesn't necessarily mean anything. Volunteers as a teacher at a charity school off Ninth, which is unusual given his . . . interests. Owns a large white house in Old Town off of Regent's Square. On Oakwood Avenue."

"You have a good memory."

"He was memorable. Largest permit number I've ever seen. Not that I've seen that many, mind you. What else do you want to know?"

Why involve the Captain of the Watch in a routine tag check? If it was of no importance, why not have a cadet handle it? He'd had those questions from the instant he'd spoken to Tavian. *Why did they risk involving her further?*

Because she might not see what a Warden is trained to see. "Wait," Caius said, paging back through his own notes. "Did you say his . . . records were up to date? Including the permit?"

"I did," Captain Drake said.

"I see," Caius whispered half to himself. The permit record stored in the Hall of Records had had been altered, and whoever had altered it didn't want the change recorded. *How far does this go?*

"What is it?" Drake asked.

He paused, thinking of how to frame his next questions. *Start at the beginning.* "What does Arion look like? Any identifying characteristics?"

She shivered in revulsion. "He's part malorum. You can tell by the eyes. I don't even want to think about how that's possible."

Caius's heart thudded in his ears. The Baron's lineage hadn't been documented on the card in the Hall of Records, and it should have been. *Particularly if his lineage carries a malorum's taint. The Brotherhood would be very interested in such a person.*

What is going on?

"He's balding. Black hair," she continued. "Average-looking. Average height. Would think he was afraid of his own shadow, that is, until you found his knife in your gullet."

I need allies. A partner, perhaps, Caius thought. *Someone outside the Brotherhood.* That last thought brought with it a renewed sense of duplicity and fear. He believed in the Brotherhood of Wardens, or he used to. The Brotherhood was honorable and just. It was beyond reproach. The Brotherhood were the guardians of the Regnum. *What if Father was right? What if Severus's doubts were valid all along?*

Caius swallowed. "I want everything you can find out about Arion. I'll pay. And you will speak to no one else of the matter."

"Forget it," she said, and folded her arms across her chest.

He tried not to let his desperation show. "Are you certain?"

"I'm not going back to that house. Or anywhere near that man. Ever again," she said. It was then that he understood she wasn't angry or insulted. She was afraid. He hadn't thought that possible before.

She said, "That house and its servants are intended to keep things *in* rather than *out*, if you catch my meaning."

He paused, not quite understanding but unwilling to show ignorance. "How do you know?"

"I know. My father was Syndicate. A street harvester with an eye for moving up to burglary," she said. "He had a Retainer, Fortis Vita."

"That isn't unusual."

"Sure. She taught me a thing or two. And that's why I'd bet my stripes Arion wasn't the one paying those Retainers," she said. "That . . . man was a prisoner in his own house."

It was a foolish move, but Caius didn't see another way. He needed her help. Unbuttoning his waistcoat, he revealed the protective wallet strapped across his chest and close to the skin. It was made of heavy black canvas sewn in quilted vertical rows. Although it was common practice for patrol wardens to wear wallets, the Brotherhood didn't want that known for obvious reasons. Wallets were issued to all patrol wardens for protection. The compartments were left to the individuals to fill. Each row of silver was sewn closed to prevent easy access. Keeping his back to the rest of the room, he used his knife to open one of the rows and heard her gasp.

Before she could utter a word, he said, "I'd be very grateful if you didn't tell anyone about this."

"Of course."

He counted out twenty sterling coins, stacking them neatly on the worn tabletop. He saw her tongue trace the edge of her lip as if she were a bloodflower addict presented with a prize sample. "Does your refusal stand?"

She reached for the silver, but he stopped her. Her hand was warm under his, and he felt a sudden charge of attraction.

"We'd best get that out of sight," she said, staring at the coins.

"Do we have an agreement?"

She closed her eyes and sighed. "Yes. I'll get what you want."

Releasing her hand, he saw her pull up the tail of her shirt and unfasten it from the bottom, revealing the smooth skin of her abdomen. The sterling coins jingled as she dropped them into a small leather belt pouch. She glanced up and caught him staring. He averted his gaze at once, but he caught her expression before he did. It was a small knowing smile and a raised eyebrow, and all at once, he was slammed with a powerful sense of desire. She let her shirt drop.

At that moment, Fran arrived with the whiskey and left the unmarked bottle without looking at or speaking to either one of them. Caius poured in order to fill the awkward silence. The neck of the bottle clinked three times as he touched it to the short glass. He stopped pouring when it was an inch and a half full. She waved him on. The short glass was filled with the amber liquid before she signaled for him to stop. The scent of fine whiskey with its rich, smoky hues wafted up his nose as he pushed the drink in front of Captain Drake.

"Do you like whiskey?" she asked.

"No."

"Too bad," she said. "They say the Eledoreans used magic to brew this stuff. It's like no other. Not even the elphs in Ytlain brew whiskey the same way. It's too bad they're all dead now." She sipped the contents of her glass, savoring its contents before swallowing. "Emily."

"What?"

"My name is Emily."

"Caius."

"Nice to meet you, Cai." She emptied her glass.

He halted an urge to lie and tell her that no one called him that. "There is no need for you to pay another visit to the Baron. I don't expect he'd be home, if you did. Particularly if he's as connected as you say."

"All right. When do you want my report?"

"We can meet here. Eight o'clock tomorrow morning."

"Can't do it."

He paused while pouring her another round. "Why?"

"I can't tell you."

"Why?"

"It's a secret." Once again, she let a hint of a smile slip across her lips.

"Fine," Caius said. "Don't tell me."

"Oh, pour me another and maybe I will."

"I thought you were angry with me."

She shrugged and patted her money belt. "It's quite possible I've forgiven you."

He held up the whiskey. He was warming up to her. "It only took one drink?"

"Tomorrow morning, I'm meeting one of the Consul's lackeys along with one Censor Fortis Crispus at the North Gate," she whispered. "To assist in an arrest. It looks like a member of Gens Aureus has been illegally smuggling nonhumans out of the city." She paused for another swallow. "Doesn't that sort of thing usually fall under the Brotherhood's jurisdiction?"

Caius put down the bottle and frowned. "It does."

"Then it would seem the new Consul has lost faith in the Brotherhood."

If so, he's not the only one. "I rather doubt that." Something in the room didn't seem right, and he couldn't place what it was until he realized the musicians had stopped playing. The alehouse felt quieter. Watchful. "I should go. I'm on duty in an hour."

"Mind if I take the bottle?"

"It's yours." Caius got up from the table, edged around it, and then buttoned his greatcoat before leaving the snug.

She stood up as well and then leaned into him. Her whisper tickled his ear. "I'll send you what I have later tonight." Then she gently bit his earlobe.

His jaw dropped.

She murmured in his ear. "We're being watched. It's best to give them a reason for our chat that they'll understand." And then she kissed him.

She tasted of sweetness gone bitter. Before he knew it, her tongue slid into his mouth. Blood rushed in his ears. His very bones shuddered with need, and he knew right then he was in over his head. *She's clever. Too clever. Do not listen to your cock. She's distracting you.* But part of him, specifically the aforementioned cock, didn't give a damn. He returned the kiss with enthusiasm. Then her lips parted from his every bit as suddenly as they had arrived.

"Now get out of here," she said.

Gasping, he exited the snug—doubly glad of his greatcoat because it covered his cockstand. The patrons roared in laughter, and the musicians went back to their work. He stumbled to the door to the opening strains of a bawdy tune called "The Warden and the Duchess of Gibson Road".

It was midnight before the remainder of his evening's duties were complete. Caius splurged on a carriage ride home. The night had grown painfully sharp and there was a metallic edge in the breeze. He suspected it was going to snow soon. The carriage stopped outside his living quarters. The wobbly step extended with a clang. Caius reached up, giving the driver a certificate of reimbursement with a small sterling note for a tip. The coach left with a rush of horse's hooves on cobblestones that echoed in the empty, lamp-lit street. Tomorrow would be an early day; he was scheduled for a morning watch shift. He hoped to make progress on at least one of his assignments in the morning.

"Would you be Inspector Fortis?" The voice was young and cheerful—a little too cheerful.

Caius threw his back to the brick wall that protected the rooming house from the street and laid a hand on his pistol until he spied the voice's owner.

A scrawny, dirty boy of eleven stepped from the shadows under the stairway. The boy wore a man's frock coat, the hem of which reached his ankles. The sleeves were rolled up and all of the buttons were missing. His feet were encased in worn boots with string laces. He held himself tall as if he were a debased noble.

"No need to worry, mister," the boy said with a sly smile that lacked a front tooth. "I'm a friend, I am." The boy smelled horrible. The stench of unwashed skin, rotting teeth, and bad tobacco grew worse as he moved closer. He stopped a few paces from Caius with a loud sniff. Caius watched him wipe his nose on the frayed cuff of his filthy coat, then reach into a voluminous pocket for a snuffbox.

* *Street harvester.* "Do you have a permit to be on the street at this hour?" Caius asked. The boy made him uneasy. His accent as well as the state of his clothes indicated he didn't belong anywhere near this part of the city.

"I do. Name is Jack, Jack McCauley. Watch captain's special

courier, I am." Pride shone over the layers of grime. "Here to deliver you a message, all private-like." The boy produced a thick, wax-sealed envelope.

Caius accepted it and then tucked it into his coat pocket.

"You got a reply, mister?" Jack asked.

"No."

"Right, then." He remained where he was, clearly waiting for something.

"Oh," Caius reached into his pocket and gave the boy a copper penny.

The coin vanished into the folds of the boy's voluminous coat. "Nice evening to you." Jack tugged at his greasy forelock, and with that, he bolted down the street at a run.

Opening the envelope, Caius found the names of every interviewee that Emily had seen. Unlike before, she'd included their addresses. Arion's was there along with a description of his Retainer, the floor plan of Arion's home, a list of known servants, and a disturbingly thorough inventory dated a year before that showed signs of having been conducted by a Syndicate thief. Emily's handwriting was measured and exact. Her note stated that more information would be forthcoming. The only indication of her earlier display of passion was her signature—a simple letter *E* and a flourish. Tired, Caius went through the gate and up the stairs to his rooms. He was halfway to bed with the candle before he realized he hadn't given Emily his address.

Syndicate connections. She's dangerous.

The memory of her warm lips burned hot, and it took quite a long time to get to sleep.

⊰ I L T A ⊱

FOURTH OF PITKÄKUU, 1784

Ilta paced the kitchen floor while Moss finished the evening's cleaning tasks. The scent of savory rabbit-and-venison stew, bread, and coffee lingered in the air. Not everyone could attend the communal meals, and this was why, in spite of winter rationing, Moss kept water heating for herbal tea, and warm soup or stew available at all hours of the night.

Malorum attacks were becoming more frequent. Still, the community struggled with the idea of breaking Eledorean Blood custom. As one of those unwilling to fight, Moss had told her that he felt it was his responsibility to feed those who could bring themselves to do so. He wasn't alone. Everyone contributed to the defence of the Hold—whether that was in casting silver into ammunition, making bandages, mixing healing remedies, or caring for the families of the injured or dead. Disagreements still occurred, and Ilta had had to step in upon occasion. Everyone was in an agitated state, after all, but largely, aggression had been directed outside the community. Everyone seemed to understand what was at stake, even the troublemakers.

For the most part, she thought. The situation between Nels and Blackthorne hadn't changed much since the fight. While there'd been no more physical altercations, the tension between them was getting worse.

"Why don't you sit down for a while, Miss Ilta?" Moss asked, taking up a broom. The sturdy handle looked fragile in his big hands. "If nothing else, it would make the task of sweeping less complicated."

"I'm in your way," she said. "I'm so sorry. It's just—"

"You are waiting for Colonel Hännenen," Moss said.

"Am I that obvious?"

"I am uncertain I would employ that specific expression," Moss said. "However, I must say that I do pride myself in possessing certain skills of observation."

She tilted her head. It was difficult to tell whether or not Moss was making a joke at her expense. In many ways, he was as hard to read as Blackthorne. Only, in Moss's case, the glimpses she'd caught from the interior of his skull bordered on the alien. Still, she sensed no ill will in him. "May I help?"

"While such would serve to channel your nervous energy into something constructive," Moss said, "I must regretfully decline. Please do not regard it as a personal slight. My trepidation is due to previous unfortunate experiences in conflict with my desire for the current state of organization within my kitchen."

She blinked and smiled. "You're afraid I'll rearrange your pots and that you'll be unable to find them again?"

"This is so," Moss said, and shrugged.

"All right," she said. "I'll sit." She perched on a bench at one of the four trestle tables. She checked the kitchen clock for the fifth time. It was after eleven o' clock.

"Are you certain Colonel Hännenen has not already retired for the evening?" Moss asked.

She felt her face grow warm—more out of guilt than embarrassment. "He hasn't been home for hours. I—I checked there first."

"Would you like a cup of tea?" Moss asked, pausing in his sweeping. "There is ample chamomile this evening, should you wish it."

"I think I would," Ilta said, and got to her feet. "I'll get it. Would you like a cup too?"

"Yes, please," Moss said.

Once the water had boiled and the tea steeped, she began to pour. That was when she heard movement in the passage outside. She set down the pot and went to see who it was. As she did, Birch nearly struck her with the door. She stumbled back, and Nels entered. Relieved to see the person for whom she'd been waiting, she ignored Birch's apology and fixed her attention on Nels instead.

"Are you all right? I was afraid of what might happen," she said. "The—the vision was so vivid." She wrapped Nels in a hug. His body stiffened the instant her arms went around him. Releasing him as abruptly as she'd grabbed him, she stepped back. "Are you hurt?" *He's been pushing himself too hard.*

"It's only a scratch," he muttered. He looked exhausted.

"You were right, Miss Ilta," Birch said. "The malorum would've had our sheep and goats if you hadn't told us to watch for them."

"I—I'm glad I was able to help," she managed to say.

The others filed into the kitchen and headed directly for the stew. Moss stopped cleaning long enough to give them welcome and to serve those who needed it. Ilta attempted to stay out from underfoot. She watched Nels wait until the others had full bowls before approaching the pot. Afterward, Moss moved around, portioning out the remainder of the bread that had been baked before breakfast. Ilta selected a slice while the others fought over the butter. Then she settled on a nearby stool and attempted patience while pretending to eat. Her stomach had been in knots all day. She'd made a decision, but wasn't sure when or if there would be a good time to act upon it.

She watched Nels interact with the others in an attempt to gauge his mood. He took off his all-weather coat, and she saw the uniform jacket underneath had been ripped. She could see a make-shift bandage above his right wrist.

Maybe tonight isn't such a good idea. "It's as cold as a wraith's ass out there," Birch said. "My feet are frozen solid."

Between mouthfuls, Dar said, "You think it's cold now? Let me tell you the story of a winter so bad that the sun froze solid."

Sitting next to Dar, Dylan grinned. "Here we go."

Freyr Ahlgren, a big redhead with freckled skin let out a disgusted noise. "That never happened."

Dar said, "My great-grandfather said it did. It happened when he was a boy. The sun froze and fell from the sky. It broke into thousands of shards. The impact left a huge crater far to the north near the Ghost Horse Glacier. Isn't that right, Moss?"

"I have heard it is true that such a geological formation exists," Moss said. "I cannot, however, substantiate any claim as to the cause."

"Do your people have any stories about it?" Dar asked.

"I cannot say," Moss said. "I left them when I was very young. I do not have any memories of those with whom I previously resided."

Ilta stopped an urge to ask *Where did you come from?* Like

many of the refugees living within Grandmother Mountain Hold, Moss didn't discuss his past. She was never sure whether or not he actually had one—or at least, one he remembered. Others let slip the odd detail, no matter how much they wanted to keep such things private, and she'd catch the odd thought. With Moss, she never did.

Dar resumed his story. "The clan gathered the pieces together, and their best blacksmith thawed the shards in a great forge fire built within the crater. The bellows was so huge, it had to be worked by fifty of the clan's strongest warriors."

"I know this story," Ahlgren said. "This is an Uplander tale. How would your great grandpa come to know it? Aren't you Waterborne?"

"I am," Dar said. "But my great-grandpa was an Uplander. His people came from a wandering clan near Ghost Horse Glacier. He had pale skin and hair redder than yours."

Ahlgren frowned. "Why would an Uplander go to sea?"

"Same as a lot of men. He fell in love. In his case, with a Waterborne girl," Dar said.

"Waterborne get far enough north to trade with Uplanders?" Sloan asked.

"The Waterborne sail all the seas, even the frozen ones," Dar said. "Can I get on with my story now?"

Ahlgren said, "Sure."

"All right," Dar said. "When the repairs were as complete as they could be, the shaman asked their best and strongest archer, Rania, to shoot the sun back into the sky. The sun is light, in spite of its size, you see. How else can it float above us? So, she created a giant magic bow specifically for the task. Using it, she was able to get the sun back where it belonged. The reindeer, seals, and forests were saved. Unfortunately, not all the missing pieces were found.

The sun turns very slowly as it travels above us. Sometimes the missing side appears. And that is why they say that there are some years when the sky grows dark, and the sun goes black."

"That's a ridiculous story," Birch said.

Dar reached into a pocket. "I assure you it's true." Then he pulled out a flat orange stone and handed it to Sloan. "Great-Grandfather gave me a piece before he died. See how light it is? See how it glows when you hold it up to the fire?"

Ilta moved in for a closer look. The others, with the exception of Ahlgren, did the same.

"That's nothing but a piece of amber," Ahlgren said.

Dar asked, "And just where do you think amber comes from?"

Everyone laughed.

Eventually, they finished eating their meal, and weariness took its toll on the conversation. Birch and his partner, Sloan, made their excuses and left for bed. With a huge yawn, Ahlgren followed not long after. Moss returned to his cleaning and breakfast preparations. The comforting sounds of chiming kitchenware filled the silence. At last, Dylan dropped his bowl and wooden spoon into the washtub to soak and with Dar wished everyone a good night. Moss sat down with some sand and began scouring. Ilta continued to wait until Nels seemed prepared to leave.

When it was clear she couldn't put it off any longer, she braved a second approach. "Nels? May I walk with you to your rooms? I'd like to talk." In truth, she wanted to do more than talk.

He paused, and his eyebrows pinched together, forming a worry line between them. "Is it another vision?"

"It's not that. It's—it's . . . something else." She smoothed the green skirt she wore when she wanted to feel pretty. She had even gone to the trouble of braiding her hair with a matching ribbon.

"All right," Nels said. Getting to his feet, he went to the exit and held open the door for her. "Good night, Moss. Thank you again for dinner. It was excellent as always."

"You're very welcome," Moss said. "May you have a most pleasant evening, Colonel Hännenen."

Nervous, Ilta picked up her healer's bag. Then she waved a farewell and followed Nels into the hall.

They walked several paces before the silence motivated her to make another attempt at conversation. "Were you able to save all of the sheep?"

"Most of them. We only lost three. We were lucky."

"What about Favia's goats? Their wool makes the softest yarn. And—"

"They're safe too."

"Oh. Good."

Halfway to his apartments, she found herself reaching for his hand. All at once, her hand began to tingle as if it'd fallen asleep. Time slowed and became disjointed. Stunned, she released him. Down the hallway, a shadowy form appeared, and she heard a ghostly voice. It faded in and out in a way she'd never experienced before.

"—wrong." "—unning—" "—a choice, but not the—"

"Gran?" Ilta asked.

At the edge of her vision, she felt more than saw Nels stop. She heard him ask a question, but he was too distant to make out the words. There was a buzzing in her ears, and her vision dimmed. The ground grew increasingly unstable.

"Gran?" Sudden weakness drove Ilta to her knees, and she landed on her left hip with a bone-jarring thump. "Is that you?" The shadow vanished as abruptly as it arrived and was replaced with an image of a wailing newborn. Its birth-matted hair was thick and black. The child's mother lay dead in a pool of blood. The vision ended in a stomach-wrenching flash of bright white light.

"Ilta? Speak to me," Nels said. He was crouched next to her. Concern overpowered the exhaustion in his voice. "Ilta?"

She blinked. "That was unpleasant."

"Let's get you to the infirmary."

"No!"

He started.

She said, "I mean, I'd rather we continued to your place. I'll be fine. I only need a cup of tea."

"I don't have any black tea."

"How about chamomile?"

"I do have some of that." He helped her to her feet. "Are you feeling steady enough to walk?"

She nodded, dusted off her skirts, and then searched for her pocket watch.

"You were only gone for a moment," he said.

"Oh. Thank you," she said, and slipped the watch back into her apron pocket without opening it. "I'm sorry."

"For what?" he asked. "Having a vision? That's part of who you are." He shrugged. Then his weary face grew sly. "Was it anything good?"

She returned his smile, weakly. "Not like that."

"Honestly, why don't you see anything useful? Like Viktor in a compromising position? Or deeply embarrassing things about Westola involving kitchen utensils?" Nels asked. "I have it on good authority that Cousin Edvard's Silmaillia facilitates all manner of court gossip. It's not fair."

"My powers revel in being uncooperative, apparently." The exchange was so effortless and comforting, so much like they'd been before that she was reminded how much she missed being with him.

When they got to his apartment, she saw the fire had recently been tended and fresh snow collected in a iron caldron was resting on the hearth. She spooned some snow into the kettle, set it on the hook, and pushed it over the flames. With that done, she settled on the rug in front of the fire, wrapped her arms around her knees, and began to consider what the vision had meant. For his part, Nels went to the next room to change.

Gran was warning me, Ilta thought. *That much was obvious. But the baby? What did that have to do with anything? And 'unning'? What does that mean?*

Nels returned. His shirt was untucked, and he'd removed his boots. The bandage around his forearm was soaked through with blood. He'd brought a tray with fresh linen scraps and the ointment she'd given to him.

"I should take care of that for you," Ilta said.

"You don't have to," Nels said. "I can do it."

Running. Gran was telling me to stop running. Ilta blinked. And then she remembered one of the things her Gran always said when she was being stubborn about something. *"That's a valid choice, Ilta girl. But all choices have consequences. Best keep that in mind. We can make things difficult for ourselves and others in the long term by only thinking of the short term. Sometimes what looks like the easy, pain-free way is a lot more destructive. Stop. Think. What is it you fear? Be brave. You can't afford not to, girl. You're too powerful. You're making a choice, but is it the best choice?"*

Her heart began to gallop inside her chest. "I want to do it for you. May I? Please?"

"All right."

She sat at his feet and took his wrist in her hands. Beginning the process of removing the bandage, she recalled the first time her Gran had given her that particular speech. She'd balked at rebreaking a patient's badly set leg bone. "Oh, goddess."

"Is something wrong?" Nels asked.

"Yes," Ilta said. "I mean no. Not with your wrist. The wound needs cleaning." She winced at the sight of the four-inch-long cut. "And maybe some stitches and plasters. Good thing that was on the top of your arm and not the other side."

Nels shrugged.

Keeping her eyes to her work, she said, "Remember when I told you that Gran was concerned about us being together?"

He nodded.

Ilta said. "She was wrong. At least, I think she may have just told me so."

"What?" Nels asked. "*That* was your vision?"

Ilta nodded.

"Isn't it the Silmaillia's job to never be wrong?"

"Do you honestly believe that, knowing me as you do?" she asked. "Just because a Silmaillia sees a future doesn't mean we're required to work to avoid it. We have to determine what is necessary to act upon and what isn't. Sometimes, an unpleasant event can't or shouldn't be avoided. Sometimes, it's difficult to know what a vision means or . . ." She shrugged. "Of course, I don't think Gran had any visions about us. Or, to be more specific, you. At least, her diaries don't mention it."

He blinked. "But she told Uncle Sakari that I'd be the savior of Eledore."

"That she did," Ilta said. "She also lied."

He jerked his wrist from her grasp and stood up. "The Silmaillia can't lie! That's—that's treason!"

"She did it to save your life," Ilta said. "I was there, remember?"

"But—"

"I also remember telling you that you shouldn't have been eavesdropping," she said.

"You were in one of your trances! How did I know you knew what you were saying?" He began to pace in front of the hearth.

"Oh, please. Don't lie. I was making perfect sense, and you knew it. You chose to ignore me. I remember. Everything. Vividly," she said. "Your uncle was about to have you murdered. There. In Gran's garden. She stopped him. And you weren't the only one she saved when she did. She knew he'd have had his men break down her door and kill everyone to cover it up. *I* knew it. He could've easily blamed the Acrasians for the whole thing. She *had* to lie."

"Oh."

"Suvi and I have been going through the histories," Ilta said. "Do you know what we found out?"

He stopped pacing and shook his head.

"The old stories are wrong. The ones you and I know," Ilta said. "Kassarina Ilmari did not banish the Old Ones on her own. She did it with the help of two others. Her sisters."

Nels didn't move. "That can't be—"

"It's true," Ilta said. "The histories changed over time. Eventually, the Old Ones vanished altogether and became a vague loathing of death and anyone associated with it. Even blood is viewed with disgust." She paused before going on. "How does it feel to have blamed yourself for a failure to fulfill an expectation you were never intended to meet? To have loathed yourself your entire life because of a lie?"

He swallowed, went back to the sofa, and dropped onto the cushions. "I don't believe it."

"The myth of the lone savior is just that: a myth," Ilta said. "At its best, it's a beautiful metaphor for the cycle of life. All is born, lives, dies, and is reborn again. A tragedy or a terrible mistake occurs, but life doesn't stop there. It shouldn't. Life continues. And one starts again from there with new knowledge. It's an important concept." She laid a hand on his knee. "At its worst, the myth of the one savior is a lie told to the powerless. 'Be good. Do as you're told. And someone will come save you from your misery.' It's also a story intended to make the oppressors feel good about themselves. It allows them to believe that they have everything not due to an accident of birth but because they are more like that lone savior and more worthy than those who have nothing.

"The truth is, all the important, necessary changes that happen occur because a *group* of people decide to make it happen. A single person simply can't. They don't have enough power."

"Oh."

"You have to stop punishing yourself for a failure that wasn't yours in the first place," Ilta said. "We need you too much, Suvi and I. And not merely because we love you. Do you understand?"

He struggled to tie off the bandage on his wrist one-handed, but she finished the knot for him.

"I'm attempting to," he said.

"Good," Ilta said. "Now I would like to bed you. If you're up for it."

"What?" He gaped. "Now?"

"Any objections?" She got to her feet and held out a hand.

He paused. "Strangely, none spring to mind."

◄ BLACKTHORNE ►

ONE

Sixth of Pitkäkuu, 1784

Blackthorne dreamed of archery practice.

He despised archery. He would rather have been assigned to working the fields. Perversely, the duke had insisted upon personally instructing him in the art of the bow. Talus had made it clear that the master did him a great honor by doing so. Blackthorne would have preferred to be far less honored. He'd been beaten for missing his aim the day before, and his body ached. Now he shut his eyes while servants fixed the target in place. He didn't want to listen to the process but knew no way to keep from it without drawing the duke's ire.

Standing close behind him, the duke bent and whispered in a loud voice that forced a stinging puff of brandy-laced breath against

Blackthorne's sore ear. "Open your eyes, Severus. Now. Damn it, you cannot sight the bow with your eyes closed. I will not have you a coward. Do it, boy."

Left with no option but to obey, Severus reluctantly opened them. There was a fresh bandage on his upper left arm. It covered the latest of a long series of wounds that had been inflicted upon him by the sorcerer. The cut underneath the bandage burned, and the substance that had been smeared into it smelled horrible, but he had learned to leave the plasters alone. He'd also learned that none of his questions regarding the purpose of the treatments would be answered. It wasn't his place to know the motivations of his betters.

His shoulder throbbed. The bow in his fist imprinted a crease in his palm at the base of his thumb. His legs were healing but still sometimes ached from having been broken. The collar had been removed from his neck at the same time. He wasn't free—that much he knew. He still bore the brand, but he no longer slept in the cell below the guardhouse. Now he lived with Talus, the duke's weapons master, in a cottage on the edge of the duke's estate.

Severus liked Talus. Talus was kind and nursed him after each excruciating visit to the sorcerer. The weapons master had even held the slop bucket while he was sick. However, not even Talus had explained what was being done to him. At first, Severus had been terrified, but since nothing could be done about it, that fear had faded into the rest of his emotional existence—a heavy, low-level weight in his chest and back, best ignored.

The only reprieve from pain and fear involved fencing, fighting, and shooting. Talus had proven to be a patient and methodical teacher. Every day that Severus was well enough to stand, they practiced with saber, dagger, musket, pistol, bow, and the basics of hand-to-hand combat. An encouraging word from Talus was like cool water on the hottest day. Severus quickly found himself focusing all his attention on pleasing his teacher. And he'd been happy for the first time in his life since his mother had vanished—that is, until the duke announced he would be taking over the archery lessons.

At first, Severus had purposely mishandled the bow in the hope that the duke would think him slow-witted and abandon the task—or, preferably, find another, more interesting subject for his attention. However, the duke had consulted Talus, and upon discovering the deception, had had him punished. It was then he knew there was no escaping archery lessons.

Now the richly decorated bow was once again gripped in Severus's hands. The duke handed him an edged arrow, and Severus saw that the same target was in place as before. He swallowed a fresh bout of dread.

An old house slave named Esa had been stripped to the waist and tied immobile to the post. Marks were painted on his chest in red and white. Esa was bound and gagged, and his darting, wet eyes begged Severus not to kill him.

Severus heard the duke once again whisper in his ear. "You are not one of them, boy. You are something else. Something more. Remember that. Now shoot."

His arms and hands made the necessary motions to nock the arrow. He saw himself pull on the string while pushing outward on the curve of the bow at the same time, but he hesitated as he had twice before. He didn't want to shoot Esa. He knew Esa. Esa, along with Brita, had looked after him after his mother had been taken away.

The cut on Severus's arm burned as the fresh scab stretched. The string dug into the leather glove on his right hand. He had no intention of killing Esa. He was resolved enough on the matter to take another beating, if he had to. At the same time, he knew he was only prolonging the inevitable. The tension in the bow began to wear against the strength of his arms, and his muscles quivered with the effort of keeping it taut.

"Do it NOW, boy!" the duke shouted in his tender ear.

Severus flinched. His fingers slipped from the string. As the arrow passed through the air, the target changed, and old Esa no longer struggled wild-eyed at the post.

The target had become Lydia, his last bed partner.

Blackthorne grabbed for the arrow with everything he had but couldn't keep it from hitting her in the throat with a terrible, quiet thump. She opened her lips to scream but instead, a cascade of blood flooded out with a horrible choking gurgle. Crimson colored her white teeth, poured over her chin. It rained down the front of the tight blue dress, instantly soaking the fabric, causing it to cling to her breasts, revealing the shape of delicate nipples beneath. The sound of her futile, staccato attempts to breathe echoed in his head.

The image was instantly cut off and replaced with another. A balding man with a gore-drenched face laughed at him. His mad pupils were slitted diamonds like a cat's. "I see you." He held up two bloody orbs of flesh in one palm and gently patted them with a finger. "Blood calls blood," he said in a hoarse wet voice.

Blackthorne sat up with a gasp and covered his ears, trying to block the images and sounds from his mind. The room was dark, and it took him a moment to remember where he was.

Lydia. He hadn't thought about her since he'd left Novus Salernum in the fall. Now worried, he hoped she was well. He also couldn't help anticipating her being available when he returned. Lydia was one of his contacts. She was also a prostitute. Originally, he'd never intended to bed her. In fact, the idea had been hers. She'd claimed that Reggie Meade, the landlord of the Golden Swan on

Headley Street, would become suspicious if she didn't play out her entire role as rich patroness of the dueling ring. At first, he thought she was joking, but he quickly came to understand she'd been serious. At the time, he decided he didn't care as long as he wasn't being charged. Lydia's services were far more expensive than he could afford, and it wasn't long before he understood why.

Gathering his trousers, he put them on in the dark and tried to clear his mind of looming dread. The nightmares were getting worse. He didn't know what to make of them. He tried to believe they were naught but a mix of bad memories and leftover fear, but it was clear they were drifting into new, more intense directions. He didn't want to think about what that might mean.

All kainen possess some form of magic. He shuddered.

His watch, nestled in its place on the bare mantel, let out a series of quiet buzzes—the sound of its vibration against its holder. *Five o'clock in the morning.* There would be no going back to sleep. *Not now.* He finished dressing and then lit one of the candle nubs.

The others seemed to be more lax in the mornings now that winter was in full force. With everyone in a state of near-constant vigilance, no one was sleeping well. More and more members of the community got a late start—not that there was enough daylight to provide much of a demarcation. Acrasian winters weren't nearly as cold and dark. Still, he was growing used to the longer nights and found he didn't mind. Deciding on a trip to the bathing niches, he gathered his things.

The passage outside was decorated with imported ceramic tiles from Tahmer. Their blue surfaces glittered with sea images lit by oil lamps during the winter months and light vents during the summer. The longer he resided in the Hold, the more impressed he became with the level of ingenuity the Waterborne possessed compared to the people of Acrasia. The Regnum's architecture followed strict styles dictated by Gens Fortis and the Emperor. Thus, everything built within the past fifty years tended to look the same—all designed to the exacting specifications of the Golden Mean, the glorification of the Regnum, and classical influences from a lost land over the distant sea. A land that no one in the Regnum had seen since the volcanic eruption and destruction that had led to the great migration.

In his experience, the Regnum gazed backward and inward. In contrast, kainen of Eledore and the Waterborne Nations fixed their vision in any direction that suited them. He liked that.

The Hold's interior was a palace, and it was well hidden by its unassuming exterior. As a result, he could only assume that the Hold had been created to serve a different intent than a Waterborne warehouse. For a start, it'd been originally constructed by Eledoreans. For another, it was too far inland to be a Waterborne property. He decided to ask Slate about it later. *Maybe even Ilta or Moss.* It suddenly occurred to him that it was nice to have someone other than Slate to whom he could turn.

The air became close and smelled faintly of sulfur, and at last, he knew he'd reached the stairs leading to the bathing niches. The steps were slick with moisture as he descended. The radical temperature difference between the passages above and the warm stairway gave him a shiver.

Ten semi-private bathing niches had been hollowed out of the walls surrounding the underground pool. Curtains were hung in each arched doorway to provide privacy. He paused to pull off his boots and stockings—he didn't wish to risk falling in with them on. The stone was warm and smooth under his bare feet. He peered into each niche on his way to the farthest and was relieved to discover he was alone. Settling into the most isolated of the alcoves, he set down his things, drew the curtain, and stripped. He placed his pocket watch on top of his folded clothes. Finally, he assumed a comfortable position on the stone ledge, or as comfortable as he could manage on hard stone.

Emptying his mind as Talus had taught him, Blackthorne focused on his breathing. He took a deep breath and slowly released it several times. Next, he concentrated on every muscle, flexing and then releasing tension. When that was done, he listened to the flow of water, letting it be his only awareness. Soon, passages from the Retainer's Code drifted to the surface of his mind. He recalled their soothing words and felt a measure of reassurance from the familiar, the known.

The First Precept: A Retainer's life is not his or her own to spend. The true Retainer exists for the master. The sacrifice of one's life for one's master is the highest honor one can achieve.

The Second Precept: Fear is the eternal enemy. Fear destroys the mind. Fear tears at conviction. Have no fear. Grant it no power. For fear prevents perfect service to one's master. Fear is the tool of cowardice.

The Third Precept: Release the things of the material world. A worthy Retainer possesses nothing—not belongings, not family, not lovers. These are fleeting. All a true Retainer requires is the orderliness of one's own mind. Even access to weaponry is unnecessary, provided one maintains ultimate self-discipline.

The Fourth Precept: The only true peace is the serenity of death. One must endeavor to maintain inner peacefulness at all times. It is only from a place of calm that one's duty can be executed with precision during the chaos of battle. Therefore, it is of the utmost importance that a Retainer be comfortable with their own mortality. Visualize death morning and night. Live as if already dead.

He finished his meditations feeling more confused and uneasy than before. Slipping into the hot spring-fed pool, he sank to the bottom, letting its warmth cover him completely—hoping his uncertainty too would be washed away.

Live as if already dead.

A Retainer exists only for the master.

Master. A slow rage burned deep inside his chest at the word. *Slate does not own me.*

I have no master. I am my own.

Masterless Retainers are without honor.

Suddenly, he felt trapped. It was at that moment he understood the foundations of his former self had worn thin. Self-contempt came on the heels of surprise. To be ambushed by this information was ludicrous. He had come to Grandmother Mountain with the intention of discarding his past, after all. It had seemed easy enough to shed the Brotherhood's lies—much as he still struggled with them. He had inwardly rebelled against the Brotherhood and the duke his whole life, but he hadn't considered how much of his identity centered on what else he'd been taught. And now . . .

Now he was terrified.

Fear is the enemy.

The only true peace is the serenity of death. One must endeavor to maintain inner peacefulness at all times. It is only from a place of calm that one's duty can be executed—

If I discard the Retainer's Code, what is left? What am I? In spite of physically abandoning his past, he understood now he'd brought it with him. Worse, he wasn't sure he would ever be entirely free of it. *Slavery of thought is still slavery.*

Which left a new, more frightening problem. He couldn't be what he had been but had no idea of what he should be. *The question is not "What should I be?" Isn't it "What do I want to be?"*

He suddenly realized why he had waited over a year to consider the consequences of leaving Acrasia—seen in terms of everything he had given up, the weightless insecurity would have been far too unsettling. The truth was that as much as he had despised his previous life, it had had the benefit of being familiar, simple, and therefore comfortable, even certain.

I have no master. Not the duke. And not Slate. I am my own.

The lack of air pressed against his lungs more urgently than his thoughts, and he used the bottom of the bathing pool to propel himself to the surface. He combed wet hair from his face with both hands. A thumb brushed against one artificially rounded ear.

No matter how much I wish it, I'll never be free of the past—of the things I've done. Nor should I.

He liked the way Ilta had treated him at the party, as if he were someone honorable and worthy. She made him feel it was possible to be that person. Of course, it wasn't the first time a woman had looked at him like that. Others had professed attraction for him before, but he had always known it had been about the duke's money, the Warden's uniform, the illusion of being human. Ilta was the first to know him for what he truly was.

I can't forget what I am. But the truth was, he didn't know what that was anymore. He had spent so much of his life being what others required that he wasn't sure he ever did know. It was as though a gaping canyon had opened beneath his feet, and all at once, he felt lost. He needed something, anything with which to catch himself. He reached out for the little leather book resting next to his pocket watch.

To lay down one's life for the sake of one's master—

He cut off the thought by punching the water. *Damn it! Stop!*

I'm not lost. I'm trapped and bound in my own beliefs! Pulling himself out of the bath, he dried off and dressed in frustration.

How does one go about discarding every single thing one has been taught? Is it even possible? Quitting the Brotherhood, that had been easy. It had been the right thing to do. *But what am I, if I am not even a Retainer? What then remains?*

I am nothing and no one.

He draped his waistcoat over one arm and took the stairs two at a time. He remembered his friend Caius with a pang. Caius would've listened to what little Severus could've told him and then put it all in perspective with a few insightful words and a kind laugh. Of course, Caius didn't know the whole of what Severus— now Blackthorne—was. A very limited number of people did.

And now Ilta Korpela has been added to that list.

Has she told anyone? Will she? What happens when the rest of them find out?

I die a very unpleasant death, that's what happens.

Visualize one's own death—

He desperately needed to think of something else for a time. The idea of facing his empty room wasn't appealing. *Not yet. Perhaps Moss is awake?*

Wet hair dripped in Blackthorne's face, and the chill in the upper passages made him shiver. He turned the corner and was almost to the junction leading to the kitchen when he spied a group descending the passage and inwardly cursed. There was no corner in which to duck along this section. He couldn't turn around and go back, and even if he could, getting caught where he could be drowned was a bad idea. The hallway was narrow enough—only two persons could fit side by side—to limit the number of attackers. He had to hope none of them had pistols. Lowering his head, he made to go past, but they'd already spotted him and blocked the way. There were three of them. Two were older, perhaps thirty or thirty-five. The last was Blackthorne's age and was missing an eye. He didn't know their names, but he knew them for friends of the Nickols brothers.

The one with the long grey beard said, "Why, look who's here, boys."

Blackthorne backed up a few paces. He pushed wet hair out of his eyes with one hand and reached for the hilt of his missing knife with the other. Inwardly cursing himself for leaving his room unarmed, he considered his options. None of them were good. He'd tolerated too much abuse from Hännenen and his troops in the past, he knew, and this was the result. He hadn't been thinking ahead. *Live as if already dead.*

It was past time for a change.

The muscles between his shoulder blades cramped, and he prepared for the worst. *I'll have to hit them hard—hard enough to convince them to leave me alone.* He didn't like it, but he had to take a stand if he was going to be of any use to Slate.

Or, more importantly, myself. "What do you want?" Blackthorne kept his voice even.

"Nothing," the oldest of the lot said. He had a craggy face with Acrasian features, dark greying hair, and black kainen eyes. He was wearing a dirty floral-printed waistcoat. "Except for you to leave and never come back."

A chorus of agreement echoed down the otherwise empty passage.

"And if I don't?" Blackthorne asked.

Floral Waistcoat said, "Then me and my boys here will have to teach you a lesson."

Blackthorne rapidly grabbed the man with the long beard by the shoulders and kicked his legs from under him. The older man landed hard on the stone floor with an alarmed grunt. Then Blackthorne placed a boot on his neck and readied himself for another attack. The others stayed where they were while their friend gasped.

"Well?" Blackthorne asked.

The other two whirled and ran.

Blackthorne turned his attention to the attacker on the floor. "Before I let you go, I want you to understand something."

Grey Beard fought to get free, but Blackthorne shifted a little more of his weight to his right foot, closing off the man's air. When he stopped struggling, Blackthorne lifted his right foot enough to allow him to breathe.

"I could kill you now and not think twice about it." Of course, that was a lie. Blackthorne would think about it a great deal—particularly after Slate threw him out, but the man on the floor didn't know that. "However, I find myself in a generous mood this morning. Consider yourself lucky," Blackthorne said. "Because if you ever come at me again, I won't hesitate to kill you. Do you understand?"

Grey Beard grunted in what Blackthorne assumed was agreement. With that, he removed his boot from the man's throat. Grey Beard scrambled to his feet and then bolted.

"You have an interesting way of making friends."

Blackthorne whirled.

Colonel Hännenen's second-in-command stood in the passage with a teapot in one hand and an empty tray in another. It had taken a moment for recognition to set in because Moller wasn't in uniform. Instead, he was wearing buckskin leggings and a loose jacket over an untucked nightshirt. He was about fifty years old, short, and stocky for a kainen. He also wore a beard, which was unusual for a nonhuman. It partially covered a deep scar on his left cheek. He looked as though he hadn't slept, which was highly likely.

"Relax," Moller said. "It's too swiving early in the morning for a pugilism contest."

"Oh." Blackthorne dropped his defensive stance.

"I'm Sebastian Moller," Sebastian said, not offering a hand in greeting. The easy tone made it seem the reason why was merely due to the teapot and tray and not any other. "You're Blackthorne?"

Blackthorne blinked and then nodded.

The scar on his face deepened as Sebastian smiled. "Are you headed to the kitchen?"

Blackthorne nodded a second time.

"Come on, then," Sebastian said. "Can't have you fighting your way to breakfast. You'll wake the Hold."

Accompanying Moller, Blackthorne didn't know what to make of his intentions. Moller seemed friendly enough, but Blackthorne had yet to have an encounter with any of the Ghost's troops that didn't start or end badly. They arrived at the kitchen without meeting anyone else. Blackthorne opened the door for Moller since his hands were full, and he couldn't help thinking that in addition to the appearance of courtesy, it also served the tactical function of forcing Moller to enter first.

Warmth from the kitchen's fireplaces and the scent of baking bread flooded Blackthorne's senses.

"Good morning, Moss," Moller said.

Reaching inside the wall oven, Moss withdrew his hand and turned. "Salutations, Captain Moller, Mr. Blackthorne. Captain, would you like something to eat? The breakfast is not quite ready, but I do have leftover cold meat pie."

"Yes, please," Moller said. "Will there be enough remaining for Mr. Blackthorne?"

"Certainly, if he wants it," Moss said. "Just enough. Shall I heat the kettle for tea? We have sassafras and peppermint."

Moller sat down at one of the tables and gestured for Blackthorne to do the same. Without a polite excuse to leave, he sat.

Using both hands to rub the sleep from his face, Moller said, "You'll have to pardon me. The last few nights have been long."

Again, Blackthorne nodded.

"How bad is it?" Moss asked.

Moller asked, "I can trust you not to tell the others?"

"Of course," Moss said.

"There were two of the monsters at the river dock last night. With the one the Colonel and the others killed in the sheep pens, that makes three in the same night. If we hadn't known about their weaknesses, we would've been overrun," Moller said. "We'll have to double the watches."

"Is that possible?" Moss asked.

"It means less sleep, of course," Moller said.

Blackthorne frowned. The likelihood of his being assigned to a watch with a few of Colonel Hännenen's troops had just become a certainty. He'd been able to convince Slate to let him serve his turn at watch alone or with Birch, Sloan, Dylan, or Dar—all of whom, if not sympathetic, at least didn't wish him harm. It'd been difficult to convince Slate. Now such selectiveness would be impossible.

Moss set two plates of cold meat pie onto the table. Blackthorne didn't pick up his fork. Instead, he considered taking the plate back to his room along with a cup of tea.

"The others will have to be told eventually," Moss said.

"I'd rather not risk spreading panic. The Council should meet on it first," Moller said. "And I don't know anything for certain. It's possible the attacks will taper off again."

"Do not count on it. The darker it gets," Blackthorne said, "the braver the malorum will become."

TWO

A weak afternoon sun shone through thick clouds when Blackthorne knelt in the snow to read the fresh, easy-to-follow trail a young buck had left only minutes before. He moved in careful, slow steps through ice-crusted snow to avoid frightening off what little game there was—as much good as that did with Colonel Hännenen tromping behind him.

Blackthorne sometimes wondered how Hännenen had avoided capture for as long as he had. *Whose idea had it been to name him "The Ghost"?* "Ghostly quiet" was not a phrase one associated with anyone who walked around in hobnail boots.

Regardless, the more time Blackthorne spent with Hännenen, the more he began to understand why the others were so loyal. Hännenen possessed a certain quality that made him a difficult person to hate. It was damned hard to resist. So much so that Blackthorne often found his fear of catching a musket ball with the back of his head slipping. Then it occurred to him that Colonel Hännenen was a kainen prince, and Eledorean royalty possessed domination magic. *And didn't Slate once tell me that charm was an aspect of their power?* An involuntary shard of frozen dread pierced Blackthorne's chest, and vigilance renewed the painful tension between his shoulder blades. *Does* Hännenen *know about me? Has Ilta told him?*

Blackthorne didn't want to reach into his pocket for his watch. It would take too much of his attention from the trail and those who followed him. Instead, he searched the clouds but didn't get a good enough view of the sun through the trees to estimate the time. *We've travelled far from Grandmother Mountain.*

Reindeer were normally plentiful. However, something was driving the herds farther and farther away from their normal feeding grounds. He had a good idea what that something was. The reindeer weren't the only animals affected. He'd noticed fewer squirrels, birds, wolves, sheep, mountain lions, and even rats. It was the first time he'd seen anything like it. *Or perhaps it's the first time I've noticed?* His experience with malorum had been restricted to urban environments, after all, and what wildlife there was within such areas tended to be less noticeable. Nonetheless, having grown used to the small, busy noises of the forest, he found the silence unnerving.

There were less than two hours of daylight remaining. In that time, they were to find the buck, kill it, and transport it back. Since it'd taken more than an hour to find any evidence of game, he didn't have much hope of success.

"Are you certain those reindeer tracks are new?" Hännenen asked in a whisper.

Before Blackthorne could provide an answer, Captain Reini replied in equally low tones, "The signs are difficult to misinterpret. Even for an Acrasian."

Blackthorne let the jab pass. He was learning to pick fights that were worth the energy of engaging—which, at the moment, meant none in present company. *I don't care what they think, anyway.*

The twisting knot in his gut said otherwise. *Ilta loves him. I like her. I must try to get along with Hännenen for her sake.*

Get along? You want to swive his woman!

She's not his property any more than you are Slates's.

If that's so, why did Hännenen's man punch you in the face for having danced with her? Forget her. She's too good for you, anyway. And did I mention dangerous?

And yet that danger seemed to only make her more attractive.

Unfortunately, since the fist fight, the unspoken antagonism between himself, Hännenen, and his troops seemed to be getting worse rather than better. Slate blamed cabin fever. Therefore, this venture had been his idea. At least Captain Reini and Colonel Hännenen were speaking Acrasian.

A behavior change of dubious improvement.

Blackthorne shivered. The clothes under his coat were plastered to his skin. The fabric was growing more and more damp, inside and out, due to the combination of sweat and melted snow. The wind came in intermittent blasts. He fervently wished he were in his apartment, next to the fire. He peered over his buttoned coat collar, turning to check on Hännenen and Reini. They seemed content to follow his lead. Unfortunately, Blackthorne couldn't see the sun in order to judge direction. What was visible in the less dense parts of the forest was nothing but a sullen grey haze. Buried under layers of snow and ice, landmarks were difficult to recognize. In some areas, the precipitation had been so heavy that arching branches formed ice tunnels. Nothing looked as it had in the fall.

He paused, spying a depression in the nearest tree. He brushed snow off the trunk. Then he bit the tip of his glove and removed it so that he could feel the surface of the bark with his bare fingers. *Northeast. We're still heading east by north of the Hold.*

Of course, what the marks he'd carved into the tree months before actually meant was: *Warning: area restricted by order of the director of Wardens. East by North 1.* He'd used the Brotherhood's notation system and then provided translations to Slate, who had, in turn, passed them to the others. Marking the trees had been Slate's idea after a winter hunting party had been lost. However, Blackthorne knew leaving such signs posed certain dangers. So, he'd compromised, opting for Warden Unit cipher without providing a literal translation. Such notices were common enough, and the director's wishes were inviolate. Therefore, none would think to question—no one in the field would be of high enough rank. Eventually, the news of formerly unknown, private hunting grounds would reach the director's ears. It was inevitable.

And then all will come unravelled. Until it did, such things were the least of his problems.

Small movements to his right brought him back to the present. As he did so, he glimpsed a flash of pale brown flank between the trees a little over a hundred yards away. He brought up his musket. Hännenen and Reini did the same. The reindeer stepped into the open, unaware. Spying more of the animal for the first time, Blackthorne confirmed it was probably the same reindeer. *Big. No antlers.* He'd learned that young bulls shed their horns in winter. The reindeer paused, sniffing the freshening breeze. They were downwind—Blackthorne had made certain of it—but he held his breath nonetheless. Reassured, the reindeer lowered its head and pawed at the snow with a hoof. When its head came up a second time, Blackthorne took aim.

A musket went off next to him. The explosion echoed huge in the unnatural quiet, temporarily deafening him. He saw the buck drop through a haze of powder smoke.

"You owe me a bottle of rum," Hännenen said.

"That bet was for a gold eagle," Reini said. "And we haven't checked your shot yet. How do we even know you hit it?"

Blackthorne didn't wait for the others. He headed for the fallen reindeer.

"It's down, isn't it?" Hännenen slipped his arm through the gun's strap and followed. "And in one shot, I might add."

"I'm waiting for confirmation," Reini said.

"How else do you think it died? Are you suggesting that it smelled you and fainted dead away?" Hännenen asked.

"You don't care for Tahmerian sandalwood?" Reini asked. "It was a First Winter gift from Taina."

"Correct me if I'm wrong, but isn't wearing scent on a hunt counterproductive?" Hännenen asked.

"Who said I applied it?" Viktor asked in return.

"That woman gets up early," Hännenen said.

"That isn't all she gets up," Reini said with a contented sigh. "She's got quite the grip."

"For the goddess's sake, Viktor, must everything be about sex?" Hännenen asked.

"That reminds me," Reini said. "I've been waiting until we were far enough from of the Hold, but now I can finally say it."

"You aren't normally this reticent. What's the special occasion?" Hännenen asked.

"After all my badgering, you and Ilta have finally made the beast with two backs! Congratulations!" The declaration was followed up with the thump of a shoulder punch.

"Viktor, this isn't the—"

For once, Blackthorne was glad to have his back to Hännenen. Still, the news hit him like a mule kick in the groin.

Hännenen asked, "Remind me again, why do I put up with you?"

"I'm your best friend," Reini said. "Also, you asked me to stand for you at the binding ceremony next week."

"And now I've a whole week to find someone else," Hännenen said.

"You wouldn't," Reini said.

"Right now," Hännenen said, "I'm seriously considering Westola for the role. She, at least, understands the word 'discretion.'"

"My, you're awfully grumpy," Reini said. "Corporal Mustonen says it's been two whole days since you've put on clothes. Isn't it about time you two left your bed?"

"And to think I could be there now," Hännenen said. "Instead, I'm out here, freezing my balls off with your ass."

"Oh. I see the problem. Are you getting nervous?" Reini asked. "This will be a permanent binding, after all. It's all right to change your mind. I understand it's common for—"

"I'm not nervous!"

"Good," Reini said. "I can't wait to tell you about the amazing stag night I've planned."

Hännenen asked, "Why am I suddenly afraid?"

Reini said something in Eledorean.

"I don't think Ilta will care much for that," Hännenen said.

The pair switched entirely to Eledorean at that point, and Blackthorne ignored the rest of the conversation in spite of hearing Ilta's name repeated. He concentrated on the buck and tried not to think about the sinking ache in his chest. *All a true Retainer requires is the discipline of one's own mind.*

He found the animal on its side, twitching. Warm blood melted the snow in bright crimson pits. The right half of the reindeer's head was a gory mess.

Reini whistled.

"In the eye," Hännenen said, holding out his hand. "Like I said I would."

"I don't know," Viktor said. "Ball looks like it hit the outer edge of the eye—"

"It's close enough to count, and you know it," Hännenen said. He wiggled his fingers. "Pay up."

Reini shook his head, reached into a pocket, and slapped the coin into the Ghost's outstretched palm. "How many times is this?"

"Twenty-two," Hännenen said. "Haven't missed once since the new smith replaced the barrel. Rifling, he calls it."

"We should have the other guns updated," Reini said.

Hännenen said, "I'll only lose my marksmanship ranking to one of the others next spring."

"I doubt that," Reini said. "You're the best shot in the regiment. Always were. I hate being forever second place. Why must the advantage go to you?"

Blackthorne attempted to not interpret that as a subtle threat.

"You'll have your own soon enough," Hännenen said. "Joking aside, the work of replacing the others has already begun. Toby will make as many as he can with the steel we have on hand. Should make more progress when Nickols brings in more next spring."

The three of them cut a sapling and lashed the reindeer to it. By the time they were finished, the clouds had gathered force, dimming an already ailing sun.

It will snow again soon. Blackthorne began to worry if they'd get back before dark after all. Bending at the knees, he picked up his end of the heavy reindeer carcass and then balanced the stripped sapling on his shoulder. Reini did the same.

The scent of fresh blood, reindeer musk, and death wafted up Blackthorne's nose. There was something both attractive and disturbing about the smell. It brought to mind the gore-filled nightmares and the entity that had haunted his dreams that morning.

He mused again upon the Eledorean private's question, *Are the malorum here because of you?*

It's not possible. Couldn't be.

But Blackthorne didn't know for sure. And because he didn't, he was determined not to dwell on it. Unfortunately, the Hold didn't provide as many distractions as Novus Salernum had. *Other than the one.* And that one distraction was something he could never afford. *Not here.* He found it ironic that no woman would've had him in Acrasia had they known what he really was, and now no woman would have him because of who he'd pretended to be.

Having taken on the rear of the load, he was happy that he wouldn't have to worry about walking with his back to Reini and Hännenen on the return journey. Shaking hair from his face, Blackthorne settled into a steady pace. Trudging through the snow, he fought to keep his mind blank. The reindeer carcass weighed heavy and awkward on him. He focused on not dropping his part of the burden and keeping the sharp knot on the sapling from digging into his neck and right shoulder. They hadn't gotten far before a foul taste flooded the back of his throat, and he was brought up short by a long, unusual howl.

Reini stopped too, and Blackthorne nearly dropped his burden into the snow when the sapling slipped off his shoulder.

That's close. Too close.

Reini turned toward the second howl. His head tilted as if focused on listening.

"What was that?" Hännenen asked.

Blackthorne felt Reini's shudder of revulsion through the sapling's length. "Malorum."

"Are you sure it wasn't a wolf?" Hännenen asked.

"I've not seen any wolf tracks in at least a week," Blackthorne said. "Have you?"

"He's right," Reini said. "We need to get home. Now."

"We can't move fast enough. Not like this," Blackthorne said. He checked the sky again. "We must make a decision. Abandon the kill or find a defensible position for the night."

"What makes you say that?" Hännenen asked.

"Malorum may seem slow, but they can move very fast." Blackthorne pointed to the reindeer. "Particularly when they smell fresh blood."

Hännenen took off his hat, shoved hair out of his eyes, and then blew air out of his cheeks. "Swiving hells."

"Which is it to be?" Blackthorne said, leaving the decision to Hännenen.

"We can't abandon the kill," Reini said, speaking to Hännenen. "Who knows when we'll be able to get another? It's almost dark all day as it is."

"Where can we go, then?" Hännenen asked, angry.

Blackthorne pointed. "There's a place to the north of here. A recess in a canyon wall a half-mile away. Could be difficult to get the kill to safety. The base is eroding, but the ledge itself is stable. There are three of us. It won't be impossible. It has the benefit of high ground. Good defence. Room enough for a fire. Some shelter from the wind. It's where I'd go."

"How do you know about it?" Hännenen asked.

"Spotted it on one of my walks before winter set in," Blackthorne said. He didn't mention that he'd mapped the area. Although Slate hadn't asked him to do so, it had given him something constructive to do and kept him out of trouble while the weather held. Blackthorne couldn't help seeing the irony of it. Such a thing was what he would've once considered "busy work". His former self would never have voluntarily done it.

Another call shuddered through the trees in a fractured

harmonic—one part whistle, one part low, shuddering wail. The sound set his teeth against one another.

"It's getting closer," Reini said.

No. They are, Blackthorne thought. He didn't want to think about why he knew the difference between one malorum's voice and another's. A bolt of terror shot him through the chest. *They don't hunt together. You know this.*

A series of hollow calls originated from different directions. *Five of them. There are five of them out there. Hunting together.*

That's impossible.

Hännenen laid a hand on the stripped sapling. "All right. You've another chance to prove yourself, Warden. Don't swive us. Do so, and I'll make sure you eat your own liver."

Ex-Warden. Heart pounding, Blackthorne handed off his half of the burden. The terrain was rough and the incline grew steeper as they went. The snow was deeper too, and all three were out of breath by the time they came within sight of their destination. The canyon face, like most rock formations in the area around the Hold, was comprised of layers of sandstone and limestone. Some rock formations were more stable than others. Unfortunately, getting the dead reindeer up the fragile slope was difficult, frustrating work.

First to make his way to the top, Blackthorne accepted the packs and other equipment he was handed and then began loading muskets with silver shot. Hännenen's gun was already loaded. Blackthorne dealt with the other two weapons. When that was done, he began inventorying his personal supply of sterling. Hännenen pulled himself up the steep slope and then turned to offer Reini a hand up.

Checking the woods, Blackthorne spied the first malorum. A second one arrived about twenty feet away from their sheltering ledge. With that, it was plain that Reini wasn't going to make it to safety.

Blackthorne made a decision. First, he shoved the dead reindeer to the farthest side of the outcropping—as far away from Reini as he could get it on his own.

"Come on, Viktor," Hännenen said. "Get your ass up here already."

"This would've been a lot easier if your swiving boots hadn't gouged out the toeholds," Reini said.

"And it would be less slippery if you had had the common sense to wear hobnails in the snow and ice," Hännenen said with a grunt.

Grabbing a musket, Blackthorne tracked the malorum using the gun's sight. The barrel was much longer than he was used to—and he now understood he'd picked up Hännenen's gun. The metal worked into the stock had a greasy, unpleasant feel against his cheek. *Magic?* It was also heavier, and the balance was different. He made the necessary adjustments to his aim while counting the enemy. Six malorum lurked in the shadows now.

Six? Something was very wrong. The darkness under the trees seemed thicker. He closed his eyes and concentrated on listening. His skin tingled, and with that sensation came the knowledge that there were seven total malorum, all waiting for their moment to strike.

That's bad. He couldn't take on all of them at once. And Hännenen and Reini didn't have the experience with malorum that he did. There was only enough silver shot for twenty rounds. He could cast more. He had the equipment, but that would take too much time.

He heard the abrupt crack of crumbling stone. His eyelids snapped open. Hännenen's curse and Reini's scream accompanied the sound of breaking bone. Lying at the bottom of the incline on his back, Reini clutched at his right leg. It was covered in dirt and rock from the collapsed portion of the ledge. Reini's face contorted in agony.

One hundred feet away, the first malorum emerged. The creature was all odd angles and sharp edges with spiny fur. It wore the remnants of an Eledorean uniform and glided toward Reini on uneven, backward-bending legs. Its alien grace reminded him of a huge long-limbed insect, and yet there was something mammalian about the creature. Blackthorne had long decided that this was what made malorum so disturbing—they were neither one thing nor the other but an unwholesome combination of many, and if he didn't know any better, he'd say the northern malorum patterned themselves upon whatever creature they first fed upon. *Or creatures.*

The monster sniffed as it crept along, drawn by the scent of blood. It moved in the light like a blind thing.

Blackthorne's heart slammed a rapid drumbeat against his breastbone. He hoped it wouldn't affect his aim. The taste of dusty tin in the back of his throat got worse. He spat to keep from choking and then took a deep, slow breath, sighting along the musket's exaggerated barrel. He didn't know for certain what Hännenen had loaded the barrel with—chances were the ball was lead. Therefore, Blackthorne had to hit the creature in the head. He wasn't as accurate a shot as Hännenen. If he missed—

"This isn't a good time for a nap, Viktor," Hännenen said. "Get the hells up here! Now!"

Reini dragged himself from under the largest rock. "Oh, shit! Oh, gods! I think it's broken." Glancing up, he saw Blackthorne with the gun and held up his hands in defence. "Wait! Don't shoot!"

Hännenen whirled. A shocked expression flashed across his face before it transformed into betrayed fury. "Wha—"

Blackthorne slowly squeezed the trigger. The butt of the rifled musket rammed his right shoulder, numbing it. Powder smoke filled his nose and dusted his lips with spent powder. The heat of the explosion warmed his bare cheeks, and he tasted gunpowder grit. The explosion muffled the sound of the malorum falling—thrown onto its back by the force of the hit. He paused just long enough to be certain it wasn't moving. Then he discarded the musket and drew his black-handled Warden's knife. He rushed to the other side of the ledge. Yanking the reindeer's skull up and back, he cut its throat and let the head drop so that cooling crimson dripped over the far side of the frozen ledge.

With no beating heart to pump it, he wasn't sure if the blood would draw the malorum off. His fears proved to be in vain. The instant the blood began its sluggish flow, a chorus of piercing shrieks split the air. The malorum grew frantic. They began to fight among themselves as if to determine who would have the right to approach first.

"Stay here," Blackthorne said to Hännenen, and pointed to the reindeer's legs still tied to the sapling. "Throw me the rope. I'll tie it around Reini. Together, we'll get him up. As soon as he's safe, pull the reindeer from the ledge. If you don't, they'll get it. Understood?"

Hännenen nodded.

"Once it's moved, get a fire started," Blackthorne said. "There's a cache of wood in the crevice. There."

"You left a stash of cut wood here?" Hännenen asked with a frown.

Blackthorne sheathed his knife and went over the side after Reini. The journey down was even more dangerous and tricky than the way up had been. Sandstone, rock, dead roots, and dirt crumbled under his feet as he went, and he landed with a bone-jarring thump that caused his still-healing leg to ache.

Reini's face was set in a grimace of agonized determination. "I can't climb. Leave me."

Blackthorne lifted Reini, shoved his shoulder under Reini's arm, and half-dragged him to the bottom of the ledge. Risking a glance over his shoulder, Blackthorne saw the malorum he'd shot twitch. Across the clearing, two malorum broke free of the squabble and skittered to where the reindeer carcass lay. Both plunged their faces into the bloodstained snow. Other malorum arrived. Another violent dispute started only thirty feet away from where he and Reini were. The ancient death stench of the creatures filled Blackthorne's nose and clogged his throat. He coughed.

The end of a rope slapped him in the side of the face. Grabbing it, he spoke to Reini. "You've got to stand long enough for me to get this around you. Can you do it?"

Reini answered by raising his arms and balancing his weight on one leg. The slightest movement clearly pained him.

"Hurry up, damn you," Hännenen said. "That thing you shot isn't staying down."

Blackthorne secured the rope with a knot and tugged. "Ready."

Together, they guided Reini up the crumbling incline. Blackthorne did what he could to avoid jostling him, but the awkwardness of the angle made it impossible. Reini's mouth was set in a tight line the whole way, and by the time Hännenen dragged him to safety, Reini's skin nearly matched the snow. The effort of keeping from screaming showed on his face. Once it looked like Hännenen had most of Reini's weight, Blackthorne began to follow.

Reini shouted and pointed.

Something heavy smashed into the ledge-wall next to Blackthorne's head. It caused yet another small avalanche, sending frozen gravel down the front of Blackthorne's collar. Reini cursed. Turning, Blackthorne drew his knife.

The wounded malorum made another unbalanced, clumsy attack. The gaping wound in its bulb-like head oozed dark ichor the color of old blood. The gunshot had torn the skin from its right cheek, and half its ruined nose was gone. White bone and flecks of fractured teeth were steeped in the gore. The malorum's features grew blurry. It began to change form, but for whatever reason, it failed to complete the transformation. Its countenance became an amalgamation of the familiar and strange. The monster's sour breath filled Blackthorne's nose as the creature hissed and bubbled. The stench of it was overpowering.

Loud howls punched the air. Bickering malorum renewed their frenzied fight to get at the reindeer. One of the weaker creatures' arms was ripped from its body. The limb slapped another in the chest before landing on the ground. Losing all reason, they began feasting upon one another.

The malorum Blackthorne shot attacked again, swiping at his stomach. He twisted out of the way. His return blow was more reflex than planned attack. The black-handled blade pierced the malorum's skin but skipped across its ribs. It grimaced and screamed. The sound filled Blackthorne's skull. Revulsion pierced deep into his bones. The urge to rip and tear at the creature was overwhelming. The malorum slammed him against the incline. The back of his head was hammered against rock, and he was stunned. A claw clamped down on his left wrist. The pain flashed up his arm and through his spine, knocking him back to himself.

"Blackthorne! Stop playing with that thing!"

Remembering his knife, Blackthorne shoved the blade into the malorum's gut. Flames blossomed from behind and above him as if in response. Someone—either Hännenen or Reini— had lit the fire.

"Blackthorne?!"

He wrenched his dagger free with a twist of the wrist and a kick. Gasping for air, he watched the monster drop. The fingers of his right hand were now numb, and his glove had been shredded. He switched the knife to his left hand. He needed to get back up the ledge, but he couldn't do it without turning his back on the malorum, and he wasn't about to do that until he was certain the thing was down for good. He kicked the monster a second time, rolling it onto its back. Then he cut its throat.

Rage took control, and he followed a powerful impulse to stab it twice more.

"It's dead, damn you," Hännenen said. "Get up here!"

A musket went off, sending a gout of powder smoke into the air. Another frenzied malorum fell, its skull shattered. Ichor and brain matter splashed a second monster. A third tackled the wounded creature.

Caught up in his rage, Blackthorne took two steps toward the crazed group before he stopped himself and backed up to the ledge. Once again, the length of knotted rope slapped him in the face.

"You can't stay down there," Hännenen said. "Grab it."

Blinking, Blackthorne put away his blade, and Hännenen pulled him to safety. Blackthorne got both legs up just as two malorum reached his former position. They sniffed the air and then fell upon their stricken friend with wild abandon. Reini sat with his back against the rock wall, reloading one of the three muskets. Four pistols lay on the rock next to his injured leg.

Hännenen squatted nearby. "Were you bitten?"

Blackthorne felt Hännenen grab his right arm. Blackthorne winced and shook it free. Standing, he didn't look Hännenen in the eye.

What did I just do? Blackthorne said, "Thank you. I'll—I'll take care of it." He still had a small amount of antivenom in his pack.

"Will they give up and leave, you think?" Hännenen asked.

"Normally, I'd say yes." Turning, Blackthorne said, "But they're normally solitary hunters. I've never seen them cluster in a large group like that before."

The spell that had overtaken the malorum ended. The remaining creatures shifted out of the steadily increasing firelight. Blackthorne counted two. Both had taken on aspects of local wild-life. The first had a raven's beak, the second the ears and mouth of a mountain lion.

Do we have enough wood to last the night? Will more of them come? Or will that be all? The flames would keep the malorum from scrabbling up the ledge. To insure they stayed away, he reached inside his pocket and carefully laid out a half-circle of six sterling coins. It was the last he had. Below, the malorum seemed to sense the offending metal and moved back a respectful distance.

Reini raised his musket and aimed.

"Don't waste the powder," Blackthorne said, and then went to Reini. The pack with the antivenom potion in it was resting at Reini's elbow. "Were you bitten?"

"You stopped it from attacking me," Reini said.

"You're lucky I didn't miss," Blackthorne said. Continuing his search in the pack, he repeated his question. "Were you bitten?"

Reini shook his head.

Blackthorne found what he was looking for and held the brown vial up to the light. It wasn't a full dose, but it was enough to keep someone from dying. *Maybe.* He'd have to ask one of the healers for more ingredients whenever they got back. *If we get back.* He rewrapped the vial and then knelt next to the fire. "How bad is the leg?"

"Bad," Hännenen said. "It's going to be interesting getting Viktor and the reindeer back to the Hold tomorrow."

Blackthorne said, "Let's concentrate on seeing dawn."

Hännenen said, "I think there's enough wood to last. If they get too close, we've also got this." He rummaged in his rucksack and produced a small cannonball the size of a man's fist. A bit of fuse cord had been forced inside the hole in the top.

"A bomb? How many of those do you have?" Blackthorne asked.

"The one," Hännenen said. "It's another of Toby's experiments. Had it with me because I thought to test it while we were out here. Didn't want to risk an avalanche or drawing attention to the Hold with the noise." He gazed up the cliff face and shrugged. "Hopefully, I won't blow off my hand in the process."

"Save it," Blackthorne said. "We may not need it. At least not now."

Hännenen gazed down at Blackthorne's half-circle of coins. Blackthorne bent, retrieving one. Hännenen accepted it and almost smiled.

"Hello? Remember me?" Reini asked. "Pain is getting pretty bad."

"Lucky for you, I brought whiskey," Hännenen said, and fished a bottle out of the rucksack. "Let's sort out that leg."

"Don't take this personally, but I'd prefer to wait for a more attractive attendant," Reini said.

"I don't think you have a choice," Hännenen said. "If it's broken, the longer we wait to set it, the more difficult it's going to be for Ilta to fix it."

"Isn't that just my luck?" Reini asked. With a wince and a hiss, he shifted until his wounded leg was more accessible.

"Don't worry. Ilta taught me what to do. It won't be perfect, but it'll be better than nothing." Hännenen stooped, carefully feeling along the injury. "Thigh looks all right. Calf is swollen, though. I won't be able to pull the boot free," he said. "Maybe we should cut it off?"

"You're not taking my leg," Reini said.

Hännenen said, "I meant the boot."

"Oh," Reini said. Then he smiled. He was already sweating and shivering. "You would ruin a perfectly good boot just to place a splint on my leg? How do you know the boot isn't performing that function already?"

"He's got a point," Blackthorne said. He retrieved a blanket from his pack and threw it over Reini's shoulders.

Hännenen looked up, and for the first time, Blackthorne felt he was being addressed no differently from one of Hännenen's troops. "I don't suppose you have any healing skills?"

The warm feeling vanished. Blackthorne tried not to look insulted. "I have no . . . *magic.*"

He watched Hännenen's expression harden in an instant. Blackthorne could almost read the thought behind his eyes. *Warden.* The hate was so potent that it felt like a blow to the gut.

"Of course," Hännenen said.

Blackthorne went again to his rucksack. He hadn't left the Hold for longer than a few days at a time since winter had started. Therefore, he hadn't bothered to unpack—not completely, and even if he had, he wouldn't have removed the item in question. He searched until his hand closed around a second small cloth-wrapped blue glass vial. "I have . . . I have something that may serve to dull the pain. However, I'm not certain of the dosage."

"What is it?" Hännenen asked with a frown.

The second vial contained a solution Blackthorne had mixed for himself the day after he'd escaped the Reclamation Hospital. Although he hadn't opted to use it, he'd still carried it with him. The mixture at its current potency was designed to kill without pain within a short period of time. To his knowledge, it had no known antidote. He hadn't had the courage to swallow it, not at the time. He carried it now for new reasons. In spite of his training—or perhaps because of it—he knew better than to think he could withstand torture at the hands of the Brotherhood for long. They were far too efficient. Nonetheless, he was determined to never betray the Hold. "It's pure bloodflower extract."

Hännenen gave him a blank stare. "What is that? Poison?"

Of course it is, Blackthorne thought. *Do I know of anything else?* He looked away. "That is its original intent."

"What?" Reini asked.

"Are you suggesting I poison Viktor because his leg is broken?" Hännenen asked.

Blackthorne shook his head in denial. "I'm not—"

"Why are you traveling with that on your person?" Hännenen asked. "Does Slate know?"

"I was only suggesting . . . I . . ." Blackthorne took a deep breath. "Miss Korpela said that the potential for harm or help is in the dosage—" He regretted using her name at once. Hännenen's expression flashed to pure hate. "Your healers use similar substances to heal. Is that not true? I was taught a different name, but—"

"I should think the difference is in more than the naming," Hännenen said. "I don't know why I bothered to ask." He found a suitable stick among the kindling and gave it to Reini. "How much of the whiskey did you get down you?"

Reini held up the bottle to the firelight. "Enough."

"All right," Hännenen said. "Bite on that stick. This is going to hurt. Bad."

Blackthorne said, "I can dilute the mixture. If the dose is small enough—"

"Tell me where it hurts." Hännenen once again began feeling along Reini's calf.

Reini's curse was incomprehensible due to the mouthful of stick.

"Viktor, be serious for once," Hännenen said. "Can you move it?"

A loud slap sounded. "Ouch! Stop that! Shit! Shit! Shit!" Reini jerked from Hännenen's grasp. "You did that on purpose!"

Hännenen stood up. "I think it's the ankle. Or the leg bone right above it."

"Fantastic," Reini said. "I'll be walking a mile on it through the snow tomorrow."

Resigned, Blackthorne moved to the far side of the ledge and watched the remaining malorum test the boundaries of the firelight.

A Retainer's life is not his own. He was light-headed. His right wrist was hot and swollen, and his left hand clenched into a tight fist around the blue vial. He closed his eyes and something brushed against his cheek and then his nose.

It took him a moment to register that it was snow.

THREE

Blackthorne huddled next to the fire, wrapped in a threadbare horse blanket. The pain in his wrist grew worse, but it served to clear his head. The stone beneath him was frigid enough to be uncomfortable. So, he'd grabbed his rucksack and used it for a pillow. Hännenen hunched on the opposite side of the fire. The collar of his all-weather coat was turned up, and his thick, knitted scarf hid his face and neck beneath his hat. He shivered with his gloved hands shoved in his armpits. Hännenen had bundled Reini in his own quilt, and Reini was now curled on his side in a fitful sleep—his injured leg stretched out at a stiff angle. Blackthorne had offered his horse blanket—in truth, the only blanket he had—but Hännenen had refused it. Followed closely on the heels of the earlier rebuff, the refusal had stung. However, Reini hadn't suffered with the pain for long before Hännenen had relented and permitted Blackthorne to dose Reini with a small amount of liberally diluted bloodflower. At last, Reini had been comfortable enough to stop groaning and sleep. That, in turn, had the added benefit of making Hännenen less antagonistic.

Normally, Blackthorne would've shared the watch with Hän-nenen and gotten some rest. They would both need their strength for the journey back, but neither could trust the other enough to do such a thing. So they sat, staring at the flames in bitter silence.

Abruptly, Hännenen began sorting through his pack as if he'd forgotten something. He unpacked a series of small items—a vial and a jar. It couldn't be for food or tea. They'd already eaten.

"What are you doing?" Blackthorne asked.

Hännenen paused, pointing to the green glass jar with the linen-wrapped cork stopper. "That is salt." He returned his atten-tion to his ruck sack and retrieved a fragrant leather pouch. Then came a brown vial. "This is clove oil." Placing that on the ground next to the pouch, he unsheathed his knife. The fire whispered and crackled to itself for some time. He stared at Blackthorne with eyes that rapidly changed from light to dark. Finally, he spoke. "In the rush, Viktor and I forgot—we—I didn't perform a purification ritual."

Blackthorne blinked. Dread flash-froze the blood under his skin. He attempted to hide his reaction, but it was clear Hännenen had spied it nonetheless.

"I would do this in private. But I don't have the option, Warden," Hännenen said, using the blade on the back of his scarred left hand. Blood quickly welled up. He let a few drops fall into the fire. The flames savored the sacrifice with a hiss. Closing his eyes, he muttered something in Eledorean. When that was done, he daubed the cut with clove oil and a clean white cloth. "I'm doing this for Viktor and myself. I don't give a shit if it offends you. Interfere with what I'm doing, and I'll make you regret it." He pressed the cloth tighter into the wound and then tied it in place using fingers and teeth.

Blackthorne leaned away as much as he dared and attempted

to control his revulsion. At the same time, he was more than a little intrigued. His mother had been a marine before she'd become a slave—a marine from Marren. It was all he knew of her past. He didn't know what city she'd come from or even her real name. The people of Marren had been sea folk with close ties to the Waterborne Nations. That, along with vague memories of singing while she created beautiful clay pots, was all he had of her. So it was that he watched Hännenen with equal parts trepidation and fascination.

Hännenen used the clove oil and a linen rag to clean the curved blade. When that was done, he used two kindling sticks to gather two small lumps of glowing embers at the edge of the fire. He collected a large pinch of the leather pouch's contents and muttered a short speech in Eledorean. Then he tossed the substance onto the embers. Blackthorne recognized the scent of frankincense. He looked on as Hännenen wiped and anointed the blades and guns with the clove oil. Then, Hännenen shut his eyes and whispered a prayer in Eledorean. He passed his knife, saber, and musket through the smoke and did the same with Reini's weapons. Each time the incense smoke dissipated, he added a little more.

The sharp dusty scent grew strong enough to make Blackthorne sneeze. He'd never cared for the smell of frankincense. It reminded him of church, and it wasn't a pleasant association.

A noise from below the ledge drew Blackthorne's attention from Hännenen. The malorum stalking the shadows were again agitated. He couldn't see what was bothering them, due to sacrificing his night vision by staring into the fire.

Unaware, Hännenen continued with his ritual. He gathered a cupful of snow, melted it, and sprinkled salt into the water. Then he prayed with his wounded hand covering the cup—again in

Eledorean. Using the mixture, he got to his feet and sprinkled the warm, salted water on Reini's head. Then he did the same to himself. He flicked the last of the saltwater in a tight circle around his friend.

"If you have no wish to be included in the blessing, Warden, you'd best get against that wall," Hännenen said, indicating the far side of the outcropping.

Blackthorne hesitated. Aside from cutting himself, Hännenen's ritual hadn't been as disturbing as all that, and Blackthorne wasn't sure he wanted to spend a very cold night away from the fire's warmth. It would mean risking frostbite. "I'll . . . stay."

Hännenen arched an eyebrow. His expression changed with a blink. "Suit yourself." Muttering in Eledorean, he traced a broad circle with the salty water until it encompassed the entire ledge. He whispered in Acrasian, "Hasta, Horse Mother, grant your servant wisdom."

As Hännenen neared the completion of the circle, Blackthorne began to feel more and more confined and anxious. At the same time, he felt warmer and safer. Conflicting feelings dredged up memories of long days sitting in church. *Magic is dangerous. Evil. Those who use it are damned.*

I certainly was never among the pure. Still, Blackthorne decided to stop watching. Taking a deep breath in order to avoid breathing in any more incense, he turned to the darkness.

As if taking it as a challenge, Hännenen continued in Acrasian. "Great Synkkanen, Mother of Death and Life, I ask for Viktor Reini that you bless this sacrifice—theirs and ours."

Blackthorne's gaze snapped back to Hännenen. Hännenen bent, gathered a handful of snow and dirt, and gently tossed it over the bodies at the bottom of the ledge.

"Bless these dead, our former enemies. Lead them safely to

their next journey, wherever that might be. We thank them for taking their part in this battle, your sacrament." He picked up the vial of clove oil and went to Reini. Anointing him on the forehead with it, Hännenen said, "Bless we who live." He moved back to the ledge and smudged a dab of clove oil on his own forehead. He hesitated and then spoke again. "Forgive me if I killed in anger or hate. Forgive them if they did the same. Judgement is yours, Great Mother. It is not mine." He paused, sighed, and murmured, "Thank you for reminding me."

Blackthorne heard the words but hardly noticed. His mind had travelled back to Virens. *All the dead.* The laughter as prisoners were murdered—shot down after digging their own graves. The memory hit him doubly hard. If it weren't for the malorum, he'd have jumped over the ledge and ran as far as he could from the sound of Hännenen's voice. At that moment, Blackthorne felt as if he teetered on the edge of madness. He didn't understand why. He clenched his injured hand into a fist, wrapping his fingers ever tighter around the pain.

"Is something wrong?" Hännenen asked.

Afraid of what he'd say, Blackthorne didn't answer. He focused anywhere but on Hännenen's face. That was when Blackthorne noticed what was happening below. "The malorum." Blackthorne pointed. "Look."

They'd withdrawn under the trees.

Hännenen glanced at the cup in his hand and then threw the last of its contents at the malorum. They retreated even farther. "Well, isn't that interesting?"

Blackthorne knew better than to believe Hännenen's words had driven them back. If religious rituals were protection, then every Acrasian pastor, priest, and monk throughout the Regnum would've been employed for that task long before. "I wonder if it's the salt,"

"Can't be the water," Hännenen said. "If it were, they wouldn't be wading in snow. The clove oil, perhaps?"

Staring at the open green jar sitting next to the fire, Blackthorne suddenly liked their chances of surviving.

FOUR

Staggering, Blackthorne dragged the frame improvised from lashed saplings and a blanket. Reini lay unconscious on the stretcher. He'd developed a fever in the night and had been unable to walk. Therefore, Blackthorne had offered to carry him while Hännenen took the reindeer's weight on a second impromptu frame. Hännenen had added the packs to his own burden. Blackthorne had offered up his horse blanket to the cause. At the moment, he wasn't as certain it'd been a good idea. He alternated between feeling too cold and too hot. His hands were blistered, and his arms and shoulders ached. His wrist was swollen, and the pain was bad. He did his best to ignore it. This plan had worked well for the first half of the journey, but it was becoming more and more difficult as time wore on. His chest felt tight, making it hard to breathe.

Weak and not a little dizzy, he pushed on. The sky was already darkening, and it was still snowing. It wouldn't be long before the malorum ventured from their daytime sanctuaries. At least the weather would help cover their tracks—not that the traces he and Hännenen were leaving would be difficult to follow. Blackthorne hated not being able to stop and take care of the trail, but he didn't have the strength or time.

Blackthorne stumbled. *I won't stop. I won't. I can't.*

"Do you need to rest?" Hännenen asked.

Blackthorne was overcome with a burst of rage. *I'm wounded. Weak. The weak don't deserve to survive, and he knows it.* He forced an answer through clenched teeth. "There's no time."

"If you drop, I can't carry both of you, the kill, and all the ryggsacks," Hännenen said.

"Don't you think I know that?" Blackthorne had been allotted the lighter of the two burdens. That knowledge had offended him from the start. Unfortunately, he hadn't been able to argue the point. His right arm was almost useless. "I'll get Reini to the Hold."

"It won't do anyone any good if you kill yourself doing it."

I'm already dead, Blackthorne thought. A long, discordant howl echoed through the woods, jolting his heart with a flash of terror. "Come on!" Somehow, he scraped together enough energy to run.

They got as far as the first perimeter before the malorum caught up to them. They'd just entered the ravine leading to the river dock. Tall pines and birches towered along the top ledges, casting long shadows in their path. Blackthorne didn't have time to sense the creature. The malorum leapt down onto Hännenen and his burden from behind, landing to the right. Blackthorne's exhausted warning was cut off by two gunshots from the trees. The malorum dropped and rolled off Hännenen. The pristine snow was painted with ichor. Three sentries hopped down from their perches to meet them—all three dressed in Eledorean uniforms. One of them used a series of loud whistles to signal that friends had reached the perimeter.

"Thank the Mother you're here," Hännenen said, gasping. "Gustafsson, get Reini. Hirmi, Isokoski, help me with the reindeer."

The sentries with torches rushed to assist, relieving Blackthorne of Reini's weight. He would've protested, but he didn't have the breath. No longer running for his life, he was slammed with a bout of dizziness. His lungs refused to obey him and squeezed shut with agonizing pain originating in his back, close to the spine. At the edges of his blurring vision he spied two more malorum. Unable to speak, he pointed.

Hännenen retrieved something from his pack and turned. "Get down!"

Blackthorne didn't have time to wonder how Hännenen lit the fuse. He threw himself onto the ground just as Hännenen tossed it at the monsters. The bomb landed at the feet of the malorum. Then came the explosion and pressure. Time became disjointed. Blackthorne couldn't hear. He felt clumps of snow, rock, and ichor land against his cheek, head, and back. The agony trapping his chest didn't stop. He smelled burned gunpowder, his own sweat, and blood. The taste he associated with the presence of malorum flooded his mouth. Someone or something tugged at his body. He closed his eyes and fought to breathe. His training had taught him to welcome death, and he thought himself immune to the fear of it. Still, he didn't want to watch himself be torn apart.

Hännenen's voice was muffled. "Laine, get over here!"

The dizziness was all-consuming. Blackthorne didn't know one direction from another. His ears were ringing. Everything was moving both too fast and too slow. Coughing, he stood up with the help of one of the others. He choked on powder smoke until, just as suddenly as it happened, the attack stopped and he could breathe again.

Hännenen asked, "Are you hurt?"

Blackthorne shook his head.

The group headed homeward, chased by a hunting pack of malorum. Blackthorne lost count in the rush but had stopped around ten. *That's simply not possible,* he thought as he used the last of his reserves to get home. *They aren't group hunters. They cannot cooperate.*

He collapsed in a heap the instant the door slammed shut behind him. The muffled sound of malorum cries echoed down the passage as they threw themselves at the wooden door.

⊰ ⊰ DYLAN ⊱ ⊱

Entering the shrine he'd created in a less-traveled corner of the
Hold, Dylan was taken aback by the presence of a woman he didn't
recognize. She was sitting on the rug positioned in front of the
seawater font with her back to him. She was heavyset, and her dark
brown spirit knots were mostly gathered high on her head, while
some spilled down her back and onto the rug. The prayer tokens
tucked into her greying braids were shaped like tiny ships. She was
dressed in a loose silk shirt dyed in greens and blues with flecks
of yellow, and a pair of brown sailor's breeches. Her feet were bare.
He recognized the intricate pattern painted into the silk as a traditional Waterborne wax-relief process his sister, Joan, specialized in.

Dylan hesitated. He didn't wish to disturb the woman's prayers, but at the same time, he was curious as to who she was. The Waterborne shrine was intended to be private. He hadn't heard of any new arrivals, much less any new arrivals of Waterborne descent. He decided to go ahead with his plans and released the bead curtain he'd been holding. The glass beads made a clattering sound like rushing water. He began replenishing the oil in the lamps around the altar. The room wasn't large—he couldn't have avoided disturbing her. Still, he attempted to be as quiet as he could.

"Good morning, little lordling," she said in perfect Ocealandic. "I've been waiting for you."

Dylan knew that voice. *Aegrir*. His heart staggered inside his chest, and his blood grew cold. He turned and tried not to gape. "Great One?"

"Thank you for the shrine. You thought of everything." She waved a hand at the font. "It's filled with seawater. This far inland, such a thing is . . . good. River water is so bland and flat." She got to her feet and held out her brown arms. "Don't stand there with your mouth open. Come. Give your mother a hug."

He obliged her. She smelled of the ocean and fresh air. Her pale eyes were the same color as Dar's, a shifting blue-green, and her skin was warm like the sun's reflection on the surface of the sea. She gave him a gentle, loving squeeze and released him. Respectfully, he stepped back and bowed.

"I apologize, Great One," he said. "I did not expect you here."

She gazed around the room, taking in the furnishings and hangings he'd used to give the space a more homelike feel. "So much rock. It is understandable."

"It is necessary, Great One."

"Because of the abominations," she said, a sad expression tugging at the corners of her full lips. "And it is about them that I've come."

"The soulbane?"

She nodded. "Sit. We need to talk."

He gathered a couple of cushions and offered one to her. When she refused it, he settled on the rug, using them both.

"Have you ever been to Ghost Crescent?" she asked.

Ghost Crescent was an uninhabited island about seventy miles south of the Acrasian peninsula. It was known to be haunted. "I haven't, but I know where it is," Dylan said. "There are many stories told about it—none of them good."

"There's a reason for that," she said. She traced a pattern in the air at her side, and a bottle and two small glasses appeared. "Long, long ago, when I was young, this world was peopled with many beings like myself. Mortals were much fewer then. Our world, this world, was linked to another not unlike our own. On it lived beings much like us. In the beginning, those beings who lived in this other place were intelligent and wise. They learned how to harness power from the land, the water, and the air. They built cities high into the sky. Their thirst for knowledge became insatiable. They abandoned wisdom and empathy in exchange for gain and control. Their desire for more took on a darkness. It became an obsession. In the process of their pursuits, they enslaved and consumed all life and all light, and yet they craved more. They asked for this world, and we refused. The light of their sun was consumed at last. Hungering in the dark, they invaded. A great war was fought. The force of it scorched and shook the very earth. Seas boiled dry, and much of the beautiful world this once was . . . was destroyed. Rifts were opened with the force of the fight. But at long last, we drove the abominations back at great cost. To do so required the united power of all the peoples and surviving beings of spirit. We closed the rifts against the other-worlders, although many of the others like me were lost. The abominations drove themselves mad in their defeat.

"Unfortunately, too much damage was done, and there are weaknesses in the closures. Each place in which one of these rifts exists has a guardian people. Each was charged to pass on the necessary lore. The seals had to be reinforced periodically. Over time, the lore was lost. The guardian peoples stopped paying attention. Other needs overshadowed their duty. Some of the . . . doorways no longer have their keepers." She uncorked the bottle, filled the cups, and handed one to him.

Dylan accepted the cup. He smelled finely crafted rum. "That doesn't sound good."

"It was to be expected," she said, taking a sip. "Mortals have short lives and even shorter memories. When memories change, mortal history changes with it. We knew the lore would be lost. That is why the seals were built to overlap and reinforce one another. They're connected. In this way, this world has been made safe for centuries. Every so often, one of the abominations forces its way here."

"The soulbane and the malorum are one and the same," Dylan said, unsurprised.

"And the more they consume, the more they become what they eat." She nodded. "One hundred years ago, one such creature crossed over. The being it first encountered was a lesser spirit. As a result, the creature was more powerful, more aware than the others. It survived and thrived in the night. It grew to know this world and its people until it could disguise itself as a mortal. It has taken leadership within the mortal country in which it resides. Since then, it has been bringing over more and more of its kind. It has been working to break the seals and remove any possible defense. It was that creature who ordered the extermination of the kainen. It is also the one who collected the water steel swords you seek."

"The Emperor?" Dylan asked. "The Emperor is one of—of them?"

"Not the Emperor. A consul," she said. "There are two consuls. And one of them is . . . this creature."

"Oh."

"There is a place—an underwater cave," she said. "It is on Ghost Crescent. This is the source of the abominations who have been infecting my oceans. The guardians there were destroyed. Therefore, you, my little lordling, must go to this island and close this rift."

Dylan blinked. "Me? I can't! I—"

"I am doing what I can," she said. "But I cannot go to Ghost Crescent."

"Why?"

"As powerful as the Acrasian consul is, that abomination consumed a *lesser* spirit. If one of its kind were to encounter and consume me . . . the result would be unthinkable," she said.

"Oh," Dylan said. He paused, staring at the contents of his glass. "How am I to do this? I don't know anything about closing a rift. Should I consult the Sea Mother? Perhaps there is someone more qualified—"

"There isn't time," Aegrir said. "The one I had chosen before you was unable to complete the task before she was consumed. I made a mistake. I sent her alone."

Dylan swallowed. "Tell me what I must do."

"You have friends here," she said.

"I do."

"They have weapons that will be of some use. The Eledoreans must give you these weapons," she said.

"How many will we need? Enough for me, Dar—"

"I must caution you against bringing your Darius," she said. "He doesn't have the necessary connection to the ancestors. He is unprotected."

"I can't leave him behind," Dylan said. "I promised never to leave him again."

"Then I will not ask you to break your oath, little lordling." She paused and gazed past his shoulder, apparently seeing something he could not. "Interesting. It seems he will prove useful. Not at the rift . . . elsewhere. On the island itself. Your Darius may go with my blessing. However, he will need to do something for me."

"I'm certain he would be honored."

"Normally, I would not permit you to speak for him, but time is far too short." She then closed her eyes and spread her arms out wide with her palms to the ceiling and began to sing.

Dylan didn't recognize the song, nor did he understand the words. Her quiet voice resonated through his entire being. It was the most beautiful thing he'd ever heard. After a time, Aegrir brought her hands together. A ball of blue light appeared. It drifted, finally resting inside her cupped palms. She stopped her singing, and then with a sad smile, she blew into her hands. The light grew brighter before it went out.

She turned to him. "I will entrust your Darius with this life. He is to protect them and nurture them, for they are the last of their kind. Neither of you is to tell anyone of their true nature. There are those who might make use of them elsewhere. This one is intended only for Ghost Crescent. Understood?"

Dylan nodded and reached his hands out. A small brown lizard with jewel-blue eyes crawled into them. "What is it?"

"The parent of Ghost Crescent's new guardians," Aegrir said. "Your Darius will know when to release them on the island."

Dylan nodded. "Thank you. How soon does this need to be done?"

"No more than two months' time." Aegrir stared him in the eyes. "And do not go alone. Take only those you trust."

⚔ S U V I ⚔

"You're sure?" Suvi asked. Her heart was thudding inside her chest as she attempted to accept what she'd heard. *I'm going to die? I can't die!* This was the first time Ilta had given her bad news since the fall of Jalokivi, and she was doing her best not to panic.

Don't be stupid. Everyone dies eventually. No matter how much one avoids talking or even thinking about it. You're a queen. Mother would want you to be brave and face this, and you know it.

She understood she must have given away the strength of her emotions when she saw Ilta wince. Suvi thought, *Get control of yourself. Now.*

Ilta said, "Nothing is certain."

Suvi frowned. *Stop. Stay alert. She's softening the blow. She'll get in the habit of not telling you the full truth, if you let her. You must be strong for everyone else's sake.* "It's okay. I'm not afraid." It was only partly a lie. "I'm not my father, you know." The remark sounded defensive even to her ears.

"Every Silmaillia is trained to gauge the character of their regent. And have been from the time of Samsa Rasi," Ilta said. "If I thought you were like your father . . . well . . . Gran wouldn't have breathed a word, and neither would I."

Suvi nodded, and the conversation died. An uncomfortable silence lingered in the air until she ventured, "So, what does one say when one is told they're going to die?"

"I didn't say that," Ilta said. "I said that if you go to Novus Salernum, it's highly likely that you'll be captured."

"There's a difference?"

"There is," Ilta said.

"Well . . . there's that, I suppose," Suvi said.

"Remember, the future isn't simple or certain. It's mutable. The act of telling you in and of itself affects the outcome."

Again, Suvi nodded. "Hopefully in a positive way." She was trying to take in everything she'd been told, but none of it was fitting easily inside her mind. *Wait a moment.* "I'm not needed in Novus Salernum. The rift is located on an island called Ghost Crescent." Dylan had approached her about the swords and about a venture to the island. He hadn't asked for her help. He hadn't needed to. She'd volunteered. "I can remain aboard ship while the others retrieve the swords."

Ilta tilted her head. "So, technically, you won't be in Novus Salernum proper. You'll only be in the harbor."

"Exactly."

"That's a fine line."

"But one I don't mind risking," Suvi said, and then paused. "What if this is one of those events we can't avoid?"

Ilta said, looking away. "I don't get the feeling that this is one of those. The visions feel more like a warning."

"You're sure?"

"As I can be," Ilta said. "Of course, no Silmaillia is perfect. We're just as flawed and just as prone to mistakes as everyone else. And this is even more so in my case."

"I'm aware. No one expects perfection from you," Suvi said. "I certainly don't."

Ilta frowned. "The truth is, sometimes I have trouble sorting out what is a vision and what is . . . reality. That's why . . . well . . ." She shrugged. "If it makes you feel better, I can conduct a more specific, personal reading for you."

Although Suvi had heard of it being done, she'd never witnessed an actual stone reading before, and while her curiosity threatened to get the better of her, she knew requesting one at this time would only undermine the tenuous line of trust between the two of them. "It's not necessary," she said, suddenly understanding that Ilta was more nervous than usual. "I know you're doing the best you can. We all are."

Ilta nodded. She still seemed jittery, in spite of the reassurance. "I had that vision or variants of it three times in the past week. Tea?"

The Silmaillia's apartments smelled of a combination of medicinal herbs and flowers. From the moment Suvi had entered the room, she hadn't been able make up her mind whether that was pleasant or not. *Ilta is your Silmaillia. Trust that you will work together to find a means of avoiding what can be avoided.*

And if it can't?

Then it can't. And your duty is to mitigate the potential for disaster. You aren't the important factor in the survival of New Eledore. Your people are. And that means you're going to have to give some thought about what happens to them when you die.

Ilta's discomfort appeared to be getting worse. Now she seemed unwilling to meet her eyes. Suvi watched Ilta fuss over whatever concoction she was substituting for tea and tried to be more . . . *queenly?*

Since when has the relationship between a regent and the Silmaillia ever been comfortable? But it could be, and ultimately, that was what Suvi wanted. Too much depended upon it. *This is a phase. We'll get through it.*

Suvi allowed Ilta to place a delicately painted teacup and saucer in front of her without showing her distaste. The Hold had run out of black tea a week earlier. Suvi hated having to settle for herbal tea, particularly chamomile. She didn't want to drink it, but one of the surviving Eledorean customs was hospitality to visitors. Therefore, for the sake of civility, she picked up the cup and brought it to her lips. All at once, she caught the scent of cinnamon and cardamom and paused before tasting it. It was surprisingly good.

Of course she knows you hate chamomile, Suvi thought. *She's the Silmaillia.* The contents of the cup trembled with a second jolt of cold realization.

"Is it all right?" Ilta asked.

Unable to decide whether or not Ilta had meant the tea, Suvi swallowed. Finally, she trusted herself to speak. "It's lovely." And it honestly was. "I'd—I'd like the recipe."

"It's not all that complex. I'd be happy to give you some for your personal larder before you leave. I made it especially for you."

"Thank you," Suvi said.

The conversation died out again and unease took its place.

"Anyone would be frightened by the news I gave you," Ilta said.

"Anyone isn't queen," Suvi said.

"You can't force yourself to not have emotions about emotional things," Ilta said, not meeting her gaze. "This is even more true of queens. I'm here to listen in ways that no one else can. Consider it part of my role as Silmaillia. You can trust me. If you don't, I can't help you, and if I can't help you, I can't help the kingdom."

Suvi felt the corners of her mouth turn up. "I have to trust you."

"In fact, the use of a souja could be considered . . . inadvisable," Ilta said. "If you look at it from another angle, your inability to shield can be seen as an advantage. If we're careful of one another's boundaries, it could make our work together easier. I—I've been doing a lot of work with maintaining boundaries lately." She blushed.

"When did you become so wise?"

"I've been studying Gran's journals, among other things." Ilta seemed a little more at ease, but she still seemed deeply uneasy.

"All right," Suvi said. "I'll work on a contingency plan for if I'm unable to resume my duties as queen after the journey south."

"I've . . . already talked to Nels about—"

Suvi's jaw tightened. "You told *Nels* before you told me?"

Ilta stared at her own hands, distressed. "It couldn't be helped. You see . . . he was there when the visions came, and I apparently said enough during the trance that he deduced what I was seeing without my telling him. And . . . and . . ." She sighed, seemingly helpless.

"Ah. I see." *This is what comes from your Silmaillia also being your bond-sister. Well, soon-to-be bond-sister.* Suvi didn't understand why she was so relieved. "And *this* is what you were so worried about?"

"I thought you'd be furious with me." Ilta's shoulders perceptibly dropped, and she now sat with her body carrying less tension.

"You're living together. And my brother is perceptive," Suvi said. "How could you prevent it? Mind you, this doesn't mean you should discuss all your visions with him first. There are a number of things he doesn't need to know. At least, not before I do."

"I'll do my best."

"Well. I'm glad that's settled," Suvi said, took another sip, and then swallowed. "Now, back to more important matters. How did he react?"

"He was very upset and confused. He doesn't want you to make the journey south."

"Too bad," Suvi said. "Dylan needs us. All three of us. We've a rift to close."

Ilta nodded.

"Have you been able to discover anything new?" Suvi asked. "Why is it that Father didn't notice there was a breach? For that matter, why didn't Saara know?"

Ilta said, "That's what worries me about Acrasia. Well, one of the things."

"One of them?"

Ilta said, "According to Blackthorne's reports, there are distinctions between the southern malorum and those we've encountered here." She glanced to the stack of books on a nearby table. "If both groups are one and the same species—"

"If? You heard Dylan," Suvi said.

"Then all the knowledge we have, the knowledge gleaned centuries ago about the malorum, is wrong. And—and if that is the case, then we have no hope of preparing for what is ahead—not without Blackthorne."

Suvi blinked. "His training may be more useful than our collected ancient knowledge. But don't we already know all that he knows?"

Ilta said, "The honest truth is, he's been fighting those things a lot longer than we have."

"Then it's long past time Blackthorne shared that training with our troops."

"Nels isn't going to like that."

"Nels will get over it, I'm thinking," Suvi said. "We'll do what we must to survive. I believe he's familiar with the concept." She waited while Ilta poured a fresh cup of tea and then took another sip. "Where have the malorum we've been seeing come from? Do you know?"

"Do you mean to ask if something was wrong with last year's seal?" Ilta asked. "This isn't your fault, Nels's, or mine. We performed the ritual correctly. It remains sealed," Ilta said. "I've no idea where they are coming from."

"They could be entering Eledore from the beaches," Suvi said. "Now, that's a terrible thought."

Ilta nodded. "All the more reason for us to get those swords to Clan Kask, and to arm ourselves. How many of our soldiers have water steel? Do you know?"

"Exactly fifty-three, including the one that Nels carries," Suvi said. "A majority of the weapons weren't in common use during the war. Blades employed by the private armies were considered the property of the nobles and stayed within their control. As for my father's army, most of them consisted of criminals and peasants. What little water steel they possessed was either passed down from one generation of soldiers to the next or from master to apprentice. The casualty rates among the Royal Army meant that very few of those blades were recovered."

"The Eledoreans took them from the dead?"

Suvi nodded. "Clearly, even an Acrasian can sense the value of such a blade."

Blinking, Ilta turned her attention to her tea.

"I'm sorry," Suvi said. "Like my brother, I suppose I'm having trouble with my biases."

"It's all right," Ilta said. "They're certainly earned."

"But you feel Blackthorne can be trusted?"

"Absolutely," Ilta said.

"Then I'll resolve myself to trusting your judgement in the matter," Suvi said. "Have you been able to find the location of the Acrasian seal yet?"

"No," Ilta said. "But I'm sure that the histories of Kassarina Ilmari recorded the locations somewhere. The only problem is translation. What we need was written in four-hundred-year-old Eledorean, and in cypher. Nels has been working on it, but stubborn as he is, even he has his limits."

Suvi sighed. "Very well. I may be of no use when it comes to translations, but I'm very good at puzzles. I'm happy to give it another attempt when you're ready."

"I'll let you know as soon as we get enough translated to make it worth your trying," Ilta said.

Suvi nodded. They both focused on their tea. Sitting in silence, for the first time, Suvi felt comfortable with Ilta.

"I wish there were any other way than going south," Ilta said.

Suvi asked, "Will you be all right?"

"I've not seen anything to indicate I won't," Ilta said. "I wish you could stay here. I wish you didn't have to risk going at all."

"Wearing a crown means more than nice dresses and parties," Suvi said. Or, in my case, going about begging for assistance for your people from rich relatives and keeping an eye out for poison and potential plots. "I know certain family members forgot that in the past . . . but I haven't."

"You do have a choice, you know."

"Actually, I don't—not if I don't wish to be like my uncle or my father or the countless other Ilmaris that allowed the kingdom to slide into ruin," Suvi said. "But I appreciate your making it seem as though I do." She kept her expression blank while fresh terror made ice of her blood. *If you can't save yourself, Nels will get you free. He'd do anything to find you. You know that.*

Even die. She blinked again. "What about Nels?"

"What about him?" Ilta asked.

Suvi set the cup on a small nearby table. Several books were stacked there in an untidy pile—all of them medicinals, from what she could tell. That was when she caught the title of the fifth in the stack. *The Transmutation of Species.* The title was written in Acrasian. It clearly belonged to James Slate.

Ilta can read Acrasian? Or is she having Nels translate it for her? "Have you seen anything about whether he'll return from Acrasia?"

"Not yet," Ilta said, looking uncomfortable. "I have to assume it means he will."

"Good," Suvi said. "And the children Freyr Ahlgren has been training, have any of them demonstrated a talent for command magic? Are any of them possible matches for Silmaillia training?"

"Not yet," Ilta said. "But many of them are too young for him to be able to determine their talent. I've told him to report to me the moment he knows anything."

Suvi nodded.

"Don't worry," Ilta said. "More children are being born. Others are being found, too. Who knows how many of our people are still living in the wilds?"

And how many of them will survive the winter and the malorum alone in the wilderness? Suvi said, "None of us will live forever." *Particularly if we're travelling into Acrasia.* "We must find successors soon."

Ilta swallowed and stared into her cup. Not knowing what else to do, Suvi did the same. The herbal mixture was sweet, spicy, even soothing in that it reminded her of the spice cake her mother liked so much. *And Nels.*

She served this tea to put you at ease, Suvi thought. *That was smart.* She listened to the small, comforting sounds of the fire and the clock while she gathered her thoughts. It occurred to her that she could hear the ticking of more than one clock. That was when she noticed that in addition to the clock on the mantel, there was a small clock on the table. *That's odd.* There were no clockmakers living in the Hold. *Not yet.* They were lucky to now have a blacksmith.

"Have you given more thought to binding?" Ilta asked.

"What? Oh," Suvi said. "No."

"But—"

"No," Suvi said. "I saw what it did to my mother. If there's one part of my life over which I want some measure of control, it's whom I sleep with."

"But— Having a partner may make your burdens easier to bear."

"Or infinitely more difficult," Suvi said. "I'm not like you. I can't let my heart lead me in such matters. As if it weren't difficult enough to find a suitable partner in life, I have added challenges. If Eledore were a viable country, I might have some power in such negotiations. However, I have none at the moment and none for the foreseeable future. In the best scenario, Eledore becomes a protectorate of a more powerful country. Worst case, I won't be safe from the Acrasians. Choosing wrong doesn't means misery. It means assassination."

"I hadn't actually considered—"

"Eledore is *my* responsibility. Surely that counts as enough mothering for any woman?" Suvi asked. "I've decided to leave the matter of producing Eledore's heirs to you and Nels."

"Oh." Again, Ilta blushed.

Suvi tried to smile. It felt good to talk to someone as she had to Piritta, even for a moment. Her best friend and former *souja* had been lost when Jalokivi fell. Her twin brother, Nels, and Dylan were her remaining confidants, but it wasn't the same. They were men. Piritta had been a sister. *And soon, Ilta will be too.* "That wasn't exactly subtle, was it?"

Ilta returned the smile. "No. Not exactly."

"Don't worry. You have my approval," Suvi said. "He's wanted this since he was sixteen."

"Maybe not in the permanent sense."

"Maybe not," Suvi said. "But you make him happy in ways that no one else has. You make him more cautious about his own welfare. And *that* makes me very happy indeed." *It feels good to have the succession sorted out at least. In case.*

"I wish I could be more reassuring," Ilta said.

"I know. It's all right. Really." Suvi paused. "Dylan said that we must get to Ghost Crescent no later than Mansikkakuu. How soon do you think we can be ready to leave?"

"Even if the snows melt before the vernal equinox, I wouldn't risk it while the daylight hours are shortened."

"The malorum." Suvi had taken to using the Acrasian name for them, largely because "Old Ones" sounded so vague and archaic. "Old Ones" were childhood myths. "Malorum" were a real problem to which there were real answers and real solutions—at least, so she hoped.

"Maitokuu, I think," Ilta said. "I guess that means you'll have some time to plan."

How am I to make all the arrangements without Nels catching on? Suvi thought. "I'm considering giving Councilor Slate all the information I have on the situation. He's right. Him not knowing everything I do about the malorum and the venture south means he's less effective as a spymaster."

Ilta tilted her head and closed her eyes. "I think that would be wise."

"Did you have a vision?"

Ilta smiled and blinked. "No. I just think that you'll need some support other than myself when it comes to Nels. You'll want him to take over in your place, I assume?"

"I will."

"He's not going to like that idea. Neither will the rest of the Hold."

"Of course not. That doesn't change the fact that Nels is next in the line of succession."

"He'll claim he's not eligible."

"He's no diplomat. But every ruler has their strengths and weaknesses. And unlike anyone else, including myself, he studied statecraft at an early age with the intent of running the country. He's the most qualified other than Councilor Slate, and I won't hand my kingdom over to an Acrasian—no matter how well intentioned and suited," Suvi said.

"Nels is . . . stubborn."

"Of course, he is. He's my twin brother," Suvi said. "However, I'm the queen. I decide. He doesn't."

"And you think he'll go along with that?"

Suvi let one corner of her mouth curl. "Who else can I leave in charge and absolutely trust to make every effort toward my return? He'll want out of that role as fast as he can manage it. Not only that, he'll do a good job. And he won't hand it off to anyone but me, no matter how much he'll want to."

"But he is going with us."

"And he's returning. I may not."

Ilta stared down at the cup in her hands and shook her head. "Are you going to tell him? Won't he need some time to adjust to the idea?"

Pouring herself yet another cup of tea, Suvi said, "And have him fight me every inch of the way? I won't have time for that, prepare for the journey, and run things. Besides, he's not like me. He does his best thinking on his feet. Don't worry. I'll leave enough instructions that he won't be lost."

"He'll be angry."

"He'll be angry no matter what, if it comes down to that," Suvi said. "I just won't be around to witness it. Lucky you. You'll be in the thick of it." She sipped her tea. "He'll forgive me eventually. He always does." *At least, I hope so.*

"I wish there were another way."

Believe me, I do too, Suvi thought. She paused, for a moment unsure whether or not to continue. The conversation was depressing enough. "I must send a message to Cousin Edvard," Suvi said. "It's time to discuss the matter of the malorum in the open—at least between rulers. Maybe that will spur some cooperation."

⚜ NELS ⚜

ONE

"Where's my dress uniform?" Nels asked, stumbling in the dark. His head was pounding, and his stomach seemed to be staging a revolt in answer to the whiskey assault from the night before. The water he'd forced down to counter it seemed to have put out the flames but didn't seem to be doing much for the gastric pitchforks. "Shit! I hung it up right here last night! To keep it from getting wrinkled. I knew I shouldn't have listened to you! I'm going to be late! I knew it!"

Viktor's languid voice came to him out of the darkness from across the room. "And yet you did anyway. Some people never learn."

"You son of a—"

"I was joking! Don't worry. I've got your back. You know I do. Relax."

In Nels's rush, he stubbed his toes on a chair and cursed. Hopping, he clutched his injured foot and wished he'd never met Viktor Reini. Nels cursed the darkness, the cluttered floor, and the fact that he hadn't stayed in his own apartments.

He'd given Ilta his rooms for the night since hers were connected to the infirmary, and she'd needed privacy in order to prepare. Therefore, he had opted to spend the evening with Viktor and the remnants of his company in Viktor's apartments. As a result, it'd been a late night of debauchery—half of which was a distant memory. "Where's the lantern? I need light!"

"Take it easy," Viktor said in languid tones from his place on the sofa. "The ceremony is hours away."

"My watch says otherwise. It's half past one!" Nels said. "Why did you let me sleep so late?!"

"I didn't," Viktor said. "And don't worry about your uniform. Mustonen took it. He wanted to clean it and make some repairs. It was looking a bit worse for the wear."

"I'll never make it in time!"

A squeak accompanied a small flood of light as Viktor flipped open a blinder on a dark lamp. Nels instantly regretted the request, grabbing his head and groaning.

Viktor said, "Take a deep breath. Slow down. You're going to be fine."

"I've exactly one half-hour to—"

Viktor placed a hand on his shoulder. "Sit. You have plenty of time. Oh! I've something for you." He snapped his fingers and began searching his pockets. "There it is. Drink this."

Nels accepted the corked dark blue bottle and then held it up to the light. "What is it?" He popped the cork, took a whiff, and pulled a face. The inside of his nose seemed to contract in pain and his eyes watered. "Oh, gods. It smells like feet. Worse, if that's possible."

"It's a special little something I had Westola put together for you," Viktor said. "Guaranteed to cure what ails you."

"By killing me?"

"Sit," Viktor said, shoving him into a wingback chair. "Stay. There's a good colonel. First, it's nine in the morning."

"But—"

"I may have reset your watch while you were sleeping."

"Viktor! You son of a—"

"It got you moving, didn't it?" Viktor went to the hearth and stirred the coals. Then he began the process of building up the fire. "Drink that quick, now. Because if you don't, I will. She refused to mix a second batch for me. Said it was likely I'd deserve what I got, and then added something about considering it vengeance for the time I faked river fever. That woman has a long memory for slights."

Nels held his nose and swallowed the foul concoction all at once. His stomach made one last riposte and then settled peacefully down. He blinked as his head began to clear. "Huh."

Viktor spoke over his shoulder. "What?"

"It's working."

"It better, for what I paid her." He pushed the kettle over the flames and then sat back down on the sofa, nearby. "Soon, there will be coffee."

"Don't tease," Nels said. "I don't think I can handle it today."

"I wouldn't joke about anything so serious on a day like today," Viktor said. "Mr. Moss may have given me a couple handfuls of ground beans last night. Before the . . . ah . . . festivities." A slow, sly smile crept across his average features. "Incidentally, how much do you remember?"

Nels paused. In truth, he remembered all of it. He knew better than to drink himself entirely senseless, but before he could answer, there came a knock on the door. Viktor staggered over and answered it. The hulking form of the Hold's head cook blocked most of the light pouring in from the hallway. He was carrying a covered tray.

"Salutations," Mr. Moss said. "I gave some consideration to your probable plight and decided it might be best if I delivered your breakfast. I understand it is considered bad luck for the bridegroom to view the bride before the wedding."

"That's an Acrasian custom," Nels said. "Not Eledorean."

"Then I apologize for my mistake," Mr. Moss said. "I hope I have not given offence."

Nels said, "Not at all. It was kind of you."

Viktor accepted the tray. "Thank you very much."

"And thanks for the coffee, too," Nels said. "Would you like to join us?"

"I deeply appreciate the invitation," Mr. Moss said. "I would be glad to join your good company. However, I find I must return to my kitchen before it is left in a most unsatisfactory condition. Please enjoy your repast, gentlemen. Captain Reini, you may return the dishes tomorrow when it is more convenient. I will see you both at the ceremony."

"Thank you, Mr. Moss," Nels said.

Once Viktor had set the tray on the table, Nels lifted the lid. The scent of fresh rolls met his nose at once. His stomach let out a loud rumble.

"Apple jam?! I thought we ran out. And fresh butter. Cheese and . . . Praise the gods, it's bacon!" He began loading a roll with as much apple jam as he could fit onto it.

"Save some for me," Viktor said, bringing the coffee. "Or I'm keeping this for myself."

The next quarter of an hour was silence punctuated with the sounds of determined eating.

"That was wonderful," Nels said when he'd finished. He leaned back in the chair, sighed, and stretched out his legs on the rug, content.

"Ahhhh! Can you have another binding ceremony tomorrow?" Viktor asked. "Better yet, once a week for the next month?"

"Spring isn't that far off," Nels said.

Viktor said, "I may wither away." He closed his eyes.

"I rather doubt that," Nels said. "By the gods, I don't want to move from this chair."

"I suspect that may upset your new wife," Viktor said. "Since I'm not sure you remember me saying it . . . Congratulations! You've been pining for that woman since before I met you. Of course, now I owe Larsson a gold falcon, drown it all."

"You bet against me?"

"Nothing personal," Viktor said. "I merely assumed she had more common sense than—"

"Piss off!"

Viktor lifted his coffee cup and grinned. "To you both. The best of luck."

Nels paused.

"Come on. I'm being serious. I'm happy for you," Viktor said. "I truly am. It's about time."

"Thank you." Nels tapped his cup against Viktor's, and they both drank.

"Let's hope that your happiness lasts. Or I'll have to resort to violence I'd regret."

"You wouldn't."

"You're right. I wouldn't," Viktor said. "But half the company would."

"That would be unfortunate for all involved."

"I'm sure," Viktor said.

Nels gazed down at the table and noticed the items on the second tray—a needle, half a wine cork, a covered bowl, and what looked like a ring with a silver disc threaded through it. "What's that?"

"The reason I woke you so early," Viktor said. "That, my friend, is your binding ring. It goes in your ear. And tomorrow ... or whenever your lady fair is ready for a few hours rest ... I'll take you to the blacksmith and have it fused closed."

Raising an eyebrow, Nels asked the question without asking. Throughout his years in the Eledorean Royal Army, he'd noticed a number of soldiers with such rings in their ears. Most of them were older. Fashions came and went in the Royal Court. Therefore, it hadn't occurred to him to inquire. There were so many other details that had demanded his attention. Lately, there'd been a resurgence of the practice.

Viktor said, "As your closest friend, the one who will stand for you in the ceremony, and a formerly bound—"

"*You* were bound?" Nels didn't bother to hide his surprise. "*You?* Permanently committed?"

Viktor looped his hair behind his left ear. The lobe was scarred. "She died the summer before you and I met. Childbirth. I lost them both."

"I'm so sorry. Why haven't I heard of this before?"

Viktor shrugged.

"Does anyone else know?"

"Only you," Viktor said. "I don't like to talk about it."

"I suppose I can't blame you," Nels said. "That must have been hard."

"It was," Viktor said. "Afterward, I did some very foolish things, which ultimately culminated in my joining the Royal Army. It was that or the noose. And well ... I never was much for hemp collars."

"Wait," Nels said. "If it's an army tradition, and you were no longer bound—"

"I had it done and then ripped it out." Viktor looked away and shrugged.

Nels winced.

"I had only begun to realize that punishing myself wouldn't bring back Aava and the baby when I received a certain offer from a korva claiming to be working for an unnamed member of the royal house. It seemed I was to keep a certain young and equally foolhardy captain from killing himself. It was a rather handsome sum."

"And how did that work out for you?"

"Not bad so far. We're both still alive, aren't we?" Viktor asked. "And that money funded a large number of illuminating evenings with Helmi, as I recall."

"I wonder what happened to her."

"She's living in Ytlain. Karlindermoor. When things were looking bad, I told her to leave Eledore," Viktor said. "She followed my advice. Set herself up with her own brothel. Smart as well as talented, that one."

Nels sipped more coffee. His head and stomach felt perfectly fine, and he felt more alert than he had in days.

"Now the time has come to impart some wisdom upon you," Viktor said.

"Really?" Nels asked. "And just exactly how long were you bound?"

"Longer than you, youngling," Viktor said.

"You're only two months older than me."

"It's not the years. It's what you've done with them," Viktor said. "Now, the first year is the hardest. You get through that without wanting to kill one another and—"

"We've been together for—"

"Living together is different than walking out together," Viktor said. "You'll see." He paused. "The next thing I'll say is . . . keep your sense of humor. You'll need it. If there's one thing I miss about Aava, it's how she could always make me laugh, no matter what. And I can't tell you how much easier that makes the worst to bear. My father used to say that having a partner in life halved one's troubles and doubled the joy." He stared into his coffee cup. "I think the one thing I'd add to that is . . . it only works that way if you have the *right* partner."

"Why, Viktor Anders Reini, I do believe you're a romantic at heart."

"Tell anyone, and I'll deny it," Viktor said. He set down the cup and bent to retrieve the needle from the tray. "Now, let's get this over with, shall we?"

"My father didn't pierce his ear. Why should I?"

"Your father was a king," Viktor said. "This is a soldier's tradition. You're lucky. You're only having one ear done."

"Why?"

"You have no other family members in the service," Viktor said and held up the earring. "One, the left one, is a gift from a friend. The right is a gift from a relative."

"Oh."

"It is an offering to the Goddess for protection. See the rune?" Viktor asked, showing him the back of the disc. "So that you can live to protect your family. I used to think it was merely symbolic." He shrugged. "We all did."

Nels asked, "Is this new?"

"It seems Acrasians weren't the first to notice the connection between the malorum and silver. Eledoreans were, perhaps, the first to forget it, however."

"When did you have time to gather the ice?"

"I didn't. Corporal Mustonen did," Viktor said. He selected a piece and motioned for him to move closer. "Give me your ear."

"I'm not sure I trust you with that needle. The way your hand is shaking, you're likely to pierce my nose instead."

"Don't be a baby," Viktor said. "It'll be over with before you know it."

Nels sat up and let Viktor apply the ice to his earlobe. "How many times have you done this?"

"Including this time?" Viktor grinned. "Once."

"Great," Nels said. "That's exactly what I wanted to hear. Why isn't Corporal Horn stabbing me with sharp objects? Doesn't he have three daughters and a son serving? And they're all bound to partners?"

"Horn isn't standing for you in the ceremony. I am."

"Why didn't anyone tell me this was— Ouch!"

"See? Done," Viktor said, daubing at the wounded earlobe with a cold, wet cloth. "Now sit still while I get the ring through."

"Hurry up. That stings."

"Stop wiggling."

Mustonen entered, carrying the dress uniform.

"I mean it, Viktor. Get it in already! It hurts."

Mustonen raised an eyebrow. His usually sober expression twitched with reined-in mirth. "Should I return and leave you two alone?"

Nels said, "So help me—"

"There," Viktor said and withdrew. "It's finished."

"—if one word about—"

"Understood, sir," Mustonen said. "Your uniform is ready."

"Good." Nels stood up.

Viktor said, "You might want to wait for a moment."

Nels felt the world tilt a little to the left and sat back down. "You may be right."

"It'll pass in a moment. Have something else to eat," Viktor said. "There's bacon left."

Nels's assaulted earlobe began to throb. He gently touched it; it felt hot. "Is it bleeding?"

"Stop handling it. Relax. The difficult part is over. The rest involves getting dressed, saying 'I do' when prompted, and standing inside a circle without fainting," Viktor said. "I understand even the most inbred of royals can handle that."

"Viktor—"

"Have some more coffee," Viktor said.

TWO

The main hall was lit with candles, and the scent of musky incense hung in the air. The furniture had been removed and stored elsewhere to make room. Ribbons of yellow and indigo were hung in loops from the ceiling and draped around the entrance. Nels wasn't sure, but it looked like the whole community had turned out for the ceremony. All were standing around the outskirts of the large circle painted on the marble floor in black, blue, and yellow. Within the circle, someone had sketched a spiral that outlined the paths he and Ilta would be walking to the center. Suvi waited in the middle, wearing what had once been their father's crown. Next to her stood the oldest living member of their community, ready to give a blessing, as was custom. In this instance, it was a sixty-eight-year-old named Eelis Saksa. He would be officiating alongside Suvi. Ilta had explained that her spiritual practice required representation from at least two genders—whether that was within one person or two didn't matter. While that could've been handled by Lieutenant Fugl Vang alone, Nels had wanted his sister to have a part in the ceremony, and that had dictated Ilta's choice.

Nels searched the crowd. *Where is she? Has she changed her mind?*

Viktor asked, "How're you doing?"

"I'm fine," Nels said. "Stop asking."

"It's going to be all right."

"Why do you keep saying that?"

"No reason," Viktor said, and looked away.

At that moment, the musicians—most of whom were volunteers from the company—began to play a slow melody in three-quarter time. Nels recognized it as a piece that he and Ilta had danced to in Jalokivi before the war. It'd been one of the rare evenings they'd had together before everything went horribly wrong. It was also one of his favorite memories, and he remembered telling Ilta something to that effect but couldn't remember when. He was focused on recalling the name of the piece when the crowd parted and Ilta appeared.

He stopped breathing.

"I told you it'd be all right," Viktor muttered.

She was wearing a dress he'd never seen her wear before. The overdress was Eledorean blue—the same as his formal uniform coat. The underdress was a pale yellow that brought out the highlights in her hair. She wore no jewelry and no gloves. Her hair was neatly piled on top of her head with curls spilling down the sides in the fashion that had been popular before the war. It wasn't something she normally did with her hair. She was more beautiful than he thought possible. At the same time, she looked nothing like his Ilta. Ilta went barefoot in the summer. All other times she wore plain boots. She climbed trees when it suited her. She was untidy except when it came to her medicines. Her stained apron pockets were filled with rocks or pretty leaves she'd found.

She gave him a shy smile just for him that began like the small light of dawn on the horizon and then grew into the brilliant, shining revelation of day. And that was when he knew it was her underneath all the finery.

Nels thought, *This is actually happening. Now.*

Until that moment, he'd been going though the motions, absolutely certain that she was going to change her mind. He knew the impossibility of her binding herself to him the way he knew the lines in his own hand. Hadn't she backed out on him multiple times? Granted, it was taking her longer to evidence her uncertainty this time, but he knew he wasn't worthy of her. It was one of the constants of his life.

That was why the reality of her stepping into the circle hit him harder than he could've imagined. His knees felt weak and his stomach seemed to plummet to the ground. The weight of it all kicked him in the gut.

"Steady on," Viktor said, and held his arm.

Nels swallowed.

"Time to go," Viktor whispered. "Unless you're changing your mind?"

Nels didn't acknowledge the question.

"I didn't think so." Viktor gave him a gentle nudge. "Off you go."

The first step was the hardest. It was as if his legs had forgotten what it was to walk. He was sure he was moving like a drunk. His stomach was clenched in a fist. It was difficult to breathe. Everyone was watching as he walked the spiral path toward the center and Ilta. Viktor followed just behind him. It wasn't long before Nels found himself standing at Ilta's side. He didn't know how he made it without tripping.

Suvi held up a wreath of evergreen and winked before placing it on his head. At the same time, Eelis Saksa set a matching wreath on Ilta's head. Ilta turned, and that was when Nels saw she was just as nervous as he was.

The musicians stopped their playing.

"Ilta Brynjar Korpela, do you come of your own free will?" Suvi asked.

"I do."

Eelis asked, "And you, Nels Gunnar Ari Hännenen, do you come of your own free will?"

Nels opened his mouth but the words wouldn't come. Finally, he choked out the answer. "I do."

"With whom do you come, and whose blessings do you bring?" Suvi asked.

Viktor said, "He comes with his friend as well as the blessings of his sister, his friends, and his ancestors."

"And you? With whom do you come, and whose blessings do you bring?" Eelis asked Ilta.

"I come on my own with the blessings of my new sister, my friends, and my ancestors," Ilta said.

Suvi said, "Then we are here to publicly celebrate the permanent joining of Ilta Brynjar Korpela with Nels Gunnar Ari Hännenen."

Nels was glad that she'd listened to him and had left off the useless titles. There was no point in calling attention to the reduced state of the kingdom. His uniform was bad enough, he felt, but Suvi had demanded he wear it. Thus, this had been their compromise.

Suvi continued, "Please join hands."

Nels faced Ilta and took her hands in his.

"As your hands are joined, so are your lives—forever linked through good times and bad," Suvi said. "Bolster one another in times of need. Share your joy. Dance, argue, and grieve together in the coming years. Speak what needs to be spoken and keep silent the things that need silence. Be honest. Trust one another. Make mistakes. Learn. And forgive. Above all, be happy. Be the closest of friends as well as passionate lovers." She wrapped a blue ribbon around his left wrist and tied it loosely around Ilta's.

Suvi stepped back, and Eelis Saksa moved forward.

Looping a buttercream ribbon around Ilta's left wrist, he said, "Be together as one tree with two large branches. Stretch for the sky. Pursue your dreams. Serve your duty. Care for your children, should you be so blessed. But never forget the one to which you are joined, for while you're separate, you're also one—nurturing each other with all that you gather on your own." He took a step back.

"Ilta Brynjar Korpela," Nels said. "I, Nels Gunnar Ari Hännenen, do swear with the gods and the goddesses and all assembled here as my witnesses that I will be your husband from this day forward. To love and respect you, to support and hold you, to join you in laughter and wipe away your tears, to soothe your hurts and be your life's companion, lover, and friend. In this, our journey together, you will be first before all others." With his free hand, he reached inside his coat to retrieve the ring that had been his mother's and then placed it on Ilta's finger.

"I, Ilta Brynjar Korpela, do swear with the gods and the goddesses and all assembled here as my witnesses that I will be your wife from this day forward. I promise to love and respect you, Nels Gunnar Ari Hännenen. To support and hold you, to join you in laughter and wipe away your tears, to soothe your hurts and be your life's companion, lover, and friend. In this, our journey together, you will be first before all others." She reached out for his free hand.

He blinked. It was the wrong one, but she was determined to put the ring on his right hand instead of the left. She gave him a distressed look. Finally, he allowed it, but when she turned to face Suvi, he made quietly made the change and hoped no one noticed.

"I, Queen Suvi Natalia Annika Hännenen Ilmari, do hereby

declare Ilta Brynjar Korpela and Nels Gunnar Ari Hännenen bound by oath and love. May their journey be smooth and their road made easy by the goodwill of their ancestors. May the gods and Goddesses grant them their blessings." She waited while the audience clapped and shouted their congratulations. "I think now is the time to start the party. Don't you?"

⊰ BLACKTHORNE ⊱

Tenth of Pitkäkuu, 1784

"I've served with Corporal Arvid Nyberg for two years," Sebastian Moller whispered, and then motioned to the big blond sitting at the table opposite Moss.

A solid two hundred fifty pounds and six feet five inches tall, Arvid Nyberg rolled up his right sleeve and rested his elbow on the table with a wide grin. Nodding, Moss accepted the challenge. Blackthorne watched Katrin collect bets from the rest of the room and frowned. He was fairly certain Slate wouldn't have approved of her behavior. However, Blackthorne decided it wasn't his business. Slate's daughter wasn't in any danger, and if Slate wanted him to be Katrin's watcher, he would've said so.

"He joined the Eledorean Army during the war. The Home Guard ran him off his land," Moller said.

Blackthorne paused, confused. *Oh, Nyberg. Pay attention. This is important.* If he would be breaking into a military depot, he wanted to be sure of those with whom he was working. His initial recommendation included Lieutenant Reini, Corporal Nyberg, Natalia Annikki, Bernard Sloan, Master Sergeant Jarvi, Birch, and Katrin Brooke. Blackthorne was uneasy about the prospect. This would be the first time he was to lead others in Acrasia, and he was particularly uneasy about Katrin being among them. Therefore, he'd asked Moller's advice.

Moller gave a sideways nod toward a human with dark skin and straight, dark brown hair. "That's Jeremiah Birch. He's been here two years. Hasn't told anyone why yet. I heard it had something to do with a woman he was involved with." Moller finished off his beer and continued. "Annikki is new. I don't know much about her. She's a grumbletonian, but she doesn't seem to mean anything by it. As for Master Sergeant Tane Jarvi, well, I've known Tane for almost as long as I've been in the Royal Army. We served in the same artillery regiment before I was transferred. He's a good man to have at your back."

"Thank you," Blackthorne said. Over the course of the winter, the Ghost's troops had been friendlier—especially Moller. That gave Blackthorne a small amount of confidence.

Soon, he wasn't sure when, he'd be asked to not only escort the Queen of Eledore into Acrasia but to break into a military depot, and not just any depot—a depot specifically owned and maintained by the emperor. If Dylan Kask was right and the consul was a malorum, then the consul would be motivated to keep those swords hidden. In fact, a malorum-born consul may have even had them destroyed. That was a possibility he hadn't brought to Slate.

Not yet, anyway. And it bothered him that no one else had considered it. It meant someone wasn't thinking clearly.

But then, Hännenen has other things on his mind, doesn't he?

Blackthorne hadn't been alone with Ilta since the wedding. His feelings on the matter were strangely empty, after the initial shock.

Moller stopped talking to watch Nyberg arm-wrestle Moss. Almost at once, Nyberg's face turned deep red and his arm shook. In contrast, Moss pressed his advantage with gradual relentlessness. He didn't even appear to be putting forth much effort.

At that moment, Moller whispered, "Would you mind if I ask you something?"

Blackthorne saw Moller steal a sideways glance. For his part, Blackthorne focused on Moss and Nyberg.

Quid pro quo, Blackthorne thought. "You may."

"Were you sparking Ilta?"

"What?" The word burst out of Blackthorne's mouth, loud enough to cause a few of the others to turn around.

Moller paused, waiting for everyone to go back to watching the match. Then he whispered, "I thought I'd inquire as to your position in the matter." He shrugged. "It shouldn't be any of my business, I know, but she's chosen Colonel Hännenen. How do I put this delicately? The potential for trouble seems . . . fraught."

Blackthorne decided to play innocent. He felt his face heat and hoped it wasn't too obvious. "I'm not sure I understand your meaning."

There was a loud thud and a howl. Moss had smacked Nyberg's arm onto the table's scarred surface. Money was exchanged is a flurry of enthusiasm. With that, a boisterous commotion started over who would be next to challenge Moss. Katrin insisted it should be her, but the others only laughed. Sloan took Nyberg's place on the stool.

The kitchen door crashed against the chair wedged against it.

"Moss? What's wrong with this door?" Slate asked.

The troops looked to Moller. Moller gave several hand signals.

Oh, shit, Blackthorne thought.

Chairs were rearranged. Ale was poured into the fire or hidden in the sideboard. Katrin stuffed wadded Acrasian paper notes into her pocket. Moss got up and gently removed the chair that had been wedged against the doorknob. With that, a confused Slate entered carrying an empty tea canister. Blackthorne stood up.

"Is something going on that I should know about?" Slate asked.

Blackthorne opened his mouth to speak.

"No, sir," Moller said. "Absolutely not."

Blackthorne decided it was wise to go along with Moller. He closed his mouth.

Slate made to scan the room's occupants. He raised an eyebrow. "Mr. Blackthorne, I wouldn't have expected to see you here."

"I invited him," Moller said.

In truth, the subject of a pre–Novus Salernum gathering had come up in a conversation with Moss. In turn, Blackthorne had asked if a small quantity of ale might be provided. He'd wanted to observe the others while their guards were down. It was a common-enough practice among Wardens in leadership positions. After that, it'd been a simple matter of asking Moller if he might attend.

Moller is covering for me? Blackthorne thought.

"You did?" Slate asked. "Isn't that interesting. Mr. Blackthorne, do you have anything to say for yourself?"

All at once, Blackthorne felt all the eyes in the room focus on him. He forced himself to concentrate on a nail struck in the mortar of the open fireplace just over and to the left of Slate's shoulder. "No, sir."

Slate moved to where Moss stored the herbal tea and opened the cupboard. He paused upon spying the tankard hidden there. Instead of asking about it, he grabbed the community tea tin and filled his empty canister.

Katrin gave out a loud hiccup and covered her mouth.

Slate changed targets. "Shouldn't you be in your room, studying your Eledorean language lessons, Katrin?"

"I—I—"

"She merely dropped by to say good night," Blackthorne offered.

"Is that so?" Slate moved closer to his adopted daughter, leaned closer, and sniffed.

The color drained from Katrin's face.

Slate retreated to the exit. "Katrin, I expect you home in a quarter of an hour."

"Yes, sir," Katrin said.

"Good evening, everyone," Slate said.

With the shutting of the door, the entire room let out the collective breath they were holding.

"Is that the last we'll see of the ale?" Birch asked Moller.

Nyberg looked hopeful and said, "You're in hot for us being foxed, anyway." Birch elbowed him. "I mean, we. We're in hot for being foxed. Pouring it out won't make it any less so."

"And navigating the main passage drunk will?" Jarvi asked. His low voice was almost a growl.

"The ale wasn't my idea," Moller said. "Don't look to me."

Moss said, "It was Blackthorne's."

Once again, everyone in the room turned to Blackthorne. He watched Katrin's jaw fall open.

He shrugged. "In for a pence, in for a sterling note," Blackthorne muttered, and swallowed the last of the liquid in his glass.

The others cheered.

Moller took Katrin's mug from her. "No more for you. Off to your room."

"Awwww!"

"No excuses," Moller said. "We're in enough trouble with your father. Go."

"Good night, everyone," Katrin said, and slipped out the door.

With Katrin gone, the others settled down to business in earnest. Blackthorne stayed until late in the evening, watching the others and talking to Moller. For the first time, he permitted himself to imagine himself a part of the community around him, and for a few hours, the bone-deep ache of loneliness was forgotten. When he finally staggered off to his apartment, his pocket watch read a quarter past one in the morning. He didn't feel the need to watch every single corner as he went. He was vigilant—to be otherwise would be stupid. However, Blackthorne felt more relaxed, safer.

He entered his empty room. Setting his watch on the fireplace mantel, he considered retiring for the evening but was uneasy about the prospect. His dreams had been getting worse, more detailed. He couldn't shake the feeling that something or someone was searching for him.

The dreams are merely tension concerning the upcoming journey. That's all. He was confident in his abilities, but Novus Salernum always put him on edge. In Novus Salernum, the memories were bad. The consequences for getting caught, worse. And this time, he would have Queen Suvi and Colonel Hännenen with him. That alone was bad enough.

The weather had been getting warmer and drier. It was a clear night, if a bit chilly. A walk might do him some good. Instead, he found himself staring at the pink quartz stone the size of his palm resting next to his watch. Ilta had given it to him a couple of weeks before the wedding. He didn't understand why he had chosen to keep it.

Are you sparking Ilta? Moller's question hung in the back of his mind like an unwanted guest. Like many Acrasians, he didn't want to believe in the power of Eledorean witches. It was illogical to belittle the existence of magic and live in terror of it at the same time, but then, he never claimed to understand everything Acrasians believed. Very little of what he'd been taught to expect of kainen matched what he had witnessed, and this was true of Ilta in particular.

Remember your place.

With that, he abandoned the idea of a walk. *Not tonight. Certainly not while I'm drunk.* Instead, he threw himself onto the bed, shut his eyes and whispered familiar lines. *Resist the temptation to cling to life. The essence of the Retainer is death. Therefore, do not dread death. Fear is the enemy. Fear incapacitates action at the crucial—*

The knock on the door gave him a start.

It's late. Who can it be? He collected himself and went to the door, hoping it wouldn't be trouble.

Instead, it was Slate.

"I'm sorry to disturb you at this hour, but we have a problem," Slate said. His face was pale. He glanced behind him. "May I come in?"

Blackthorne stepped back, allowing Slate inside, and closed the door as quietly as he could.

Slate said, "There are two individuals that I need for you to get out of Acrasia when you go. This means you'll have fewer people for the military depot, but it's important that you get them out."

"Who are they?"

"The first is May Freely. The second is Mallory McDermott."

Nodding, Blackthorne offered Slate the only chair.

"Then I will get them for you."

"There may be a third individual, but I don't know her name, not yet. Mal hasn't told me."

"And he's sure of this person?" Blackthorne asked.

"He says he is."

"And if this other person should prove otherwise? Is he prepared for what may happen?"

"Mal knows what is at stake," Slate said. "Bring him back with or without this other individual. Whatever it takes. He's a good man. Like you, he's saved many lives. I won't leave him to hang."

Not to mention torture. If he spies for Slate, the Brotherhood will be very interested in what Mal knows. Blackthorne nodded. "Are you certain he can wait?"

"He says he can," Slate said. "And I trust his judgement."

"If he's already in the Brotherhood's hands by the time we get there—"

"If that's the case, you'll have to leave the city at once." Slate looked away. "I won't be sure of our contacts at that point. Any of them."

✤ DRAKE ✤

ONE

Novus Salernum
The Regnum of Acrasia

18 February
The Twenty-Second Year in the Sacred Reign
of Emperor Herminius

The scent of baking bread drifted across the room. Drake kicked off the warm blankets and sat up. She snatched her trousers from the cold floor, threw them on, and then jumped back under the covers to finish buttoning. "Oh, Mithras! It's freezing in here."

"Good evening to you, too," Mallory said. His rich voice drifted over from the fireplace. He was dressed in breeches and the white long-tailed linen shirt he'd slept in.

For the most part, she mentally added with a smile.

His skin appeared a shadowy gold in the firelight, and his dark brown hair was bound in about a hundred little braids—a popular style among the Waterborne Nations. In the year that she'd known him, she'd never asked if he were Waterborne. As Watch captain, she made a point of not asking him personal questions. In any case, she suspected he wasn't. His family could've originated in Eledore, Tahmer, Kaledan, or the now-defunct Marren. It didn't matter to her either way. She was of mixed race herself. She simply didn't look it. That wasn't anything like a rarity in Acrasia, no matter how much the officials wanted to pretend otherwise—particularly among the common folk.

"It's evening already?" she asked, and stretched under the blankets. She'd taken two whole days off from the Watch. To have spent most of the first sleeping felt decadent. She told herself that Benbow had things under control. He'd been in charge before, and he'd been a Watchman for far longer than she had. It was winter, after all, the slowest time of the year for the Watch. She'd sent her last report to the Brotherhood, and they'd finally stopped their visits. There'd been no more bodies to clean up, either—not for some time. She wasn't sure if she was unhappy about that. In any case, the Watch House had become as quiet and dull as Benbow had predicted. Grown weary of listening to Jaspar's farts and eating Gilmartyn's sorry excuse for cooking, she'd decided to take leave of the Watch House. It'd been two months since her last visit with Mal. She was, after all, overdue some personal time.

Of course, she'd have to pay a rather expensive, secretive visit to the apothecary afterward. She wanted a baby even less than she wanted a husband.

Mal raised a perfectly arched eyebrow. His face was handsome and he had deep green eyes. At the moment, his hair was pulled back into a thick ponytail with a strip of bright red silk. He didn't wear his hair like that very often, although that was popular among the elite. With his ears exposed, she could see the tips were pointed.

"Care for something to eat?" Mal asked.

"What's on offer?"

"At the moment?" He straightened to his full height, toasting tongs in hand, and deposited a slice of warm bread on a fine white porcelain plate. "Chocolate and toast."

"My favorite."

"Come sit by the fire, then."

"It's too chilly in here for that."

"You've had enough laying about, lazybones," he said. His voice was cultured in contrast to her own. "And you're escorting me to Lady Marca's salon tonight. You've an hour to get ready."

She groaned. "I'm not going anywhere."

"Oh, yes, you are. I need you. You're the only way I'll get in," he said. The curfew restrictions could only be avoided by nobility, the Brotherhood, and the Watch. "And you agreed. Remember?"

"I've brought nothing to wear."

"That's quite all right," he said. "*I* have something. And if I've nothing that will suit, Lydia most certainly will. She won't be needing any of the available gowns for a few months."

Drake inwardly winced at the mention of Lydia. Lydia lived in the much more elegant apartments next door. A close friend of Mal's, Lydia shared his profession, but since Mal didn't entertain men, he had far less business than she did.

She couldn't stop herself from asking "Was she arrested?"

"Much worse," Mal said. "She's pregnant. Which is odd. It's not like her to be so careless."

"Oh." Changing the subject, Drake moved to the stuffed chair angled in front of the fireplace. "I suppose I'm to be trussed up like a prize turkey?"

"Honestly, I don't understand your need to wear trousers."

"I'm a damned Watch captain, not a pampered lapdog," she said. "I work for a living."

"So does Lydia. And pampering is underrated." A smile curled the corner of his wide mouth. "Trust me."

"You know what I mean. Well?"

"In answer to your question, yes. You'll have to wear a dress." Mal tucked a thick quilt around her and then handed her the plate of toast.

"Oh, Mithras," she said. "Why do you do this to me? I'll never be taken seriously, you know."

"Someone must civilize you. I'm stunned your mother never did."

"I didn't have a mother." They both knew she was lying.

"There are certain advantages in not being taken seriously, you know. As a Watch captain, it may even work in your favor. Someone might slip up. Say something they shouldn't."

"The Watch doesn't involve itself in the affairs of nobility." She thought again of the Brotherhood and suppressed a shudder. "They have their own law. And you know it."

"Then why worry about what they think? Anyway, tonight isn't for your benefit," Mal said. "It's for mine. I'm presenting Lady Marca with a new painting, and it will be more advantageous to do so in front of witnesses." He winked.

"You finished it?"

He nodded.

"Can I see it?"

"Sure." He crossed to the studio door behind her.

The scent of turpentine wafted into the room. Strangely, she liked that smell. She couldn't have said why. She supposed it was the association with Mal. The message birds he kept in the studio made soft cooing noises.

"This is new," she said, indicating the dinnerware. "It looks Eledorean."

"Ytlainen, actually. The set was a gift from a friend," Mal called from the studio. "Although Fortis would have us believe it's a new process they invented. Porcelain has great strength and yet it's thin and light." He continued to rummage around. "Hold it up to the light. It's translucent. Isn't it beautiful?"

She drained the cup and did as he suggested. It seemed to glow as firelight filtered through. There was a nautilus-shell emblem of Gens Fortis clearly stamped on the bottom in black. Fortis, like the other four predominant gentes, had areas over which it lorded power. All legitimate businesses—and, frankly, even the illegitimate ones—held guild memberships, and the guilds were controlled by the five gentes. Fortis regulated the medical, scientific, and arts ventures. It also oversaw prostitution, which was but one of the reasons why Mal didn't retain as much of an income as one would think at the prices he charged. He maintained two guild memberships.

"What's taking so long?" she asked. It occurred to her that if he'd just finished a painting, it shouldn't take this long to find. She stood up, keeping the quilt wrapped around her.

"Stay there," he said. "I'm only letting in one of my birds."

He was oddly strict about anyone entering his studio, and although she'd known him for a year and his house was fairly spacious by her standards, she'd only ever seen the one room—the room where he conducted his more social business. His studio was, he'd explained, his private sanctuary. No one was allowed to enter. No one. She respected his wishes, and it was a sign of how much he trusted her that he'd let the door remain ajar while fetching the painting.

"Hurry up," she said. "You're letting in the cold." In truth, she was more frightened of a malorum discovering the open window. She didn't want an attack to ruin their evening.

"Don't be an infant." Metal clattered against glass as the sash thumped closed. The windows in the front of the house were silver-mullioned and fitted with pocket shutters. She imagined that the rooms at the back of the house were less expensively secured.

She poured herself another cup of hot chocolate. The chocolate pot had been painted with golden nautilus-shell swirls. It was beautiful and expensive. She knew exactly what kind of friend would've made such a gift. She didn't let it bother her. Mal was what he was—like she was. *Much like we all are*, she thought with an inward sigh. That was one of the things she liked most about him. He didn't present complications. She liked Mal quite a lot. She enjoyed his company. She didn't need anything more than that.

An image of an earnest face, black hair, brown eyes, broad shoulders, and a Warden's uniform came to mind.

"Got anything to drink?" she asked.

Mal closed the studio door one-handed. In the other was a three-foot-wide by a little over two-foot-tall canvas. "Isn't that what I served?"

"You know what I mean."

"I need you alert. You've hardly touched your toast. And here I went to all the trouble of making it for you."

"If I wanted a lecture, I'd be visiting my mother."

"You don't have a mother, remember?"

"Oh, right."

He leaned the canvas against his chair, carefully resting it so that the furniture's padded bulk was between it and the fire. She contorted herself in order to get a good look at the painting while he went to the tallboy where he kept his liquor.

"Don't touch it," he said. "I only finished it the day before yesterday. The paint is still wet."

The image was a foggy landscape executed in gauzy pastel hues, bordering on the monochromatic. The hills, trees, clouds were all done in faint but cool blues, greens, and browns. The sun itself, seen through blurry atmospheric conditions, was painted in a smudgy soft warm gold. The painting lacked detail. Close up, it looked like nothing but a series of indistinct brush strokes, but when she sat back in the chair, it formed a valley at dawn. Emotions she couldn't name clogged her throat.

The musical tinkle of glass came from across the room as Mal made a selection from the rows of bottles inside the upper half of the tallboy. "Do you like it?" he asked.

"It's . . . amazing." She finally pinned down the unfamiliar emotion blurring her vision. *Hope.*

A small, fragile smile appeared on his lips. "I hope she buys it."

"She's an idiot if she doesn't."

"Thank you." Genuine warmth colored the words.

"It's too bad it isn't larger."

"What do you mean?"

"We could pretend to walk into it together and forget everything else for a while."

"Why, my dearest Em, you have quite the imagination."

"Oh, shut up, damn you. Just bring the bottle already."

"Which one?"

"I don't care."

"Since you're buying, let's go with the brandy. It's a nice one."

"Nice is worthless to me."

He winked. "That's not what you said a half-hour ago." He opened the bottle and made the requested adjustments to her cup. "What's got you in a mood?"

"I'm not in a mood."

He set the bottle down to breathe and arched an eyebrow at her.

She debated not saying anything but knew she would talk to him anyway. It was one of the many reasons she'd come to see him. He listened. And if she didn't talk to someone about what was bothering her, she'd do something she'd regret. "Have you associated much with Wardens?"

Mal blinked. It bordered on a flinch. "Me? Are you serious?"

"I'm afraid I am."

He shrugged. "Beyond the census? Not if I can help it. And not that I should tell you even if I did. You know the rules."

"I wasn't asking about your other clients."

"Weren't you?"

"You don't entertain men."

"I never said never. Preferences don't always dictate one's clients in my business," Mal said.

"Then you do?"

"That isn't any of your business. And why would you ask a thing like that?"

"I apologize and withdraw the question."

"Thank you," he said. "Now, why do you want to know if I associate with Wardens?"

"Something has happened."

"Did one of them forget to pay for a horse and lacked a solicitor or coin to sort it out?"

"Don't be ridiculous," she said. "I . . ." She let her sentence trail off unfinished. It was possible that she was putting him in danger by saying anything to him. On the other hand, she supposed he held a large number of secrets, and if he were inclined to reveal them, he would've been dead long before. "I made an arrest yesterday."

"That isn't all that unusual, is it?" He got up and, as if in search for something to do, moved the painting across the room. She couldn't see his face, and it bothered her.

"Not particularly," she said, continuing. "But there were Wardens present."

"Is this your way of telling me that you've taken up census collection in your spare time?" The question was hard—much harder than she'd heard from him before.

"Absolutely not. I'd never do such a thing." Suddenly, she didn't feel quite so comfortable, because she knew it for a lie. She would bend with the prevailing wind. Everyone did who wanted to survive. "I—I didn't have a choice in the matter."

"That's what everyone says. I thought I knew you. I thought—"

"I know; just . . . listen."

He paused and nodded. He didn't turn around to face her, but he didn't order her out of his home, either.

"Someone has been smuggling nonhumans out of Acrasia," she said. *Did he just twitch?*

"If half the stories are true, there's always someone smuggling nonhumans out of Acrasia."

Don't make anything out of his reaction, she thought. *You pass for human. He doesn't. This affects him more than it does you. He's bound to be more sensitive.* At that moment, she began to understand just how far her defenses had slipped around him. "It was an innkeep. A member of Gens Aureus. They took her away."

"I thought you were there for an arrest. Why isn't she in your custody?"

"I was told to make the initial contact, but—"

"The Wardens took care of the rest."

She nodded.

"Why are you telling me about this?"

"Before she was taken away, she mentioned one of Lydia's . . . acquaintances."

"Who?"

Drake paused. "Ricci. Octavia Ricci."

"Oh."

"Did— Do you know her?"

"You know I can't tell you that."

She couldn't help noticing he sounded frightened. "Look. I'm telling you this so that—so that you can do whatever you need to protect yourself."

"You honestly think I've been smuggling nonhumans out of Acrasia?"

She laughed. "How stupid and paranoid do you think I am?"

"We're nonhuman, you and I." He finally turned. "We're all paranoid, Emily, no matter how much money we have. None of us are safe. Not even Watch captains. We're paranoid, or we're dead." He only used her first name when he was being absolutely honest with her.

I pass, and you don't. It's different for me, she thought. But she also knew he was right. The only difference between them was that she had the luxury of pretending otherwise, and the ability to reap those benefits. *Which only serves to make living more dangerous.* Those who attempted to pass and failed were particularly detested and punished in kind. *I can't forget myself. I can't.* She thought again about Caius. "I only wanted to warn you. They may come calling. I didn't want you to be . . . surprised."

"Thank you," he said. His expression was genuinely grateful. "I'll even pretend it was entirely for my sake that you told me."

Her face heated, and she looked away.

He sat down and took her hand. "Don't worry. They won't find a connection between myself and Octavia. That inn only handles women, and Octavia doesn't frequent my circles."

"Will you tell Lydia?"

"And risk questions from the Brotherhood?" he asked. "You
don't know Lydia. She has quite a few friends in high places. For all
I know, she may even have been the one to turn Octavia in. They
share a particularly generous client. Octavia might have decided to
cut out her competition. Particularly now that she's . . . indisposed.
It would be like her."

Drake nodded.

"Time to fill the bath," Mal said. He retrieved the copper tub
from the studio and arranged it inside the stately stone-carved fireplace.

"Whatever for?"

"You're not getting out of tonight's little party. I need you
cleaned up." He opened the cistern located a few paces away. "Count
yourself lucky that I'm heating the water first."

"Well, all right. But only if you join me," she said.

"Of course," Mal said. "Someone has to see to it you scrub
behind your ears, my little heathen."

TWO

Drake exited the coach and attempted to ignore her anxiety. She'd never attended a salon before, although she'd heard about them. It was one thing to imagine; the reality was quite another experience. Upon setting foot on the cobblestones, she gritted her teeth with a hiss. The street felt like rounded ice slabs through the bottoms of the thin kid-leather slippers. Her feet were painfully cold in no time. Mal gave her an arched eyebrow, and she stopped hopping from foot to foot at once. *Why insist upon my wearing these flimsy things? No one would see my boots under all these skirts,* she thought, but knew better. *Why can't women wear actual shoes?* Once again, she battled a powerful ambivalence toward women's fashion. A part of her couldn't help enjoying the sumptuous feel of silk against her skin and the softness of kid leather on her feet. At the exact same time, she hated the impracticality of it all. She huddled inside the velvet hood of her cloak and hoped they would get inside quickly.

Of course, "inside" was relative. The evening entrance to Lady Marca's estate, like that of all the great houses, was underground, well guarded, and brightly lit. The affluent areas of Novus Salernum were riddled with tunnels and subterranean roads. Some were intended for servants and deliveries. Others, like this one, were created to circumvent curfew, as legally such roads were considered indoors. In this way, coaches rarely exposed their wealthy passengers to the nighttime dangers aboveground.

The hollow percussion of horse hooves and wagon hardware overshadowed the muted strains of string instruments. Both echoed off the tunnel's walls while guests were greeted by well-dressed footmen. All of their faces were as dark as their linen ruffles were white. The passage was wide enough to accommodate two coaches at once. However, it wasn't big enough to diffuse the smell. The tunnel reeked of greasy lamp oil, unnamed filth, mildew, and horse dung. Night-blooming flowers growing beyond silver-plated gates lent their perfume to the mix. From the moment their rented coach had entered the tunnels, Drake's jaw muscles had tightened at the sight of the myriad of lamps and torches. She wondered who paid for it but could make a good guess. Gallons upon gallons of lamp oil were being wasted to shield the rich during their nightly revels. Meanwhile, the poorer sectors of the city fought to survive in darkness.

Hold your temper. Don't ruin Mal's evening. A grim smile curled the corner of her mouth. *Think of this as his opportunity to fleece as many of the bastards as he can.*

Expensive Retainers waited at the ornate gates like menacing shadows. Rows upon rows of potted hothouse plants and trees formed an ordered garden close to the house's entrance. With no natural light, she considered how long the greenery survived and how the gardener managed such a feat in the first place. She supposed no one cared, provided they lasted the night. *On the other hand, the pots are probably moved aboveground during the day by an army of slaves.* She imagined the backbreaking work it would require and swallowed yet another bout of resentment.

The footmen checked invitations at the door. Drake waited to join the line of guests until after Mal had paid the coachman and his Retainer. She hid under the dove-grey velvet hood of the cloak Mal had loaned to her, and dreaded shedding it. The form-fitting borrowed dress was fashioned from delicate powder-blue silk. It fit almost perfectly after Mal's deft alterations, although it was too small in the bust and smelled faintly of its owner's perfume. The stays also pinched her ribs, making taking a deep breath a challenge. She hated wearing stays and had almost refused to let him cinch her into them. It'd taken a great deal of thorough coaxing from Mal, but since she wasn't being charged for said motivation, she hadn't minded a bit. *Perhaps a little pampering isn't so bad.*

Just get this over with without tripping on your skirts or starting a fight, she thought. *Enjoy the expensive food and liquor. You aren't likely to see anything like it for the rest of your life.* She felt like a stranger to herself, clad as she was. The clothes restricted movement, let alone the thought of protecting herself. She found the sense of vulnerability more annoying than the stays. Mal had insisted she leave her weapons behind, but she'd secreted a silver knife in her pocket hoops nonetheless. She would've brought a pistol, but it simply wasn't possible or practical. She entertained herself by counting security flaws and estimating the worth of various guests and their jewelry—a habit born of her childhood. She could've made a fortune in silk handkerchiefs alone. Such thoughts were reassuring. Mal could change her clothes, but she would keep some aspects of herself no matter what.

"All right, Em," Mal said. "Time to earn your keep."

"You don't keep me," she whispered, irked by his use of her first name outside of their sanctuary. "Supposedly, I keep you—at least for tonight."

"Most here aren't aware of art's seedier side," he whispered back, and winked. "They actually think I earn my keep with my brush."

She arched an eyebrow at him.

"My *paint* brush," Mal said. "It's best to maintain their illusions." He offered her his elbow. "Shall we?"

She looped her arm through his and then handed off the invitation card to the footman. The music drifting through the open doorway faded away and vapid party chatter took over. Apparently, Mal was a regular. The footman didn't so much as blink, and they were ushered into the entry. She was relieved of her cloak, and they were led to the room where the salon was being held. Candles and lamps blazed in the huge room. Two stately fireplaces, one on each end, kept the chill and damp from the air. Their painted screens protected guests from stray sparks. Richly dressed nobles with fine crystal goblets or porcelain plates in hand clustered together around food or conversation. They chatted and laughed with others who clearly didn't belong in such a setting—like Mal and herself—as if nothing were out of place. In spite of this, an aura of genteel daring permeated the room.

One or two individuals spared her an eyebrow of refined disdain, and she checked her appearance in the closest mirror for whatever sign had advertised her lack of status. It took her a moment to understand that it was her open awe. She decided not to care.

Burning beeswax, incense, perfume, and cigarillo smoke helped boost the atmosphere of refined creativity. A new group of musicians finished their preparations and began playing. Their music was Tahmerian—all jovial violins, mandolins, harpsichord, drunken woodwinds, and deep, dull drums. Three half-dressed dancers, two female and one male, gyrated in filmy silks. Silver coins and bells displayed in their hair and on their skin jingled as they danced. Their feet were bare on the cold white marble floor. Their dance was as foreign and lost in the lordly setting as she was.

"Can we go home now?" she asked Mal, hating herself for her unease. Her uniform provided a certain amount of protection. The rules for behavior were distinct, and she knew them well. In this dress, she wasn't herself. While that was fine when she was alone with Mal—she relished that aspect of their time together, in fact— in this room, it was anything but.

Mal squeezed her hand. "Stop scowling."

"How does she get away with it?"

"Whatever do you mean?"

"None of this falls within Fortis's rigid artistic standards. You know, those standards you complain about so much."

"She is Lady Marca. That's how," Mal said. "Isn't it wonderful?"

"I don't know that 'wonderful' would be the word I'd use to describe it."

"We should present ourselves to the hostess. Are you ready?"

"No."

"Right. Time to fix that. Stay here." He briefly abandoned her in order to fetch two crystal goblets. Lazy bubbles drifted in the pale pinkish wine. "Best I could do on short notice. They won't bring out the stronger stuff until later. Drink up."

She swallowed the pale pink contents of both glasses in one gulp apiece. The light taste carried a hint of sweet, while the memory of bitter lingered on her tongue. He abandoned the delicate crystal flutes on a nearby table. With the wine still burning in her throat, she let him tug her through the crowd. He didn't stop until he'd located the hostess, who chattered in the center of a large group of admirers.

Lady Marca was younger than Drake had expected—a year or two younger than Drake herself. Her features were flawless, and even Drake had to admit she was a beauty. Masses of silky black curls were artfully arranged on top of her head and tied with some sort of purple wrap. Clusters of diamonds and pearls set in silver were draped around her throat. On the surface, Lady Marca was everything Drake hated about noble women. However, within a few moments, Drake detected a carefully monitored intelligence behind Lady Marca's eyes—intelligence and a hidden strength. Drake recalculated her estimation. Lady Marca was no spoiled, thoughtless child, at least not in the sense that Drake had come to expect. For a start, Lady Marca lorded over the room with no visible male backup. Her husband was nowhere in sight. Drake began to wonder what dangerous games Lady Marca played at to maintain her power. Patient, Mal waited until Lady Marca turned away from the dandy at her side and offered her hand. Mal kissed it while half-hiding the canvas behind his back.

"Mallory McDermott, you're late," Lady Marca said. "I should be very angry with you."

"But you won't be," he said.

"You've brought me a gift?" she asked.

"I have." Mal presented the painting with a flourish.

Drake prepared herself to hate the woman. Mal's art, like many of those who lived and worked in the Creeksbend area of the city, didn't always fit within the guidelines dictated by Gens Fortis. Drake expected a dismissive wave of the hand. Instead, Lady Marca let out an appreciative gasp.

"Oh, Mallory. It's incredible. I adore it."

"Careful," Mal said. "It's still wet."

"Then you shouldn't have risked damaging it by bringing it tonight."

"A promise is a promise," Mal said.

"I'll take special care, then." Lady Marca moved away. "Everyone!

You must see Mallory's latest effort! Isn't it divine? Come. I'll have it put on display, and you can tell me what you see." After the painting had been deposited on an easel and a large number of admirers were shepherded in front of it, a lively discussion of its merits and flaws began. Lady Marca didn't retreat until the conversation had been sufficiently established. Finally, she returned to Mal's side, smiling. "It's even better than the last. You must take something for it."

"Being able to present it to you here is payment enough."

"I insist." Lady Marca tugged a servant aside and whispered in his ear. She turned to face them once again, and Drake felt her take her by the arm. "Mallory, you've been rude. I regret that I have joined you in this offense. Aren't you going to introduce me to your friend?"

"Emily Drake," Mallory said. "This is Lady Marca."

"I apologize, Mistress Drake, but Mallory's art takes away my sense," Lady Marca said, and then leaned toward Mal. "She is lovely."

Liar, Drake thought.

"What sort of artist is she?" Lady Marca asked.

"She isn't." Mallory gave her one of his most mischievous smiles and lowered his voice. "She's a Watch captain."

"And you brought her here? Why, Mallory, that's positively shocking," Lady Marca said with amused approval, and then whispered just loud enough for Drake to hear. "I love her already."

"I thought you might," Mal said.

Lady Marca placed a hand on Drake's arm. "So, you have a taste for dangerous art? Don't worry, dear. Your secret is safe with me."

This wasn't for Drake's benefit, she knew, but for Lady Marca's. If the guests knew a member of the Watch was present, they'd flee in droves and that would spell the end of any future salons. Of course, if Drake's superior knew where she was and that she wasn't here to make any arrests, there would also be grave consequences. *We both have something to lose.*

"Would you two care to join me for dinner?" Lady Marca asked.

"I leave that question entirely up to Em," Mal said. "She was to have my undivided attention this evening."

Uncomfortable, Drake nodded permission nonetheless. Anyone with power enough to openly thwart Gens Fortis was someone Drake didn't want for an enemy. *Besides*, she thought, *she's Mal's patron. I can't damage that relationship for him. I won't.*

Drake and Mal were introduced to a new group. Intent on listening, she limited her responses to smiles and nods. All in all, Mal's intent of securing more financial backing appeared to be successful. Still, it annoyed Drake that regardless of guild membership, Mal's work wouldn't have been noticed without Lady Marca's enthusiastic support. His signature was on the back of the painting and not the front. None of these people would acknowledge him, nor would his name be spoken aloud outside of this room. If any of them came to him for a commission, they'd do so in private. Ultimately, while Mal's work might become popular and might bring him a certain amount of wealth, it would never be enough to make him more than relatively comfortable. Whereas if Lady Marca were to sell the gifted painting, it would fetch a handsome price. What angered Drake most was the knowledge of all that it had cost him to get this far.

While Mal was intent on conversation with one of the other guests, Lady Marca turned to her.

"Mistress Drake, would you mind if Mallory and I left you for a moment?" she whispered. "I've something that I'd like to discuss with him. I promise not to take too much of his time."

"Feel free," Drake said. And with that, she was abandoned in a sea of strangers. Uncomfortable, she made excuses and drifted to a quiet corner. She knew herself for a pessimist at heart. She didn't buy into the Regnum's self-aggrandizing claims surrounding mercantilism. A social system entirely dependent upon trade was far from egalitarian. The gentes hoarded power, worthiness, and money in the same manner that nobles of other countries hoarded power, worthiness, and land. Freedom was not, in fact, freedom if it required purchase. She felt the same way about morality, which was why she'd chosen not to care about either.

An attractive young man with long dark hair approached. She was about to tell him to go away when he said, "I didn't expect to see you here."

It took her a moment to recognize Fortis Caius. "You're out of uniform."

"So are you," Caius said. "Your hair is different."

Mal had spent a quite a while taming her locks with a pair of hair tongs. It wasn't in her to bother with such things. "It is." She suppressed an urge to ask if he liked it. With alarm, she remembered Mal. *It will be all right. Mal will be gone for a while, and I don't want to be alone. Just make sure to get rid of Caius before Mal gets back.* "What are you doing here?"

Caius smiled and nodded at an elderly guest from across the room. "I'm here because of my father. Displaying a rebellious streak makes family events during the winter holidays more tolerable."

"The father of a Warden patronizes deviant art?"

"You're assuming he approves of the Brotherhood."

"He doesn't? Then why did you join?"

"Why did you become a Watch captain?"

She hushed him and checked to see if anyone had heard.

"Don't worry," Caius said. "No one here cares about the Watch. That's for other people. So? Why?"

"If you're a woman, there aren't many opportunities within the Syndicate that don't involve earning your keep on your back," Drake said with a shrug. *And I didn't want to end up like my mother.*

Caius said, "This is the Regnum. There are no restrictions preventing—"

"Syndicate membership isn't cheap. And even street harvesters are particular about who they allow within their ranks. Women are charged twice as much as men. This is true of all guilds, with a few . . . exceptions. It was less expensive to buy my stripes. And the only reason that was the case is because no one thinks women would want such work." She noticed his cheeks had grown pink. "Is something wrong?"

"Not at all."

"You're offended?" she asked. *He's a Warden. You know what that means. If he knew what you really are, he'd—*

"I never took you for an insurrectionist."

"And I never took you for an uptight traditionalist. Apparently, I'm mistaken," she said. "Excuse me. I have to go."

He reached out for her arm. "Wait."

"Why?"

"I'm sorry. I didn't intend insult. May we try this again?"

"Is there a reason why we should?" At that moment, she caught sight of Mal. He was talking to someone who looked familiar. It wasn't until the other individual had turned around that she understood why her heart had stopped. "Oh, Mithras."

Caius blinked at her profanity. "What's wrong?"

"That's him. *Arion.* What is he doing here?"

Caius shrugged. "Perhaps he's interested in deviant art and music. Quite a few people are."

"Let me go," she said. *Mal is talking to Arion. Mal. My Mal.*

"You can't say anything about his license. He can have you killed for—"

"Don't you think I know that?" She pulled free of Caius's grasp. She wasn't thinking about anything but getting Mal away from the hunter. *He may only target children, but that doesn't mean he wouldn't kill Mal if given a chance.* She'd forced her way between them before she'd given thought to what she'd say.

"Hello, Em," Mal said, smiling. "This is—"

"I know who he is," Drake said. She searched the room for an excuse to pull him away and her gaze lit upon the painting on its easel. "Mal, someone has a question about your work I don't feel I can answer for you."

"Oh," Mal said. "Very well. I . . . er . . . It was nice to meet you, my lord."

Arion nodded. Again, his manner was subservient, even frightened. Drake fled with Mal before Arion could catch her eye. As they walked away, she could feel Mal's rage in the tremor of his tensed muscles.

"What in all of Sandrion's Hells was that about?" Mal asked between clenched teeth.

"I'll explain later," she said. "Just . . . stay away from that man. He's dangerous."

"Really?"

"I'm serious, Mal. *Please.*"

Mal said, "If you say so."

"I can't explain right now," she said. "It's connected to something I'm working on. Something to do with the Watch and the Brotherhood."

"All right, I trust you."

"Good."

"But you're telling me later. I don't care what means I have to undertake to get it out of you."

Drake placed a hand on Mal's arm. "That sounds . . . costly."

He leaned in closer to breathe into her ear. "It might be, but I'll make it worth the price. I promise."

The proximity of his mouth sent a pleasant shiver through her body. "In that case, I think I could spend one more night in your company."

"Glad to hear it, my lady."

"Don't spoil the moment."

Lightly brushing his lips against her throat, he whispered, "Yes, ma'am."

"Mistress."

"*Mistress*."

They spent the rest of the evening with Lady Marca and her other guests, but Drake found she couldn't avoid Caius's gaze. It was clear he had questions regarding her escort, but she was intent on never answering them.

⊰ BLACKTHORNE ⊱

EIGHTH OF MAITOKUU, 1784

Blackthorne hauled bundles of supplies onto the sloop *Clár Oibre Rúnda* while the others finished their goodbyes. It gave him something upon which to focus his nervous energy.

It was six o'clock, and the sun had crested the horizon an hour before. While their numbers had dramatically decreased as summer approached, Colonel Hännenen had wanted to be certain the malorum had retreated before setting out. The first part of the journey would be to meet the Clan Flounder frigate *Star* in the port of Wyeth. The journey would take four days, sailing east on the Kristallilasi River. Blackthorne dreaded the prospect of stopping. He didn't want to tour the ruins of Eledore. It would bring back too many memories. He hadn't served long in the war, but it had been long enough.

In spite of himself, Blackthorne couldn't shake the feeling that he didn't know the whole of the plan regarding Novus Salernum. He wanted to believe otherwise. Unfortunately, after the business with the new weaponsmith, he found such trust difficult to muster.

It is a Retainer's duty to—

You aren't a Retainer. You never were. Retainers have contracts with their masters, indentured or not. You have no contract—

—Masterless Retainers are without honor—

You gave up everything in order to be your own. You have a choice.

He realized with a start that he'd been avoiding not only the anxiety of discarding everything but responsibility for having made certain decisions. *I could have said no to this journey,* Blackthorne thought, testing the idea. *I still can.* But he knew he wouldn't. Just as he knew he wouldn't discard the Retainer's Code. *Not now. Maybe not ever.* This, in and of itself, was a choice, and for some reason, being aware of that made him feel better. *Is it possible to keep the Retainer's Code and all that goes with it but view it from a different perspective? Until now, I've followed Talus's interpretation without question. What if his isn't the only approach?*

Blackthorne set down the bundles intended for the larder in the galley and retraced his steps through the narrow passage to the stairway.

Focus on the path in front of you. Nothing of import exists in the past. Contemplating the multiple implications of that line, he almost walked into Slate, who was making his way down the stairs.

"I'm sorry, sir." Blackthorne made room for Slate to pass.

"I was waiting on the dock. Weren't you going to say goodbye?" Slate asked. He had a coat looped over one arm and was carrying a couple of bundles in the crook of the other.

Blackthorne blinked. "Do you have final instructions, sir?"

Slate said, "Actually, I wanted to give you something." He

unfolded the coat and held it out. "We can't have you freezing to death before you get to Novus Salernum."

Stunned, Blackthorne didn't move. *A gift?*

"Go on. Take it," Slate said. "Put it on. I need to know now if it fits. It's a bit late for Emilius Arnason to make alterations, but he assured me that he could guess your measurements well enough."

Blackthorne had put on every article of clothing he owned in preparation. Given the threadbare state of his overcoat, he'd even cut a hole in the middle of a horse blanket and had thrown it over the top as if it were a cloak. It functioned well enough, and it kept his hands free. In addition, it'd circumvented the need to pack.

His cheeks heated as it occurred to him what he must look like to the others. *Is it a gift, or is it charity?* He hadn't given much thought to his appearance, because he wasn't having to playact during their journey south. He was only to be himself—whatever that was, for the time being. Therefore, he'd been focused on practicality alone.

"Is something wrong?" Slate asked.

"No, sir." Caught between his tattered pride and obvious necessity, Blackthorne still didn't move.

"If you cannot accept the coat as a gift from a friend, consider it partial compensation for services rendered to the community," Slate said.

"Yes, sir." Blackthorne lifted the horse blanket over his head and removed his threadbare coat. He knocked his hand on the low ceiling in the process. The narrow passage wasn't the best place to change. Still, he was grateful that Slate had chosen to present the gift to him in private.

He shrugged on the new coat and found its heavy warmth a near-perfect fit. Unlike its predecessor, it didn't restrict his movement. He could reach his weapons without fear of tearing the seams. "Thank you, sir."

Slate squinted. He wasn't wearing his spectacles, and the cloudiness in his eyes was gone. "Feels all right?"

"Yes, sir."

"Good," Slate said, and nodded, pleased. "I want you to know how much I appreciate what you've done—what you're doing now. I'm not sure I've expressed that enough. I should've done a better job of that."

"It's all right, sir."

Slate said, "The truth is, I've grown rather fond of you, as has Moss. He sends this and apologizes for not saying goodbye himself." He gave him the bundles. "Open them later."

"Please give him my thanks."

"I will." Slate stole a glance up the stairs behind him. "One last thing. Would you—" He paused, seemingly embarrassed and distressed. "Would you look after Katrin for me? See to it she doesn't get into trouble?"

There had been a great deal of consternation surrounding the inclusion of Katrin Brooke. Officially, Colonel Hännenen had made the original recommendation because, while what remained of the Royal Eledorean Army contained a large number of pickpockets, thieves, and rogues, none of them had the requisite skills to quietly break into an Acrasian building. That is, Brooke, a former street harvester, was the Hold's only resident Acrasian lockpick.

Unofficially, Blackthorne had suggested her first. However, Queen Suvi had decided to tell Slate that it'd been Nels's idea. Blackthorne wasn't entirely sure the ruse had worked.

"I will do everything I can, sir." *Everything within my power,* he thought.

"Good. Good," Slate said, somewhat relieved. "Good luck, Severus. Come back alive." He put out a hand.

Blackthorne blinked at the use of his real name. "She will too, sir. You've my word." He took the man's hand and shook.

"Thank you. I can't tell you how much that means to me. I—I know she'll be safe with you to look after her." Slate released Blackthorne's hand and went back up the stairs.

Blackthorne gathered his things and followed after. He took a moment to examine his new coat in better light. Styled in the Ytlainen fashion with big cuffs and a high collar, a great deal of thought had been put into its design. It was made of black wool, and tall as he was, it was long enough to cover the tops of his boots. A second layer of wool draped over his shoulders like a shawl and could be used to form a hood in foul weather. He straightened under its welcome weight and felt warm for what seemed the first time in months even though it was May.

The gardens had been planted, and fishing was now practical. Beef, however, was a distant memory. The cattle that Moller had stolen from the Acrasians were long gone, and the wild reindeer that normally supplemented the community's stores had been scarce until recently. For his part, Blackthorne didn't care if he saw another onion or turnip for the rest of his life.

It is good to be leaving this place.

Leaving his baggage on the deck, he went back to work. This time, his thoughts were lighter. He decided he liked the feel of the vessel beneath him more and more. He'd never traveled by ship before—even one as small as *Clár Oibre Rúnda*. That was, when he thought about it now, a little unusual for someone who had been raised Acrasian. However, the duke didn't care much for boats and had generally left the overseas travel to underlings.

At last, the loading was finished and the passengers boarded.

Colonel Hännenen and Ilta, his wife, went below at once. The queen, her bodyguard, Jami Rautio, and the Waterborne ambassador, Dylan Kask, went about their tasks, piloting the small ship away from the hidden dock and into the river. Lieutenant Viktor Reini was assisting Darius Teak high up in the rigging. This left Blackthorne, Katrin Brooke, and Natalia Annikki to fend for themselves. For his part, Blackthorne moved to the front of the small ship. He hoped to stay out of the way of those who had work to do. He left Annikki and Katrin talking together at the ship's side.

Blackthorne took a slow, deep breath in an attempt to relax. Early spring was cold and hard inside his lungs, even painful if he weren't careful. The days had steadily grown longer and warmer. His new coat was a bit heavy for Eledore in summer, even the start of summer, but he couldn't bear to take it off. The overcoat would be just right for the evenings. After some consideration, he concluded it was definitely too warm for Acrasia. He didn't care. He stood at the front of the ship, out of the way of the sails and ropes, and felt the wind push against his back. He savored the sunlight cast upon his face—the way it reddened the skin under his eyelids as he turned toward it. He spent most of the morning with the wind blowing his hair in his face, watching the river.

His senses had grown sharper during his stay in the Hold, particularly his hearing. That disturbed him. He didn't understand how or why, but he'd even felt the change when spring and then summer had arrived—particularly spring. He had no need of an almanac. The energy in the air or the earth had been different. That difference sang under his skin and hummed in his bones, making him restless. By May, getting out of the Hold had become an imperative. If he'd remained behind, it would've only meant trouble. He had *had* to get out.

"First time on a ship?"

Blackthorne turned and saw it was the Waterborne named Darius.

His hair was done in braids that had grown longer since Blackthorne had first met him. They were now gathered in a short queue at the nape of Darius's neck. Blackthorne had to tilt his head down a little in order to look him in the eye.

Blackthorne nodded.

"Do you want me to show you where you're bunking?" Darius asked.

Blackthorne blinked. It wasn't even noon yet.

"So you can store your things. It's going to rain soon. Everything will get wet," Darius said, and pointed to the coat. "And aren't you hot?"

"Oh." Blackthorne collected his rucksack from the deck.

"Come on," Darius said. "I'll show you."

Following Darius down the steps, they left what Darius referred to as the gun deck and made their way to the lower deck. Eventually, they arrived at a small room lined with bunks.

Darius pointed to the bunk on the bottom left. "That's yours. You can store your baggage in the locker underneath." He opened the small cabinet tucked under the bed. "See?"

"Thank you," Blackthorne said. He stowed his bag inside, and with some small reluctance, he removed the overcoat, folded it, and put it away.

"*Clár* is a sloop. So, we'll be a bit cozy. Normally, that wouldn't be a problem. A couple of us could sleep on the deck, but that might not be wise."

"The malorum," Blackthorne said.

"Exactly," Darius said. "Queen Suvi and Jami are taking the captain's cabin. Dylan and I will be in the first mate's. Nels and Ilta will have the bosun's and, well . . . the rest of you are in here, the crew cabin. You going to be all right on the left with Viktor? Natalia and Kat will be on the other side. A canvas divide drops through the middle. See? That halves an already-small space, but the divider will provide some privacy. Although canvas walls don't do much for the snoring or the late-night chatter."

Blackthorne indicated it would be fine.

"It's almost time for lunch," Darius said. "I need to get everything ready. I could use some help. Would you mind?"

"Not at all," Blackthorne said.

They went to the galley together, and Blackthorne set out the plates and tableware. While he'd no experience in doing so, years of instruction in table manners made the task of arranging the weighted cups and plates simple. The room was warm due to the oven, and it wasn't long before Darius ventured from the stove to open the portholes to allow in some air. Blackthorne could smell bread baking. Stooping over yet another place setting, he sensed someone move close to him. In such a cramped space, it wasn't difficult to catch the scent of winter roses, rosemary, and mint. It also told him who was near without turning.

Ilta. His heart was struck with a freezing bolt of something too close to terror. All at once, his skin felt tight, and his mind flooded with conflicting thoughts. *Go away. You belong to him. You've made your choice. You're going to get me killed.*

Please stay.

She would only use you for a cocksman.

What does that matter? Has anyone done anything else? Almost against his will, he captured the smell of her in his lungs as if it were the only part of her he could hold. *I couldn't compete with Hännenen even if I wanted to. What could I have offered her? That fight is done. Speaking to her now is suicide.*

A Retainer must consider themselves already dead—

I want to live, *damn it.*

Suddenly, the prospect of living in a confined space with her so close seemed infinitely stupid. *Walk away—*

"I like this ship. She's beautiful, isn't she?" she asked. He could hear nervousness in her tone, threatening to knock her voice off balance.

What does she have to feel uneasy about? He didn't look her in the eye. *Why is she here?*

She turned and asked Darius, "What's for lunch?" through the narrow doorway.

Oh, Blackthorne thought. Heart drumming a forced march, he continued with his work. From the corner of his eye he saw she was wearing a blue day dress. Her cheeks and nose were a healthy pink.

"Cold meats," Darius said. "Bread and cheese."

"What kind of meat?" Ilta asked.

"Reindeer. Viktor and I hunted a fresh one yesterday," Darius said. "Since it was partly my kill, I was able to convince James to let me have part of it for the trip."

"Sounds good," Ilta said.

"Will Nels be joining us?" Darius asked.

"I doubt it," Ilta said. "He's in his bunk."

"Is he sick already?" Darius asked.

She shook her head. "I keep telling him he'll be fine, but he doesn't trust it."

"The river is calm. He should eat something while he can," Darius said. "He can't starve himself the entire journey."

"That's what I told him," Ilta said. "But he's stubborn. I'll bring him something after we eat."

"So, that means there'll be eight for lunch," Darius said. "I'll switch off with Dylan at the wheel."

The noon meal was uneventful, as was dinner. Blackthorne managed to keep to himself by spending most of his time on the upper deck. He learned a few things about sailing from Dylan and Darius, both of whom were much easier to talk to than the others. Katrin had taken to trailing behind Jami and Natalia. Viktor, like him, tended to keep to himself for the most part.

This, Blackthorne thought, *is going to be a very long journey.*

❧ DRAKE ❧

ONE

"What are we here for?" Benbow grumbled. "Can't the army handle a few nonhumans?"

"Shut it, Benbow," Captain Drake said.

She laid a hand to the River Sector's wet stone wall. Behind her, five Watch volunteers waited. Looking through the iron gates, Drake watched the nonhumans crowding into and out of shops. Nothing seemed different. Women and children waited in lines as with pinched, resentful faces, rushing to collect purchases before the curfew bells rang the end of the day. Still, she could sense something was wrong.

Suddenly, she understood what it was. *Where are all the young men?* She spied one or two, but nowhere near as many as she would've seen last spring.

Rain fell in sheets, and a cold breeze swept through the gates. The clock tower in the Commons rang four o'clock.

Drake said, "Army is paying extra. Expecting trouble, I suspect."

"How much trouble?" Benbow asked.

Benbow is getting more inquisitive, Drake thought. "Enough. But not too much."

"All the more reason to be at home in bed," Benbow said. "You planning on sharing that extra pay, or are we to be happy in the honor of being volunteered?"

"You'll get your cut," Drake said. "Don't you worry."

A drum accompanied marching feet in rain-dampened echoes. Drake waved her ten Watchmen against the wall to let the army pass. Her orders were to hang back, and at the first sign of trouble, they were to shut and lock the gates.

She counted twenty soldiers as they marched past in orderly parade formation. *That's quite a few for a recruiting party,* she thought. Ten of the men assumed positions under the clock tower at the center of the shabby Commons park while the others proceeded to herd nonhumans into the square. The lieutenant ripped a broadsheet from the side of the tower, wadding the paper in his fists with a frown. A private assembled a camp table and stool before the sergeant took his seat on the wooden stage. A ledger, paper, ink, and several quills were set on the table's surface. The lieutenant rang the bell on the side of the tower three times, the signal for an official announcement. Then he unfolded a piece of paper and began reading in a loud voice as the residents reluctantly gathered.

"The Regnum of Acrasia calls upon her sons to serve and protect her from the northern threat."

"I thought the war was over," a nonhuman with greasy black hair said.

The lieutenant ignored the statement and read on. "When each name is announced, form a line to the right and report to the recruiting sergeant. The following honored beings are summoned to military service in the Glorious Army of Acrasia: John Alder, Hakon Balder—"

"Hakon died last fall," someone said.

"—Eric Frigg, Kelder Mielikki, Mikael Pellervoinen . . ." The recruiting lieutenant's voice pierced the air like a steady death knell.

Muted cries of despair mixed with grumbles of outrage as each name was read. Regardless, a line began to form in front of the sergeant, who handed the first recruit a quill and pointed where he was to put his mark on the ledger book. Nearby, Drake overheard an older woman as she grabbed a young man's sleeve.

"Don't go," she said.

"I have to. You know the law," he said. "It's this or work. And I don't have work to excuse me from service. Don't worry. This way, I'll come back a citizen."

"If you come back," she said.

He didn't seem to hear her. "I'll be qualified for guild membership."

Surreptitious motions from those along the edges of the crowd were enough to tell Drake something unpleasant was definitely on the way. The lieutenant doggedly continued to the bottom of the list, unaffected by the sullen atmosphere. As he reached the end, a mud clod exploded on the clock tower three feet above his head.

Next to Drake, Gilmartyn suppressed a laugh. Somewhere in the crowd, someone didn't.

In response, several soldiers drew their muskets, but the lieutenant signaled for them to stand down. Two additional mud clods rapidly slammed into the tower. The lieutenant ordered the sergeant to pack. However, before he could comply, the barrage intensified. Mud slapped the recruiting sergeant's face. Incensed, the sergeant grabbed a musket from the private standing next to him and shot a nonhuman at the front of the crowd.

For a moment, no one moved. Then a cry of grief and outrage pierced the air. It was followed by chaos. Most of the crowd fled for safety, but another part of it surged forward in a rage, ripping at anyone and anything in its path. Drake saw and heard musket fire. Again, it brought the crowd up short for a few moments. Then they pushed forward. The soldiers didn't have time to reload. Within moments, the lieutenant and twenty Acrasian soldiers vanished in the roiling mass.

Drake hesitated. Her orders were to wait to lock down until the troops were through the gates. However, she didn't think the troops were going to make it out. If the mob could overtake twenty trained soldiers, then ten Watchmen didn't stand a chance.

Fresh blood painted the cobblestones. Bloody uniform parts and weapons surfaced in the form of trophies waved in the air. The mob spread toward a guard tower, and Drake had the bad feeling they weren't going to stop with the officer and his troops.

Drake grabbed half the heavy iron gate with both hands. "Benbow, Jasper, get the other side. Gilmartyn, help me. The rest of you make damn sure no one gets out that isn't a soldier. Shoot anyone who tries to stop us; you got it?"

The clock tower toppled with a loud crash, the bell clanging as the broken timbers fell. Screams and angry howls intensified, and shattering glass from the shops mixed in the chaos. Flames appeared in doorways, and Drake had hardly budged the gate when she spied a bloody form crawling out of the crowd. A filthy and starved-looking elph stood over him with a paving stone. The soldier on the ground looked up, and she knew him at once.

"Emily! Help! Please!"

Hayden? When did he sign on with the army? Without thinking, Drake drew a pistol and fired at the elph. She missed, hitting another in the back instead. Hayden vanished within the mob. Her brother's gory hand stretched out from the churning mass.

"Benbow, get the damn gate shut!" She thought, *I'm going to regret this.*

She rammed her pistol into her belt and drew her knife. Then she ran through the gate and into the crowd. She kicked two elphs aside and dove for Hayden's arm. Grabbing his sleeve and pulling, she scrabbled one-handed for better purchase. Everywhere, people were screaming in pain, anger, and fear. Smoke clogged the air as buildings caught fire. The smell of burning timbers mingled with the stench of unwashed bodies. Someone kicked her in the side. A rock crashed onto the cobblestones inches from her head. She felt hands groping for her pistol. She struck out with her knife hand without looking. Again she yanked on Hayden's arm. Finally, she got a hold on him and pulled him to his feet. His relieved face was a mask of blood. One arm hung at a crooked angle. She staggered toward the gates but was brought up short by the gates swinging shut.

"Benbow! Wait!"

Benbow paused only to show her his ugly teeth by way of a smile and a farewell salute as the chains and locks were thrown into place.

He's taking a promotion. All this time, he waited. I gave him my fucking back! A fierce sense of rage and betrayal welled up inside her. If she could've willed the gates open, they would've swung wide fast enough to pin Benbow to the stone wall. "Goddamn you, Benbow! Open that damn gate! I'll swiving rip your heart out and eat it if it's the last swiving thing I do! My father's Syndicate, you asshole! He'll—" A numbing blow to the back of her head cut off the last of her threats.

⇥ BLACKTHORNE ⇤

Clár Oibre Rúnda proved to be a swift and agile ship. Even after keeping to the Acrasian coast for a healthy distance, she made the journey to Novus Salernum in record time. They arrived on the evening of the twentieth, but since the harbor wasn't open due to the city curfew, they'd dropped anchor and waited for morning several miles offshore. Upon arrival, Blackthorne accompanied Dylan Kask to register Clan Flounder's ship *Clár Oibre Rúnda* with the assistant harbormaster. Dressed in borrowed clothes in order to play the part of a merchant of the middling sort, Blackthorne took charge of haggling. The standard negotiations resulted in a satisfying drop in harbor charges. He handed over the requisite fees, and no questions were asked. It was an auspicious start.

So far, Blackthorne thought.

"That was . . . expensive," Dylan said. "I don't think I've ever seen a dock fee like that before. No wonder it's standard practice to avoid overnight stays."

"We didn't want an inspection, nor did we want an unsecured night-berth. We didn't bring enough troops, and the *Clár* isn't designed to be secure against malorum," Blackthorne muttered as they made their way back through the crowds around the docks.

"Understandable," Dylan said. "But you-know-who won't be happy."

Colonel Hännenen isn't particularly happy about anything right now, Blackthorne thought. *And he won't be until his sister is home safe.* "Everything has a price here. You know this. The extra fees mean that we do what we need without notice, and we can come and go whenever it suits us."

"I suppose I should be glad that we won't be here for longer than two days," Dylan said. "Where to next?"

"The Broken Crown," Blackthorne said. "I'm to meet with a friend of Councilor Slate's. His name is Mr. Sparrow."

"That doesn't sound like an assumed name at all," Dylan said.

Shrugging, Blackthorne said, "It is how these things are done. I can deal with the matter myself, if need be. Have you changed your mind about coming along?"

"Absolutely not," Dylan said. "It's been years since I've seen anything of Acrasia."

Blackthorne nodded and paused outside their destination. There was a line outside the door and two Watchmen conducting an inspection of identification papers. He didn't recall seeing a line outside a pub before.

That is not a good sign, he thought. "In that case, watch our friend Mr. Sparrow. Tell me if you see anything strange. Particularly if he seems nervous."

"Will do," Dylan said.

When it came their turn, Blackthorne produced his falsified papers. Dylan handed over his own for inspection.

"What's going on?" Blackthorne asked the Watchman.

"Nothing to worry about, mister. As long as you got your papers, and you do." He gave the counterfeit papers a cursory check and handed them back.

"Who are you looking for?" Blackthorne asked.

The Watchman shook his head. "Was a big row a week ago. They're looking for the one that started it. A writer by trade, I understand. Goes by the name Libertas. Writes about elphs being equal to humans. How war with Ytlain won't solve nothing. Says the games were invented to trick the poor into suicide for the pleasure of the rich. Mad shit like that. You're free to go inside."

"Oh. Thank you," Blackthorne said, and kept his face as blank as possible.

The Broken Crown smelled no different from all the other public houses in which Blackthorne had conducted various business since he'd entered the Academy. The main difference between it and the others was that the Broken Crown specifically catered to nonhumans. Not that such a thing was rare; it was only that Blackthorne hadn't often frequented such places.

At this hour, he and Dylan had their choice of tables. Instead, Blackthorne scanned the room and then headed to one of the occupied few. The man sitting there was wearing a grey coat and eating his breakfast alone. There was a blue sparrowhawk feather pinned to his collar, and he was positioned so that he could easily see the front door—a not-uncommon decision in this place. He didn't look up.

Blackthorne changed his posture, assuming a slight hunch and bending his knees a little in order to appear shorter, and tucked his hands into his breeches pockets. "Mr. Sparrow?" He lowered the pitch of his voice. "I understand we have a mutual acquaintance in the export business."

Mr. Sparrow finally glanced up from his meal and motioned for them to sit. "I am. You are Mr. Aldar, I presume?"

"I am," Blackthorne said.

"I was told to expect you," Mr. Sparrow said. "But the message didn't mention a water sneaksman."

Dylan frowned, obviously getting the impression that he'd been insulted.

He isn't wrong. "Mr. Flounder is a good friend," Blackthorne said.

"I don't know if you're aware, but things have changed a mite bit around here. Watch are poking their beaks into things more often than people like. And more often than not, the Brotherhood follows right behind. Folks are growing more cautious. Perhaps I should start with him," Mr. Sparrow said, and pointed at Dylan. "I don't like Waterborne."

"I understand the need for more thorough circumspection. However, Mr. Flounder can be trusted," Blackthorne said.

"I've only your word for that," Mr. Sparrow said. "And I don't know you all that well."

"Your concern is that my friend is connected to the Brotherhood?" Blackthorne asked.

Mr. Sparrow shrugged.

Blackthorne leaned toward Mr. Sparrow. "Since when has the Brotherhood worked with Waterborne magic practitioners?"

Mr. Sparrow blinked and then gave Dylan another hard look.

"Mr. Flounder, indulge me," Blackthorne said without turning away from Mr. Sparrow. "Please give our friend a demonstration. Nothing too overt. We don't wish to upset the patrons or draw too much attention."

Dylan paused and then nodded. Moving closer, he stuck his

index finger in Mr. Sparrow's ale mug and closed his eyes. After a while, its pewter surface began to sweat with cold. A frost began to form and spread onto the table's wooden surface.

Mr. Sparrow's mouth dropped open.

"That's more than enough, Mr. Flounder," Blackthorne said.

Dylan withdrew his digit and leaned back. As he did, there came the tiny sound of ice cracking and melting.

"May we continue?" Blackthorne asked. "My time is limited, and my patience has worn thin."

Mr. Sparrow nodded. The open fear in his expression didn't abate, and he kept his gaze on Dylan as if the Waterborne weathermaster had drawn a weapon.

"In addition to the . . . package that I have for your employer, I also have need of two wagons capable of handling a heavy load and four of your strongest men to assist. They will be required for a few hours. I will pay for your discretion. Can you accommodate us?" Blackthorne asked.

"Mayhap I can," Mr. Sparrow said.

"And the price?" Blackthorne asked.

"Hold on. Your . . . brothers have all been kainen." Mr. Sparrow stopped eating and gave Blackthorne a hard stare. "You don't look kainen."

Blackthorne frowned. "I was told the look of my sterling would be more important. I've had quite enough of—"

Mr. Sparrow waved for a barmaid. "Let's not be hasty. We'll have a drink. Talk it over. What'll you have?"

"An Ytlainen porter would suit me fine," Blackthorne said.

Mr. Sparrow smiled, and his shoulders dropped just a little. He sniffed. "You've fine taste in ale, sir. However, porter is a bit too fashionable for folks around here. You'll have to settle for plain grog or ale."

Blackthorne had his doubts as to the state of the water in this place. "Ale will be fine."

"Seems we can do business after all. Times being what they are, you can't fault a man for being cautious."

"I suppose not."

Mr. Sparrow rested a stubbled chin on his hand and studied Blackthorne's face again. This time, it seemed more out of curiosity than hostility.

"The wagons belong to a friend, understand. Rent price isn't mine to set. But I'm sure my friend is willing to give a discount in honor of certain political sentiments," Mr. Sparrow said.

Blackthorne nodded.

Setting his wooden spoon on the table next to the empty pewter bowl, Mr. Sparrow reached into his coat and brought out a clay pipe. "A hundred will do."

"That's impossible," Blackthorne said. "I could *buy* what I need for that."

"But not the additional labor," Mr. Sparrow said.

"Mr. Flounder, we're leaving," Blackthorne said, and got up to go.

"Come. Come. A counteroffer is customary." Mr. Sparrow filled the pipe with tobacco and lit it with a match from the table.

"I thought you said you couldn't set the price," Blackthorne said, pausing.

Mr. Sparrow blew out a mouthful of smoke. "You not being what I expected, thought I'd start ahead of the price. No harm in a little profit on the side."

Blackthorne sat back down. "I can pay fifty."

"Fifty? Why, those wagons are practically new. And labor isn't cheap—especially *discreet* labor."

"Right, sixty-five. That's all I have," Blackthorne said. "I can't ask my employer for more."

"Sixty-five it is. See? Wasn't all that bad, was it?" Mr. Sparrow leaned back against the bench and smiled. His missing teeth didn't help to make his expression friendlier or more sincere.

"Where are they?" Blackthorne said.

"Begging your pardon, but I want to see the color of your sterling first." Mr. Sparrow shrugged. "You got your instructions; I've got mine."

Blackthorne put a hand inside his coat, pulled out a leather folio, and carefully opened it, giving Mr. Sparrow only a glimpse of the contents.

"Your money does have a nice shine."

As Blackthorne put away the folio, he caught Mr. Sparrow's meaningful nod to someone across the room and pretended not to notice.

Mr. Sparrow said, "You got permits? Permits will cost extra."

"Permits will not be a problem. Thank you for your concern."

"No trouble."

"The wagons?"

"You in a hurry?" Mr. Sparrow asked.

Blackthorne said, "I believe I did mention that time was of some concern."

Mr. Sparrow nodded. "Meet me at the coach house on Archer Street at half four."

Standing, Blackthorne shook Mr. Sparrow's hand. "That will do."

As he and Dylan walked away, Blackthorne felt Dylan tug on his sleeve.

"He's not alone. I'd expect friends," Dylan said.

"I suspected as much," Blackthorne said.

"Why did he think you'd be kainen?" Dylan asked.

After a pause, Blackthorne said, "Perhaps he's used to dealing with another group of Slate's associates?" *One of Hännenen's troops?*

*A friend of Nickols? Who knows? Slate has other contacts. He doesn't
tell me everything.*

"Ah."

"There's going to be trouble when we get there," Blackthorne
said with a frown, and held the door open for Dylan. "Let's get back
to the ship."

They headed to where *Clár* was temporarily docked. Climbing
aboard, Blackthorne handed off the signal flag that granted access
to the secure part of the wharf to Darius Teak. While Darius went
about the business of posting the flag, Dylan piloted the ship to her
designated berth. The whole process took several precious hours
of daylight.

While the ship was settling into her assigned berth, Blackthorne
met with Katrin, Lieutenant Reini, and Natalia Annikki to review
the plans for later in the afternoon. Jami Rautio would remain on
board with Queen Suvi and Colonel Hännenen. Once the ship was
moored, Blackthorne gathered his weapons and his false identity
papers. Then he collected Kat and Lieutenant Reini and headed
for the exit. Blackthorne wanted to test Kat and felt the situation
would be safe enough to do so. If she proved a problem, it wasn't
too late to leave her onboard during the more intense operation.
The next day would go much smoother if the authorities didn't
notice the weapons were missing until *Clár Oibre Rúnda* was long
away with her prize.

He nodded to the guard stationed at the secured dock enclosure's exit. Kat followed behind with Reini. Both wore the clothes
of a Waterborne ordinary seaman. As kainen, it would make them
less noticeable or suspicious—particularly Reini.

It wasn't long before the rough-and-tumble public houses and
warehouses of Old Mercatur Road gave way to more reputable
dwellings. The sour saltwater and sewage stench of the wharf was

left behind them. A warm wind ruffled the hedges lining the street as they made their way north. The comforting scent of burning coal heating the houses hung in the air. The crowds thinned as they traveled farther away from the markets.

A black cat suddenly scurried across the road, and Katrin yelped.

"Calm yourself," Blackthorne muttered between his teeth.

"I'm sorry," Katrin said.

"There's no need to be nervous," Blackthorne whispered.

"No need at all," Lieutenant Reini added, keeping his voice low. "We'll be hauling stolen Eledorean swords without a permit. And the local authorities have a reputation for asking questions with nooses."

"Stop trying to scare me," Kat whispered. "You weren't Syndicate. Do you know what they do to nonmembers caught operating on Syndicate territory?"

Reini grinned, traced a slow line under his chin, and raised an eyebrow.

"That may be where it ends," Katrin said. "But it most certainly isn't where it starts."

Blackthorne didn't see a need to interrupt. Katrin seemed to be holding her own well enough.

When they were a street away from their destination, he signaled to Reini. Reini nodded once and dropped behind with a nonchalant glance into a shop window. Blackthorne and Katrin continued on. He hoped Reini wouldn't run into any trouble on his own.

Archer Street ran at an angle up a hill. In addition to the coach house where they were to meet Mr. Sparrow, the cobblestone street was home to a smithy, several stables, and a mail-coach office. The closer they got, the more intense the smell of horse dung and smithy coal became. The coach house was two doors down from the corner and consisted of three buildings set into a C shape, one of which had a steeple. All three buildings squatted behind a new iron fence.

Blackthorne and Katrin walked the opposite side of the street. Blackthorne did everything in his power to project the appearance of a citizen out for nothing more than an afternoon's stroll. He strode past the main entrance with no apparent intention of stopping, glancing at the trees and down several alleys as if he were a stranger taking in the sights. Katrin seemed to catch on to the ruse quickly enough. As a result, the knot in his stomach loosened.

When the two of them had completed the circuit and reached the main entrance the second time, Blackthorne stopped at the empty archway bisecting the front building and peered through the gate. There was no one in evidence, but he knew better than to assume that was the case even if he couldn't smell the guard's pipe smoke from where he hid a few paces away.

Speaking to the empty coach yard, Blackthorne said, "I'm looking for Mr. Sparrow."

A young man with a scant beard and a patched waistcoat emerged from the doorway to the left and stepped up to the bars from behind a pillar. He had a lit pipe in one hand. The stem appeared to have been chewed. "You Mr. Aldar?"

"I am," Blackthorne said.

"Said you was a rum one. Said you might be a bit early. Mr. Sparrow's in the stable, making sure all's ready, sir."

Blackthorne focused on listening and felt the familiar tingling on his skin. His stomach clenched in a fit of nausea just as the gates opened with a squeak. He had only just entered the courtyard when he brought himself up short. *There are two others here.* He felt Katrin walk into his back.

"Something wrong, sir?" the young man asked.

"I don't believe I'm familiar with your friends," Blackthorne said.

The young man smiled. Blackthorne noted that he was missing his front teeth. "That's just Pete and Bert. Long as you're polite, you got nothing to worry about from them."

"In that case, they won't mind if I wait here until they step into the coach yard where I can see them," Blackthorne said. "It's only polite."

Two men emerged from the side building. One had a broken nose. Both were armed. Neither looked the sort to worry much over manners even if they knew what manners were.

"Well, then, is everything to your liking, your lordship?" The young man executed a mocking bow.

"Not entirely, but it'll suffice," Blackthorne said.

The young man laughed.

Blackthorne continued through the archway, and as the gate clanged shut, he hoped Reini was in position. *Too late to worry about it now.* Blackthorne stopped in the center of the coach yard and slowly slid a hand under his coat. Then the man he knew as Mr. Sparrow exited the stables and sauntered toward them at a leisurely pace with both hands in his pockets.

People who keep their hands hidden usually mean trouble, Blackthorne thought with a small amount of irony.

"You got my money?" Mr. Sparrow asked.

"I do, indeed. Where are the wagons?" Blackthorne asked.

"How do I know you aren't a Brotherhood spy?"

Blackthorne sighed. "Now, what would a spy want with your wagons when so many are available around the wharf with a flash of a badge?"

"Not the wagons he'd be wanting but the friend that owns it, and we both know it."

Blackthorne remained still.

"I need confirmation you are who you say you are." Mr. Sparrow's eyes narrowed.

"Again? I should have thought the watchword I provided in the Broken Crown as well as my friend's credentials proof enough," Blackthorne asked.

Mr. Sparrow said, "Maybe we had a change of heart."

"It's a bit late for second thoughts, isn't it?" Blackthorne asked, straightening his posture and flipping the front of his greatcoat back.

At the sight of Blackthorne's drawn pistol, Mr. Sparrow's eyes went wide. Pete and Bert went for their weapons.

Blackthorne said, "I wouldn't do that if—"

A shot hit the ground near Pete or Bert's feet. Both froze where they were.

"Is that you, Mr. Reini?" Blackthorne asked.

"That it is." Reini's voice drifted from the roof. "Lovely view from up here. There's a young lady who probably should be warned to keep her shade drawn. She was somewhat distracting. I almost shot your man Pete's nose off. Or is that Bert? Hard to tell, since I was left out of the introductions."

The shutters lining the second floor windows swung open with an echoing bang and now they bristled with the barrels of six muskets.

A female voice called down. "Well, isn't this something?"

Blackthorne sighed. "Look. If you've changed your mind about dealing with us, that's fine. Just let me speak to May Freely, and then we'll go on our way."

"That depends. Do you know Erkki Jarvela?" the woman asked.

Blackthorne paused. His heart beat three times fast while he tried to recall faces and names. *He's one of Hännenen's men, isn't he?*

Katrin cleared her throat. "Ah. I do. Well, I know of him, anyway."

"Tell me, girl, what color is his hair?" the woman asked.

"Well, that's a tricky question. See, in the summer, the sun bleaches it blond. Winter, it's a light brown. So, I guess it'd depend on when you saw him last. He's got a saber scar high up on the outside of his right thigh, though," Katrin said.

"Right, then." The barrel of the woman's musket vanished. "I'm coming down. Pete, Bert, put away those weapons and offer your apologies."

Turning, Blackthorne stared at Katrin as her cheeks grew steadily pinker.

"I saw him in the bathing niches once. Not like I meant to. It was an accident." Katrin looked away. "You going to tell Papa Slate?"

Blackthorne turned so that he could see Reini and motioned for him to stay where he was. "I should think not," he muttered to Katrin. *I'm relatively certain he wouldn't want to know.*

The woman who entered the coach yard was short and plump. Her brown hair was anchored to the top of her head in a round knot with haphazard pins. Loose curls spilled down her neck in willful bunches. Her skin was slightly darker than his own. Gripping the barrel of her fowling piece in her left, she offered a tanned, ink-stained hand to him.

"You can call me May, Mr. Aldar." May smiled. "Let's finish up in my office. I've about had enough of shouting. Good thing the Watch is touring elsewhere right now, or we'd be up to our necks in bother." She walked to the building on the right with a rolling gait and threw open the door. He and Katrin followed her inside.

The entrance led to a narrow hallway and a simple staircase. To the right and left were closed doors. Blackthorne suppressed an urge to check them for enemies. As a result, the muscles between his shoulder blades tightened and wouldn't let up until he'd reached the second floor and could stand with a wall to his back.

"Sorry about the reception. Was expecting the Nickols boys and got you instead," May said, leading the way to a cluttered room with shuttered windows. "The Watch and the Brotherhood have been on alert. There've been a few riots lately. It seems the people are growing tired of the wars."

Gazing around the room, Blackthorne began to understand why Slate had asked them to make space on the ship for one more.

A printing press hulked in the far corner, and the air smelled of ink, reheated lead, and paper. Every flat surface was covered in paper. One-sheets hung from lines strung across the room like clean laundry. Their bold headlines declared the Regnum culpable for various atrocities. Each flyer pointed out the fallacy of the games as a pathway to citizenship, the lack of representation in the Senate, corruption in the Church, the need for equality, and the moral and economic effects of slavery. Each and every one was signed with a familiar name.

He waited long enough for the door to shut, and they were assured of what privacy could be had. "*You're* Libertas?"

May turned from the closed door and smiled. "It's possible that I might be."

It occurred to Blackthorne that May's manner of speech had acquired a formality it hadn't possessed in the coach yard. *You aren't the only one who wears disguises.* "I thought Libertas was a man."

May said, "And I thought Libertas was a goddess."

"Yes, but—"

"I'm university-educated?" May asked, and shrugged. "Women are permitted education, Mr. Aldar, even nonhuman women— provided they're able to pay the extra costs. This is Acrasia, after all." Her friendly face acquired a sneer. The sarcastic expression vanished almost as fast as it appeared. "It's possible you are supposed to believe that Libertas is male. It makes it much easier for someone like me to hide in plain sight." She held out a hand. "You have something for me?"

Blackthorne handed over the folded envelope hidden inside his shirt. She opened it and silently read the contents. Her full lips moved as she did so. At last, she reached the end and refolded the letter. "It's always nice to hear from my former teacher. It's heartening to know that he's doing well where he is. However, I find I must decline the invitation."

"You can't," Blackthorne said. "You said yourself that Novus Salernum is becoming far too dangerous."

"Others face danger," May said. "Yourself, for example."

"Still—"

"Please express my thanks and gratitude to your employer," May said. She went to her wooden trays of type and ran her fingers over the metal letters. "No matter how attractive the offer, no matter how frightened I might be, I must stay and do my part. It's too important. He has his role in this war, and I have mine."

"And what if words no longer suffice?" Blackthorne asked.

She gave him a grim smile, plucked a letter from the tray, and held it up. "Then typesetter's lead makes good bullets." Returning the little rectangle to its tray, she continued. "Now that that is done, shall we discuss the wagons and labor? What do you need them for?"

Blackthorne hesitated and then decided May might be of assistance. "We'll be breaking into a military depot—one with a certain amount of security. We'll need to get in, get out, and load everything onto our ship in broad daylight. All preferably without causing a great deal of notice."

"I see," May said. "Then you'll want Mr. Sparrow, Ian, Carl, and Mandy. They can be trusted."

Nodding, Blackthorne said, "Thank you. We'll take one of the wagons now. I would like your people to meet us at the location with the other wagon at the appointed time. Afterward, I'll need them to help us unload the cargo onto the ship."

May said, "I think we can accommodate your needs."

"Then we've an agreement," Blackthorne said. He gave her the date, time, and locations.

"That's a secured dock," she said.

"It is," Blackthorne said. "They'll have to meet me in the loading area near the ship. You'll have the second half of your fee once my cargo is safely onboard."

"Fair enough. Now let's go downstairs," May said. "We'll have a look at the wagons."

Blackthorne was the last to enter the stable. Two large wagons with four horses hitched to each were parked in the coachway. Katrin was giving the lead mare of the first team a rub on the nose and dodged just in time as her harness-mate, a black gelding, craned his neck for a nip at Katrin's leg. Unsuccessful at venting his temper, the black dipped his head and then bit the dapple mare on the shoulder instead. She gave out a startled grunt and jerked the bridle out of Katrin's grasp. Blackthorne ended the quarrel by firmly steering the mare's head away.

"Are you sure about those two? If you ask me, it looks like they'll tear each other apart long before pulling that wagon," Katrin said.

Mr. Sparrow walked over and placed a soothing hand on the black's flank before speaking. "Always like this before a start. They'll settle in fine once you get going."

Blackthorne inspected the wagon. "Will it handle the load?"

May said, "Should be strong enough for your purposes."

Blackthorne nodded. "It'll do." After giving the harness a cursory check, he pulled out the leather folio and paid May in Acrasian notes. "That's thirty-two sterling now and thirty-three at the dock for a total of sixty-five, plus an extra five for your trouble."

May's smile broadened. "Pleasure doing business, Mr. Aldar. And good luck."

Blackthorne swung up onto the driver's bench and gestured for Katrin to follow, but she was stopped by a hand on her arm.

"One last thing," May whispered, and bit her lip. "Would you mind taking a letter to our mutual friend? Can't exactly send it Eagle Post."

"We wouldn't mind at all," Katrin said.

May handed her a letter, and Katrin tucked it inside her shirt as Blackthorne had done. Once Katrin had climbed up next to him, Blackthorne shook the reins. The coach lurched as it pulled into the yard, and stopped. Blackthorne paused long enough for Lieutenant Reini to join them before racing through the archway.

Blackthorne leaned toward her. "You should give me that letter. It's dangerous."

She asked, "Don't you trust me?"

"I do." Blackthorne frowned. "However, I told your mentor that I would get you home safe. In which case I would prefer to be the one bearing the majority of the danger."

Katrin said, "I'm good at hiding things. Don't worry."

"All right," Blackthorne said. He decided it wasn't worth under-cutting her confidence. "The letter is your responsibility."

"Thanks," Katrin said, and then paused. "I'm sorry I didn't draw my pistol in the coach yard. I . . . I froze. I won't do it again."

Blackthorne considered what to say. He had to be careful. Much would depend upon her later. "By not acting, you did the correct thing. The situation may have escalated even further had you done otherwise. In any case, you spoke up at exactly the right time."

Katrin nodded.

"Don't be hard on yourself. No one knows how they'll react in situations like that, no matter how much they wish or claim otherwise. It takes practice, like anything else. I have faith that you'll do fine when you're needed."

⇥ DRAKE ⇤

"I feel like shit. No, I'm not drinking that. Get it away from me. It's disgusting," Drake said. Her refusal was uttered in a darkness so intense that she couldn't see her own hand in front of her face. She ached in places she didn't think possible. That was bad enough. What was worse was that she was afraid, and more than anything, she hated being afraid.

Mal's disembodied voice replied, "You've been injured. You should drink something."

"That's what I asked for," she said.

"You need water," Mal said. "Not alcohol."

"I'm a grown woman, not a child. I'm capable of knowing what I need and what I don't," she said. "Where are we? How long have we been here? Why is it so dark?"

There was grit beneath her palms and cold, smooth stone against her back and buttocks. The air was chilly and ever so slightly moist. Somewhere, water dripped. As far as she could tell, she and Mal were hiding alone with a young woman and her baby. Due to the bits of conversation she'd been able to overhear while pretending to be asleep, Drake had found out that the woman was a former whore. The baby, a girl, wasn't hers.

Years of street harvester training taught Drake not to rely upon the obvious. Mal and the woman and the baby had been gone when she woke the first time. That had been very bad. However, she hadn't had a chance to explore what she'd come to think of as her cage. Her swollen ankle had prevented her from doing much more than eat, shit, and sleep.

At the moment, the woman and the baby were gone, which was good. The child's crying made the ache in Drake's head worse. *Never mind the stink of its clouts.*

"You're going to tell me you don't know where we are?" Mal asked. "Weren't you the one with the rough past?"

There don't seem to be any guards. This place is small and underground. It was difficult to think beyond the pain in her head. "We're in a bolt-hole."

"We are," Mal said. "A very expensive one. Solid rock all around. Don't worry. There's not a chance of malorum. The entrance is laced with silver. Get some rest. We'll be here for a while."

"Light a candle or something," she said.

"I'm sorry, Em," Mal said. "I know how you feel about—"

She snorted.

"—the dark, but there are no candles or lanterns here. This place has rules, and we will abide by them," he said. "Not my choice. But the rules are in place for everyone's safety, including yours."

Not a legal bolt-hole, then, she thought. "Why aren't we in your apartments?"

Mal paused. She could hear him stop breathing. "Emily, can I trust you?"

He used my name. "You're serious."

"I'm very serious. More serious than I've been with you before," he said.

"That depends," she said. "How much money is in it?"

"Come on," he said. "I know you aren't as hard as you pretend."

"It's a hard swiving world," she said. "Everyone is out for themselves, no matter what they claim."

"Not everyone."

"Everyone that survives," she said. "Or are you going to tell me that you sell your paintings and give the money away to the poor?"

"I am the poor."

"See?"

"Em, please. This is important."

"Why are we talking about this?"

"Because I'm leaving Acrasia with Sondra and the baby, and I want to know if you want to come with me," Mal lowered his tone to a whisper.

Oh, Drake thought. *This is not going to be a good conversation, is it?*

"There's nothing left for you here," Mal said.

"Don't do this," she whispered, following his example. "You don't know who is listening."

"We're alone," he said. "I know we are. I paid a great deal to make sure of it."

"Then why are we whispering?"

"Em—"

"More money can always be arranged," she said. "You have to know that."

"The people that own this particular bolt-hole are people I trust with my life."

Oh, shit. Oh, damn his blood. He's involved in something I don't want to know about, isn't he? She swallowed. Her throat was raw, and her head pained her worse than before. Her eyes burned with tears she didn't want to cry. "I'm thirsty, damn you."

Invisible hands positioned a tin cup of water so that she could drink. The cup's rim pressed against her cheek. "Give me that." She pried it from his grip and sipped. The gritty water was warm and tasted flat. "Only you would buy a bolt-hole and not bring any whiskey."

"I didn't say that."

"Then give me the bottle."

"After we talk."

"I can't have this conversation without a strong drink, damn you," she said. *Perhaps more than one. Maybe even an entire alehouse full.*

"All right," he said. "Give me a moment to find it."

She heard him shuffle or crawl—whichever it was, she no longer felt his warmth next to her. Shivering, she felt around for the blanket that she'd shed earlier. When she found it, she pulled it over herself and tried very hard not to think about the sorts of things that lived in dark, damp places. Bad memories lurked in corners of her mind that she hadn't considered in years. *You're not six. This is not your father's bolt-hole, and Mal is not "Uncle" Billy.* An involuntary shudder coursed through her body. *That cursed man is dead. You killed him. Remember?*

It took him a while, but Mal finally returned with what smelled like whiskey. She heard him pour it into something.

"You don't have to do that," she said. "I'm happy to drink from the neck of the bottle."

"I need you sober."

"Why?" She moved close to him.

He slapped her hand away from the front of his trousers. "I'm being serious. We have to talk."

She sighed and then whispered, "Why would you want me to go with you?"

"I don't think it's any surprise that I like you," he whispered back.

"And I like you too," she said. "But that's a very different thing from—"

"It's more than—than . . . I like you a great deal."

"You do?"

"You can be honest. I need to know the truth," he said. "How much do you like me?"

Giving the matter strong consideration, she paused. "I like you more than anyone I know."

"Enough to give up a life that you no longer have?"

Again, she hesitated. She definitely didn't want to lie. *Not to Mal.* She didn't think she was capable of love. She'd worked too hard to cut that emotion out of herself. At the same time, Mal was the closest thing to a friend she had. "Maybe?"

"That's enough for me."

She felt the corners of her mouth tug upward. "I don't think you're aware of the kind of people I know. That's not really saying much."

His hand travelled up to her cheek and she pressed against it, snuggling into the curve of his palm. More than anything, she needed reassurance, and she hated herself for it.

"What do you want from me, Mal?"

"Honestly?"

"We're being honest, aren't we?"

He shifted even closer and breathed into her ear. "The truth is, we're both kainen. You pass for human. I don't. I care a great deal for you, but if I am to leave . . . I—I need you, Em."

"I see." Another ache, this one inside her chest, joined the inventory of pain. Suddenly, she was very glad he couldn't see her face. "I assume you have proof?"

"I do," he said. "I have it with me, in fact."

You care about me but you're willing to blackmail me? "How did you find out?"

"I have my ways."

"That doesn't answer my question." There was real anger in her voice, and she didn't bother disguising it.

Again, he paused. "I'm very selective of my regulars. I always have been. I have to be careful. I'm a cocksman. I don't know if you're aware of how dangerous an occupation that can be."

"You had me investigated?"

"Of course I did. A *year* ago, when it became clear you were going to be a part of my life. I won't risk becoming emotionally involved with someone who—who has certain connections."

She took a long, deep breath. There was only one place where Mal could've gotten that information. *The Brotherhood of Wardens Records Library.* "So, you paid a *Warden* to look into my background?"

"Not a Warden," he said. "But someone with access to their records, yes."

"I see."

"It's funny that you should keep using that phrase when we're in a pitch-black bolt-hole."

"What am I supposed to say?"

"Say you'll come with me. To Greenleaf at the least. You can go that far, can't you?" he asked. "You've always wanted to leave the city for a few days."

"This isn't the same thing, and you know it. You're asking me to help you illegally flee the Regnum," she said. "I'm a Watch captain, damn it."

"Not anymore," he said. "Benbow is Watch captain in the Sisters."

"I wouldn't be surprised to hear that." The sudden burst of rage was strong enough to make her jaw ache. Sipping the whiskey, she considered her situation, using brutal equations. *I could go with Mal. I could vanish. No more payments. No more watching over my shoulder.* She took a breath. *Well, no more than usual, I suppose.* "Tell me, did you arrange it?"

"NO! I—"

"Good."

"—I'd never do that to you. You have to know that—"

"All right, calm down," she said. "I had to ask."

"Let me point out a fact you appear to be missing," he said. "I've known this about you for how long, and I've never mentioned it before?"

"That only means you're intelligent enough to wait for the most advantageous moment to use information."

There was another silence between them.

He said, "That suspicious nature of yours is going to get you into trouble one day."

She harrumphed and tightened her grip on the tin cup until her fingers hurt. "I wasn't suspicious enough, it would seem." *Benbow, you swiving bastard. You are going to be very swiving sorry your mother ever lived long enough to squirt you out of her cunt.* One of the things she'd prided herself upon was patience when it came to revenge. There was a saying among the street harvesters: *Sit by the sewer ditch long enough, and the body of your enemy will float by.* "You're avoiding my question. You know I won't give up asking. You might as well tell me the rest. Did someone pay you to retrieve me? If so, I need to know who."

"We aren't like that. We never were."

"Aren't we?" she asked. "Did I or did I not give you silver in exchange for sex for the past year?"

The only sound was his indrawn breath.

That was too far. You need him every bit as much as he needs you, and you know it. "I'm so sorry. I don't mean it," she said. "I'm just really swiving angry right now." She threw the empty cup against what she hoped was a wall.

It hit stone with a tinny clang that seemed huge, and then rolled off to her left, by the sound.

"I can't say I blame you." He moved away from her.

She flinched. *He's retrieving the cup. He isn't going to murder you. Relax. Mal isn't like that. He doesn't have it in him. Isn't that what he's been telling you?*

Can it be possible that he is what he seems?

Everyone is awful. It's only a matter of time before they show their true selves. "Can I have some more?"

"That depends," he said. "Are you going to throw it at the wall? We only have three of these, you know. And this one's dented. They're going to charge me for that."

She asked the question she'd been too injured to ask before. "How did you find me?"

"When you didn't show up for your appointment . . . well, first I was angry, and then I got worried. I heard about the riot. I was afraid for you. So, I searched for your father."

"You did?"

"I did."

"And he didn't rob you, beat you, and then send house breakers to—"

"He told me what happened," Mal said. "He was worried for you too."

She let out a snort. "Was probably angry I wouldn't be sending him any money this month."

"He's your father."

"And?" she asked. "Did he tell you he blackmails me?"

Mal was silent.

"I thought as much," she said.

"Your brother is dead. I thought you should know."

"Oh." She paused. She didn't know how to feel about that. She hadn't been close to her brother since she was too small for him to make money from. So, she changed the subject. "You entered a sector on lockdown because you need me to get you as far as Greenleaf?"

"No, Em," Mal said. There was a delay of a few heartbeats before he continued. "I—I did it because I was worried for you."

"I'm supposed to believe that?"

"Whether you believe it or not doesn't change the truth, does it?" She could hear the pain and longing in his voice. "Is it so hard to believe you're worth caring for?"

She felt him place a hand on her arm and lean against her.

Sensing his discomfort, she reached for and squeezed his hand. "I wish like hell I could believe you."

"I wish like hell you could too."

She sighed. Her eyes were burning again. She wiped at her cheeks. "I'll go."

All at once, he wrapped her in his arms. "Thank you. Thank you so much. You won't be sorry. I'll paint something just for you. And you can do whatever you like with it."

"There'll be paint and canvas where you're going?" She hugged him back.

"You expected me to leave something as important as my paint-mixing supplies behind?"

That is so like him. He flees for his life with a bag full of oils and pigments. "Did you remember to bring clothes?"

He let out a small, amused huff.

She asked, "Do you know where you'll go after Greenleaf?"

"I do." He squeezed her once and withdrew. "But I don't think I'll tell you yet."

Reaching into the darkness, she felt around until she had his face in both of her hands. "Smart and attractive." And with that, she kissed him. "Hmmm. I suppose we should find something to do in the meantime."

"You're feeling better?"

"Your whiskey numbed the pain somewhat," she said.

"You don't like making love in the dark."

"I'll make an exception this once," she said. "Just . . . be careful."

"I'm always careful, my love."

"Stop the stupid honey-dipped lies," she said. "Just give me a good hard swiving. I don't want to be able to walk for a week."

"That's one of the things I love about you, Em," he said. "You're as smooth as a corncob."

❧ CAIUS ❧

ONE

Caius rallied his patience by studying the family portraits in Duke Aureus's main entrance hall. Although it was spring, the temperature had grown steadily colder with the sinking sun. He was grateful for being allowed the honor of waiting inside the house rather than on the back doorstep. After his latest discussion with Huntmaster Warden Aureus, Caius knew the interview with the duke was merely another of a long series of futile gestures. The rogue would continue leaving bodies in obvious places, and for reasons Caius didn't understand, nothing would be done about it.

Hopefully, Dalton will have useful information this week. Not that he'd had any for some time.

Polite laughter and orchestra music filtered through the house from the ballroom. He ventured another ten feet or so farther down the crimson runner. It'd been years since he'd been inside the duke's home. Not much had changed over the years, with the exception of a new addition to the rows of paintings.

A younger version of his missing friend, Severus, stared back at him from the canvas. He had thick hair cut in the Academy style and grey eyes. Severus had always seemed deathly somber; even on the first day at the Academy Caius had noticed him as the freshmen cadets had assembled in the main yard. The other fifteen-year-old students had been boisterous and jubilant about their selection. *Not Severus.* He had stood apart, observing the rest of the class like a wizened campaigner. It had been strangely disquieting, and Caius had thought then that Severus was destined for great things.

Archiron isn't that far. Why hasn't he sent even one letter? Is he alive? Surely, if they were going to execute him for striking a Huntmaster, they'd have done it in the Rehabilitation Hospital. Why go through the motions of reassigning him?

Caius never did find out what had happened. Severus was reticent under normal circumstances. Thus, when Severus had returned, he had refused to speak of it. In spite of his curiosity, Caius hadn't pried. If there were anything Severus needed to discuss, Caius trusted he would do so. As Severus's only friend, he knew it was what was expected. However, Severus appeared to have vanished. In truth, a big part of the reason Caius had been willing to risk traveling so far, so close to curfew, was to inquire after his friend. *Surely, the duke knows something.*

The sound of a heavy door sliding open brought him to the present with a jolt.

"I understand you are here to see that my inventory permits are in order?" Duke Aureus was dressed in a red-and-black silk brocade evening coat with gold trim and matching trousers tucked into his boots. His face was flushed as though he'd just finished dancing. Like his son, the duke was tall. His eyes were grey and his hair was wavy, but that was where the resemblance between father and son ended. The duke's hair was auburn, and he was heavier than Severus ever would be. The duke stood less straight, and his gestures were broad, sweeping. Depending upon necessity, Severus could sit in a room for hours before being noticed, but the duke seemed to take command from the moment he entered.

"Your Grace, I am Fortis Modius Caius. You probably don't remember me. We met once after graduation. Severus was one of my classmates." Caius extended a hand for Duke Aureus to shake.

An instant passed before recognition replaced uncertainty. "Caius? Yes. Now I remember. I recall Severus spoke well of you. You were his friend, were you not? Welcome." He accepted Caius's hand and appeared to relax as he smiled. He glanced to the portrait that Caius had been standing in front of. "I would much prefer a quiet conversation with a friend of Severus's, but I regret I cannot neglect my guests."

"I apologize for the inconvenience, Your Grace. Perhaps another time. If you would show me to your records, I can complete my task and be gone." Caius bowed with a nod of his head. His instructions were to detain the duke as little as possible.

"This way," Duke Aureus said, pulling the sliding door closed behind them and then leading Caius up the stairs and into the left wing of the house.

Silver-plated doorknobs decorated each door, not merely the front entrance. The carved crown molding along the ceiling was layered in gold and silver leaf. Furnishings imported from distant corners of the Regnum filled the rooms.

The duke said, "It has been some time since I've had news of my son. Have you received any word?"

"I'm afraid not, Your Grace." Caius attempted to contain his surprise. "His new responsibilities must keep him very busy."

Ultimately, he felt he understood Severus well enough to remember the duke would've been the last person to receive a letter. Not that Severus spoke much of his family over the years. However, it had said a great deal that he'd remained alone at the school during holidays. So much so that Caius had extended invitations to his friend, which had resulted in their spending the last three years of academy holidays together with his family. Caius's mother had expected some sort of acknowledgment for taking care of the duke's son, Caius knew, but no recognition had been forthcoming.

Duke Aureus entered his private study, pulled a book off the shelf, and then handed Caius the ledger. Moving to a cabinet behind the writing table, he offered Caius a glass of brandy.

"No, thank you, Your Grace," Caius said, and then opened the ledger.

The splash of pouring brandy accompanied pages and pages of inventory figures, names and dates. If Caius were truly here to find a discrepancy, he would confiscate the duke's entire records library. However, with Duke Aureus, such measures were considered unnecessary, particularly since he enjoyed close ties with the director of Wardens. In any case, Caius seriously doubted the duke was smuggling nonhumans out of the city. It simply wasn't something a duke would get involved in.

After a quarter of an hour of patiently scanning the figures in silence, Caius closed the ledger. "I believe I've seen enough, Your Grace."

"Are you certain the Consul would be satisfied with such a cursory check?" the duke asked with a meaningful smile.

The Consul is involved? Or is the man making a joke? Caius said, "I believe I have followed my orders."

Duke Aureus set down his brandy glass and accepted the ledger book from Caius, reshelving it.

"Second only to the Emperor himself, you'd think he had more important matters to tend to, or perhaps more effective methods with which to harass a rival in the Senate," the duke said. "If you wish, my overseer can prepare the inventory for inspection."

"Should it become necessary, I can return at a later date," Caius said.

The duke nodded. "I've heard good reports of you from the director. You have a reputation for precision, even if your methods are somewhat out of the ordinary. How go your duties?"

Caius's heart sped up, and he tried not to stammer. "Fine, Your Grace."

"I understand a rogue hunter has been disposing of his kills in the North End. Am I correct?"

Caius paused. While it wasn't out of the ordinary for someone with the duke's connections to be aware of such matters, one didn't normally discuss them outside the Brotherhood or the Watch. However, he decided he risked nothing speaking to someone whom the director had already informed of the situation. "Yes, Your Grace," Caius said. "However, the rogue seems to have moved his activities outside the city. The last body was found on the High Street, a day's ride from the Kylmapuro River."

"That far from Novus Salernum? How do you know it's the same rogue?"

"The eyes were removed with the same type of knife, and another note was found."

The duke stopped pacing, and Caius could have sworn the man was frightened. "What note?" the duke asked.

❋ 560 ❋

The casement clock standing against the wall by the door ticked as Caius stumbled over his thoughts. *Was I wrong to discuss the situation with the duke? I'm in too far to stop now.* He took a deep breath. "There are three so far. All written on a page torn from a hornbook."

"What do the notes say?" The duke moved closer, standing over him, and the conversation began to take on the air of an interrogation.

"Nothing that makes sense, Your Grace. Rhymes. I believe the verses are from a children's prayer book," Caius said.

The duke frowned. "Why hasn't the director been made aware of this?"

"Surely, the director has had access to my reports," Caius said, starting to sweat. *Something isn't right.*

The duke turned away, pacing the room. After a few moments, he paused. "Perhaps he didn't divulge every detail to his old friend. It is understandable, is it not?" His relaxed expression didn't match the intensity of his gaze.

"I suppose so, Your Grace."

The duke smiled. "You've no need for concern. I will speak of this to no one," he said. "However, my guests are certain to be wondering where I am. Perhaps you can return another day and we can discuss your days at the Academy."

"Yes, Your Grace." Caius hoped the invitation was only a cordial lie. He was certain he didn't want any more of the duke's personal attention. He followed the duke through the house to the main entry with an uneasy feeling. When the soothing thump of the front door signaled an end to the visit, Caius blew air out of his cheeks and checked his pocket watch. It read a quarter to ten. The moon was nearly full in a sky beleaguered by strengthening storm clouds. A hired coach pulled up, and a hurried lady exited in a blue silk evening dress and a fine wool cloak. Her hands were concealed in a fur muff. Her maid followed, carrying several bags, while the footman dealt with the trunks.

Caius stopped to help the maid and approached the coachman once the unloading was finished. "Would you take me to the Green Dragon alehouse on Porter Street? I'm willing to pay you."

The driver squinted and his bushy brows bunched. "Isn't that near Gibson Road?"

"It is."

The driver gave Caius's uniform a second look and glanced again at the house.

I came from the front door. He saw me.

"Right, then. No need for payment, sir. I'd be happy to take you. Be there in no time."

After the footman closed the door, Caius settled on the padded bench inside and tugged up the collar of his greatcoat. The storm's first snowflakes drifted past the window before he pulled the shutter closed.

The trip from the duke's estate off Regent's Street to the Green Dragon took half an hour. By the time Caius exited the coach, the snow was falling steadily. The alehouse's clientele watched him order hot tea with nervous expressions, but since he made no move to arrest or kill anyone, the crowd eventually returned to their amusements.

The appointed hour came and went, and Caius decided to give Jack an hour before giving up. Caius spent the time going over the conversation with the duke. After ordering a pint of porter, he stared into the tankard as if the answers to his questions were in the bottom. He only pretended to drink.

Is it true that the director didn't know about the notes? If it is, who's interfering? Huntmaster Warden Aureus? Why? Who is the rogue?

*And why is Baron Munitoris Arion always unavailable? Is he the one?
What is his connection to Gens Aureus?*

Outside, the storm rattled the bull's-eye panes, and the
landlord placed more coal on the fire. When the tower clock in
the square struck a quarter past eleven, the wind slowed and the
Dragon emptied. At half past eleven, Caius assumed he'd been
duped and stood up to leave.

The alehouse door swung open and two high-ranking
Wardens entered. They scanned the empty smoke-scented room
before making their way toward him. A shiver traced a cold finger
up his spine. He heard the landlord drop a tankard with a loud
thump. Caius knew the two Wardens on sight but hadn't spoken
to either before. Both answered only to the director and were most
often seen transporting offenders to the Rehabilitation Hospital.
Inspector Warden Aureus Martin was short and muscled where
Inspector Warden Aureus Thaddeus was tall and gaunt. There was
a vivid white scar on Thaddeus's left cheek under his eye.

*How did they know I would be here? Did they intercept Jack
Dalton? What could they want from me?*

Thaddeus was the first to speak. "The director wishes to see you."

"Yes, sir. Now?" Caius asked.

"If it is convenient," said Martin. His voice was low and commanding, suggesting that Caius's convenience was actually of little
concern.

Caius got the barkeep's attention with a wave of his hand, left
enough money on the table to pay for the porter he hadn't drunk,
and slipped on his greatcoat. Dread gathered in his belly. "Am I to
know what this is about?"

"The director will inform you," said Thaddeus. His face was
unreadable. The scar on his cheek pointed to an almost-colorless
blue eye that didn't match its darker twin.

Caius left the alehouse with the Inspector Wardens, embarking on the long walk back to Regent's and the Academy without exchanging further discourse. The wind might have lost its enthusiasm but the snow had not. Caius kept his hands in his pockets while his stomach twisted. *I must've offended the duke. Or perhaps I'm in trouble for having divulged information about the rogue?* In five years of training, he hadn't once been inside the director's mansion. Caius suspected that this wasn't the preferred way to see it. He went over the conversation with Duke Aureus in his mind as he walked and came to the conclusion he shouldn't have brought up the rogue to the duke at all.

After passing through security at the front gates, they arrived at the director's home. One of the Inspectors opened the front door without knocking. A fifth-year cadet jumped up from a small writing table in the main passage and saluted. Caius returned the salute, as did the two who flanked him. Inspector Thaddeus signed the record book. The interior of the director's mansion was more understated than that of Duke Aureus's. There were no paintings on the cream-colored walls, and the silver plate decorations were limited to door handles and window frames.

"You may go in, sir. The director is expecting you," the cadet said, motioning to a black door on the left.

Caius approached the door with an increasing sense of terror. He put a hand on the doorknob and took a deep breath. He wasn't much for praying—regardless, he scrambled to remember a few lines before opening the door.

Leather-bound books lined wood-paneled walls, and several decorative lamps shed yellowed circles of light. The director was seated at a large mahogany writing desk, writing in an open record book with a blown-glass quill. He looked up from his record entry and smiled a predator's smile. His face was narrow with pale skin stretched tight over high cheekbones. Piercing eyes stared out from deep sockets, and the lamplight cast shadows on his face that made Caius think of a skull. The man's uniform jacket was immaculate and void of insignia, with the exception of the small pewter eagles on his buttoned collar.

"Thank you for visiting on short notice. Please sit. I will be with you in a moment," the director said.

Caius settled on the big leather chair. Sweat slid its way slowly down his sides from under his arms. He attempted not to fidget. The director wrote briefly, put the glass quill in its holder, blotted the page in the record book, and closed it. Caius couldn't read what was written on the cover.

"The rogue hunter was apprehended and disposed of this evening. I wish to extend my personal thanks. Your methods, while unorthodox, have proven useful. You are promoted to Captain Inspector and will be provided a new residence, which I expect you to take full advantage of within the week."

Caius blinked. *How is that possible? I thought I was the only one looking into it seriously.* "Yes, sir. Thank you." He allowed himself to breathe. "May I ask who made the arrest?"

"Inspector Wardens Aureus Thaddeus and Aureus Martin. Do not worry. It was your investigation which led them to the culprit. You'll receive full credit."

The director's men. The investigation was being tampered with, but no longer. Caius felt the tension in his shoulders loosen. "Who was the one responsible, sir?"

The director's face could've been carved in stone. "Her name was Lady Quinta Serena. She was a courtesan."

None of my suspects were female. It's doubtful she could've left the handprints on the victim's necks. A woman's hands would be too small. Might they have been affected by weather conditions? On such a scale? I must check my notes. What if the director is protecting the real culprit? But why would he do such a thing? What's going on?

You will be provided a new residence, which I expect you to take full advantage of within the week. The director's words gave him another chill. *Provided my notes haven't been meddled with as well.* "Thank you, sir. If that is all, I will not trouble you further." He got up from the chair, trying not to seem in too much of a hurry.

The director held up a hand. "There is one more item I wish to consult with you about."

Caius stopped where he was. "Yes, sir?"

"As a Warden, you understand the threat malorum pose to the Regnum." The director laced his fingers together on the surface of the writing table.

Caius nodded. While their numbers weren't as excessive as the Acrasian people were led to believe, those with malorum taint were appearing more frequently in higher levels of society and government. He didn't want to dwell on how that was possible, let alone happening, and this disturbing trend was causing anxiety among the nobility.

"The new theory is that malorum are evolving. Changing. Individual malorum more advanced than the whole have always existed." An expression of distaste contorted the director's face. "It is a complicated matter. The Acrasian Regnum is a free nation, after all, and plebeians should profit from hard work. They do require a great deal of motivation to overcome their slothful natures. However, it is my belief that certain rewards should be reserved for humans. The Senate's policy of acceptance in regards to wealthy nonhumans will turn our passion for freedom against us."

Clearing his throat, Caius risked a comment. "What of nonhumans who are loyal to the Regnum?"

"Nonhumans don't have the mental capacity for complex concepts such as patriotism, self-sacrifice, and the common good."

Caius didn't agree but wasn't about to admit it.

"The new Consul is attempting to convince the Emperor to disband the Brotherhood. If he succeeds, the Regnum will cease to be a haven for the human race, and it will be the Senate's softness that brought us to it!" The director brought a fist down on the writing table. "Unorthodox methods are in order, Inspector."

Uncomfortable with the display of rage, Caius shifted on his feet.

The director got up and walked to a shelf. "I do apologize, *Captain* Inspector Fortis. Can I count on your support and cooperation?"

"Yes, sir," Caius said, feeling uneasy.

The director stared at the row of books before speaking. "His Grace, Aureus Severus. Do you know him?"

Caius blinked and tried to control his anxiety. "We are—were close friends, sir."

"Have you communicated with him recently?"

"No, sir." *What does Severus have to do with any of this?*

The director nodded and placed a hand on the shelf. "Indeed." There was a pause before he continued. "I may have need of your expertise in a delicate matter. You will be required to follow orders implicitly, no matter how challenging or unusual. Would you be willing to do so?"

There was only one way to answer that question. "Yes, sir."

"I thought you might. You may leave. I will contact you when you are needed," the director said, only then turning to face him. The director's face was once again unreadable.

Caius saluted and left. The Inspectors who had escorted him there were no longer waiting in the main passage. The cadet saluted before Caius made his way to the door. It had stopped snowing, and he headed for home, absorbed in thought. He splashed through slush puddles as he walked.

He hoped Severus wasn't in trouble again. Severus had always done what he was told when he was told to do it with an exacting, unquestioning air that had been almost frightening. Caius had often taken it upon himself to broaden his friend's horizons, to get him to think beyond orders—even to have a bit of fun. It had amused Caius to think that between the two of them, Severus had been more committed to his Academy studies and yet had been the weaker student. Still, Severus's devotion to duty hadn't saved him from the Rehabilitation Hospital.

The director's voice echoed in Caius's head. *You will be required to implicitly follow orders, no matter how challenging or unusual. Would you be willing to do so?* Caius had answered yes because one didn't say no to the director's requests, but Caius wondered what the director may have meant. *How might Severus be involved?* Severus simply wasn't the type to associate with nonhumans. He avoided entanglements with them as if they disgusted him.

Anyway, if it were something so simple, why would the director ask me for help? Has Severus betrayed the Brotherhood? Or is the duke the problem? Is the duke smuggling nonhumans out of the city after all? What does the duke have to do with the rogue?

At half past one, Caius reached the stairs leading up to his apartments. He was exhausted but removed his greatcoat and uniform jacket at the hearth. He understood he wouldn't be sleeping. *Not tonight.* And he remembered the evening with a sense of dread. He lit the oil lamp on the mantle with a long match. Then he headed to his study, lamp in hand, and opened the door. What he saw rooted him in place on the rug.

The wall where he'd kept his notes on the rogue hunter

was blank. Tiny holes left behind by absent pins were the only indication that anything had been there. His fists clenched. He knew he should drop the matter—that pursuing it further would only bring trouble he didn't have the money or power to combat. However, the director had ordered someone to break into *his* home and steal *his* notes. The thought of it made Caius's stomach knot and his jaw clench.

You are to be provided a new residence, which I expect you to take full advantage of within the week. The reason for the promotion and seeming reward was obvious. The director wanted him where he could be watched. Somehow, Caius had stumbled upon something the director of Wardens, Aurum Atticus, didn't want known. Once again, Caius was being warned off.

He stared at the wall, and its emptiness filled him with cold rage. It was then that he knew he wouldn't abandon the investigation. He wasn't a frightened cadet anymore.

He was a full Captain Inspector Warden.

⧏ BLACKTHORNE ⧐

Novus Salernum
The Regnum of Acrasia

Twenty-Third of Maitokuu, 1785

He decided to make the journey to Mallory McDermott's residence on Tyler Street alone. The others were preparing for the afternoon's venture, and after two weeks of sharing tiny spaces with Reini, Blackthorne needed some time to himself. He didn't like the memories living under such conditions dredged up.

It was an hour after dawn when he decided a private breakfast at the Golden Swan before meeting with Armas Frost would be a good idea. His dreams, always bad when he stayed in Novus Salernum, had been particularly unpleasant. The North End was some distance from Old Mercatur Road, enough so that hiring a hackney would be worth the savings in time. Dressed as his former self, he had small difficulty convincing the driver that he was good for the fee, but that issue was resolved with a half-payment up front.

Andrew Blackthorne, duelist, was an identity he hadn't used in months. His forged papers were in order. Slate had seen to that. However, Blackthorne couldn't shake the bad feeling he'd woke with. Gazing out the window, he saw that the townspeople seemed fearful and movement through the streets was hampered by periodic security checks by the Watch. They were squatting on Novus Salernum like a broody hen. That was bad enough. Then he spied a Warden Unit and his stomach did a flip.

He reached the Golden Swan at a quarter to eight. Strangely, it was one of the nicer establishments in which he did business— when Reggie Meade bothered to clean the floor. The outer walls of the place were dark brown, and the small glass panes in the door and windows were decorated with the occasional bull's-eye. Today, the cobblestones out front had been swept clean and washed. He entered the common room and selected a table in his usual corner. With the exception of a few patrons who'd obviously not yet gone to their beds, the place was empty. Taking a seat, he signaled to Hattie, the barmaid, and ordered his breakfast. He'd swallowed all of two bites of his fried fish when he spied Armas.

Slipping onto the booth bench across from him, Armas said, "Back again, I see?"

Blackthorne nodded a greeting and continued eating his fried fish.

Armas waved Hattie over. "And how was the dueling in Archiron? Profitable?"

"Profitable enough," Blackthorne said.

It was Armas's turn to nod. Hattie arrived with a second plate of fish, and the two of them remained silent until she left. Watching Armas's face for any sign of trouble, Blackthorne once again thought the man resembled a stray tomcat.

Armas's hair was a thatch of sandy blond and grey pulled

back from his ugly face in a halfhearted ponytail. Long scars sketched lines from either corner of his mouth and deep into his cheeks, widening a stubborn frown. Half of one pointed ear was missing. Armas had seen the sand of the arena and lived to claim citizenship.

Taking a quick glance around the common room, Blackthorne registered something he hadn't given much thought to before. Having lived most of his life in Aerasia, he'd been accustomed to seeing smallpox scars, missing or twisted limbs, and syphilis skin lesions. However, one winter among kainen, and the sight bordered on a shock. It was then that he understood why humans had called the kainen "the beautiful ones" or "the shining ones." It wasn't because kainen happened to be more attractive than humans. It was because they had more effective healers.

Armas reached into his coat, retrieved a small, flat item wrapped in dirty cloth, and pushed it across the stained table. "Had some trouble getting ahold of that. Use it wisely. Won't be able to get another for some time."

Blackthorne partially unwrapped the item. Inside he found a palm-sized pewter disk engraved with a skull and crossbones. The back of the disk was marked with a number. It was a replacement for the one he'd had to leave behind in August. That seemed a lifetime earlier. "Thank you." He paused. "Have you seen Lydia Corey?"

"You hadn't heard?"

Blackthorne shook his head.

"Died last summer. Childbirth. I heard the baby was yours."

Swallowing the bite of fish before he could choke, Blackthorne then took a sip of grog. When he recovered, he said, "Couldn't be."

"Are you sure?" Armas asked. "She seemed fairly certain."

Blackthorne didn't say anything. He knew too well it was possible. "What happened to the child?"

"Mallory McDermott took it in," Armas said. "Said something about a debt."

"I've a message for Mallory," Blackthorne said. "Was going to deliver it myself."

"Don't bother," Armas said, frowning.

"Why not?"

"He's not home." Armas went back to eating his fish. He seemed to be speaking more to his plate than his tablemate. "He's not the only one. Jori and Niemi have gone missing. Niemi was behind on his payments to the Syndicate. So, I can guess where he went, but Jori was clean. Wasn't the type to rabbit, either. There's a lot of your friends gone missing these days." He reached into his mouth with a greasy finger and dug out a fish bone. He wiped it on the table edge and took a swallow of grog.

Has the Watch stumbled upon my network? Or is it the Brotherhood? Or did Jori and Niemi have dealings with others? Did someone talk? Blackthorne's heart galloped.

"Also, Reggie was seen talking to a Warden a while back. Nothing came of it then, but who is to say all these things aren't connected?" Armas shrugged. "Thought you should know."

Blackthorne cleared his throat. He hadn't seen Reggie yet. That had seemed odd. "Anything else?"

"Word is, someone's dumping dead kainen on the street. Takes their eyes first."

Blackthorne felt the hair on the back of his neck and arms stand on end. *The nightmares.*

It's a coincidence. One can't have anything to do with the other. He wiped sweaty palms on his thighs.

"Been keeping the Brotherhood a bit busy, that one. Not sure I mind when it comes to that," Armas continued. "Brotherhood are bastards. You wouldn't know nothing about them, now, would you?" He paused in his meal long enough to narrow his eyes.

"I would not. How is it you do?" Blackthorne asked.

"If the middling sort are blind and dumb as sheep, it don't make the rest of us so." Armas tore apart another piece of fish before stuffing it in his mouth. "You sure you don't know nothing?"

"I am certain," Blackthorne said, lying.

Swallowing, Armas wiped grease from his chin with the back of his hand. "Reason I'm asking is a rogue's an easy way of getting rid of folk that get inconvenient. With Mallory, Jori, and Niemi missing . . ." He shrugged again. "Seems I heard you got connections with the Brotherhood. Seems I heard it from Nickols's brother. Jacob Nickols is my cousin by marriage, see. He's got a lot to say about you."

Damn it.

"Caution is only thing keeping some folk alive," Armas said with a shrug. "Knew your name wasn't Andrew for a while. Pretty sure it ain't whatever it is the Nickols boys know you by, neither. I'm thinking you're not a plebe, no matter how you dress. Not of the middling sort, neither—not that it matters to me. This business. You deal with all sorts. You get things done. Things that need doing."

Blackthorne stopped breathing. *He knows who I am. What is he going to do about it?*

What can he do? He's in every bit as deep as I am.

"Jacob, though, he's been through a lot. Month stint in one of the Brotherhood's body holes is enough to unhinge any man. Follow that up with watching your family fed to their dogs, and, well . . . we'll just say he goes a bit unreasonable-like around Wardens. Ex-Wardens included. That's Jacob.

"Me? I been watching. You get the job done. No airs about how much you're owed like some folk. Even got our Laila out safe, pregnant and all, and that can't have been easy. Can't say I'd have you to meet the missus for supper, myself, but I do trust you within certain bounds."

Blackthorne opened his mouth, but Armas held up a hand.

"So, I'm here giving you a warning," Armas said. "Someone been sniffing around, asking questions. Someone with Brotherhood connections. And with Jori and Mallory gone missing . . . well, I suggest you get done what needs doing, forget Andrew Blackthorne ever lived, and get out of Novus Salernum real quick 'til things cool off, you got me?"

"Did the Brotherhood come for McDermott?" Blackthorne asked.

"Don't know," Armas said. "I just know he's gone."

Have they taken Mallory McDermott? Or did he leave? I have to know. But they're looking for me—or Andrew at least. Blackthorne nodded, with his heart slamming inside his ears.

Armas leaned in really close and whispered, "Now, you get out of here. You stink of the Black, and it's unsettling my stomach."

Standing, Blackthorne dropped enough sterling to cover his meal as well as a little extra for Armas and abandoned the rest of his breakfast. He needed time to think. He also needed to know what had happened to Mallory McDermott. He wasn't as concerned with Jori. Jori, regardless of Armas's assumptions, was far from clean. Jori could take care of himself. But Mallory . . .

Blackthorne left the Golden Swan and began the walk to Tyler Street. He'd gotten as far as the row of shops on Monti Road when the implications of all that Armas had told him slammed him. He covered by pretending to gaze into a window display.

I've a child. He laid a hand against the glass for support. *I don't even know if it's a boy or a girl.* He'd been so careful from the moment he understood the duke had wanted him to sire offspring. It'd been the duke's obsession. As a result, Severus had sworn to never do so—even resorting to searching for and finding a nonhuman apothecary rumored to have healing powers. The man had told him such a request was unusual—his clients for such things were women—but it was certainly possible, provided a strict regimen was followed. And so, Severus had taken care to follow the instructions and dosage given. No matter how sick the concoction made him.

That is, until he'd become Andrew Blackthorne. At that point, it'd been too dangerous to return to the apothecary. Living in the Hold, he couldn't bring himself to speak with Ilta or the other healer. The matter was too embarrassing. When Lydia had approached him, he'd assumed she would take precautions. She was a prostitute, after all.

I've a child.

How could she know it was mine?

Does it matter? There is a motherless child, and you may be that child's father. She believed you were, in any case. Isn't that enough? Are you willing to abandon them as you were?

Lost in thought, he didn't realize he wasn't alone until he felt a tap on his arm. The low gravelly voice that accompanied it was so familiar that the danger didn't register until he'd involuntarily straightened as ordered. There was only one person who had spoken to him in that tone, paternal and commanding.

"They frown on napping without renting space around here. Be hip-deep in orphans otherwise."

Blackthorne's eyes snapped open. A man with thick grey hair and reproachful steel-colored eyes stood next to him. He was dressed in loose-fitting black clothing. Blue-stained gladiator scars lined his right cheek.

Talus.

"Didn't they teach you any better in that ridiculous school?"

Talus asked. "A novice harvester could've lifted your money and run off before you'd opened your damn eyes."

Blackthorne placed one hand closer to his pistol. Out of habit, he attempted to cover the move by running the other hand through his hair. "How long have you been there?"

"Long enough to be certain of who you were," Talus said, keeping his voice low. "You look like something a lion fed her cubs. Have to admit, the beard threw me. You've lost weight. Always heard that Wardens made enough money to dine like princes. Maybe that was an exaggeration." The crow's feet grew more pronounced around Talus's eyes as a half-hidden smile appeared from beneath his bushy beard.

Taking a chance that Talus wouldn't make a move for a weapon yet, Blackthorne quickly scanned the street for the duke. *That's all I need.*

"His Grace isn't here. He's staying at Baron Munitoris's country estate. He sent me into town to make some purchases," Talus said. He hesitated. "Aren't you supposed to be in Archiron?" He seemed surprised but not alarmed.

Archiron? He thinks I'm still in active service. Why didn't the duke inform Talus that I'd been dishonorably discharged? His Grace certainly had enough money and connections with the Brotherhood to create whatever fabrication suited him. *But why would he go to the trouble? Or is it possible the duke doesn't know?*

On the other hand, Talus may have already sent for the Watch. He might be stalling.

"Damn you, you've been gone a year, and no one's had so much as a letter," Talus said. "Is your assignment that secret?"

Stunned and disoriented, Blackthorne didn't speak.

"You're close-mouthed as always," Talus said. "Aren't you going to say a damn thing?"

It wasn't like Talus to be deceptive. The only tricks he engaged in were those used in the arena. If the Brotherhood or the Watch were on the way, he would have said as much.

Blackthorne bargained his fate and those of the others. "I have come only to make a report and must return to my post as soon as possible."

Talus appeared to accept the excuse and nodded. He glanced across the street. "You can drop your hand from your pistol now." He smiled. "Don't play innocent; I taught you that move before your balls dropped. Why are you so edgy?"

"I'm operating under another identity."

"Ah. I had no idea the Brotherhood went in for that kind of thing. I wondered why you weren't in uniform."

Unable to think of any other means of distracting Talus from further questions, Blackthorne decided to ask his own. "How is His Grace?"

Talus seemed startled by the inquiry but wrinkled up his face in another smile. It was less enthusiastic. His eyes took on a guarded look. "He is his old self. There was a big to-do at the big house last week. Doesn't seem to get on well with the new Consul. But that won't surprise you."

Blackthorne nodded as if he cared.

Without waiting for encouragement, Talus continued with all that had transpired in the last year: new additions, births, and the state of the crops. In truth, Talus was the only person from the estate Blackthorne cared about. After what he'd been through, he couldn't help finding it heartening to meet with some aspect of his former life and find it unchanged. *And not awful.*

"Do you remember Kukka?" Talus asked.

"I do," Blackthorne said. Kukka had been one of the duke's favorites. She had also been Blackthorne's introduction to women.

The duke had sent her to his bed the week before the Academy. Kukka was pretty and fun-loving. Blackthorne hadn't known her well, but they had spent two days together while she had systematically taught him everything she knew.

Talus continued without taking his gaze from the street. "She's dead. A week ago. Ran away three weeks before. Brotherhood found her and brought her back. I had to lash her to the post. What a waste," Talus said. He delivered the news as if the duke's prize calf had taken a turn for the worse.

Blackthorne shivered. *Would you show any more remorse if it'd been me, old man?*

I must get out of here. "It has been good to see you, but I must be on my way," Blackthorne said. "Please send my regards to His Grace."

Talus nodded. "I understand. You've your duty. Mithras willing, I will see you when your assignment is complete. If not . . . Die well, Severus."

"I will." Even though he had not done so in years, Blackthorne had to stop himself from adding the "sir".

With that, he shook Talus's hand and walked away. Blackthorne knew Talus was watching and didn't look back. The sense of relief as the crowds drifted between them was powerful. He continued on his way as dread ran a cold finger down the back of his neck. *I must hurry.*

He'd have gone back to *Clár Oibre Rúnda* but for two things. The first was Mallory McDermott. Mallory was a good man and had risked much to save the lives of many. Determined to help, Blackthorne couldn't leave Novus Salernum without knowing where the man might be. The second reason was the child, and the child was with Mallory.

Arriving at the respectable redbrick building that had been

Mallory's residence, Blackthorne went to the front door and knocked. A young man with dark brown skin, dressed in a footman's uniform that matched the green curtains, answered.

"Can I help you?" he asked.

"Is Mallory McDermott at home?" Blackthorne asked, already knowing otherwise. However, the servant's reply might provide information with which he could start a search.

"Master McDermott is not," the footman said. His stony expression didn't reveal distress of any kind. "Would you care to leave a calling card?"

The Brotherhood haven't been here, then. That's good. Blackthorne didn't show his relief. "No, thank you." He decided to take a chance. "Is Miss Lydia Corey receiving visitors? My name is Andrew Blackthorne. I've been away for some time and—"

Sorrow passed over the footman's face. "I—I . . . Can you wait here?"

"I can."

"And your name again?"

"Andrew Blackthorne." If Lydia had named him the child's father to Armas, it was highly likely that she'd told others, and if that were the case, it was possible those living here who more than likely shared Lydia's profession would be willing to tell him where the child was.

The footman vanished behind the closed door. Blackthorne turned and, leaning against one of the white columns that were set on either side of the front stoop, watched the street. Coaches, riders, and groups of pedestrians passed—none gave the redbrick house and its visitor the slightest interest. He didn't notice any Wardens among them. That wasn't unusual in this part of the city.

Finally, the footman reappeared. He opened the door wide. "Would you please come inside? Lady Melissa will see you now."

Blackthorne feigned confusion. "Is Miss Corey unavailable?"

The footman said, "It would be best if Lady Melissa explained the matter to you. Won't you please come into the receiving parlour? She will be with you in a moment."

He followed the footman into a parlour outfitted with expensive mahogany furniture, a large Ytlainen rug of muted reds, blues, and greens, and green printed wallpaper depicting country scenes. He sat perched on the sofa not far from the door. The footman bowed and left. It wasn't long before Lady Melissa appeared. She was beautiful, voluptuous, and pale. Her hair was light brown and styled in a tousled knot on top of her head that didn't take away from her beauty. She wore a modest buttercream yellow day dress with white underskirts.

He got to his feet.

"Mr. Blackthorne?"

Bowing, he said, "I am. And you are Lady Melissa, I presume?"

"Please, resume your seat," she said. Turning, she addressed the footman. "George, could you bring some tea?"

The footman nodded, bowed, and left, closing the sliding doors behind him.

"I apologize for making you wait," she said. "It is rather early in the day yet."

"I'm sorry for calling at an inappropriate hour," Blackthorne said. "I can return at a—"

"I'm afraid this can't wait. I—I have some rather unfortunate news for you," Lady Melissa said. "It's about Lydia. She's—she's dead."

Blackthorne let some of his discomfort show on his face. "How?"

"Childbirth, I'm afraid," Lady Melissa said.

There came a knock and the footman returned with the tea. He set the tray on a sideboard and left.

Lady Melissa went to the tray. "Would you like some tea?"

"No, thank you," Blackthorne said. "I should probably leave you to your—"

"There is something else I need to tell you, Mr. Blackthorne. Something important," Lady Melissa said. "Lydia was a good friend of mine. We . . . entered our profession at the same time, you see. In fact, Lydia, Mal, and myself bought this place together. We confided in one another as much as someone in our line of work can. She placed a great deal of trust in you. As did Mal. I hope it wasn't misplaced."

"What are you saying?"

"What I'm about to tell you . . . well . . . let's say that your response is important." She poured herself a cup of tea, applied milk and sugar, and then resumed her place in the upholstered chair opposite. "The child was yours."

"Was?" He felt the corners of his mouth turn down.

"Is. She's a girl."

"Where is she?" Blackthorne asked.

"Not so fast," Lady Melissa said. "What are your intentions?"

Blackthorne hesitated. *What* are *my intentions?* He hadn't thought much about what he'd do once he had found her—only that he didn't want her left on a rubbish heap as was so often the case with unwanted children. *What am I to do with a baby?* "I—I don't—"

"You don't know?"

"I don't know how to take care of her," he said. "I know nothing of babies."

"I see." She frowned.

"I must be honest with you," Blackthorne said. "I had heard that Lydia was gone. I only heard it an hour ago. I came here to—to . . ."

"To what?"

He looked away. "To get the child."

"Why?"

"I had thought to take her with me," Blackthorne said. "But now I'm not so certain that is wise."

"I see." She took a sip of her tea. "And why shouldn't she be with her father?"

"I don't know how to care for a baby."

The frown didn't budge from her mouth. "First-time parents often don't."

"How well do you know Mallory McDermott?"

"Well enough to know that you, he, and Lydia were involved in a certain illegal operation. One involving nonhumans," Lady Melissa said.

Blackthorne blinked. *Shit.* "I—"

"It's all right. You're safe," Lady Melissa said. "I've been helping for some time. They simply didn't include you in that knowledge."

"Oh." Blackthorne sat back down and attempted to slow his heart. "Good."

"That still leaves the child. Do you want her or not?"

This time, Blackthorne didn't hesitate. "I do." *I must be mad.*

Lady Melissa released a breath she apparently had been holding. "I'm relieved to hear you say that, Mr. Blackthorne. It tells me a great deal about you."

"It does?"

She took another sip of her tea. "It says you are the person Lydia said you were. She . . . liked you a great deal."

"She did? I thought—"

"You thought she had sex with you merely because that reprobate Reggie Meade expected it? My, my, Andrew—I hope you don't mind if I use your first name—I would've taken you for many things, but gullible isn't one of them."

"Does she have a name—my daughter?"

"She does," Lady Melissa said. "I named her Lydia, after her mother.

Although 'Lydia Blackthorne' seems a rather odd combination."

"My name isn't Andrew Blackthorne. I'm sure we both know that."

She smiled and emptied her cup. Then she returned to the sideboard for more. "Are you certain you wouldn't want any tea?"

"I'm certain," Blackthorne said. "I don't have long."

"Are you planning on vanishing?"

"You are in danger."

"A woman in my profession often is."

"That isn't what I mean," Blackthorne said. "Several of my contacts have gone missing, including Mr. McDermott. It's possible that the Brotherhood may come calling."

"I see."

"We need to make sure that—"

"Mal left the city and took the wet nurse and your daughter with him," she said. "He said he would attempt to make contact with you in Greenleaf."

Blackthorne felt the tension in his shoulders and back release ever so slightly. "I'm very glad to hear that. However, just in case, I would like to go over his apartments and Lydia's as well. That way, I can remove anything the Brotherhood might deem of interest."

"That sounds like an excellent idea," she said. "You seem to know a great deal about the Brotherhood."

"I do."

"I suspect I shouldn't ask why, should I?"

He ignored her question. "In addition, I would like to go over any statements you might make to them. There are specific phrases they will be listening for, phrases which you should avoid," Blackthorne said.

"When should we start?"

"Now," Blackthorne said. "I wasn't lying about having limited time. Let's start with Mr. McDermott's apartments. We can talk while I work."

⊰ DRAKE ⊱

Emily Drake didn't know how much time had passed before the three of them left the bolt-hole. She didn't own a watch. Such things were a luxury for the rich. The chimes of the sector clock in Seven Sisters Square had always been good enough for her. Not that she'd have been able to read a watch in the blackness of the bolt-hole. The whole situation was disorienting. She felt the mental ties mooring her to her former life loosen. It was frightening, but it was also freeing. So, she did something she never did.

She indulged in living for the moment without looking for the angle.

It wasn't too long before Mal tied a handkerchief over her eyes and she was led out of their hiding place. The woman and her baby were with them. He insisted Drake keep the blindfold on until the three of them had been bundled inside two leper's-coffin boxes. The woman and the baby were in one box. She and Mal were in the other. No one spoke during the process. She was given no clues as to where they were or where they were going—outside of the smell of horse manure and old hay. The journey through Novus Salernum's gates had been the most stressful part of the venture. Terrified that the baby would scream at the worst possible moment, Em held her breath—not a bad idea in and of itself, she'd had to admit. The inside of the gritty, sticky box stank of rotting corpse. She understood by the stench, they truly were inside of a coffin used to transport dead lepers. Therefore, she spent most of her time trying not to imagine what they were lying in. The air inside the enclosed space grew increasingly stale in spite of the air slits in the sides—supposedly designed so that the guards could check the coffin's contents without exposing themselves to the disease. Unfortunately, the same slits were angled and too narrow to see anything but the sides of the wagon. Much of the time, she thought she was going to vomit and then smother. If it hadn't been for Mal, she wouldn't have made it longer than a quarter of an hour.

I'm never getting this stink out of these clothes. They'll have to be burned.

When they finally reached their destination—a vacant road outside the city walls—she'd had to replace the blindfold before climbing out. Her legs were so stiff, she didn't think she could walk. She heard Mal pay their benefactor in silence.

She couldn't help being impressed. Every person involved was disciplined, every aspect of the venture well practiced and designed for minimum risk. At the moment, she was aware of what was happening only due to the sounds of clinking silver.

They've done this quite a bit. And here I'd thought the stories of a safe way out of of the Regnum were myths. "I've never wanted a bath so much in my entire life," she said, removing Mal's handkerchief when he finally gave her the signal. She then proceeded to rub yet another cramp out of her leg. At least her ankle was no longer swollen and could accept a bit of her weight.

She saw the woman with the baby for the first time and recognized her as one of Mal's friends. She was young, perhaps seventeen, and wearing a filthy dress that may have once been blue. Her hair was brown and her pale face bore all the marks of kainen ancestry. She gave Em a grateful smile and returned her attention to the baby.

"I've got something for you, Em," Mal said, and handed her the crutch he was holding.

They think of everything, Em mused.

"When we reach Greenleaf. I promise," Mal said, "I'll join you in that bath."

"Is that a threat or a promise?" she asked, and kissed him.

"Start walking. We've a long way to go."

Glancing down at her crutch, she asked, "Don't you mean 'hobble'?" She attempted another kiss, but he turned away.

"Walk first," Mal said. "Fornicate later. I've just spent a whole day and a half with you lying on top of my balls. I think I've had enough for a while."

She caressed his rump. "We could find a nice hedge while Sondra feeds the baby, and I could take a turn on bottom."

"Oh, no, you don't." He removed her hand. "We have to make it to Greenleaf in three days." He gently shoved her. "Move along."

"Three days? On this? All the way to Greenleaf?" She hopped for a bit before he swept her up in his arms. The ease and grace with which he did it made her feel giddy. She'd forgotten how strong he was.

"We've a horse waiting for us," Mal said. "Three farms down the road."

Careful, Mal. You just gave away something. Or is he trusting me? "Why do I need a horse when I could just ride you?"

"Really, Em? Is there not a moment you don't think about sex?"

The horse turned out to be a docile, tired old mare with a sway-back. The poor creature's spine made for uncomfortable riding, given that there was no saddle, only a blanket. Still, it was better than limping all the way to Greenleaf. Her armpits already ached from using the crutches.

The journey north involved a great deal of riding, walking when the horse tired, and hiding from coaches traveling along the road-way. The mail coaches were the worst, with their horns blaring and the rush of the galloping horses. It was difficult to get off the road before being run down, let alone hide. It wasn't long before she was exhausted and grumpy—even the baby seemed to be doing better. Mal was in a hurry—so much so that he was reluctant to sleep. She wasn't sure as to the reason why, but she had an idea. It wasn't until they had to dodge a Warden Unit by ducking under a bridge and standing in the stream that she decided it was time to get more information.

Mal had his hand over the mare's nose while the Wardens and their dogs crossed above. The young woman—her name was Tyra—held on to the sleeping child and shivered. Cold stream water soaked into Em's boots. She was terrified, she was itchy, and she didn't think she'd ever get the stench of rotting leper out of her hair. She was growing very tired of her situation. She couldn't tolerate the lack of control any longer.

"We'll go slow and follow the stream up into Greenleaf," Mal whispered after the last of the Warden Unit had passed. "Hopefully, they'll be long gone by then."

"Won't someone else see us?" she asked.

"That's just a risk we'll have to take."

She put a hand on his arm. "It's time. I can't do this anymore."

"Time for what?"

"It's time for you to tell me what's going on," she said. "I've been very patient, but we're nearly there, and you've not told me why you left Novus Salernum. I want to know. I have to know. How do you know these people? Why are they being so . . . helpful? You can't be buying them. I know you don't have that much money."

He hesitated. "I think you know already."

She finally voiced her suspicions. "You're the one the Brotherhood have been looking for," she said, feeling her heart sink. "The one that's been smuggling nonhumans out of Acrasia."

He shrugged. "Not the only one. But one of them. Yes." Taking a few hesitant steps from under the stone bridge, he craned his neck in order to check that the road was clear. "Let's go."

"Where are we going?"

"I told you, Greenleaf."

"All right, *who* are we meeting?"

"Why do you want to know?"

She put a hand on her hip. "What if we're separated? Where am I to go? It's not like I can turn around and go back home at this point, is it?"

Mal's dark brows formed a straight line. "I suppose you're right. His name is Dacian Frost. We're to meet him at the Ribbon and Saber."

"Before the bath or after?"

Looking into the sky, Mal seemed to judge the time. "Before. I hope. I don't want to stay there any longer than we have to. It's dangerous."

Em made to smell herself and scowled. "Then I hope your friend has a strong stomach and isn't squeamish about nits."

"You can always rinse off in the stream."

"Tempting. Although I'm not sure the town downstream from Greenleaf will be happy when I kill off all the fish."

"Come on. We're almost there."

They waded up the stream, sticking to the highest bank. Sour mud sucked at her boots. Mal took a turn carrying the baby. Drake pushed through duckweeds, spiderwebs, and willow branches and was glad it was early summer. The stream was obviously spring-fed. Her teeth were rattling inside her head by the time they reached a spot that Mal felt confident of climbing in secret. It helped that it was getting dark. She supposed most people would be home. Although she didn't know if there was a curfew this far north. She hoped not.

Finally, he led the dull-eyed mare up the steep slope up onto the road a mile from Greenleaf's gates. This she understood by reading the stone marker sunk into the earth nearby. The three of them trudged on in silence. The water sloughing off their clothes and bodies was the only sound to disturb the singing of the frogs and crickets.

The road led them in a broad arc. Greenleaf's walls broke the horizon. Soon, Drake spied the torches bolted to the towers on either side of the big wooden gate. Unfortunately, she could see something else, too. Four men dressed in austere black uniforms. Two of them held the leads of no less than six large, sleek-looking hunting dogs. The animals were resting on their haunches, waiting for the command to give chase.

A Warden Unit, Em thought. Terror squeezed the air from her lungs. "I don't suppose there's any point to running, is there?"

"I'm so sorry, Em. I did my best." Mal continued leading their horse to the gate.

They were fifty feet from the gate when the Wardens

surrounded them. Their leader stepped in front of Em. He wasn't wearing a hat. His long dark hair was pulled back in a tidy queue so tight that the roots of her own hair ached in sympathy. He was taller than she was but shorter than Mal. His nose was narrow and pinched, and his face was set in pale, disdainful dignity.

She resisted an urge to shove a knife into it.

The Warden gave each of them a long, hard stare and seemed to settle upon addressing her. "Do you have identification?"

Mal straightened. "I don't."

"I didn't ask you, elph."

She reached into her pocket for her papers and was relieved to find that they hadn't suffered too much damage in the journey. "What is this about?"

Mal stooped to whisper in her ear. "What are you up to, Em?"

Numb, she handed the Warden her documents as if she'd done so a thousand times. In truth, she probably had.

He flipped through them, bored. "We're searching for a prostitute named Mallory McDermott. We understand he's traveling with two women matching your descriptions. One of them with a baby."

Oh, god damn it all to hell. She turned to Mal and kissed his cheek without looking at him. Then she took a deep breath and did the thing she always did, no matter how hard it was to do so. She felt calm, but she couldn't breathe. "I am Watch Captain Drake of Novus Salernum. This is the man you're looking for."

"Em?" The shock and betrayal in Mal's voice were almost too much for her to bear.

Almost. "He's been running a smuggling ring. I've proof. He's been smuggling elphs out of Novus Salernum."

Tyra burst into tears as the Wardens grabbed Mal and tied his wrists together.

"Em! Em, please! You can't do this!" Mal shouted.

The Wardens gathered around Mal. She stepped back and watched as they punched and kicked her friend.

"I'm sorry," Drake said. "If it's you or me, I pick me."

They didn't stop beating him until he ceased moving.

❈ BLACKTHORNE ❈

After speaking with Lady Melissa, he'd decided to make some minor adjustments to the plan. That way, should the worst happen, the odds of at least one of the wagons arriving at the docks with its cargo were higher. Just in case, he drew a map and made certain everyone knew how to get back to the ship from the depot. He also told Reini and Annikki they would be in charge of the other wagon and they were to take a different return route.

"This will take longer," Reini said with a frown. "The Evans Circle gate is farther from the ship."

"I know," Blackthorne said. "It would be best if both wagons didn't go through the same checkpoint."

Annikki stole the map from Reini. "Makes sense to me."

"Give that back," Reini said.

Raising an eyebrow, Annikki tucked the paper underneath her shirt and walked out of the crew cabin.

"Good thing she's on our side," Reini said.

The sky was overcast, and it had begun to rain when Blackthorne set the brake and then climbed down from the wagon bench. The bad weather meant a tighter schedule. The curfew would be earlier today. He didn't like it, but there was nothing he could do about it.

He adjusted his tricorne so that big, slow raindrops wouldn't slap him in the face. A casual glance down the street told him the area had been deserted for the noonday meal. In his experience, military staff didn't tend to lag when it came to mealtimes. He'd surmised that this would be even more the case for personnel given loosely supervised assignments—particularly if the assignment was guarding a warehouse in a less-populated part of the city. Unfortunately, he didn't see Mr. Sparrow and the other wagon. *Not yet.* But he knew May to be reliable and trustworthy.

He signaled to Katrin, and she collected the reins, ready to drive the team away should something go wrong. As for Reini and Annikki, he'd let them off two streets back. Both would make their way to the military depot via back alleys and roofs. It was their task to neutralize security behind and around the warehouse. According to the information Armas had sold Blackthorne, today and at this time that would mean three guards in addition to the two at the entrance, but the total number of guards could be as many as eight.

In the distance, a clock tower chimed the hour. Stalling, he counted the rings.

Noon, Blackthorne thought. *Time to begin.* Misfortune was always a factor, and just before an assignment he often found himself wishing for some celestial patron. *Not that I know of any that would have me.* He took in a deep breath and strolled toward the two bored guards dressed in Imperial Army uniforms. They were sitting at a makeshift table made of emptied crates, eating their lunch. The stout one tapped out his pipe in preparation for filling it with tobacco. Both ignored Blackthorne until it was apparent he would disturb their meal. The leaner and younger of the pair got to his feet.

Blackthorne caught the scent of burning tobacco as the older guard used a tinderbox to light his pipe.

The younger guard laid a hand on his pistol and took several steps toward Blackthorne. "Mister, this here is a restricted area. So you can get back up on that wagon of yours and keep on going wherever it is you're going."

Assuming a subservient attitude, Blackthorne also altered his speech—slowing and softening it with drawn-out, rounded vowels. "I'm sorry. I don't mean no trouble. I seem to be lost," he said, holding up a slip of paper and pretending to read from it. "Do you know where Hodge Lane is?"

"Hodge Lane?" the younger guard asked. "That'll be the Hodge Lane in Jester's Court? Or the Hodge Lane in Perryston?"

"There are two?" Blackthorne asked.

The older guard spat and then sighed. "From down south, are you?"

"How'd you know?" Blackthorne asked.

The older guard let out a disgusted harrumph, rolled his eyes, and muttered something about country bumpkins over the pipe-stem clenched between his teeth.

Blackthorne flipped the paper scrap over and squinted. "Oh, there it is. Yes. Jester's Court."

"If it's Jester's Court you're looking for, you're a good ten miles in the wrong direction," the older guard said. "You need to go south and—"

Annikki eased from the corner of the building and positioned herself behind the older guard without his noticing. She moved with a silent grace that matched Reini's. Just like Reini, she was strangely difficult to focus upon. Blackthorne's gaze kept sliding away from her—not that he wanted to concentrate upon her. Doing so might give her away, but he found even keeping his awareness of her in his peripheral vision difficult.

In one quick, smooth movement, she looped a leather thong around the older guard's neck. At the same moment, he let out a startled gasp.

The younger guard began to turn. "What the—"

Stepping between the younger guard and the sight of Annikki's attack, Blackthorne punched the younger guard in the throat. Then he grabbed the choking man, placed a hand across his mouth, and slowly eased him onto the ground, where he stepped on his neck.

With that done, Blackthorne again signaled to Katrin. Then he spied the bloodstains on Annikki's clothes.

"I thought I said to handle the situation quietly and neatly," he said.

She shrugged. "No one screamed."

"And where's Reini?" Blackthorne asked.

"He stayed behind to clean up the mess," Reini said from the roof. He lowered himself onto the makeshift table and then hopped down. He scraped the remains of the guards' lunch from his boot onto the cobblestones and addressed Annikki. "You're welcome, by the way."

With everyone accounted for, Blackthorne turned his attention to the bodies. Dragging the guard he'd killed by his feet, he deposited the man next to the crates and propped him up against the building.

"Are you implying I should thank you?" Annikki asked Reini.

"It was *your* mess I was cleaning," Reini said, grabbing the second body under the arms.

"Whatever makes you say that?" Annikki asked, and took the dead guard's feet.

Hefting the body, Reini asked, "And I suppose those two guards bled all over the side of the building by themselves?"

"It could've been a tragic toenail-clipping accident. You never know what an Acrasian might do," Annikki said. "Who am I to judge if they decided to use their knives upon themselves instead of their meat?"

"They were eating bread and cheese," Reini said.

"The ginger one had a knife," Annikki said.

"It was dull," Reini said.

"You actually took the time to check?" Annikki asked.

Katrin asked, "Are korvas always this noisy when they flirt?"

"Just get the door open," Blackthorne said, and waved her on. "Be quick about it. We don't have much time."

Kneeling in front of the door, Katrin reached inside her jacket and produced a rolled piece of black cloth. She paused to examine the rectangular block of steel with its doorknob and keyhole. "The army sure does trust its Syndicate contracts. Wish I'd known that when I lived here. My whole brood would've lived high," she muttered to herself. "This place is begging to be hit."

"I've an idea," Reini said, holding up an iron ring with a key on it. "How about you use this?"

"Where did you get that?" Katrin asked.

"It was in that guard's pocket," Reini said, and pointed to the older guard. "Makes sense. He's the guard in charge, after all."

"How do you know he's in charge?" Annikki asked.

Reini pointed to the embroidery on the bottom of the older guard's sleeve. "Corporal." Then he pointed to the younger guard. "Private."

BLACKTHORNE

Katrin reached out for the key. "Let's see if it fits." She placed the key in the lock and turned it. Then she opened the door with a flourish.

It was at that moment that Mr. Sparrow and his three friends arrived with the sound of rattling wagon hardware.

"Right on time," Reini said.

"Reini and Katrin, you're with me," Blackthorne said. "Annikki, you stay here. Get the wagons in position. Arrange them to cut down on the time it'll take to load them. I'll send Katrin out when we've got access to what we need."

Annikki nodded. She turned to Reini. "Good luck."

"Thanks," Reini said. "You too."

The interior of the warehouse was a big open space with an arched ceiling and large wooden support posts. It smelled of gunpowder and oiled steel. Most of the building's contents were piled, stacked, or otherwise organized to the right and left, creating a broad open space in the middle. Both sides were sectioned off into shallow niches lined with shelves and racks. The first few areas consisted of foodstuffs, but soon those gave way to racks of rifles, ammunition, and cannon. Blackthorne couldn't help thinking that the building was relatively empty for a military depot—that is, until he noted the racks of dusty wine bottles and good cheeses. The last third of the building consisted of a walled-off area and a narrow hall to the left. The door to that section was padlocked.

Once more, Katrin assumed a position on the floor next to the lock. "I don't suppose you have another key, Viktor?" she asked. "I'd like to know if you're going to spoil my fun." She untied and unrolled the cloth bundle.

"Not this time," Reini said.

Katrin slid a couple of delicate tools out of the pouch. "This looks like the same style lock Julian used to teach me my trade. That can't be. It was an old model back then."

Reini peered over her shoulder. "Well?"

"I give it a count of twenty, and that's being generous." She turned her head and grinned.

"Twenty seems a long count," Reini said.

"Fifteen, then," she said. "Here we go."

Blackthorne paced, trying not to listen to Reini's counting. When he reached fifteen, Blackthorne heard the lock snap open. Katrin took the hardware off the chain and pushed the door open.

"Ha! I've still got it," she said, and then gathered her tools.

Reini helped her get up off her knees. They both stepped back.

"I don't know; I almost reached sixteen," Reini said, teasing.

"I'd have done it in ten," Katrin said. "Only, I'm not used to working with a nosy korva staring over my shoulder, is all."

Stepping to the open door, Blackthorne was brought up short by a soft noise. He noticed that Reini froze at exactly the same time. They both turned to the source of the sound. When Blackthorne focused, he thought he could make out what sounded like an animal panting.

"Get inside and close the door," he said, keeping his voice low.

"What?" Katrin asked.

"Do it. Now," Blackthorne whispered.

"It's a dog," Reini whispered.

Blackthorne blinked.

"Oh, that," Katrin said. Once again, she reached inside her jacket. "I've got this."

Reini said, "Here it comes."

A large black-and-tan mastiff loped into view. Its black nose seemed to have been pushed into its jowly face. It gave the impression of being anything but friendly. It lowered its head and let out a deep, rumbling growl.

Katrin slowly knelt down. "Hello, sweet puppy. Who's a good

dog? Are you hungry?" She held out a treat that looked like dried meat.

The dog didn't approach. It remained where it was and continued its threat. Blackthorne did his best to remain perfectly still. He didn't care for dogs, particularly big ones. He kept his hand on his knife, ready to draw it.

"Shy one, are you? Here," Katrin said. "I'll put it on the floor for you." With a steady hand, she scooted the treat across the floor.

The beast sniffed the air over the tidbit.

"Go on. My friend Darius made it special," Katrin said. "And it's all yours, boy. Looks like you won't even have to share."

Slowly, the mastiff went to the treat and lapped it up with a great, sloppy tongue. It appeared to enjoy the flavor for a few moments before settling onto the floor and yawning, displaying a distressing number of teeth. Then the dog stretched out, closed its eyes, and stopped moving.

"You poisoned it?" Reini asked, clearly disturbed by the idea of harming an animal.

"It's asleep," Katrin said.

As if to reassure Reini, the mastiff let out a wet snore.

"Oh," Reini said. "Good."

Katrin said, "You'd swear you two had never broken into a building before. Anyone with any sense keeps dogs. That is, if they want to keep their belongings."

The interior of the locked room revealed an ink-stained desk littered with ledgers and various recipes. A bottle of ink and a shaker of sand rested on top, along with several goose quills and a penknife. The other half of the room was crowded with long wooden crates. Blackthorne snatched up a nearby crowbar and pried open the nearest. Even in the dim light, he could see it contained what they'd come for.

Katrin reached inside and pulled out a scabbarded blade. The other swords let out a few clanks as they resettled. Reini took the sword from her and drew it. A look of awe spread across his plain face.

"It's water steel, all right. So beautiful," he said. "And light. It weighs nothing."

Blackthorne said, "Katrin, get the others. Let's start loading."

Katrin nodded and left, stepping carefully over the dog.

That thing is going to be a problem, Blackthorne thought. But he didn't want to risk moving it.

Reini began to knot the water steel saber to his belt.

"Put it back," Blackthorne said.

"Why?" Reini asked. "It's an *Eledorean* blade. I've a right to it."

Blackthorne said, "Because you're nonhuman in Novus Salernum, and nonhumans do not carry weapons within the bounds of the Regnum—not without a very expensive permit. One that you do not possess. In any case, such a thing will draw attention. And attention is something we cannot afford."

"In that case, I suppose it can wait until we're back on the ship." Reini reluctantly returned the sword.

"Sooner we start, sooner this is over with," Blackthorne said, moving into position and lifting an end of the crate.

Reini grabbed the opposite end and lifted it from its former resting place. Mr. Sparrow and the others entered the room and shifted around so that Blackthorne and Reini could get past with their load. Blackthorne indicated the crates with a sideways nod. He let Reini be the one to walk backward. Blackthorne stepped over the sleeping mastiff and felt his balls clench in defense as he did so.

The loading took up the estimated hour, but at long last, the crates were in place. The dog slept through the entire process. After making sure that all was put back to rights—he had to demand that Annikki replace the bottle of wine she'd stolen—Blackthorne told everyone it was time to leave.

"Reini, Annikki, you're both with Mr. Sparrow's load," he whispered. "In case he gets any ideas."

Nodding, Reini tapped Annikki on the arm, and they both climbed onto their assigned wagon. Mr. Sparrow, Ian, Carl, and Mandy assumed places on the back. They drove off.

Blackthorne waited for Katrin to go before using the key to relock the warehouse door. With that done, he returned the key to the dead guard's pocket and then tossed the assassin's token onto the body. At last, he boarded the wagon and took the reins from Katrin.

She gave him a crestfallen expression. "I wanted to drive the team."

"Maybe later," Blackthorne said, disengaging the brake. He made a clicking sound with his tongue in the back of his throat and urged the horses to move with a flick of the reins. Ever since he'd learned of his daughter, Lydia, his orders to protect Katrin had acquired a certain intensity. He wasn't certain what to do about it.

Katrin was unusually quiet on the journey back to *Clár Oibre Rúnda*. He had the feeling that she was holding her breath. He found himself doing the same. With the midday meal finished and curfew shortening their day, the people of Novus Salernum flooded the streets in an attempt to finish their duties before dark. The ebb and flow of wagons, riders, and pedestrians slowed the return journey more than Blackthorne had hoped. He watched the crowds for signs of trouble.

A wealthy woman made her way down the street in a blue silk dress. She entered a shop with the hood of her pale gray cloak pulled down to shade her eyes. A few strands of long blond hair escaped from beneath the velvet. Next, he spied a fat gentleman wearing gold rings, exiting a coffeehouse. He was hatless and his wispy hair blew in the wind as he stumbled. Two urchins darted out. One walked into the man and a second child passed behind. Both were gone in an instant.

"What are you laughing at?" Blackthorne asked.

Katrin motioned to where the gentleman had been. "That was what Julius used to call a 'bump and tumble.' The older child walks into their intended victim—bumps him, see. At the same time, the smaller brood member cuts the man's purse from the opposite side," Katrin said. "They did it perfectly. Julius would've been envious."

"Who is Julius?" Blackthorne asked.

"He was my Brood's Guardian. You know, the leader," Katrin said. "I wonder if he's still alive."

"How old was he?" Blackthorne asked in a fit of uncharacteristic curiosity.

"Twelve, I think," Katrin said. "He wasn't sure. Thing is, after a certain age, the Syndicate starts to take notice. If they think an orphan is good enough, they'll recruit you. If not, well . . . there are no grown-up freelancers."

As they began to approach the northern part of the harbor, the rotten-nut stench became stronger, until it overpowered the normal wharf damp and old-fish smell.

"What is that?" Katrin asked, holding her nose.

Blackthorne shouted over the rattling of the wagon. "Coffee barge lost its cargo in the north canal a few days ago."

Half the reason Novus Salernum was a prosperous port was the natural harbor formed by Pafioro Bay. The other reason was the system of canals connected to the sewage system. It rained a great deal in northern Acrasia. The canals kept the city from becoming a disease-ridden bog.

They crossed a bridge that took them out of the Gibson Road area and spanned one of the canals, and came to a line of people, wagons, and horses at the gates to the northern warehouse district. Dockmen, ships, and barges of various shapes and sizes were all around. Beyond the first set of docks squatted ten warehouses in a chaste row, each painted prim white and trimmed in red and black.

Church Tithing Warehouses, Blackthorne thought. He gave the darkening sky a worried look. *It's getting late.*

A wagon loaded with wine barrels joined the unmoving line behind them. It wasn't long before several wagons filled with various goods did as well.

"Wonder what the holdup is?" Katrin asked.

Torn between sending her to find out and keeping her at his side, Blackthorne decided to wait. Whatever was ahead, they couldn't leave. They were now boxed in. He hunched under his dripping tricorne and hoped they would get to the ship before dark. They'd not rented their berth for another night. Hännenen was eager to get his sister far from Acrasia. Blackthorne was suddenly glad of having taken the precaution of the second wagon and hoped the alternate route was less congested.

The Gibson Road clock struck the hour.

Katrin frowned. "How did it get to be three already?"

Out over the bay, a large bank of menacing storm clouds clustered. The city's population began its rush for the gates or the safety of home against the setting of the sun. Alehouses and shops not licensed to remain open after curfew ejected clientele and shut their doors. Two Wardens arrived at the checkpoint. One remained among the crowd. The other strolled down the growing line. Periodically, he shouted to those waiting to prepare their identification documents.

Blackthorne's hands tightened on the reins.

"What do we do?" Katrin whispered.

"Nothing. You have your papers and I have mine. We wait," Blackthorne said. "But if anything happens, you are to abandon this wagon and run. Do you hear? Make your way to the ship however you can. I'll meet you there."

"Why can't we run together?" Katrin asked.

He couldn't tell her that the Wardens might be there for him. He was afraid she might do something loyal and stupid. "I may need to distract them," he said, "in which case it will be safer if you are far away from me."

"I won't leave y—"

"Do not argue with me," Blackthorne said in his coldest tone.

"But—" She stopped as the Warden walked past without even glancing in their direction.

Blackthorne hissed, "You will do as you're told, or you'll never go on another of these assignments. It won't be my word that bars you. It'll be your father's."

Katrin swallowed. "All right."

The line moved a few feet and halted again. The narrow alley running between the last of the Church Tithing Warehouses and a Brocchus East Tahmer mercantile building came into view. Gazing down the garbage-cluttered length of it, he could see that the offices went on for several blocks before ending. The taste of dusty tin flooded Blackthorne's mouth at once. He spat in disgust as his heart began to thud in his chest. He scanned his surroundings for the cause. As he did, he spotted a four-year-old girl with dark hair and wide eyes dressed in a ragged brown dress at the mouth of the shadowy alley. A fresh bruise darkened the pale skin under the child's swollen right eye. The orphan was crying piteously as adults ignored her in their rush to get home. Recognizing the ploy for what it was, he wheeled away. His stomach turned. *That might have been Lydia were it not for Mal.* The thought was foreign and unwelcome.

Katrin made a small, panicked sound. "Where's her guardian?"

Blackthorne looked at the child. Her bony hand grasped coat hem after coat hem, only to be brushed off or shoved away in contempt. No other orphans were near, all having already taken to their rented bolt-holes.

Katrin turned in the seat twice. "How can they pretend not to see what was happening? How could they leave her to die?"

Frowning, Blackthorne took a closer look. It was possible that he'd been wrong after all. That was when he detected signs he knew he would find. Behind the girl in the advancing shadows, something shifted—a something that crept with the caution and grace of a predator stalking prey.

"I can't watch and do nothing." Katrin leapt from the seat.

"Katrin! Don't!" Blackthorne reached for her arm but was too late.

As Katrin ran to the alley, the orphan seemed to withdraw into it in despair. Her cries became sobbing wails.

Setting the brake with a curse, Blackthorne looped the reins around the handle. He abandoned the wagon and sprinted after Katrin. Inside the alley, the light was almost gone.

Katrin held out a hand to the orphan and got down on one knee. "Hey, don't worry. I see you. You're going to be all right. You can come with us. You're small enough, no one will mind."

She was inches from the child when Blackthorne snatched Katrin away and then dropped her. She landed on her back in the filthy street with a yelp. He threw himself in front of her and drew his Warden's knife. A long black leg lashed out from behind a pile of broken crates, slicing through the sleeve of his coat and sending stinking refuse tumbling. He felt the stinging burn of the cut, but the pain wasn't too bad. *Not yet.* He'd had time to hope that the wound wouldn't slow him, when the rest of the creature emerged from its hiding place. Its hulking spidery frame towered over him.

The malorum's head was that of a kainen but for the uneven insect-like mandibles that consumed the bottom half of the face. It was covered in black hair as coarse as porcupine quills and stank of the grave. It took a lurching step toward him on four bent thin legs, roaring its frustration.

Blackthorne sensed more than saw Katrin scuttle from under his feet—not taking the time to get up from the ground.

Lunging at the malorum, Blackthorne shouted, "Get back to the wagon, Katrin! Now!" He had to keep the thing from risking the light and leaving its lair. If it did, he wasn't sure he could hold it off. Acrasian malorum were fast and they could jump. He attacked again, this time connecting. The cut traced a wounding line across the creature's face. It flinched back as if burned, and howled in pain. He took that moment to reach into his inside coat pocket. When he had what he needed, he threw down four silver coins, one at a time. Each one rang out against the worn and broken cobblestones.

The orphan was lying on the ground to his left and on his side of the uneven line of coins. Rain had soaked the little girl's filthy hair, plastering it to her dirty face. Water pooled in the hollows of her open, unseeing eyes. Her white, translucent skin carried a hint of blue laced with the faint mottling of broken blood vessels. He wasn't surprised to know that what had appeared to be a bruise was actually the beginning bloom of grave rot.

The dead orphan's mouth opened. "Mama?"

At the edge of his vision, Katrin got to her feet. She gasped, whirled, and ran for the wagon. The malorum hissed and gurgled, edging around the line of coins—testing for a weakness in the defense. Blackthorne pressed his attack as far as he dared. At last, the malorum retreated to its lair beneath the piled garbage with a wet snarl.

"Mama?" The child's small dead face stared back at the black-ened clouds with eyes that didn't blink the rain away.

He unsheathed his saber with his other hand. Nothing could be done about the coins—not without risking the creature's return—but he could do something about the dead child. He cut the orphan's head from her body in one powerful stroke that grazed the broken pavement stones. The pitiful cries ended at once, and with that done, he backed out of the alley. He considered four sterling a small loss and returned to the wagon.

The line had progressed fifty feet while they'd been in the alley. Their wagon was now an obstacle. The others waiting behind shouted their exasperation. He waved to them in acknowledgment and stepped up onto the wagon. Freeing the reins took two tries, and he released the brake with trembling hands.

Katrin sniffed. "I almost—she was—was—"

"It was a decoy," Blackthorne said, keeping his voice as even as he could. "Are you hurt?" When they'd caught up to the queue, he reined the horses, and once again they waited.

She stood up and tried to brush the street muck off her trou-sers. "I'm all right. At least, I think so." She resumed her seat with a shiver.

"Good," he said, and resisted an urge to give reassurance. In truth, he didn't know how without sounding reproachful. It would only make matters worse.

"That—that could've been me." She clamped a hand over the sob that forced its way out of her mouth.

Blackthorne stared for a moment before he awkwardly patted her back twice. "There are only a few more ahead of us. We're almost back to the ship. Hold together a little longer."

She sniffed and then took a deep breath as if to calm herself. "You're hurt." She pointed to the bloody rents in his sleeve.

"It's a scratch. I'm fine."

Katrin nodded and wiped her wet face with her soggy coat sleeve, not that it dried anything. "I'd—I'd feel better if you let me bandage it now."

They both knew an open wound was more likely to draw malorum. Blackthorne understood he couldn't deal with it himself without help. In any case, he recognized an unspoken apology when he saw one. "All right."

He slipped his wounded arm out of his coat, and she dug around in her bag until she produced a scrap of cloth that might suffice. By the time the queue moved, his arm was securely bandaged and dressed.

The wagon in front eased forward a few more feet. As they got closer to the front of the line, another Warden began his walk along the waiting row of wagons. And then the one thing that Blackthorne had dreaded for more than a year finally happened. The Warden in question glanced up at him, and Blackthorne knew the face. His heart staggered inside his chest, and his blood became ice.

Caius.

At once, Blackthorne turned away and hoped with all his might that he wouldn't be recognized. He stopped breathing. Caius paused. Blackthorne leaned close to Katrin and whispered in her ear.

"I want you to get down and pretend to check the back of the wagon," he said. "If anything happens, slip into the crowd at the gate. Get out of sight. Walk through like nothing is wrong. Hear me?"

Katrin's eyes went wide, but she gave him a slight nod. Then she climbed down and made her way to the back of the wagon.

"Excuse me?" Caius asked.

Shit. Shit. Shit. Blackthorne pretended not to hear. He glanced up at the sky and then started checking under the seat as if looking for a tarp to cover his cargo.

"Sir? May I see your identity papers? Sir?"

Swiving hells. That's it. I'm done. Blackthorne nodded and reached inside his coat. Keeping his head down, he made to hand them over.

"Severus?" Caius asked. "Is it you?"

"Name is Dacian Frost, sir." Blackthorne kept his voice low and a bit hoarse as if speaking were painful.

"I could swear . . . Can you turn and face me, please?" Caius asked.

Blackthorne turned to the back of the wagon and mouthed one word to Katrin. *Go.* He waited until she'd gone to comply with Caius's request.

"Severus! It *is* you! I thought it—"

Jumping off the wagon, Blackthorne shoved Caius with all his might. Caius fell backward onto the cobblestones. Blackthorne ran around the wagon and made for the alley. Drawing his dagger, he prayed the malorum lurking there was still nursing its wounds and didn't have a short memory.

The sounds of high-pitched Warden whistles followed him as he sprinted for his life.

⊰ S U V I ⊱

Playing cards with Nels in her cabin, Suvi detected a sudden, hectic rhythm to the pace of the dockmen's work echoing off the interior of the secured docks. She pretended to muse over her cards. The small mound of black pebbles resting on the table in front of her represented all the "valuables" in play. She'd already knocked Jami and Dylan out of the game. Jami hadn't lasted long. She never did, not having much patience for five-card-bluff. Nels was down to resorting to IOUs, but Suvi had a feeling he'd picked up on some fresh nuance. He'd won the last two tricks.

On the other hand, it's possible he's been leading me into a false sense of security. He's sly that way. She controlled a small smile at the thought. Her brother was a skilled player. "What time is it?"

"I've no idea," Nels said. "I left my pocket watch in the Hold.

It's still not working right after the last ocean voyage. When is your Mr. Slate going to recruit a watchmaker? At this rate, I may never get that thing repaired."

She knew he was being facetious.

"I'll find out," Jami said, and slipped from the cabin.

That left Suvi alone with her twin brother. Dylan had joined Dar in getting prepared for taking on the stolen cargo. The block-and-tackle hoist had to be ready for lowering the load into *Clár Oibre Rúnda*'s hold. They would need to do so in a hurry, if they were to leave before curfew.

Thunder rumbled somewhere far off. It'd been a gloomy day, from what she could discern from the confines of the cabin. They'd been playing cards to the light of the oil lamps. *Again.*

Jami returned. "Dylan says it's nearly four, and they've not returned yet. Says inquiries are being made regarding our remaining here for the night. What's your answer?"

"We've another four hours before curfew," Suvi said. "What's the harbormaster's problem?"

"Dylan says that curfew will be early," Jami said. "Incoming storm."

Suvi silently cursed all Acrasians and their grubby, grasping natures. "I assume the harbormaster wants to collect a late departure fee?"

"Says he'll need at least a hundred fifty sterling to keep the gates open," Jami said.

"Swiving hells," Nels said in Acrasian.

"I know this game," Suvi said. "That's merely his starting price." She laid her cards face down and stood up. "I'll take care of this."

"Send Dar," Nels said.

"I'm sick to death of this cabin," Suvi said. "I could use a breath of fresh air."

"That would be unwise," Nels said.

Suvi motioned to her current ensemble—boy's breeches and a white linen shift. She was also barefoot. "Because so many Acrasians would look at me right now and think, 'Oh, look! It's the Queen of New Eledore!'" She strode over to the cabin door. "I'm bored. A bit of playful negotiation will make me feel less like cargo."

"Then I'm going with you," Nels said.

Suvi looked over her shoulder. "Uh-uh. You're staying here."

"I am not," Nels said.

"I've a question," Suvi said. "Just how many kainen are known to be wandering around with pale blond hair, Mr. *Ghost?*"

Nels sat back down, muttering a long string of curses in Acrasian.

"I understood that," Suvi said. "Doesn't calling to question my parentage also say something about yours?"

"Your Acrasian is getting distressingly good," Nels said.

"It had better be," Suvi said. "Negotiating harbor fees in Eledorean isn't exactly an option. Jami, bring the wallet."

She left the cabin with Jami in tow. When she got to the main deck, the first thing she did was stretch her arms high in the air. It felt good to not have a cabin ceiling hovering low over her head.

Dylan appeared at her side. "What are you doing up here?"

"Someone needs to negotiate for more time with the harbormaster," Suvi said, and stared out the huge open sliding door that was used to secure the private harbor. It was raining, and heavy storm clouds clustered on the horizon. She frowned. "You sure it'll be wise for us to go out in that?"

He glanced at the clouds. "Dar and I have sailed in worse."

"That wasn't the question I asked," Suvi said.

"I can get us underway," Dylan said. "The storm may even be to our advantage. That is, if it doesn't get any worse."

"How's that?" Suvi asked.

"If I nudge it just so," Dylan said. "I can use it to cover our leaving. The Acrasians definitely won't want to follow us."

Suvi gazed at the clouds. "All right. Sounds like a plan. Let's go talk to the harbormaster."

Dylan raised an eyebrow.

"Mr. Blackthorne hasn't returned," Suvi said. "Who else can convince our friends to keep the gates open with less than fifty sterling?"

"Don't cut the price too deep," Dylan said. "We don't want suspicion to fall on us after the fact."

"Why would that matter? We'll be gone," Suvi said.

"You're forgetting," Dylan said. "We're *Clan Flounder*. Such a thing would make it more difficult for future family business."

Sighing, Suvi nodded. "You're right. I'm sorry. I wasn't thinking. I've been too long in that musty cabin."

Dylan said, "*Clár Oibre Rúnda* isn't musty."

"I didn't mean to insult your girl," Suvi said. "She's beautiful and fast and—"

"About to save your skin," Dylan said, and pointed to the loading area. "They're here."

Suvi frowned. "I only see one wagon."

"No doubt the other is on the way," Dylan said. Then he shouted, "Dar? Is everything ready? We're about to be very busy."

Suvi went to the gangplank and met the harbormaster waiting on the dock. He was a balding Acrasian with a red face and an impatient air.

"Good afternoon, madam. Is Mr. Frost here?" the harbormaster asked.

"He has been unavoidably detained," Suvi said. "He has, however, left me in charge until he returns. I am Tabitha Sternchaser, First Mate of Clan Flounder's *Clár Oibre Rúnda*. May I be of service?"

The harbormaster made to scan the ship's deck, apparently for someone with more authority.

"Let me assure you, sir," Suvi said, "I am in charge." She hoped that would be enough to convince him. She didn't want to resort to command magic. *Not yet.*

He paused. "Miss Sternchaser, I'm here to inform you that the rent on your berth is expiring in a half hour."

"I understand that you're willing to grant my ship an extension," Suvi said.

Frowning, he said, "That might be . . . costly. The storm—"

"I am authorized to pay seventy-five sterling," Suvi said.

"The fee is one hundred, plus an extra fifty for keeping the gates open after curfew," he said.

"Curfew is at least four hours away," Suvi said.

"Curfew is contingent upon available daylight hours," he said in a bored tone. "The coming storm has reduced those hours. This is a secure facility. In the event a malorum gains access, my employer would be liable."

Suvi hesitated. "Seventy-five for the extension and twenty-five for the gate fee." She moved aside as Viktor Reini and a gentleman she didn't recognize walked past while carrying an oblong wooden crate. Three more crates followed the first. "We won't be here much longer, I assure you. The delivery we were expecting has arrived."

"One hundred and fifty," the harbormaster said. "I have other responsibilities that I should be seeing to, Miss Sternchaser."

Unfortunately, she only had one hundred thirty sterling with which to work. "One thirty."

He frowned. "How much longer will you be? I must close the gates in three quarters of an hour."

"As long as it takes to load our cargo," Suvi lied. In truth, they would have to wait until Mr. Blackthorne arrived with the second wagon.

The harbormaster seemed to judge the speed with which the wagon was being unloaded. Natalia Annikki and another woman moved past with yet another crate.

Suvi took the opportunity to seemingly bump into the harbormaster. In the same instant, she lowered her voice and charged her words with a discreet amount of magic. "Fortunately, ours is not the only ship running behind its time. You will be happy to accept one hundred and thirty sterling. Say so now."

The harbormaster blinked, and his expression grew distant. "Fortunately for you, *Clár Oibre Rúnda* is not the only ship running behind," he said. "I will be happy to accept one thirty. Thank you for your business. The gates will be closing in three quarters of an hour."

"Very good. Except you will wait to close the gates until after we have left harbor," Suvi said. "You will not remember the name of our ship, nor any details about us, or our cargo."

"I won't remember," he said, nodding.

"Now smile and shake my hand. Accept your fee, and go about your business," Suvi said, and released his arm.

Jami opened the wallet and counted off the paper notes. The harbormaster smiled, accepted the money, and wandered off with a slightly confused expression.

Jami whispered, "Are you sure—"

"I had to buy us some insurance," Suvi said. "We may be cutting this one closer than we would like."

"And if Mr. Blackthorne doesn't come back?" Jami asked.

"He'll return in time," Suvi said. *Please, return in time.*

"You should consider leaving him," Jami said.

"And what of Katrin?" Suvi asked. "Councilor Slate won't be happy about us abandoning his daughter."

"You do make a point," Jami said. "We could come back for them."

"Just how do you plan on finding them?" Suvi asked. "Will

you volunteer to search the streets of Novus Salernum for an ex-Warden and a former street harvester?"

Jami paused, seemingly to give the matter some thought. It was then that Suvi spotted Katrin sprinting down the dock, a panic-stricken look on her face.

Katrin staggered to a halt. "Is Blackthorne here?" She was gasping.

"Where's the wagon?" Jami asked.

"We—we left it," Katrin said, bending at the hips and grabbing her knees. "He told me to run. He said he'd meet me here. Isn't he here yet?"

"Not yet." Suvi asked, "What happened?"

Straightening, Katrin said, "They stopped us. The Brotherhood were checking identification at the entrance to the wharf."

Shit. That's not good, Suvi thought.

"Someone recognized him." Katrin looked like she was going to start crying. "He *told* me to leave him. I didn't want to."

Suvi whirled and headed up the gangplank, leaving Jami to collect Katrin. "Dylan?"

Dylan paused. He had one hand on the rope attached to the cargo net. "Yes?"

"How much longer?" Suvi asked.

"This is the second-to-last load," Dylan said. "Viktor is paying Mr. Sparrow."

"Good," Suvi said. Biting her lip, she turned back to the docks. Blackthorne was still nowhere in sight. *If the Brotherhood are after him, he's as good as dead.* "Get everyone onboard and get ready to weigh anchor."

Dylan nodded.

Suvi stared at the harbor entrance. *Come on, Mr. Blackthorne. Get your ass back here.*

⊰ BLACKTHORNE ⊱

TWENTY-SECOND OF MAITOKUU, 1785

Heavy rain rapidly soaked his clothes where his all-weather coat didn't reach. Thunder roared and the wind picked up. He bolted down several muddy alleys as fast as he dared, making his way northwest and staying out of sight. It was already too late for him to slip out of the city and into the surrounding countryside. The curfew would have all the gates closed in less than a quarter of an hour. No one would be allowed out—not unless they were a Warden or, he thought sourly, a leper. He didn't have any of the requisite passes and badges such a ruse would require, nor had he packed his Paulus disguise when he'd left. A rented bolt-hole was an option. However, this late in the day, it was likely that only the most expensive had vacancies remaining. That said, he did not like the idea of being confined to a small space with only one exit, nor the idea of trusting strangers motivated by greed. Both seemed less than safe bets, and he was gambling with high stakes—not all of them his own.

What happens to little Lydia if I don't meet Mallory McDermott in Greenleaf?

Something had changed in him from the moment he'd learned he had a daughter. Suddenly, his life—his *beliefs* had been thrown into a vastly different perspective. Unanswered questions by the hundreds had been stacking up against his internal barriers. The choices he'd made gained new weight—even his interactions with Katrin had come into a fresh awareness.

Passing through Rosacollina, he paused in the doorway of a closed shop to catch his breath, take inventory, and formulate a plan. He pressed his fingers against his chest, felt along the stitched rows of the Warden's wallet he wore under his shirt, and counted the coins stored there. More than half of the pockets were empty— just over the recommended amount. That was good news. He was also fairly certain he'd lost the Wardens who'd given chase. While they had signaled for assistance, he hadn't seen any evidence of further pursuit. That was something, at least. In addition, the fact that Caius had been shocked meant that Caius hadn't expected to see him, not in the city.

Perhaps they haven't made the connection between Blackthorne and Severus. Not yet. That was also good news. He hoped they never would. The Reclamation Hospital was a dire enough prospect without adding a thorough interrogation on top.

He returned his attention to his situation. Ultimately, his best option was to hide, and he needed to do so in an area he knew well—one to which the Brotherhood wouldn't expect him to run— if they were indeed searching for him. Best of all, an area that would provide a great many places to hide.

The duke's estate. He tried not to consider the irony.

He stepped out of his temporary shelter and into the press of hurried crowds. As he did, he caught a glimpse of black uniforms with silver detailing in the corner of his vision. He looked again. *Wardens.* He turned his face away and prayed they hadn't spotted him. Ducking and making his way down the street, he kept to the densest groups when possible. Using that technique, he was able to get past yet another canal bridge and that much closer to the duke's estate. Unfortunately, he spied yet another cluster of Wardens. He eased into a corner between two shops for cover. Panic spurred his heart, but then he reminded himself of the time. It wasn't unusual for the Brotherhood to make such a showing at curfew. The display of power reminded the common people that curfew compliance was of the utmost importance.

Clock towers and church bells began to ring out warnings across the city, signaling the start of curfew. The streets emptied at once. There were a few stragglers like himself. However, in the more affluent northwest sector, most were citizens holding permits and licenses, and enforcement was more lax. Counting on this as he had so many times before, he assumed an attitude of confidence. Still, the final part of the journey was made via back alleys when possible as well as the back of a coach that fortuitously lacked the customary footman. He hopped down upon arriving at Regent's Street, thankful of the coachman's inattention. The duke's estate was now only a few hundred feet distant.

He'd gotten as far as the corner of His Grace's property when the shrill notes of a Warden Unit's whistle sent a bolt of ice down his spine, and he shuddered. *One long. Three short. One long.* Having served in a Warden Unit, he knew that pattern. It signaled the start of a hunt. Some poor bastard was about to be torn apart by the Brotherhood's war dogs. He suppressed a shudder.

I must get off the street now.

Turning left, he took the servant's access road that ran along the southern edge of the property. As he did so, he searched for a specific spot along the broken glass–topped rock wall in the gathering darkness. It was the one area he knew to be free of glass. He'd created the access himself when he'd first thought to run away. That had been before the Academy, not long after his first visit to the twisted healer. He hoped against hope that no one had discovered it and replaced the shards or filled the indentations in the wall itself. It took him a few tense moments to find the familiar hand- and toeholds. Wet from the rain, the stones were slick, and his injured arm ached as it accepted his weight. He felt a warm trickle down his right arm. Still, he managed the climb up with only a small amount of trouble. He slipped down the other side, landing in a patch of soft, damp clover. Relief ran cool in his veins, and he leaned back against the stone to once again catch his breath.

Ahead, the duke's estates stretched out for two hundred acres—a vast display of wealth within the city's confines. A thick forest populated the grounds, which hadn't been pruned into ornate gardens by slaves. Echoes of the Warden Unit's whistles were blunted by the thick stone at his back. Having explored the area thoroughly as a child, Blackthorne set out among the trees with confidence. He headed for the main road with the intent of locating one of the gardener's tool sheds. It would have the benefit of being dry. Better yet, he knew of a specific building where hay was stored in a loft for the strawberry field. The plan was to keep to the edge of the road just in case. It was a risk, but it would shorten his journey. He'd allowed himself brief regrets for the unfortunate soul who had garnered the Warden Unit's attention when he was brought up short by the clang of the chains at the front gate.

He slipped behind the trunk of a nearby tree, his heart already galloping.

It's not the Warden Unit. It's only the duke returning from a visit or an errand. It's not—

A long howl cut short hope.

They're here for me. They've been hunting me all along. He swallowed. *How did they find me?* Gazing down at his throbbing arm, he spied the one thing that he'd been ignoring since the incident at the gate. He'd bled through the bandage. A new wave of panic slammed him. In reflex, familiar words drifted to the surface of his mind. He grabbed them like a drowning man, and they slowed the beat of his heart like a prayer.

Discard all that ties one to life. Thus, no cowardice can interfere in the crucial moment, and there will be no hesitation in the instant between life and death.

The ideal Retainer lives as if already dead. They are the master's sword and nothing more.

Please don't let it be the dogs. The thought burned his cheeks. His shame lasted a few heartbeats before he forced it down and away and the familiar safety of deadened emotions returned. *Live as if already dead.*

The numbness didn't last. *I have a daughter.* And suddenly, everything he'd once believed rang hollow. He finally understood that none of it fit the person he now was. A sense of wild panic overwhelmed him. Unsure of what to do, he recalled something he'd overheard Colonel Hännenen say to one of the new recruits. Blackthorne wrapped a fist around the terror and transformed it into cold rage. *Anger, at least, is more useful than fear.*

He concentrated on strict control and silence. A tingling sensation sprang up all along his skin, and his stomach clenched and twisted. For the first time, he allowed himself the question that he'd been trying hard not to ask. *What if I am like Reini?*

If so, I can use it to my advantage. I may yet have a chance. I know their tricks, but they do not know mine. I will be who I am now, not what I was. Maybe that will be enough.

With that, he focused on moving quietly through the trees. He found his earlier trail and retraced his steps. It wouldn't fool them for long, but it would buy him time. When that was done, he knelt in the darkness and waited. He needed to know how many enemies he was up against.

Use whatever it is you have. In desperation, he paused and listened. Unsureness sent a shudder of fear through his heart. He'd hidden from who and what he was for so long that he wasn't confident he could call upon his magic, if indeed it was magic after all. And then the knowledge came to him as it always had.

One Unit. Made of eight Wardens. Two dogs.

He breathed out his relief.

They haven't released the dogs. Perhaps they won't?

I've a chance. No matter how small that chance was, he was glad to have it. *For Lydia's sake. I'm all she has.* As a former Warden, he knew too well the fate of orphan girls left on the Regnum's streets—particularly kainen. Even though her mother had been human, it was highly possible that Lydia had inherited certain telltale traits from her father.

He held his breath as the Warden Unit drew near. One of the Wardens murmured to one of the others. He couldn't make out the words, but the tone was at once familiar.

Waiting for the Warden Unit's steps to fade before Blackthorne slipped back into the woods, he loosened the oiled leather strap on his knife. Then he started off in the direction the Wardens had gone.

His only chance of survival would be to separate them from one another and attack each individually. *Leave the kennelmaster for last.* He hoped there were only eight. The usual number for a Hunt was four: a commander, lead tracker, and two on each flank, but the actions of the lead suggested a training session. If so, then there was a chance they wouldn't release the dogs, and the Hunt tagging him might consist mainly of cadets. If he was lucky, he might elude them altogether. He didn't want to consider what would happen if he wasn't.

Catching up to the lead Wardens, he found the pair puzzling over the last of the false trail. The younger was a third-year, by the insignia on his greatcoat—no more than seventeen or eighteen years old.

It had been nearly two years since Blackthorne had last hunted. However, that didn't seem to matter. It was as if the proper actions had been permanently fixed in his bones along with whatever it'd been that the twisted healer had put there. He felt a strictly controlled part of him thrill at the prospect of a kill, and for a moment, his thoughts drifted to the nightmares.

Not now. Think about it later.

Using a pine tree for cover, he gradually eased into position. When finally ready, he whistled the signal indicating the target was approaching. He watched the two Wardens split apart as he knew they would, one on each side of the false trail. His stomach did another lazy roll as he moved without a sound. Finding his first target waiting behind another tree, he slipped behind the instructor and struck. His hand clamped over the man's mouth. Then he rapidly forced the head back at an angle. The knife pierced the neck just below the Warden's ear. A gout of blood pulsed out of the wound. Blackthorne turned away and eased the dead man to the ground.

He exchanged coats with the body before it had finished twitching.

As he buttoned the uniform coat, he carefully watched the woods around him. He found it troubling that there had been no response after his first whistle. The commander couldn't be far, and neither could those flanking. Without that signal, there was no indication of where they were. However, until he resolved the immediate threat, he couldn't risk waiting and listening for them. The cadet would expect to see his instructor. *Get it over with.*

Blackthorne whistled the all clear from the former instructor's location. With that, the cadet stepped into view. Blackthorne waited to a count of fifteen. When no other Wardens emerged, he secreted the knife in his sleeve and pulled up the bloody collar of the stolen greatcoat to mask his face. He strode from his hiding place as though nothing were wrong.

The cadet smiled. "While I was standing in the tree line, I think I spotted more prints, sir. Do you think he doubled back?"

Blackthorne jabbed the cadet in the Adam's apple with an elbow. Then he knocked the boy to the ground, cutting his throat before he could call out. Dragging the body into the trees, he screened it from the path by placing it behind a fallen trunk. The young cadet's head rolled to the side, and a blood-soaked church medal slipped over his collar. The third-year's innocent brown eyes were open, staring out in surprise.

Only the fit survive. He swallowed a surge of self-disgust. *You don't believe that. You never did.* He focused on confusing the tracks in the drying mud.

Distant thunder rolled through the city. The wind shoved the tops of the trees around in noisy swirls. The clatter of the leaves made him think of surf crashing into the beach. He checked the sky. The lumpy clouds were an angry gunmetal green. He recalled that Dylan Kask had been a Waterborne weathermaster.

Magic?

Does it matter?

He returned his attention to the task at hand. The blood on the ground would be obvious, particularly to the dogs, but at least he could make it difficult for them to deduct what happened. When he was done, he leaned against a tree and shut his eyes.

All was quiet. The knowledge of where the others were came to him in a strong twinge of nausea. He spat and then moved east of his current position. He found the alpha flank exactly where he expected it to be. The cadet had his back to the open while searching the mud. The second instructor was twenty-five yards away, his view temporarily blocked by a large bush.

Blackthorne didn't hesitate. He attacked, digging his fingers into the cadet's neck, then crushing and twisting the larynx. Once again, he concealed the fresh corpse in silence and melted into the trees.

"Cadet Fortis, report." The order came from Blackthorne's left.

Damn it. He'd hoped to have more time to get into position.

When no reply came, a warning pierced the woods. It was followed by a rapid muster-check, and Blackthorne answered in the stead of one of the missing. He glanced down at the damp ground. The hash marks cut into the heel of his boot left clear prints exactly as intended. His gaze traveled to the bottoms of the dead cadet's boots.

Two chevrons.

His heart stopped. *They've changed symbols.*

"You've performed excellently, but haven't you forgotten something?"

Blackthorne drew his saber and whirled to meet the speaker. As he did, he felt a hard blow on the outside of his thigh. He staggered to keep his footing.

Six Wardens stepped from the trees. All had weapons at the ready.

One sighted a crossbow on him while a second reloaded. He recognized the Captain at once, and his heart dropped into his stomach.

Caius had changed little since Blackthorne had last seen him. His hair was longer, and the Captain's tabs on his collar were new.

I have to kill him. Talus would. Blackthorne swallowed. *I'm not Talus.* In a blink, all hope vanished. Gazing down at his leg, he spied the crossbow bolt buried in his thigh up to the black fletching. The pain flooded in.

"Never could convince you of the merits of archery," Caius said, and took a few hesitant steps forward. "You look terrible," he whispered. There was an expression of genuine concern on his face.

Why doesn't he get on with it? Blackthorne thought.

Two older Wardens moved to flank Caius. One was tall and lean with mismatched eyes and a thin scar running down his cheek. The other was shorter. Stockier. *Thaddeus and Martin.* Blackthorne couldn't suppress a shudder. He checked his right. It was clear. *I can run.*

"You wouldn't get far." Caius's manner became official, and his voice louder. "Care to guess what the bolt was coated with?" He waited for the answer.

When none came, Caius whispered, "You always did have trouble with toxin studies, Severus."

I am not Severus. Not anymore. Blackthorne felt everything around him make a sickening shift. *Poisoned.* He assumed he had about a minute of consciousness remaining and desperately tried to think of some means of taking advantage of it. However, his perceptions had already begun to slow, and his thoughts were sluggish. A jarring impact to his knees awakened an explosion of pain from the wound in his thigh. He bit back a scream. Mud coated the side of his face. He rolled onto his back and blinked. When he next opened his eyes, a black sky laced with branches whirled above.

Lightning flashed. For an instant, every color was brilliant and full of life. It formed a beautiful backdrop for Caius's blurred, worried face. Blackthorne saw the shine of a silver-laced blade in Caius's hand.

At least it won't be the dogs. In spite of his training, Blackthorne had thought he'd be afraid, but he wasn't. He was glad of the time he'd been able to buy for the others. They would've sailed from the harbor by now. It saddened him that he'd be leaving Lydia without a mother or a father. He prayed to a god he didn't believe in that Mallory McDermott would get her to the Hold safe. At least she had that chance. He wouldn't be leaving anyone else behind who would grieve him. He made what peace he could with that knowledge and lifted his chin, welcoming the blade.

Die well, Severus.

Caius stooped closer. His face grew more conflicted. He glanced to his side and then whispered, "I have my orders. I can't go against them."

Blackthorne wanted to tell Caius he understood, but what came out of his mouth was, "See to your back."

He saw Caius flinch, and the last thing Blackthorne felt was the cold edge of a silver knife under his ear.

⊰ CAIUS ⊱

"How long will the director be away?" Caius asked.

It was the fifth time in the span of two days that he had questioned the officer posted outside the director's gate. In each instance, Lieutenant Aureus had given Caius a bored look and a vague answer—the most recent of which had been punctuated with an impatient frown.

"The director is currently in Archiron," Lieutenant Aureus said in a firm voice, this time offering more.

"I understand," Caius said. "And when is he due to return?"

Lieutenant Aureus hesitated.

Caius gave him a determined look. *You know damned well I'll be here every day until I get an answer.*

He whispered, "Late next week. I'll leave a message that you wish to see him."

Was that so difficult? "Thank you," Caius said. "Now, if you would please add that it is in regards to Inspector Aureus Severus, I would be grateful."

At the mention of Severus's name, the lieutenant's expression became more guarded. Caius could've sworn the man was extremely nervous, even fearful.

What has he heard? Caius considered asking but knew he'd get nothing.

The lieutenant bowed. "The director will be informed, Captain Fortis." There was less indifference in the lieutenant's tone.

Caius nodded his thanks and left. There was nothing to do but return to the infirmary and wait for Severus to wake. *And perhaps when he does, he will tell me what in the hells is going on.*

When he'd been given his orders, he'd been told that Severus had been spying on a group of smugglers under the guise of being one of them. Apparently, the group had expanded beyond the illegal sale of nonhumans to Tahmer or Massilia. They were indulging in treason. Caius's orders had been to track and capture Severus so that Severus could report to the director without arousing suspicion. In order to maintain appearances, Caius was to act as though the capture were legitimate.

It had been a shock to see Severus so ragged, no matter how much it fit the director's story. Still, he was determined to go through with the action. It wasn't until Severus had spoken that Caius had been certain something was wrong.

See to your back. With that, the first seeds of doubt had been planted. However, when the bodies of the cadets had been discovered, his hunch had been confirmed. He'd known Severus from the time they were both boys. He wouldn't kill without need. He had to have honestly felt he was in danger. Caius wished he'd known more. He wished he'd been able to speak to Severus alone. *But with Martin and Thaddeus tagging my heels, there wasn't a damn thing I could have done about it, anyway.*

And that was another thing that bothered him. Why had the director sent his men? Caius was known to be Severus's friend. Surely, couldn't he be trusted to get Severus home safe?

Severus had lived among the smugglers for more than a year. Have the nonhumans corrupted his mind with magic? Was that why he killed the cadets? There were so many questions.

He hurried across the frozen practice grounds to the infirmary. He'd needed the walk. He hadn't slept in his own bed since returning from the field. Aware of Severus's feelings regarding surgeons, Caius had been sleeping in a nearby chair—not the most comfortable arrangement. However, he'd not been able to convince the attendant to bring a folding bed.

Two days since the arrest. And Severus hadn't opened his eyes once.

He's thinner than he was. Did I miscalculate the dose? Or is the physician deliberately keeping him unconscious? Caius didn't like where that thought led.

He nodded to the cadet stationed at the reception desk and headed to the private room where Severus slept.

"Sir?"

Caius halted. "Yes?"

"Your friend has a visitor," the attendant said. "His brother. Perhaps you should allow them a moment...."

Severus doesn't have a brother, Caius thought. He bolted down the hallway and threw open the door to Severus's room. As he did so, he tripped over the gore-strewn remains of a junior surgeon in a huddled mess on the floor. The surgeon's face was an eyeless mask of blood and meat. *Exactly like the rogue hunter's kills.*

A bleeding bowl had been upturned on the floor. Its contents pooled on the scrubbed wooden floor. The wall above Severus's bed was streaked with crimson. A balding, slope-shouldered man stooped over the bed.

"What are you doing?" Caius asked.

The man turned. He was holding a bloodstained Warden's knife. He smiled. There was something very wrong with his eyes.

He's malorum.

Caius launched himself at the creature. They both crashed to the floor. Caius landed on top. Scrabbling for the malorum's wrist, he twisted, but his opponent was strong. The malorum bucked him off, turning his hips. Caius slammed down painfully on his elbow and then his side. He had just long enough to think to continue rolling before the knife arced past his face. The malorum howled and stabbed again. Caius felt the blade catch his clothes as he turned his body away from the blow. While his attacker was over-extended, he rammed his head into the creature's ear with all his might. The malorum pitched sideways. Caius freed his own knife at last and plunged it into the creature's side. Its mouth fell open. It blinked and a secondary membrane nictated over surprised eyes. A chill oozed through Caius's body.

Slashing with his Warden's knife, he cut the creature's throat before it could recover and attack again. Another gout of crimson painted the blood-soaked floor. He staggered to his feet, intending to check on his friend. Above Severus's bed was a message daubed in gore. Like the message he'd found months before, each letter R was reversed.

It read: *I'm the heir. You're the spare.*

"Got you, you bastard—in spite of your friends," Caius said, wiping his face with the back of his forearm. "I got you." *Why would the attendant think that thing was Severus's brother? ?*

Panicked footsteps echoed down the hallway outside as he thought to search the malorum's greatcoat pocket, retrieving the identification papers. He stuffed them inside his coat. Then he went to Severus's side. He appeared to be alive and unharmed. One arm protruded from under the covers; the bloodletting incision in his arm oozed.

Two surgeons and three Wardens burst into the room.

"What is the meaning of this?" a surgeon asked. "What did you do?"

"I prevented that thing from murdering my friend," Caius said. "Why didn't anyone stop it from entering in the first place?"

One of the older Wardens pulled the surgeon into a corner. The others checked the bodies and began the process of taking them away. Caius felt more than saw a presence at his elbow.

"What are you doing here?"

Turning to the speaker, Caius saw it was Aureus Thaddeus. "I came to see Severus."

"Report."

"The surgeon was dead when I got here. It attacked Severus; therefore, I killed it," Caius said.

Thaddeus's face remained blank while he listened. One of the surgeons bandaged Severus's elbow while surgeon's assistants began cleaning the room.

"Why would that thing come here? Why would it tell the attendant he was Severus's brother?" Caius asked.   .

"I'm sure I don't know. But you've had very little sleep, and you've just been through a shock," Thaddeus said. "Go home. Get cleaned up and have a decent meal. We'll take over from here."

"But Severus—"

"Will be fine. Thanks to you," Thaddeus said. "I must ask you to leave now."

"We will take care of him," Aureus Martin said.

Caius hesitated. *That's what I'm afraid of.* He nodded and reluctantly stepped back.

Two surgeon's assistants entered carrying a third wooden stretcher. This time they went to Severus's bed.

Caius blocked their way. "Where are you taking him?"

"We have orders to take him to the Reclamation Hospital, sir."

"But he's obviously still ill . . ."

Aureus Martin said, "Get out of the way, Fortis."

"Why? What has he done, sir?" Caius asked.

"It's for his protection. You saw what happened," Aureus Martin said. "Now go."

Helpless, Caius watched them bundle Severus up and then exited the room. He went to the cadet at the check-in desk. The cadet glanced up from a text secreted in the center drawer before pushing it closed. When Caius made no move to reprimand him, the cadet appeared to relax.

"Who is the surgeon in charge of treating Aureus Severus?" Caius asked.

"Let me see, sir." The cadet checked a record book. "It says Inspector Surgeon Aureus Augustan, Managing Surgeon, Research Group Seven."

A research surgeon and another member of Gens Aureus? "Thank you." Caius left, intent on finding Augustan. But first, he stopped to check the papers he'd stolen off the malorum. The name listed on the record was Munitoris Arion. *He was the noble whose records Captain Drake was sent to inspect—the one that I've been unable to interview.* He crammed the documents back into his coat before anyone could see them.

I'm not meant to know about Arion.

First, do what you can to help Severus. Then worry about the rest. The surgeon was the only one who could stop the transfer. He got halfway across the parade ground before he was brought up short by a thought: *What if Augustan already knows? What if this is being done on his orders? What do I do then?*

He continued, arriving at the Hall of Records before he was aware of where he was going. *There's no harm in looking up Inspector Surgeon Aureus Augustan. There might be something in the unrestricted records.*

Unless the record has been altered. Caius attempted to not think the worst as he entered the building. Then he did something he had never done before—he didn't sign in. Instead, he bribed the cadet at the desk and the sentry at the door. He reached the stairwell with the sinking feeling that he had crossed a line he'd never imagined he'd cross. After passing the Warden stationed on the second floor, he was ten sterling poorer, leaving him with two coins and less than a hundred in paper notes with which to breach the records of a brother Warden.

He went to the record cabinets along the far wall, intending to get through the least intimidating aspect of the problem. He couldn't find anything on Munitoris Arion. That was not surprising. What was interesting was the surgeon Aureus Augustan. Caius discovered his name listed in the scientific journals. Augustan was widely published, and it took several minutes to gather the volumes. Most of the articles were twenty years old and related to plant hybrids, the recording of unusual leaf shapes and flower colors. Some progressed to other topics like smallpox immunity, but almost all pertained to the reproductive systems of plants.

What on earth could a botanist want with Severus?

When he tired of reading essays arguing plant propagation

and trait inheritance, Caius approached the Warden Librarian's desk. He recognized the librarian's curly brown hair and crooked nose with a jolt. He was both relieved and embarrassed, knowing what he would have to do next. "I see congratulations are in order, Tolerans Cornelius."

Cornelius smiled and nodded. "Successfully completed the exams three weeks ago. Knowing the director didn't hurt." He paused, seeming to catch Caius's serious mood, and changed to a more professional tone. "What may I help you with?"

"I'm not certain you would wish to be involved."

Cornelius leaned closer and peered at Caius. "Is it that serious?"

Caius nodded.

"For you?" Cornelius whispered, and then shrugged. "Ask."

Hesitating, Caius finally sighed and reached for the contents of his pocket.

Cornelius put a hand on the desk to stop him. "Don't."

Caius slumped in defeat. *Cornelius doesn't take risks.*

"There's no need for you to pay," Cornelius whispered.

Caius was surprised to find a sympathetic expression on Cornelius's face.

"My friend, whatever you seek must be very important if you, of all people, are willing to attempt a bribe," Cornelius whispered.

"I need what you have on Munitoris Arion and . . . Aureus Severus."

Cornelius pursed his lips in a silent whistle. "The last is an extreme request."

"I told you that you wouldn't wish to be involved."

Holding up a hand, Cornelius said, "Don't despair yet. Let me think."

Caius looked away, checking the room. Two other Wardens were doing research. Both appeared engrossed in their work.

Cornelius cleared his throat. "Bring me a record drawer. It doesn't matter which."

Caius did as Cornelius requested. When he returned, the librarian was gone. Caius set the record drawer on the desk and waited. The room was quiet except for the tiny rustling sounds of cards being flipped, the scratch of a pencil or the occasional chair being shifted. Every noise, no matter how small, echoed throughout the room. He breathed in the familiar scents of the library. Once, those smells would've meant comfort to him, but now they gave him a far different feeling.

What am I doing?

A quarter of an hour passed before Cornelius returned. His footsteps echoed through the library like the tick of a clock. He turned the file drawer around, shuffled through the record cards with one hand, paused, and then casually inserted several new ones amongst the old.

Bent over the file drawers, Cornelius whispered, "Both sets of files are closed. This was all I could obtain without risking more than my stripes. Have them back to me within a quarter of an hour."

"Thank you," Caius said. "I'm in your debt."

He carried the file drawer containing the new cards to an isolated table and sat down. The information printed on the first two cards consisted of Severus's school records and wasn't of much interest. It wasn't until he reached the fifth card that he found something significant. *Reference Project Testudo. Inspector Surgeon Aureus Augustan, Managing Surgeon, Research Group Seven. All other records Director's Eyes Only.*

He sat up straighter in the chair and flipped backward through the cards to the first set.

Munitoris Arion. Also Aureus Arion, Project Testudo. Inspector Surgeon Aureus Augustan . . . All other records Director's Eyes Only.

Caius felt his heart drop into his stomach. *Maybe Severus had a brother after all.*

They can't have shared the same mother, but if they are half-brothers, that would mean . . . Duke Aureus fathered a child on a malorum? That's revolting.

Wait. Aureus is a vocal supporter of racial purity. He'd never—

Caius's eyes burned, he was tired, and his neck ached. He set down his graphite holder and pinched the bridge of his nose. When he opened his eyes, he glanced at one of Augustan's books. It was open. *Propagation. Hybrids. Trait inheritance. Purity of strain.*

Project Testudo.

Surgeon Aureus Augustan is a research surgeon.

The room grew cold as Caius felt the blood drain from his face. *What have they done to Severus?*

He heard someone cough and glanced to the librarian station. Cornelius gave him a meaningful look. Quickly jotting down the information from the card, Caius then returned the drawer to Cornelius.

"Did you get what you needed?" Cornelius asked.

"I think so," Caius said. "Would you happen to have access to anything pertaining to a Project Testudo?"

Cornelius shook his head. "I pulled all the related files I could. Duke Aureus's records were sealed as well."

"Thank you, Cornelius." *Director's Eyes Only.* Caius cleared his throat. "You won't—"

"Tell anyone about this? And get myself busted down to cadet after all the work I've done?" Cornelius whispered. He moved the file drawer closer, removed the cards, and then concealed them in a pocket.

"Thank you again," Caius said.

Cornelius said, "You're welcome."

Caius checked the duke's nonrestricted records, and after finding nothing significant, he headed for home, his mind packed with information that made no sense. *If Severus is part of a scientific experiment, why send him to live among kainen? What do malorum have to do with any of this?*

We lived in the same dorm room for ten years. He handles silver. Daylight does not harm him—

Hybrids. Trait inheritance.

Why create Arion, a malorum who passes for human?

The new theory is that malorum are evolving. Changing.

When he arrived at his new apartments, he exchanged a wave with the Warden watching from his station across the street. He was becoming used to seeing the director's spies. Since they made no attempts to hide, Caius assumed they were only being used as a reminder. Now that Arion was dead, Caius wondered if the guards would increase or simply vanish.

Severus is in the Hospital now. There's nothing I can do to help him.

Am I sure I want to?

See to your back.

Perhaps he was trying to warn me away. Severus was a good friend. A brother. In the years they had trained together, they had saved one another's lives. If Severus wasn't human, he deserved a chance to explain. *Is it actually important to me that he's human?*

Severus acted human. He was honorable. Truthful. Honest. Loyal. Intelligent. All the things malorum weren't, and all the things some humans couldn't aspire to.

Malorum are evolving. Changing.

Locking the door to his apartments behind him, Caius went to bed and then spent an hour studying the crown molding before finally falling into an uneasy asleep.

❧ DYLAN ❧

ONE

Clár Oibre Rúnda, two-masted Sloop-of-War,
Clan Kask, Waterborne Nations
Ninety Miles off the Ghost Crescent
Aegrerian Ocean

3 June, 1785

Waking alone before his watch, Dylan knelt and then settled his hipbones onto his ankles for his morning prayers. He, Suvi, and Dar had been rotating the four-hour watches since leaving Acrasia. Having served in the Eledorean Royal Navy long before becoming queen, Suvi was eager to take a turn at watch. Unfortunately, the three of them were the only experienced sailors on board. The others took turns as well, but Dylan didn't trust them at the helm. Dar had taken the middle watch, starting at midnight, which meant that Dylan was to serve the morning watch starting at four, and Suvi would take over at eight when he rang eight bells.

The cabin Dylan shared with Dar was cast in shadows from

the lone lantern. The fishy scent of burning whale oil joined the other homey ship smells. To his right, two of the little brown lizards peered down at him with their bright blue eyes from over the edge of the hammock. There were now seven of them living in the cabin. For the most part, they stayed near Dar whenever possible—unless he was outside their quarters. Then they tended to linger on or around Dar's sea chest. They didn't seem to care for the messenger cages. The tiny lizards made no sound, and for the most part, they kept to themselves, but they still took some getting used to. An intelligence lurked behind their azure gaze. They got into everything, much to Dylan's dismay, but Dar said they were merely curious and intended no harm.

Praying isn't easy with seven sets of beady eyes looking on, Dylan thought. They didn't seem to understand the need for privacy. It didn't seem to bother Dar as much as it did him. Dylan didn't enjoy having an audience to their lovemaking. Something would have to be done, and soon.

Two more lizards peeked over the hammock's edge. There was now a row of blue eyes staring at him.

Dylan shifted his weight, closed his eyes, and tried to ignore them. He focused on the feel of Dar's wool rug beneath him. It made a thick and comfortable padding, even if it was a little scratchy. Outside, gentle swells rocked the ship. The wind seemed to be steady and blowing in a useful direction without need of his magical assistance. His stomach gave out a rumble. Breakfast wouldn't be ready for another five hours, if past history was anything to go by. Nels and Viktor both tended to sleep late, and it was their turn to take over in the galley. The tea water wouldn't be heating, not unless Suvi was up—a distinct possibility these days.

Dylan breathed deeply and concentrated on imagining his

breath traveling up and down his spine. He did this twenty times, up and down, and then he felt ready to begin.

The first law of magic is thus: Energy does not vanish. It transforms. All are born of water. All shall return to—

"This is a good ship. She's sound. Well built," Aegrir said. "She's small, but she is also fast and nimble on the water. I like her name, too. *Clár Oibre Rúnda*. Clever. A good Ocealandic name."

He'd known it was Her before he'd opened his eyes. Her voice had a resonance that was unmistakable. "Great One?"

Aegrir was wearing the same guise as he'd seen in the Hold—a heavyset, middle-aged woman. Her long, dark brown spirit knots were streaked with grey. As before, the prayer tokens tucked into her braids were shaped like tiny ships. He tried not to notice that they numbered fewer than before. Her loose silk shirt was now blue and black with flecks of yellow, and her sailor's breeches were navy. As before, her feet were bare.

The little lizards hopped down from their perch and scurried to her outstretched hand. She smiled. "I see our friends are happy and thriving. You two have taken good care of them."

"Thank you," Dylan said.

"We don't have much time," she said. "You're getting close to Ghost Crescent."

He nodded and waited.

"Drop anchor in Dragonsjaw Cove," she said. As she spoke, she began to pet one of the lizards. To Dylan's surprise, it let out a soft hum. "From there, follow the waterfall to its source. Your predecessor was heading in that direction when I lost contact with her. I suspect the rift is somewhere along the river's length.

"One more thing," she said, and placed a small token carved from jet in the shape of a sea horse on the rug next to him. "Wear this for me."

He gazed down upon the little carving and swallowed. The sea horse had several meanings among the Waterborne. The main ones were good luck, protection, and steadfastness. However, the oldest stories told how the sea horse protected the souls of those who died at sea as they passed through the abyss. "Thank you, Great One. I am honored by your gift."

"And this is for your Darius," she said, setting a second sea horse on the rug. "I can't very well send you two into danger without a blessing." She gave him a genuinely warm smile.

"Thank you," Dylan said. "Thank you very much."

"Be careful, little lordling," she said. She began to grow less substantial. "It would grieve me to lose you so soon." And then she vanished.

Above, someone rang eight bells. The lizards scurried off to new hiding places.

Time for morning watch, he thought, picking up both amulets. He would give Dar his at the watch change. Other than a bright red bead that he'd given to Dar when they'd committed to one another, Dar hadn't earned any tokens. This, a gift from the goddess Aegrir, would be Dar's first. Dylan felt the corners of his mouth turn up. It was a great honor indeed.

TWO

Dylan dropped anchor in Dragonsjaw Cove five hours later and hoped the name was merely an allusion to its shape on the nautical charts and not something more literal. It appeared to be safe. *So far.* Gazing out past the bowsprit, he decided Ghost Crescent was among the most beautiful islands he'd ever seen. The sky was cerulean, and the ocean around it practically glowed bright turquoise— that is, until it hit the shallows, where the white sand washed out aquamarine to a pale blue. The island itself was hilly, even mountainous, and painted in shades of green, indicating thriving plant life. The winds blowing across the hills were scented with the perfume of fresh jasmine and honeysuckle vine. A majestic waterfall plunged from the heights of a nearby cliff onto the rocks below. The ocean was clear enough to reveal every creature, rock, and plant on the ocean floor.

That was the disturbing part.

Without the clear water, he'd have missed the wreckage off *Clár*'s port side. Inspecting the remains with his glass, he judged that it'd been a much smaller sloop. He attempted to make out details that might reveal the ship's name or clan, and failed. Aegrir had sent someone else, all right. And he had a hunch that that someone's ship was now at the bottom of the Dragonsjaw.

Dylan turned his glass to the white beach. It wasn't long before he spied the remains of a rowboat littering the otherwise spotless sand. It wasn't clear what sort of creature had destroyed it, but based on the bite marks, whatever it was had to have been huge. In spite of this, there was no sign of any tracks.

It must have been some time ago. He searched the beach for any other sign of life and found none. It didn't make him feel any better.

Did the creature attack while the lone Waterborne Leaudancer was in the boat? Or did it seek out vengeance later?

If the first Leaudancer couldn't even make land without being attacked, what was the point in sending replacements? *Has Aegrir sent us on a suicide quest?* He lowered the glass and stared into the water. Jet the dog trotted across the boards, her nails clicking. She leaned her black body against his left leg. Then she sniffed the air, pointed her nose at the island, and let out a low, rumbling growl. He reached down and gave her a soothing pat. She looked up and softly whined.

We're here, Lady Aegrir, Dylan prayed.

Having left the helm, Dar stepped to his right side and slipped an arm around him. Dar's spirit knots had grown longer since the start of the voyage, Dylan noted with some relief. They now brushed his lover's earlobes. Dar had been taking his religious training more seriously of late. He still didn't rank much higher than an acolyte on his own, but he was studying and progressing. The two of them had taken the time during the morning watch to sew the sea horse tokens into one another's hair.

Maybe it will be enough, Dylan thought. *Maybe that, combined with his training and his ties to me and mine, will be strong enough to protect him.* He couldn't have told Aegrir how grateful he was for the addition of Dar's gift, but he supposed she already knew.

"This place makes my skin creep," Dar said, moving away and pulling his hair into a stubby ponytail high up on the back of his head. He tied it with a leather cord.

Dylan thought the style accentuated his lover's cheekbones nicely.

He took Dar's hand and squeezed it gently in an attempt to be reassuring. "Why is that?" He didn't like Ghost Crescent either. The island's beauty made its intrinsic wrongness even more difficult to reconcile.

"See how clear the water is?" Dar asked, and pointed at the shoals.

Dylan nodded.

"There's nothing living in that water, not within three hundred feet of shore," Dar said. "What does it mean?"

It means we've a chance of reaching the shore without sinking, at least. Dylan hesitated, poised to ask another question.

"I'm not staying behind," Dar said. "Don't you dare even ask."

"No one else other than Suvi can handle *Clár* alone," Dylan said without much conviction. "And Suvi *has* to go."

"No. That's my final answer. There. Argument ended," Dar said. "Shall we get the jolly boat in the water?"

"After breakfast. I suppose it can't be put off," Dylan said, glancing at the flawless sky. "We've only ten hours of daylight in which to find the rift and get back. I'll wake the others."

Dar frowned, raised an eyebrow, and then whispered, "So She didn't give you a more exact location? Just 'somewhere along the river'?"

Dylan shook his head.

"The gods never do make these things easy, do they?" Dar asked, treading dangerously close to blasphemy.

"I suspect She gave me all the information She had," Dylan said. "It's not as if She can risk exploring the matter Herself." Dar had been the one person to whom he'd told everything. Suvi only needed to know certain aspects of the matter.

Dar said, "All right, who stays with the ship? We'll have to leave someone behind. I don't trust this place. And neither should you."

"We'll leave Katrin in charge," Dylan said.

"She'll hate that," Dar said.

Dylan shrugged. "She is the least qualified to go."

At fifteen, she had yet to manifest her magical powers.

"You want to leave her here alone?" Dar asked.

"Unless you can convince one of the korvas to stay," Dylan said. "And I rather doubt that's going to happen. Not that it will do much good if we don't return. None of them know the first thing about sailing."

Dar paused. "I'll prepare a few messages. That way, Katrin can send for help if need be."

Katrin had shown herself to be a quick study, and she had been picking up the odd sailor's skill during the voyage, but they both knew she couldn't handle *Clár*—not alone, and certainly not during rough weather. While it was summer, there was no guarantee that the seas would remain calm.

"We'll break the bad news at breakfast," Dylan said. He lowered his voice. "Have you thought about how you'll transport our little friends?"

"Viktor is loaning me a ryggsack," Dar whispered. "They'll be safe there until it's time to release them."

"I suppose we should get below, then."

Nels and Viktor were already in the galley, preparing breakfast. Taking a deep breath as he passed, Dylan caught the scent of a mouthwatering combination of trout, fried potatoes, onions, bacon, biscuits, and coffee. They'd laid in a store of coffee beans in addition to the tea while they were in Novus Salernum. Nels had demanded it.

Suvi was already awake and mocking her brother for his limited cooking skills. Nels was explaining how he was accustomed to a campfire and not a stove when Dylan continued down the hallway to roust the others. He was sitting at the table, eating his breakfast with the entire crew, less than a quarter of an hour later. He waited until everyone was finished to break the news to Katrin.

"Why me?" Katrin asked, folding her arms across her chest.

"Someone must stay behind with Jet," Dylan said, feeding the dog a bite of bacon under the table. Jet's soft, sloppy tongue explored his fingers for every possible morsel. It tickled.

"You want me to stay here with the dog?" Katrin asked. "I'm not a baby."

Stuck, Dylan knew he couldn't voice his reasons without making Katrin feel worse. She'd been keeping to herself, and they'd all been allowing her the space she needed—such as there was on a little ship. She'd been sensitive lately, not that he blamed her. No one did. But he had a feeling that didn't matter.

"This is because of—of Blackthorne, isn't it?" Katrin asked, frowning at her empty plate. "It's my fault. He's probably dead. And it's *my* fault."

Sitting next to her, Ilta laid a hand on Katrin's arm. "You aren't to blame. Blackthorne knew—we all knew the risks."

Katrin said, "But if I hadn't tried to—to—save that dead orphan—"

"I didn't know malorum could do something like that," Nels said. "And that trick must have worked before, or the thing wouldn't have continued to employ it. Any one of us would've done the same."

Katrin stared. "But you never lived in Novus Salernum. I did. If I hadn't forgotten—"

"Then the two of you would've been stopped at the gate," Viktor Reini said. "And you wouldn't have been able to get away. And we would be short two people on this venture instead of one."

"Something else to consider . . . Blackthorne is also the only one of us who can possibly survive in Acrasia," Dylan said. "None of us knows the Brotherhood like him. He'll probably be waiting for us at the Hold. Great abyss, he's probably there now, wondering what's taking us so long to get back."

"Ultimately, someone must remain to guard the ship," Suvi said. "What's to keep a malorum from coming aboard while we're away? The swords in *Clár's* hold must make the return trip, Katrin. Do you understand how important that is?"

"Oh." Katrin blinked back what Dylan was certain were tears.

Suvi continued. "Trust me, what we're asking won't be easy. You'll be left here alone. We may not be able to get back before dark. If that happens, you'll be alone overnight."

Katrin's expression changed from disappointment to fearful resolve.

"Don't worry," Dar said. "You'll have Jet with you. She's Waterborne. She senses magic, and she knows what a soulbane smells like. She'll protect you and keep watch when you can't." He spoke to Jet. "Won't you, girl?"

Jet barked as if in agreement. Dar being Dar, Dylan was fairly certain it was.

Dar slid off the bench and called Jet over to a corner. While everyone watched, he spent a few moments with his forehead resting against Jet's black head. Then he gave her a hug and a few scritches behind her short, floppy ears just where she liked it most. "You're a very good, very brave dog, Jet. I love you."

Jet licked him in the face, and Dar laughed. He wiped the slobber from his cheek and got to his feet. "Katrin, come with me. I need to show you how to take care of the birds while I'm away. And how to send one for help if need be. Will that make you feel better?"

"That would be great," Katrin said.

Dar headed for their cabin with Katrin following behind. "The gull will know to come to me. The frigatebird is trained to find the nearest Waterborne ship. And the last, the albatross, will fly to the Hold and Councilor Slate. Got that?"

"Which one is which?" Katrin asked.

"I'll show you," Dar said.

Nels and Viktor got up, collected the dishes, and began cleaning the galley. Dylan decided to go up to the deck and give the island another look before he packed. Suvi decided to go with him.

She checked to make sure they were alone before she whispered, "Do you know where the rift is?"

"Not exactly. The only map of the island doesn't contain any details. And, well . . . I've never been here before," he said. Both statements were true. He'd checked the charts over and over before they'd arrived. Pointing, he continued. "But we should start at the top of that hill and follow the waterfall to its source. I understand the rift is somewhere along the way."

Suvi asked, "Do you know if it's salt water or freshwater?"

Dylan muttered a curse. "I hadn't thought to ask." In truth, he hadn't. He'd merely assumed that since Aegrir had known about Suvi and the others, she'd also taken into account the limitations of their powers. "I'm not sure anyone knows. No one has visited the island and lived in a very long time."

"I'll hope for freshwater," Suvi whispered.

I will too. Although I might not be as powerful, Dylan thought, *and I've a feeling I'll need as much power as I can muster.* Then he had another unsettling idea. "What about Nels?"

"What about him?" Suvi asked.

"He can't swim," Dylan said.

"He'll be fine," Suvi said. "He can dog-paddle."

"Have you told him the rift will be underwater?" Dylan asked.

Suvi asked, "And ruin the fun of watching him squirm? Not on your life."

"You're pure evil," Dylan said.

"Not really," Suvi said. "I know my brother. He's at his best under pressure. And this way, he won't have time to let his fear get the better of him."

At that moment, Nels emerged from below. "What are you two conspiring about?"

Assuming an innocent expression, Suvi said, "Nothing."

Nels gave her a look that said he didn't believe her for one moment.

"You want something," Suvi said. "What is it?"

Viktor and then Ilta came up the ladder next.

"If there are malorum on the island, I thought we should make use of the water steel blades when we go ashore," Nels said. "But only if you—"

Viktor threw his hands in the air. "Yes!"

"See to it that everyone is issued one," Suvi said. "Myself included."

"There's only one problem with that," Ilta said. "I don't know how to use a sword. And even if I did, using it would mean breaking my Healer's Oath."

Nels said, "I've already taken that into consideration." He held up one of two heavy leather pouches. "This, my love, is for you."

Ilta accepted it with two hands. "What is it?"

"Silver dust." Nels turned to Suvi. "No insult to your combat skills, but this is ... well ... just in case."

"And here I thought you'd spent all that time below being sick," Suvi said.

Grinning, Nels said, "Not even close."

Ilta elbowed him.

"Ow!" Nels rubbed his side. "You'd wound me before we leave?"

Suvi said, "What about Katrin?"

"She'll have silver musket balls—whatever we can't carry," Nels said. "She's an excellent shot."

Suvi said, "You think of everything."

"I try," Nels said.

Suvi got up on her toes and kissed him on the cheek.

They were underway by five bells. Rowing the jolly boat to shore with the help of Viktor, Jami, and Dar, Dylan couldn't avoid a sense of foreboding. He didn't have premonitions like Ilta. So he tried not to read anything into her expression as they neared the shore. As if that weren't enough, Nels and Viktor were quiet. That disturbed Dylan more. Over the winter, he had witnessed how the two of them reacted to danger in multiple instances. He'd never seen them be silent before.

Of course, that may be due to Nels being on a ship, Dylan thought.

Nels had one hand clamped so tight onto the gunwale that his knuckles were white.

At least he isn't sick, Dylan thought. Over the course of the voyage to Acrasia, Ilta had managed to cure Nels's seasickness. Of course, he still hadn't developed a taste for sailing, but Dylan supposed some people never did.

The bottom of the boat scraped sand as they reached the shore. Lowering himself into the waist-deep water, he was glad the cove was so clear. He didn't want to think about beaching the rowboat in murk. *Not on this island.*

After they had hauled the boat far enough from the tide, Dylan straightened as a small, brightly colored bird fluttered past. It landed on Dar's shoulder.

Dar turned his head. "Why, hello, little one. Aren't you friendly?" He encouraged the blue, green, and black bird to perch on his finger.

Dylan said, "That's a scallop parrot."

Gently petting it, Dar said, "It is. And you're a long way from home. What are you doing here?"

The bird rubbed its head on Dar's finger a few times and then resumed its place on his shoulder.

"You seem to have made a friend," Suvi said.

Dar shrugged. "If she's willing to stay, I don't mind. She could prove useful."

Dylan blinked. He looked closer at the bird. It was difficult to know the gender of a scallop parrot, but if Dar said the bird was a female, then she was—

The bird tilted her head and winked. Then she made impatient rocking movements as if to say *Hurry up*.

Dar laughed. "I guess that means we've another member of the party."

"Fair enough," Dylan said. That was when he noticed that everyone, including Nels, appeared to be waiting for orders—*his* orders. "Oh, no. Don't look at me." He pointed to Nels. "You've more experience at this sort of thing than I do. It's why I brought you here."

"And this is a Waterborne island," Nels said. "Your ship. Your venture. Your decision."

"And my decision is for the experienced soldier to take the lead," Dylan said. "You're familiar with tactics involving small bands fighting against larger numbers of enemies. I make it a point to know when to leave matters in expert hands. This is one of those times."

Nels frowned and looked away. He hefted the ryggsack on his back. "You do remember I lost the war, right?"

"And you forget that I've seen you fight malorum," Dylan said. "My decision stands. If at any point I disagree with you, I reserve the right to override your authority. This is a Waterborne island, after all."

"I'll accept," Nels said. "But I have one condition."

"And it is?" Dylan asked.

Nels glanced at Ilta, and Ilta nodded as if agreeing. "If the question concerns my sister's safety," he said, "I can't let you take responsibility."

Dylan shrugged. "We agreed to as much before Suvi set foot on board *Clár Oibre Rúnda*. Done."

Then Nels spoke to the others. "Viktor, you're at the front with me. Dylan, you're next. Annikki, you take the rear. Dar is in front of you. Suvi and Ilta are in the middle with Jami. Load your pistols now. With silver shot. We're not taking any chances. Are you all right with that, Dylan?"

Dylan nodded.

Pointing at the cliff, Nels traced a path through the trees and up the hillside. "The woods don't look too thick on either side of the hill. We'll try going up the west side first. The light will last longer. Viktor, did you bring the rope?"

"I did," Viktor said.

"Just in case, we'll run this rope from the front to the rear," Nels said. "I don't trust that incline, and I don't know the terrain. I'm tying it to my waist. Natalia will do the same. The rest of you, keep one hand on it if the ground becomes too rough. We don't want anyone falling, but we may be attacked. You may need more mobility. We're going in quiet. Natalia, Viktor, you know what that means. The rest of you, if you notice something, tug the rope. No shouting. Got that?"

Dylan nodded.

"Guns loaded? All right, Hasta help us," Nels said. "Let's go."

They picked their way up the incline. Under the trees, the ground was soft beneath the soles of Dylan's boots but for the occasional stone. The forest smelled of damp earth, moss, and moldering leaves. Sunlight filtered through the branches. Birds chirped, and small animals crawled in the underbrush. It was warm, and it wasn't long before he'd grown tired of the stinging gnats. The breeze died under the trees, and the angle made walking a chore. The push uphill grew tiring. He stumbled and caught himself with the rope.

Stopping, Nels looked back as if to check on him. Dylan got his footing again, and when Dylan nodded, Nels continued.

At long last, they reached the summit of the cliff. Nels indicated that they'd take a quick rest. Dylan wiped sweat from his face and sat. The others did the same. The trees bunched on either side of the river. The air was thick with mist. Water roared all around them as it rushed past in its race to the ledge. The wind was strong, shoving the trees. The gnats dissipated. Dylan felt sweat cool on his skin as he gazed back toward the ship. It seemed so small and far away. Seabirds called out to one another as they flew overhead, not that he could make out the sound over the water.

Nels untied the rope, gave it to Viktor, and motioned upstream. Dylan nodded as if in answer. With that, they continued inland, following the edge of the river as they went. Dar reached out and, grabbing his hand, held it for a few miles as they walked. Dylan could see he was spooked. The farther inland they ventured, the less lush the undergrowth appeared. Even the animals grew quieter.

They stopped to rest for a while after hiking for a couple of hours. It occurred to Dylan that he hadn't seen one seabird land since they'd left sight of the beach. They seemed to know to keep their distance. There were no animal footprints along the riverbank. He couldn't see any fish. No snake burrows. Nothing. That was very unusual. Worse, the air had acquired a flatness that he remembered experiencing only once before.

On Sunset, he thought. *When we found the soulbane.*

"We must be getting close," Nels whispered. He drank from a water canteen.

"You feel it too?" Dylan asked, keeping his voice low.

Nels nodded. "I don't like this place. It's too . . . dead."

"You liked it before?" Dylan asked.

"I didn't say that," Nels said. "The thing I don't understand is, the trees, the plants—"

"No new growth," Dylan said, and pointed. "See?"

He'd noticed it as they were walking up the hill. The undergrowth was lifeless. The whole island was slowly dying. The idea that such a thing was happening to such a beautiful place made him sad. He wondered what it must have been like before the soulbane had blighted it. *What will it be like closer to the rift?*

When Nels called an end to the rest, everyone got back to their feet. Dylan gave Dar a quick kiss.

"What's that for?" Dar asked.

"Luck," Dylan said.

"If that's the case," Dar said, "then I think a more enthusiastic kiss is in order."

Once again Dylan kissed his lover and attempted not to think of it as the last. *That's getting to be a habit*, he thought.

When Dar released him, Dylan stepped back. The little blue bird on Dar's shoulder made a happy noise.

They moved on for another couple of miles, and as they did, the progression of dying vegetation grew more and more pronounced until only the oldest of trees remained, and even they appeared to be sickly. Gradually, the ground began another incline, and ahead they could see another hill. It was at this point that Dylan began to notice the dank smell, and that the water, once clear and sparkling, had grown murky. Even the wind had died.

"We're almost there," Dylan whispered. He'd kept his voice low, but even so, his words carried farther than he'd expected.

Nels nodded.

They soon reached a place where the vegetation had died back to form a clearing. All around them was bare black earth. Ahead, a large pool of water stretched out. It measured about a half mile at its widest point. What looked like steam drifted up from its surface. Swirls of utter blackness curled within the water. On the other side of the pond, the hill rose up another four hundred feet, and at its base was the entrance to a cavern.

Dar knelt and opened the ryggsack he'd been carrying, releasing the lizards. They scattered into the edges of the clearing.

Nels frowned at the water. "No."

Viktor said, "It's not as bad as—"

"I am not getting into that," Nels said. "Not happening."

"Come on," Suvi said, "you're going to tell me you're afraid of a little bit of water?"

"I'm not afraid," Nels said.

"Then what's the problem?" Suvi asked.

"You swiving well know the problem," Nels said.

Suvi said, "You can—"

Something moved within the shadows of the cave. In the dying woods all around them, half-formed creatures emerged. The one commonality between them was an abundance of long, thin, spiny legs, flat, round, black eyes, and jagged mandibles oozing poison. Dylan tried not to look too closely as he counted. He stopped at fifteen.

"Fortunately, that will not be necessary," a woman's voice said. "This is where you end as the other did before you."

The figure in the mouth of the cave was a thin, older woman with pale grey skin. Her dark brown hair was close to her scalp. It crowned her head in uneven tufts as if she'd once had spirit knots and every one had been burned off. Dylan recognized the face and felt his heart sink into his stomach.

The Leaudancer Aegrir had sent before, he thought. *I think I'm going to be sick.* "Angelique?"

The thing wearing Angelique's corpse tilted its head. The movement lacked the grace of a living person. "I think that is what I was called. Angelique Lachance. Yes. That's it."

In that moment, the scallop parrot burst into the air from Dar's shoulder and shot high into the sky. The thing that was Angelique watched it fly off and frowned. The barrel of Nels's musket lowered. The explosion echoed off the hills like a thunderclap. A cloud of spent gunpowder erupted from the gun, and the thing wearing Angelique was struck in the chest.

Now, a familiar voice said inside Dylan's head, *the water.*

He looked down at the pool and knew at once what to do. He knelt down in the river mold and put his hand into the brackish pond. All at once, the water leapt away from his touch, exposing the soft muddy bottom. He was nearly overcome with the stench of moldering mud and rotting fish. The feeling of heavy, deadened atmosphere became nearly unbearable. A strange buzzing sound, once muffled by the weight of the rotten water, filled the air. It came from a horrible black gash in the center of the pond. The blackness oozing from it had the consistency of insubstantial mist. As he watched, it formed into tentacles and reached out for him.

Standing nearby, Ilta stuck a hand inside the leather bag she was holding and threw a handful of silver dust at it.

The earth shook with the force of the thing's howl.

At the edge of his vision, Dylan saw Nels swing the butt of his musket into an encroaching malorum. Viktor shot it with his pistol, and the creature dropped half-seen through an added layer of small-arms smoke.

"Viktor, this is where I leave you," Nels said, dropping his musket and grabbing his sister's hand. "You know what to do."

Viktor whirled to face the next creature. "Annikki! Jami! To me!"

Dylan glanced over at Dar. "I love you."

"And I love you, but I'm staying here," Dar said, concentrating upon the darkening sky. "Don't argue."

"I won't," Dylan said past a painful lump in his throat.

"Keep fighting, drown you," Dar said. "Remember, I've got your back."

"Don't you die either," Dylan said.

"I've no intention of doing so," Dar said, looking him in the eye at last. "Now go."

With that, a huge mass of squalling seabirds descended upon the clearing. Dylan hesitated long enough to see them strike several of the soulbane at once, knocking them down with the force of their trajectory. Then he stepped onto the exposed pond muck. The awful mud sucked at the soles of his boots for two paces before Ilta joined him.

She tossed another handful of glittering dust on the wet ooze. "That works better than I'd hoped."

Sword drawn, Nels moved into position behind them with his back to Ilta. "You doubted one of my plans?"

Dylan sensed Suvi's presence behind him. It was reassuring to have her there. With that, he concentrated with all his will on widening the gap in the rising wall of horrible water. Shadows swarmed inside, curling around the barrier of air and not gaining any purchase. It was now high enough that he lost sight of Dar and the battle on the other side of the water. The sunlight flickered as wave after wave of birds attacked. Easing with the group toward the crevice, Dylan could feel his energy being sapped. The nearer they came to their destination, the more power was required to keep the malorum at bay. Finally, they were in position. Ilta got down on her knees and began to recite the words of an Eledorean ritual. Her words were lost in the rush of water and vengeful birds as she threw silver dust into the crack. Then she drew a white-handled knife and plunged it into the muck at the base of the mud-slimed crevice.

No longer able to divide his attention, Dylan began his own ritual in an attempt to rally his resources. He closed his eyes. Just as he did, he felt someone touch his shoulder. A flood of extra energy flowed through the touch, bolstering his flagging power. He turned to look. Suvi gripped his shoulder with one hand and her brother's arm with the other.

"We're stronger together," Suvi said.

Dylan nodded. *So it would seem.* Glancing down, he noticed that either Suvi or Ilta had sketched out a wobbly protective circle around them with the silver dust.

Ilta got to her feet and took Nels's hand before placing the other on Dylan's left arm. He suddenly felt comforted and strong—a part of the more powerful whole.

He shut his eyes once more, confident that the others would protect him while they each played their part.

The first law of magic is thus: Energy does not vanish. It transforms.

All are born of water. All shall return to water. He took a deep breath. He felt himself merge with the elements forming the wall. Where the shadowy spirits brushed the barrier, he sensed an unpleasant stinging sensation that grew more potent with each contact.

He also sensed Aegrir's presence. She was still distant, but it was reassuring to know that she fought along with him.

Raising his hands, he bent his knees and anchored himself in the foul mud. He moved with slow grace, shifting his weight from one leg to the other and back as he traced the patterns in the air that gave Leaudancers their name. He slid his right foot ever so slightly forward, taking care not to break the circle of silver.

The second law of magic is thus: The tide which goes out shall return, bringing with it all energy collected in its wake. This time he gradually shifted his balance forward and then back. In the same instant, he pushed out and then drew his palms together in front of his chest. He didn't let them touch but kept them ever so slightly apart.

The third law of magic is knowledge. Understanding brings empathy, connection, and control. Ignorance is the enemy. It is the weakness of sand against the tide. Learn from all the world and all those that dwell within it. Above all, know thyself.

He slowly breathed in and out again, feeling his connection with the earth beneath his feet and the sky above.

May the Mother of All Waters bless the souls circled in her holy embrace this day, for all are worthy. I, Dylan Kask, beseech the Great Lady Aegrir for her favor. I make this request for Darius Teak, Suvi Hännenen, Nels Hännenen, Ilta Korpela, Viktor Reini, Jami Rautio, Natalia Annikki, Katrin Slate, myself, and all of those who could be harmed by the forces intent upon destroying this island. I weave the winds and dance the seas with the intent of the best outcome for those touched by my will.

Then he shoved his arms forward and used all the magical energy he'd gathered to shove back the entities throwing themselves against his barriers.

Thunder shook the ground. He heard rock cracking as the earth continued to shake. It was difficult to remain on his feet, but he managed it somehow. The earthquake seemed to last forever, but it finally stopped. He looked at the crevice and saw that it was now shut.

Once again, Ilta broke contact, got down on her knees, and began mixing silver dust with the mud. "Suvi, Nels, help me. We have to pack this into place all along the edges of the rift."

Dylan felt the loss of power at once.

"Won't it wash away when the pond water flows back?" Suvi asked.

Ilta said, "Not if I set it, it won't."

"Whatever you're going to do," Dylan said, "please do it, already. I don't know how much longer I can hold the water back."

The others moved fast, mixing the mud and covering the rift. It wasn't long before they had the entire area covered. Ilta then set a hand deep into the silver-laced clay and murmured a few words in Eledorean. The seal began to set.

Worried that he might lose control before she was finished, Dylan closed his eyes and concentrated. The wall of water began to droop. At the same time, the entities swirling within it started to fade away—their connection to their home world gone. An ache settled into the back of Dylan's skull. He pressed his lips together in determination. He could feel his legs trembling.

"All done," Nels said. "All ashore who's going ashore."

Dylan nodded. "You . . . first."

As the others reached the riverbank, the last of his strength gave out. The water closed over him. In the resulting roar, he thought he heard Dar scream. The water slammed him into the muddy bank and forced all the air from his lungs. For a panicked instant, he lost track of which direction was up, but he burst to the surface before finally drowning. He half-filled his lungs with air before going down again. Eventually, he clawed his way to shore, lay down on the beach, and passed out with Dar's hand on his back.

⊰ BLACKTHORNE ⊱

ONE

The Regnum of Acrasia

June 1785

Hard, cold stone pressed into his face and the left side of his body. This close to the worn flagstones, the damp, sour odor of old filth filled his nose. It would've made him sick if he'd had the strength to be. Instead, he lay on the floor, shivering, while he gathered the will to move.

They left me my clothes this time, he thought. *Small mercies.* The time before, they'd only left him his rage to keep him warm.

He wasn't entirely certain where he was. The Brotherhood had multiple Reclamation Hospitals throughout the Regnum. That said, he was sure he was in a Reclamation Hospital. He recognized the signs. Wardens guarded the door. The cell itself had no windows. No bars. An iron door with a closed slot at the bottom was the only access to the outside world. It was his only light source as well. The narrow room was only five feet wider than the iron bench mortared into the smooth wall.

He didn't know how much time had passed since he had been captured, because he didn't know how long he'd been unconscious. Of course, the light under the door never varied. He kept track of the meal deliveries and had begun etching marks into the cot frame with a spoon. He could've been in the cell a week or months. There was no way of knowing for certain.

He tried not to let that disorient him. That was what they wanted. It was part of the all-too-familiar process used to break him.

Four marks. He'd been awake five days. He concentrated on remembering to scratch another hash mark into the wall hidden close to the cot's edge. If they spied the cuts, they would punish him again. Then someone would sand the entries into oblivion and along with it his sense of time.

What preyed on his mind foremost was that in spite of the beatings, no one was bothering with questions. It was as if anything he could tell them was deemed unimportant.

He shifted painfully from his side onto his stomach. Waiting until the agony receded, he then crawled to the shelf serving as his bed. It took two tries, but he finally pulled himself onto it and took inventory of his injuries. There was a stabbing pain in his thigh from the crossbow bolt, but it was healing. The rest of his body ached from deep bruises. One eye was swollen shut. However, he didn't think anything was broken. The eye worried him, and he hoped he wouldn't lose it.

He closed his good eye and tried not to think about what they wanted from him. However long he'd lain on the cold floor, it'd been long enough to develop cramps in his neck and leg. He waited out the pain before moving. For a few minutes, his only coherent thought was that he needed to sleep. At last, he awkwardly tugged the thin blanket around himself and attempted to rest, but his pains wouldn't let him.

His feet were freezing. They had stolen his boots and stockings while he was unconscious. His watch, the sterling, the forged papers, and even the knotted string he used to judge distance in the wild—they'd confiscated it all.

Thoughts drifting, he hoped Katrin and the others were safe and that the other wagon had reached its destination. As for Caius, Blackthorne wasn't sure how he should feel. Betrayal was obvious, but he kept seeing his former friend's expression.

I have my orders, and I can't go against them. Blackthorne understood that sentiment. Considering the situation, it was likely he would've done the same thing had their roles been reversed.

He didn't cut my throat. Blackthorne didn't know if Caius had done him any favors. Soon, his jailers would drag him up the stairs to the main floor of the Hospital for another round of rehabilitation. The thought of it already frightened him more than death.

The director has to know what I am by now. Surely, they won't waste resources rehabilitating a kainen.

It was illogical to keep him alive, yet they did. That meant he had something they wanted. *But what?* It wasn't information, or they would've begun the interrogation by now.

His thoughts ran the curve of his skull, returning to the point of origin. He dredged up images of Lydia, but it brought no comfort. *She's dead now.* He considered the fate of his daughter and felt marginally better. *Did Mallory McDermott get her to the Hold? Is she safe?* Mallory was intelligent and resourceful. Blackthorne told himself that she was in good hands.

Did I buy the others enough time to flee the city? Or were they captured? He tugged the blanket tighter under his chin and shivered. An even colder thought forced his good eye open. *Were the Wardens I found the only ones tagging me? Did they tag the others as well?* Again, he mentally counted the Warden Unit—those that he'd killed and the survivors.

Ten. It was an unusual number.

Why haven't they asked me anything? Why haven't they killed me? He let out a careful, frustrated sigh. His ribs hurt, but now, at least, the pain was manageable. He needed a distraction from worry. He needed rest. His situation wasn't anything new, after all. He had been through this before. *Many times before.*

His mind was muzzy while he struggled to recall what he used to do to keep from focusing on the pain and fear.

Meditation. He supposed Talus had taught him some things that were useful.

Blackthorne didn't feel he could sit up, not comfortably. He carefully rolled onto his back, took a deep breath that made his bruised ribs ache, and attempted to empty his mind. Out of habit, he whispered the first words from the Retainer's Code that came to him. "A Retainer is not bound by family, friends, or lovers. There is only duty—"

What duty? Duty to whom? To what? Weary of the endless questions, he lay on the shelf, searching for anything that might substitute. That was when an Eledorean poem floated to the surface of his mind.

Early in the year, Moss had decided to take on the task of learning Eledorean. He'd said he needed someone with whom to practice. Deciding that learning Eledorean might be useful, Blackthorne agreed. In the process, he'd begun to pick up pieces of Eledorean culture. He hadn't gotten far before the ill-fated journey to Novus Salernum, and in truth, he remembered very little—the alphabet, a few snatches of poetry. The fragment that sprang to mind had been a love poem. He remembered it because Moss had asked quite a few rather amusing questions about it.

Let me be your warm earth, in darkness—

A loud squeal and clank from somewhere on the other side of the door cut short his trance. Footsteps soon followed. His stomach did a lazy, queasy flip, and as he often did, he knew the identity of two of the four individuals approaching.

Turning to face the wall, he pretended they would stop at another cell, but the knelling of keys against the outside of the iron door dissolved false hope. His heart rammed his breastbone. He decided to pretend to sleep. *I will not fear. I will not give them—*

The door opened with a shrill protest that vibrated along the stone wall. Blackthorne knew without looking that Duke Aureus Corvinus stood in the doorway. The thought of him made Blackthorne's stomach twist in a knot of fury. The second man he hadn't expected to see ever again.

Aurum Atticus, the director of Wardens.

Blackthorne felt something inside him erode into nothingness, and the poem vanished from his mind as if it had never been.

Welcome it like a lover, for the lover does not bring terror. In this way, fear cannot splinter one's heart from duty. Grow numb. Feel nothing. Discard all that ties one to life. Thus, no cowardice can interfere in the crucial moment, and there will be no hesitation in the instant between life and death.

But he was afraid. *I am no Retainer.*

Damned if you don't make a pathetic kainen, too.

He heard the group crowd into the cell. Chairs were set in place. The director dismissed the guards in a low mutter, and the door shut with an ominous clang that sent another shudder through the wall.

"I know you're awake, Severus," the director said. His voice was deep, with a slight nasal quality. "I will not fall for such a simple ruse."

Blackthorne opened his good eye and sat up. Then he struggled to position himself on the shelf with his back against the cold wall. The pain of moving was intense, but he had no intention of showing it.

And that's your first mistake, he thought. *Pretending to be unaffected will only make them press harder for what they want.* But the rage in him didn't care. He made fists of his hands and held tight to his anger. It was the very last thing he had of his own, and he used it to beat back his terror.

His Grace, Duke Aureus Corvinus, stood next to the director, behind two tall wooden chairs. Clearly, there wasn't much room for him to sit.

Blackthorne thought he understood why the duke was present. It was the presence of the director that worried him the most. With the exception of certain required social gatherings, Blackthorne had rarely seen the man.

The duke smiled. "It is good to see you, son."

Always the pretense. Blackthorne bit down on the profanity that his throat threatened to vomit up. It would be a pointless use of his scant energy. *I'm in a Hospital cell, and he wants to play at happy family for the sake of the director?*

Blackthorne refused to acknowledge the greeting. Instead, he combed stiff blood-soaked hair from his face with his fingers, gritted his teeth, and focused on the wall just beyond the duke's right arm. He didn't get up from the shelf, only sat up straighter. His ribs protested.

"I know you don't believe me," the duke said, "but it is nonetheless true."

Maintaining his silence, Blackthorne attempted to cross his arms over his chest without wincing.

"It seems you haven't changed your attitude. Although you

appear to have undergone a rather dramatic transformation," the duke said. "Have you been eating?"

Why don't you ask my jailers? Blackthorne thought.

"You've had enough of the niceties, I see," the duke said. "I'll get to the point, then. We wanted to ask you a few questions."

At last, Blackthorne thought. *Something with which I can work.* He felt the feather touch of relief. He could find out what it was they wanted from him. And that knowledge might bring him a small amount of power.

The director rested an arm on the back of the second chair and looked away as if the proceedings didn't interest him in the slightest. However, he held himself too still, too quiet, and that alone told Blackthorne the man was very interested indeed.

The duke edged his way into one of the chairs. Then he folded his arms across his chest. Noticing this mirroring of his own actions, Blackthorne placed his arms at his sides. *Swive you, old man. I'm nothing like you. I'm not yours. I'm my own.*

"Where have you been living?" the duke asked. "We found the room in that disgusting public house."

The Golden Swan, Blackthorne thought. *I hope Armas got out before the Brotherhood arrived.*

"Dueling? Really, Severus, I would've preferred that you not risk your person so," the duke said. "You're too important an investment for that."

Yet not important enough to avoid this place? Blackthorne stopped himself from rolling his eyes.

"Thank you for the cache of swords, by the way," the director said. "Our enemy wanted to keep them from circulation among the Brotherhood. You've done your country a great service by liberating them. Still, your actions raise a number of questions. The first being: who did you steal them for?"

Staring at the wall, Blackthorne didn't so much as move.

"We understand that you've been away for the winter," the duke said. "I assume that you've been outside the city. If you'd been in Novus Salernum, the Brotherhood would've found you."

Blackthorne decided not to give an answer to that question either. *Not yet.* He had no intention of mentioning the Hold, and he would use every trick he knew to avoid doing so. Therefore, he would have to let them pry a lie or two out of him. The most difficult part would be keeping the story consistent. *Start simple. The simple lie is easiest to remember.* Maintaining a deception would be difficult when his mind was muddled with pain. He'd already planned the whole story he'd feed them. He didn't delude himself with the idea that he wouldn't break. Breaking was inevitable. Everyone broke. The only hope he had was that the director would give up asking questions before he finally did.

The duke sighed. "You had a great deal of silver on your person when you were found—far more than that barman paid you to fight in his ring. Where did you get it?"

"Who paid you to steal those swords, Severus?" the director asked.

Blackthorne decided it might be time to speak. *Let that be the first lie.* "I stole the money like I stole the swords. I didn't have a buyer. Not yet."

"Is that so?" the duke asked, and leaned forward. "I understand your desire to protect your cohorts. They have been paying you a great deal, after all. Your loyalty, however misplaced, is reasonable. The punishment for such an offence is rather . . . lengthy and painful, I understand. In any case, you need not concern yourself. We are already aware of a number of your contacts."

He's bluffing.

"Your friend Mallory McDermott has been rather forthcoming," the duke said.

Blinking, Blackthorne struggled to keep his expression blank. *They have my daughter.*

"Ah, it would seem that you care about someone after all," the duke said.

It doesn't mean Mallory told them about her, Blackthorne thought. *It's possible he didn't say anything about that. And if he didn't, where is she now? Dying of exposure?* "I don't."

"I know you, Severus," the duke said. "I raised you, remember?"

You mean you had Talus do it for you, Blackthorne thought. *It isn't the same thing.* And in that moment, he understood he'd do anything to make certain little Lydia was safe. It didn't matter that he'd never seen her.

"What if I told you that you had an opportunity to save your friend?" the duke asked.

"I'd say you were lying," Blackthorne said. "He's dead already."

"Oh, I beg to differ," the duke said. "He's very much alive."

"You forget. I know you, too," Blackthorne said, his mouth forming a sneer. "I know when you're lying. You open your mouth to speak."

The duke hopped to his feet, nearly upending the chair in the process. He raised a fist, and Blackthorne leaned toward the blow.

"Stop," the director said. "This is going nowhere, Corvinus. It's my turn to reason with him."

Lowering his fist, the duke shook hair from his eyes and resumed his seat.

"There is something your father has failed to mention," the director said. "McDermott wasn't alone when we found him. He was with a Watch captain, a wet nurse, and a baby. McDermott claims the child is yours. It seems the mother, a prostitute, died while giving birth."

"Is this true? Are you the father?" the duke asked.

Blackthorne didn't answer.

The director continued. "Understand we mean the girl no harm. Far from it. We merely need to verify her parentage. It's important to our work."

"Please, Severus," the duke said. "The fate of the Regnum could rest upon it."

At last, Blackthorne looked the duke in the eye. He focused all his rage and hate on the man. The duke returned the gaze, and they sat challenging one another in a tense silence.

When it became clear Blackthorne wasn't going to volunteer an answer, the duke shrugged. "That can wait for the moment. There are ways of determining her parentage ourselves. All we need to know is if you have fathered more children."

Blackthorne ground his teeth in shame and disgust. *Again, it comes to this. Next, it will be the interrogation about how many times I bedded her mother, and how long had we lain together.*

"Well?" The duke shifted closer.

Ignoring the screaming pain in his ribs, Blackthorne leaned forward once more. He tried to give the impression that he was about to give the desired information. However, he borrowed a phrase from one of Hännenen's soldiers instead. "Why don't you swive a reindeer?" he asked, and then he showed his teeth.

He had never said anything like it to the duke's face before. The feeling of freedom and release in it was overwhelming. *It's nothing but futile bluster.* But at least he'd finally had the courage to say what he had always wanted. He wasn't going to cower in silence. *You don't own me anymore.*

A muscle in the duke's jaw clenched, and Blackthorne knew that it was only the director's presence that saved him from a beating.

"You picked up an insolent attitude during your furlough," the duke said.

The director said, "Perhaps the time has come to tell Severus what he truly is. That way, he will know what is expected and why."

"I am the kainen who graduated second in your precious school of the pure," Blackthorne said.

The director smiled, unsurprised. "And who do you think allowed you in the gate?" He paused, seeming to wait for the weight of his words to penetrate. "Even with everything that foul magician was able to achieve, certain inferior traits always tell." He turned away in disgust. "You are only the means to an end."

"You are an experiment," the duke said.

"You wanted a kainen that could pass for human." Blackthorne's teeth were clenched together so tight he could barely speak.

"Shut up, boy. Listen," the duke growled. "There once was a noble race of men who came to this land from the east—"

"The Purus. The Academy teaches that myth to the first-years," Blackthorne said, and spat. "I'm familiar with it."

The duke frowned. "You may have been kainen once, but you are no longer. The old race will be reborn even stronger than before, and you will be its progenitor."

The director raised a hand. "Academy surgeons and naturalists discovered years ago that humans exposed to smallpox in a controlled manner survived immune and with minimal damage," he said. "They avow that the same effect can be achieved with magic. However, during the trials, it became apparent that pure humans could not withstand the treatment process. Therefore, another means was developed." He made to examine his fingernails. "You have been inoculated against magic. You have also been inoculated against malorum poison. If the magician did his job, these immunities will be passed to your offspring."

Blackthorne felt his mouth fall open.

"You are of far inferior stock to those who will come. They will be the soldiers we need to combat the malorum problem," the director said. "It is fortunate, but you weren't the only suitable subject your father had to offer to the project. However, you are the only issue of your dam to endure the treatment whole."

Unbelieving, Blackthorne attempted to understand what he was hearing.

The duke took over the conversation. "You and one other were the only ones to survive. Arion's mother was half-human, and he was . . . damaged. Not only was he mentally incapacitated, but he had some rather unfortunate proclivities that made reproduction impossible. He is, alas, no longer with us, making you the last. A few years ago, there might have been a girl, but we lost your mother and the child during the birth. We've been unable to locate another suitable surrogate. Nonhumans of the appropriate coloring are difficult to locate."

"My mother was alive when Talus told me she was dead?" The question slipped out before Blackthorne could stop it.

"As poor material as you are to work with, we could not risk her polluting you further," the director said. "Therefore, she was removed."

Talus lied. Blackthorne had never doubted that Talus was the duke's man, the perfect Retainer. The old gladiator had killed, even tortured without question, without compassion. Talus could be cold and brutal, but until this moment, Blackthorne had thought he'd never been more cruel than necessary. *I thought I could trust his word, if nothing else.* "I will never again serve the Brotherhood."

"You will do as I order you," the director said. "Corvinus sold you to me to use as I see fit when you were ten. I own you."

Blackthorne felt his lungs constrict, and he began to feel

light-headed. His heart hammered at the insides of his chest. The wound in his thigh throbbed in rhythm with his heart. His vision narrowed to that of the cell floor.

He heard the duke say, "I informed the director of your reluctance to breed. He suggested you be released. He felt that eventually, you would follow your destiny. His theory proved correct, it would seem."

The director said, "Not only will we resurrect the old race but assure the eventual extinction of nonhumans. Your children will reproduce quicker. Their superior traits will eradicate those with whom they mix."

A chill passed through Blackthorne's body. He wanted to be sick. He felt more than saw the duke move closer.

"If you father more children, we will agree to keep your friend McDermott alive," the duke said.

The director said, "Ultimately, we need only wait until your daughter grows old enough to reproduce."

"Then why don't you kill me?" Blackthorne asked.

"We have learned that redundancies are desirable," the duke said. "Therefore, our only requirement is that you mate with others of our choosing. We will make arrangements for the offspring. You will have everything you need."

Pain in the center of Blackthorne's fists brought the cell back into focus. He glared at the wall. "Will I have to wear the collar? Or would that only be a formality?"

The director placed a hand on the duke's arm. "Whether you agree to the terms or not is of little consequence. At this moment, you're being awarded the option of avoiding rehabilitation."

They will strip you of everything that makes you who you are. They will drive a spike through your brain and leave you to drool. None of this will stop them from using you as a breeding stallion. Blackthorne swallowed and shut his eyes. He fought to keep from being sick.

A knock sounded on the door, and he heard the guards remove the chairs. It was followed by the duke's steps in the passage outside.

"Give the matter consideration," the director said. "You have until our next meeting."

"I want proof," Blackthorne said. "I want to see both of them. I want to talk to Mallory McDermott."

The director smiled. "I will make the arrangements."

"I won't commit rape for you," Blackthorne said. "I won't—"

The lock turned with a heavy finality. Blackthorne lay in the dark a long time before sleep came. When it did, he dreamed of Lydia, his daughter's mother. None of the dreams were pleasant.

TWO

The knots of agony squatting in different corners of his body combined forces. He let them consume conscious thought. There came moments when the cell was unbearably cold and others when it seemed stifling. As he lay facing the wall, alternately sweating and shivering, he was aware of food being shoved through the slot at the bottom of the door at intervals. He didn't remember doing it, but at some point he had stolen a pewter spoon from an uneaten meal. He awoke from his fever clutching the spoon in a bloody hand. It was when he saw what he had scratched onto the wall in his delirium that the last of the numbness finally retreated.

I reserve no faith for hope.

He knew the rest. *Death is more certain than love. Yet hope shines.*

The lines wrenched up what seemed now another person's memories. One night when he couldn't sleep, he'd decided to practice what he'd learned from Moss. He had opened the book that the cook had loaned to him and flipped to a random page. Then he had translated it letter by letter. When he had registered its meaning, it had given him a chill. He wasn't certain if he had interpreted it correctly or not—he honestly didn't want to know. He liked it as it was. He touched the uneven Eledorean letters with hesitant fingers.

There came a loud bang as a bolt on the outside of the door was thrown open. He found it alarming that he hadn't heard the guard's approach and didn't know who would enter. He faced his enemy and attempted to hide the verse by resting his back against it. The action was irrational. The line had been carved into the wall; eventually, they would see it. Still, he couldn't stop himself. The words felt solid and comforting there, like a friend in a desperate battle.

His jailer entered the cell with yet another bowl. He seemed surprised to see Blackthorne awake. "Will you eat? If not, my orders are to force it upon you."

"No need," Blackthorne said. His voice came out in a weak croak that sounded strange to his ears.

The guard nodded and set the bowl on the floor. "I will tell the director." Then he dropped a slice of brown bread into its contents and left.

Steadying himself with one hand on the wall, Blackthorne limped to the bowl. The stew had the consistency of greyish glue, and yet it managed to smell appealing. Grateful no one was watching, he devoured it two-handed and wiped the bowl clean with the bread. After emptying the dented water pitcher, he felt alert for the first time in days. His right eye seemed to be functioning almost normally. And although breathing was painful, his ribs were better too. Even the bolt wound had healed. At some point before he had been dumped in the cell, someone had stitched it closed with waxed black thread, and the bandage and sticking plaster had come loose. When he removed the filthy bandage, the exposed flesh was scarred. He pulled the torn trouser leg together against the cold.

I must get out of here. And if McDermott is alive, I must take him and the child with me. How?

An opportunity will come. Have faith. He thought of the poem that he'd carved, and a corner of his mouth twitched.

It suddenly occurred to him that he should keep limber so he could run if the need arose. After testing his legs, he thought he might manage a short distance, provided he prepared. *But that isn't enough. Not anything like it.* He had to assume that he'd have to carry little Lydia. He might even have to help McDermott walk. *If they didn't lie about his being alive.*

Blackthorne began with stretches; his cell was too small for much more than that. He pushed himself as far as he could stand. Sadly, it wasn't long.

When the guard came for the pewter bowl, Blackthorne exaggerated the extent of his injuries. If the guards thought him too weak to attempt escape, they might become careless. Once free, finding his way north would be simple. *Provided the others escaped.* The only way to be certain was to go back to the Hold. Thinking of the Hold brought up memories of his time there. They'd taken his freedom from him. *Again.*

He clamped down on a powerful surge of grief with tightened fists, and his palms sent sharp bolts of pain up to his elbows.

Escaping the Hospital was his first priority. His chances increased if he was moved from the cell, and the odds fell to nothing if he was rehabilitated. Therefore, there was no other option than to cooperate. With that, he practiced saying the words without choking on them.

The director returned two days later, assuming meals were delivered in regular intervals. Blackthorne spent the hours between stretching, getting what exercise he could, and eating.

The director entered and gave Blackthorne an expectant look.

"Where's McDermott and the child?" Blackthorne asked.

"I would have your answer first," the director said.

Glaring at the floor, Blackthorne attempted to cover his fury with a defeat he didn't feel. "I will do as you wish."

Sounding pleased, the director said, "I suspected that would be your answer."

Blackthorne waited for the director to sense the lie. It was then that he understood that living among kainen had affected his expectations.

The director turned to the open door. "Bring them in." He stepped out, apparently in order to make room for the visitors.

Mallory McDermott shuffled into the cell with his head down. Manacles circled his ankles and chains rattled around his bare feet. When he had limped to the far side of the room, a tired woman entered, holding a small child with wide kainen black eyes and thick black hair. The baby was fussing.

The director said from the doorway, "I can be merciful, you see."

"I want to talk to McDermott," Blackthorne said.

The director motioned toward him. "Feel free."

"Alone," Blackthorne said.

"I will permit it," the director said.

The woman held out the child.

That is my daughter, Blackthorne thought. *I'm responsible for her. She's a living person, and she's my daughter.*

"Take her," the director said. "I wish to see how she reacts."

At that moment, it occurred to Blackthorne that he knew nothing of babies. "I don't—"

"You hold her like this," the woman said. "One hand under her bottom and one on her back. Fortunately, she's old enough that she can sit and hold her own head up. See?"

Blackthorne accepted the baby, and as her weight settled into his arms, the child stopped her cries at once. A shocked expression passed over the wet nurse's face.

"Isn't that interesting?" the director said.

Holding the child as carefully as he could, Blackthorne asked, "Why?"

"The baby hasn't stopped crying since we brought her here," the director said. "Until now, McDermott is the only one who has been able to console her. It's one of the reasons he's still alive."

Oh, Blackthorne thought.

Little Lydia had her grandmother's eyes, her father's hair, and her mother's ears and chin. Her skin was the same shade of tan as Blackthorne's own. *This is my daughter.*

The wet nurse moved to take Lydia away.

The director said, "Leave her for now."

"Yes, sir," the wet nurse said.

"You may go," the director said. "Return in an hour."

The woman bowed and left.

"I want to talk to McDermott in private," Blackthorne said.

"Very well," the director said. "You have a half-hour." The door slammed shut.

Blackthorne made room on the shelf—the only surface on which to sit—and offered it to Mallory. "How bad have they hurt you?"

Mallory lifted his head. His face was a mass of bruises. "Bad enough." His speech was affected by swollen lips. He sat; his eyes didn't meet Blackthorne's.

"Can you run?" Blackthorne asked.

"Absolutely."

"Good."

Baby Lydia squirmed in his arms. She seemed intent on facing a different direction. He attempted to permit her the freedom to do so without dropping her. She wiggled until she could lay with her head on his chest and face Mallory at the same time. Then she waved a hand in the air in Mallory's general direction and gurgled. The noise communicated contented sleepiness. Something in Blackthorne's chest warmed and twisted.

"I'm . . . sorry," Mallory said.

"About what?" Blackthorne asked. "It is I who should apologize to you. You wouldn't be here but for me." He swallowed and gazed down at little Lydia. He could only see the top of her fuzzy head. She smelled of fresh linen and mother's milk. "In fact, I should thank you for taking care of little Lydia. I owe you a great deal for that."

"Why?" Mallory asked, the shame obvious on his face. "I gave you up. I told them everything I knew." He lowered his voice to a whisper. "Except about where Slate is. That is because I don't know."

"None of that matters," Blackthorne said.

"It doesn't?" Mallory asked in self-disgust.

"You're alive," Blackthorne said. "A man has to do whatever he must to survive."

The baby in his arms suddenly sat up. In that moment, he noticed she seemed rather somber for someone so young. *On the other hand*, he thought, *how would I know?* She laid one hand on his face, grabbed a handful of beard with the other and tugged. Sharp pain exploded in his cheek. "Ouch."

McDermott gave him a sad smile. "You'll have to watch out for that. At this stage, she'll grab anything she can and put it in her mouth."

"You speak as if you know a lot about babies." Blackthorne moved little Lydia's hands from his face, and she snuggled back into his arms with a yawn.

Mallory's full lips curled into another sad smile. "In my line of business, babies are a—uh—hazard, you could say."

"The spy business?" Blackthorne felt one side of his mouth tug upward.

"No. The other business," Mallory said. "The one that pays my rent."

"I thought you were a painter."

The expression on Mallory's face instantly reminded Blackthorne of Viktor Reini whenever he spoke to Colonel Hännenen. "Seriously? You're going to tell me you didn't know I was a cocksman?"

"Oh."

"You didn't?" Mallory hugged his ribs and began to laugh. "Oh, Mithras, my ribs. I can't— It hurts too much. I—"

The baby started awake.

"I thought you were Lydia's . . ." Blackthorne cleared his throat and attempted to soothe her back to sleep. "Business manager."

Wiping under a bruised eye, Mallory said, "Lydia didn't need anyone to manage her. In fact, she owned the building. I was her tenant."

Blackthorne hesitated. "Only her . . . tenant?"

"Only," Mallory said. "We didn't share clients." He paused. "Most of the time. I'll admit, she did send me the occasional lucrative referral. But I only resorted to that when I didn't have any other choice."

A more complete image of Mallory's existence began to emerge. "I see."

"Not because I didn't enjoy it," Mallory said. "Men are simply more dangerous. Particularly men in power. And most of Lydia's clients were very rich indeed. Not that there aren't licenses for such things, but they're extremely expensive for someone like me." He shrugged. "That more than anything is the reason why events at molly houses are so often conducted in disguise." He shrugged.

"Between the two, I prefer women. They're more fun." He frowned and winced. "Most of the time."

"Ah."

"Anyway, Lydia was a good friend," Mallory said. "I couldn't let her baby die. Besides, she had a lot of feelings for you. She said you were more than you seemed. She was certain you'd take in little Lydia." He gazed at the wall across from him. "She always was a good judge of character."

"Oh," Blackthorne said, not knowing what else to say.

Once again, he looked down at his daughter. She burrowed in his arms again in the search for a new position. She wiggled and twisted until she was lying on her back with her head cradled inside his elbow. She blinked up at him and smiled.

That warm feeling returned. At the same time, his ignorance of babies now loomed like a mountain. *Even if I had thought to do so, leaving Mallory behind is impossible. I don't know how to take care of her. He's been doing so for months.* "How—how old is she?"

"She was born on the thirty-first of March," Mallory said. "She's four months old today."

Blackthorne blinked. "It's the thirty-first of July?"

"It is," Mallory said. "Since you wanted to speak in private, I assume you had something to talk about other than the baby?"

Whispering, Blackthorne said, "When I escape, I'm taking you and Lydia with me."

Mallory asked, "And how do you propose to do that?"

"I don't know," Blackthorne said. "Not yet. Do you know if we're still in Novus Salernum?"

"We are," Mallory said. "In fact, this place is under the Warden Academy."

Good, Blackthorne thought, feeling the tension in his shoulders loosen. "How far is your cell from mine?"

"I'm next door," Mallory said. "They killed Tyra, and it's my fault. If I hadn't—"

"Who is Tyra? The Watch captain?" Blackthorne asked.

Mallory scowled. "No. Tyra was Lydia's wet nurse. The Watch captain was Emily Drake, and if I ever see her again I'll—I'll—" He seemed to choke on his own rage. Then he clenched his fists until he got control of himself. "She's the reason we didn't make it to Greenleaf. She turned on me."

"I see," Blackthorne said.

They sat in silence for a few moments before Mallory ventured further. "Well?"

"We can escape," Blackthorne said.

"How?"

"Let's just say you aren't the only one with a . . . past. That said, not only have I escaped before," Blackthorne said, "but I've been planning on such an inevitability from the first day at the Academy."

Mallory's eyes widened. "You're a—"

"Ex-Warden," Blackthorne said. "You'll need your strength. I won't be able to carry you in addition to Lydia. And I'm not leaving without you."

Mallory lifted an eyebrow. "I wouldn't have expected such sentiments."

You aren't the only one, Blackthorne thought, and gazed into his daughter's eyes.

She smiled and made a happy noise. Then she tightened her grip on his finger and began to gum it. For some reason, he didn't mind the slobber.

"She really likes you," Mallory said. "It would seem she's as good a judge of character as her mother was."

It would be nice to think so, Blackthorne thought.

The keys rattled in the lock.

"I'm glad we had this chat," Mallory muttered with a fearful look on his face. "But I'm afraid it's time for me to go."

"Remember what I said," Blackthorne whispered. "Cooperate as much as you dare. Whatever it takes to avoid more injury. I need you whole."

Mallory nodded. "Don't drop her on her head. Keep her warm, but not too warm. Keep her bottom clean. And feed her when she's hungry. She'll sleep when she needs to. The rest will work itself out. At least, until she's old enough to walk and speak. After that, all the rules change."

"Good to know," Blackthorne said.

"Let's hope we both live to see her become a woman," Mallory whispered.

The door swung open, and a guard led Mallory away.

The director stood in the doorway, frowning at the baby in Blackthorne's arms. "She's sleeping," Blackthorne said. "I would like more time with her if it's possible."

Frowning, the director nodded and slammed the door.

Baby Lydia jerked awake and squeezed up her face in what he could only assume would be a scream.

"Shhhh," he said. "It's all right. You're safe. I'm here. I won't leave you. I promise." He held her tight and rocked her in what he hoped was a soothing manner. He didn't think he'd ever felt so powerless and yet happy in his whole life.

Her expression relaxed, and she waved a hand in the air. He gave her his finger again, and again she grabbed it. She pulled it to her mouth, closed her eyes, and sucked. He thought she might be hungry, but she fell back to sleep.

THREE

Blackthorne said, "You said you'd bring Lydia today."

"I thought we'd have a chat first," the director said. "I have questions that remain unanswered. I have been generous. I've permitted you to meet your daughter. Now I would have your cooperation. Where were you last winter?"

"Archiron," Blackthorne said.

"I rather doubt that," the director said. "There is no evidence of your having been there."

"How would you know? How many times do you think I've been to Novus Salernum?" Blackthorne asked. "Once? Twice? How about twenty times?"

The director's eyes narrowed. "You're lying."

Blackthorne shrugged and told the truth. "You're right. It was more like thirteen."

"Where were you last winter?"

"Archiron."

"You should reconsider your behavior. I do not believe it is within your power to deny me anything." The director frowned. "I have your child. I understand nonhumans can become quite pliable when they perceive that their get are in danger."

He's only goading you. He won't see her harmed. They need her.

"You're thinking that I need her alive," the director said. "And you're correct. To study, if for no other reason. However, no one said her existence need be comfortable. It might be interesting to observe her with a malorum."

Blackthorne's hands curled into fists, and his heart beat fast. *Think, damn it. He won't hurt her. He needs her.*

"One more time," the director said. "And if I don't like the answer, I'll see to it that you'll be sorry, I promise you." His lips formed a thin line of anticipated satisfaction. "Where. Were. You?"

Hanging his head, Blackthorne considered a fresh lie. Something close enough to truth but not so close as to send the Brotherhood looking in a profitable direction. "Wyeth. I was in Wyeth."

Wyeth was a port. Through Wyeth, one could access the Eledorean river systems or hire a Waterborne ship. The director would expect him to have sold those he'd helped to flee the Regnum. And he'd already decided that this would be the lie he fed to them.

"And where is James Slate?" the director asked.

Blackthorne didn't answer. He had to at least feign resistance or he wouldn't be believed.

"Do I need to mention that I not only have your daughter but your friend McDermott?" the director asked.

"Don't."

"Don't what?" the director asked.

"I can't give you that information," Blackthorne said.

"Why not?" the director asked. "I'm not interested in illicit slave trade. The tax revenue loss is of no concern to me."

That was a lie, and Blackthorne knew it. The Brotherhood

received a percentage of all recovered funds—and recovered slaves would most definitely result in a profit. Of course, being a lowly Warden without rank, he wasn't supposed to know that, because the revenue in question was divided among the higher-ranked Wardens. The director was at the top of that particular financial equation. However, the highest-ranking nobility also received a percentage of recovered funds. And Warden Aurelius Aureus Severus, recognized son of Duke Aurelius Aureus Corvinus, would most certainly be aware of this fact.

Apparently, the director forgot that, Blackthorne thought. *Or is he playing some other game?*

"I have more important responsibilities," the director said. "The Regnum is in danger from the malorum threat. That is our top priority. By giving us the swords, you have already assisted us in this endeavor—possibly more than you'll ever know. There'll be no charges against your Mr. Slate. That is, as long as you keep your agreement and produce more offspring."

Blackthorne hesitated. This was important. He had to sell it. He also had to hope that the opportunity to get himself, baby Lydia, and Mallory out would come before the director could get a report back from Wyeth.

"Give me what I want, Severus," the director said. "Do so, and you will have unlimited access to your daughter."

"And I can see Mallory again?"

"Today, if you like," the director said.

"He's . . ." Blackthorne paused. He glanced away as if ashamed. "He's in Wyeth. We meet in a tavern called the Red Boar."

"Good. Cooperative. You always did possess a certain base intelligence." The director moved to the door and knocked on it. "I will see you soon." He exited the cell, and the bolt slammed back into place.

One day, I'll kill you, Blackthorne thought at the door. Taking a deep breath, he conserved his rage. He would need the energy for what lay ahead.

Sometime later, a guard arrived with more food. The guard watched him eat before returning his boots and the greatcoat Blackthorne had taken from the dead Warden. It was apparent they were making ready to take him to what Blackthorne assumed was his next prison. He shrugged on the coat with exaggerated care and noticed someone had stripped it of insignia. *Dishonorable discharge.*

He almost laughed. The gesture was entirely for appearances; he knew they weren't going to go through with an execution. He was glad to have the coat, regardless. After he had suffered the cold for so long, its heavy warmth felt luxurious. He slipped the spoon into his pocket and finished tugging on his boots. A pewter spoon wasn't much of a weapon, but it would have to do. He'd have surprise, at least.

The guard left and relocked the door. Blackthorne waited and listened for footsteps indicating who would come for him next. If he managed to overpower the guard, finding Mallory would be easy. The problem would be in locating baby Lydia. Blackthorne had no idea where the director was keeping her.

It wasn't long before he heard the guard return. He was accompanied by the wet nurse.

They're bringing Lydia.

Blackthorne waited on the shelf while the guard opened the door. The wet nurse entered with little Lydia in her arms. When he accepted the child she turned and left. Quickly, Blackthorne laid Lydia on the shelf as far from the edge as he could manage. Then he jumped up and flung himself at the door before the guard could lock it again. The door slammed into the guard, knocking him back. The wet nurse screamed. Blackthorne launched himself at the guard, knocking him off his feet and onto the ground. Then he drove the handle of the pewter spoon deep into the man's eye. The guard fought, clawing at Blackthorne's hands. Blackthorne used all his rage to ram the now-slippery handle farther into the man's eye socket. He didn't stop until the guard's struggles ceased.

The door at the end of the passage flew open. Blackthorne grabbed the dead guard's knife and got to his feet. A second guard drew his knife and charged toward him. The wet nurse flung herself against the wall. Blackthorne ran past her, meeting the second guard a few feet away. The guard stabbed at Blackthorne. Blackthorne grabbed the guard's wrist left-handed and ducked under the man's arm. Then Blackthorne plunged his blade into the guard's throat. Warm blood poured over Blackthorne's hands. The guard choked and then went limp.

Glancing back, Blackthorne saw the wet nurse trembling with her back to the wall. Her eyes were wide with terror, and she didn't seem to be inclined to move. He went to the door at the end of the passage. Pausing there, he listened.

No one. Not yet. He gently pushed the door shut and returned to the wet nurse.

"Please," she said, and shook her head. "Don't."

He briefly checked to see that Lydia hadn't rolled from the shelf. She was sucking on her fist and lying where he'd left her. He motioned for the wet nurse to enter his cell.

She started to cry.

"I won't hurt you," Blackthorne said. "Just get inside. Look after the baby."

This time, she did as he asked.

"Blackthorne?" It was Mallory.

"One moment." Blackthorne searched the dead guards for the keys. It wasn't long before he found them and unlocked Mallory's cell.

"Get Lydia," Blackthorne said while he took care of the manacles on Mallory's ankles.

Mallory nodded. His bruised face looked a little grey. As soon as he was free, he retrieved the baby. Blackthorne locked the wet nurse inside.

"Now, help me get these bodies out of the way," Blackthorne said. "We haven't much time."

They dragged the dead guards into the other cell and stripped them of their weapons. Blackthorne offered Mallory a knife.

"I don't know how to use it," Mallory said.

"Take it," Blackthorne said. "I need to know you have it. In case we're separated. Neither of us knows what time it is. It could be dark out there." Then he checked the bottoms of the dead guard's boots.

Mallory swallowed. "Malorum."

"Exactly," Blackthorne said. "That blade is a Warden's knife. It's laced with silver."

After Mallory accepted it, Blackthorne sat on the shelf and took off his right boot.

"What are you doing?" Mallory asked.

Blackthorne checked the guard's boot and then made a few quick adjustments to the pattern carved into his own. "They'll be tagging us. If my boot prints have the same marks as theirs, they'll have a more difficult time finding us."

"Oh." Mallory blinked. He set baby Lydia on the floor, measured his foot next to each of the dead guards', and proceeded to steal the taller guard's boots.

"Are you certain you want to do that?" Blackthorne asked. "The punishment for wearing Warden's boots without being a Warden is—"

"They can only execute me once."

"Point," Blackthorne said. Then he helped Mallory tug the legs of his trousers over the tops.

"Their shirts are linen, right?" Mallory asked.

"I believe so," Blackthorne asked. "Why?"

"Lydia will need fresh clouts."

"The wallets, too. The sterling will come in handy," Blackthorne said. *For multiple reasons.*

As it turned out, the shorter of the two had a wallet that was almost full. Blackthorne made Mallory take that one. "This, too," he said, handing off a pistol. "Hide it inside your shirt. I can't carry all these weapons. It won't look right, not if I'm to be your guard."

After accepting the pistol, Mallory swaddled baby Lydia with one shirt and then fashioned a sling out of the other. Once the baby was secured to his chest, he stood up.

Blackthorne raised an eyebrow in question.

"If we're attacked again, I want both hands free," Mallory said. "I might be able to do something other than stand there and gawp. Besides, she'll make it easier to hide the weapons. And she's more apt to stay quiet this way. Tyra said babies found being able to hear a heartbeat soothing. It worked the first time." He glanced down at the swaddled bundle. "Don't worry. I won't do anything stupid. I don't think I could kill anyone even if I had to."

"Loop the manacles over your wrists," Blackthorne said, grabbing a cadet's tricorne from the dead. It would help with the disguise. He didn't have time to put his hair into a regulation pigtail. "Don't lock them."

Increasingly glad he'd decided to take Mallory with him, Blackthorne checked the hallway before ushering him outside. Then Blackthorne locked the door behind them. There was nothing he could do about the blood in the hallway, but checking the cell might slow down pursuit. "There isn't much time left. Follow me."

When they got to the end of the passage, he put out the lamp there. The hallway was plunged into darkness. He pushed Mallory to the left of the door. In that way, it would hide him and the baby should there be more guards.

"Don't move from there until my signal." Blackthorne quietly unlocked the door using the key and peered through the crack.

No one in the next hallway. It wasn't unusual. Most prisoners at this level weren't in much shape for escape attempts. He eased through and checked the next part of their journey. Then he gave Mallory the signal. In this way, they progressed along two levels of stairs and turned to the left. Blackthorne caught his first glimpse of the outdoors from the darkened windows lining the top of the passage when they reached the ground floor. The strength of his disorientation momentarily made him dizzy.

I was certain it was morning. However, waiting to transfer him until after dark made sense; a student curfew was strictly enforced. Of course, it didn't apply to those on duty. Nonetheless, there would be fewer witnesses.

Across the dark courtyard, one guard waited next to a coach-and-four with shuttered windows. Blackthorne heard the rattle of horse tack as a restless mare shook its head. A young Academy graduate he didn't recognize sat on the bench next to the empty driver's seat.

Blackthorne gazed into a clear night sky before turning and muttering, "Stay close. Say nothing. And keep your head down. If no one is inside the coach, get inside. If someone is inside, climb onto the footman's rest. I'll handle everything else." He made as if to check the manacles around Mallory's wrists.

Together, they approached the coach. Before they got too close, the guard put up a hand.

"Report, Cadet Lucrosa," the guard said.

Luckily, half the school is Gens Lucrosa. Blackthorne kept his chin down, hoping the shadows would obscure his face. He pitched his voice higher than normal. "Was ordered to take this prisoner to the coach, sir." He didn't stop moving but kept walking toward the guard.

The guard frowned. "I didn't receive any orders stating that McDermott would be moved."

"I'm only doing what I was told by the officer in charge, sir," Blackthorne said. He laid a hand on his knife.

"We'll just see about that," the guard said. "Wait here, boy."

What? Blackthorne thought, not believing his ears. "Yes, sir."

The guard strode past, grumbling about command and disorganization. Once he was gone, Blackthorne led Mallory to the coach. Throwing open the door, Blackthorne saw that no one was inside.

"Get in," he whispered to Mallory.

"Hey, Warden Munitoris said to wait," the cadet on the driver's bench said.

Climbing up, Blackthorne said, "Change of plan." And then he cut the cadet's throat. He shoved the body off the bench and hopped down. Lifting the dying cadet by sticking his hands under his shoulders, Blackthorne dragged the body around the coach. Then he got Mallory to help him get it inside. Blackthorne propped the body up in the corner. He knew they would have need of it at the gate.

"Mallory, can you drive a coach?"

"I can drive a wagon."

"Good enough," Blackthorne said.

When Mallory had settled onto the driver's bench, he reached down for the brake. "For the record, my friends call me Mal."

Assuming a place next to Mallory, Blackthorne asked, "We're friends now?"

"Anyone who kills three guards to get me out of prison qualifies," Mal said, and snapped the reins.

"You have high standards. You must not have many friends."

"Only the ones that count."

When they were within a few yards of the exit, Blackthorne jumped down from the moving coach and ran to the gate. He shot the gatekeeper before he could draw a pistol. Mallory stopped the coach as Blackthorne tore the key from the gatekeeper's hand. He rammed the key into the lock and shoved the gate open just as Warden Munitoris shouted his displeasure from across the parade ground.

"Go!" Blackthorne shouted at Mal. "I'll catch up."

After Mal steered the coach through, Blackthorne swung the big iron gate shut and locked it. With that, he whirled and sprinted down the empty street. He grabbed the handle on the footman's perch and pulled himself up. Then he shouted over the rattling of the coach. "Mal!"

Mal spoke over his shoulder. "Yes?"

"Do you know how to get to Old Sarath Road from here?" Blackthorne asked.

"I do," Mal said.

"Don't stop until you cross Rickens Bridge in the North End."

"Got it."

At Rickens Bridge, Blackthorne told Mal to get inside and put on the manacles. Then Blackthorne arranged the dead cadet so that he appeared to be sleeping. The ruse wouldn't hold up to a closer inspection, but he hoped he could avoid one. He blew out the lanterns inside the coach.

"Here's what we'll do." Blackthorne pointed at the dead cadet. "He'll be your guard. Your job is to keep Lydia hidden and to appear too injured to be a threat. Keep the chains visible exactly like before. Don't speak. Leave that to me. Understood?"

Mal nodded.

Blackthorne inventoried the rucksacks that had been left under the driver's bench. He found a couple of tinderboxes, tools for casting ammunition, two canteens, changes of clothes, identity papers for a Cadet Warden Ardon, and best of all, a silver token with the director's initials on it. That, plus a substantial bribe, would get them through the city gates. Otherwise, they would have had to wait until morning, and he wasn't confident of avoiding the Brotherhood that long—not within the city. Somewhere in the distance, a clock tower struck the hour.

Three, he thought. *We'll need to hurry. When daylight comes the Brotherhood will have every checkpoint covered from here to Wyeth.* Of course, the advantage of a coach was that they wouldn't need to stop for the night. Provided they didn't meet with any highwaymen on the road, they could travel as long as he could stay awake. *Nor will we be going to Wyeth.*

One thing at a time. The gate first. He pocketed the papers and the token. Untying his shirt, he used the knife to cut open a number of the pouches in the Warden's wallet. He counted out five sterling crowns. *Should be about right.* He had to be careful. Not enough, and the guard might talk. Too much and the guard might become suspicious. He tucked the coins into his uniform pocket. With that finished, he took up the reins and released the brake. *Let's get this over with.* He assumed the demeanor of someone with every right to be where he was—he was, after all, a Warden.

He adjusted his tricorne. *Cadet Warden.*

The coach rattled down streets that were for the most part

empty. They weren't entirely alone, of course. Nonetheless, the lack of pedestrians, produce and poultry delivery wagons, shoppers, and merchants—the city's lifeblood—shortened the journey to the north gate. He slowed the coach to a stop and assumed a haughty posture. He waited impatiently until a portly sergeant with thinning braids on either side of his face approached. He appeared tired and walked with a familiar rolling gait. With a shock, Blackthorne recognized Sergeant Fisk.

"Curfew is in effect," Sergeant Fisk said. "Mail coaches and official government business only."

Blackthorne looked down his nose at Fisk, which was easy enough to do from his perch. "This is official business. The Brotherhood's business. We're transporting a prisoner by the director's order."

Fisk looked like he wanted to spit but didn't dare. "Papers."

"My papers aren't important," Blackthorne said. "The director's order is."

"I'm in charge of this gate," Fisk said. "And I say the papers are important."

Blackthorne glared at Fisk. "Very well." He reached into his pocket and produced the dead cadet's papers.

After accepting them, Fisk began flipping through the pages of official seals.

"This is the identification you're looking for," Blackthorne said, and flashed the silver disk.

Sergeant Fisk's reaction was both dramatic and instant. "Oh, I see." He coughed and handed back the papers. "If you don't mind, I'd like a closer look."

"Feel free," Blackthorne said, and handed it off. "I am also authorized to make a donation to offset your trouble."

This news had another dramatic effect upon Sergeant Fisk. It was obvious that he'd seen this one at least once before. He coughed and then smiled. "Ah. I—yes. Very good," he said, giving back the director's personal token. "How much, exactly?"

Recognizing the glint of greed in Fisk's eye, Blackthorne reached into his pocket. "Would five be enough?" He produced the coins.

Fisk's eyes got wide. "Silver?"

"Is it enough?" Blackthorne asked.

"Well, I suppose so," Fisk said.

After Blackthorne dropped the coins into his outstretched hands, Fisk ordered the gate opened. Blackthorne urged the horses through.

The blast of a mail-coach horn echoed off the hills. Heeding the warning, Blackthorne kept the horses to the right side of the road until the mail coach roared past to the gate. He pushed the horses as hard as he dared for five miles and then slowed to a walk.

He was never so happy to leave Novus Salernum in his life.

FOUR

Blackthorne decided to leave the coach in a field a mile outside of Byrint. It was along the way to Greenleaf, which was, if the director had believed him, their expected route. After removing anything valuable and defacing any markings that might trace it to its original owners, they unhitched the horses and set the coach on fire. No one in the area would find such a thing unusual. It was the typical action of highwaymen without Syndicate backing, of which there were increasing numbers outside of the Regnum's larger cities. He felt bad about the cadet not getting a proper burial, but it couldn't be helped. There was no time. He used the light from the flaming coach to check the horses' shoes for markers, and finding nothing that would stand out, they took three of the horses and rode the last mile toward Byrint.

It was dawn when they reached the outskirts of town. Baby Lydia hadn't slept well in the noisy, bone-jarring coach. In addition to being tired, she was hungry and making her displeasure known. Byrint was too small a town for anything as refined as a sanctioned house of prostitution, and there wasn't time to inquire about a wet nurse. In any case, two ragged men carrying a motherless baby and traveling without a wet nurse would kindle far too much curiosity from the townsfolk. Therefore, they turned off into the hills. In the end, Blackthorne left Mal and Lydia hidden away in an abandoned shepherd's shed before riding into town alone. There, he sold one of the horses and bought a saddle, saddlebags, some tack, several blankets, and a few days' provisions. Following Mal's recommendations, he also acquired oats for porridge as well as the ingredients for mash. He bought a small basket of strawberries on a whim with the idea that baby Lydia might like them. He certainly had as a child.

Rushing through the buying and selling, he didn't focus as much as he normally would have on conservation of their resources. He wanted to get back as soon as possible. Although experienced in the art of smuggling people out of Acrasia, he found he was anxious about leaving Mal and Lydia alone—more so than he'd ever been with the others. He wasn't certain this was a good sign. Still, the twisting in his gut didn't stop until he'd returned and found Mal and the baby safe.

Little Lydia was not happy and making her opinion on the matter of delayed feeding times clear to one and all. That made Blackthorne glad that he'd been able to locate a hiding place far from the road. Curiously, her bright red face and the accompanying screams pulled desperately at something inside his chest. He picked her up and attempted to soothe her while Mal prepared her mash. It seemed to work. Her face resumed its previous light tan, and she drooled all over his finger as she attempted to nurse from it. She had grown frustrated with the lack of forthcoming milk when Mal took her from him.

She didn't like the mash at first but eventually accepted the substitute for the expected mother's milk. She stopped her crying and resumed the wide-eyed solemnness Blackthorne had witnessed when he'd first met her. The reserved dignity strongly contrasted with the remnants of mash and slobber soiling her clothes and bonnet. Lying on her stomach while Mal rinsed his hands, she pushed herself up onto all fours and began to rock back and forth.

"Looks like that one is going to start crawling soon," Mal said. "She's a quick study."

"Are babies always this messy?" Blackthorne asked.

"Generally," Mal said. Kneeling, he pulled up the back of Lydia's dress and tugged at her clouts.

Blackthorne sniffed. "What is that smell?"

"That, my friend, is a dirty clout," Mal said, pulling a face. "And she's made quite the deposit this morning."

"Ugh." Blackthorne started to move away.

"Oh, no," Mal said. "You're her father. This delivery is all yours."

Hesitant, Blackthorne said, "I've no idea how to change a clout."

Mal said, "If you can kill Wardens with impunity, you can manage a napkin and pilch."

"I didn't mean to imply that I didn't wish to learn," Blackthorne said. "You've already taken on far more of her care than is equitable."

Mal raised an eyebrow. "To be fair, you've been busy making sure none of us gets dead."

Blackthorne shrugged. "She's my responsibility, not yours."

"I'm glad to hear you say that," Mal said. He picked up baby Lydia and flipped her onto her back. "Come on, little girl. Help Uncle Mal show your papa how it's done."

The process of folding and knotting a clout was simple enough. The matter only became stressful with the addition of the pins. Lydia squirmed a great deal, making the matter more dangerous than was comfortable for Blackthorne. However, he finished the task at last, and she was clean and ready to travel. While he took care of obliterating as many traces of their presence as he could, Mal packed their belongings.

It won't help if the Warden Units bring the dogs. And they will bring the dogs. I have to find a stream. "You'll take the horse with the saddle," Blackthorne said. "I'll take the other." He'd only bought the one saddle because he'd wanted to appear as if he were alone.

"But—"

"You'll be in charge of the third horse," Blackthorne said.

"And baby Lydia?"

"She'll ride with me. When we ride. I want to walk for the first mile. I'll have to cover our trail."

Mal nodded and smiled. "Let me show you how to bundle her, then. She'll need her arms and legs free to move."

In the end, Mal decided to strap Lydia to Blackthorne's back. It made more sense. He'd need to access his weapons, and Blackthorne didn't want to risk her getting hurt. His chest was a more likely target in a close-quarters fight.

The sun was high in the sky when they made their way to the crossroads. Blackthorne intended to head southwest to Gullblad. From there, he hoped to book passage on an Ytlainen ship that would take them up the Andallopp River to the Finger Lakes. After that, he and Mal could cut north overland to Grandmother Mountain and the Hold. He wasn't entirely sure what he'd do after getting Mal safe. Blackthorne briefly considered that it might be better for Lydia if he were to leave her with the others at the Hold. The Brotherhood would be hunting him. Therefore, he was a danger to everyone with whom he made contact. At the same time, he felt her warm weight on his back and knew he couldn't do it. He was all she had.

She swung her legs and gurgled happily. "Ba-ba-ba-ba."

He started. "She's speaking?"

Mal said, "Testing the waters, I think. They all do that."

Something tugged at Blackthorne's ponytail.

"She's got your hair again," Mal said.

"Won't she choke?" Blackthorne reached back to rescue his ponytail but she had quite the grip on it.

"Here," Mal said and freed the now-damp hair. Then he handed him the tricorne. "Looks like you'll need this a while longer."

Blackthorne tucked his hair up inside the cadet's hat. "I—I should've purchased a rattle or something."

"And give away that you've a baby traveling with you in a town the Brotherhood are sure to question?" Mal said. "Her fists will be entertaining enough for a while."

Nodding, Blackthorne stepped out into the sunlight. They finished with the packing and then gathered the horses to begin the long walk west. Testing his new center of balance, Blackthorne did something he hadn't allowed himself to do since he'd escaped the Reclamation Hospital the first time. He began to consider the future in larger increments than a few months. All those times he'd delivered children to worried parents, he'd never comprehended the depth of their joy or their terror. He was always outside of it. That wasn't the case any longer. And that wasn't all. With a shock, he understood he no longer felt adrift. That was the moment he understood he needed Lydia every bit as much as she needed him.

A painful lump formed in his throat and his chest tightened. *A Retainer is not bound by family, friends, or lovers. There is only duty to one's Master.*

I am a father now. The weight of overwhelming responsibility was now a welcome one. He was a skilled Retainer. It was all he knew how to be, but that didn't mean he couldn't be a father as well. He decided to make a few revisions to his previous beliefs—revisions that were all his own.

A Retainer is bound by family, friends, and lovers. He let that first change shift and then anchor itself in his brain. It felt perfect and right.

"You're awfully quiet," Mal said. "Is something wrong?"

Blackthorne cleared his throat. "No. Everything is all right— or will be." For the first time in his life, he meant it with every fiber of his being. He listened to his daughter's cooing and was happy.

He had a great deal of thinking to do.

ACKNOWLEDGMENTS

No novel gets written in a vacuum. When it comes to creativity, lived experiences with other human beings over the expanse of one's lifetime are grist for the mill. Other author's works, both fiction and nonfiction, are a professional writer's best education. This is why I try so hard to remember my influences. It's important to give credit where credit is due. Education is precious.

Nonfiction is a passion for me. It keeps my brain working and feeds my muse, but then, I always did enjoy school—not the exams and the bullying, mind you. The *knowledge*. I love learning, questions, and expanding my experience. At the same time, I'm human, and I don't always absorb all the details. Therefore, there are no doubt quite a few blunders contained in this novel. That isn't the fault of anyone listed. Trial and error are how human beings learn best, and we can't learn from mistakes we don't claim. Thus, the errors are mine. It's a shame that so many people these days seem incapable of admitting when they're wrong, let alone when they've made a mistake. Human beings *need* mistakes. They're what make us wiser. And you don't become wiser without radically changing your mind from time to time. I don't know about you, but I want to be like Yoda when I grow up—lightsaber and all. (*Although, I'll give a pass on the green muppet skin and big ears. However, speaking in Frank Oz's voice might be fun.*) Of course, that assumes I'll grow up. I probably won't since I kind of reject most of what our society feels being a grown-up is about, but that's a whole other essay.

So, here goes. . . .

Many thanks to Tempest Bradford, Nisi Shawl, Mary Robinette Kowal, and Cynthia Ward. The Writing the Other workshop was instrumental in making this novel work. If you're a writer and can't afford to attend, definitely pick up Nisi's and Cindy's *Writing the Other: A Practical*

Approach. It's a great place to start diversity education. Another workshop I attended was Revolutionary Writing/Writing for Social Change run by Steven Barnes and Tananarive Due. I learned quite a bit in both workshops and made valuable contacts. Diversity is an important aspect of worldbuilding. If all the characters that people your world look and act exactly the same, it stops being a believable place. Unless you *want* a flat, white-walled world. That has its uses too. (See Ray Bradbury's *Fahrenheit 451*.) The point is to make conscious choices, not unconscious ones. Racism, sexism, homophobia, ableism, religious bigotry . . . we're all soaking in it from the day we're born. As a result, every human being has internalized that shit, including myself. I want to use my superpowers for good. That's why I choose to work hard on my biases. Nonetheless, I feel like a gardener forever yanking up weeds by the roots. There's always something I've missed and don't see until the leaves shoot up from the dirt. That's just the way it is.

One of the things I definitely want to bring up here is that much of Blackthorne's little red leather book is heavily influenced by *The Hagakure: The Book of the Samurai* by Yamamoto Tsunetomo. I wish to state up front that Blackthorne's interpretation (and the Acrasian Regnum's) is absolutely wrong. I wanted to demonstrate how philosophies and teachings could be warped when taken out of context. (Yes, cultural appropriation.) Blackthorne's little red leather book is his Bible, in a way. So, he does what many people do with the Bible—he takes things out of context. I chose the template I did because I'm a martial arts student (Kendo, Wing Chung Kung Fu, and currently Hakkoryu.) As a semi-pacifist hippie type, I greatly appreciate the teachings of martial arts. The heart of it is nothing like what Blackthorne demonstrates. (Unless you're a Cobra Kai from *The Karate Kid*, and if you are . . . yikes.) Part of being a genre writer is looking at such things, twisting them, and then turning the volume knob to eleven. I'm sorry if I've offended an entire culture as a result of playing with that idea. Nonetheless, know that I know the difference between what the real text says and Blackthorne's interpretation. You should too.

Books: *The Art of Blacksmithing* by Alex W. Bealer; *The Craft of the Japanese Sword* by Leon and Hiroko Kapp and Yoshindo Yoshihara;

Samurai by Harry Cook; *The Samurai* by S. R. Turnbull; *The Sword of No Sword* by John Stevens; *The Book of Five Rings* by Miyamoto Mushashi; *The Art of War* by Sun Tzu; *An American Plague: The True and Terrifying Story of the Yellow Fever Epidemic* by Jim Murphy; *Plague, Pox, and Pestilence* by Kenneth F. Kiple; *The Age of Homespun* by Laurel Thatcher Ulrich; *The American Revolution* edited by John Rhodehamel; *Founding Brothers* by Joseph J. Ellis; *The Writer's Guide to Everyday Colonial America* by Dale Taylor; *Everyday Life in Colonial America* by David Freeman; *The Human Predator: A Historical Chronicle of Serial Murder and Forensic Investigation* by Katherine Ramsland, PhD; *A Sea of Words* by King, Hattendorf, and Estes; *1811 Dictionary of the Vulgar Tongue* by Captain Grose; *A Narrative of a Revolutionary Soldier: Some of the Adventures, Dangers, and Sufferings of Joseph Plumb Martin; Incidents in the Life of a Slave Girl* by Harriet Jacobs writing as Linda Brent; *Heart of Oak: A Sailor's Life in Nelson's Navy* by James P. McGuane; *London 1753* by Sheila O'Connell; *After the Revolution: The Smithsonian History of Everyday Life in the Eighteenth Century* by Barbara Clark Smith; *Common Poisonous Plants and Mushrooms of North America* by Turner and Szczawinski; *Revolutionary Medicine 1700–1800* by C. Keith Wilbur M.D.; *A Modern Herbal Vol. I&II* by Mrs. Grieve; *The Prince, The Art of War*, and *The Discourses* by Machiavelli; *Common Sense* by Thomas Paine; *SPQR* by Mary Beard; *Moby Dick* by Herman Melville; *If The Walls Could Talk: An Intimate History of the Home* by Lucy Worsley; *The Gathering Wind: Hurricane Sandy, the Sailing Ship Bounty, and a Courageous Rescue at Sea* by Gregory A. Freeman; *On Combat* by Dave Grossman; *Invisible Man* by Ralph Ellison; *Barry Lindon* and *Vanity Fair* by William Makepeace Thackeray; and *The Encyclopedia of Combat Techniques* by Chris McNab and Will Fowler. Also, all the Patrick O'Brien books I could get my mitts on, as well as some Jane Austen. It takes a lot of reading to screw things up the way I do. ;)

I want to send out a big, big thank-you to Enid Crowe, who took several days out of her work week to take me around the Ulster Museum—which, if you're unfamiliar with it, is an Irish village pieced together with actual old buildings transported from all over Northern Ireland. The village itself is designed with the Edwardian period in mind, but many of the buildings are far, far older, like many things in Ireland. Walking the paths between the farms and other buildings was the closest thing to time travel I've ever experienced. Go there, if you get the chance. They have a post office, police station, a working linen farm, linen looms, churches, cottages, a school, a coal scale ... it was amazing. That tour helped so much to make the late 1700s and early 1800s real for me. The Giant's Ring and the canal were amazing too. Also, thanks to Ian for driving me all around and telling stories. You're an inspiration. (*And I still want that Eggplant/aubergine parmesan recipe.*) Seeing all the things in living color that I'd been studying in black-and-white was incredible. And walking the walls of Derry was amazing—never mind the trip to Long Kesh and Newgrange. Brian, thanks for setting up the tour with your cousin Mickey, and everything else you did for me. It was kind of backward to go to Ireland *after* having written about it, but one day there will be more Northern Irish stories. One. Day. Thanks to my friend Shelly Rae Clift for taking me to the locks and the fish ladder in Seattle, WA. Thanks to Melissa Mead Tyler and Brian Tyler for hosting and for being such great friends. More thanks to Cherie Priest for that amazing tour of Lookout Mountain and the surrounding battlefields as well as the spooky stories. Thanks for the coffee, the company, and for tolerating my silly cannon fixation too. Many thanks to Chris Levesque for his on-the-spot military expertise, Shecky Betai—the best, most fun copyeditor I've ever had, Barry Goldblatt my wonderful agent, Joe Monti my editor, my good friend Ben Fritzler (and awesome DM) for checking my gay, and to Ela Sjunneson Henry for her kind instruction regarding writing blind characters. Sensitivity readers are vital, if inclusion and diversity are going to work—that, plus an awareness that white, straight people aren't always the most appropriate persons to address certain topics. There's so much I've learned and am still learning. I promise not to stop trying even though it's frightening and risky. Creativity is dangerous, after all. Thanks for your patience, dearest readers.

Lastly, thanks to my husband Dane aka the Viking—my best friend and my lover. I truly wouldn't be doing any of this without you, my love. Here's to the adventures to come.